LOVE AND SACRIFICE

BY

TOVE FOSS FORD

INSPIRED BY AN IDEA FROM BRIAN D. FORD

SECOND BOOK OF THE PROPHECY SERIES

This book is a work of fiction. Names, characters, businesses, places, events and incidents are either the products of the author's imagination or used in a fictitious manner. Any resemblance to actual persons, living or dead, or actual events is purely coincidental.

http://www.eirdon.com

ISBN: 978-0-9981549-3-0

DEDICATION

To all who have known the red flame of love
and the white flame of sacrifice.

BOOK ONE

THE MIDDLE CONTINENT

PROLOGUE

At the center of The Sea of Grass, Tharan-Tul, Great Shaman of the Thrun, sat on a hilltop by the dying flames of his fire. His gnarled hand smoothed an area of fine gray ash.

He waited, listening, closing his eyes.

They came – the whispering voices rising from the Sea of Grass. They sighed and sang of past and future.

Tharan-Tul drew three interconnected circles in the ashes with his forefinger – Ascendance, Balance and Descent.

He drew his runes from their small leather pouch and passed them from hand to hand, the worn bone discs clicking together softly. His mind called to the Spirits at The Light At The Top Of The World to help him see clearly. He cast the runes across the drawn circles.

He frowned.

The rune of the Winter Sun was in the uppermost circle, Ascendance, but the other two had fallen together in the adjacent circle of Balance. The third circle, Descent, was clear.

Not a bad sign, but unexpected.

Could Light Of The Winter Sun ascend so soon? The runes of Reflection of My Friend and Light Brighter Than The Sun had fallen under another influence, when before, all three of the chosen children's runes had always been unified in one circle.

The whispering voices sang that this was the near future he was seeing, not the present.

Sweeping the fragile discs together into his hand, Tharan-Tul replaced them in their pouch, then erased the circles in the ash. Sitting back on his heels, he looked up at the night sky.

The prophecy might yet come to pass, despite the division between the chosen children he had just seen. They could be reunified. There was still time.

In the interim, there was much to be done.

THE SHADOWS, MORDANIA

I

GLADDAS DALMANTHEA VISITS THE SHADOWS

Ifor Trantz, former Mordanian spy, was riding home from a day of hunting when he saw a woman burdened with a particularly large portmanteau trudging along the road from The Shadows' railroad halt. He frowned. No visitors were expected today. This was a serious breach of security.

Ifor urged his large black gelding forward and rapidly overtook the figure toiling along in the dust of the midsummer road. As he got within earshot, it was obvious that not only was the woman toiling along, she was swearing expertly as she did so.

"Gladdas, you old biddy," Ifor grinned as he drew even with her.

Piercing eyes as dark as his own glared up under heavy, shapely eyebrows.

"Retribution for those tight shoes you sold me will begin," Gladdas Dalmanthea, the only female freelance spy and assassin on Eirdon, snapped.

"Gladdy, that was twelve years ago," Ifor chuckled, sliding from his horse's back and taking the portmanteau from her without a by-your-leave. "My back was so bad that day, it's a wonder I didn't sell you hobnail boots."

"They would have pinched less," she retorted as he began securing the portmanteau to the front of his saddle. "Don't think I'm going to flop around behind you on that grundar you call a horse," she continued.

Ifor smiled to himself and tied the portmanteau behind his saddle instead.

"Should we leave her to cope with the dust and heat, Blackie?" he asked his very large saddle mount.

"You call your horse Blackie?" Gladdas Dalmanthea asked sarcastically.

"Makes sense. He's black," Ifor responded laconically. He remounted and crooked a booted foot for her to step onto, pulling her upward to sit sidesaddle before him. He pretended not to hear her involuntary sigh of relief. She had walked almost halfway to The Shadows from the halt on an unpaved road – a difficult journey on a hot day, particularly for a woman wearing very citified shoes.

They were silent until they rounded a bend in the road and the great estate house called The Shadows came into view.

"Good gods!" Gladdas Dalmanthea burst out. "Is that Menders' little hut in the woods?"

Ifor grinned to himself. The Shadows was as striking as it was imposing, four stories of elaborate Old Mordanian architecture. It soared against the sky, its onion-domed turrets frosted with decorative painted woodwork. Sixteen years of loving restoration and maintenance had made what was once a neglected, near-ruin into a gracious home for nearly seventy people – including Princess Katrin Morghenna, second Heiress to the Throne of Mordania

"That's it," was all Ifor said.

"It's incredible – but not worth Menders staying out here in this wilderness," Gladdas sniped.

"He didn't have any choice about it, if you'll remember," Ifor rebuked gently. "These days it's far from a wilderness. You're just grumpy because you were shuffling along in the dust. What brings you out, Glad?"

"I thought I would take a look at the place I'm exiling some of my best operatives to for the next three years," she responded, still staring at the house and grounds as Blackie strutted along.

The grounds of The Shadows were at their summer best, green lawns sweeping up a gentle slope to the house. A lake on the right side of the curving oval drive shimmered in the sunlight, ringed with purple flag flowers and lilies. An extravagant rose garden nestled against the south side of the house – a dense forest of old growth trees guarded the sunlit gardens adjacent to the massive house. The display of light and shade was dazzling.

A small, blond man sauntered out onto the massive front steps of The Shadows, shaded his eyes and stared in their direction. Ifor waved before the man darted back inside, to emerge a few seconds later with a pair of binoculars. He surveyed them and dashed indoors again.

"Gone to tell Papa?" Gladdas sniped.

Ifor smiled, but he pinched her waist just hard enough to get her attention.

"Now then, Glad – we're happy to have you, but if you'd let us know you were coming, we would have met you at The Halt," he chided gently. "What's more, I could have come and brought you over from Erdahn on the boat. That would have saved you the two-day delay the trains have been having outside of Rondheim."

She groaned and he could hear the weariness in the sound. She leaned back against him. He wrapped a big arm around her waist affectionately. They had known each other for more than twenty-five years and nothing she threw could rattle or offend him.

"You may take me back on your boat," she finally said as they started up the drive to the house.

The blond man reappeared with a companion who wore dark spectacles and thigh length black hair held back with a decorative clip. He peered through the binoculars held out to him by the blond fellow and laughed before he waved.

"That is Sir Slippery Eel?" Gladdas Dalmanthea asked in astonishment. "Last time I saw him, he looked like a naughty schoolboy!"

"It's been a very long time," Ifor observed. "Since before he went to deal with the Surelian Problem nineteen years ago? You haven't run into him since then?"

Gladdas shook her head, staring at the men she knew were Aylam Josirus, Lord Stettan, who went by the name Menders and Kaymar Shvalz, his second in command – first cousins to each other and second cousins to the Queen of Mordania.

"No, it never came up. I spend a lot of time in Artreya now," she answered distractedly. "And that's Kaymar. The last time I saw him he was a child – albeit a frightening one."

"He still is at times." Ifor smiled at her description of the mercurial man he had been bonded with for eight years. "I believe you'll find that he's quite grown up – for the most part."

Gladdas laughed outright and Ifor smiled. Now her visit would go well, and she wouldn't appear on the doorstep at her worst.

Two heads popped out of a second story window – those of a golden-haired young woman and a striking young Thrun man.

Gladdas glimpsed startling blue eyes on the woman and dark spectacles, like Menders', on the man before the heads popped back out of sight and excited conversation could be heard.

"The Princess, I presume?" she said. "I hope she doesn't expect curtseying."

It was Ifor's turn to laugh.

"Glad, you have no idea – absolutely no idea," he said, swinging off the horse and lifting her down to the steps, where Menders came forward and to her utter amazement, embraced her like a long-lost sister.

***

"Gladdas Dalmanthea – here?" Eiren asked, her eyes wide. She had just come home from teaching at The Shadows Academy.

"Indeed," Menders smiled. "Turned up on the train and had walked halfway here from The Halt when Ifor rode by."

"In this heat? The poor thing!" Eiren rose in alarm, going toward her medicine cabinet.

"She'll be fine. She's already had a bath and changed and is now being regaled by Borsen and Katrin, who are showing her the wood carvings throughout the house." Menders smiled and sprawled across the bed.

Sixteen years ago, Menders had come to The Shadows at the age of twenty, having been appointed guardian of the newborn Princess Katrin. He had been Mordania's foremost assassin during his youth. His unconventional and daring disruption of an attempt to infiltrate and conquer Mordania by the nation of Surelia had earned him the nickname "The Surelian Solution." Then, at the Queen's command, he had vanished from the world with the infant Princess and became Head of Household at The Shadows. There he had met Eiren Spaltz, daughter of one of the tenant farmers.

Eiren had attended teachers' college through the patronage of Menders and Doctor Rainer Franz, Princess Katrin's personal physician. She was now the headmistress of The Shadows Academy, now a prestigious institution she had founded as a one room school in an unused building on her father's farm.

Eiren and Menders had lived as man and wife for some eleven years, though Menders' commitment to Princess Katrin precluded his marrying. They had raised Katrin as their daughter and also acted as parents for Menders' nephew, Borsen and Hemmett Greinholz, now a graduate of the Mordanian Military Academy and the Captain of Princess Katrin's Personal Guard.

"Why do you think she's appeared here without a word of warning?" Eiren asked, selecting several bottles from the chest despite Menders' reassurances that Gladdas Dalmanthea would be fine.

"That's my clever girl," Menders smiled admiringly, interlacing his fingers behind his head. "She turned up here dressed absurdly for anyone traveling. She does nothing by chance and normally would never get on a train in the getup she was wearing – purple silk dress, open-fronted laced shoes with high heels. She was deliberately appearing as a novice traveler, disguising herself well."

Eiren came and sat beside him.

"What do you think she wants?" she asked, a line of concern showing between her eyebrows.

Menders reached up and smoothed the line gently.

"My dear, Gladdas Dalmanthea is impossible to predict," he answered. "Something is afoot, but we won't know until she divulges it. That will be in her own good time."

Borsen and Katrin both burst into laughter on the floor below.

"All seem to be getting along well," Menders smiled, sitting up. "I take it our young people are moving Glad along this way."

"I'm actually going to meet Gladdas Dalmanthea," Eiren said a little breathlessly. Menders looked round at her.

"My dear, you aren't nervous!" he exclaimed.

"I'm not sure," Eiren managed.

Menders took her hand, shaking his head.

"You've heard far too many blood and thunder stories from Kaymar," he said firmly. "Glad is very good at what she does and in her day, she was a ruthless and efficient assassin. But like me, and like Kaymar, that is not the sum of her. You'll be able to talk shop, because Gladdas runs a school for young women in Artreya. Some of them do become spies and even assassins, but most are trained for clerical or managerial work. Those with talent for the arts receive appropriate training. They're poor girls who would have no opportunity for education or advancement otherwise."

"Like a certain red-haired farm girl?" Eiren smiled, her eyes kindling with interest.

"I think this red-haired farm girl would have become a great teacher whether or not a certain assassin with bad eyes and a baby girl under his arm turned up at The Shadows," Menders laughed.

"And now, darlings, you must introduce me to your brave Mamma," a powerful and distinguished woman's voice said from the stairwell.

"Don't forget our debonair Pappa," Katrin responded, laughing.

"My old friend, Sir Slippery Eel? He's an old tune!"

With that, a refreshed and transformed Gladdas Dalmanthea appeared in the doorway of the suite that was home to Menders, Eiren and Katrin.

In reality, she was an anonymously plain woman, but Gladdas had acquired the ability to transform her appearance to anything she wanted it to be. Now free of road dust and being confined to a second-class railway carriage, she had taken on her favorite persona – refined but worldly, a trifle sarcastic but kind, elegantly but casually dressed in a beautiful but simple deep red dress. Perhaps it was the persona closest to her true self.

She smiled as Eiren came forward, reached out and took both her hands.

"Well, my dear," Gladdas pronounced. "Yes, you have to be the one who set that Therbalt character on his ear. Well done!" She embraced Eiren suddenly, murmuring something to her.

Eiren laughed aloud.

"I had Kaymar and Ifor there as well. Without them, things would have been very different," she replied.

The year just past had involved a plot against the Royal Family, cooked up by a flamboyant character who called himself Lord Therbalt. This danger kept The Shadows in lockdown status for months. Eiren had been approached by Lord Therbalt while she was attending a teacher's course in the capital city, Erdahn. He had feigned romantic interest while attempting to winkle information about The Shadows from her.

Ifor Trantz and Kaymar Shvalz formed a counter plot to eliminate Lord Therbalt. Aided by Eiren, who spent weeks luring Therbalt along with promises of information about the floorplan of The Shadows, their scheme culminated in a late-night meeting in a garden with Kaymar impersonating Eiren. A case of mistaken identity allowed Therbalt to escape with his life – but not before Eiren's knife had opened his cheek from his ear to the corner of his mouth. He had fled to Surelia. From his stronghold there, Therbalt launched a tide of assassins on The Shadows.

Eventually, Kaymar went up against the worst of these assassins, a Surelian sadist named DeLarco. Though he took the thrashing of his life, he and Ifor managed to eliminate DeLarco and found information in his belongings that led Menders' operatives to Therbalt's Surelian hideaway.

A bomb was detonated in Therbalt's townhouse headquarters, but Therbalt himself narrowly escaped and effectively vanished from the face of Eirdon. His network of spies was destroyed. It was easy to believe the threat from Lord Therbalt had been eliminated.

Menders hoped that Gladdas' sudden appearance at The Shadows had nothing to do with the vanished Lord Therbalt.

***

"But of course, my dear! My girls receive a thorough education no matter what final course they choose to follow," Gladdas Dalmanthea said firmly. "Education is vital. Ask your Mamma and she'll agree with me. It opens the mind to possibility."

"But I chose not to go on with school," Borsen protested. "I think my mind is open."

"You've thought of nothing but sewing from the moment you left school?" Gladdas asked.

Borsen's elegant eyebrows went up over the rims of his clear indoor glasses.

"Well – no. I read books with and talk about them with Uncle. Auntie suggests ways to improve my writing, though it never seems to get much better no matter how much I work at it."

"And mathematics?" Gladdas accepted another glass of wine from Menders, never taking her eyes off the slender young man with the heavy Thrun accent.

Borsen grimaced. "Never cared much for it," he admitted.

"Surely in making a pattern you would use mathematics."

Borsen's eyebrows went up again.

"You could say – using measurements, yes. Geometry, I guess," he answered. "Kaymar had to help me with that. He's the advanced mathematics master at The Shadows Academy. He worked out ways I could see how geometry worked for fitting patterns."

"And that, my dear little frog, is exactly what education is for – to help you, to enhance your life. That's the way we educate my girls, in ways that make sense. Why have them memorize and then gabble over some endless poem? They need to learn things that help them to be independent women."

"Don't your girls learn literature, Aunty Glad?" Katrin asked, looking over the top of her current favorite book.

Menders had to smile. In the three days of Gladdas' visit so far, Katrin and Borsen had begun calling her Aunty Glad, while Hemmett, when off duty, referred to her as Sweetheart. It was hard to believe the affable, interested and outgoing woman who obviously enjoyed spending time with the young people had been the scourge of many a Mordanian assassin, Menders included.

"Of course they do. It's a vital accomplishment. Did your dear Pappa force you to memorize and recite long sagas?"

"Of course not," Katrin replied.

"Because?"

"Well… because I wouldn't like it."

"And that's the only reason?" Gladdas' eyebrows were inching up her forehead.

"No," Katrin ventured. "What point is there to being able to recite sagas? To understand them, to be able to analyze them, yes, but just parroting them accomplishes nothing."

"Absolutely. Tell me, does your Pappa have you learn things you don't like?"

Katrin colored slightly. "Of course," she said. "I don't care much for mathematics or grammar, but I have to learn them."

"Well, that's a mercy," Gladdas replied. "Borsen, what do you do that you don't like?"

"Sew on buttons, make sheets and kill chickens," he answered instantly. Katrin laughed out loud at the incongruous list, but Borsen didn't.

"Are you the chicken executioner here?" Gladdas smiled at him.

"It's supposed to be shared," he answered levelly. Katrin stopped laughing. She hated killing chickens and made sure to disappear whenever Cook wanted chickens slaughtered for dinner, leaving the nasty task to Borsen.

"So how do you deal with your distaste for these jobs, my little frog?" Gladdas put a hand over Borsen's.

"Best to get it over with. Do it well, do it with dispatch," he answered crisply. "Buttons will always need to go on clothes, people will always need sheets and if you want to eat chicken, someone has to kill a chicken. I can sew a button on so fast you can hardly see me do it and I've worked out efficient ways to sew sheets by machine. I use my pistol to dispatch the chickens. It's cleaner and the chicken never knows what hit it."

Gladdas smiled and patted his hand, then engaged Katrin in conversation over her book, effectively defusing any discomfort between the young people.

Menders, who had been listening from the next room, smiled and looked over at Eiren.

"Impressive," she mouthed. Menders nodded. Gladdas, in a fairly innocuous conversation, had just learned a great deal about both Katrin and Borsen. Doubtless she would store it away in her prodigious memory and use it if she ever needed to analyze the actions of either of them.

***

Menders waited while Gladdas took her time sauntering down the aisles of one of The Shadow's greenhouses. It was ablaze with roses borne on very young plants. During his sixteen years as Head of Household at the estate, Menders had researched and implemented many improvements, among them three greenhouses. They not only provided a head start for spring plantings, but also housed a small assortment of fresh winter vegetables, most welcome during the bitterly cold, snowbound months of Old Mordania's winters. Having a controlled growing environment sparked his interest in developing rose cultivars. This brilliant display was the result of many years' careful planning and cultivation.

Gladdas paused by a very dark red rose and inhaled.

"Man of many talents," she pronounced. "This is exquisite. Have you named it?"

Menders raised his eyebrows.

"I was actually considering naming it after you," he answered.

She shook her head.

"As lovely as that would be, I want no light on me right now. It's unlikely a cultivated rose would draw attention, but not entirely so. Call her Dark of the Moons. Dark and very rare."

"Perfect," Menders answered. It was apropos. Eirdon's two moons were almost never dark at the same time.

He leaned against a potting bench, crossing his ankles and arms.

"Why are you here, Gladdy?" he asked.

"Multiple reasons."

"When is anything you do for a single purpose?" he smiled.

Gladdas laughed to herself. Then she turned to him and he knew she was ready to stop playing the role of unexpected houseguest.

"Who will you have as your second here while you and Kaymar are away?" she asked bluntly.

"Haakel." Erlen Haakel was a longtime friend, an ex-assassin as were many of Katrin's unofficial guard, known at The Shadows as Menders' Men. He was one of the senior men and had been at The Shadows since Katrin was four years old. Before that, Haakel had been one of Menders' study mentors at the Mordanian Military Academy when he'd arrived there at the age of eleven, sadly behind his contemporaries thanks to a series of incompetent tutors. Haakel was a widower, devoted to The Shadows' family, brilliant and dependable.

"Not a bad choice," Gladdas said quietly. "But not entirely what you'll need."

Menders waited, saying nothing. Gladdas was akin to his cousin Kaymar, tending to fill silences in conversation.

"You need me here," she continued. "I need to be away from of Artreya for an extended period. I couldn't be here all the time, of course, since I'm moving my school to Samorsa indefinitely and will need to be there at times."

"And why do I need you here?" Menders asked levelly.

"Erlen Haakel is a good man," she responded. "Normally he would be all you require, along with my people who are going to stand in for you and the rest of the family. But he's not equal to something out there right now."

"Our friend Therbalt?" Menders felt a cold sweat breaking out under his shirt, despite the heat of the greenhouse.

Gladdas snorted.

"That freak has gone to ground somewhere far, far away," she answered. "No money, no network. No trace of him. What I'm talking about is in Artreya. They aren't actively after Katrin, not as of yet, but the best thing you can do is get her anonymously away from here. I would need to be here to support her double. She's one of my best operatives. I don't want to lose her, and I don't want your home endangered."

Menders pushed away from the bench and began to prowl up and down the greenhouse. Gladdas waited.

"Individual or group?" he finally asked.

"It's a group," she answered. "Their goal is to have Artreya invade Mordania, but that's some time off. In the meantime, they have their sights set on the Queen and Princess Aidelia. They know of Katrin's existence, but they're not interested in her at the moment. If they should manage to eliminate the Queen and Aidelia, they'll come after her."

Menders stopped pacing, shook his head and removed his glasses, massaging his eyes wearily for a moment. Then he looked up at her.

Gladdas had seen his eyes before. They were such a light grey that from a distance they appeared to be entirely white except for his pupils. Even so, they were always a shock, as he wore darkened spectacles almost constantly to protect them from the light. They were a continual trial to him and prone to infection. They frequently ached and his vision was poor in full light. Conversely, he had night vision a langhur would envy.

"Do you know their timeline?" he asked.

"A couple of years out from any assassination attempt on the Queen. I've informed Thoren Bartan at the Palace, of course – and now you. Between the three of our networks, we can put a stop to this in time. But I wanted to speak directly to you – as well as meet this marvelous family of yours."

Menders started prowling again. He was startled when she put her hand on his arm. His hearing was sharp, but she had moved soundlessly.

"Aylam, you're about to make some terrible decisions because your emotions are running away with you," she said briskly. "Do not do this. Take a breath and use your brain, not your heart. And if you get stubborn with me, I'll throw you on the ground."

Menders had to laugh and shook his head.

"Yes, Mama," he responded. "You are correct. Now, there must be another reason why you want to be here and why you came here secretly."

"They know who I am."

Menders blinked.

Gladdas Dalmanthea's true identity was an incredibly well-kept secret. She had a plethora of aliases and names. She moved entirely in the shadows and always had, both when she was an active assassin and afterwards, as she built one of the largest and most effective spy and assassin networks on Eirdon.

"One of my girls has gone over to these people," Gladdas explained. "That's why I'm moving the school to Samorsa to protect the girls. She knows everything – locations, people. I need to disappear. Considering how well you disappeared sixteen years ago, I thought this might be just the place to start."

"It is," Menders said firmly. "Let's go talk to Haakel."

ARTRIM, MORDANIA

2
PROGRESS

Menders and Doctor Rainer Franz sat astride their saddle mounts, watching a train shunting at the new Artrim Station. A railroad spur had recently been extended to Artrim, the closest village to The Shadows. It was one of the last Mordanian trains they would see for a while. With Gladdas Dalmanthea's operatives settled at The Shadows, preparations for the family's departure to Surelia were being expedited in the face of the information she had given Menders.

Their interest had been drawn by the locomotives, which were new and larger than any they'd seen before.

The world was changing and Mordania was changing with it. Here in this isolated corner of the country, change was perceived as something remote, experienced through letters and newssheet articles. It was not something affecting daily life.

"Nothing like those pretty little green engines that used to haul the trains," Doctor Franz said with a smile, looking intently at the steaming locomotive. "This is impressive, but I was fond of those little toys, with the spoked wheels and copper trimmings."

Menders nodded silently. The small, dark green engines that had carried him with Katrin and a household of six to The Shadows sixteen years ago were no more. In their place rumbled larger, workmanlike locomotives with black iron boilers trimmed with gleaming bronze, their wheels and underworks painted a uniform dark red. They moved at enormous speed, leaving behind the lingering smoke of chabron, the hard, hot-burning coal mined only in eastern Mordania.

The Northern Mordanian Railroad was expanding rapidly, bringing rail travel and commerce to formerly isolated villages and communities. Mechanized industry had arrived in Mordania, rising from burning coal and boiling water, propelled by great iron wheels. Cities reverberated to the pulse of machinery while coal smoke smudged the skies the color of old lead.

Although Menders was impressed by these recent technological advances, he was not innocent enough to believe the rapid progress was entirely positive.

"We'd best get on," he said as the locomotive was coupled with the rearranged carriages and boxcars. "I'd like to be home in time for dinner."

"Indeed. They assured me that everything is ready," Franz replied, reining his big bay gelding around.

Demon, Menders' farlin, snapped at the big, gentle horse as a matter of course. Menders dealt out a slap to the animal's serpent like neck, but Fatboy, Franz's gelding had matters well in hand. He bared his teeth at Demon and shook his head, as if remind the evil-tempered animal of the day he's finally had enough abuse and grabbed that slender neck in his teeth, shaking his head viciously.

"You'll bite that bastard sheep if he ever nips you again, won't you?" Franz laughed, patting Fatboy's shining neck.

Menders couldn't help smiling. Franz babied his horse like nothing he had ever seen – overfeeding him, doting on him, grooming him until he gleamed.

As if he'd read Menders' mind, Franz said, "I'm going to miss this fellow while we're gone."

"I thought of bringing all our saddle mounts, but it would be a terrible process for them," Menders answered. "I don't even want to think of how Demon would carry on."

"Gods no," Franz said fervently.

Menders laughed to himself. Doctor Franz was one of the original household sent to The Shadows on the night Katrin was born. He was Katrin's personal physician but also cared for the entire household, as well as for all The Shadows' tenant farmers and many other families spread out across the district. He was courageous and infinitely caring in his medical practice, but he could find no love for Demon, a rangy, wickedly intelligent, slope-backed farlin with jaggedly sharp teeth and a fiendish temper.

As they neared the village square, their errand to pick up medical supplies was pushed to the back of their minds. Red and black bunting hung about the square. A small military band played marching tunes and the latest example of mechanized warfare was the focus of all eyes. Franz and Menders reined in their mounts and watched the rally from some distance away.

The machine was roughly shaped like an oversized suit of iron armor, riveted together and articulated at the joints, with large metal tracks turned by multiple wheels where the feet of the suit would be. It towered thirty feet above the square. Gun sponsons bristled from the front, sides and top. Steam and smoke rose from twin funnels on the back and from inside came an occasional hollow clanging, like the metal of a cooling stove. A small knot of weary, oil-stained engineers fussed and swore about the machine, clambering up, into and out of it again through many hatchways.

Menders had heard of these contraptions. They were officially called 'Land Tanks' but were commonly referred to as 'Steam Soldiers'.

Mechanized industry had spawned mechanized warfare. Guns of increasing size, with the ability to hurl an explosive shell as far as forty miles, were lauded as a great step forward for all mankind. They were hauled into battle by steam tractors, not horses. Contraptions with no purpose other than causing mayhem and death were turned out by the thousands in the newly built factories. There was no end to human ingenuity when it came to thinking up novel ways to murder by mechanical means.

"That's right, lads!" a much-decorated Regimental Sergeant-Major boomed from a small wooden dais beneath the machine. "Step up and feast your eyes upon the latest mechanized marvel in the history of warfare! By taking up the Queen's florin, you could captain one of these fearsome fighting machines! Strike fear and terror into the hearts of Mordania's enemies as you roam the battlefields in command of the very latest and most modern method of killing yet invented!"

"That's for those of you who are tired of killing with guns, grenades and poison gas," Menders muttered with obvious distaste.

"You don't care for modern warfare, then eh?" Franz replied, lighting a small cigar. "Odd attitude for a military man."

Menders gave him a look.

"Special Services operatives are hardly drum-beating military types," he answered. "I don't care for any form of warfare. There are people who will look upon this monstrosity as a great and good thing. Those same people would call me a barbarian because I'm an assassin."

"You mean were an assassin, don't you?" Franz enquired.

"Do you stop being a doctor if you stop practicing medicine?" Menders asked.

"Of course not."

"Exactly."

Franz thought about this, then said, "I think people have trouble with the idea of assassins, because they make killing so… personal." The big, blond man had never been able to become blasé about assassins, though he was Menders' closest friend and lived at The Shadows surrounded by men who had been either spies or assassins.

"Of course we do," Menders replied, watching the crowd pressing closer to the Steam Soldier, oohing and aahing at the bronzed barrels of the fire throwers and the gaping muzzles of the cannons. "That's the whole point. I never had to destroy a town and kill countless people to get one man. I could slip up to him and hand him death. He'd never see me coming and probably not feel a thing. But let the army take this thing here and go kill ten or twenty or a hundred or a thousand and so long as it's impersonal, then that's all right."

"I see your point."

"The old ways were better," Menders continued sourly, turning Demon and riding away from the square. "Sometimes I read about the new mechanization and think we're verging on a new age of wonders. Then I see something like this contraption and I wonder what in all the hells we are doing to ourselves? What sort of a world will Katrin inherit, if she becomes Queen?"

"I think all we can accurately predict about the future is that it will be different from today," Franz said.

"Yes. That's what worries me."

THE SHADOWS, MORDANIA

3
VILLISON

And that's all of them, with one exception," Hemmett said, sitting back in the chair across from Menders and crossing his legs.

Menders looked closely at the young man.

Hemmett had come to The Shadows at three years of age. He was the son of Katrin's official Guard, Lucen Greinholz and his wife, Zelia. A rambunctious and strong-willed child, he was overindulged by his aging parents to the point of being extremely unappealing to anyone else. He had gravitated toward Menders, who gave him structure and standards for his behavior. Over time, Hemmett had become a son to him.

Hemmett was Katrin's closest friend and companion. He would take the role of her older brother during the family's tour of the Middle Continent and Artreya. He'd attended the Mordanian Military Academy and graduated with highest honors only that year, taking his long-coveted role as the head of Katrin's Personal Guard, which had been assigned to her when she turned sixteen.

The wild little boy had grown into a radiantly handsome giant of a man. Possessed of an antic sense of humor and a quick and active mind, he was going to be very successful in his chosen profession. His choices of members for the military Guard to be assigned to Katrin were excellent – so far.

"Why does the exception make me think I'm not going to like this?" Menders asked warily. Most of the men Hemmett had chosen were tried and true. Many were members of the unofficial unit known as Lucen's Men, which had been assembled by Menders years ago when it became obvious that the single Guard assigned to the household would not be sufficient security for the Princess. Hemmett had also requested a couple of young men he'd known at the Royal Military Academy. They had excellent references and records.

"Because I want Villison," Hemmett answered calmly.

"No." Menders shook his head. During the years Hemmett was at the Academy there had been far too many off-color stories about Villison and his antics. He had taken six years to get through the five-year course and graduated at the absolute bottom of the class, squeaking through with one point above a failing grade.

"I disagree. I'd like to present my reasons for wanting him." Hemmett's handsome face was impervious beneath his curling, russet-brown hair.

"I imagine it's because you were friends," Menders said.

"Not entirely, though that is a factor in my reasoning," Hemmett answered with blunt honesty. "A summary refusal is not like you, Menders. You can't think that I want him here simply because we were friends, because if I thought like that, I'd request half a dozen fellows who wouldn't be suited for the job at all."

Menders thought for a moment.

"All right. State your case, but that doesn't mean I'll change my answer," he ordered briskly.

"Villison is not stupid, though his terrible grades would make you think he is," Hemmett began, uncrossing his legs and sitting forward on his chair. "He doesn't have a military mind. Given his own choice, he would never have gone to the Academy."

"And you want him for a military unit?" Menders said sarcastically.

"Yes."

"Hemmett…"

"Indulge me, Menders," Hemmett interrupted, a cold edge on his voice that made Menders blink. He nodded, deciding to let Hemmett speak his piece.

"Villison has an originality of mind that keeps him from being a good, obedient military man," Hemmett continued. "This very originality makes him incredibly valuable to me, considering we are not dealing with a typical military situation here."

"Specify," Menders prompted, curiosity pushing his misgivings aside.

"Menders, he can find out anything, procure anything, bribe anyone. If you want to know who's gambling, ask Villison – because he's running the games. Want contraband? Villison knows how to get it. Need to know gossip or dirt on anyone – he's your man. Need someone bribed? Ask Villison to do it. He's a slimy little weasel in a lot of ways, but he's a damn loyal slimy little weasel."

"Now I'm interested, but not entirely sold on the idea," Menders admitted.

"I'm not finished. If I were in a situation where I needed help, I would want him there," Hemmett continued. "He's a not a model soldier but he's a staunch ally and friend.

"We got sent on maneuvers once with one of the wonder boys from the latest war – some commissioned prat who never went through the Academy at all. Pappa bought his commission. He had the luck to get a good battalion. They won a battle, he got all the credit. They'd send these bastards to teach the cadets."

"I remember that type of thing well," Menders nodded.

"So here comes Mister Fancy Pants Lieutenant to lead us on an exercise," Hemmett went on. "He's holding the map upside down half the time. We're tromping around in circles in a pine forest, where the trees all look alike. I'm trying to intercede a bit before we end up marching to the next town ninety miles away, at least to get him to hold the map right side up. He keeps telling me that the land isn't right, when it's obvious he can't read a map.

"What happens then but I step in a hole and sprain my ankle. I'm afraid it's broken, it looks it, and I absolutely can't walk on it, not even with my boot on. The rule is, if a boy gets injured on maneuvers, he's sent back to the Academy. If the injury is severe enough, the maneuver is called off entirely. So, I'm thinking thank gods, I'm out of this now. For the sake of the others, maybe the Lieutenant will use this as an excuse to stop.

"Next thing I know, he's ordering the rest of them to leave me there alone."

"What?" Menders nearly shouted. Hemmett nodded.

"Yes – leave me there alone. They'll pick me up on their way back. We're so lost at that point that I know he'll never find me again. I can't walk and don't any idea where the hells we are.

"So even though the rule is 'never leave a man behind', our brave leader is just about to do that, as if the enemy is lurking right behind the horizon and it really matters that a bunch of twelve and thirteen-year-old boys pretend they're in a war. He doesn't even arrange for them to rig a litter and haul me along. He's just going to leave me there by myself with a leg that looks broken."

"Hemmett, why didn't you let me know this happened?" Menders said angrily.

"Because I can take care of myself – and I had help," Hemmett replied. "Now, stop interrupting me, Papa.

"What do all the militarily trained cadets do? They line up and proceed to start following this fool, leaving me lying there, no water, no food, my leg probably busted all to hells. Ready to march along like nice little sheep – except for Villison. He steps out of line, comes over and stands by me.

"Idiot Boy Lieutenant comes storming over, starts screaming at him to get back in line. 'Never leave a man behind, sir,' Villison says very respectfully. Now, this was the Loot's chance to remember the rule and do something, correct? Nothing doing. He's an officer! He can't be wrong. He screams and screams at Villison to get back in line. Every time he squawks, Villison just says 'Never leave a man behind, sir'.

"So, the bastard pulls out this riding crop he's carrying around, even though it's not uniform issue, and starts belting Villison with it. It's one of those Surelian racing crops, something I wouldn't hit a grundar with. It's cutting right through Villison's jacket. At the time, Villison is still just a little fellow but he stands there with tears running down his face at the pain and keeps saying 'Never leave a man behind, sir' every time this bastard hits him."

Menders stood abruptly and started pacing the room, clenching and unclenching his hands.

"Finally, the Lieutenant slashes Villison across the face with the crop. It lays his cheek wide open. The Lieutenant is screaming about how he's going to have Villison flogged, court martialed, all sorts of grundar shit. Villison stands firm and says, 'Never leave a man behind, sir' one more time.

"Off goes the Lieutenant with all the little sheep following in his wake while Villison stays behind with me."

"He left you there? He abused a cadet with a riding crop and then he walked off and left you there?" Menders said furiously.

"As sure as I'm sitting here in all my bigness," Hemmett grinned. "Villison used his shirt to wrap up his face and then he got his shoulder under my arm. He pulled out his compass and somehow we limp along, him bleeding and me howling with every step because my damn ankle hurts so much, until we come to a road. Pretty soon a wagon comes along. The people in it see our uniforms and wounds and are horrified that a war has started up in their own backyard. They heave me into the wagon, Villison cuts my boot off and it's back to the Academy with both of us."

"What the hells did the Commandant say about this?" Menders seethed, settling in his chair again, his face stony.

"Menders, he yelled for hours," Hemmett grinned. "Turns out the Lieutenant got everyone completely lost. They were out in the woods overnight because he wouldn't just settle down and stay put. When they were finally found by the real Army platoon that had to be sent after them, turns out the Lieutenant had hit several of the other boys when they got scared and started crying. Some of them were only eleven, after all. They all confirmed my story.

"Villison had fifteen stitches in his face and I spent a week on my back and most of the rest of the term on crutches. You could hear Sir screaming at the Lieutenant for half a morning. Not long after that the Lieutenant got sent off to the next skirmish with Artreya and ended up where a bunch of shells hit him."

Menders drew in a deep breath and let it out slowly.

"I wish you had let me know about this, Hemmett," he said.

"No point. It would have stirred everyone up here to no avail and Sir took care of it. My point here is not an incompetent fool of an officer, Menders. It's Villison. He's not one to march along behind an officer no matter what. He questions the military mentality. I don't consider that a bad thing. If I were in combat, yes, I would want people who wouldn't question my orders because I would give the best orders I could. But in the situation we have here, mingling an official Guard with covert operations, I want men with me who can think on their own and who will be unswervingly loyal to the point where they will question me if they think I'm wrong.

"If Villison could take what that fool dealt out when he was only fifteen and puny because he knew he was doing the right thing, I'll trust him with my life, with Katrin's life – with anyone's."

Menders sat there, contemplating what he'd been told.

"You've convinced me of his loyalty to you," he eventually said. "But you must admit some of the stories you've related about him are not enticing. A lot of them were about pranks. I don't want endless practical jokes going on here."

"A lot of that came from boredom and because he liked getting Sir riled," Hemmett answered.

"If he was bored in Erdahn, what makes you think he won't be bored here?"

"He hated school," Hemmett answered, unperturbed. "He doesn't like living in a city either. He's a second son, Menders. He would have loved to stay on the family estate, but big brother got that and has produced a total of four sons. Vil will never inherit the old family sod. So, his Mamma got it into her head that he had to follow in his Pappa's footsteps in the military, ignoring the fact that Pappa got his head blown off in battle. Vil didn't belong at the Academy, but every time he got sent down or Sir would try to tell Vil's Mamma he didn't belong there, she'd sob and carry on and kiss his fingers for all I know. Sir finally just relented and kept him on."

"Ah." Menders remembered how that same Sir had arranged it so he could stay at school during recesses while his father was still alive, so he didn't have to go home. Most of the time it had been as the guest of Sir himself. "Your letters always made it sound as if Villison caused so much trouble at home that his mother didn't want him there."

"I think one thing fed another, truthfully," Hemmett shrugged. "She couldn't cope with him and he played up because he knew it. He's a loving son and she dotes on him. He didn't have any choice about being in the Army, Menders."

"Yes," Menders sighed. "Some of us didn't." He turned his chair to the window for a few moments and looked out at the orchard.

"Let me tell you why his scores were so low," Hemmett said. "It wasn't that he didn't know the answers – he did. He's very bright. But he just wouldn't spit them back, because he could see other ways to do things. Very often his solutions for the test problems weren't orthodox, but they made a lot of sense. Once there was a test question about invading an island – how big the island was, how many people were on it, what defenses they had, where the towns were, yakety yakety. You were supposed to diagram your invasion. Well, everyone drew merrily away, arrows pointing everywhere, but Villison wrote one line and went on to the next question. Come to find out, he's put 'I would not invade, I would blockade the island and starve them into submission at a great saving of the lives of my men.'

"Well, Sir threw a fit, called him into his office and ordered him to explain. Villison said that it would be the most efficient way to obtain the goal of taking the island, with the least loss of life. Sir asked, 'What if the island is self-sufficient – would you just bob around on the ocean like a bunch of corks indefinitely?' Villison told him that from the size of the island and the population figure given, there was no way it could be self-sufficient, that it would be a matter of a couple of weeks before they would have to surrender.

"He'd applied what he knew about farming and his family estate, you see, instead of just spitting back an answer he learned in tactics class – and it was the most correct answer of all, Menders. That's how he thinks. I need that, because I do not and cannot think that way. To protect Katrin, I will need men who can think in all sorts of ways."

Menders barely kept from smiling. Villison's answer would have been his own. He was beginning to understand a bit more about the famous Villison.

"If you will personally guarantee his behavior I'll allow it," Menders said. "On trial, mind you. If buckets of paint start falling off doors onto people's heads, or pillows start exploding, he goes."

Hemmett nodded and stood.

"Thank you. I'll need you to pull a string or two to get him released from his posting, but it shouldn't be difficult if you contact Commandant Komroff. And I'm very glad I was able to present the case to you convincingly, without giving you his letter of recommendation for Vil."

Menders glared at him.

"You had a letter from the Commandant recommending him and you didn't just give it to me?"

Hemmett grinned.

"Menders – I wanted you to take my word on it," he said. "You've been a very good father to me since I was three and I appreciate everything you've ever done for me – but if we're to work together, I need to know you accept me as a man. That means respecting my opinions and judgment. I'm able to state my reasons for wanting Villison in Katrin's Guard without a note from the teacher."

Menders blinked at the rebuke. Hemmett was absolutely right.

"All right," he said, rising also and extending a hand to Hemmett. "I'll have him released from his posting to be reassigned here. And if you would, I would appreciate seeing the Commandant's letter, though I did base my decision on your words alone."

Hemmett shook his hand furiously and dropped a letter on the desk. He then looked at the clock.

"My turn on the roof," he said. "Thank you, Papa." He saluted and turned with beautiful precision and strode out the door with comical effect, as he was dressed in casual clothing and barefoot.

Menders picked up the letter, shaking his head.

My dear Menders,

It is with some amusement I write this recommendation for Corporal Villison to be included in the Guard of Princess Katrin. Captain Greinholz has conferred with me at some length about his choice of Corporal Villison for this post, as at first appearances, it is an extremely eccentric one.

Though Corporal Villison has a most dismal school record and a reputation for being a prankster and rebel, I can personally attest that he is a young man of considerable courage and character. As Captain Greinholz will doubtless tell you, Villison has both an original turn of mind and an enormous capacity for loyalty. He would have been a candidate for Special Services if it had not been for the interference of his mother and his academic performance, which to first appearances is poor, though his low marks are more the result of consistently offering original solutions to problems rather than the standard answers that are expected on exams.

It is my belief that Villison would be a valuable addition to the Princess' Guard. He is steadfastly loyal to Captain Greinholz and will keep his less desirable qualities in check if asked to do so by that same officer. He has my highest recommendation for this very unusual posting, as he is in every way, a very unusual man.

Your "father",

Morschal Komraf, Commandant

N.B. – *As Hemmett would say, if you were up to your eyeballs in shit with bullets flying all around, would you want someone who worries about keeping his uniform up to standard or someone who would help you to safety and not worry about protocol? Villison has never worried too much about spit and polish, Menders, but he has never left a man behind and never would. He will be considered cannon fodder by the regular Army. I hope you will be able to make use of him. He is, in many ways, very like the young man you used to be.*

***

A week later, the infamous Corporal Villison was standing in Menders' office.

He was absolutely not what Menders had expected. He'd had a notion of Villison being a Hemmett double, big and brash. Instead, he was small, wiry and very unprepossessing. A long, tight scar, courtesy of the riding crop in Hemmett's story, puckered his left cheek, giving his face a wry asymmetry and perpetual squint. His eyes and hair were dark and his skin was swarthy.

How the hells does he ever carry a soldier's pack, Menders thought. It would weigh more than he does. But this same young man had heaved Hemmett out of a pine forest when Hemmett was a mammoth fourteen-year-old. Small men could have enormous strength, as Kaymar Shvalz and Borsen could both testify.

"Have a seat, Corporal," Menders invited cordially, indicating the chair across from his desk. "We don't stand on a lot of ceremony here."

"Thank you, sir," Villison replied, waiting until Menders was seated before sitting himself.

"Menders will do. This is a home, Corporal, not a military installation. Uniforms aren't worn in most circumstances. No-one calls the Princess or me or anyone else here by title unless circumstances require it."

Villison nodded.

"I wanted to talk to you alone, without Hemmett, because I will admit that I still have misgivings about having you here," Menders continued bluntly. He was pleased to see that Villison didn't flinch. "Where have you been posted?"

"Forsham," the young man answered.

Menders flinched. Forsham, a fort on the Upper Peninsula of Mordania, had recently been the site of an unexpected skirmish between an Artreyan battle cruiser and Mordanian troops present on the ground. For months, Artreyan patrol boats had cruised by the fort on the shore. Like clockwork, a Colonel Murcheson ordered Mordanian soldiers onto the open beach to fire at the boats with their rifles. The patrol boats would respond with a few rifle-fire salvos and go their way.

Then one day the patrol boats were replaced by a battle cruiser.

Colonel Murcheson ordered his men to remain in position in the open, even though the cruiser was shelling the beach and the Mordanian soldiers were armed only with rifles. He might as well have sent them out with flyswatters. They were mowed down by the dozens.

"And how did you survive that debacle?" Menders asked.

"Took myself and my men the hells away from the beach," Villison replied bluntly, looking him square in the eye. "We weren't going to sink a cruiser firing at it with rifles."

"No," Menders said quietly. "And what happened to you for doing that?"

"Fifty lashes, administered day before yesterday," Villison answered, with no more inflection than if he'd mentioned he'd been given a demerit for talking in class. "If there'd been more high-ranking officers left alive, they would have had me shot for it. I was lucky because it was another Corp who oversaw the flogging and he's a mate of mine. Had them take it easy."

Menders ground his teeth. The only man in the situation who had behaved with any sort of common sense and Murcheson had him flayed alive.

"Have you seen a doctor?" he sighed.

"No, sir."

Menders rose, indicating for Villison to stay seated. He went to the door and called out to Franz, who appeared almost immediately. He had been wild to finally lay eyes on the legendary Villison of Hemmett's letters home from the Academy.

"Would you take a look at Corporal Villison's back?" Menders said coolly. Villison stood, shucked off his uniform jacket and shirt, and turned his back to Franz.

Franz blanched. Menders wanted to, but Villison deserved better than that.

"This is a mess, son," Franz said. "I'll get my bag." He exited Menders' office quickly.

"Look, I'm not going to give you the lecture I started out to," Menders said suddenly. "All I ask is that you don't make any pillows explode or set up practical jokes all over the house. Mind your manners and language around the ladies and children. I don't care if you gamble and swear in the Men's Wing, but please don't set up a casino and beggar my tenant farmers or romance the local girls in an unchivalrous manner. Those are the house rules for all men living here. Always remember that this is the home of many people, not a boarding school or a bivouac. That's it in a nutshell, Corporal."

"Why did you tell me to drop the titles and keep using mine?" Villison grinned.

"Because I'm set in my ways," Menders replied wearily. Seeing that torn back made him feel very old and very exasperated. It was typical of everything he hated about Mordania and the people who ran it.

"Well, be that as it may, I wanted to let you know how grateful I am to be here," the young man said as Franz came back into the room and opened his bag. He extracted swabs and several bottles, settling to work on the open slashes on Villison's back. "That skirmish was enough to make me wish I'd just given them the answers they wanted on their exams and graduated higher in me class, or that me mother had let me go to Special Services training. I won't let you down, Menders. I'm no paragon, but it's important to remember that our boy Hemmett does love to embellish a story."

Even though Franz was swabbing his back with something Menders knew stung like all the hells, he grinned, the taut scar pulling his left eye into a comical wink. Menders found himself grinning back. He shook Villison's wiry hand and left him to Franz, going into the hall to make Hemmett stop prowling around like a caged langhur.

"He's one of your Men," Menders said as Hemmett looked toward him. "He's to behave, as I said before. He's being patched up by Franz. Apparently, he was flogged a couple of days ago."

"Yes, I know," Hemmett answered, looking relieved. "Thank you, Menders."

"He's not to be your second," Menders said.

Hemmett kept his counsel.

THE SHADOWS, MORDANIA

4
COOK'S PARTICULAR SPOON

"Let me stir," Borsen laughed, reaching for Cook's particular spoon.

"That you will not, you'll make hash of it," Cook laughed back, turning her back to him, stolidly stirring a pot of simmering sugar syrup.

"Let me!" Borsen tried to reach around her for the oar like spoon she treated like a treasure. It was the mainstay of her kitchen arsenal, used for everything from ladling stew to stirring yeast starter for bread. It was also her favored weapon, brandished at people who interfered with her cooking and used to rap the knuckles of those who attempted to snitch food from pans.

"Oh, let him," Katrin teased from her vantage point on the other side of Cook. "It's a long time off the boil. He'll get bored long before then."

"Not me," Borsen retorted. "I want a turn!" He feinted at the spoon again, managing to get a grip on the handle.

"Now see here, you young demon," Cook exclaimed, giving the spoon a vicious wipe on a kitchen towel before turning toward Borsen and swiping at him with it. He dodged, laughing, and reached for it again. Cook giggled and swung the spoon playfully.

There was a sharp cracking noise. Borsen's face paled as he stared at the forefinger of his left hand, which was bent sharply in a very wrong and sickening direction.

"Grahl's teeth!" Cook gasped, jerking the spoon away in reflex. It caught Katrin squarely in the right eye.

"Ow!" She jumped back, lost her balance and fell. Her eye throbbed.

The spoon clattered on the tiles as Cook tried to help both of them.

"My poor darlings," she gasped, trying to pull Borsen close while hauling Katrin up off the floor. "I barely touched him with it. He reached… I never meant to hit him…"

Katrin shook her head to clear it and reached out for Borsen's hand.

"It's broken but good," he said almost calmly.

"I'm so sorry, sweetheart," Cook groaned, looking at the distorted finger in dismay.

"You hit him?" Varnia Polzen shouted, appearing in the doorway. Varnia supervised the housekeeping staff at The Shadows. "And the Princess?" The young woman stormed across the kitchen. She took in Borsen's finger and Katrin's rapidly swelling eye.

"Now you see here, my girl," Cook bristled. "There was no wrongdoing, we were only playing…"

"Playing that broke his finger?" Varnia's voice rose toward a shriek. "You don't miss a chance with that damned spoon and now look what you've done!"

"Varnia, she didn't…" Borsen began, clutching his injured hand to his chest, his face creased with pain.

Varnia had hit her stride. Though her usual demeanor was taciturn, she had a hot temper. Any perceived threat to Borsen brought it out. She'd come to The Shadows from her father's nearby bleak, unfruitful farm at the same time Borsen had been apprenticed to The Shadows' tailor. Varnia had developed an intense protectiveness toward Borsen over the last three years.

"Can't you understand that he's frail, that you can't bash him with a spoon you could row a boat with?" Varnia shouted, grabbing Cook's shoulders. Her years of hard work on her father's farm gave her a grip like iron but Cook had been kneading bread and stirring enormous pots of food for decades. She had arms like a blacksmith. Varnia found herself sprawled on the floor with a bruised bottom and a spinning head.

"You bitch!" she yelled, scrambling to rise.

"No-one move."

Menders was in the doorway. Katrin saw his eyes flicker over the scene and unaccountably found herself starting to snicker, though she was shaken and her eye was watering copiously. They must look as if they'd been brawling. She caught Menders' eye, then looked pointedly at Borsen.

She was shocked when Menders' face went gray as he took in the broken finger. Varnia was picking up momentum, rising from the floor in a rage. Cook was barely holding her ire but Katrin could see a vein pounding in her temple as she crossed her arms and faced Varnia down.

"You see here, young woman," she said in a low, grating voice, "I love both these children as my own and I wouldn't willingly do any harm to either. I've been here caring for Katrin and everyone else since we all were sent out here. Borsen is as dear to me as my own son. Yes, it was foolish to be horsing about in the kitchen, that I'll give you, and now they're both hurt as a result. Nothing was done in anything but a bit of fun. You get a grip on that temper of yours and fast. I'm still in charge in this kitchen and I won't be coping with tantrums."

Menders stepped in front of Varnia as she went for Cook. He said nothing, pointing adamantly to the door. Varnia glared for a few moments, meeting Menders' white-eyed gaze boldly. Then she bolted away.

Cook sighed suddenly and groped her way to a stool.

"I swear on my child I never meant to hurt them," she said, her voice suddenly weak.

"Of course not," Menders answered, patting her shoulder fondly before going to Borsen. Katrin was inspecting his finger while he said, "At least it wasn't my drawing hand."

"Don't be brave, it hurts to break a bone," she answered. Menders looked at the finger again, maintaining his composure this time.

"That's nasty, but Doctor Franz will put it back right," he remarked heartily, thankful that the bone hadn't gone through the skin.

"I swear it barely touched him," Cook quavered. Borsen and Katrin nodded agreement.

"All right," Franz said, coming into the room with a breezy smile. "What now?"

Katrin felt relieved until she saw Varnia come in behind him. Her face was pinched and white, blotched with red patches. Katrin could see her hands trembling.

Franz was pointedly ignoring Varnia's currents of rage. He inspected Borsen's finger.

"A dose of ramplane and I'll fix that good as new," he said, using a clean towel to wrap the hand loosely. Somehow Katrin knew it was to hide the hand from Borsen's – and perhaps Varnia's – sight. "Let me take one look at your sister's eye and then we'll go to my office and get started."

"It's nothing. I'll just look like Kaymar for a while," Katrin murmured as Franz leaned over to study her injury. He smiled. Recently one of Kaymar's explosives had misfired and he was sporting two black eyes and singed eyebrows. Franz patted her on the shoulder, told her to put some ice on her eye, then took Borsen away with him.

"How could it just give way like that?" Cook asked desperately. "I only touched him. He grabbed at the spoon, otherwise it wouldn't have touched him at all. It was just a graze, I swear it."

"He's fragile," Varnia hissed viciously. "Even an idiot can see that…"

"I told you to leave this kitchen," Menders interrupted. "Go, now, to your room and stay there until I send for you."

"I won't," Varnia retorted. "I'll have it out with her."

Menders turned and faced her. Katrin felt the room go cold.

"No-one here is unaware that Borsen is fragile," he said in a grating tone. "I appreciate your concern and your love for him, but you will not have it out with anyone. Go to your room or leave The Shadows."

Varnia nearly retorted. Then she turned on her heel and stalked out of the kitchen.

The neglected pan of sugar syrup boiled up and Menders turned swiftly, pulling if off the fire before it went everywhere.

Doctor Franz set Borsen's finger with a minimum of trouble, but the young man's frail constitution quailed under the shock. He ended up in bed for several days with a slight fever and general fatigue. Katrin spent much of her time with him, playing games, talking and reading. Her eye had swollen into a pugilist's pride and she'd felt pretty rattled for a day or two as well. She welcomed the chance to lounge around and rest.

Their invalidism kept them from full awareness of the storm that had erupted in the household.

Varnia was, apparently, one for grudges. As far as she was concerned, she was in open warfare with Cook. Being young and driven entirely by emotion, Varnia started one confrontation after another. Cook, on the other hand, became intensely defensive. She tended to face Varnia down with her particular spoon in hand, which only fanned the flames of the young woman's anger.

"Why don't you just send Varnia back home?" Katrin asked in exasperation after Menders had to interrupt lessons to quell yet another noisy squabble between the two women.

"Because this is her home," Menders answered tersely. He sighed and removed his glasses, pinching the bridge of his nose between his thumb and forefinger.

"Varnia hasn't had the privilege of a good upbringing," he said after a moment, his voice less harsh. "She was raised on that ghastly place without a mother, without any sort of love or tenderness. She loves Borsen as if he was her own child and she's reacting as a mother – a wild, savage mother with no proper breeding – would when perceiving a threat. Cook is reacting as a woman who has managed, without intention, to injure two children from the Royal Family. If word of what happened got back to Court, Cook could be summoned and executed."

"No, Menders!" Katrin gasped. "It was only play!"

"I know," Menders responded. "But we live with reason here. There is no reason at Court. It's unlikely word would travel there, but Cook is understandably anxious. So, she lashes back at Varnia when ignoring her would be the most effective thing to do."

"Hard to ignore," Katrin sighed. Varnia was so intense, always keyed up as if she expected to be attacked any minute.

"She's always so ready to fight," she continued, trying to think the matter out.

"Give some thought to what might have made her that way." Menders picked up the Surelian text they had been working with. "She was not given your advantages of a loving home and people with patience and education around you. Varnia has had to fight, for many reasons. I'm as fed up with this situation as anyone, but we have to be enlightened in how we deal with her."

"Yes, Papa," Katrin whispered, looking at the book again.

Doctor Franz held a meeting of the household and explained that Borsen had very brittle bones as a result of being severely malnourished as a child. He would have a high risk of fracture all his life and would have to curtail his physical activity. He had to give up the tumbling and hand fighting techniques he had been learning with Menders' Men. He was grappling with the decision to continue riding or not.

This made Borsen quiet and withdrawn, which only fueled the flames of Varnia's anger. The arguments and confrontations between Varnia and Cook became daily occurrences.

"If it hadn't happened and we didn't know about how frail his bones are, he could have ended up with much worse than a broken finger!" Cook shouted in the kitchen one day. "Perhaps that was a blessing!"

"You took a swing at a little boy with a great stick of wood!" Varnia shouted back. "Don't try to make it sound like a favor!"

"Get out of here!" Cook's voice resounded into Menders' study and Katrin watched as he clenched and unclenched his fists and rose mechanically. She trailed along in his wake.

"This is going to stop," he said sharply as he reached the doorway of the kitchen.

Both women started and turned toward him. Cook colored with embarrassment. Varnia's chin went up defiantly as she met his gaze.

"Varnia, I want you to stay out of the kitchen altogether unless you are specifically asked into it by Cook," Menders continued, walking over to her. "I have to be able to trust the two of you to manage peacefully together when the family is abroad. You'll have to convince me that will happen or I'm going to find another situation for you. If I can't, you'll have to return to your father's farm. Cook has been here since we first came to The Shadows. We can't do without her. Much as I'd hate to do without you, the household could manage."

Katrin was surprised to see Varnia's eyes widen slightly. She'd been so steely and forceful since Borsen's injury. Then Katrin saw the Polzen farm in her mind.

It was a freeholding bordering part of the eastern border of The Shadows. Varnia's father was the worst kind of farmer – callous, negative and convinced that his way of doing things was the only way. His continual crop failures and thin, sickly animals told another tale.

There were four grown, uneducated, half-savage sons from Mister Polzen's first marriage who did little about the farm unless they were driven to it by their father brandishing a stick or strap. Varnia, the child of Polzen's second wife, was years younger than her half-brothers.

There had been an ugly confrontation between Mister Polzen and Menders early in the family's stay at The Shadows. Menders had ridden by the Polzen farm and seen a cow down in the barnyard. He'd assumed it was dead and waiting for disposal – until the stricken animal moved slightly, groaning in agony, her swollen tongue lolling from her mouth into the pool of blood she lay in.

When Menders found him, Polzen said the cow had suffered a breech calving and was being left to "take her chance". When Menders insisted the animal be put out of her misery, Polzen said a bullet wasn't going to be wasted on her.

It had ended with Menders shooting the suffering cow himself and avoiding the Polzen place afterwards. A few years ago, he had offered to purchase the farm, but Polzen refused. Drab, dreary, badly kept with neglected animals, that farm was the stuff of nightmares to Katrin. No wonder Varnia had looked away from Menders.

"Go on now," Menders said, gesturing gently for Varnia to leave the kitchen. The tall young woman walked away rapidly, her face averted.

***

From Menders' Journal:

The complications of this summer have me anxious to get away on our journey. Though there is now a tense silence between Cook and Varnia, it is far from a peace. Thankfully Franz has now removed Borsen's splint, replacing it with a soft, stiffened bandage to support his injured finger.

I am never at ease with any injury to my children, but this incident has me shaken. Seeing how easily Borsen can be severely hurt is unnerving, for more reasons than one. Being a young man, he has been exploring his freedom. That includes going out on his own, mounted on his pony or his gentle little farlin, Sweetheart. Unfortunately, now we know a fall from either could be catastrophic, considering Borsen's fragile bones.

Borsen has decided to continue riding – and I have to applaud his courage though I quail at the thought. He is an excellent horseman but has no desire to deal with difficult animals, always choosing gentle and obedient mounts. That will be some protection for him. Still, when one rides, it is not a matter of if you fall, but when you fall. It is inevitable. The worst fall I ever had was from a gentle, old horse that was standing stock still. I hadn't double checked the saddle girth, which was not properly buckled. I wasn't alert, the horse was practically asleep – and suddenly the girth failed, the saddle slid, and I fell off onto a fence, breaking my collarbone and acquiring a terrific black eye and concussion that kept me in bed for a week.

For something like that to happen to my boy and the possible repercussions – I can't even countenance that. Not now that he's left the starving, abused waif he once was far behind him.

Seeing him now – small but strong, muscular, graceful, to say nothing of courageous beyond anything I would have expected from a soul so crushed for so long – the idea that something as unlikely as horseplay with a woman of nearly fifty would snap his finger in two makes me shudder.

Yet he doesn't. He laughed about it even as he stood there with his finger bent where it shouldn't be. Just as Katrin tried to joke about her badly broken arm two years back and how Hemmett made his amputated toe into a comic prop, claiming to no longer be able to count to twenty. My brave children – each one of them now less than whole, less than perfect – as the Prophecy fortells.

No. I will not entertain that Thrun Prophecy, not even here in the privacy of my journal. My dear children <u>*will*</u> *choose their own paths. Hemmett and Borsen are free to go whichever way they will. Katrin, of course, is limited by her rank, but there may be alternatives to that in the course of time. I know I have done the right thing by keeping them ignorant of the great Prophecy, of the three children who will change the fate of Eirdon. Prophecies have a way of becoming self-fulfilling if people know about and believe in them.*

And now there is another child in need standing at my door – Varnia. Angry, damaged, distant, difficult. I would like to send her to Gladdas' school, where her considerable intelligence and drive could be trained in a direction other than domestic work. This would open great opportunities for such a strong and driven young woman – but if it was even suggested that she leave here, thus leaving Borsen, I know she would react viciously. She might even go back to that farm of her father's.

So, what to do for this difficult one? I keep looking for an opportunity, a window, where I could reach beyond that bristling carapace. Eiren tries, with gentle kindness, but gets nowhere. Katrin is friendly but Varnia remains distant. Borsen is the only person who ever sees her as she truly is – and that is not enough. Her wounds are deep and they have not healed. She's grown armor over them, while they fester underneath.

Enough for tonight.

***

Cook looked around the kitchen again, though she knew her particular spoon was nowhere to be found. She'd searched every drawer, cupboard, cabinet and pantry. It had been in its usual place the night before, lying in solitary splendor on the butcher block. In the morning, it had been gone.

She'd asked the family and drawn a blank. But unless some enormous spoon-stealing rat had carried it off in the middle of the night, someone had taken it.

Cook sighed and poured herself a cup of tea, settling at the big kitchen table.

Her initial fear after Borsen's finger was broken had ebbed when it became obvious that word wasn't going to find its way back to the Palace. It had been a fairly baseless terror in the first place, but no-one in the service of the Royal Family in Mordania was entirely free of fear at any time. The Queen was weak and ineffectual while the Council that truly ran the country was corrupt and erratic.

However, the real threat came from the Queen's oldest daughter, Princess Aidelia, first Heiress to the Throne of Mordania. She was now twenty-one years of age and had been wildly mentally unbalanced since birth. She reveled in cruelty and sadism – and had been known to intervene in the punishment of prisoners, demanding that they be tortured or executed in the cruelest manner. The stories were dark and twisted, best not dwelled upon.

Cook knew Menders had been openly defying the Queen's commands for years and that Kaymar was one of her protected Courtiers and had her ear – but still, having injured two Royal children left her in a vulnerable position. That fear had led her to an inappropriate reaction to young Varnia's rage. It had also led to these weeks of grudge holding and simmering resentment.

She suspected Varnia had made her particular spoon disappear. Part of her wanted to let it go without comment, but it was her most valuable kitchen tool. She cooked for one hundred people at times and you couldn't do that stirring with a small wooden spoon!

Cook rinsed her empty cup and paused, looking out the window for a few moments. She had come to The Shadows with Menders and Princess Katrin and had weathered many difficulties and dramas with them. She'd treated both the baby Princess and twenty-year-old Menders as if they were her own children, even though Menders had been a famous assassin at the time, before the Queen had made him Katrin's guardian.

They'd just weathered a terrible year, leading up to this summer, when a plot to remove the Queen and place Princess Aidelia on the Throne had posed a terrible threat to Katrin. Menders' Men had caught many hired assassins trying to get close enough to burn the house or find a way into it. None of that had unnerved Cook as badly as Varnia Polzen's fury over Borsen's broken finger.

With sudden decision, Cook removed her apron and left the kitchen. A quick foray into the wing that housed most of the household staff produced nothing. Varnia was not in her room. It didn't take long to discover she wasn't in the house.

It was a quiet time of day, with breakfast over and preparations for supper complete. The midday meal was a matter of every man for himself – there were always pots of soup or stew simmering in The Shadows' kitchen, bread and cold meats were available, leftover food abounded. Cook was free for a few hours.

She slipped out the Rose Garden door at the end of the Men's Wing and looked around.

At first, she saw no sign of Varnia. Then Cook realized what she had had assumed was one of Menders' cultivated rose bushes in bloom was actually glimpses of the young woman's deep red dress. Varnia was sitting on a secluded bench, almost completely obscured by foliage.

Cook walked forward slowly, wanting to gauge Varnia's mood before speaking to her. Then she stopped short.

Varnia was weeping – not as a young woman would normally cry, easily and freely, but fiercely, her fists clenched against her eyes, her jaw moving as she ground her teeth. She was trembling, each sob making her entire body shudder. The sounds she made were muffled but terrible, the moans of an animal dying slowly in a trap.

Cook retreated immediately, closing the Rose Garden door silently behind her. She cogitated for a moment, then made a beeline to Menders' office. The door was welcomingly ajar, and she popped her head around it.

"I'd like to take out the pony trap for a few hours, my dear," Cook said as Menders looked up from paperwork on his desk. "I have time to go for a gossip round – with you leaving so soon, there won't be so many times I'll be able to manage while you're gone."

"Of course," Menders answered, rising immediately. "I could use a walk, so I'll give you a hand."

He offered her his arm as they went down the broad stone steps to the oval drive, then sauntered toward the stable. Halfway there, Cook stopped short.

"I don't have a thing to give Demon," she said. "Poor boy, he'll be disappointed."

Menders laughed and stepped over to a lanar tree drooping with ripe fruit. He plucked several of the golden ovals and returned to Cook, putting them into her hands.

"We couldn't let him be disappointed," he smiled.

At the stable, Cook went right to Demon's stall while Menders took out one of the ponies and hitched it to a little tub like, two-wheeled cart. Demon snaked his long neck over his stall door, greedily eying the lanar fruit.

"Who's a good boy?" Cook asked delightedly as he made odd murmuring noises and nibbled at the fruit with his sharp, doglike teeth. She scratched between his lop ears while slipping one fruit into her pocket for the pony. Demon noticed and shook his head protestingly.

"Greedy grumps!" Cook scolded him. "You have all these! Begrudging one for the poor pony who's to do all the work today while you laze around here in the cool. For shame!"

Demon took his cue and quirked his head quizzically, making his eyes large and innocent. Cook could hear Menders snickering to himself as he finished harnessing the pony. Demon had his tricks and a bad habit of kicking and biting, as well as the intelligence to know how to devil people. He certainly deserved his name, but he had never so much as snapped at her. She felt no fear of him and was sure that was why he never misbehaved to her. Menders didn't fear him either, but he and Demon were like two rough young men, always thumping and teasing each other.

"All right then, you can have some more when I get back," she promised while Demon put his head on her shoulder and batted his eyelashes at her winningly. "I have to get moving now and find out what's troubling the other difficult creature living here with us." She ignored his mutterings as she walked away.

Menders helped her into the trap, handed her the reins and then watched as she drove briskly away down the drive.

***

Menders rose from his desk and prowled across his study, his jaw clenched. He was obviously struggling to control his temper.

He stared out the window for some time before he turned toward Cook. His anger had ebbed, sadness and pity taking its place.

"I had no idea," he said to Cook. She nodded agreement silently, swallowing hard.

"I assumed that there had been abuse, of course," Menders continued. "It's a given, considering her behavior and defensiveness. And those half-brothers of hers…"

Cook nodded again, trying not to picture the loutish, primitive young men.

"How long ago did her mother die?" Menders asked.

"Mistress Hertzoff says when Varnia was ten years old," Cook answered. "She's been doing all the woman's work on that farm ever since, until she came here when we took Borsen in."

Menders perched on the edge of his desk, drawing in a deep breath.

"I know Polzen is callous to his livestock and it's obvious he is to his children as well," he said in a low voice. "But to let a sick little boy 'take his chance' rather than send round here for Franz? Leave a young girl to care for a child sick to death? I had no idea there was a small child on that farm."

"The boy's birth carried off the mother. Varnia raised him. And from the day he died as she tried to nurse him, she's never said a word to anyone about him." Cook dabbed at her sore, red eyes with her handkerchief. It had been a tearful afternoon.

Menders was silent, letting his mind sort the information Cook had brought home from her "gossip round" – a tour of the village and a couple of estate houses, where she knew the citizens, cooks and housekeepers. It was an excellent way to keep tabs on the happenings in the area. The ladies who ran the households knew everyone and formed a network as complex in miniature as Menders' own far-reaching web of contacts, spies and informants.

Unfortunately, clan or neighborhood loyalties and a sense of minding one's own business led to silence at the wrong times – but Cook could jolly just about anything out of anyone.

"Now we know why she's so attached to Borsen," Cook said softly. "That's what I was coming to. She's acting like a mad girl because she can't bear the idea of being parted from him. You must take her with you."

Menders raised his eyebrows, nodding thoughtfully.

"If she'll come," he mused.

Cook snorted and stood up.

"Don't you doubt it for a minute," she said. "He's her heart's blood. I saw it in her eyes when she was about to tear my throat out when I broke his finger. And really, my boy, shouldn't that young creature have a chance to see the world, considering what her world has been? Why not let her stop working, as she's done all her life, and go along with the other young ones?"

Menders smiled, feeling some relief from the thoughts flooding his mind since he had heard Cook's terrible story about Varnia and her younger brother. He must take some action against the father, but that could wait for now. More importantly, he needed to speak with Eiren about adding another member to their traveling party at very nearly the last minute – and he needed to speak to Varnia.

"Won't it be a problem for you, without a housekeeping supervisor here?" he asked as Cook prepared to return to her kitchen.

"Between myself and Miss Gladdas, I'm sure we can find someone to fill in," she answered briskly, checking her face in the mirror to be sure all signs of tears were gone.

Menders almost laughed as she left the room. Cook and Gladdas Dalmanthea would make a formidable team. Good thing they had gotten along from the outset!

***

"I'd like a word with you," Menders said kindly when he found Varnia sorting out the linen closet in the Men's wing.

She looked up warily, her face pale. Realizing she was terrified that he was going to send her away from The Shadows, he sighed to himself. He continued quickly, to relieve her suffering.

"I would like to invite you to come along with us when we go abroad," he smiled, taking a pile of linens from her as her grip loosened from shock.

Varnia's defensiveness and ferocity were completely absent.

"Do you need me to care for Borsen?" she asked, her voice small and distant.

"No. His finger has healed well. We want you to come because you're of an age with the others and we should have asked you before. I'm sorry we didn't, and I hope you can overlook that."

"I never expected to be asked," Varnia responded. "I'm the housekeeping supervisor, not family."

"I would say that your caring so deeply for Borsen qualifies you as family. You also care about Katrin. Are you determined to find a way to argue? Don't you want to come?"

"To see the world?" she said, her face suddenly lighting up. She looked as if she might even smile – and Menders realized he had never seen Varnia smile.

"Absolutely. If you'd like to attend classes with Katrin and Borsen, you may. Or you may discover things on your own. You may see the world however you like."

Varnia smiled and Menders didn't need her to answer aloud.

***

Cook closed the Rose Garden door behind her. A quick look-round located Varnia sitting on what must be a favorite bench, the secluded one behind the rose bushes.

She made sure the young woman had the opportunity to see her coming so she wouldn't startle, but Varnia was intent on something she was sewing. Cook would wager everything she had that it was a bit of lace being applied to the bodice of a new blouse.

Eiren had gone into action the moment Varnia accepted the offer to accompany the family on their journey to tour the Middle Continent and Artreya. Varnia sewed well and had some nice dresses in addition to her serviceable work clothing, but she had nothing up to the standard she would need for this journey. So Eiren bundled Varnia, Katrin and to her immense surprise, Cook onto the next train, with Menders, Kaymar and Ifor along for security. They had spent the next five days in Erdstrom, the large city some fifty miles north of The Shadows, outfitting Varnia and picking up supplies and odds and ends for her journey.

Varnia was speechless when ushered into the dress shop of a woman Kaymar privately referred to as Madame Intimidation. Cook noticed that Varnia was bedazzled by flounces and ruffles. She was impressed when Madame gently advised the girl away from having everything look like a pile of doilies.

"My dear, you are a distinguished young woman, tall, slender and striking," she explained, taking Varnia's arm and turning her toward a mirror. "Your style should always emphasize your elegance, your height and the long lines of your figure. These are your assets, along with your eyes and the angles of your face. If you put ruffles across your figure or up around your chin, you will lose those things. We will give you ruffles, but at your wrists, long graceful ruffles to show off your exquisite hands. The rest we'll leave to the cut of your dresses."

"But I love lace," Varnia blurted.

Madame laughed outright. "Lace you may have, but we'll show you how to use it," she replied. "We don't have time to do the sort of appliqué work that I will show you, but Mistress Menders tells me you are an expert seamstress. You'll be able to enrich your dresses with lace, my dear. Now, let's take your measurements."

The packages of Varnia's new clothing had arrived earlier in the day. Initially she refused to open them publicly, but Kaymar had teased and threatened to model the clothing himself until she finally gave in. Cook would never forget the look on the young woman's face as she smoothed the elegant garments and at Kaymar's urging, held them up for everyone to see.

And now she was sitting there in the late afternoon, carefully applying a bit of lace to a bodice, as Madame had shown her. She was wearing her hair as the hairstylist in Erdahn had done it, swirled up on top of her head with volume around her face. It drew out her slanted, Old Mordanian eyes, clear gray and lively. What a difference from the way she had always scraped her hair back so tightly!

Varnia heard Cook's footsteps on the path and looked up.

During the time in Erdstrom they had been carefully courteous, but were so busy with shopping and other outings that they had really not spoken directly to one another.

As Cook approached, Varnia moved toward one end of the bench, making room for Cook to sit down. She did so and then pressed a small, soft package into Varnia's hand.

The girl looked astonished and stared down at it.

"That's for you to put on a special dress," Cook smiled. "Go ahead, have a look."

Varnia fumbled the packet open and then slowly drew a length of exquisite Fambrian lace from the folds of paper. It glistened in the summer sunlight like a silvery cobweb.

She didn't speak.

"I wore that on my dress when I married Tomar's father," Cook explained. "It was passed down from my grandmother, to my mother to me. I took it off the dress after the wedding – we didn't intend a wedding dress to be worn only once and put away, but the lace was far too fine to risk. Lace like that was usually passed down from mother to daughter, but I had a son and his father was killed in one of the wars when he was just a tiny baby."

Varnia's eyes were on the lace but she was listening closely.

"The years went by with work and raising Tomar by myself. By the time I married Mister Ordstrom there was no chance of more children. When Tomar married, his wife had her own family heirlooms. So, this is for you."

Varnia swallowed.

"I'll never marry," she whispered.

"It doesn't have to go on a wedding dress," Cook replied. "I'm sure you'll have many lovely dresses over the years. You could move it from one to another, with your sewing skill."

Varnia nodded slowly. Her eyes, sparkling with tears, met Cook's.

"What is your name?" she asked, her voice husky.

Cook smiled. "I've been Cook so long it seems like I forget," she answered. "Mister Ordstrom calls me Vee, but my name is Valdema."

"Thank you, Valdema," Varnia said, smoothing the lace against her deep plum colored skirt. It stood out frostily, every thread intact and perfect. "And for telling Menders I should go abroad with the family."

"You should go. You're young and you're free. What better time to see the world, eh? For all the stay-at-home I am now, I used to long to travel when I was your age. But I married at seventeen – we married young in those days. Tomar was born by the time I was eighteen and life kept going by. I'm content here now, but you deserve your chance just as much as Borsen, Katrin and Hemmett. Go away from here, where there's been so much pain and find some happiness, my dear."

Varnia smiled at her.

"I didn't take your particular spoon," she said, and actually chuckled.

"I know you didn't," Cook replied. "I suspect that devil of a Borsen did and hid it away somewhere. I've set Mister Ordstrom to carving me a new one. It'll take a while to break it in and get it comfortable like the old one, but that's all right. Now then, fold that away so it doesn't get spoiled and then you come and give me a helping hand in the kitchen. I want a Surelian flip cake for the dessert and no-one can beat one so light as you can."

Varnia rose after wrapping the lace, extended her hand and helped Cook up from the bench.

5
CORPORAL CONTRABAND

Villison walked briskly up the drive, an enormous duffel slung over his shoulder. He banged cheerfully through the front door, stopped off at the kitchen to sample what Cook had on the range and ask her to marry him for the fifteenth time, much to Mister Ordstrom's glee. Dumping the duffel on the floor, he proceeded to unwrap some of its many bundles and share them around.

"Gods, where did you get these things?" Cook trumpeted, staring at what Villison was laying out on the kitchen table next to her piles of cut vegetables. "That's Surelian brandy. It's contraband, boy!"

"I got it in Surelia, of course. Where else would I get Surelian brandy?" Villison replied.

"You went to Surelia? You've hardly had enough time to get there and get back!" Cook was standing, arms akimbo, looking Villison up and down, as if she was expecting him to say that he'd flown there. "There wasn't even a train through here at the time you left!"

"Sure there was."

"There certainly wasn't! The train wasn't due until two days later," Cook insisted.

Menders could hear them clearly. He left his paperwork behind and started toward the kitchen, intensely curious about whatever the hells Villison had been up to.

"Cook dear, there was a freight train through right after I walked off the place," Villison explained patiently. "A good run and jump and there's my ride to the coast in a comfortable freight car. I'm sure my hundred and thirty pounds didn't make them burn up much extra chabron. If you're appalled by my crime, I could always mail them a few pieces to make up my fare."

"Boy, you'll be the death of me," Cook said blankly.

"If you don't want the brandy for the kitchen, I'll give it to Sawbones," Villison grinned.

"Now then, don't be hasty," Cook said, snatching up the bottle.

"A woman after my own heart. Don't drink it all now, remember to save some for the Winterfest cakes," Villison teased, revealing another bottle. "Now you can't have this one, it's for Sawbones. I was going to give this other one to Menders, but I observe that he don't drink much. Since I have something else for him, I'll give it to Hemmett's pa, he likes a drink in the evening. Now here's what I got for my Princess. What do you think of that, Cook dear? It'll look a treat around her neck." He held up a strand of Surelian firestones that made Cook goggle.

"Villison, this is all contraband!" she declared.

"Well of course it is, old darling," he replied with satisfaction. "Don't worry, I paid for it all."

"With a soldier's wage?"

"No, with the money I made from the contraband I took over there, Mordanian wine, kirz, waterstone jewelry. I'm a scoundrel but I'm not a thief. All that contraband nonsense is stupid anyway. Why shouldn't we be able to buy things and bring them here?"

"Villison, are you insane?" Menders asked from the doorway.

Villison answered calmly. He'd obviously known Menders was standing there but had never given the slightest indication.

"No, just a shrewd businessman. I've been trading in contraband for years, on my own time. I've got no time for ridiculous laws. It'd help both countries a treat if we were able to trade freely, but some folks just don't see it. Here, I don't think you have a Surelian hunting knife with a firestone handle, do you?"

Villison tossed a wrapped bundle to Menders and merrily continued unpacking, unfurling another strand of gems, this time Surelian smoke sapphires.

"I thought these just the color of your lovely Eiren's eyes, so they go to her," he pronounced gloatingly. "And this here is a little pistol for me good mate Hemmett, wherever he is, probably out chasing women. Take a look at this beauty, Menders." He unwrapped an impressive handgun and displayed it. Menders took it, feeling as if he was trapped in a bizarre dream.

"This is a Surelian Barga & Sincta 44.04," he said incredulously. "They're illegal!"

"Not where I got it. Don't act like you're not a man of the world, Head of House, it don't become ya," Villison grinned. "Now then, I've got a nice bit of Surelian silk for Little Man, who's upstairs hunched over his sewing machine, I'll take bets on it, and a box of them sweets our Kaymar is so mad over. He can fight with his man over who gets the best ones. The rest of this will pay for me next trip to Fambré, where I'll sell it all and come back with more goodies." Villison ended his rapid patter by hefting the still bulging duffel and heading off toward his room. Menders followed in his wake.

"Where is old Hemmett anyway, I want to shock him into speechlessness with his prezzie," Villison grinned, heaving the duffel onto his bed and retrieving the gun from Menders.

"He's taken Katrin over to the school," Menders replied. "Villison, you have to know that I'm concerned about this."

"Eh well, no need to be. I been doing it for years," the little man answered contentedly. "Where do you think Sir gets his Surelian brandy from?"

"Commandant Komroff knew you were doing this? You were doing this when you were a cadet?" Menders said in astonishment.

"Sure! Been doing it since I started at the Academy. Slip out during a vacation break, pop over to Surelia, do my buying and selling, pop back over to school, easy as you please. Then next break, over to Fambre, sell and buy, back home again. No-one ever suspects a little innocent cadet now do they? They think me pack is full of apples for me to gnaw if I get hungry." Villison chuckled to himself and began stowing his various parcels around the room.

"Now that I'm a proper Mordanian soldier, no-one stops me at customs when I come back home. I just walk through, very upright and correct in me uniform," he continued. "In Surelia, well, I've been bribing those officials for so long it isn't funny. They know me by sight and wave me on. No danger of me bringing trouble here, Menders, or I wouldn't do it."

"I can't have Katrin's safety risked, Villison, you know that."

"Yeah, I should say, being as I'm one of her Guard," Villison grinned, no sarcasm or disrespect in his voice. "It won't come here, that I promise. My word is as good as gold. Ask Hemmett, if you won't believe me. Problem is, Menders, you've read all that stuff Hemmett used to write when he was all carried away with how funny things were. Some of it was tripe and lots more was exaggerated. You're also used to being father to half the young folks here, but I don't need a father. I had a good one, though he died too young, and I had a loving nursey and a damned nice Mamma too, though she never knew just what to make of me. Always said I was her darling little changeling boy.

"So, let old Vil be about his business and know I would never do anything that would endanger my Princess. If they ever do come after me, you don't know nothing – but trust me, nobody's coming after me, not with what I know of real contraband smuggling, including the Queen's bloody Chamberlain, puffed up Surytamian twit."

Menders sat down in one of Villison's chairs and eased the door shut.

"You're joking," he said.

"No sir, I'm not," the young man answered, climbing up on the bed. He settled against the headboard and laid out three parcels he'd left out of his duffel. "He's been running contraband for years, most of the Council too. One of the reasons they keep passing policies against trade – they're getting bloody rich off of it while they hurt all the little businessmen who could be doing much better if they could trade in foreign goods. I'm small time if they ever decide to put heads on pikes. Very unlikely that is too, considering how the country is being run."

"How do you know these things about the Chamberlain and Council? I knew about it but how do you know about it?"

"I been around and about, I get to know who people are."

Menders shook his head. "No, Villison, that's not how you know them. You wouldn't have had time to know that much, getting information that way."

"Ah, smart fellow," Villison grinned. "All right, me father was the Earl of Barlwaite."

"What?"

"Do you really think a little street sparrow with an Artreyan accent you couldn't cut with an axe would be at the Mordanian Royal Military Academy? Menders, you shock me, old fellow," Villison grinned, having shifted from his lower class Artreyan accent to an upper crust Mordanian twang in the blink of an eye. "I'm higher born than you are, Lord Stettan."

Menders burst out laughing. He couldn't help it. He'd been completely duped.

"Here, let me take that from you before you drop it and shatter the handle," Villison grinned, holding his hand out for the parcel Menders was still clutching. "Didn't Hemmett ever tell you?"

"No, the bastard," Menders gasped.

"Ah well, he figures it's my business," Villison said, shifting back to his Artreyan street drawl. "Actually, this is the way I really talk. Learned from me nursey, who took care of me because me big brother, Roley – Rolant, really, but we call him Roley – was a sickly child. Poor Mamma was busy with him and doctors and suchlike most of the time. I can sound as high class as you wish, but it's more natural for me to talk like this. I'm a Lord meself. It's an extinct title, no land or income. Me family's got a ton of useless titles to share around, Roley had to take two so they were used up. I do have an income. Roley arranged one for me because he felt that bad about inheriting and me not supposed to have one pennig."

"Then why the Army? Why military school when you were so miserable there?"

"Wasn't miserable, just not interested. I would have liked Special Services. I think I'm cut out for it, but it just destroyed Mamma to think of me being trained as an assassin, though what she thinks soldiers do I'm not sure. Throw flowers at each other, maybe. Nice woman but not very bright. I thought the Army would be a good way to make connections, and I was right. It's just that I find it boring, like school. So, I made me own life outside of it all."

Menders stood and walked over to the window, while Villison occupied himself opening one of his three parcels, extracting a nice length of Surelian lace and spreading it out on the bed cover. He started in on the next bundle, obviously unperturbed by Menders' silent cogitation. An expensive bottle of perfume was revealed and set beside the lace.

"I need someone like you," Menders said. "I'm tempted to take you with us to Surelia and wherever else we go, but I need you here. Can you work with Haakel and Miss Dalmanthea? Do you get along? And can you combine working with them with your regular Guard duties? Security won't be that vital with Katrin gone but it must be maintained consistently."

"Love them like family," Villison said contentedly. "Haakel's a good man and I live for the opportunity to polish Gladdy's boots. I can do both. Keeping more than one ball in the air at a time is me business. And as you see, I got reason to stay here." He unwrapped the third, smallest parcel and revealed a jewelry box. He flicked open the lid to display a Surelian greenstone ring set in heavy gold. He handed the box to Menders.

"Petra?" Menders asked, admiring the ring. It was stunning.

"Of course, in time. I'm not about to bump Mister Ordstrom so I can marry Cook," Villison chortled. "It's early yet, but I won't be jaunting off to Surelia again while you lot are travelling, so I'm thinking ahead. She gets the lace and perfume now. I don't expect to be disappointed, but all ladies deserve a courtship before settling down."

Menders handed the ring back, feeling as if his head was spinning. Petra was one of The Shadows' secretaries. She came from one of the estate farms, had attended Eiren's first school and was Katrin's close friend. He'd offered for her to travel with them, but she had declined. Now he knew why.

"She is quite young," he said. "I feel as if she's under my protection here…"

"Petra's hard on twenty. Your lady was a good bit younger when she came home with you," Villison replied.

Menders gave top marks to how rapidly this unlikely young man accumulated information. He'd only been at The Shadows for two months and he probably knew everything about everyone. He would rattle on to people and before they knew it, they were jabbering right back. He was disarming and came off as not paying much attention to you, when everything he heard was being stored away as securely as the packages he'd stashed all around his room.

Why am I trying to give this fellow advice, Menders thought. He's miles ahead of the pack. He's had a detour or two, out of misplaced pride, but if Hemmett trusts him so implicitly, who am I to distrust him?

Villison, thinking that Menders was still doubtful about his marriage plans, looked over at him with that lopsided grin pulling his left eye shut.

"When I see something I want, Menders, I get it – and I keep it. Petra's safe with me, no fear. I'd never hurt her. I'm ready to settle down and Petra likes me. She wants to start a family and so do I. She'd always be taken care of. I have the means to keep her very well indeed."

"How many peccadilloes of Hemmett's did you take the heat for?" Menders asked blandly.

"Some. Hemmett didn't get into too much trouble," Villison grinned. "He had to work too hard to keep his grades where they were. It was important to him to be first in the class. Not to say that he wouldn't throw out the occasional idea for mischief or get into it. I wanted him to keep a clean record, so yeah, I took the heat for him.

He would look out for me later, because he knew he would get this posting. That doesn't mean I was using him, now. I'd walk into a bullet for Hemmett. We wanted to work together. It was the best way to be sure we'd be posted together."

"I'm glad you're here, Villison," Menders said. "Now, can you compile all the information you have about the Council, people at Court and the like, and give it to Haakel? This is the sort of intelligence we need."

"Absolutely. I have some of it written down already," Villison answered, clambering down from the bed. "I'll put the rest together and give it to him, as well as anything else I find out."

"Ho, Villison!" Hemmett could be heard bellowing in the hallway.

"In here!" Villison answered. A moment later, Hemmett stuck his head around the door.

"Hello Menders," he grinned. "Back from your nefarious expedition, Subordinate? Getting scolded by the boss man?"

"No, informing him of things you didn't bother to," Villison grinned, tossing Hemmett the gun. "That's for you. Don't say I never give you nothin'."

Hemmett goggled at it. "That's a beauty! Thanks!"

"Remember me when you find some pretties while going around the world and I'm holding the fort here," Villison answered.

"Not a worry, I will," Hemmett replied, gloating over his gun. Villison picked up the parcel he'd given to Menders and held it out.

"Come on," he grinned.

Menders took it and peeled back the wrappings, managing not to gawk openly at the incredible knife it held. The blade could split a hair. Intricate designs had been engraved in the blade, and the handle was carved from Surelian firestone, a rare gem that was simply not exported to Mordania.

"Do you know how to invest money?" he asked, turning quickly to Villison.

"Not really, but more than willing to learn," the young man replied.

"Good. You'll give me information, I'll give you information. You shouldn't limit yourself to contraband running, not with your mind." Menders put out a hand and shook Villison's.

"You know what means more to me than anything?" Villison said as he pumped Menders' arm. "That you said you were glad I'm here before you opened that little prezzie. Sir was right about you."

Hemmett smirked. Menders raised his eyebrows in query.

"He said you were the one man on the planet I would never be able to buy," Villison said. "You just proved him right."

THE SHADOWS, MORDANIA

6

CAPTAIN GREINHOLZ AND A DAMSEL IN DISTRESS

Lorein Spaltz waved once more to her best friend, Rivka, as they separated at the road leading to the Spaltz estate. It was school picnic day, the end of the school term. They had stayed late in the afternoon and then helped Mistress Menders and the other teachers clear away.

It had been a wonderful day, the best picnic day ever. Katrin was there since she taught at the school, but most of the rest of the people from The Shadows were there as well.

Menders had designed a terribly difficult scavenger hunt and was merciless in seeing to it that the correct items were found. Borsen ran a pony ride for the little children while several of the Men ran other games. Kaymar Shvalz had been the Fool in the ducking booth. No-one managed to throw the ball accurately enough to duck him all day, until Menders crept up on his hands and knees while Kaymar yelled and hooted, taunting all the children who were desperately flinging balls at the target. Menders rose up suddenly and hurled a ball so hard it made the air ring with its impact on the bullseye. Kaymar went into the water with an enormous splash, swearing.

Best of all, Hemmett Greinholz was home from the Military Academy after graduation. He had refereed all the foot races and games. Lorein entered one of the races and ran until she could hardly breathe. Because she was plump-bodied with long thin arms and legs, running wasn't what she did best. She'd had the glory of having Hemmett declare her the winner and pin the ribbon on her dress! Rivka jealously tugged one of Lorein's braids in retribution. They both thought Hemmett was beautiful.

Now Lorein slung her shoes, laces tied together, around her neck. She took time to make sure they didn't ruffle her blue-ribbon prize and began to skip up the long dirt road toward her home. She didn't run easily but skipping was second nature to her. Her lanky legs ate up the dusty road at a great pace until she came down hard on a stone with her bare right heel.

She ended up rolling in the dust, howling in agony, grasping the offended foot. It hurt so badly she expected to see an enormous hole in it. Inspection showed it to be bruised. The purple mark was already showing.

Lorein sat in the dirt and sobbed, rocking over her foot. It was already so swollen there was no way she could stand on it. She was almost a mile from home. Mamma insisted that she walk back and forth to school as much as she could, because she didn't believe in girls being weak, spoiled little misses. Lorein liked walking, because it gave her time with Rivka and she didn't have to worry with seeing to her pony at the school, which gave her more time at lunch and recess to play with the other girls. Now she wished she had her pony, fat old Pinky, with her.

How was she going to get home? She couldn't possibly crawl, and she couldn't stand on the foot, no matter how hard she tried. Mamma had never let her make a great deal out of every little injury, like some girls who sobbed over a cut finger, but this was very bad.

Lorein looked around and saw several large sticks nearby. She could use one of them as a crutch! She crawled over, grabbed one and managed to get to her feet. The stick gave way the moment she tried to put weight it, tumbling her back into the dirt. The sticks were old and dried out.

She rolled over in the dust and reached for her shoes. Perhaps she could put on the right shoe as a splint. No, her foot was too swollen. What was she going to do?

Suddenly she heard hoofbeats approaching and wondered who it was. Usually only the people from The Shadows came along this road, as a shortcut to the village. It might be Borsen. He was always going over to the village to pick up supplies. She hoped so. Borsen was comfortable. It wouldn't be the first time he'd given her a ride home.

It was a bigger horse, she could hear now, not Borsen's pony. It might be Doctor Franz or Menders. Doctor Franz was jolly, and she wouldn't mind being rescued by him, because he would make a joke out of it all and keep Mamma from scolding about not wearing shoes. If it was Menders it would be even better, because he was so dashing and mysterious, but would also keep Mamma from fussing.

For all he looked stern, Menders knew how little girls could get into situations like this, since he'd raised Katrin from the day she was born.

She could see the horse now and breathed a sigh of relief. It was Ifor Trantz's big black gelding. She liked Ifor. He was shy and quiet, but very kind and patient. He'd taught her to play DeGratz when she was laid up for weeks with aching fever and had stayed at The Shadows because her parents were also ill and couldn't take care of her. All the children called Ifor the Big Bear because he looked sort of like one, but he wasn't a fierce bear.

Oh no.

It wasn't Ifor! It was Hemmett, in his uniform with his cromar slung behind him on the saddle! He must have borrowed Ifor's horse since he had no mount of his own at The Shadows. He was probably on his way over to the village tavern for the evening, where Mamma said he chased after women who weren't good enough for him. Lorein always imagined Hemmett chasing them in the street, playing tag, though she knew that wasn't really what Mamma meant. And no woman was good enough for Hemmett, except maybe Katrin, but he couldn't marry her. He was too handsome and brave and wonderful for any of those silly village girls!

Lorein began scooting back into the dusty ferns at the roadside, suddenly desperate not to have Hemmett see her here, covered with dirt and crying with the pain in her foot. She wanted to go home, but she didn't want wonderful Captain Greinholz to see her wallowing in the dust like a worm!

"Ho there, Firefly!" The horse stopped beside her and Hemmett was looking down at her, using the nickname he'd given her when she was a white-haired little baby whose hair glowed in the faint light of dusk. "What's wrong, honey?" He was down off the horse in a flash, crouching beside her in the dust. "Has someone hurt you?"

His voice was fierce and Lorein understood he was afraid someone had caught her and interfered with her.

"No, I hurt my foot on a rock," she gasped and saw the relief that went through the big, handsome soldier.

"Here now, let me see," he said, carefully lifting her foot while keeping her skirt over her knees so her bloomers wouldn't show. He whistled when he saw the now-black bruise spreading over the sole of her foot.

"Good thing I came along, Firefly," he said. "What happened?"

"I was skipping after I left Rivka and stepped on a sharp stone," Lorein sniffled. Hemmett looked around.

"This fellow, I'll warrant," he said heartily, picking up a big pointed stone. He heaved it far up into the woods at the side of the road. "We'll get him out of the way, so he doesn't hurt any more little feet. Some cold water and ice are what you need, so let's get you home. You won't be winning any more footraces for a while." He gave her his handkerchief. It had his initials and class insignia on it. She knew Mistress Menders had stitched a dozen of them up for his graduation gift. She waited until he turned his back to steady the horse, and tucked the unused hanky in her pocket, so it wouldn't get dirty, then wiped her face rapidly with her skirt.

Hemmett lifted her onto the horse and got up behind her after tucking her shoes and books safely away in his saddlebags. Oh, it was too romantic! Borsen would have heaved her up to cling like a monkey behind him. Hemmett was holding her in front of him, sidesaddle, like a lady in an old picture riding in front of a hero! Oh, Rivka would be so mad! She'd probably slap Lorein over it, but it would be worth it! She was so full of glory over riding with him that she hardly heard the funny stories he was telling her.

Mamma was waiting on the front steps, looking worried, but she smiled when Hemmett waved as soon as she spotted them. She gasped over Lorein's foot and hardly scolded at all except to remind her why she owned shoes. Hemmett carried Lorein into the house and set her on the sofa while Mamma sent for ice and water and tended her bruise.

Hemmett kept saying funny things about sending away for a foot she could use while this one got better. His jokes took away a lot of the hurt, because she didn't think about it. Pappa came from his study and made jokes too until Lorein was tired with laughing. Then Mamma helped her change while the men went into the solarium for a cigar before dinner, Hemmett's trip to chase unworthy women apparently forgotten in favor of taking dinner with them.

He stayed for dinner and into the evening, talking to Pappa and Mamma, but including Lorein as well, though she didn't know much about politics and military things. Then he played the cromar for her, saying it was magic music that would make her foot heal faster. Mamma and Pappa listened too. Mamma always said Hemmett's playing was a credit to Menders' teaching.

When it got late, Hemmett offered to carry Lorein up to her room. Her eyelids were drooping though she was struggling to stay awake, because she wanted to savor every moment he was there. Pappa accepted thankfully. He could carry Lorein, but it would be slung up over his shoulder like a huge baby, because he wasn't nearly as big and strong as Hemmett. But Hemmett carried her upstairs as if she was light as a feather and not the tallest in her class.

He set Lorein on her bed, saying he would stop in next time he passed to see how she was doing. Then he bade Mamma good night and she could hear him going down the stairs, speaking to Pappa and then going out the door.

"Oh, wasn't he wonderful?" Lorein said to Mamma, who was getting her nightgown and hairbrush.

"He's a very fine, kind young man," Mamma agreed. She began brushing out Lorein's long, white blonde hair.

"I'm surprised Katrin isn't in love with him," Lorein said cautiously.

Mamma smiled. "Love is a strange thing," she replied. "It's as well too, because Katrin wouldn't be permitted to marry Hemmett because he's a commoner. Katrin's life is limited in a lot of ways, my girl. People think it's a great thing to be a Princess, but she can't just marry anyone she wishes, even if she did want to marry Hemmett."

"Why would anybody not want to marry Hemmett?" Lorein sighed blissfully. Mamma laughed.

"Love is a strange thing," she repeated. "At one time people couldn't believe I didn't want to marry Menders. The heart loves where it loves."

Lorein thought about that when the room was dark and she was falling asleep. People were always saying she would grow out of being awkward, with a tubby body and thin arms and legs, like a frog. They said she would look like her mother, who was very beautiful indeed. Even Mamma said it and she didn't flatter.

Maybe one day when she didn't have a frog body and wasn't eleven years old. Maybe when Hemmett didn't love Katrin any more.

MORESBY, MORDANIA

7
THE REVENANTS

"And what are you two very diligent young people studying?"

Dorlane Cheval-Shvalz, Princess of Fambré and the mother of Kaymar Shvalz paused on her way from her sumptuous gardens to the Moresby estate house to observe the dashing Hemmett Greinholz and the tall and intense young woman, Varnia Polzen, bending over a book open on the verandah table before them.

Hemmett rose immediately and bowed to her. Dorlane observed that Varnia watched Hemmett closely, standing herself and curtsying awkwardly. We must correct that, Dorlane noted to herself as she smiled and returned their courtesies with a head-bow, then went to take the young people's hands.

"I'm helping Varnia with her Surelian," Hemmett smiled, indicating the textbook.

Dorlane gazed at him in amazement and then laughed aloud.

"Dearest, when the blind man leads another blind man, they both fall off the cliff!" she said, patting Varnia's hand. "Of all the people who speak Surelian here, Hemmett is tutoring you?"

There was a muted 'haw-haw' from Hemmett.

"Now, Your Highness, who better to help her than someone else who struggles with the language and needs a brush-up?" he countered. "On top of that, I don't intimidate her."

Varnia said nothing, but raised an eyebrow and nodded.

Dorlane pondered that for a moment.

"You may be right," she conceded. "However, I have heard you speaking Surelian, young Captain. You will teach Varnia a terrible accent."

"Right now, I'm just trying to understand the grammar and realizing that saying everything with a Surelian accent isn't speaking Surelian," Varnia said wryly while Hemmett snickered.

"Oh-a you cutta me to the heart-a, beautiful-a sanorina," Hemmett told her.

"I am not beautiful, I'm striking," Varnia retorted, smothering a smile.

"Grammar will only confuse you," Dorlane declared. "You don't learn your native language by studying grammar. You learn it by hearing it and speaking it."

"You see-a, beautiful-a sanorina?" Hemmett asked winningly. Varnia shook her head at him.

They were visiting Kaymar's family on their estate, Moresby, prior to sailing for Surelia later in the summer. Moresby had once been part of the massive Stettan land holdings which belonged to Menders' family. Kaymar and Menders' fathers had been brothers. Over the years Kaymar's family had visited The Shadows many times. They had prevailed upon Menders to return the visit before embarking on the world tour that promised to stretch to three years.

Suddenly Dorlane held up her hand for silence, straining to hear.

"Kaymar is shouting at someone," she said tensely.

Varnia was immediately alert, listening so keenly that she quivered like a racehorse in a gate.

"Borsen went down there to sketch," she gasped and bolted away toward the road at a breakneck pace.

"Try to catch her!" Dorlane cried as Hemmett raced after the fleeing girl, hard pressed to gain on her. Dorlane dashed in their wake, holding her skirts up out of the way of her feet. The gods only knew what Varnia was running into.

Kaymar's shouting in the distance had roused the household, family and visitors alike. Ifor rushed down the steps and brought Varnia to a halt.

"Kaymar can take care of things – you mustn't rush into the unknown," he told her as she tried to pull away.

Menders was suddenly there, followed by four of Menders' Men. They immediately spread out and blended into the scenery, moving toward Kaymar's voice, checking every shrub and tree on their way. Eiren ran down the wide house steps and put her arms around Varnia, who was still determinedly fighting against Ifor's gentle grasp on her shoulders.

"Let me go! He may be hurt!" she hissed.

"Stop dear!" Eiren pleaded. "Kaymar is there. I could see from my window. Some people stopped and were talking to Borsen and Kaymar ran right over..."

"I don't believe it!" Princess Dorlane had reached the front lawn where they stood. "I haven't seen them in this neighborhood in years."

Varnia stopped struggling and stared at the fantastical group of people who were approaching, followed by a caravan of colorful wagons. Ifor almost released her, thought better of it and kept his hands on her shoulders protectively.

"Dorlane," Eiren whispered, "are they?"

"Revenants," Dorlane answered firmly. "They must have been after Borsen."

Varnia gasped, staring at the approaching procession.

The Revenants were itinerant people who roamed the roads of many nations. They dressed peculiarly, in oddly clashing colors and styles. Many of the women affected elaborate hairstyles and wore dramatic and flashy cosmetics. The Revenants sought out and traded for peculiar pieces of metal, bits of what appeared to be ancient machines that were occasionally turned up in farmers' fields or found in rockslides and remote places. Often they appeared and disappeared from a district without anyone seeing them coming or going.

It was also said that The Revenants stole children. This was why they were feared and despised. Many a child had been frightened into good behavior with suggestions that The Revenants might just take a naughty boy or girl.

The people coming up the road were led by a swaggering, smallish man who was wearing an improbable clash of colors – bright yellow trousers of very full cut, a brilliant green plaid waistcoat topped off with a scarlet frock coat and tattered black top hat with a blazing orange ribbon round it. He wore unmatched shoes. Each strutting step revealed similarly disparate socks.

Menders abandoned his search of the grounds and positioned himself at the base of the front steps of Moresby, while the members of his family gathered behind him.

The leader of The Revenants halted some ten paces from Menders.

"I be Tellyn Fein, Magic In The Eyes," the Revenant said, bowing slightly to Menders.

Menders said nothing. Eiren and Hemmett exchanged a startled glance – only the residents of The Shadows and the Thrun knew Menders' Thrun name. How could this peculiar tramp be aware of it?

"Or should I speak of you as 'Weaving Man'?" Tellyn Fein continued.

Menders' eyebrows went up.

"What do you want here?" he asked brusquely.

"One moment," Tellyn Fein responded, turning toward Princess Dorlane. He bowed elegantly. "Madame, be you not the owner of this house? I would not slight you in this conversation."

"My nephew, Menders, is the head of our family," she responded graciously. Tellyn Fein bowed to her again and turned back to Menders.

"We stopped to offer a place with us to Reflection Of My Friend," Tellyn Fein said, using Borsen's Thrun name. "He has declined. He be not harmed – see, there he be, coming this way with your cousin." He gestured gracefully toward Borsen and Kaymar, who were hurrying toward them across the sweeping, manicured grounds.

"You tried to take him?" Varnia's voice rang out stridently. She shook Ifor's hands off her shoulders, stepping toward Tellyn Fein.

"Miss, we do not steal children and Reflection Of My Friend be not a child," Tellyn Fein answered gently, smiling at her with tenderness. "Sometimes a child who be not loved or who be neglected and abused, we will include in our family. Sometimes a child who be more than those around him, who does not fit in, wishes to travel with us. But we do not include children who are cherished, who are happy. Only those who be not."

"That sounds like taking a child to me," Hemmett blurted.

"Does it, Light Brighter Than The Sun?" Fein smiled. "A child neglected, starved, deprived of all that a child needs?"

Menders had been watching the conversation silently, but as Hemmett began to argue with Tellyn Fein, he interrupted.

"That's enough for now, Hemmett."

Hemmett looked rebellious, but obeyed.

"Tellyn Fein," Menders began, but suddenly the Revenant leader looked over Menders' shoulder toward the house.

"Light Of The Winter Sun," he said reverently. He and the other Revenants bowed low. The curtain of one of the wagons was drawn back by a thin white hand.

Katrin had come out onto the steps. She had been asleep in her room; she found the heat in this southern portion of Mordania sapped her energy. The commotion must have wakened her. She wore her wrapper and her golden hair was loose, reaching almost to the ground, catching the sunlight like a glowing cascade.

"How does he know our Thrun names?" she asked, coming down the steps and standing beside Menders.

"That is something I would like to know," Menders said, his voice steely, his eyes never leaving Tellyn Fein's.

"Perhaps we know the one who gave them to you?" Tellyn Fein smiled.

After a moment, the corners of Menders' mouth quirked upward slightly. The obvious, which in the heat of the moment, he had missed. Tharak Karak, High Chieftain of the Thrun had given all The Shadows family Thrun names – and surely these traveling people had run across Tharak.

"But we didn't know you were here until we were much closer. Petrahvah felt Reflection Of My Friend and led us his way." Fein indicated a Revenant woman who stepped forward. Her clothing swirled and billowed around her, seemingly weightless – as she herself seemed to be. She didn't seem to walk on the ground. Her hair stood out around her head and the air around her seemed to crackle. She curtseyed toward Menders, Katrin and Princess Dorlane.

"Why Borsen?" Katrin asked, fascinated by the woman's moving garments.

"Because of his talent and his will. But the time for him to join us has passed," Tellyn Fein answered gently.

"Where were you?"

Varnia's voice, breaking hoarsely with emotion, made even the completely composed Tellyn Fein start. Everyone turned to see that she was trembling and pale, her eyes shimmering.

"If you take children who aren't loved, who are neglected, where were you? Why didn't you take us? Why didn't you take him?"

"We did not know in time for him," Tellyn Fein answered. "You were on your journey to where you be now and where you be going. I be sorry, but that be not with us."

He stepped toward Varnia, his hands deliberately held in full sight of them all. Kaymar countered, moving toward Varnia as well, a knife held before him.

"Put that away," Fein murmured. He moved one hand so quickly it was a blur – and Kaymar's knife was on the ground. Tellyn Fein had disarmed one of the world's most accomplished knife fighters so quickly that it seemed like magic.

He reached Varnia, whose head was up as she struggled with mighty emotions.

"Anger has served you well," Fein told her gently as Kaymar retrieved his knife and slid it into its sheath, never taking his eyes from the Revenant. "It has given you strength and sustained you. But now, dear girl, it be damaging you. It be time to let your anger go and learn other feelings. You be where you should, with the people you should be with."

Varnia almost retorted, then looked at the ground.

"Head up, My Fierce Hawk," Tellyn Fein suggested, using the Thrun name that Varnia had never accepted or acknowledged when the High Chieftain gave it to her. "Eyes ahead. Keep walking forward."

He turned back to his caravan of people and wagons. The curtains on the lead wagon moved again and the thin, white hand pointed down the road. Fein turned to Menders.

"We will leave you now," he said. "We will meet again while you make your journey – we will be watching, but we would never bring harm to you. It be for other reasons that we watch."

He bowed low to Katrin again, while The Revenants did the same. Then he strutted forward, leading his procession away.

***

Borsen perched on the edge of the enormous desk where Menders was seated. Kaymar and Ifor, as well as Doctor Franz, Hemmett and Kaymar's older brother, Dorsen Shvalz, were ranged about the luxurious study of Moresby. Borsen was recounting his encounter with Tellyn Fein and The Revenants.

"They never seemed at all threatening," Borsen said in answer to a question from Ifor. "Tellyn Fein spoke to me in Thrun. At first I was surprised – then I remembered it's rather obvious that I might speak Thrun."

Menders smiled. Borsen was the son of his illegitimate half-sister, whose mother had been Thrun. Very little of Borsen's Mordanian heritage showed. He was almond-eyed and raven-haired, with dark golden skin and a haughty nose. He wore a traditional Thrun-style jawline beard and thin moustache and let his hair grow as long as it could, as the Thrun – and for that matter, Menders, who was one-quarter Thrun himself – did.

"It didn't take much daring espionage to divine your heritage, that's true," he said. "What else did he say? Did any of the others speak to you?"

"No. They just came close. The woman whose clothes float touched my hair. It crackled when she did. Fein introduced himself and said, 'Would you like to come with us? We travel all over the world, looking for wonderful things – and sometimes we fly.'

"And you said?" Menders prompted.

Borsen smiled and looked at the floor.

"I didn't say anything. I thought of everyone and touched the watch-chain you gave me – and I saw that Tellyn Fein knew I didn't want to go with them. Then Kaymar started screaming and that was the end of the conversation."

"You wouldn't have been happy if they'd snatched you," Kaymar replied waspishly.

"There was no danger of that," Borsen refuted him quietly. "They weren't trying to force me to go with them. I believe Fein when he says they don't take children. They just seemed sad that I wouldn't go."

"Borsen, they were all around you…" Kaymar retorted.

"Do you really think I couldn't have held them off?" Borsen asked him. His voice was low and respectful, but it had a steely edge that made Kaymar stop fuming and look startled. "I had my gun and several knives and I'm sure they knew it. I would have liked to talk to them for a while."

"Sometimes we fly," Ifor quoted, diverting the tension building between Borsen and Kaymar. "I wonder what Fein meant by that."

Menders raised his eyebrows, then removed his dark glasses and rubbed his eyes gently.

"There are the lighter than air balloons being experimented with in Fambré," he answered. "They usually fail. I can't quite see The Revenants having one."

"Perhaps the fellow was speaking figuratively," Doctor Franz suggested. "Or he could have even been mistaken. From his speech, it was obvious Mordanian isn't his native language."

"Yes, his accent was very odd," Dorsen Shvalz added. "I couldn't place it."

"Perhaps from Chetkinkev."

The men immediately rose, turning toward the study doorway in surprise. All of them bowed to Princess Dorlane. Menders took her hand and settled her in the chair he'd vacated, then perched next to Borsen on the edge of the desk.

"What do you mean, Mahmay?" Dorsen asked curiously.

"When I was a girl in Fambré, many people from all over the world visited the Court," she responded in the measured and captivating tones of an accomplished storyteller. "There was a man – we children called him The Mysterious Visitor – who spoke in the way Tellyn Fein does. Listening to Fein speaking brought back many memories of those days. I finally realized why."

"Did this man actually say he was from Chetkinkev?" Kaymar asked incredulously.

"Indeed," his mother answered with a smile. "He made no secret about it."

Menders looked pensive.

"What language did he speak in Fambré?" he asked her.

"Fambrian – and I anticipate where you're going, Menders. He made the same odd use of the word 'be' when speaking of the present, but he did it in Fambrian, using the word 'esta'. Our friend Mister Fein did the same thing in Mordanian."

"Only in present-tense," Doctor Franz added. "When he spoke in past-tense, he used 'was'."

"I'm hardly a linguist," Kaymar said, his pique with Borsen and The Revenants forgotten as he became intrigued with the problem and his mother's story. "I certainly haven't heard every language in the world, but I've never heard anyone use 'be' that way."

Ifor shook his head. "I'm more of a linguist than Kip, but I have to agree," he added quietly.

"I thought that people who tried to go to Chetkinkev ended up being thrown into the sea in jars – their heads at least," Borsen said incredulously.

"Those are the ones who try to go in. From what we could tell in those days, Chetkinkev had no problem with their own people going out," Dorlane smiled.

Chetkinkev was a nation located in the far north, to the west of Artreya. It had been an enigma all through history. It was entirely closed, and no-one knew what the nation or its people were like. Nature had supplied it with natural defenses in the form of sheer, high cliffs around its coastline, which had been enhanced by monstrous battlements built by its citizens.

No-one had ever traveled to Chetkinkev and come back to tell the tale. Ships were dashed to splinters on the cliffs if they ventured too close. Those who managed to swim to shore and scale the cliffs and battlements re-appeared in the legendary "jars" – waterproof containers holding the heads of the intrepid and curious. No-one had expressed an interest in exploring or invading Chetkinkev in a very long time.

"Well, you know they say the only way to get into or out of Chetkinkev is to… fly."

Kaymar had spoken flippantly at first, but faltered at the end of his sentence.

"Sometimes we fly," Borsen said softly, quoting Tellyn Fein's words. He looked at his uncle.

Menders nodded and then rose, putting his hand on Borsen's shoulder.

"Son, I want you to keep an eye out for our friends while we travel," he directed. "If they attempt to speak to you, go ahead and have a conversation. I don't feel they are any danger to you or any of us – but be prepared."

"Always, Uncle," Borsen said, patting the holster under his jacket where his pistol – small and bejeweled, but deadly – was at hand.

"Same for the rest of you," Menders added, looking at the men around him. "And Princess Dorlane, if you should remember more, or hear something of interest – you know where to find me."

"I will bring you all the tea party gossip," she smiled.

"Very often a serious and valuable source of information," Menders responded, only half-jokingly.

***

"Who do you think Varnia was talking about?" Katrin asked, looking from Hemmett to Borsen.

"Cuz, I don't know," Borsen responded. "I would know if anyone does, she's become like a big sister to me."

"Varnia is very closed in," Hemmett added. "I don't think she wants us to know. Since I've been working with her on Surelian, she's been a little more forthcoming, but for the most part, she's a fortress."

"Aren't you curious?" Katrin asked in frustration.

Both young men looked startled.

"Not really," Hemmett replied. "Men don't analyze as much as women do."

"If she wanted me to know, she would tell me." Borsen pulled out his watch and made a point of looking at it. When Katrin began to speak again, he frowned.

"Katrin, have some sensitivity," he cut her off brusquely, his Thrun accent thickening, as it always did when he was upset. "You know what that farm she came from is like! You've seen her father and those pigs-turned-to-men that are her half-brothers. Use your imagination and understand why she doesn't want to play true confessions about it!"

"But she said something about 'him' – who?" Katrin protested.

"We don't know." Borsen said with finality. "Leave it!"

Katrin was about to flare up at him. She and Borsen usually got along very well, but they could clash. Some of their confrontations had become legendary.

"The Captain of your Guard says we will leave this topic, Your Highness," Hemmett interjected, respectfully but with force. "We will wait for Varnia to tell us in her own way – or not."

Katrin felt a prickle of tears in her eyes. She turned and started to walk away.

Hemmett took several quick strides and put his hand on her arm, stopping her.

"I know you mean well, Willow," he said gently. "But you always want to rush in and sometimes – sometimes that's the last thing you should do. Just be a friend to her."

"She's difficult to be a friend to," Katrin answered.

"I'll grant you that. But you're equal to it. We've got three years. I imagine you'll be able to get through her prickles by the time we get home. Now come on, let's talk about what we're going to do in Surelia."

He put an arm around her shoulders and led her back to Borsen.

***

Kaymar, Baronet Shvalz, Prince of Mordania and Fambré, lounged on a divan in his mother's solarium at Moresby, leisurely lighting a brandy-cured cigar. They were slender, elegant and unbelievably fragrant and potent.

Kaymar knew if he waited long enough, the person he needed to speak with would find him.

He was sorting through the itinerary before him and the rest of his family. They would be embarking for Surelia within days. He, Ifor and Menders had gone over every detail minutely, but Kaymar's mind never rested – not even in sleep.

This made him an excellent security man. He had been Katrin's personal bodyguard since she was four years old. Prior to that, he was the second most lethal assassin in the Queen of Mordania's service. Only Menders, during his own career with Special Services, had bested him.

Menders, however, had managed to eliminate over two hundred enemies of Mordania in an explosion. Kaymar had dispatched all his marks individually. This had pushed him over the edge of sanity. He had never truly recovered and coped with his personal demons as a matter of daily routine.

At times, he went mad, unable to sleep for days on end, talking to trees, walls, people and things only he could see. Most of the time, his madness was under the influence of his considerable will and he functioned normally, ignoring the voices in his head and the hallucinations lurking in the corners of his eyes.

Now thirty, Kaymar was comfortable in his own skin. He had been bonded with Ifor for almost a decade and their union was happy. He was content with his position in Menders' household – second in command, official escort and guard for Katrin, liaison between The Shadows and the Mordanian Royal Court, spy and assassin who could be dispatched anywhere at any time. This journey abroad was a new challenge. He was waiting for someone who had valuable information to come and talk to him.

He was in the process of trying to blow one smoke ring through another when he heard her coming.

"My little Kipper, you are smoking in here with my plants," Princess Dorlane proclaimed with amusement.

"It won't harm their lungs one bit, Mahmay," he answered, rising respectfully.

She opened the door leading to the garden and then seated herself opposite him.

"And now, what do you wish to know?" she asked.

Kaymar was used to his mother anticipating his wishes and didn't pause to marvel at it.

"Fambré," he said bluntly. "What is the true situation there?"

She hesitated, then looked away at the garden.

"Ugly," she finally said. "The present king is as foolish as his brother, who was deposed during the Revolt when I was a girl. Callous about the poverty there. Never carried out the promised reforms."

"What about organization? Are there rallies or protests?"

"Not as of yet, but it won't be long."

"Damn!" Kaymar, finished with his cigar, dropped the smoldering end on the tiles and extinguished it with his foot.

"You must watch Katrin at all times and take great care if you do travel to Fambré," Dorlane continued. "There is terrible danger if she is recognized."

"No-one there could know Katrin," Kaymar replied, turning from where he had been prowling around the sunny room.

"There are those who knew her mother."

Kaymar was so astonished that he sat back down on the divan.

"I see her mother frequently. I can't say there is a close resemblance," he rebutted her.

"Now. I'm talking about then. Their hair and eyes are not the same colors, but there is a marked resemblance in their features and their bearing and mannerisms. There are people who would make the connection almost immediately."

"Royalty or commoners?" Kaymar pulled out a notebook and pencil and began to write.

"Royalty. If you travel incognito, you would be safer, but there is always going to be a chance she'll be known. Her mother traveled widely in Fambré and knew most of the highly born families."

"I need names," Kaymar instructed briskly. Dorlane rattled off a list of names familiar to him as members of the Fambrian Royal Family and aristocracy – the few who had remained or had returned to that nation after the Revolt and Terror.

By the time she was finished, he was concerned. They had no plans to have Katrin anywhere near the Fambrian Court, but it would be possible to run into any of these people if she went into the major towns or cities.

"Not much point in taking her abroad if we have to start striking places off the list," he sighed.

"Take her for a tour of the country areas. There are plenty of picturesque sights, wineries. Take her to the Laval district, where they make the perfumes. She would love that."

"Not a great deal left in the museums in Fambré after the Revolt," Kaymar mused, scribbling away. "That could be a reason not to bother with the towns."

"Lacemaking in the Velmar Mountains – Varnia would be most happy there."

"Mahmay, you're going to salvage what could be a disaster, aren't you?"

"I cannot go there myself and never will be able to. But I know my country. Use a plain carriage, wear simple clothing. Keep the visit short – possibly go for short stays during the children's school breaks." Dorlane became very interested in a nearby plant and started to pinch off dead leaves, grooming it as she would a pet dog.

Kaymar saw a glitter in her eyes – tears. He put the notebook down and knelt before her.

"My dearest Princess mother," he said gently, "you know my past work has required disguising myself – and I'm good at it. I can disguise you so that no-one in Fambré would ever recognize you. It would be delightful to have you come with us. Don't you wish to see it again?"

She smiled slightly, avoiding his eyes. After a moment she shook her head.

"No, Kip," she replied, "and not because I am fearful of being recognized. I would probably be quite safe if I was. The Royal Family and aristocracy are quite open about themselves at this point.

"What I would not be able to bear would be the remembrance of all that happened, of the screams and the torches – the terrible hatred of the peasants and the things they did because of that hatred.

"It's poisoned ground for me. Best to visit Fambré in my dreams. Then I am a happy little girl playing in a beautiful and safe land. My real world is here."

Kaymar put his arms around her and held her close.

Moresby, Mordania
Leptham Dock, Mordania

8
Embarkations

"Ah, the very two young ladies I wanted to see." Princess Dorlane was standing in the doorway of the Moresby solarium, where Katrin and Varnia were bent over a dress of Katrin's. Varnia was showing Katrin how to apply lace to the bodice of one of her dresses. Both girls looked up in surprise.

As they rose to curtsey, Dorlane waved them back into their seats.

"This is one place where I allow no formality," she laughed. "It is my favorite sanctuary. Kaymar loved it as a child because he could be a wild thing in here. He would pretend to be a langhur, growling and leaping around while I tried to read."

Katrin laughed aloud and Varnia smiled.

"Now then, what pretty work," Dorlane exclaimed, perusing the dress that was being transformed. "If you weren't leaving tomorrow, Varnia, I would beg you to use this technique on some of my dresses."

Varnia flushed slightly and nodded.

"I've prevailed upon Menders to come by Moresby again when your journey is done, so I would ask if you would consider it then," Dorlane continued.

"Of course, Princess," Varnia whispered.

"Not in here. I am Dorlane, this is Katrin, you are Varnia. Now, I want to give you both gifts, for going away with. How wonderful to be going to see the world when you're young and free!"

"Why don't you come with us?" Katrin asked excitedly.

Princess Dorlane patted her own right hip.

"A fall a few years back finished traveling for me," she answered cheerfully. "But here at Moresby, I have the entire world. It's always there, no matter how small or restricted the place, if you only know how to look. Something to remember when cooped up on a rainy day."

She laughed and patted their hands, then produced two packages from her capacious dress pocket. She put them on the sewing table in front of them.

"Don't be polite. Open," she directed grandly.

They took up the prettily wrapped parcels and opened them to find two daggers, their sheaths and handles jeweled and embellished with repousse work and gold decorations.

"I can't possibly accept something this valuable," Vania gasped.

"And risk my wrath?" Dorlane laughed.

Katrin had her dagger out of its sheath and was inspecting the blade.

"This is beautiful!" she exclaimed. "Is it Samorsan?"

"Well done!" Dorlane answered. "Indeed, it is. There is a story of these two knives. Would you like to hear it? I warn you – it is not all pretty."

Katrin put the dagger back into its sheath. Varnia looked intently at Dorlane.

"As you know, I am a Princess of the Royal Family of Fambré," Dorlane began. "I was the niece of the King. My mother was his sister. Growing up at the Court was wonderful for my sister and me – we were shielded from the less savory things that went on there. Being children, we saw it all as magical and splendid.

"But the King, my uncle, was a weak and foolish ruler. He ignored the fact that the people of the country were poor. He felt they were of no import. Only great matters of state, arranging marriages for his children, Court entertainments and hunting mattered to him. The trials and difficulties of what he called 'the common people' concerned him not at all – though in any nation 'the common people' *are* the nation."

Katrin nodded. Menders had taught that from the time she first sat on his lap to have stories read to her. Varnia looked fierce.

"I'm sure you both know the story of the Revolt of Fambré and of the time that followed, The Terror," Dorlane continued.

Both girls nodded. History classes at Eiren's school had been part of their educations. Eiren thoroughly analyzed the Fambrian Revolt with the students. Katrin was plagued by nightmares after reading about The Terror, a time when members of the Fambrian aristocracy and royal family were hunted down, tortured and killed by common people who had been taxed beyond endurance and treated as less than human by the wealthy.

"My dear Pappa was a military man," Princess Dorlane continued after a moment. "He was more aware of the situation in Fambré than my mother, who had been sheltered all of her life. He wanted to leave Fambré and go to Samorsa or Barambos but Mahmay wouldn't hear of it.

"He came back from a mission to Samorsa with these daggers – they are ladies' daggers and were commonly carried at that time. Very dashing and glamorous. We were astonished when Pappa gave them to us and Mahmay said that he was silly. He insisted we learn to use them and had us practice every day with him. We thought it great fun and very dramatic at first. We became quite skilled. We learned to throw them at targets as well. I was best at fighting with the knife, my sister was far better at hitting the targets.

"My sister was fourteen and I was sixteen when The Revolt began. Pappa moved us quickly to our country estate and for a while, things seemed to be secure. Then he moved us again to a small cottage near the ocean, in the middle of the night. We didn't know it then, but the King had been captured and executed by the leaders of the Revolt. Our Pappa was trying to arrange an escape by sea and needed us at the seaside so we could be taken away to safety.

"We had a few servants with us at first but then they ran away. We were alone, the four of us, and only Pappa with any idea of how to cook and keep house. Mahmay was bereft away from her friends and family at Court. She did not know if they were dead or alive. Pappa spent hours every day on the beach, watching the sea with his spyglass to see if the boat arranged to come for us was on the way. He always insisted on our knife practice, no matter how unhappy or tired we were from trying to keep the house clean and gathering wood for the fires.

"Things had changed so much. Now, if we complained or protested that we didn't want to practice with the knives, Pappa was very stern and wouldn't indulge us. He made us work for hours on our skills. We began to hate the sight of these knives and told each other we should hide them and say we'd lost them. Foolish, but we were kept so in the dark at the time. We had no idea of the danger and the condition of the country."

Katrin reached out for Princess Dorlane's hand. Varnia swallowed audibly.

"The terrible night came. Pappa had been down by the shore all day, peering through his glass. He finally came rushing into the cottage, shouting that we must leave, the boat had come. He said there was no time to take anything with us, that we had to run as quickly as we could. When my sister tried to pick up her case of jewelry, he took it from her hand and threw it on the floor. He asked us if we had our knives. Once he saw they were strapped around our waists, he told us to run – to run down to the sea, not to stop, not to look back.

"His voice was terrible. When we hesitated, he bellowed for us to go, to run, that he and our mother would be right behind. We were so shocked that we ran out of the cottage.

"Then we stopped and looked back.

"Our father had picked up a gun and was handing another to our mother. Though this was frightening, what terrified us was what we saw coming toward the cottage – a huge line of torches moving up through the fields and woods. They threw a flickering, reddish light as they drew closer to the little cottage. We knew those two guns would be no use against so many.

"The torchlight was enough by then that our father, looking out the door, could see us standing there, transfixed.

"'Run! Run to the sea!' he shouted desperately. 'Run to the sea!' His face was terrified. It was then we knew our parents were buying us time with their hopeless attempt to fight the people who were coming.

"We did as he bid. We ran, our dresses catching on branches and rocks. But we had been seen. Then we heard our father's gun and his voice as he shouted to us again to run to the sea."

Princess Dorlane paused and closed her eyes for a moment.

"You don't need to finish," Varnia whispered.

"Oh, but I do," Dorlane answered. "The people with torches had seen us and some of them gave chase. We could hear our father screaming – and then our mother. His voice was silenced right away but hers went on and on..."

Varnia began to shiver. Princess Dorlane reached out and took her hand, gripping Katrin's fingers with sudden strength at the same time.

"I saw that my sister had her knife in her hand and drew my own. We turned and fled toward the shore, but we were too late. Men raced up to us and laid hands on us.

"I swung my knife at the one who had grabbed me, slashing at his hands and face again and again. Pappa had never told us that some men will continue to fight even though wounded. I slashed and stabbed, but I could smell the drink on him. He probably wasn't feeling a thing. I could hear my sister fighting nearby and that gave me strength, though the man was grappling with me and trying to get my knife. I was tiring – fear will give you strength for a while, but it saps you too.

"He finally managed to trip me. He fell on top of me and began squeezing the wrist of my knife hand. I managed a couple of slashes, but my strength was gone. He got the knife from me and I was certain he would kill me. I tried to fight him but could barely move. He was very big and heavy, you see.

"He began cutting at my dress and I realized what he was doing. I found strength then and hit him in the nose with my fists. He roared and rose up in pain – and then my sister threw her knife as true as she did during target practice. It struck his throat and a great surge of blood ran down. I scrambled up and took my knife from him – and between us, we finished him. My bold sister had already killed the man who attacked her."

"Good!" Katrin burst out. Princess Dorlane smiled grimly and patted her hand.

"We saw more men coming, their torches bobbing along in the dark. We turned and ran together across the dunes and down to the sea.

"The lights of a ship were not far! We ran toward it, screaming for help. The men with torches were on the beach, slow as they ran across the dry sand, but moving faster when reached the firm wet sand by the water. I had lost my shoes and the shells and rocks cut my feet. My breath hurt at every gasp but the knowledge of what those men would do kept me going as fast as I could run.

"Suddenly men appeared from the direction of the ship, caught us up and pulled us into the water where a small boat was waiting. They scrambled in and dragged us in as well. The men at the oars pulled as fast as they could while the men coming with the torches ran into the water after the boat. The water is shallow on that beach. They reached the boat and were clawing at it, but the sailors were stronger. They beat those men with their oars until they sank into the water. Then they began rowing and soon had us out of their reach.

"The peasants howled after us, screaming that they would kill us, roast us on spits. The sailors kept asking about our parents, if they were on the beach as well, if they needed to try to find them.

My sister and I were trying desperately to get our breath. She was wounded from her fight with the man who had attacked her. Seeing how she was bleeding with a sailor binding up her wounded arm, I realized I was covered with cuts and bruises myself.

"Then I looked at the shore. Where our cottage had stood, there was a brilliant blaze. It was then I knew our parents were dead."

Both Katrin and Varnia were speechless at the horrible tale. They exchanged glances, then looked back at Princess Dorlane.

"And you wonder why I tell you this terrible story," she said, coming back from somewhere far away and smiling faintly. "You are both going out into the world and though that is wonderful, it can also be dangerous. I know Menders has taught you both to defend yourselves, but sometimes young women simply do not see or suspect danger. They can make foolish choices, foolish mistakes. I seek to arm you, both with your knives and with the knowledge that the world as you know it can change in a moment. Live fully, but be aware."

Both girls were silent and Princess Dorlane sat very upright.

"And to finish," she said firmly, "I will tell you how life continued to spin out. My sister and I were taken to Samorsa and cared for by the Royal Family there. We were related you see – if you're part of a royal family, you're related to every other one. They're always marrying one another. We learned the truth of The Revolt and the terrible slaughter of many people – all the royalty and aristocracy, but many other people also. Once people get the taste for killing and cruelty, it is difficult to make them stop. Fambré was in chaos for many, many years. It is troubled still.

"My sister, Princess Charina, met the Prince of Hetzophia and is now the Queen of that exotic land. I met a Prince of Mordania – your cousin Kaylen, young Katrin. He was Menders' uncle. I married him and came here to Moresby and had my two wonderful sons. Life went on, despite the tragedy and pain of my last days in Fambré."

"I never think of Mordania as having Princes," Varnia said quietly. "It is always ruled by a Queen."

"Yes, from the days of the great Glorantha," Princess Dorlane agreed. "Always Queens with no kings or princes in sight. No boy children in the immediate Throne line allowed to live – a terrible thing, in these modern days. But thankfully male children who are more distant from the Throne are not killed, and so we have Menders, Kaymar, Dorsen and my Dorsen's little boys as well. Borsen is also a Prince of Mordania, though from the wrong side of the blanket. They don't make much of it, particularly Menders, but they are royalty and Princes at that."

"Now, my dears, keep those knives by you on your world tour – and be good friends to one another. The spirits of my sister and I will go with you."

Katrin hugged her impulsively and Princess Dorlane laughed out loud.

"That's the other lesson here – life goes on and it can be good, if you seek the goodness. Now, Varnia, show me how you do this delicate work. I am going to try it on some of my own dresses!"

***

Kaymar wove through the crowd on the deck of the Carmathia, a wine glass in each hand. He moved with a grace that was almost reptilian. It was fascinating but strangely repellent to the people who watched his progress. He looked at none of them, but Menders, waiting by the deck railing, could tell Kaymar was amused.

"Don't frighten our traveling companions," he said wryly as Kaymar reached him and handed him one of the glasses.

"I'll give them something to talk about," Kaymar smiled. "And here come our charges, just on schedule."

Katrin and Borsen ran toward the opposite rail. They were followed by Varnia and then Hemmett.

Menders made eye contact with a young man across the deck, who moved unobtrusively nearer to the young people, but stayed out of their line of vision. They were intent on the spectacle of the ship being made ready to leave and the people waiting on the dock below.

***

Katrin rushed to the rail of the steamship.

"Look at all the people!" she exclaimed. Borsen laughed and handed her a paper streamer that could be tossed down to observers on the dock.

"Pick a likely young man, hold the end of the ribbon and throw that down to him," he directed.

"Oh, who?" Katrin laughed, scanning faces.

"I've found mine," Borsen grinned, holding tight to his streamer.

"Here Varnia," Hemmett said, offering a streamer to the young woman. "You were stampeding here so fast, you forgot to pick one up."

"Who would I throw it to?" she asked sharply.

"Anyone you want," Hemmett laughed. "Don't give me a glare. Ah, I see just the sweetheart I'll bestow mine upon."

He whistled shrilly, until a curly haired young woman looked up in his direction. He blew her a seductive kiss and held up his paper streamer for her to see.

She laughed and held out her hands.

Borsen tried his best to jostle Hemmett as he tossed the streamer to his temporary sweetheart, but it was like a puppy trying to upset a warhorse. Hemmett stood a foot and a half taller than his diminutive friend and was honed to physical perfection by years of military training. He laughed a hearty 'haw-haw' and threw the streamer directly into the hands of the lady below.

Varnia was looking around, forgetting to guard her expression. She was fascinated by the sounds, colors, the throngs of people on the deck and on the shore. The scent of seawater mingled with smoke from the ship's funnels. The ship vibrated slightly from the thrum of its engines. Overwhelmed, she looked at the crowd, her paper streamer clutched in her hand.

Borsen waggled his eyebrows at someone below and flung his streamer down. It was caught by a handsome young gentleman who Katrin realized had been looking up at Borsen the entire time they'd leaned on the railing.

"He likes you," she grinned. "Are you sorry it's too late to do anything more than throw a paper ribbon to him?"

"Safest way to flirt is when they're too far away to do anything," Borsen laughed. "What about you?"

Katrin scanned the mob below. She tossed her streamer indiscriminately.

It was caught by a red-haired man with a distinctly unlikeable face. He began looked up the length of the streamer to its source. His expression was so repulsive and sneering that Katrin drew back, moving into Hemmett's shadow.

"Ugh," she said.

"Did you catch a pigfish, Willow?" Hemmett laughed. He pressed another streamer into her hand and pulled her around to stand on his other side. "Toss it out again, but aim this time. No point in slinging it out any old how."

Katrin shook off the feeling of repulsion she'd formed about that man. He hadn't even seen her. The streamer could have been from anyone. She wasn't going to let that brief jarring contact spoil a thing.

She wasn't even Princess Katrin Morghenna of Mordania, second Heiress to the Ruby Throne any longer. They all had new identities and she was Emila de Cosini, daughter of the wealthy Surelian merchant, Erco de Cosini. She was not going to have to worry about being a princess for three years!

She stepped back up to the rail and tossed out her streamer, letting the breeze decide where it would land despite Hemmett's advice.

It was caught by a handsome sailor, who saluted smartly and held the end of the bright red streamer aloft with a grin. Katrin scanned the crowd quickly, but saw no sign of the red-haired man with the evil face. Good!

Varnia leaned on the railing beside Katrin and gently let her ribbon pay out, down, down, into the hands of a ragged little street boy hanging around the dock to see the ship set out. He giggled with delight and capered a bit, looking up with a sweet smile, excited to be chosen. He waved and Varnia waved back.

Suddenly Katrin's sailor pointed vigorously at his own left ear. Before Katrin could ask Hemmett what that meant, the horns and whistles of the ship blew in a deafening cacophony.

Katrin and Varnia both jumped, while Borsen and Hemmett laughed at them. Both young men had traveled by ship to Surelia before and enjoyed their superior knowledge very much. Hemmett's loud laughter blended with the music of the band on the shore as the huge fans thrashed the water to foam and the boat moved away from the dock.

The four streamers stretched out and quivered until, one by one, they broke and drifted down into the water.

"I've left Mordania!" Katrin cried excitedly.

***

Eiren had come on deck for their embarkation and was as excited as Katrin. She had traveled between The Shadows and Erdahn, as well as to other towns within Mordania, but this was her first international voyage. She was overjoyed to see how happy Katrin was, how Varnia was smiling openly and the antics of Borsen and Hemmett as they teased the girls good-naturedly.

"Wonderful to see them all so happy," she smiled, leaning against Menders' side. He wrapped his arm around her waist.

"Indeed it is," he replied. "Glad I didn't insist on using our own boat?"

"Yes," she said firmly. "For all the reasons we've discussed and more. Seeing Borsen able to enjoy being on a ship and not hanging over the back railing, being horribly sick, is well worth the extra surveillance."

Originally, Menders had planned to move their party from Mordania to Surelia on The Shadows' steam launch, which was regularly used to cross The Gulf of Mordania between The Shadows and Erdahn. It was a great improvement over taking the train, which often involved serious delays due to weather. But when Menders had proposed the plan of taking the launch to Surelia, Ifor, who usually piloted the vessel, shook his head.

"The Gulf and The Sea of Surelia are two different things," Ifor had said deliberately, in his low, heavy voice that sounded like two slabs of lead being knocked together. "You're in very deep water there. You can have massive waves come up quickly, there are squalls. Borsen wouldn't be the only person who was seasick, that's a surety."

Menders had bowed to Ifor's expertise. Ifor was from Southern Mordania fisherfolk and knew the ocean well. His own father had been lost in a squall on The Sea of Surelia, which led to him being sent to the Mordanian Military Academy at twelve, where he had become a successful spy with a genius for codes and languages.

So, they were testing the safety of having Katrin travel on a public vessel. Menders' Men were positioned all over the Carmathia, all watching the four young people. Ifor was nearby, holding the leads of the four massive boarhounds accompanying the family. The dogs were pets, but their faithfulness and ferocity made them effective guard animals as well. Kaymar was watching and occasionally patrolling. The young people were too intent on their new experience to notice. It was a delight to see Katrin so happy and fascinated by everything around her.

"How is our other young lady doing?" Menders asked Eiren, snagging a glass of wine for her from a passing wine steward.

"Quite well, I think," she answered, sipping it and then looking at him in amazement. "My dear! What is this?" she asked. "It's wonderful!"

"The Surelians call it Dreams of Angels," Menders smiled. "To be taken in very small quantities."

"Yes, it's powerful," Eiren agreed. "Varnia is warming up a bit, but she's still a very closed book in many ways. She'll definitely need our support."

"That's why she's here," Menders replied. "I see she gravitates toward Hemmett – is there something there?"

Eiren shook her head decidedly. "No and never will be. They aren't attracted in that way. It's that big heart of his, seeing someone who needs protection and friendship, but who pushes it away. The perfect knight."

Menders smiled, but had to admit she was right. Hemmett had a tenderness toward anything in need of care, be it a baby bird or a hostile and defensive young woman.

"Is she interested in attending the university with Katrin and Borsen?" he asked.

"Nothing definite yet. She was a diligent but average student," Eiren replied, referring to the years when Varnia attended her school after hours of chores on her father's farm. "She may not find going to university as alluring as Katrin does."

"We'll let her set her own course." Menders took Eiren's arm and guided her over to the railing, where they joined the younger set in watching Mordania grow smaller in the distance.

LEMHOS, SURELIA

9
FREEDOM IN A SUNBURNT LAND

Dear Petra,

We're just finishing our first week of university classes and since it's so hot here I can barely move in the afternoons, this is a perfect opportunity to write to you. Other than the heat, things are wonderful!

Hemmett, Borsen and I go to the University on weekdays. Borsen and I are taking art studio and art history and all three of us are taking a Surelian military history class because Hemmett was interested. He's acting as my bodyguard and has to sit through the rest of our courses, so we felt it was only fair to do something he was interested in. Actually, the military class is quite fascinating. I wish I could say the same for art history, which is a crashing bore. Borsen and I wanted to drop it, but Menders is making us finish. He says life involves a lot of situations where you have to tolerate things, that we can learn something from the class even if the professor isn't as fun and interesting as the art studio professor is.

Art studio, on the other hand, is hilarious. The professor moved Borsen and me into a small group of students who have advanced art skills. He's a very dramatic Surelian, given to fits of temperament. When the class began he didn't like Hemmett just sitting in the back of the room, being a bodyguard. So, he insisted that Hemmett join in. Now Hemmett draws like a grundar and has no interest in trying to be artistic. He declined but the professor threw a tantrum. Hemmett had a terrible time trying not to laugh while this little, bald Surelian in a smock shouted and stamped his tiny feet in their Surelian road-slappers.

So, after the professor fussed enough, Hemmett went to an easel that was turned slightly away from the class. He picked up a brush and started painting away. Professor was very happy, beaming, rushing around the room and criticizing everyone. Told me I make so much mud of my paints that he expects to see toads hopping out of it. Told Borsen that his sketch looked like he'd used the wrong end of the pencil (if you're good he criticizes you mercilessly, if you're not, he's very kind.) Then he went to Hemmett, who was looking very artistic, brandishing his brush with great dignity.

Well, I've heard about someone throwing a Surelian Fit and now I've seen it. The professor yelled and stamped and called Hemmett names. He took away the palette and hit him with a paintbrush, with Hemmett haw-hawing all the while. Turns out he had painted a bunch of stick figures holding hands, a sun with a smile on it and stick flowers with little faces on them, like a three-year-old would.

So, the professor rumpussed for a while but then started to laugh and pinned the "painting" up on the wall. Hemmett is now banished to the back of the room and not forced to produce art.

Best thing of all about going to the University is that we take lunch in little cafés or restaurants nearby, or bring a picnic and eat it in one of the public parks! You may shrug this off but for me it's wonderful.

You see, Menders has been very careful and he's found that no-one knows we're away from The Shadows. He talked to me right before we registered for classes. He said things were safe enough for me to go to school with only Hemmett and Borsen – no Kaymar, no Menders' Men shadowing us! We can go to museums and shopping too!

I still can't go out completely on my own, as Varnia can, but it's been so much fun. We even had beer to go with our sandwiches the other day! Don't tell on us now.

The villa is beautiful, long and rambling with many balconies and a large green vineyard, gardens and those stunning umbrella trees all around. The five men who live here all the time are very nice. They were assassins at the same time Menders was, but they all had terrible experiences and their minds gave way. They need a very stable environment and predictable routine.

There is a housekeeper here, Madame Spinta, who is perfect for providing routine because she's one of those people who is utterly inflexible. She's a paragon: the house is perfect, the grounds are perfect, the meals are perfect. The only problem is that she hates Borsen because he's Thrun. He takes it in stride. Since Menders doesn't want to upset the residents here, he doesn't come down on her as he would if she were at The Shadows and treating Borsen badly.

You asked how Varnia is doing in your last letter – she decided against going to the University this term. She was going to, but then Menders realized she was upset about it and told her that she could see Surelia in her own way, that she wasn't required to attend. Since then she's been a lot more relaxed, and spends a lot of time going on walks alone. I asked her what she does and she said she just observes the people and how they live. She also likes to go to museums and galleries by herself. She doesn't lose her temper much, but I can see she's ready to take a swing at Madame Spinta for being rude to Borsen.

You must let me know the moment Vil asks you to marry him! I know you wouldn't have said anything if you weren't sure of it, so now it's a matter of when. I'm sure you know what's best, it's just that you haven't known him that long. He's so funny and nice, I'm sure you'll be happy. How funny to think that we're getting old enough to be married!

It's really getting hot now and my head is starting to pound. Eiren is out looking for some cooler clothing for us and finding out what Surelian women do for underwear. We're sweating right through our corsets every day and they make things that much worse – that and our long hair. The women here wear theirs long, but up in all sorts of elaborate styles. I pin mine up, but it makes the headaches even worse.

Time for a cold bath and a lie down with a wet cloth on my head. Write to me soon!

Love,

Katrin

Dear Vil,

I saw that Katrin had a letter going out to Petra and wanted to let you know your old mate and commanding officer has not snapped his cap, letting Katrin go to University with no-one but Borsen and me to watch over her.

Menders hit upon the idea and I think it's a good one. Katrin has always hated being watched and shadowed. When she was a little girl she used to try to run away from her guards all the time.

Once when Kaymar was sick with melancholia but still guarding her, she ran from him and was caught by Menders. There was a great to-do, because Menders was so mad at her taking advantage of Kaymar's illness that he was about to spank her. Kaymar came running after her and ended up spanking Menders, so to speak. They had a bloody great fistfight in the road, Katrin ran away to the house in terror and Menders ended up with a black eye so bad he had to lie around for almost a week. Kaymar looked like someone who got caught in a gristmill.

So, Menders cooked up a way to have it seem that Katrin is going around with just Borsen and myself or with me alone as her official bodyguard – but all the while we're being shadowed by Kaymar or another one of the Men. She's all giddy at the idea of eating at cafés and going to class that she doesn't even notice them. So far, so good.

It's ghastly hot here! We're all back from the University for the day. Time for a cold wash and a nap. I admire the Surelian custom of a good sleep during the hottest time of the day. Poor Katrin just wilts with the heat and I'm starting to think she's never going to get used to it. So off to splash at my washstand.

Let me know when you ask Petra the big question and here's a hint – she's already figured it all out, so don't sit around too long.

Your best mate,

Hem

***

Varnia settled on her favorite bench on the deeply shaded patio and looked out at the rows of grape vines covering the hillside that sloped down from the villa. She had a book in hand that had been left for her by Menders.

When they'd first come to the villa, she'd found herself at loose ends for the first time in her life. She'd known relentless work from the time she could carry things. By the time she was ten, with her mother dead, she was doing all the woman's work on her father's farm. She'd gone from there to The Shadows at eighteen and had soon become the housekeeping supervisor. Her days had always been flooded with physical activity and work.

At first taking long walks around Lemhos had been enough to keep her mind occupied. She loved exploring the small side streets, seeing how the people lived, enjoying a freedom and leisure she had never known. She didn't have to small talk or curtail her wandering for anyone else's wishes. The Surelians were friendly but polite and could tell she wanted to keep her distance. They went about their business without feeling impelled to engage her in conversation.

In time, she was familiar with the area and her walks didn't satisfy her active mind any longer. She began visiting the famous museums, but found herself at a loss, as she was unable to read the Surelian exhibit plaques. Her knowledge of art was limited, so other than a general appreciation of what she considered pretty paintings, she felt confused.

One afternoon she ventured into the villa's library, hoping to find a book that would occupy her interest. She had seen the even larger library at The Shadows, of course, but had never ventured to look into the books – she always had far too much to do. Now she found this library daunting. She had no idea how the books were arranged. Many were on subjects she knew nothing about – others were in languages she did not know. Entirely humbled, she left the room packed floor to ceiling with books behind.

The next day, Menders saw her sitting on the patio, raising the hem of one of her dresses to the shorter Surelian style, which was much cooler and more comfortable. He came over, complimented her work and then took a seat opposite her.

"I ran across a couple of books that might be of interest to you," he said quietly. "I've put them on the table in the hallway outside your room, if you'd be interested in having a look at them."

Varnia nodded silently, indicating permission when he asked if he could smoke a cigar. They sat together without speaking, she stitching, he puffing – both of them comfortable with silence.

Menders had left her a simple travel guide to Lemhos and a novel based in Surelia. She'd already scanned a few pages of the novel and was anxious to read it. The travel guide was the sort of book to carry with her when she was rambling around the town.

She opened the novel and became absorbed immediately. The late afternoon air was cooling, and the patio became even more shadowy as the sun began to set.

Varnia dropped the book as someone withdrew the pins from her coiled up hair, letting the long locks drop to the ground. She was so frightened her breath came short as someone stroked the long fall of her hair.

"Mina, I'm so glad I found you," a man's voice whispered. "You stayed away for so long, I thought I would never see you again. Darling Mina."

Movement behind her, then one of the five permanent residents of the villa walked around in front of her. Varnia was frozen in place as the man smiled – and then the smile faded.

He blinked and then stepped back.

"I'm very sorry, young lady," he said, looking embarrassed. "I thought – I thought you were my Mina. Your hair is so like hers. I'm very sorry."

Varnia forced herself to smile, but was unable to speak. She had never heard him coming up behind her – and though he was quiet and seemed gentle, he was mad.

She was used to Kaymar, who was also mad – but his madness was under his control almost all the time. The five unfortunate men who lived here at Menders' villa were not under control and needed very careful handling.

"Good evening, Starnor."

Varnia had never been so glad to hear Menders' voice. He stepped through the glass double doors from the villa dining room just as if he was having a casual look around his domain. The mad ex-assassin smiled suddenly and turned away from staring at Varnia as if he couldn't really understand why she wasn't someone else.

"Menders!" he exclaimed, as if he hadn't seen Menders in years, though Varnia had seen them speaking in the vineyard earlier that afternoon. "So good to see you! I was just speaking with this young lady. I thought she was someone else."

"This is Varnia Polzen," Menders said conversationally, but with a firm note beneath the polished courtesy. "She is traveling with us."

"Oh yes. Miss Varnia, I'm very pleased to meet you," Starnor said, smiling at her just a little too enthusiastically. He seemed agitated and worried. "Menders, have you seen Mina? It's been a long while since I've seen her. It's very late for her to still be away from home."

"I believe she'll be coming in by the side gate," Menders answered conversationally. "I saw her in town only a little while ago and she was coming this way."

"Please excuse me, I have to meet her," Starnor said breathlessly, then rushed away across the darkening vineyard toward a gate on the far wall.

"I'm sorry about that," Menders said gently, sitting across from Varnia. "I never thought… Mina was his wife. She died years ago. She had raven black hair like yours, very long – like yours. Seeing you from behind must have reminded him. He had that trick of pulling out her hairpins. Drove her to distraction with it sometimes."

"He startled me," Varnia said, dusting off the end of her long tail of hair before she began to coil it up again.

"Yes," Menders answered. "He's harmless, has been known to do it to other women with black hair. It's easy to distract him – he won't even make it to the gate before he forgets why he's going there. Watch him – see? The moment something catches his attention, he forgets what he was doing. Poor Starnor. He was such a bright and funny fellow."

"What happened to her – to Mina?"

Varnia was startled to find herself asking the question. She was accustomed to a strict code of minding her own business. Menders didn't seem at all surprised or displeased.

"It's an ugly story, so I'll make it brief," he answered. "Someone Starnor was assigned to shadow and assassinate discovered that plan and arranged for a group of Surelian assassins to enter Starnor's home. Mina was there, alone. They killed her. It wasn't a swift or merciful death. Poor Starnor came home and found her. His mind broke entirely and he's never recovered."

Varnia said nothing, images flooding her mind, no matter how brief Menders' story was.

"If I believed he was a threat to you, I would take action immediately," Menders told her after a moment. "If you're uncomfortable about him, please tell me and I will make arrangements to have him watched when you're out here."

Varnia thought for a moment.

"I'm not afraid, now that I know," she replied. "I see how you distracted him. You don't need to do anything."

"You'll let me know if that changes – if you feel frightened or worried?"

Varnia nodded. She was watching Starnor, who had been distracted by the evening's first fireflies. He was holding out his hand to them.

"Some of us don't seem to break," Menders said quietly. "There have been times when I thought breaking like Starnor would be so much easier than enduring. Escape from some things would have been most welcome. I wonder what makes people different in that way."

Varnia was startled. She'd always seen Menders as extremely competent and controlled, able to rise to any challenge, always calm in the face of crisis. Was he admitting that he had his own troubles, his own memories that he buried and avoided – as she did?

Menders rose after another moment.

"I'll leave you to your book," he smiled, walking away in Starnor's direction

***

"It's coming along," Doctor Franz said enthusiastically, flexing Varnia's right arm gently. She saw him regularly when he was with them in Surelia. It seemed that stopping work could cause a formerly active joint to protest. For her, it had been her right elbow.

When they first left The Shadows, she could hardly sleep because of the pain. Her elbow had swelled suddenly, stiffening so badly she could hardly bend it.

She'd followed Franz's recommendations to the letter and now had very little pain. It would take time, he said, but time was something she had in abundance.

"Continue as you have, and I think you'll have no more pain after another couple of weeks," Franz smiled. "Anything else giving you the miseries?"

Varnia shook her head. Then she looked right at him.

"Yes? The piercing eyes look right into my soul," he teased.

"Starnor – he came up behind me the other day and pulled out my hairpins. I wanted to know if there is any special way I should treat him."

"Hmm. Yes, Menders told me about that. Now you know he might play that little trick, you won't be likely to startle or scream – those are things that could frighten him and set him off. He isn't violent, but he can get into crying fits that go for days if he isn't given ramplane to calm him."

"Should I tell him that I'm not his wife?"

"Just turn your face to him if he does it again. She had blue eyes – yours are gray. He'll see that right away. That gives him a chance to understand that you aren't Mina." The doctor rearranged his instruments for a moment.

"What you need to understand, Varnia, is that Starnor can't come back into our world but we're able to step into his. When he becomes fixated on finding his wife, it's best to go along as if she will be coming through one of the gates – just as Menders did."

"But isn't that like teasing him?" she ventured.

"It would seem so, but to him, she is still alive, just beyond his range of sight. She's out for a few minutes, or she's late coming home. We used to try to explain to him that she was dead, but every time it was like he was finding her dead for the first time. He would be in agony. We know now that he will never be well again. His sickness is far too deep for anything we can do for him. So, we go to where he is for a while, where Mina is just on her way home or will be here soon. He starts to go to the gate, gets distracted and forgets about finding her for a while."

They were silent for a moment.

"Perhaps he gets distracted because he really knows she's dead and not coming back," Varnia said suddenly.

Doctor Franz raised his eyebrows and nodded.

"I wouldn't be the least bit surprised," he replied. "He knows, deep down, that Mina is dead. He found her body. But over the years, no-one has been able to help him accept it or live with that knowledge. Perhaps he simply can't. When a man is devoted as he was, and his line of work leads to his wife's murder – that is a guilt that can destroy. His mind has found a way for him to avoid that knowledge."

Varnia thought about that for a while.

"If you're interested in this sort of thing, I have some books you can read," Doctor Franz offered.

"Yes," she answered. "I would like to know more about this kind of sickness."

"We don't know much," Franz said. "Illness of the mind is a very new science. I'll be off to The Shadows within a couple of weeks – the books I'm thinking of are in my office there. I'll bring them back for you. You might also think of taking some classes here at the University next term – there are some that deal with this subject. You might have to scurry to keep up, but it would be of interest, I'm sure."

She smiled and rose.

"Run on with you," Doctor Franz laughed. He was the only person here in Surelia who knew that Varnia absolutely despised school. Though she knew he'd like to see her at the University, she also knew he would bring her those books.

LEMHOS, SURELIA

10
MANY VOICES WHISPER IN A SHOUT

"I truly believe she's deaf," Eiren said disgustedly.
"Stupid is more like it," Hemmett grumbled, thumping down his beer mug.

The topic, once again, was Madame Spinta and her treatment of Borsen, who was absent from the table, which was set out under the grapevine shaded patio that evening. He'd endured an insulting diatribe from the housekeeper, who accused him of everything from having weaseled his way into the family to having lewd designs on Katrin. When she called him trash from the streets Borsen finally lost his temper and stormed off, even avoiding Menders' attempt to stop him. That meant it was really bad, Katrin thought, because Borsen adored Menders.

"She absolutely refuses to hear," Menders sighed, his jaw tense. "I'm considering taking a house elsewhere."

"It might be the best thing to do," Eiren agreed. "I'm appalled at her viciousness toward Borsen."

"This is absurd," Katrin snapped abruptly.

Everyone at the table fell silent, staring at her. She tossed her head.

"Well, it is," she asserted. "Here you are, in your own villa, Menders, considering moving to a house that isn't yours because of her madness. We're all sitting around fussing about this woman's terrible behavior and Borsen's out somewhere frying his skull in the sun when he should be here with us! Who does she think she is?"

Menders was obviously squelching a smile.

"That question has crossed my mind, little princess. Madame Spinta is very inflexible and unfortunately, Borsen has become her target."

"Oh, stop trying to analyze her nonsense," Katrin interrupted heatedly.

Hemmett grinned to himself and poured a glass of beer for her, pushing it across the table. "Have this, Willow, it's cold."

Katrin sipped it slowly, but her temper didn't cool. She was not going to let some old vulture of a housekeeper ruin this trip. She glanced over at Varnia, who was also furious. The older girl met her gaze.

The foundation of Madam Spinta's prejudice against Borsen was the annual diaspora of Mordanian City Thrun into Surelia. City Thrun had left their traditional nomadic lifestyle to pursue what they believed would be easy living in Mordanian cities. When they encountered the almost universal Mordanian hatred of their race and found no-one would employ them, they turned to theft, begging and prostitution out of desperation.

City Thrun kept one Thrun tradition – migration to greener pastures with the seasons. Any City Thrun who could scrape passage on a ferry made his way to Surelia in late autumn, escaping the bitter Mordanian winter, much to the consternation of the Surelians. The Surelian crime rate skyrocketed in the winter months, until springtime, when the City Thrun returned to Mordania.

"I know it's frustrating and that it seems as if I'm doing nothing, Katrin," Menders explained. "In other circumstances, I would just go and have it out with Madame Spinta – you know I would. But that would upset the men who live here."

"I've tried talking to her too, darling," Eiren added gently. "She does not hear that Borsen is no threat to you and very dear to us all. It would be best for everyone if we left."

Katrin nodded – and then stood up very suddenly.

"No, it wouldn't. I'm going to have a word with her myself."

"Katrin, it's probably best not to," Menders began.

"Is she a Mordanian citizen?"

"Yes, she is," Menders answered, looking puzzled. "Her Surelian name is from her late husband."

"If I've got to be a damn princess, at least I can have the comfort of being able to issue a command," Katrin declared. "I won't scream or shout. No-one will hear me. This is going to stop."

"Yes." Varnia's voice was low, but intense. Katrin looked at her again. Varnia nodded back.

Not waiting for anyone to tell her otherwise, Katrin turned and walked quickly into the house, making a beeline to the room Madame Spinta used as an office.

She rapped briskly at the door and entered. Madame Spinta looked up, startled. She scrambled to her feet and managed an awkward curtsey.

"Yes, Your Royal Highness?" she asked unctuously.

"Madame, I am very angry and disturbed by the way you have been treating my cousin, Borsen," Katrin said as majestically as she could, keeping her voice icy and drawing herself up to her full height. "You will treat him with the respect that he deserves."

"I only look to your welfare, Your Highness," Madame Spinta oozed. "In such a matter, someone who is your elder is a better judge..."

"Perhaps you forget I'm a Princess of Mordania," Katrin interrupted, feeling her eyes burning into Madame Spinta's. The housekeeper tried to maintain her place in their staredown but failed, letting her eyes drop.

"You're in danger of being taken advantage of by that piece of trash," the woman muttered.

"You live in your own world, Madame," Katrin replied harshly. Stunned, the woman looked directly at her for the first time.

"Borsen is not interested in women. Borsen is interested in men. He's a nancyboy. He would not sleep with me if I paid him to!"

"Wh… Why didn't anyone tell me that?" Madame Spinta gasped.

"For the gods' sakes, you've been told dozens of times! You've upset my cousin and made accusations against him that are completely unfair and that show how small and mean your mind is." Katrin was infuriated. She kept it in check, channeling her rage as quickly as she could to come up with words that would work with this obtuse woman.

Madame Spinta stared up at Katrin, who suddenly felt ten feet tall.

"Menders is considering moving from this house, but he's forgetting just whose house it is and that you are here as his employee," Katrin drove on. "I'm sure he could find a housekeeper who would be more polite to members of his family. Borsen is his nephew. There is no doubt about it. The Highest Chieftain of the Thrun has confirmed it."

"A savage?" Madame Spinta blurted, her tone snide. She'd found her foothold. Her prejudices made her bold.

Suddenly Katrin understood why Menders and Eiren wanted to retreat. Talking to the woman was like trying to carry water in a sieve. No matter how hard you tried, you accomplished nothing and became exhausted in doing so.

She began to leave the room, ready to give herself the satisfaction of banging the door for the noise it would make. Then she stopped as if frozen.

Something was gathering in her, a force, an energy, a whispering – voices. Voices of women, very faint and distant. They spoke in words she did not know or couldn't clearly hear, but she knew what they meant.

Katrin had heard them before, from the time she was very small. They had saved her once, when a woman sent to kill her walked up behind her and pointed a gun at her while she was making soap.

You are a Princess! This woman is nothing, not of us, petty and small. We gave our blood, in battle, in childbed, to make this nation! We kept the Royal Line alive to create you. Do not let this paltry sum sway you. Show your blood, girl!

The voices were inexorable and could not be denied or ignored.

"I am Princess Katrin Morghenna of the Royal House of Mordania, Second Heiress to the Ruby Throne." Katrin heard herself speaking in a low and terrible voice. She felt her spine draw erect. Her neck straightened, so that only her eyes were inclined downward to Madame Spinta. Her blood was roaring in her ears and battle cries were echoing in her head.

"My mother is Queen Morghenna VIII. Her mother before her was Queen Morghenna VII, called The Terrible. I command you to show respect to all members of my household, including my brother, Borsen of the Thrun Royal House. Should you fail at any time to follow this command, I shall inform my mother, The Queen. Then you shall be at her mercy."

After a moment, Madame Spinta, whose eyes were huge and round, curtseyed to the ground.

Katrin felt the clamoring voices dying away. She began to wonder just what she had done.

Through the window behind Madame, she saw Borsen, looking dumbfounded, his mouth hanging wide open. Standing with him was Doctor Franz, apparently just back from Mordania, similarly at a loss.

"By your command, Your Highness," Madame Spinta fawned. To Katrin's complete disgust, she sounded happy, as if she enjoyed being threatened and given royal commands.

"That is all," Katrin wound up briskly. She turned, not bothering with the protocol that would have her offer her hand and raise the woman from her curtsey. She got out of the office but not before seeing Franz and Borsen fleeing toward the patio, hands over their mouths to choke back laughter.

In the hallway, Katrin leaned against the wall. Her head was still spinning. She was shaking.

After a moment she returned to the vineyard, where from a distance she could see Franz and Borsen re-enacting her conversation with Madame Spinta. Franz was declaiming grandly and Borsen was cringing, completing the performance with an awkward curtsy, pretending to remove his drawers from his backside afterward. Hemmett was rollicking around, roaring at the top of his voice. Katrin went to them.

"She'll likely leave you alone now, Borsen." She couldn't help smiling because he was laughing helplessly.

"Oh Cuz, if only you could have seen it. You were magnificent, but she – that great swooping flop to the floor and the 'By your command, Your Highness'. The mighty Madame Spinta!"

Menders looked up at Katrin, his eyes twinkling behind his glasses.

"Did you hearken to the voices of your ancestors – Katrin, what is it?"

She'd felt herself go pale at his words and her sight dimmed. Before she knew it, he was on his feet and she was in his chair. Menders and Doctor Franz bent over her.

"It's just the heat," she said loudly enough for the others to hear her, then whispered, "I need to talk to you about something later," in Menders' ear. He nodded and handed her a glass of water.

"Let's hope this settles the issue," Eiren said quietly. She firmly changed the subject, though Borsen and Hemmett had been having a wonderful time bowing toward and away from each other, being sure they collided, declaiming that they were truly majestic and regal.

"I'm also thinking that at the next university break, a visit to Fambré would be a good idea," Menders added. "It's much cooler there – we can get away from the heat for a while."

"With that I concur," Doctor Franz smiled, removing his cravat and unbuttoning his collar.

Later, when the sun was low, Menders and Katrin lingered at the table. She told him about the voices and the way she felt filled with power while they were speaking.

"No wonder you went gray when I said that," he responded quietly, taking her hand. "What a peculiar thing."

"Do you think I'm mad? Years ago, I asked Kaymar about it because I've heard them at other times. He didn't think so. He said it didn't sound like the madness he has."

Menders shook his head.

"You're no more mad than I," he replied. "Katrin, I don't know just what might have happened but I'm sure worrying about it would be pointless. Perhaps you did respond to your ancient lineage. You were certainly provoked enough to do so. There are many things that are not explainable, little princess. Best to simply let it pass and get on with life."

"Has anything like that ever happened to you?" Katrin asked. She was still very shaken. Menders went very quiet.

"Yes," he finally said. "And no, I don't know why. Best to put it from your mind, my dear. We'll hope it keeps Madame's behavior in check. Now, it should be time for dinner, so let's go in and get on with the evening." He helped her up and she took his arm. They started toward the house. Then Menders stopped her and turned toward her.

"My dear, I'm proud of you," he said gently. "Thank you."

LEMHOS, SURELIA

II
LETTERS TO HOME, LETTERS FROM HOME

Dear Vil,

Many thanks for your letter describing your wedding, but you're still a rotter for not waiting until I could stand up for you. After all, I'm only going to be away for three years. You could have held off that long (sure, with your baby big enough by then to give you away himself.) I wish you the very best of all things in your marriage and for the little Villison on the way, who had better be named Hemmett or Hemmettina or there will be big trouble.

Both Katrin and Borsen are doing so well here that we're probably going to extend our stay for an additional six months, which is fine with me. Surelia is great fun, even if I don't speak their language well. All a handsome fellow like me has to do is utter a few Surelian words, look at the women like they're the most beautiful creatures in the world, sigh a bit and they fall all over you. The wine is good too.

We're off to Fambré in a couple of weeks. Menders wants to get Katrin out of this heat. It makes the rest of us tired but she's downright sick a lot of the time. Gets these headaches, real skull splitters. Menders thinks the higher altitude and drier weather in Fambré will be helpful and says it's a lot cooler there.

I'm also looking forward to Barambos. Menders is going to get us over there as well before we leave the Continent. I'd like to have a long look at Samorsa too, but Katrin's all wild to go to Artreya, of all damn places. I truly look forward to visiting Mordania's enemy. Every Artreyan I've ever run across has been a complete bastard. Can you imagine being in a whole country full of them? Blah blah cobblestoned streets, yakety yakety the opera, art galleries, museums, humpty bumpty blah, the great culture, cough.

Who gives a grundar shit? I'd rather see the Samorsan Games any day. As if there aren't plenty of cobblestoned streets in Mordania that we have to go to Artreya and put up with the gits to see the cobblestones there? Culture doesn't make any sense, my friend.

I was glad to hear all has been quiet and that Hemmett's Men are managing well and getting along. Don't let Menders' Men try to boss you. Some of the old guard get a bit above themselves. If there is any real trouble, let me know. I can shoot across on the next boat and be there within a day or so.

My love to Petra and everyone at The Shadows.

Your friend and commander,

Hemmett

Dear Petra,

I was so glad to get your letter about the wedding! I do wish we could have been there, and I wish you much love and joy. I was so happy to hear about the baby too. How are you ever going to be able to wait for seven months until it's born? I would die of impatience. Your wedding dress sounds lovely and I'm glad Vil shined his boots!

Borsen and I have been very busy at the university. I added two classes in philosophy this term and like them very much. My art professor has set us some very difficult assignments but we're plugging away. Borsen continually impresses the professor. I could be consumed with envy because he's better than me, but he's so sweet I can't be jealous.

Borsen has been working with a Surelian tailor too, to everyone's amazement. He went into the tailor's shop armed with his Tailor's Certificate and apprenticed himself, though he isn't doing apprentice work. The tailor was amazed at Borsen being a Guild tailor at such a young age. Borsen says he's learning a lot. So, every day after his morning classes he hops on this funny little horse Menders looked out for him and goes cantering off to slave away. To think he used to be afraid to look a goose in the eye! The girls at the university are all curious and want introductions to him because he's so good-looking. Poor things, he's oblivious to them and they think it's charming shyness and try harder.

I wish you could send me some snow like you sent the autumn leaves you pressed! It's so hot here, even in what should be the middle of winter! I'm better able to deal with it now that Eiren found us some very light undergarments, and we had some dresses made with the hems higher than we wear them in Mordania. I feel like I'm thirteen again in such a short skirt.

We're going to Fambré during our term break and might go back later to stay a while. I want very much to see it, but I can't get that story Princess Dorlane told Varnia and me out of my head. Hemmett says there's unrest there now, but Menders wouldn't take us if there was real danger.

I can't wait to see Artreya, but Menders is not in a hurry to leave here since I got Madame Spinta to stop abusing Borsen. To think all anyone had to do was go in and put on the Queen act! Some people like to feel inferior, I guess. I would never tolerate it.

I hope that you aren't having morning sickness. Let me know what it's like to be pregnant, I'm that curious. Love to you and Vil and everyone. Let me know all that happens.

Love,

Katrin

Dear Gladdy and Hake,

Thank you for forwarding the information you've received about the latest hostilities between Mordanian and Artreya. Such exchanges are so commonplace now that they are treated as background here in Surelia. I have been able to find very little accurate information about it. Rest assured – if need be, I will forgo traveling to Artreya altogether. It would be a huge disappointment for Katrin and Eiren, who are both wild to see it, but their safety is far more important than their curiosity.

Please be sure I get any and all dispatches Bartan sends you. The news you have given me regarding Aidelia is unnerving to say the least. I suspect her actions are directed by a third party, as they have been whenever she's appeared in control of herself in the past.

All has been well here. Eiren loves the villa and all the time we can spend together. The children are thriving, learning and above all, enjoying themselves.

Borsen encountered a Surelian viper when he was running around the vineyard the other day and vaulting over the vines (which may I add, is forbidden, the devil). The snake was most annoyed at this activity (I can sympathize with the snake here) and struck at him. Borsen, accustomed to our sluggish northern reptiles, tried to elude it. He was enormously startled when the viper proceeded to pursue him diligently. He finally dispatched it with his pistol. He dragged his grisly kill, longer than he is tall, up to the house, where it was admired by one and all before he and Hemmett skinned it, as Borsen is determined to have a pair of shoes made as a trophy. Hemmett, concerned about waste, suggested we eat the meat. Varnia offered to prepare a meal from it, but was vociferously voted down by Katrin, Borsen and Eiren.

Such are the restful days of my sojourn in the south, accompanied by screams of fear, louder screams of fear, bellows of outright dismay, gunshots, whoops of triumph, loudly pronounced assertions of victory over all evil reptiles, cries of approbation and amazement, shrieks of disgust and revulsion and excited questions as to what would be the better way to cure a snakeskin, pegging it out to dry or submerging it in a basin of piss. Borsen considers me the authority on all topics. My days are so idyllic, I feel as if I'm floating on clouds of blissful rest.

Hardin and Vogel send their best wishes and are doing well. They find the work here restful and were much amused by the viper incident. This is heartening, as you know both were very fragile at the time we formed Menders' Men. Starnor, Simmonds, and Hermann are as well as can be expected. Very unexpectedly, Varnia has quite a rapport with the more damaged residents and they enjoy her reading to them or speaking with them.

I will close for now, as I have been called to dinner three times and Hemmett is threatening to feed my portion to the dogs.

In friendship,

M

Dear Tomar, Mirin and all the little tailors,

You should have seen the enormous snake I shot in the vineyard the other day. He was seven feet long and had fangs as long as my little finger. I was walking around the vineyard when he struck at me and met his sudden end at my hand.

Hemmett and I have skinned him and have his hide stretched out on pegs where the dogs can't get to it and once that's done and I've softened it I will have shoes made from it. I could probably get a belt and moneybag from it as well, it's that large even though Hemmett says that's only because I have tiny feet. He's only jealous because they have to use the hide of an entire borag to make boots for those deformities he calls feet.

I have informally apprenticed myself to a Surelian tailor here. I went in and asked him if he would take some unpaid help and told him about myself and my skills and explained that I wanted to learn about Surelian tailoring. I expected him to chase me from the shop but instead he plopped a piece of cloth, needle and thread on the counter and told me to show him a seam, a buttonhole and a simple hem.

No challenge for such a smart boy of course and within the hour he was explaining the secret of Surelian linings to me. They hang them differently from the way we do, and their method leads to less tearing and twisting so it will be a very useful thing to know. In return I showed him some things he didn't know about his sewing machine, which he isn't using nearly as much as he could.

The Surelian style in men's jackets has a deep cut front and wasp waist at the moment and you can be assured I have ordered no less than six of these for myself, being a young man of means and a small waist. When I return to Mordania, I will dazzle all and copy the style with my own notions for making it more wearable.

The trouser style of the moment is quite loose cut in the leg with a very tight cuff and high tight waist with pleats, in keeping with the wasp waisting on the jackets. Stunning if you are built like Kaymar, Uncle or myself but ghastly on anyone built large. Ifor tried a pair on the other day and laughed so hard he was staggering all around the tailor shop and the tailor was furious and drove him out. With his blocky build he looked like a grundar wearing pants. Kaymar on the other hand has purchased three such Surelian suits and is devastating in them, though he was beside himself when Hemmett spilled an entire plate of Surelian shellfish in red sauce right down the back of the suit he had just had made in white silk. He tore it off right away and after soaking the suit in cold water and repeated scrubbings and sun bleaching it looks new again. Kaymar refuses to be anywhere near Hemmett when Hemmett has food in hand now.

It's good to be tailoring again. I have missed it. I'm afraid a life of leisure and continual playing and amusement wouldn't be very good for me and I'm glad to have some work to do. I'm going to try to do the same sort of thing when we're in Artreya, though I will say frankly that I don't think much of Artreyan fashion and all that absurd braid they slap on top of everything, thinking it gives their poorly cut and fitted clothing dash.

I miss all of you very much. Hugs all round.

Borsen

Dear Mama, Papa and Everyone,

Thank you so much for your letter of last week. Bertel brought the mail to us and told us the additional news that Sana has had to close down school because of the extremely snowy weather. Let us hope that it will not be a closed winter. It's very hard to even contemplate snow and ice when there is not so much as a frost on the ground in the mornings here. The days are very warm to hot and the nights not much cooler. Poor Katrin is still suffering from the heat and we're sure at this point she is not going to become acclimated, though she's been more comfortable since we found lighter clothing for her

In answer to your question, Varnia is improving a great deal. At first, she was quite withdrawn, once the excitement of the journey on the ship was past and she found herself here where most people do not speak Mordanian. Menders and I have worked with her on Surelian and included her in some of our activities, as she was unwilling to try the University. She gravitates to people who are older and is more comfortable with adult pursuits. It will be a matter of time for her to come out of her shell. We make sure she knows we are available should she need help or wish to confide anything.

We will be going to Fambré within the month and I will write at great length about all we see there. Menders, in particular, is wild to see some of the old buildings and famous gardens – as am I!

I hope all of you are well, and look forward to your next letter.

Love to you all,

Your Eiren

My dear Menders,

Just a quick note to let you know that there is no further news from the Palace. Apparently, the Queen is as usual. Aidelia continues to be somewhat in control of herself. The Council has turned away from taunting Artreya for the time being and are once again targeting the Thrun. I have gone ahead and sent a load of firearms and ammunition to your estate, Stettan, for Tharak. There have been no reports of attacks on Mordanian ships by Artreyan forces, or anything else for a couple of weeks now.

We all continue well here, though it is very quiet with the heart and soul of the house away. The various dispatches from Bartan and other branches of the network are enclosed with this. Take care, my friend.

Hake

Dear Sir Slippery Eel,

I shall be able to meet you in Fambré, as I am due to make a visit to Samorsa to see how my school and the girls are faring. I'll be able to speak with you in more detail then.

We have a problem. No danger to Katrin, so don't be fearful. My former operative has come to light to some people in my network. Her intentions are not good, but they are directed at me, not at the Royal Family.

More in Fambré. Take care, my friend. My best to your family.

Gladdy

LEMHOS, SURELIA

12
NIGHT WATCH

In one movement, Varnia woke, rose from her bed and rushed out of her room, not hesitating long enough to take her dressing gown or step into her slippers. She rushed down the hallway outside her room, her breath coming short.

She didn't stop until she had let herself out onto the patio. It was definitely cooler there. She went to her favored bench and tucked her bare feet up under her. Pillowing her head on her arms, she tried to make the nightmare images fade.

After a moment her breathing quieted. She became aware of a gentle voice speaking to her.

"Varnia, I'm right over here in the corner."

She looked up, brushing her tumbled hair back out of her eyes.

A match was struck, and she could see Menders seated in the big wicker corner chair, wearing his dressing gown.

"I'm sorry, did I wake you?" she asked hoarsely.

"No, I was already up. I'm a bit of a night owl," he answered. "But, so we don't wake everyone by talking across the patio, I will take a closer seat. Would you care for your dressing gown?"

She nodded mutely. He went and was back in a few moments, bringing her gown and slippers. Then he settled himself across from her, where the night light in the hallway illuminated him faintly.

"Nightmare?" he asked gently.

Varnia was fastening her gown and stepping into her slippers. She nodded, not speaking aloud.

"I'm acquainted with them," Menders went on. "Can you do with a drink?"

Varnia was about to refuse but then nodded. Menders rose a second time and disappeared into the house. He returned with two glasses of a sweet wine he knew Varnia favored.

"Now then, that will help you get back to sleep," he said, claiming his seat again.

She shook her head.

"I never do – not once I'm awake from a nightmare," she said after taking a sip.

"We'll see. Is it a nightmare you have often?"

"Yes. I won't talk about it."

"You don't have to. I'm sure, like mine, it has to do with your past."

She looked at him curiously. She knew Menders had been born into the Royal Family. He was wealthy and powerful. He was also kind and fair. He led a happy life.

"Doesn't seem like I should have nightmares, does it?" he asked, startling her. "But there are things from my childhood that still come and torment me in dreams at times. I wasn't raised by my parents, you see. My mother died when I was born. My father was no father at all. He hated me. I was toughened by nurses and then later by tutors. That meant cold sleeping quarters, sparse food and beatings. I used to run away from home quite a bit and would hide with Tharak's family nearby."

Varnia's racing heart calmed as she took interest in Menders' words. She watched as he paused to light a cigar. The fragrant smoke was comforting to her, for some reason.

"Even so, I doubt that would be the stuff of nightmares for me," he continued, crossing his legs and leaning back in his chair. "Not the kind that drive you from bed. A bad dream is one thing. You wake, you're frightened for a moment, you realize it was only a dream, turn over and go back to sleep. A nightmare is something entirely other, isn't it?"

"Yes," she replied softly.

Her own were terrible, very real re-livings of episodes in her past. When she woke they often went on for several moments and she couldn't tell where the edge between nightmare and reality lay. Her only recourse was to flee and stay awake for the rest of the night.

"Varnia, I know you can keep your counsel," Menders said after a moment. "Only two other people know what I'm about to tell you – Doctor Franz and Kaymar.

"I had a tutor when I was only about eight years old who seemed very kind at first. He never beat me as the others and my nursemaids did and he didn't give me a great deal of memorization to do. He certainly didn't teach me much, but acted more as a friend, playing games with me, letting me read and draw as much as I liked.

He never reported my visits to the Thrun to my father, who hated me going there.

"He had an ulterior motive and I was far too young and innocent to understand what he was doing. When he tried to become intimate with me, I reacted with complete horror. I fought away from him and ran to my father."

Varnia closed her eyes.

"I got to my father's study, but was so terrified I couldn't say a word before the tutor came after me with some excuse that I had run out of the nursery after a nightmare.

"My father reached down where I was trying to hide beside his chair, grabbed my wrist and handed me over to that vile man. I would even go so far as to say he was bright enough and corrupt enough to have a good idea as to what was really going on. He didn't care. At that moment, I learned what it is to be completely helpless."

Menders puffed his cigar for a moment while Varnia waited silently. She knew Menders was putting absolute trust in her and wanted to show that it was deserved.

"He raped me. For almost two years he was there at Stettan and I was his object he used for his own pleasure. He knew there would be no punishment or retribution. I think I would have gone mad or even taken my life if I hadn't had Tharak and his clan to run away to – and Tharan T'ul, who taught me how to endure such a situation through mental discipline."

Varnia could feel how difficult it was for him to speak of the horror in his past. She rose without thinking, went to him and held her hands out to comfort him.

Menders smiled and took them.

"Many years have passed since then," he said. "I don't have the nightmares very often and when I do, I have the tools Tharan T'ul gave me in my mind. I'm able to take control no matter how terrible the nightmares are. I know it's been over for many years, that I have a good life and a wonderful family. I know I'm safe and in control."

"I'd like to know how to do that – so long as I don't have to tell you what's in my nightmares," Varnia said.

"You don't have to. One day you may want to confide them to someone – and that can help, but not always. You're the first person I've voluntarily told the story to. Franz figured it out from things I said during a fever. Kaymar deduced what happened because he ended up with the same tutor. I have to say that having told this story is making me feel even more in control."

"Can you teach me the things Tharan T'ul taught you? I'd like to be in control of the nightmares – and being angry."

"That's why I've told you these very personal things," Menders answered. "Yes, I'll help you. You're doing very well with the anger on your own, but I hate to think of you not being able to go back to sleep after a nightmare or being so in the grips of terrible things in the past. You're a disciplined person, so it won't take you long to learn how to take control, even when you're in the middle of a terrible dream."

Varnia, for the first time completely comfortable with him, sat beside him.

"What can I do to go back to sleep tonight?" she asked earnestly.

"First, finish your glass of wine," Menders replied, smiling as she retrieved it and sat down again. "Also, you've already come out of yourself a great deal since you woke. You've become interested in someone else's story and turned away from your own. So, when you lie down again, let yourself believe that you are in control. Don't do it as if you're issuing a command, but as if you're comforting a child who is frightened. The dreams cannot hurt you. If they come again, you will wake, realize they are only dreams and go right back to sleep."

Varnia smiled peacefully and drank some of her wine.

"You should have had many children," she said.

"I do. Katrin, Hemmett, Borsen – they openly call me 'Papa'," Menders replied proudly. "There's Kaymar – he was young enough and so in need of help when he came to The Shadows that he became one of my boys. A couple of the younger Menders' Men are that close as well. There were problems they struggled with that I could show them the way out of. Though they officially call me Menders and 'sir' they have also been known to call me 'Pa'. Tomar's children have always been like my own. The stablemaster's little boy calls me 'Dranpa', which knocked me off my high horse about looking youthful."

Varnia laughed softly.

"When we're back in Mordania, I'll introduce you to the man I consider my father," Menders smiled. "He's the Commandant of the Military Academy. It was from him I learned the concept of being a parent to many, even though you may have no children of your own."

"I'd like that," Vania smiled, finishing her wine. Her eyes actually felt sleepy. She rose, and Menders rose with her.

"Remember – you control the dream. You can always wake and find reality before you go back to sleep," he reminded her.

She put her hands out to him again and he took them.

"Good night, my brave girl," he said, looking into her eyes.

She felt that he was removing all the darkness from her mind with his gaze. She felt some of her heavy burden lifting.

"Good night," she said softly, releasing his hands. She went to the doorway, but felt impelled to turn to him.

"Papa," she whispered before she went into the house.

Menders heard her return to her room and went to the edge of the patio to see the night sky.

A movement above him only made him smile and shake his head. He looked to see Kaymar climbing down an ironwork pillar covered with grapevines, his bare toes clinging to the stems. A quiet rustle and Menders' cousin was beside him.

"You're as bad as a mandequan," Menders said, comparing Kaymar to the highly intelligent and meddlesome monkeys of Surytam.

"It's been a night for bad dreams," Kaymar answered, taking his own cigar case from his dressing gown pocket. "I heard you chatting with her – well done. I've been aware that she has these nightmares very often. She usually huddles out there and shivers until dawn and then is snappish and surly the entire day after."

"She'll overcome that, given some guidance," Menders replied. "I've never found the opportunity to speak with her about it before. She's apt to mistake any attention from a man as an advance."

"Don't I know. Tried to take her arm the other day and I thought she was going to bite my hand off." Kaymar shook his head. "It had to have been really bad, Cuz."

"No doubt. I've sent word to Hake to get those bastards off that land, no matter what he has to do. I don't want them near The Shadows with so many youngsters around now."

"Well played. They're a blight on the place." Kaymar handed his cigar to Menders for a puff. "Now the question for me, is to try to get back to sleep or give up and expect to be cranky tomorrow."

"We'll try a stroll around the vineyard. Distract the mind," Menders answered.

FAMBRÉ

13
SULLEN, SUSPICIOUS EYES

"I thought we might travel in the public cars," Katrin said in surprise as Menders ushered their group down the crowded railroad platform toward the private cars at the end of the train.

"It's an overnight trip. I doubt you'd enjoy trying to sleep in an upright seat with everyone snoring around you," Menders smiled in reply.

"Hemmett will snore us awake anyway," Katrin teased, slewing her eyes around toward Hemmett, who snorted at her like a pig.

"More pleasant and safer," Menders said firmly.

Katrin smiled and nodded. He meant that nothing was going to change his plans and that he wouldn't entertain any arguments.

Kaymar nodded at the carriage guard and swung aboard. They waited as he meticulously searched the car, climbed on a chair to open the overhead hatch and then vaulted up out of sight. He reappeared on the top of the car, looked keenly around, then rapidly crossed his eyes at Katrin, who laughed aloud.

Then Kaymar's gaze riveted into the crowd. He looked right at Menders and then back at whatever had caught his attention.

"Hemmett," Menders said softly. Hemmett stepped forward and took Katrin's arm. Borsen flanked her other side and Ifor stepped up behind her. Doctor Franz and Eiren turned and scanned the crowd along with Menders.

Katrin was trying to see around everyone, but suddenly Kaymar was there in front of her.

"Up you go, Cuz, it's all clear," he said, smiling. He took her free arm and up the steps she went into the carriage.

"May I look?" she asked him.

"Of course – it's our friend, the Revenant," he answered, standing at the carriage window with her.

Indeed, Tellyn Fein was standing in the crowd further back on the platform. Menders was heading in his direction.

"What could he be doing here?" Katrin asked.

"I'm sure Menders will find out," Kaymar replied.

She watched as Tellyn Fein nodded to Menders and Menders returned the compliment. The two men spoke sedately for a moment or two – then, to her surprise, Menders led the Revenant over to where she was standing at the window.

Tellyn Fein bowed and then looked up at her. She noticed his eyes were a clear light green.

"Light Of The Winter Sun," he said gently. "I would speak with you for a moment, but waited until you were aboard, for your safety."

"What did you want to tell me?" Katrin asked curiously.

"While you be in Fambré, listen with your inward ear," he said, drawing closer to the window and lowering his voice while projecting it in such a way that she could hear every word. "The ear that hears the Queens of Mordania. If there comes a time of roaring silence while you be in Fambré – you must leave then. You are the one who can hear – if you will listen."

He bowed again and began to move away.

"Mister Fein!" Katrin called. "Please wait!"

He turned back to her.

"How did you know – about the voices?" she asked.

"Revenants have ears everywhere," he replied, giving her a sudden, mischievous grin. "Be not afraid. Just listen with the inward ear and should the silence roar – you and yours must leave Fambré."

Katrin frowned in frustration. Tellyn Fein laughed aloud.

"We will be watching," he told her. Then he walked rapidly away through the crowd.

***

Oddly upright stone hills with massive boulders tumbled around them dotted the landscape of northern Fambré. They were a complete novelty to the entire party and the young people hung out the windows of the train carriage, remarking and pointing.

"Those look like – Uncle! Look! There are Giants here!" Borsen turned from the window and beckoned to Menders.

There was a general scramble as everyone tried to claim a window. They were all familiar with the ancient stone sculptures known as Giants in northern Mordania, but to see them here, south of the equator, was an enormous surprise.

"One of them looks just like the hand you sketched Hemmett, Borsen and me sitting in, Papa!" Katrin said excitedly to Menders as the train chuffed by the huge hands, feet and faces thrusting up from the soil.

"And so it does," Menders agreed, giving Kaymar a friendly shove aside and helping Eiren to the place he'd occupied at the window. "I wish we could stop for a moment… Hemmett, if you pull that emergency cord, it will be the last thing you do!"

A haw-haw from the end of the car, where Hemmett was claiming a window for himself answered him. The train went on without interruption. Menders ignored Hemmett's teasing and pulled out his binoculars to get a better look at The Giants as they passed.

"That Giant's face jutting up out of the ground – I'll swear that's the same nose as the one near The Shadows," he said, passing the binoculars to Eiren.

"Definitely," she agreed. There was a consensus as everyone considered the partially exposed face that seemed to watch them as they rode past. The Giants near The Shadows included a stone nose that was exposed. Seeing the same feature on an entire stone face was eerie.

"They look to be carved of that same stone as these odd hills and the boulders," Doctor Franz observed. "Could it be possible they were carved directly from one of the smaller hills? The proportions are such that it could be possible."

"But with what tools?" Ifor asked, using his own binoculars to look back at The Giants. "As far as we know, those sculptures are ancient. How could ancient men have carved those figures out of tons of rock? There are no other ancient sculptures so sophisticated."

"They always seem to be close to roads or railways," Kaymar added. "The road near The Shadows is an ancient one – supposedly the route Glorantha took to drive out the Surelians."

"Really?" Katrin looked at him, her eyes wide. "I didn't know that!"

"It's one of the legends, that Glorantha took the road down the coast – and it is an ancient road. When we're back home I'll take you down toward Rondstein. There's a place where part of the road washed out and rather than repair it, new roadwork was routed around it," Menders told her. "You can see there are different layers of roadwork with different materials."

"But Giants way down here? How could ancient people make the ones in Mordania and then go all this way to make more Giants here?" Katrin asked.

Menders could only shake his head.

"The Giants have confounded many scientists and historians," Eiren said. "We should keep watch for more of them, maybe even keep a record of any that we see."

Katrin, now that The Giants were fading into the distance, ransacked her bags until she found her journal. She sat down and started scribbling.

Menders smiled and escorted Eiren back to their seats.

"I think her world just became a lot larger," he said softly.

"Indeed," Eiren agreed, smiling as she watched Katrin's industry. One of their regrets was how Katrin's title circumscribed her life. Her childhood had been frustrating, once she was old enough to understand how her life differed the lives of other children.

There had been true danger to Katrin many times in their early years at The Shadows. She was barely six months old when the Queen sent a certain Madame Holz, Royal Head Nurse, to assure that Katrin was properly "toughened", a cruel regimen of deprivation and punishment inflicted on the children of the Mordanian aristocracy and the Royal Family. Supposedly, toughening created strong individuals. Instead, it produced bullies, masochists and broken souls.

Menders dispensed with Madame Holz once she refused his offers to finance her retirement abroad. He even tempted her with the deed to his Surelian villa – the penultimate move in what had become a game of cat and mouse with the sadistic nurse. Upon her refusal of his final offer, a swift kick from the Surelian Solution sent Madame Holz down the stairs, eliminating that problem.

That was the beginning. Over the last sixteen years, there had been various coup attempts where Katrin, the Queen and Princess Aidelia were targeted by assassins. For Katrin to safely leave The Shadows to attend Hemmett's graduation, Menders had to order the elimination of a number of Mordanian aristocrats and members of the merchant class. Menders' Men, teamed with covert agents from the Palace and Gladdas Dalmanthea's Girls, had spread out across Mordania's capital, Erdahn, on the eve of the graduation ceremonies.

In the course of one spring night, their combined forces put an end to a number of people who had spent years plotting to kill the Queen and her two daughters.

Menders sighed to himself. The amount of effort and stress invested in the past year had been staggering. He was approaching his thirty-seventh birthday and felt the toll far more than he once would have. He'd never taken killing or ordering someone to kill lightly, but as he grew older, it became an increasing burden

"Such a sigh, Mister Shvalz," Eiren teased him, using his family name while putting her hand over his.

"I'm not Shvalz, that's the blond fellow over there," Menders teased back, indicating Kaymar, who was keeping watch on the connecting doors between their carriage and the one ahead while appearing to lounge in his seat beside Ifor.

"Oh, I heard you were one too," she smiled.

"Menders is good enough for me," he answered.

"Then I'll call you Mister Menders," Eiren smiled.

Menders realized he was being a killjoy while she was trying to keep things happy and light. He gave himself a mental shake and looked over at Katrin. She was still working eagerly over her journal, chatting with Borsen, who had come to sit beside her.

"You may indeed, Mistress Menders." He put an arm around her shoulders and pulled her close as he pointed out the first of the purpling luxen flower fields in the distance.

"And there's where we'll be for a few days," he told her. "Right in the middle of the perfume industry."

Eiren smiled and leaned her head against his shoulder.

***

"Incredible," Ifor murmured, holding the dogs' leads as he, Kaymar, Katrin and Borsen paused on a hilltop and looked out over the most spectacular scenery any of them had ever seen.

Fragrant luxen shrubs laden with deep purple, fragrant flowers were wedged into every arable inch of a very rolling country scene. They foamed around massive boulders and fallen trees, covering almost all the ground down to the wildly crashing Great Southern Ocean. A few fields of yellow mustard broke the undulating waves of purple. A backdrop of craggy, deep blue mountains, the "spine" of this southernmost peninsula of Fambré, completed a stunning landscape. The scent of the luxen was dazzling.

Dara, Katrin's boarhound, whined to be released from her leash so she could run, but Ifor spoke gently to her.

They had found the atmosphere of Fambré was conducive to visitors allowing a very large dog run free over farmland. Dara was trained not to harass livestock, but she was safer restrained.

Katrin was horrified by the poverty of so many Fambrian people. She'd seen poverty in Mordania, of course. At The Shadows Menders improved the lives of the tenant farmers and was open to helping anyone in the district who asked, but farming in the far north country was difficult and most farmers lived on a fine edge between solvency and disaster.

There were also poor people in Mordania's cities. Katrin had seen them when she visited Erdstrom or Rondstein. Their situation was even worse. She was ashamed of this and wished she had the power to change things. She was also ashamed of her mother, who never left the Palace and obviously had no notion of the terrible suffering in her own nation.

All that was as nothing compared to Fambré.

The countryside was beautiful and Katrin had loved visiting the perfumeries and wineries. Everywhere she turned, some scene would make her heart throb with the aching beauty of it all. But the moment they neared a village or town, the crowds of beggars were everywhere. Their clothing was undefinable, gray clumps of ragged cloth. Many had terrible sores, infected eyes, huge lumps on their jaws speaking of unattended, abscessed teeth.

The poor children were pitiful, sluggishly animated skeletons. Swollen bellies, like Borsen's when he first came to The Shadows, were everywhere. The mothers who held the starving babies were silent and staring.

The first time Katrin encountered this, she handed out every pennig she had within moments, then saw that everyone in their party was doing the same thing. The poor people mobbed them, hands outstretched. When the money was gone the beggars swore and turned away, while those fortunate enough to have received something ran toward food carts or shops.

Katrin wept as she desperately searched her pockets and purse for anything to give a mother with a baby – a girl younger than herself who cradled a pitiful bundle of bones Katrin wasn't even sure was breathing. The mother's whispered pleas for help needed no translation as Katrin turned her bag and pockets inside out, searching for anything she could give. Doctor Franz stepped up and handed the poor girl the last money he had with him. Then Menders herded everyone into the hotel, where the door attendants, which Katrin found later were at every hotel to keep the beggars out, rapidly closed and bolted the doors behind them.

The hotel manager tried to apologize for the crush of beggars, but Menders cut him off brusquely and hustled everyone upstairs to their suite. There Katrin sank down on the sofa and covered her face with her hands. Her head was spinning, and she felt violently ill.

"Here Cuz." Borsen sat beside her with a cold, wet washcloth and moved her hands away from her face. He wiped her forehead and cheeks and then cleaned her hands, which reeked from contact with the hands of the people in the street.

"Oh Borsen – how? How can people let that go on?" she asked.

"When you're that poor – you're an object to them. Or invisible," he answered quietly. "You aren't anything more. People can get used to anything, Katrin, and the people here have gotten used to those poor souls in the streets."

Varnia, who could make a pot of tea faster than anyone on Eirdon, came over with a cup.

"No protests," she said firmly, putting it down by Katrin. "You drink it."

Kaymar was going through his pockets. Then he shook his head.

"I gave away everything I had, including my watch," he said with a mirthless laugh. "I am so glad I couldn't talk my mother into coming with us. If she'd seen that, she would have died of sorrow."

"Or she would have gotten roaring mad," Varnia snapped. Kaymar raised his eyebrows.

"She might at that. She can wield a pretty wicked sunshade when she gets riled enough, as my arse can testify," he replied.

Katrin was horrified to hear herself laugh at the image of Princess Dorlane walloping Kaymar across the backside with her elegant sunshade. Though there was still a hard, painful knot in her chest just below her collarbone, the laughter eased some of the hotness and pressure in her head.

"It wasn't a family watch, was it?" Eiren asked, coming in from her room.

"No, just a frippery," Kaymar assured her. "Ifor will get me another, as soon as he sends to the bank for more cash."

"That's where Menders has gone – to have a draft drawn. I'm glad he transferred funds here before we left Surelia." Eiren sat on the other side of Katrin, deliberately picking up the cup of tea and handing it to her.

"You need to drink this," she insisted. "It will help."

"Have you ever…" Katrin asked, her voice shaking so she couldn't continue.

Eiren shook her head.

"No, nothing like that," she answered. "Some of The Shadows' farmers were desperately poor before you came to live there, and Menders organized things properly. There was hunger and disease, but everyone who had something helped out and there were always game and wild foods available. The situation here is abominable."

Katrin sipped the tea. It did make her feel better. Doctor Franz came over and put a couple of drops of ramplane in it. Her breathing eased and the pain in her chest went away. The love and attention should have comforted her, but all she could think was that those people in the street had no comfort or help.

Menders insisted on an early dinner and bed for them all. Everyone was on edge and upset. Kaymar kept stalking to the window and looking out. Katrin couldn't bring herself to. She wanted to snatch up everything of value in the hotel suite and run out into the street with it, to give it to those in need. She choked down what dinner she could and was grateful for the warmth of her bed.

She wanted to ask why those people were given no help, no charity or means to help themselves – but she knew the answer. Those who had the power to change things, to make things better, to ease the lots of those desperate and starving people, simply did not care. And in Fambré, that meant the King.

The next morning, she woke late to the sound of Menders tapping on the door and then letting himself into her room. He carried a cup of coffee and a plate with a pastry on it.

"Good morning, little princess." Putting the breakfast on the bedside table, he sat on the edge of her bed. He took out his wallet and counted out some bills – the amount she had received as her monthly allowance from her account when they arrived in Fambré.

"No – I gave my money away freely," Katrin protested.

"I know. We all did. But practicality says we need money while we're here – otherwise, we'd be unable to pay for food or lodging, we couldn't move about. Going without it would do nothing for the starving mobs out there. I will make arrangements to provide some help for them."

Katrin sat up further against her pillows, curious.

"What I plan to do," Menders went on, "is to locate places in the country we can rent for a few days or weeks at a time. I'd like you to see something of Fambré, Katrin."

"Haven't I seen enough?" She picked up the dish with the pastry and felt no desire to eat it.

"No," Menders answered firmly. "Though traveling is usually associated with pleasant experiences and beautiful sights, that isn't all I want you to take away from this journey. Sometimes facing the cruel truths about human nature is part of being exposed to new experiences. I would be doing you a disservice to buy tickets on the next train out of here – though I will admit that was my initial impulse."

Katrin bit into the pastry and washed it down with a swallow of coffee. Both were excellent. Her appetite, always very strong, began to come back.

"Menders – what can be done for those people?" she asked.

"We have little power here – no, we have no power here," he answered. "It isn't like life at The Shadows, where I can intervene when people fall on hard times, doing it anonymously if they're proud. We aren't citizens and we can bring no pressure on the King."

"I'm a Mordanian Princess. Could I speak to the King? We're related through Princess Dorlane."

She was startled when Menders' eyes filled abruptly with tears. He cleared his throat and flicked a finger under his glasses, wiping at his eyes.

"I'm very proud of you for thinking of that, but I can't take the risk of someone at the Fambrian Court seeing your resemblance to your mother," he replied, removing his glasses and taking out a handkerchief. "Anonymity is your greatest protection, Katrin, particularly here."

He perused her with the intent gaze that his uncorrected vision required if he were to focus at all.

"Considering what I know of the King, it would do no good," he continued. "He might be amused. Like his brother before him, he does not acknowledge the situation in Fambré. Because of this, he will go the way of his brother, at the hands of these people. After seeing the situation here, it will be sooner than anyone outside of Fambré expects."

"I feel terrible holidaying here, Menders."

"Think of it as education then," he answered. "You're a member of a Royal Family. There is a lesson to be learned right in front of you. It's easy to say, 'help them', but how? How to go about it? What must change? These are the things to ponder, little princess."

He replaced his glasses and stood. "Finish your breakfast – there is more where that came from. Then we'll plan what we're going to do. I'll take you along when I go to make a donation to a feeding station that is being set up as we speak."

"Did you do that since yesterday?" Katrin asked in amazement.

"I sought out people who already work to help the poor here," he answered. "I've made it possible to extend their reach. Kaymar will contact his mother, who can alert those in the aristocracy here who would like to avoid a second Revolt and Terror."

Katrin had gone with him that day and seen the hall being outfitted to feed many. Menders made a large donation and pledged more, as well as more from people in Mordania. She admired the kitchen being set up and spoke with the handsome, intense priest of Galanth in charge of the operation, Abbot Fahrin.

"Could you arrange a place where they can wash and perhaps clean their clothing?" she asked. "Is there a doctor who could see them?"

"We can do these things – one of my brother priests is a doctor," he answered, looking at her closely.

"I would like to donate the cost," she explained. She drew out her purse, taking out a generous sum.

"So much?" he asked. "How do you come by this?"

Katrin laughed a little. "At home I make soap and sell it. I also help my brother manage our goats and sell the milk. My father helps me invest my profits," she answered. "I haven't been milking while we're traveling, but I do have a milkmaid's hands."

She held them out for his perusal. Abbot Fahrin took them, turned them over and back, saw the strong muscling and tested her grip jokingly. He laughed along with her.

"Indeed, you've milked many a goat," he agreed. "Thank you for your help. It is cherished. It means more when the person giving has worked for the money, though I will take any donations to help our desperate brothers and sisters. Let me show you where we can make arrangements for them to wash."

Since then, they had stayed in homes and small travelers' inns in country locations. They still saw many poverty-stricken country people, but they had, as Eiren said, access to game and wild foods and were able to grow gardens. They were poor, but not starving. It was the villages and towns with few resources to be scavenged where the horrible starvation and desperation reigned. Katrin didn't want to imagine the misery that must be going on in the densely populated cities.

Now Katrin stood on the hillside, looking at the breathtaking view. She was able to enjoy it, despite knowing that her donation and Menders' were drops in the bucket. Still, those they helped were helped. Perhaps they were doing some lasting good.

"Let's walk for a while," Borsen suggested, reaching for his own boarhound's lead. "Give the dogs a little exercise. We can keep looking at the sights."

The shifting colors and light kept them occupied for a good half mile, but then Kaymar drew up shortly.

"Time to go back," he announced, sounding cheerful.

"We haven't eaten yet," Borsen protested, but then followed the line of Kaymar's gaze. He shortened Magic's lead and turned immediately.

Katrin saw a large group of men gathered around another man who was standing on a stone, speaking loudly.

"Now, Katrin," Ifor commanded in a low tone. Though she was intensely curious, she turned away, taking Dara's lead. She could hear the man speaking, but the wind was against him and she couldn't make out his words.

As they walked briskly back along the country road, they saw a large group of men heading their way. Katrin made sure her knife and gun were easily accessible and noticed the others were doing the same. They were very simply dressed, nothing to single them out as royalty. They had the boarhounds. It wasn't the first time they'd met

Fambrians while out walking. The thing to do was to remain calm and smile.

The men did not give way on the road but Kaymar and Ifor easily led Borsen and Katrin around them. Ifor, who spoke Fambrian so well he was often mistaken for a native, bid the men good day and asked where they were going.

Not one of the men answered. They walked by, every head turning as they stared at Kaymar, Ifor, Borsen and Katrin with sullen, suspicious eyes.

"Cross country," Ifor said quietly once the men rounded a curve in the road and left their sight. They ducked into a field of tall luxen plants and were grateful the purple, claustrophobically close shrubs made them disappear from view as they made the most direct route back to their inn.

14
SECRET MEETING

A modestly dressed gentleman and lady made their way up a street in Turano, a city in southern Fambré, obviously tourists looking for a particular place. They goggled at several impressive buildings and statues and exchanged glances over objects in shop windows until they finally located their destination, a small travelers' inn on a side street that catered to the less-than-wealthy tourist.

The gentleman ushered his lady inside with such care and pride that passersby assumed she was his bride and they were on their honeymoon. They certainly weren't a couple long married! Nice to know some people still considered Fambré a honeymoon destination, despite all the trouble nowadays.

The inn was dark inside, with a noisy saloon and dining room. The gentleman looked around while the lady inquired of the barkeeper if a certain person was available.

A lady with a weary face rose from her table, having spotted them. She beckoned, and they went to her, the gentleman's companion embracing her like an old friend. They were the perfect picture of a favorite student visiting a beloved governess she had outgrown.

"Would you prefer to take luncheon in my suite?" the governess asked. "The dining room is very noisy at this time of day."

All agreeing, they climbed three flights of stairs, traversed a small, darkish hallway and finally reached their destination, a modest apartment of the type rented by the month by single men or women who did not make enough money to buy a cottage. The governess primly saw the newlywed couple in, then closed and locked the door behind her as she followed her guests.

The gentleman rapidly checked the tiny balcony and all closets and rooms, while the governess poked a broom handle under all pieces of furniture. Her ex-student laughed silently and helplessly as they made sure no-one was in the apartment.

"I hate caps," Gladdas Dalmanthea said, divesting herself of her matronly headgear. "Beautifully done, you two. You were so callow, I barely knew you."

Eiren removed her prissy little veiled hat, her auburn hair flashing in the sunlight venturing in from the balcony.

Menders removed his topper to reveal his hip length hair braided and wrapped around his head for concealment.

"Charming coiffure," Gladdas guyed him.

"It pulls like all the hells too," he added, unpinning the coil and unbraiding it. "I hope you meant it when you said you had food up here. It smelled like they were roasting rat downstairs."

"They probably are. Decent food is that rare in the poorer markets," Gladdas told him. She produced a spread of cold, smoked meat and cheese from a small chest standing on a table and handed Menders a bottle of wine to open. Bread and buns were retrieved from another cupboard.

"This is not from a rat meat market, but brought over from The Shadows," she announced. "Eiren, this was one of Menders and my techniques for meeting clandestinely when we were young folks going about our assassin work, if we needed to exchange information. Meet very publicly, go up to a room together. My favorite time was when we dressed as a priest of Grahl and a priestess of Grune."

"Everyone was so stunned they would never have thought of listening at the door," Menders grinned, uncorking the wine and taking a seat. "That was the time we went over information for so long we fell asleep on the bed, where we had our maps and papers spread around. The next morning Gladdy opened her eyes, saw me just opening mine, squeaked like a squashed mouse and fell right off her side of the bed."

"I've bragged for years that I slept with Menders," Gladdas said, cutting slices of bread while Eiren laughed helplessly.

The meal passed in similar banter and Gladdas' queries about the younger set and how they were weathering their trip to Fambré. When Eiren told her about how upset Katrin had been over the street beggars, she sighed.

"It's ghastly," she said. "I was a young girl when the Revolt and Terror took place and I remember how horrified people were as they read about it, placing the blame on the Revolutionists and peasants who rose up. But seeing these poor people in the streets, it's easy to understand. It won't be long. I hope you will be leaving soon."

Menders nodded.

"There isn't much reason to stay longer," he replied. "Kaymar and Ifor were out with Katrin and Borsen the other day and saw what looked like a meeting of peasants. Once they start to organize, there will be trouble. Not being able to take Katrin into any large town or city means we've nearly run out of things to see."

"I'll sleep easier once we're away from here," Eiren added. "You can feel the anger growing."

"Good," Gladdas agreed, her voice crisp. "Now, if we're finished with lunch, time for the matter at hand."

"Go ahead, Glad," Menders smiled, beginning to gather up dishes, gesturing for Eiren to remain seated.

"I've recruited Lucen Greinholz as an agent around The Shadows," she said, pouring herself another half glass of wine. "He knows everyone in the area. His manner is so innocent and deceptively simple that people talk very freely to and around him. As I'm sure you know, he is not particularly innocent and is certainly not simple."

"Lucen has the best ears I've ever encountered," Menders agreed. "He doesn't like to be in the spotlight and prefers a quiet life, but he's invaluable in hearing things others miss."

"He's found someone whom I suspect is my turncoat operative in disguise," Gladdas went on. "Heard about her in Rondheim when he went down with Villison after some supplies. Vil weaseled around and got nothing, but Lucen went into a bar frequented by military men and bought several rounds, got them all singing and best of friends – and the tongues loosened nicely. We don't know exactly where she's holed up – no-one seems to – but she has been seen around town posing as a fruit vendor.

"Lucen jollied them around until he found she's been steering conversations toward The Shadows. All 'ooh-aah', the poor little street seller wantin' t' hear about t'quality." Gladdas lapsed into a lower class Mordanian accent that made Eiren smile.

"What does she want to know about The Shadows?" Menders asked, offering Eiren more wine and then topping up his glass.

"Asking about the people at the house – scouting to see if there's anyone new staying there. In other words, looking for me. One of the reasons I'm now here and intend to stay a distance from The Shadows for a while, much as I like it there."

"Gladdas, what caused this animosity?" Eiren asked, her forehead wrinkled slightly in concern.

Menders shook his head and Gladdas looked over at Eiren.

"Dear, there is no animosity. This is business. This young lady – her name is Alazaria Fentez, she's Samorsan by birth – was my foremost protégée. She's a chameleon, can appear ugly, beautiful, anything in between, absorbed languages lightning fast and sounds like a native in all of them. She has no loyalty to any nation, having left Samorsa as an infant. Through various catastrophes, she ended up in an Artreyan orphanage by the time she was four. Terrible experiences, deprivation – she came to my school at the age of eight, a very intelligent but very unfeeling and unchildlike little girl. No amount of kindness or inclusion helped. She was a law unto herself, very like Kaymar when he was an assassin.

"Alazaria had no interest in training for clerical or managerial work. She had a natural talent for espionage and I tried to keep her directed that way. I was afraid, considering her lack of empathy and compassion, that it would be disastrous for her to undertake assassin work.

"She picked it up. Where, I don't know. I refused to instruct her and repeatedly told her the reasons why. But she found she made more money eliminating targets – and money is the only thing Alazaria loves."

"And that's what's driving her now?" Menders asked as Gladdas fell silent.

She nodded, rose and walked to the window. Menders noticed she approached it from the side and looked out from the wall end of the curtain, remaining unseen to any observer outside.

"Alazaria cares nothing about governments. I doubt she has much understanding of governmental or political policy. She certainly had no interest in such topics while she was still in school," she answered. "She wouldn't care if Morghenna VIII stayed on the throne forever – but she'd kill her in a brace of shakes if someone gave her enough money to do it."

"The worst sort of assassin there is." Menders sat back in his chair and looked anxiously at Eiren. "Not even a sadist like DeLarco, who kills for pleasure, is harder to stop."

"She's been offered an enormous sum to eliminate me." Gladdas turned toward them. For a woman who could make herself appear dazzling, she was suddenly haggard and despairing.

"Attempts have been made to pay her off to leave me alone – but this faction is determined to be rid of me and my network. They seem to have infinite funds. I've been working against them for years. Their ultimate goal is gaining control of both Artreya and Mordania."

"Anyone who managed that would control the entire world," Eiren said softly.

"Yes – and they have the wherewithal to manage it," Gladdas answered. "My network and several others have been fighting them off and on for years. That includes our hero here, though I'll wager all the coins in the bottom of my bag he's never told you about it."

She quirked her features slightly and suddenly was the flippant, sophisticated Gladdas Dalmanthea who arrived at The Shadows on a hot summer afternoon. She reclaimed her seat at the table.

"I don't tend to talk shop much in the family quarters," Menders chided her gently. "Too many youthful ears around, estate business, school matters. Incredibly wealthy people who want to rule the world aren't dinner table conversation, Sister Glad. But to be honest, Eiren is not ignorant of what my network does. In fact, she's a very valuable resource to me, because she often sees sides of issues I miss – or blind myself to."

"You've learned to accept your limitations," Gladdas remarked with a smile.

"And so have you," Menders answered. "Shall we finish the wine?"

Glasses replenished, Eiren looked from one of them to the other.

"Menders has always said assassins must have some ideal they believe in," she said. "In his case, it's Queen Clearheart's phrase, 'I protect the future of Mordania'. It was Kaymar's youth and lack of any guiding ideal that led to his mental breakdown."

"I remember it well," Gladdas nodded. "He was a terribly sick boy in those days."

"So, what is yours?" Eiren asked bluntly. "You don't have strong ties to Artreya – not that I've seen."

Gladdas took a sip of wine, obviously phrasing her response.

"No. I'm not Artreyan by birth, though it's a good enough country," she eventually replied. "I have no true allegiance to any nation, but I do to Eirdon itself and the people who live on it. My work as an assassin – and I am not one now, I'm far too old – was always dedicated to preserving a certain degree of peace on this planet. Certain balances have to be maintained to do this. Certain factions must not attain more power – others must not rise to power. People are far too fond of war and the money they gain from it. That has been my fight."

"And much bloodshed and misery has been turned aside," Menders added, his voice suspiciously husky.

"You've done the same," Gladdas replied, her own voice tightly controlled. "Aren't we sentimental! Now then, here is where I am going from here and where I plan to be – and when – unless it must be otherwise." She handed Menders a folded sheet of paper. He read it quickly, then put a match to it.

The sharp smell of burning paper engendered action. They rose and began preparing to leave, Menders swiftly braiding his hair to go under his hat, Eiren donning her headgear and fluffing the veil that darkened her hair and obscured her face. Gladdas pulled on her hated cap, quirked her features again and was suddenly a worn, retired governess, living on her savings in an obscure inn.

LOUVIS, FAMBRÉ

15
TELLYN FEIN

Katrin smiled delightedly as Menders ushered her into a little shop on a side street of Louvis, a perfume manufacturing town in northern Fambré. It was shop typical of the region, with local products and crafts, some groceries, assorted ornaments and doodads as well as the usual counter full of locally made perfumes. She loved to poke about in such places.

Kaymar held the shop door open for Varnia, teasingly tweaking her scarf as she walked by.

"Don't buy the place out," he grinned when she jerked around to look at him. Varnia tried to scowl but failed. It was hard to scowl at Kaymar when he was being winning. Varnia had discovered the joys of shopping and sometimes overbought her strict, self-imposed budget.

Menders nudged Katrin, who was already absorbed by a collection of charming glass boxes holding solid perfumes. She looked up to see the proprietor bowing grandly to her near the curtained doorway of the shop's back room.

Smiling, Katrin bobbed a curtsey in reply – and was stunned when the man stood up and was Tellyn Fein, devoid of his Revenant garments.

"A thousand greetings, Light Of The Winter Sun," he said.

Katrin was saw that Menders and Kaymar were scanning the shop and bolting the front door.

Tellyn Fein opened the back room for Kaymar, who ducked inside, then came out and nodded to Menders.

"Mister Fein wishes to speak to you," Menders said quietly to Katrin. "You may go with him."

She stared at him for a moment.

"It's all right," he murmured gently, smiling slightly. "I've already spoken with him several times. It's safe, but we don't have long."

Katrin found herself near at the rear wall of the shop's back room with the leader of The Revenants. Menders and Kaymar stood with their backs to them, watching the front door. Varnia was watching one of the windows.

Tellyn Fein smiled and handed her a slice of candied ruby fruit from a barrel nearby, first breaking off a piece and eating it in front of her.

"Mister Fein, I trust you," she protested.

"Still, always a good idea. Always be sure, my dear."

Katrin bit into the succulent delicacy, wondering how he knew it was her favorite – or if his choice was entirely chance.

Suddenly she was acutely aware that nothing Tellyn Fein did was by chance.

"Have you heard them?" he asked, his voice very low, sitting on a tall stool across from her, rubbing his knees as if they ached.

"Who?"

"Keep your voice down. The voices. The Queens."

"The… how do you know? Did Menders tell you?" She stared at him.

"No. We know you hear the voices at times of great danger or trouble. What you hear be the voices of the dead Queens of Mordania. Your grandmother, The Terrible, who was my friend. Clearheart, the bravest one, even the Great Glorantha. Did you not know?"

"They – they never introduced themselves," Katrin gasped.

Tellyn Fein laughed silently.

"I be having you on the back foot," he murmured after a moment. "If you be part of The Revenants, you be taught how to listen to the ones who have gone before. But now that be no matter and there be little time. Have you heard them the last few days?"

Katrin was shaking her head – then she hesitated and listened.

"Yes!" she whispered after a moment. "They are there. I've been busy and not in danger – but now that I listen for them, I hear them, as if they are very far away. No words, just a whispering. Like hearing the ocean in the distance."

He looked grave.

"Now you must be vigilant," he said, all humor gone. "You must be aware and listen. When there comes a roaring silence, you and yours must leave Fambré – but not until then. It is vital that you remain until that moment."

"Why?"

"There be a balance in this world and others. You being here in Fambré at this time is vital in that balance," Tellyn Fein said, his light green eyes holding hers. "Should you leave too soon, all will be lost."

"Have you told Menders, so I can alert him when it comes?" Katrin was feeling frantic. She didn't make the decisions for their party.

"Shh. They say they will not listen to us, but I know assassins. To not listen be nearly impossible for them. Menders knows nothing of it and you must keep it that way. Say nothing until the time or all be lost." Tellyn Fein slid down from the stool and stood before her.

"But why would he listen if I suddenly insisted we leave?" she whispered in frustration.

"You must take command at that time. This you must."

"All right." Katrin could say nothing else. This intense, strange man would accept nothing else.

"Thank you. Now, before they lose their patience and come in." He strode across the room and bowed her out into the shop again.

Menders and Kaymar turned, their faces expressionless. Katrin smiled as if she and Tellyn Fein had been exchanging frivolous gossip and went over to Varnia, who had turned away from the shop window and was looking over some gloves.

"I be standing in for my friend, the shopkeeper," Tellyn Fein said smoothly. "What may I help you find?" His face was smooth and innocent, as if he had only just been born.

BOUVAIS, FAMBRÉ

15
A ROARING SILENCE

Katrin walked arm in arm with Abbot Fahrin, the priest of Galanth who ran the feeding station in Bouvais, the first town she had encountered in Fambré, where the mob of beggars had so horrified her. The family had come full circle and were here to have easy access to the train when they decided to return to Surelia.

Or when the roaring silence said they had to leave. Katrin thought about her conversation with Tellyn Fein a great deal. She listened to the distant whisper in her mind but heard no distinct words, not as she had when the woman had come up behind her with a gun at The Shadows, determined to kill her.

She had spoken softly in her room a few times, saying, "Grandmother?" or "Clearheart?" There had been no reply – only that incessant susurrus far away.

Menders had not asked about her conversation with Tellyn Fein. This impressed Katrin. Fein must have laid down the law to Menders. That would have been a sight to see. Menders was kind and loving, he was goodness itself, but he was also in charge of the family and their safety. He must implicitly trust the Revenant – and for that matter, Katrin – to be so accepting of their secret discussion.

Kaymar was another matter and kept setting up situations where Katrin might confide in him. She finally said, "I can't tell you and that's that!" He stopped then, but she could tell he was about to die of curiosity.

As far as she was concerned, she hoped the roaring silence never came.

"And this is our new area for mothers and children," Fahrin explained, ushering her through yet another doorway. "They can have a place to rest or sleep, there is water and soap for washing. The doctor comes daily and, of course, there is food."

Katrin looked around at the women and children, remembering that desperate mob, the outstretched hands and the mothers clutching skeletal babies. The women and children here were far from plump and healthy, but they could be clean and had food to eat. She and Menders had done something to help them – and now, through the efforts of Princess Dorlane, money was pouring in from Fambrians who had resettled in Mordania and other nations.

Suddenly Katrin recognized a face. She unlinked her arm from Fahrin's and went to a woman sitting on a low cot, holding a baby in her arms.

"How is your baby?" Katrin asked as the young woman looked up at her. She was the mother who had broken Katrin's heart that first day as she held up her nearly dead child in desperation.

The mother spoke in Fambrian, her dark eyes lighting up in her haggard face. She held the baby girl out to Katrin, who nestled her in the crook of her arm, adjusting her little dress.

"She remembers you – she will never forget you," Fahrin translated. "You handle this little one as if you've had many of your own."

"On our estate there are many babies and I help at my mother's school as well," Katrin smiled. The baby, though thin and weak, had rallied beautifully and was smiling up at Katrin. She had beautiful brown eyes that looked enormous in her gaunt little face.

"Have you considered this as work for yourself?" the priest asked earnestly. "You are genuinely interested. You truly care for these people."

"Are you asking me to be a priestess?" Katrin laughed.

"No, that is not your path – but to work with and for the poor? That is something you would love."

Katrin rubbed the baby's belly gently, eliciting a healthy belch.

"Possibly," she said after a moment. "There are – circumstances." She kissed the baby and gave her back to her mother, who smiled again and blessed Katrin in Fambrian.

Menders strolled in with Eiren. They had been talking to some of the people having meals in the adjoining room. Katrin delightedly showed them the baby.

"I was asking your daughter if she would like to work with such people," Fahrin said. "She has a great heart and affinity for it."

"Very much so," Menders agreed, making Katrin start. "She is invaluable at home, when there is need among our estate tenants. I'm very proud of her empathy and caring."

"It would be something to consider," Eiren added, smiling at Katrin's astonished face. "This has been an excellent opportunity to learn."

"You see? It isn't just the foolish priest," Fahrin teased gently, extending his arm for Katrin to take. "Come and see the new laundry facilities we've been able to arrange with a gift from Princess Dorlane."

Katrin took his arm and smiled up at him.

***

From Menders' Journal:

Things seem less tense here in Fambré during the last few weeks, though we are still vigilant and maintaining a very low profile. We are staying outside Bouvais, having migrated back toward the north of the country after Kaymar, Ifor and the children stumbled upon that meeting in a field further south. We are a short carriage ride to the nearest train depot from here.

The plight of the beggars in Bouvais has markedly improved with the combination of the efforts of Princess Dorlane and ourselves. So far there are six feeding stations in Bouvais, manned by the priests and priestesses of Galanth and the priests of Grahl. The results are obvious. The atmosphere is far less threatening than it was.

How easy it would be to change the situation here – yet the King and Court see nothing. Of course, they never venture outside, other than to travel to another of the pleasure palaces by night, so their movements are not seen – they think. How idiotic can a ruler be?

And why do I ask such a rhetorical question? The Queen of Mordania is far from a magnificent example. She hasn't walked outside the Palace in a decade or more. There are beggars and City Thrun dying all over Erdahn and she doesn't even know it.

Time for a change of topic, as my temper is running away.

This morning Katrin asked me if priests of Galanth could marry. She was quite intrigued when I told her they could. Apparently, Abbot Fahrin is making quite an impression – and why not? He's charismatic, decent, caring and handsome as the morning. Intense in a manner that captivates Katrin. It's obvious he's half in love with her.

And why shouldn't he be? She's intelligent, compassionate, involved and absolutely lovely. I could see them working together happily. He is older, but he would ground her – and she would calm and rejuvenate him. There is that connection there, that spark. I know it well and I can see it in others.

And I must take her away from what might become her first love, which could ripen into a strong marriage. Because of who she is – I can't write about it today.

Kaymar just came in. He says all is quiet on the streets and from informants. So, no rush to leave just yet.

***

Katrin was telling everyone at the dinner table about assisting Doctor Franz at the Galanth feeding station that day when she suddenly felt dizzy. She closed her eyes.

When she opened them, the room was silent. Everyone was looking at her worriedly and she could see Menders and Eiren speaking, but she heard no words. It was as if someone had put a huge glass box down over her, forming a vacuum.

Then it came.

The whispering on the edge of her consciousness grew, towered and then crashed over her in a terrifying roar of voices.

There were millions of them, shouting, screaming, warning! Far more than dead Queens of Mordania – these were a multitude, all who had died in the Revolt and Terror, all who had died in the endless wars that swept across Eirdon. It was so intense it would crush her skull!

She stood abruptly, staring at nothing. Hemmett was up, his hands on her shoulders. She could see his lips moving, but heard only the crushing battery of that multitude of voices.

"Go now! Go now! They are coming to kill!"

Katrin recognized that voice! It had warned her of the woman with the gun standing behind her at The Shadows last year. It was harsh and rough, an elderly woman's voice, cutting through the shrieking multitude. Katrin was sure it was her grandmother, Morghenna the Terrible.

"Yes," she gasped. Suddenly she could speak and move again.

"We have to go! Now!" she shouted in a voice that rivaled The Terrible's in her prime. "Don't question me! Do as I say!"

She ran for her room, followed closely by Menders, who must think she'd gone mad. She tore her cases out of the closet. They were mostly packed. Menders had ordered everyone to keep their belongings packed in case they needed to leave quickly.

The voices swirled around her head like a whirlpool.

"Katrin, just let me know what is happening," Menders protested.

"We have to go. We must go now! The poor people are rising up and they are coming! I know where we need to go – they're telling me where we need to go. We need horses and two carriages to move fast and we must go to the sea! Not to the train, that would be a target. East, to the sea!"

To the sea! Run to the sea!

A man's voice, thick with terror and love rang out above the screams in Katrin's mind. Princess Dorlane's father's last words to his daughters.

She flung her cases open and began hurling her things into them.

"Katrin, I'll listen to you," Menders began. "Just…"

"There is no time!" she cried in frustration.

She turned to him. The voices were everything now. She could hear the women's voices, the Queens.

"Command him, child! You must! He is your guardian, he is your father by love, but you are a Princess of Mordania and your orders are above his! Now! THERE IS NO TIME!"

"I am Princess Katrin Morghenna of Mordania!" she shouted at Menders. "I order you to do as I say! We will go now to a port on the eastern shore and return to Surelia!"

He looked as if she'd hit him with a board.

"This is to save our lives! Do as I say, Lord Stettan!"

Menders blinked and ran out of her room. She could hear him shouting commands, then Hemmett taking up the chain. They were running to their rooms. Someone left and went toward the inn stables for horses and carriages. Good!

Katrin slammed and locked her cases, carrying them into the hall. To save time, she opened a window and heaved them down into the street. She turned to find Varnia right behind her.

The older girl did the same, dropping her cases to the pavement. She leaned out the window.

"Smoke," she said tersely. She turned to Katrin and checked to see if the knife that Princess Dorlane had given her was in place around her waist. Their eyes met, and they clasped hands. No words were necessary.

"All out into the hallway, ready to go downstairs!" Katrin shouted suddenly as the family emerged from their rooms. Doctor Franz took over dropping the cases from the window as Katrin hustled the others into the hallway.

"Darling, what is happening?" Eiren asked, looking closely at Katrin.

"Something I was warned of – the poor people are coming to kill. It's another Revolt. We have to go now!" Katrin answered.

She heard hooves ringing against paving stones.

"They're here!" Hemmett said from his vantage point near the hallway window.

"Downstairs!" Katrin commanded. They clattered down, out into the street and were portioned into the two carriages by Menders. Horses were provided for Hemmett, Menders and Doctor Franz to save weight in the carriages, so they could move fast. Ifor and Kaymar, the best drivers, sat on the carriage boxes.

Suddenly Fahrin was there, having run over from the feeding station. He found Katrin's window and reached up, taking her hand.

"There have been huge uprisings northward as well as to the south," he gasped. "Don't go to the train."

"We're not. We're going east to the sea," she answered firmly.

"Go fast down the Louvis Road and do not stop for any reason. They've already been there, so you'll be safe. They're on their way to the Capital."

"What about you?" Katrin asked, suddenly no longer impelled by The Terrible.

"I feed the poor. I will be safe," he answered. "Go now! Go, my dear!"

"Go along the Louvis Road!" Katrin shouted to Ifor. As the carriage moved forward, Eiren looked back through the rear window.

"Oh, my gods," she gasped. Everyone turned.

Torches, thousands of them, were moving toward the town of Bouvais through the fragrant fields of luxen and along the roads, an endless shifting constellation of individual flames. In the places they had been, fires roared into the sky.

Fahrin ran alongside them until they reached the feeding station. Amazingly, it was lighted, and priests were dishing out food to the endless stream of poor people who came at all hours. Of course, Katrin thought, that will identify them as helping the poor. It will keep them safe.

"Be careful," she called to him.

"I shall," he answered. "Write to me."

Then he rapidly blew her a kiss, smiled and went inside.

***

Katrin stood at the railing of a small fishing trawler. It was past midnight, after their desperate race to the eastern shore through what the peasants of Fambré had left behind in their deadly path. Dismembered and burned corpses lay thick on the sides of the Louvis Road; buildings and crops were ablaze. Their journey had been silent except for the clattering of horses' hooves and the rattling of the carriages.

The family was safe. Menders had exchanged a huge sum of money for them to be taken to the nearest Surelian port near a train station. Everyone had gone below immediately, exhausted and emotionally shattered by what they had seen.

Eiren had kissed her silently and to Katrin's surprise, Varnia did the same. Doctor Franz cupped her face in his hand and smiled. Kaymar touched her shoulder and Ifor kissed her hand. Hemmett hadn't needed to do anything more than smile at her, his eyes full of tears. Borsen had been the only one who spoke.

"Good night, my mighty sister," he whispered in Thrun.

She remained on deck alone, letting sea spray and mist clean her skin. Her clothing reeked from the stench of the fires they had passed. She knew either Kaymar or Ifor was watching her, but they left her to herself. She was utterly exhausted, and the voices of the Queens were gone.

Then she knew, without hearing him approach, that Menders was there.

"My little princess," he said softly, putting his hands on her shoulders.

Katrin realized she had been fearful, deep down, that he would be hurt or angry because of her commands. Now she heard the pride in his voice.

She turned into his embrace, resting her head against his shoulder. She was too weary for words.

Menders held her close, watching the three brightest stars in the constellation called The Weaver.

THE SHADOWS, MORDANIA

17
TROUBLE FOLLOWS LIKE A DOG

Gladdas Dalmanthea, Erlen Haakel, Corporal Villison and Cook were seated around the partners' desk Menders had moved into his office at The Shadows when he first took residence. Originally, he had chosen the desk so Katrin could sit opposite him with crayons and paper, then later with schoolwork or sketchbooks. Now it allowed Gladdas to sit opposite Haakel and work with him on the management of the estate and Menders' Men – when she wasn't teasing his life out, to his great amusement.

Gladdas had hidden on the Middle Continent for over a month, shifting her location repeatedly. She was certain Alazaria Fentez had followed her flawlessly and was only kept from carrying out her mission to eliminate her former mentor by Gladdas' effective use of the many safe houses she owned. She got away from her last bolt-hole disguised as a carriage driver.

That caper had shaken Alazaria off her trail for several weeks, giving her the opportunity to meet with Menders and Eiren and then return, by a circuitous route via Surytam, to The Shadows.

Three weeks had been free of any sign of Alazaria, but then an informant reported a young woman recently hired as a nursemaid at an estate near Erdstrom making inquiries about the mistress at The Shadows.

"Could just be a nosy young miss," Cook suggested. Gladdas had included her from the first – Menders had let her know that Cook's domestic connections in the area were invaluable for backstairs information.

"It could," Haakel agreed. "But I still want it investigated."

"It has to be entirely without her knowing – which I don't believe can happen." Gladdas leaned back in her chair tiredly. "Not considering the operative Alazaria has become."

Gladdas' journey had been exhausting and even with days of rest, she was tired. Subterfuge was wearing on the mind and body.

"Has to be difficult with one of your own doing this," Cook said sympathetically. Her quiet sagacity struck a nerve.

"Yes, it is," Gladdas answered, all roleplay gone. "And no-one knows better than I how intelligent – and how lacking a soul – Alazaria is."

"I haven't felt anything outside. Not as yet."

The voice was old, yet powerful, deep enough to rival that of Ifor Trantz. The four seated at the desk turned toward an oversized armchair in a shaded corner.

Lucen Greinholz, sent to The Shadows with the original household as Katrin's Guard, was reclining comfortably where he could see through the office window, which looked out at The Shadows' orchard. He was a huge man, standing seven feet tall.

He had retired from service years ago, once Menders recruited Menders' Men – and he had done so gladly. He much preferred functioning as The Shadows' gardener and woodsman.

He knew the estate intimately and claimed to feel what was happening on it through the soles of his feet as he walked across the land. His instincts had been right so often that no-one scoffed anymore when Lucen claimed, with a smile, that something was afoot.

"I've seen nothing when out early in the morning," he continued. "No signs in the woods of anyone watching or moving about."

"Nor me," Villison added. "We've been keeping double patrols with Hemmett's Men and Menders' Men are doubled up as well. I think if she's around, she's keeping her distance."

Haakel looked at Gladdas, whose face was frozen in careful neutrality.

"Glad, this needs to come to an end – a favorable one," he said. "Do you want us to take action or do you want to deal with it?"

Gladdas showed all the animation of a stone statue for at least a minute, while Villison and Lucen waited calmly and Cook began to fidget. Erlen Haakel settled back in his chair. He was accustomed to the intensity of people in his business and had worked for many years with Menders, who always deliberately thought out things before making a plan.

"I can't deal with it alone," Gladdas finally admitted, her face falling into lines of defeat. "Running from her all these weeks let me know that. I haven't been an active assassin for more than ten years and I'm too old. Alazaria is twenty-three. She's fast, she's strong and she'll never turn aside. I need help."

Only Haakel knew what it took to make Gladdas admit this in front of others. He smiled at her and reached out, putting his hand over her clenched ones.

"We'll help you," he said. "We'll get a plan set and begin going after her. That will alert her to the fact that we're aware she's in the locality and it might drive her here – or it could drive her away."

"It will drive her here. I'll face her here," Gladdas said, her face gone as cold, white and hard as marble.

THE SHADOWS, MORDANIA

17
LUCEN

"Letter from Menders," one of the Men said, handing an envelope to Haakel. "Came over fast. He sent Petroff back to be relieved."

Haakel nodded, tearing the communication open. He read fast, while those at the breakfast table for the Men's' sitting watched him intently. His face didn't show the effect the words had on him, but his hands tensed.

"There was an uprising in Fambré," he said, filling in the rest of Menders' Men. "They're safe. They avoided the mobs and got out on a fishing trawler."

"Ifor would have been in his element," one of the younger Men joked weakly, referencing Ifor's love for fishing.

"That he would," Haakel smiled. "They're back in Surelia with no harm done. The newssheets are due on today's train and should have news of the uprising. Menders says it was eventually quashed, but there was enormous loss of life. It won't be long until there's a full-scale Revolt again and that fat fool of a King will be deposed."

He looked at the Men around the table.

"Volunteer to replace Petroff? Three months with the family in Surelia. Menders isn't going to move them for a while. He wants to let the young ones settle down and feel safe."

Haakel went back to breakfast, but scanned the disturbing letter again. He was surprised at Menders staying so long in Fambré, which sounded like more of a tinderbox than anyone in Mordania suspected. Then, things might have seemed outwardly calm, though the terrible disparity between the wealthy and the impoverished had been blatantly obvious from the outset of their journey.

Of course, the uprising had been sudden. Menders would never had kept Katrin within reach of harm if he'd had any suspicion such a thing would occur.

Sometimes it was best not to try to decipher Menders' motivations. Haakel had accepted long ago that his one-time student was deeply complex – and sometimes inscrutable.

***

Lucen walked through the misty woodlot at a leisurely pace, using a pocketful of variously colored thumbtacks to mark trees. Black signified a tree that should come down as soon as possible. Red indicated a tree to be taken down in the spring. Green meant a tree that bore watching and might improve enough not to be cut. He tapped each carefully selected tack into the tree trunks with the butt of his broad bladed axe, which he always carried when working in the woodlot.

He wasn't one for breakfast most days and liked to spend the early morning out and around the grounds. He'd been handed a letter from his son, Hemmett, that morning and enjoyed reading it while drinking from his bottle of hot coffee that his wife, Zelia, made up for him every day.

Knowing Hemmett and the rest were out of Fambré was a relief – and the mystery of how Katrin knew that the peasants were coming was interesting. Lucen had known her since the day she was born. She had not been a typical child at any point in her life.

She had been an exceptionally bright infant and little girl, with a bad bent for mischief and misbehavior as she grew toward her teens. It was easy enough to understand. The child didn't like being restricted as a Princess was, even under Menders' very loving guardianship. It was a sad thing to put such a burden on a child and Menders had done all he could to give her freedom.

As she grew into a young woman, a lot of her mischief calmed down. Lucen thought again of Hemmett's description of Katrin calling Menders "Lord Stettan" and giving him a royal command that ended up saving everyone's skin. He would have loved to see that.

Lucen chuckled to himself and then looked toward the house. Motion had caught his eye.

It was Gladdas, following her usual routine of a ramble in the garden after a light breakfast. She was a strong woman but very worn down by running from the young woman assassin. She usually throve on company, but was seeking solitude lately.

Lucen rose, rubbing his bad knee, the result of two members of Queen Morghenna VIII's Court dueling in the Great Hall of the Palace shortly before Princess Katrin was born. A ricocheting bullet had struck Lucen, then a Palace Guard.

Palace Physician, Doctor Franz, refused to remove the bullet or amputate Lucen's leg, which all the other quacks wanted to do. Lucen regained his ability to walk but could never stand to attention for hours on end again. He ended up sent to The Shadows with the original household assigned to Menders and the little Princess.

Lucen began marking trees again, keeping a steady eye on Gladdas, keeping his mind on something else. His feet were talking to him and had been for a while. Something was afoot.

He remembered coming here to this house. Menders, a stripling of twenty for all he was the greatest assassin in the world, a newborn baby girl, Doctor Franz, Cook and Lucen's own family, his wife and three-year-old son, Hemmett made up the household.

Lucen had become a father unexpectedly after marrying in later middle age. His wife, Zelia, had been married previously but had never conceived. They were delighted with an enormous, healthy baby boy – and found out just how tired they could be as new parents with Zelia in her late forties and Lucen in his mid-fifties. He had been lying about his age for years to retain his position in the military.

Hemmett was intelligent and strong willed. Zelia believed any misbehavior on his part would eventually be outgrown. If Lucen disagreed and wanted Hemmett disciplined, there was an argument. Hemmett learned rapidly how to pit one parent against the other. By the time he was three years old, he was a holy terror and was running the family to suit himself.

The new Master of the Princess' household wasn't going to have Hemmett running The Shadows – and Lucen was glad of that. Menders was kind and caring to the little boy, but set firm rules for him that he upheld unflinchingly. Before long, though Hemmett was still a handful and would be for some years, he was a happier and more tractable child. Zelia was relieved and Lucen was eternally grateful to the younger man for stepping in.

It never bothered him that Hemmett became strongly attached to Menders. Lucen knew his son's love for him was deep and true. Menders had given the boy every advantage and opportunity, including getting him entry to the Mordanian Military Academy where the young man had graduated as a Captain, becoming the commanding officer of Katrin's Personal Guard. That was something Lucen and Zelia would never have been able to provide – nor this wonderful tour around the Middle Continent and possibly beyond.

There it was again, a presence, something here that normally wasn't. Lucen stepped behind the shelter of a small thicket, his brown clothing making him disappear. He moved nothing but his eyes, scanning, watching Gladdas, who had wandered to the edge of the woodlot. Lucen knew where she was going – there was a chatterbird nest in a particular stand of saplings.

He waited as she checked on the nest, then was attracted to a thunder tree, its flower buds red against the late winter sky. She gazed up at the display and Lucen reflected, not for the first time, on just how much this lively woman loved beauty.

Suddenly Gladdas went stock still and moved her head very slowly toward her left – but Lucen had already sensed the invading presence. He also turned his head with the slowness of a lizard, wanting to bring the intruder into view.

By design she was out of Gladdas' line of vision. An early flush of green buds in the underbrush at the edge of the woodlot hid her. Her fawn shirt and trousers matched the early spring landscape perfectly.

Lucen flicked his eyes toward the Menders' Man on the roof, then realized this young madam was out of his view as well. She was using the budding shrubs to good advantage. If she was armed with a pistol, any attempt on Lucen's part to alert the guard would lead to Gladdas' death.

The young woman in the underbrush crept toward Gladdas, who was looking around her more overtly. She saw nothing, but she knew her executioner was there – oh yes, she knew.

Mirroring the young woman's movement, Lucen eased toward Gladdas, staying behind cover, grateful he insisted on sticks and leaf litter being removed from the woodlot regularly. He could move in silence despite his size, if he didn't become impatient. He'd learned it from Menders years ago, in this very woodlot as they'd worked together to keep the original household warm, endlessly cutting wood to feed The Shadows' fireplaces and stoves.

Lucen breathed evenly, moving only when the young woman did.

Gladdas was backing toward the house, keeping her eyes on the woodlot, scanning, looking for her pursuer. Lucen knew she was hoping her movement would draw attention from the house, that the Man on the roof would notice her peculiar method of travel. He glanced at the roof.

The Man there was watching and had his gun up. Good!

Suddenly the young woman, now quite close to Gladdas, stood boldly upright. She was hidden from the Man on the roof by a tall evergreen tree. Lucen knew she had planned this meticulously.

She was close enough that if Gladdas ran, she would overtake her in a couple of strides. If Gladdas drew her knife, the same thing would happen. She had stalked as successfully as a Surytamian crocodile and was closing on her prey.

She didn't know that by being so intent on Gladdas she had neglected to notice she was being stalked as well.

"Alazaria – you don't need to do this," Gladdas said, her voice very calm. "If it's money you want, I have access to plenty here. Lord Stettan has a great deal of money in the house."

Alazaria Fentez didn't speak, only moved gradually closer to her quarry. Gladdas was trying to prompt her into conversation, to distract her.

Another quick glance at the house let Lucen know Villison was aware of the situation. He was at the Rose Garden door, his gun in hand and another on his hip, but he knew Fentez was close enough to kill before he could get past the door and fire. The Man on the roof was aiming at the wrong part of the woodlot, unable to see what was happening.

"Alazaria – please. What does this give you other than money? Didn't we try to give you every opportunity and advantage? Is this about nothing but money?" Gladdas' voice was tightening, betraying emotion.

The young woman, well trained, continued advancing on her teacher, a long dagger held low. If Villison came through the door, she would strike. She had seen him, but had no fear. She kept moving infinitesimally closer to Gladdas, their eyes locked.

Like a snake stares at a bird it's going to attack, Lucen thought. But that means she has not seen me.

Four swift steps brought him close. Startled, the young woman turned toward him. She saw him coming, axe raised behind his left shoulder.

Their eyes met, even as she raised her knife to strike him. Her eyebrows went up slightly, calmly, as if to say, "well played."

Lucen swung the axe at the full length of his arms. Sunlight touched the blade as it removed Alazaria Fentez's head. He saw Gladdas close her eyes at the fatal blow.

Villison exploded out of the door, gesturing to the Man on the roof to lower his weapon. He was closely followed by Cook, who was tearing her apron off.

Gladdas opened her eyes and looked at Alazaria's headless body. She sobbed aloud.

"Oh gods, why couldn't I help her?" she cried. "Why this?"

Lucen stepped forward as Cook flung her apron over Fentez's body and head. He put an arm around Gladdas as Cook embraced her.

"Don't look, Miss Glad," Cook said, turning Gladdas away from the body. "It's all that could be done, dear. There's some you can't pull from the fire, no matter how hard you try."

***

Gladdas collapsed and couldn't leave her bed. Haakel wrote to Menders, who sent Doctor Franz to see her.

After examining the distraught woman, Franz sat across from Haakel in The Shadows' office.

"It's to be expected," he said without his usual verve. "This woman has been stalking her for over a year. You know what it is to have someone hunting you with the intention of doing you in. Combine that with horror over the way Fentez was stopped and guilt because the child she tried to help turned out as she did. Emotional collapse. The only thing I can recommend is rest and support. If I give her something, it could make it worse, or she could become dependent."

So Gladdas spent her days escaping through sleep, only to wake to endless, tearless guilt. She had little interest in food. She wanted only to quench the exhaustion that was dragged at every fiber of her body.

Doctor Franz lingered for weeks until she ordered him to leave her alone. He spoke with the group who had started to call themselves "The Hub" – Haakel, Villison, Lucen and Cook, who were running The Shadows as a group.

"I don't know if there's a point in me staying," he said, gratefully accepting a cup of coffee from Cook. "It might be making her even more resistant. Gladdas Dalmanthea is a powerful person. I never dealt with her, but I've heard a great deal from Menders and the other men here. Short of hauling her out of bed bodily, there's little I can do."

"If you tried, it would be most unwise," Haakel replied, not smiling. "Men who have laid hands on Gladdy have been very sorry they did. She doesn't kill them, but she comes painfully close."

"I think the poor thing just needs rest," Cook countered. "That situation was a terrible strain on her – and seeing the girl killed. I know Lucen had no other choice, because she would have killed them both in seconds, but Miss Glad loved that girl and tried to raise her. Mother love isn't always logical."

"No Cook – and you're right, rest is part of what she needs," Doctor Franz replied. "But she also needs some exercise and she needs food. She's resistant to my suggestions, so I think I'm going to make the trip back to Surelia to rejoin the family. Why don't you see if you can interest her in food?"

"That I can manage – and no invalid pap either. She needs real food," Cook said stalwartly.

"Exactly!" Franz smiled. "Invalid meals aren't doing anything for her appetite. I know you'll find something to tempt her into eating. Who can get her to exercise?"

"I'll deal with it. I caused this situation."

Lucen, usually silent during these round table sessions, spoke softly but his voice carried a serene authority that put a stop to further discussion.

***

Gladdas sensed movement in her room and woke abruptly, her assassin's instinct placing her instantly in time and place. She looked directly at her wardrobe, where Lucen Greinholz was going through her dresses.

Before she could ask him what the hells he was doing, he took out a dress, held it up for a moment and then laid it out on the bed.

"That's a pretty one," he said, giving her a smile. "Get up now and put it on. I want to take you somewhere." He left without another word.

Gladdas sat up against her pillows, blinking a little. She saw her washstand bowl filled with hot water, steam rising from it and from the pitcher beside it. A towel and fresh cake of soap were placed conveniently next to her hairbrush and comb.

Undecided whether to be amused or angry about this invasion of her privacy, Gladdas spent a few moments looking at the dress he'd laid out on the bed. A brief inspection revealed shoes ready on the floor. Lucen hadn't gone so far as to select her underwear – or perhaps she'd wakened before he had a chance.

She realized that for the first time in weeks, she had not seen Alazaria's death in her mind at the moment she opened her eyes.

Gladdas knew when to take action. She swung around, letting her legs dangle for a few minutes before padding down the bedstairs. As she approached the washstand, she could smell lemons – Katrin's soap, made in the shed behind the house by the Princess of Mordania.

That girl could make a fortune off the things she makes in that shed, Gladdas thought, picking up the soap and inhaling the delicious scent. She'd been presented with an assortment of creams, lotions, shampoo and perfume by Katrin upon her arrival at The Shadows. They were always on the dressing table in "Aunty Glad's room" as Katrin and Borsen referred to her suite. So was a beautiful set of towels fashioned by Borsen and embroidered by Eiren.

One look in her mirror made Gladdas pick up her hairbrush. As always, straightening and smoothing the strands made her mind clear.

Within half an hour she was bathed and dressed. She was tying the lace of her left shoe when Lucen tapped at the door. He entered the room carrying a tray with two cups of tea and a platter of eggs, fried ham, sausage and pastries.

"I'm not one for breakfast most days, but I could do with a cup and a bite," he said, going to her table as naturally as if he walked into her room all the time with food in hand. "Thought you'd be feeling pretty hollow by now."

She'd been sure she wanted nothing, but the scent of the sausage was as enticing as Katrin's lemon soap had been.

Gladdas found Lucen an excellent breakfast companion because he didn't spend time in chitchat. She was able to eat and drink her tea in peace, watching the sunrise pale into daylight, golden sun shafts slanting through clouds.

"Now then, the gig should be ready," Lucen announced when Gladdas turned down the offer of another pastry. "It's a pretty morning, but cool, so best to wrap up." He perused her outer garments, selecting a cape with a hood. He held it out for her.

Gladdas caught herself smiling when her back was turned to him, wondering if he was going to actually put the hood up on her head, as if she was three years old.

He didn't, but escorted her to the front door where his patient horse waited, hitched to a comfortable, high-wheeled gig.

Gladdas felt a jolt of dread, fearful that Lucen would take the south curve of the oval drive, which would lead them near the spot where Alazaria was killed. The big man guided the horse along the northern curve instead. Soon they were on their way down the road that passed the Spaltz farm.

"I need to pick up something from Mister Spaltz on the way back, but we won't drive around with a quarter pig now," Lucen smiled as he waved to the red-haired farmer, Eiren's father.

"And where are we going?" Gladdas asked.

"Outside of Artrim," Lucen answered briefly. "Snowflowers are coming out, see them? Did you know Menders used to call Katrin Snowflower when they first came here? Gods, he was just a boy himself."

"Not entirely," Gladdas responded. "I knew him then."

"Well, no. He did some very great things. He also went through some terrible misery when he was just a little lad. I had the nursing of him when we hadn't been here long, and he got his eyes infected. He was sick as a dog for weeks and once it looked like we'd lost him. He had terrible delirium and trying to keep him quiet and under control was like fighting with a threshing machine. Both Franz and I had black eyes and busted lips." Lucen chuckled. "He got past it, however. Trot on, General."

They were quiet for a while, but then Gladdas' curiosity got the better of her.

"What miseries did Menders cope with as a child?" she asked.

"No secret really. Terrible father, had the nurses, governesses and tutors 'toughen' him. You know about that madness, of course."

Gladdas did indeed.

"I've had girls at my school who were abused like that," she sighed. "Broken children."

"Aye. That's what's wrong with the Queen you know. They broke her spirit. I was a Palace Guard when she was just a girl. Beautiful young thing, but no spirit. Even then she was depending on drink to cope with things. Now, well, she's just as weak a woman." He shook his head. "But Menders – he had something that made him powerful, despite all that. He used his misery to become strong. The odd one can, but so many never recover from a childhood horror like that. Now then, here we are."

He spoke gently to the horse while Gladdas looked around.

They were near the beautiful Temple of Galanth, patron goddess of mothers and children. It was a fairly new building, close to Artrim, but it had a centuries-old graveyard, full of strange tombstones and other sculptures marking the mortal remains of people long forgotten. It was still in use, with more modern memorials in evidence on the fringes furthest from the Temple.

Lucen helped Gladdas out of the gig in a courtly way and then tucked her hand into the crook of his arm.

"The ground's a bit uneven, what with the frost heaving it up," he explained. "We're not going far, but best not to twist an ankle."

He was true to his word. Fewer than thirty steps brought them to a fresh grave with a brand-new stone.

"I wanted you to know that we put her here," Lucen said very gently, patting her hand on his arm. "I had the stone hurried along, so she wouldn't be here without a marker."

Gladdas read, "Alazaria Fentez – She Was Loved" before the tears finally flooded down for the first time since the young woman's death.

***

"I was just so afraid she'd be put in that little corner graveyard at The Shadows," Gladdas said, once she had regained her composure.

"We would never do that," Lucen answered, taking out his pipe and tabak pouch. "Those there are people who didn't deserve as much. One is Madame Holz, used to be the Royal Nurse. Wicked, loved toughening children. She treated poor Princess Aidelia cruelly and helped to drive her mad and she had charge of the Queen when she was small. She was sent out here to toughen Katrin but got very drunk one night, fell down the stairs and broke her neck."

"Do you believe that's what happened in a house where Menders watched over that child?" Gladdas asked, giving him a look.

"That's the official story, on the death certificate and all," Lucen answered blandly, lighting his pipe. "Then there's the one called

Mister Enigma – some fellow dressed as an Ephraemite jumped up out of the bushes one night and went after young Kaymar with a knife. Kaymar killed him in a brace of shakes."

"How odd," Gladdas remarked. "Did you ever find out who he was?"

Lucen shook his head. "He had nothing to identify him except an Ephraemite pendant. We have no idea who he was looking for or why he attacked Kaymar."

"Wrong man to attack."

Lucen nodded and puffed in silence for a while.

"Sometimes there are no answers," he finally said. "Like young Alazaria here. I saw the look on her face when I was swinging the axe around. She looked like she admired what I was doing. Sometimes people want to be stopped, Gladdy. She was not just being professional. She was like a stalking animal. I've lived for years among men who used to be assassins. They didn't stalk their targets like prey."

Gladdas said nothing for a long time. When she did speak, she looked out across the gravestones and kept her voice unnaturally neutral.

"When Alazaria came to our school, she never showed emotion, but that wasn't unusual. Very often the girls who were traumatized kept that sort of cover. After time and beginning to understand that they are safe and protected, they come out of their shells. Then we can help them.

"Alazaria never came out of her shell. No matter how much care, love and attention was given her, she always stayed locked away. I was a fool. I've known for a long time that I was, but what was I to do, turn her out on the streets? So, I excused things, explained things.

"We always had pets at the school, because it's the girls' home. Taking care of the animals and playing with them helped so many of them. The girls loved their pets. But after Alazaria came, from time to time there would be a dead puppy or kitten, usually suffocated. She was the only child who didn't play with the animals.

"I made myself believe the animals died naturally, but deep down, I knew. I just kept believing she could be helped. I tried. Gods, how I tried."

When Lucen knew she was finished, he gestured toward the gravestone.

"You gave all you could," he said. "She couldn't take it, for reasons we will never know. Still – she was loved."

They drove back to The Shadows in almost complete silence, broken only by their brief stop at the Spaltz farm to pick up the meat Lucen had mentioned on the way out. At the house, Lucen left the horse and gig at the stable and then turned to Gladdas.

"I think you should check on those chatterbirds and their nest," he said. "I'll come along with you."

She hesitated for a moment and then took his arm.

Walking to the nest was not as terrible as she thought it would be. At first, she refused to look toward the place where Alazaria died, but then she allowed herself to be curious – and turned her head that way.

It was just part of The Shadows' woodlot. Something tragic had happened there, but it held no curse and hosted no ghost.

"There's the mama," Lucen said quietly. "Let her feed the little devils first." He indicated the nest, where the female chatterbird was busily stuffing squawking chicks.

"She hadn't even laid eggs the last time I looked!" Gladdas said in surprise.

"Life went on," Lucen answered. The chatterbird doled out the last of the worms she had brought and looked toward Lucen and Gladdas. She cocked her head to one side cheekily and gave voice to the talky sounds that had earned chatterbirds their name. Then she flitted away after more provender for her brood.

They drew close to the nest, which provoked a sudden upthrust of pointy, gaping little beaks, accompanied by frantic squawking.

"We have nothing for you, little gluttons!" Gladdas laughed – and was surprised that she could laugh.

"Ah, my prescription has worked," Lucen said with gratification. "Now I suggest my next one. When you have your feet a little better under you, I think it's time you went home. You need to get back to your school. Menders and the family will be along to Samorsa quite soon, just in case those people send anyone else after you."

"I might ask him to lend me Kaymar or another Menders' Man for a while," Gladdas said. Then she looked around.

"Yes," she said. "I would like to go home."

She turned back to him.

"Thank you, my friend. You are a brilliant man."

Lucen chuckled quietly.

"Just an old soldier who's been through many campaigns and nursed a lot of hurt men back up onto their feet," he answered. "Whenever you're ready, I'll set up one of my men to accompany you to Samorsa. Now, I'm going to go and see if Zelia needs help turning the mattresses today."

He began to ramble toward the house, but then turned.

"Meant to let you know – Menders has offered for you to come here with the school. They could help you get set up here if you want. And we all want you to know that we love you and you'll always have a home here."

"Don't make me cry," Gladdas answered crisply, though she smiled. "I want the school in Samorsa because there are much better opportunities for women there. It's best for the girls. But it's nice to know I have another home here as well."

Lucen bowed elegantly to her, his ultimate compliment and then went to turn the mattresses.

PORTOS, BARAMBOS

19
THAT SHINING STONE

Borsen and Katrin were hanging out of the train carriage window, agog at the spectacular landscape of southern Barambos and the exquisite ruins of temples built entirely from white marble.

"Just another pile of white rocks," Hemmett teased from his seat, gently tapping Borsen's backside with his foot.

"I want so much to see them close up!" Katrin said, turning and swatting at him. "Just because you've been here before doesn't mean we have to act bored!"

"No abuse of the military," Hemmett laughed. "I promise I will take you to every fallen down temple you want to see."

"It's not only that – the way the cliffs and mountains are split in half and tumbling down into boulders is incredible! I wonder why it's like that here."

"That's a topic to research," Menders answered her, coming back from where he had been reading to Eiren at the other end of the carriage. "There are a number of theories. My favorite is the postulation that this part of the Middle Continent was covered with glaciers eons ago. When they retreated toward the southern pole, they carved out this landscape."

He joined the two young people at the window, pointing out how the cliffs were split in many places, as if ice had formed in a crevice, expanding and breaking the mountain into spectacular rifts and clefts.

"That's how the Baramban people came upon marble – it is exposed in thousands of natural quarries, easily accessible. Nowhere else is marble used so much in building," Menders told them.

He saw Borsen smile delightedly. He had been entranced by marble ever since he'd written a touching little essay during his year at Eiren's school, while he was still living with his abusive father and indifferent stepmother. Borsen had described sheltering from rain with his mother at the foot of a large statue of a "lady hero" when he was a tiny child. His badly spelled, nearly illegible description of the statue being made from "shining stone" identified it to Menders as the monument to Glorantha, the first Queen and unifier of Mordania, which stood in the capital city, Erdahn.

It was not long after Borsen had written that essay that he had come to The Shadows as a tailor's apprentice – and within a couple of months, Menders realized that the boy was his nephew. A trip to Erdstrom for Borsen to be fitted for glasses to correct his terrible vision had also introduced him to marble used in building, as the lobby and bathrooms of the hotel they stayed in were lined with it. Borsen had fallen in love with the stone and could study its patterns for hours.

Now he was in the place where most of the marble used on Eirdon was quarried. All his artistic sensibilities were alerted as he gazed at the ancient temples reflecting the late afternoon sun.

Menders smiled and put a hand on Borsen's shoulder.

"It will be too late by the time we reach Portos, but I think a visit to the Temple of Fiora and a stop by one of the quarries would be a good way to spend tomorrow," he said. "The Temple is unusual because it isn't constructed from the white marble you've been seeing today, but is a combination of pink, black and gold-veined stone. The quarry I'm thinking of is green veined white marble. A small town overlooks it, with viewing areas where you can look right down and see the work going on."

"That really is a sight," Hemmett said, rising and standing by Katrin. "Sir made a point of taking us there. There's a good restaurant there too."

Borsen smiled and said nothing, wringing his hands a little as was his habit when he was overwhelmed with emotion.

***

Borsen moved quietly away from Hemmett, Katrin and Varnia, who were exclaiming over a particularly beautiful wall of yellow marble with veins of gold. The afternoon sun had touched it, making it radiate light.

Menders watched as Borsen reached out to touch a gold marble pillar, then slowly walked into the next room. A small shift of position gave him an unbroken view of his nephew as he began exploring on his own.

Menders was aware that Borsen was immensely moved by the beauty of the Temple of Fiora and the marble used to construct it. He was nearly speechless and seemed frustrated by the chatter of the others.

Borsen approached a wall of lustrous pink marble lining the sanctuary of the goddess Fiora. He reached out slowly and ran his fingers over the polished surface. Then, to Menders' surprise, he removed his glasses and leaned over to press his cheek against the stone.

Borsen never took off his glasses unless he was sleeping. His childhood had been spent in a state of virtual blindness as well as extreme poverty. Once his vision was corrected with spectacles, his response to being without them was panic, as if he was immediately rendered small and helpless when they were not on his nose.

Now he leaned against the wall as if he was listening to the stone. He was perfectly still.

Menders sensed Varnia behind him and turned slightly, motioning to her for quiet. Her forehead was wrinkled with concern.

"What?" she mouthed soundlessly.

"I'm not sure," Menders mouthed back. He reached out and tucked her hand into the crook of his arm. He had come to understand the depth of this young woman's devotion to Borsen – any perceived threat to him upset her terribly.

They waited until Borsen stood upright and slid his glasses back onto his nose. He turned, saw them and smiled, in no way discomfited that they had seen his odd behavior.

Katrin and Hemmett had joined them.

"What's wrong?" Katrin asked, her voice tight.

"Nothing," Borsen said, laughing a little. "Did I look so very strange?"

"I thought you might feel ill," Varnia said worriedly.

"No. I felt… I had an urge to lean against the marble, to listen to it. I was trying to call up an old memory."

Menders smiled, remembering Borsen's essay.

Always quick, Borsen grinned at him.

"Uncle knows," he said. "When I was a tiny little fellow, my mother and I were in Erdahn and saw the statue of Queen Glorantha. I was fascinated by the stone. When I took off my glasses and leaned against the marble just now, the memory came back to me. I can remember what my mother looked like. My memory of her had faded over time. While I was leaning against the marble, I could almost hear her voice. I was close to something infinite for just a moment."

He and Menders exchanged a smile.

"I don't want her to fade, my lovely mother," Menders said gently, quoting from Borsen's essay.

"She'll never fade again," Borsen answered.

***

Katrin pounced.

Varnia started at her companion's sudden movement and Kaymar, who was escorting them on a shopping trip, laughed out loud.

"And she finds something pretty!" he announced, well accustomed to her enthusiasm in shops.

Katrin shook her head, turning around. She had pulled a man's walking stick from a rack.

"Going to take up carrying one like Glad?" Kaymar teased. Gladdas Dalmanthea occasionally used a walking stick, courtesy of a knee she'd injured on a mission many years ago.

"No – for Borsen," Katrin explained, holding it out. "It's too short for me. Kaymar, give it a try." She handed it to him.

He inspected it first.

"Very nice," he said appraisingly. "Well spotted, Cuz!"

The stick was made from the very strong but light, striped wood of the bowerbriar tree peculiar to southern Barambos. The shaft was carved intricately in a pattern of twining vines, with mischievous, tiny faces peeping through the leaves. It was topped with a smooth, shining white marble orb, veined with dark green.

Kaymar studied the hardware below the knob, made a sudden twisting motion with his hands and drew a slender sword blade from the shaft.

"Very nice indeed," he said, his voice tinged with covetousness.

"You may not have it," Katrin decreed.

"You're right. It's too short for me as well, but it would be perfect for Little Man," Kaymar appraised.

The shop owner, sensing a sale, came over.

"You missed," he said, holding his hand out for the stick, smiling. Kaymar sheathed the sword and handed it over. The man demonstrated another secret – he turned the lower part of the shaft and revealed a hidden tube flask, ready for the beverage of choice of the carrier.

"And this!" he continued enthusiastically, unscrewing the knob and showing them how the marble globe had been hollowed out and filled with metal. "Lead! Very heavy! Bad men threaten, *bop!* Right on head! They leave you alone."

"Just the thing!" Kaymar laughed. "A sword, a lead-loaded handle, a flask for his kirz and beautiful to boot. He can guard his chastity from bad men with its bopping power. Do you have any more?" he asked the shopkeeper, who hurried him over to the rack.

"Don't get one like this," Katrin warned him.

"Give me a little credit for consideration, Katrin," he responded wryly, pulling a very different stick from the rack.

Katrin turned to Varnia, who was trying to disguise her disappointment that she hadn't happened on the stick first.

"Why don't we both give it to him?" Katrin asked, her face glowing with happiness. "From his sisters."

Varnia swallowed several times before she trusted her voice.

"Yes," she answered huskily, smiling as Katrin handed her the stick. "Isn't it lovely?"

"One thing…" Katrin turned toward the shopkeeper. "The marble – from the quarry down the road?" she asked.

He bobbed his head enthusiastically.

"Yes, from the Portos quarry. Made right here. Portos famous for the carved walking sticks."

"Perfect!" Katrin smiled at Varnia. They had seen Borsen nearly ecstatic at the quarry when they visited it, somehow asking questions of men who spoke no Mordanian or Surelian, while Borsen spoke no Baramban. But he managed, and they showed him many things about the stone, even teaching him a little about how the stone was cut. He'd been covered with white marble dust by the end of the excursion and was now at their hotel, getting ready to go to dinner.

They got back to the hotel in time to change, then rushed down to the lobby where everyone was waiting for them. Borsen was standing at the wide double doorway, looking out over the tumbling mountains and valleys that stretched as far as the sea in the distance. He was startled when Katrin and Varnia walked up behind him, and turned, his top hat in his hands.

"We have a present for you!" Katrin announced as Varnia held out the paper wrapped stick to him. Borsen looked puzzled and then laughed softly as he reached out for the stick.

"Thank you, my dears." His powerful, small hands unwound the paper – then he was silent as he looked over the exquisite carving and cupped his hand around the marble knob.

"It has a sword and a flask inside," Katrin told him.

At that, Borsen smiled.

"It's absolutely beautiful," he said, the words coming slowly, as they always did when he was emotional. He kissed each of them on the cheek and then turned, stepping onto the verandah of the hotel, putting on his hat and giving the walking stick an experimental twirl before planting it on the floorboards and leaning on it as he looked out over the mountains.

Menders looked at Borsen's silhouette against the bright late afternoon sunlight – the perfect evening suit and topper, the elegant lines of the young man's small figure, one arm outstretched to rest atop the slender walking stick.

He had a feeling of time moving, shifting beneath him like sand on a beach. It was not an unfamiliar sensation. He'd encountered it before when Hemmett appeared before him in full dress uniform at his graduation ceremony, when Menders had seen him as a grown man for the first time. Now it had come for Borsen.

"My lost and found boy," he whispered. "So soon."

PORTOS, BARAMBOS

20
BORSEN'S TURN

From Menders' Journal

A very unexpected request from Borsen today. As I handed out the various travel documents for our journey to Samorsa the day after tomorrow, he asked if he could stay behind in Barambos for a while.

Borsen has proven before that he's capable of managing on his own. His trip to Erdstrom to take the examination to become a Guild tailor was solo, at his request. He stayed in Erdstrom for a week, living in a hotel and taking care of all his affairs admirably.

But this is a foreign country – albeit a friendly one. Borsen doesn't speak the language and he wants to spend time looking at the various marble quarries. This entails some risk, as all of them are not the carefully kept tourist attraction that the one here in Portos is. He could be injured – and even if he dresses carefully to avoid attention, there is always the possibility of him being robbed.

Eiren and I have talked this conundrum over. Like me, she wants Borsen to have his freedom and strike out on his own, but she also sees the potential danger. If I could have Kaymar stay with him, I would be completely confident, but that wouldn't be letting him be an independent young man, which it is high time he should be able to be.

Fussy old Papa Hen! I'll talk to Franz and Kaymar.

Menders unaccustomedly tossed down his pen and walked away without corking his ink bottle. He rapped a code on Kaymar's door as he passed on down the hall to the suite Franz was nested in.

"Ah, Head of Household, looking dire!" Franz announced as Menders poked his head in after knocking. "Come in. I know exactly which of your chicks has ruffled your feathers."

"Now see here," Menders said abruptly, though he was inwardly amused at Franz's teasing. It was simply part of his nature and was never taken to heart.

"Don't slam the damn door in my face," Kaymar added behind him. Menders looked around to see that he was scowling.

"Were you napping?" he asked with just the right touch of sarcasm.

"I was trying. Katrin and Varnia are giggling and jabbering so much I figured I might as well come in and listen to you squawking."

"For Grahl's sake!" Franz exclaimed, rising from his comfortable chair. "No, don't you dare sit there, go on the sofa. Here, I'll give you a drink. You're like a petulant child sometimes."

He poured a brandy and handed it to Kaymar, who stretched out on a short sofa and looked somewhat mollified. Menders shook his head and settled in the other easy chair.

"Now then, I imagine Borsen has announced his plans to you," Franz said. "Yes, he told me what he wants to do, asked if there was anything he needed to consider regarding his health if he stays behind on his own. I gave him a clean bill of health and told him not to tumble into any quarries."

"I knew what he was thinking about, though he didn't ask me directly," Kaymar added. "He's absolutely enchanted with that blasted marble." He pulled out his cigar case and offered one to Franz, who accepted. Lighting his own, he puffed for a moment and then looked over at Menders.

"The answer to your question is that I don't know."

"And my question?" Menders shot back testily.

"You want to know if he should stay here by himself. That's the question any concerned parent would ask," Kaymar replied. "Thing is, I simply don't know, from a security point of view."

Menders nodded.

"Franz – I know we've discussed this a number of times – do you have any further clues about his age?"

When Borsen was hired as an apprentice for The Shadows' tailor, it was assumed that he was around Katrin's age or a bit younger – at the time, thirteen years. He'd been the size of an eight-year-old due to years of malnutrition, and his undisguised joy at being among people who cherished him, particularly after Menders realized he was his nephew, made him seem younger than thirteen.

As time passed and Borsen confided in both Menders and Kaymar about his childhood, particularly the death of his mother, they came to doubt their original estimate of his age. He had no idea of his birthdate, either year or day, but as he worked at The Shadows and began to formulate a plan for his future as a tailor, he showed a maturity and determination that outstripped the age he'd been assigned.

"Unfortunately, boys aren't like horses – I can't look for a particular tooth and know that he's over a certain age," Franz replied. "Judging by his physical maturity – he could be anywhere from eighteen to twenty. No baby fat in his face, strongly muscled, physically mature. Like all Thrun, little body hair, so that's no gauge. I think worrying about his physical age is pointless – what is he capable of handling mentally?"

"He's already handled burdens that would break most people," Menders said softly.

His companions became very quiet.

Borsen had been with his mother as she starved and froze to death during a bitter winter in Eastern Mordania. His father had abandoned them months before. He returned when he heard the mother was dying and forcefully carried Borsen away. He'd tried to push Borsen into acting as a lookout while he broke into houses, but discovered that the boy could hardly see. After that, he'd had no use for Borsen and the Thrun woman he lived with barely fed the child. Until Borsen came to The Shadows, he'd been skeletal with a swollen belly, and picked through garbage bins behind stores and restaurants, looking for scraps.

"We know he's mentally capable," Kaymar said, breaking the silence. He sat up, all business.

"Cuz, I'll give this to you as a professional. We need to put the fact that we all love Borsen aside and look at this objectively," he began. "I'm confident in his ability to stay here for a few weeks and then board the proper train to travel to join us in Samorsa. Borsen's capabilities do not concern me. He's a prodigious young man, be he sixteen or twenty-two, either of which is possible.

"What does bother me is the fact that he will not have a soul to turn to should something go wrong. The people here are easygoing, but he doesn't know the language and very few of them speak any Mordanian or Surelian. He's become known in town since we came here and many of the people seem to like him. He's a favorite at the quarries, here at the hotel and in the hotel bar."

Menders nodded.

"I think there are resources here, if he needs help," he added to Kaymar's appraisal. "The hotel management speaks Surelian. That's a plus. The local sheriff could be informed and asked to be aware that he's here alone. Same for any clergy at the temples."

Franz nodded, intrigued by the way the cousins worked together, building on each other's ideas and opinions.

"Now I'll point out the grundar in the room." Kaymar took up the thread. "He's tiny. We know that, of course, but we're used to it. We don't see him as vulnerable, but that is a sad truth. I was very glad when Katrin happened upon that walking stick. I'd have never thought of it, but it's the ideal weapon, because he loves it and is never without it. We know he's always fully armed, but the truth is, should a big man ever get a good grip on him, Borsen would lose the fight. I doubt he weighs much over a hundred pounds."

"About a hundred and ten," Doctor Franz nodded.

"After my run-in with DeLarco, I'm well aware of how Borsen would fare if anyone much larger ever got hold of him," Kaymar continued, referring to his nearly fatal fight with the assassin who had been given contracts on the entire Shadows family. "He wouldn't have a prayer."

Menders stood and paced across the room, clenching and unclenching his fists.

"Yet he seems inspired – as if something is taking hold inside of him," he said. "He told me that ideas for the establishment he wants to found in Erdahn are crystallizing in his mind. Those are his very words. I can't quash that, but yes, I see all the dangers and they terrify me. But we're agreed. He is definitely of age. It was out of courtesy and love that he asked me about this. I can't forbid him from it."

There was silence as Menders made another circuit of the room, staring at the floor, every line of his body taut with tension.

"All right then," Franz refereed. "We've laid out all the problems and I believe we're all aware of terrible possibilities as well as Borsen's resourcefulness and maturity. Now we need a solution."

Menders turned to Kaymar.

"As you are his other foster father, I defer to you," he said quietly. "You have the ability to be more objective about the children than I can be."

Kaymar looked startled for a moment, then gathered his thoughts.

"By chance, I think I know what to do," he ventured. "I had sent for a new Kaymar's Man, Willem Robbins, to join us here for a tour of duty with us in Samorsa, relieving Jorgen. Borsen has never met him because Willem's been based in Artreya. He's due in on the train from Surelia tomorrow.

"I can assign him here instead, to guard Borsen covertly. It would be real help if there should be any trouble – and I can trust him to be discreet and not give himself away. He's good."

Menders looked so relieved that Kaymar laughed a little.

"I know it's duplicitous and that we should just tell Borsen that he's being guarded – but I've seen that inspiration in him as well. He has big dreams and I'd like to see him achieve them. This strikes me as the best compromise we can make, Menders."

"Then we make it," Menders said decidedly. "Do you concur, Franz?"

"Absolutely. It's a relief to know someone will be here with him. What he doesn't know won't hurt him."

"All right, fellow hens, now I'm going back to my nap," Kaymar drawled, rising from the sofa.

***

Borsen walked jauntily down the road toward the stables, ready to claim his saddle mount for the day. He wanted to visit two nearby quarries and was getting an early start, his lunch in a rucksack, his pistol and knives at his waist and his walking stick in hand.

He'd been on his own in Barambos for a week now and was thoroughly enjoying himself. He loved his family but sometimes the enclaved situation that went along with being close to royalty grated on him – as it sometimes did on Hemmett.

At first, he and Hemmett considered staying behind together, but then realized it would cause difficulties with Katrin's security if Hemmett wasn't available to take his duty shifts. Hemmett had confided secret plans to beg extra time in Samorsa, as he was wildly interested in the schedule of sporting events advertised in the city of Sarnovilla.

A cacophony of enthusiastic braying could be heard and Borsen laughed out loud.

The favorite beast of burden in Barambos was not the average saddle horse, but sturdy animals referred to as "little donkeys" by locals and tourists alike. They hauled loads and people and were legendary for their sure footedness on the steep tracks leading down the mountains into the quarries. Horses and even mules couldn't be trusted to safely scale those near-vertical tracks.

On his first trip to the stables, Borsen had been approached by one of these little donkeys. It was a chipper and cheery gelding and it seemed to fall in love with Borsen at first sight. He laughingly took it out the first day. By the time they arrived back at the stable that evening, Borsen was more than ready to pay the owner to allow him to reserve the donkey indefinitely.

Borsen asked the donkey's name but the stable owner registered confusion and shrugged. So Borsen nicknamed the little creature Boss, because he was one for taking over when circumstances required it.

If they approached a rough and steep portion of a trail, Boss would carefully take the bit between his teeth, effectively taking Borsen's guidance out of the equation. He would find his way down confidently and carefully. As soon as they were clear of the dangerous area, Boss would release the bit and let Borsen guide him again. If other donkeys approached Borsen, Boss intervened with much head shaking and braying. If a person approached that Boss didn't recognize, he went on guard alert and stood in their way, showing his teeth and laying his very long ears back.

Best of all, Boss had learned a trick where, when his rider took out the lunch parcel, he would hold it delicately between his teeth until the preparations for his own noon meal were done. When Borsen offered Boss a nosebag, he would release the parcel and enjoy his own meal, always finishing it in time to beg bread crusts from his rider.

The owner of the stables was delighted to rent Boss so consistently and also rejoiced that Borsen was so small.

"Good for donkey," he said every time Borsen turned up to take Boss for the day. He made signs to indicate Borsen's size and that the light weight was good for Boss' back. Considering the way some of the donkeys were loaded up with marble or very large tourists, Borsen could understand.

He loved seeing the quarries, but after getting away from the ones that hosted the sightseers, he found the way the donkeys were loaded very disturbing. They were hardy and tough, but they were also very small. Often, they were loaded until they struggled along. Seeing unskilled, heavy riders bouncing on their backs was even worse. Once or twice Borsen tried to protest the treatment of the animals, but his inability to speak Baramban gave the listeners the opportunity to act as if they didn't comprehend his gestures, shrugging dramatically and turning away.

Borsen knew from the family's experience in Fambré that too much protest would not help matters for the donkeys and could bring danger his way. He tried to content himself by showing Boss a wonderful time. His success was underscored by the animal's unswerving devotion.

"I think we'll go to the quarry where they cut the yellow marble with gold veining," he told Boss as the animal inspected his pockets, knowing one of them would hold sugar. "Then that will be the end of quarries. There aren't any others close enough to visit from here. I do want to go to some of the workshops. The priest of Grahl arranged for me to visit one when they're matching slabs of marble. I want to see how that's done."

Boss had found the sugar and was pawing the ground, bobbing his head up and down.

"You're a clever fellow. Here you are." Borsen held out the sugar cubes. Rather than licking them right up, Boss always nibbled delicately away, taking one at a time.

Soon they were jogging away down the road toward yet another quarry.

A young man emerged from some scrub brush nearby and, as he had done every day for two weeks, immediately rented a donkey and followed at a distance.

The owner of the stable watched and shook his head. People from outside of Barambos were very strange.

***

Dearest Sister Varnia,

My weekly note to you and I hope it finds you happy and well. I am finished my tour of the quarries and am going now to workshops to learn how marble is matched. This is for when my establishment is built. I want to have marble lining the walls in the lobby, maybe bathrooms and other places too. I need to know how it is hung and how they match it, so it looks like one continuous piece.

I am worried about my little donkey friend, Boss. He is so sweet, and I hate to think of him being used to haul huge loads of marble or huge people after I'm gone. He's been a good friend.

I hope you are finding much to see and do in Samorsa. I am expecting to be done here soon and will let you know when I will be there.

Love,

B

***

Willem Robbins shifted his weight in exasperation, then used a focusing technique to calm his temper and went back to watching over Borsen Menders.

The young man had been described to him accurately – small, attractive, prone to fixate on activities for long periods of time. However, no-one had mentioned that he would go into a business and end up taking an apprentice's tasks on for an afternoon. At the moment, Borsen was in a marble workshop, helping a crowd of swarthy Baramban men match sheets of marble. He didn't speak a word of Baramban, they didn't speak a word of Mordanian, but they managed to talk a great deal, with gestures and dumbshow making up for their lack of linguistic expertise.

It was Borsen's third day of matching marble and Willem was weary of the assignment. Worse, the donkey was wise to him and made attempts to come over and get better acquainted. Willem had taken to carrying a pocketful of Barambos taffy. Tossed to the donkey, it kept him from braying by keeping him busy chewing. All Willem needed was to have to report to Kaymar Shvalz that his cover had been blown by a donkey.

Borsen finally stopped crawling around on the floor of the workshop, peering intently at the slabs of marble as the men shoved and budged them this way and that, then made a great flurry of marking them and storing them away. He left the workshop so quickly that Willem barely managed to take cover. Borsen swung up onto the donkey's back and they jogged merrily away while Willem scurried to his own hidden rented mount.

***

Borsen slid off Boss' back and led him toward the rental stable. He hated to say goodbye, but he'd done all he wanted in Barambos and he really needed to move along to Samorsa to join the rest of the family.

Boss had sensed Borsen's mood and was particularly sweet, leaning his head on Borsen's shoulder or nuzzling his hair.

"I know, funny fellow," Borsen murmured to him. "I hate it to end, but I can't just stay here forever looking at marble." He rubbed the little animal's muzzle and then handed the reins to the stable owner, exchanging a few words of thanks.

Willem Robbins watched from behind the stable as Borsen turned and began to walk toward his hotel. He moved to the edge of the road as a carriage rumbled up in a cloud of dust and a group of burly Artreyans, men and women climbed out.

Their idea of speaking to someone who didn't speak Artreyan was to raise their voices and within seconds, the stable yard was ringing with clamoring voices.

"We want some of the donkeys, the famous ones! Going down to the white cliffs to see the sunset! Got some that don't trip and fall?"

The stable owner was trying to sort out the four different conversations that were being shouted at once and handed Boss's reins to a very rotund woman.

"Nice fellow, all ready to go," he said distractedly before hurrying to the barn to get more donkeys for the sunset party.

"Oooh, how do I get on this animal?" the woman shrieked. Willem realized the entire group was the worse for drink. The woman hauled on the reins. Boss began to bare his teeth and back away.

Willem flinched at the idea of that woman or any of the party getting on the back of the little donkey. She must outweigh Borsen by a hundred pounds and she obviously had no idea how to handle a saddle mount. One of the Artreyan men took the reins and smacked Boss on the neck.

"Come along, you," he said, hauling the animal toward the mounting block.

"I'm sorry, sir, I'm afraid there's been a mistake. This is my donkey," Borsen said, having walked up quietly. He reached around the man and took the reins.

"Here, who are you?" the man said aggressively.

"Prince Fasal of Hetzophia," Borsen said pleasantly, walking away to the stable door with the donkey trotting anxiously beside him.

Willem shifted his position in time to see Borsen handing over a sum of money to the stable owner, who was staring at him as if he was insane. Then he shrugged and tugged on the reins of three donkeys, leading them over to the sunset party.

Borsen stroked Boss' nose and then walked away with him toward the hotel.

***

Borsen negotiated a stall for Boss at the hotel livery and then paid a visit to the train station. After considerable argument, during which he said that he'd be more than glad to take the donkey in the private car with him, he acquired a stall in the equine car for saddle mounts. He was leaving Barambos the next day and Boss was going with him.

After removing his marble dust covered clothing and taking a quick bath, Borsen felt no urge to eat dinner. The scene with the drunken Artreyans had upset him terribly. Though he had rescued Boss, he thought sadly of the other donkeys. The idea of that heavy woman heaving herself onto Boss' back from a mounting block was the stuff of nightmares to a horseman.

He sauntered out of the hotel in the twilight, looking over to where Boss was grazing in the hotel pasture. The donkey sensed his presence and raised his head. Borsen walked over before Boss could begin to bray and disturb the entire hotel.

"Cook always says that pulling one out of the fire is better than letting everything burn," he said softly to the donkey, who laid his head along Borsen's arm and closed his eyes. "But I always think of the others. There are so many, all over the world. I can only help a few."

Boss sighed mightily, making Borsen laugh out loud.

"You're right, brooding over it isn't going to help a thing," he said. "Let's go down to the cliffs and have a look at the moonlight on the marble, shall we? Just don't tell Uncle I rode you bareback with only your halter."

Willem Robbins swore inwardly as Boss jogged away down the road toward the scenic cliffs and began to cut across country on foot, keeping donkey and rider in sight.

The sun was down completely when Borsen reached the cliffs made up of pure white marble. Both Eirdon's moons were rising and near full. The cliffs reflected the light exquisitely, giving the surrounding landscape a bluish glow.

"It's all around us," Borsen said to Boss as he slid off the donkey's back and let him graze freely, knowing he would stay nearby. "I don't know if you can feel it, but marble makes me feel very safe, very protected. It vibrates through my bones."

Willem watched, sheltered behind a tree, as Borsen looked at the glowing cliffs for several minutes – and then began to sing.

He had a fine, high tenor voice and had obviously been trained well. The language was not familiar to Willem, but he knew Borsen was Thrun.

"Thrunar a'a' Thrun
Parantela a' Thrun,
Thanzant camo Tharala,
Tharala a'a' Thrun."

As he sang, he began to dance, a slow and steady measure with intricate footwork. Boss looked over at him and then came close, staring at Borsen's moving feet.

The song began to speed up, as did Borsen's dancing. Boss, intrigued by this new game, began to circle Borsen, who laughed aloud and encouraged him.

"You can dance," he told the donkey. "Everything can dance!"

He jumped slightly, and the donkey pranced away, then came back curiously. Borsen jumped again, but followed the donkey as he skipped away again. Within moments, the donkey was prancing around, capering with Borsen as he sang.

"Tharala a'a' Thrun
Thanzant camo Tharala
Parantela a' Thrun
Thrunar a'a' Thrun!"

He finished song and dance with arms outstretched, looking at the glowing white cliffs and taking a deep breath. Then he turned to his donkey dancing partner and bowed low.

"I think you were in a circus before you ended up at that rental stable," he told the animal. "You're a fine dancer. No, I don't have any sugar, but we need to go back now to be in time for the second dinner sitting. We'll walk back, you've been ridden enough today."

What a strange little man, Willem thought, though he was immensely amused. He's all they briefed me on and more – generous, somewhat impulsive, kind to a fault.

Borsen took hold of Boss's halter rope and then turned and looked directly at Willem.

"Are you coming with us? The second dinner sitting will be starting in about the time it takes to walk back to my hotel."

Willem was so stunned that he simply stepped out of the shelter of the tree trunk.

"How long have you known I was there?" he asked abruptly.

"I've known you were following me ever since the rest of the family left for Samorsa!" Borsen answered with a laugh.

Willem was speechless.

"Don't feel bad – I've lived with the family for years now and Kaymar taught me everything you know," Borsen continued. "I'm something of a Menders Man myself, though Katrin doesn't know and shouldn't be told. I knew that my uncle and Kaymar would assign someone to watch over me. I'm glad you were there this afternoon when I took this fellow away from those Artreyans. They were just drunk enough to be belligerent, but I got away fast enough."

"Damn!" Willem shook his head. They hadn't told him that!

"I'm starving. Let's go, unless you want to go without dinner. And you don't have to go back to that fleapit you've been staying in – there's an extra room in my suite and then you can travel on to Samorsa with me tomorrow. I'm taking a private carriage. Uncle insisted. You can keep me company."

Willem found himself hugely enjoying Borsen's company at dinner and through the next day, when they boarded a private train carriage after settling Boss in his stall.

"I'll be with the family in Samorsa for three months, but then I'm being sent to The Shadows," he replied to Borsen's query as they had an enormous lunch in the carriage.

"Then I think I'll send Boss back to The Shadows with you," Borsen explained. "If you agree."

"Of course. He's a mild little fellow. I'm sure by the time I'm done in Samorsa we'll be good friends."

Borsen nodded, having silenced himself by biting into his fifth drumstick. Willem couldn't imagine how such a small person could eat so much.

"I don't want to try to take him into Artreya," Borsen finally said, picking up his wineglass. "With the situation between Artreya and Mordania unpredictable, I would hate to leave him behind if we left quickly."

"Understood."

"You don't mind nancyboys, do you?" Borsen asked next.

Willem laughed.

"No – if I did I wouldn't be sitting here. I'm not nancy, but being in Special Services, I know many. The military deliberately recruits them for spy and assassin training, you know."

Borsen nodded, helping himself to another ladleful of soup.

"Yes, the perception that nancies aren't family men, all that," he replied. "So, we'll be friends with no problem. That will be fun in Samorsa, since you're so close to the ages of the younger set. You won't have to hide in the weeds."

"Good," Willem said with conviction.

***

Menders and Kaymar were standing on the balcony of the family suite at the Casone Brandoza in Saronilla, Samorsa. Borsen was expected and the train had come in a short while ago.

"I'll be interested in seeing how Willem managed," Kaymar said, lighting a cigar and exchanging winks with a man passing in the street below. Menders gave him a nudge, disguising laughter.

"Now, now," Kaymar chortled. "He winked first."

"Ifor will pound you," Menders teased.

"He'd have winked too. Wait a minute…"

Kaymar squinted as he looked down the busy street. Menders, knowing his eyes weren't equal to the task, picked up the binoculars he had ready and began to scan in the direction Kaymar was looking.

"Where?" he asked.

"I'll be damned." Kaymar reached for the binoculars, then snorted.

"They're together!" he snorted. "Borsen caught him. We taught him too well." He peered again.

"Menders – look, I can't tell you." Kaymar burst out laughing and handed the binoculars back to his cousin.

Menders looked.

"Well, it seems we've acquired a donkey," he said dryly.

SARONILLA, SAMORSA

20
SEVEN SPICES

"The Knot of Youthfulness" or "The Knot" for short, as Kaymar had started calling the young people, now a group of five, were making their way through an open air Samorsan market. With Hemmett, Borsen and Willem in attendance they were incredibly free to go about. Katrin went into places she'd never dreamed of – little theatres to see risqué musical shows, tiny restaurants and taverns, strange shops full of spices and exotic dried fruits. They went to the many popular sporting events and yelled themselves hoarse for their chosen competitors.

Now the colors and scents of the market were dazzling them. Somewhere ahead food was cooking, the tantalizing scents making their mouths water.

"Look!" Varnia exclaimed, indicating an enormous tower of dried Samorsan peppers strung on skewers. "Those are the ones Kaymar loves, aren't they?"

Hemmett blinked as the odor of the peppers reached his nose and eyes.

"I should say. They're deadly hot just smelling them. Let's get him some. You mark the spot, Willem, so we can send him back for more."

The peppers secured, they went on to a spice stall. Katrin was delighted – she loved to learn about spices that could be used in her soaps and perfumes. There were many here she knew nothing about. The woman behind the counter enjoyed telling her the names and letting her sniff each different powder.

Samorsa was very cosmopolitan and most people spoke a smattering of several languages. The Knot was never at a loss to communicate with the widely varied Samorsan people, between Willem's carefully tutored Military Academy Samorsan, Katrin's quick ear and Hemmett's universal language of smiles, winks and bonhomie.

The woman behind the counter was very dark skinned, darker than anyone Katrin had ever seen. She had luxuriant, curly black hair that cascaded exuberantly from its scarf binding. Her lovely black eyes snapped and sparkled as she spoke. She wrapped Katrin's purchases deftly, using brilliant orange paper that matched her stall's draperies and roof.

"Where is that cooking smell coming from?" Katrin asked, her stomach growling as she was continually bombarded with savory fragrances.

"That is from the restaurant of my mother," the woman replied, gesturing. "Chetigré's, it is called. Go there and she will make food for you that uses all these spices. Ask for her Seven Spice Soup!"

"I'm ready to eat my shoes," Willem said suggestively.

"You would find my mother's soup much nicer," the woman replied, her eyes meeting his sassily. She flirted as naturally as she breathed. Willem pretended to fan his face and she laughed heartily before handing him a free sweetbark stick.

"Now I've been left out!" Hemmett protested, leaning on the counter, his flirtation mode in full force.

"Oh, poor big man, to be so badly treated by Luntigré" she commiserated. "Here, I will give you sweetbark as well, so you will not cry." She handed a stick to Hemmett, leaning so close that she could kiss him – but didn't. A moment later everyone had a stick and were much amused by Hemmett's protest that they weren't nearly so beautiful as he and didn't deserve any presents.

"Are you married, Luntigré?" he asked, lowering his eyelids at her.

"The daughters of Chetigré do not marry!" she proclaimed, nibbling on a sweetbark stick of her own. "We are free women, proud and strong. We love where we like!"

"Do you like what you see?" Hemmett asked, his voice low and husky.

"Maybe I do."

His devastating seduction was quashed as Borsen prodded him in the backside with his walking stick, making him squeak and jump into the air before wheeling around to take a swing at Borsen's head. Borsen jumped away so fast that Hemmett missed by a mile and started laughing.

"We're starving, Fathead," Borsen taunted.

"The children are dragging me away from you, Luntigré," Hemmett sighed.

She only laughed and turned to another customer.

A short walk brought them to a brilliant red and orange restaurant, the source of the scents that had teased their appetites as they walked along.

"Oh, let's try it!" Katrin cried. She was immediately seconded by Varnia, who was mad for anything having to do with cooking. The three young men were already bustling them inside.

They found themselves in a room bursting with color – reds, oranges, greens, blues, yellows everywhere. Flower boxes were in every window, overflowing with purples and pinks. Brilliant swaths of cloth hung on the walls. It should have been a clashing mess. It wasn't. It invited you to look, to sit, to eat and drink.

"And who is here to eat with me?" a woman's voice said off to their right.

The five young people turned.

This is majesty, Katrin thought, trying to take in all that was Chetigré. She was large and strong, heroic in build. Not as dark as Luntigré, she had a proud bearing tempered with hospitality. She could rival Tharak Karak, Highest Chieftain of the Thrun for presence. She would also put Katrin's mother, the perpetually drunken Queen of Mordania, to shame.

Her clothing was as colorful as her restaurant, covering the spectrum of yellow from butter to tawny. It complemented her dusky skin perfectly.

But of most interest to Katrin and Varnia, Chetigré's hair was cut very short.

Both young women had been fascinated to find that most Samorsan women cut their hair. Though Surelia was even warmer near the coast and far more humid, making long hair most uncomfortable, Surelian women coped by wearing a variety of tied up and pinned styles with their hair high on the tops of their heads. In Samorsa the society was much more free, with women owning their own property and businesses, even holding important positions in government. Chin length hair was the norm, with some of the more daring ladies sporting closely cropped styles.

If Chetigré's hair was any shorter, she would be bald. Katrin shivered a bit, imagining it, while Varnia reflected on how it would be very practical and comfortable in a hot kitchen.

"Madame, we were told by Luntigré that you are the best cook in Samorsa," Hemmett said with a bow.

"Luntigré is a foolish child, because Chetigré is the best cook on Eirdon," the big woman laughed. She curtseyed to them and they responded. Katrin saw the woman look at her closely as she rose, recognition kindling in her eyes.

Hemmett introduced them all by their aliases and Chetigré ushered them to a table with a view of the busy street.

"Now, I heard something about seven spices?" Hemmett said suggestively.

"That is my famous Seven Spice Soup," Chetigré nodded. "It is made from chicken, cream and seven spices. I've had grown men cry in appreciation when they try it. Will you have it all around? Then you may decide on the rest of your meal."

As their hostess went toward her kitchen, Katrin leaned close to Hemmett's ear.

"She might know who I am," she whispered.

He nodded. "I noticed. We'll watch."

The soup came and "The Knot" sniffed in appreciative anticipation. When Chetigré returned to the kitchen, Borsen swiftly exchanged portions with Katrin, his habit when they ate at a restaurant. He ate a spoonful.

"Eat!" he pronounced, immediately scooping another spoonful into his mouth, nodding to Hemmett.

As they did, cries of approbation went up.

"It's marvelous!" Willem said, barely taking time to breathe between swallows.

"Oh Varnia, what do you think the spices are?" Katrin exclaimed.

Varnia paused.

"Comina for certain," she appraised. "Possibly sweetbark? The rest – oh, don't make me keep talking!" She went back to her soup while Katrin and Hemmett giggled and nudged each other as they ate.

"Now then, what do you think?" Chetigré invited as she came back to the table. "No-one is dead? You see, Chetigré would never poison anyone with her food. If I wish to kill someone, I would use a gun."

"I have to take care," Hemmett said simply.

"I know. I know who you are by your eyes, Your Highness. They are your father's color, but your mother's shape and kindness. I will not tell a soul. I keep many secrets."

"You knew them?" Katrin asked in wonder.

"Indeed. Many years ago now, and sometime I will speak to you about them, but for now, it is time to eat! Tell me how you like my Seven Spice Soup!"

"It's superb," Borsen said, speaking for the first time since he'd started eating. "I would like a second bowl."

"There are many more dishes to come," Chetigré warned him.

"I will do justice to them all, but I want another bowl of your magnificent soup," Borsen answered, giving her his most brilliant smile.

"And you shall have one for that smile, pretty man."

"Madame, what are the spices?" Varnia asked, wiping her mouth.

"Chetigré is my name," the big woman smiled. "The spices are comina, sweetbark, orangeweed, bay, gentle herb, tymus and a bare touch of Samorsan hot pepper. Cooked with chicken in broth, cream, onions, garlic, salt and pepper."

"But salt and pepper are nine spices!" Varnia protested.

"Pah!" Chetigré put her fists on her hips and tossed her head. "Salt and pepper – they are a given! You like cooking?"

"Yes, very much," Varnia answered.

"I have a cooking school, where I teach those who wish to become great cooks," Chetigré told them. "Perhaps you would like to come and learn some tricks?"

"Yes!" Katrin and Varnia spoke simultaneously, looking at each other in delight.

"I see myself gaining twenty pounds," Hemmett laughed. "But I'm willing to take the risk to keep you young ladies safe."

"We will feed him until he's very fat," Chetigré laughed. "And now, for the rest of your meal – give me your orders, please."

***

Dear Valdema,

I hope this finds you and Mr. Ordstrom well. Everyone here is fine, except for Kaymar, who actually managed to raise a blister on his lip eating the hot peppers the Samorsans grow. He felt very sorry for himself for some days.

I wanted to let you know that I have a chance to go to a cooking school run by a famous cook known as Chetigré. I have had her food several times and I think it would be a great thing to be taught by her. I would be so glad to bring you some of her recipes and show you her cooking methods. Katrin will be going too.

I hope you think this is a good idea. Please let me know.

Your friend,
Varnia

Dear Varnia,

Silly girl, of course you must go to this school. I hope you didn't think I would believe you were going to take over. You need to learn all the skills you can, and I have heard of this Chetigré. She is famous all over the world. I would be proud to have her recipes coming out of the kitchen here.

Everyone here is well. Miss Glad has gone to Samorsa and been gone for some time. You will likely see her there. Ask to see her school. She thinks you might be interested in some of her classes.

Ordstrom had a bad spell with his back a while ago, but a warmed sack of bran on it worked it out. One of Tomar's little ones had aching fever a month or so back but is right back to being a wild thing now.

Take care of yourself and keep your eyes open for every opportunity.

Love,
Valdema

SARONILLA, SAMORSA

21
WE REMEMBER

Menders' eyebrows went up eloquently. "Chetigré! I had no idea she was in Saronilla. The last time I ate at her restaurant, she was in Parita," he said.

"Do you know her?" Katrin asked excitedly.

"Everyone in Special Services did. We traveled a lot, you know, little princess," he smiled. "So, you and Varnia want to go to the cooking school?"

"Can we?"

"I will need to take a look at it and you would have to be escorted."

"Hemmett has volunteered and is looking forward to gaining some weight," Katrin smiled.

"I'm sure we can manage," Menders smiled. "So, you want a break from universities?"

"I didn't really think about that. The chance to do cooking with someone like Chetigré is something I don't want to pass up. It would be a change and I could go to the classes with Varnia. Since she doesn't want to go to university, it's something we can do together. She really wants to go."

"I have no objection." Menders sat back in his chair on the balcony and looked out over the city of Saronilla. "This journey isn't about acquiring a university education. You should try anything you feel interested in, Katrin, particularly here. You can study anywhere, but there are things to see and do in other countries that are unique."

Katrin smiled and poured herself another glass of lemonade. She was glad for a break from art study. She loved it, but things were becoming repetitive. She could draw and paint on her own.

"Menders, Chetigré recognized me," she said abruptly, the issue that had hung in front of her all day coming to the fore.

"Yes, Hemmett and Willem told me," he answered calmly.

"She says she knew who I was because my eyes look like my mother's. She knew my mother – and my father." She watched him closely.

Katrin knew Menders despised her mother. He considered the Queen to have abandoned her younger daughter. There was never a letter or birthday gift from her. Katrin had only seen her once, when she was commanded to Court at the age of eleven.

She had been presented to a heavy woman wearing the armored, jewel encrusted red dress that was the official garment of Mordanian queens, along with false, pointed teeth and a hideous red wig. The Queen questioned Katrin closely about her studies, said she resembled her father and then dismissed her from the Throne Room.

For this reason, Katrin felt no affection toward her mother. When she was younger, she often felt resentful, but once she saw the spiritless, weary woman, the resentment fled. Sometimes she felt sorry they didn't know one another, but life was full and busy, and she had plenty of family around her.

Menders was silent. He was often very deliberate before speaking.

"It would stand to reason," he finally replied. "Your mother did tour the Middle Continent when she was a young woman, before Morghenna the Terrible became ill and she had to return to Court. It is entirely possible they went to Chetigré's during that tour. I'm quite sure your father was with her. He had been assigned to the Palace at the time she embarked and would have been in her entourage."

"May I speak with Chetigré about them?" Katrin asked tentatively.

Menders blinked and looked directly at her.

"Of course," he replied gently. "I have nothing against you knowing about your parents. I don't care for your mother because she has remained distant from you. But I don't know her. I've met her twice – the night you were born and the time she ordered you to Court. I only spoke to her the second time and that was only to answer her questions.

"You should talk to Kaymar," he continued. "He knows her well. He's one of her protected Courtiers. She arranged his release from Special Services. He seems to like her quite a bit, though he regrets her inability to stop drinking. He'd be glad to tell you about her."

"I will," Katrin smiled.

***

"I care a great deal about your mother," Kaymar said bluntly. "She isn't evil, Katrin. She's suffered a great deal at the hands of others and it damaged her terribly, but she is not a bad person. Unfortunately, she was weakened by the abuse. She drinks far too much, and I don't think anything could change that at this point."

"Was it Madame Holz who abused her?" Katrin asked, finally voicing a question that had haunted her for years. She knew about the short tenure of Madame Holz at The Shadows, where she had been sent to begin the toughening regimen on Katrin when she was only six months old.

Kaymar nodded. "Holz and other nurses, governesses. You can't begin to imagine what toughening does to most people, Katrin. It isn't just the physical punishment – it's the squelching of everything. It degrades the person's spirit to the point where they have no self-will.

"Your mother has tried, but a corrupt Council got into power and took control of things after your grandmother, Morghenna the Terrible, had a stroke. She had no ability to speak or rule – but she was a living Queen. By the time she finally died, and your mother was crowned, the Council was entrenched. She would have had to give orders to have them removed by any means possible, which would have meant a killing spree, essentially.

"She couldn't make the decision to do that. By then she had been drinking heavily for some years. She retreats somewhere within herself. Nothing can hurt her there. Nothing reaches her."

Katrin settled against the back of the park bench and thought about that.

She had never thought of her mother as a victim. When she had thought of her, it was to wonder why she made no contact. Kaymar's words were making her think of other possibilities.

"What does she think of Aidelia?" Katrin asked, feeling an inward shudder at the memory of her older sister. Aidelia was mad, refusing to bathe or allow her hair to be washed. Katrin had encountered Aidelia when she was at the Palace. Aidelia tried to scratch Katrin with her jagged, black to the quick fingernails, hissing that she would kill her.

"She's despairing about her at this point. She's tried for years to find some doctor or medicine that would help Aidelia. Once in a great while, Aidelia begins to make some sense and doesn't seem so hopelessly mad – but it never lasts."

Katrin shuddered inwardly. She could feel sorry that her sister was mad but the memory of her clawing and threatening ran deep.

"Does my mother ever ask about me?" she asked, her voice very soft.

"Yes."

They were silent for some time. Kaymar finally took out one of his cigars and lit it.

"Why do you think she doesn't see me?" She'd finally voiced the question that had plagued her all of her life.

Kaymar didn't answer at first. He took several puffs on the cigar and then turned to look at her. His blue eyes, so like her own, were very stern and kind.

"Perhaps it's because she wants to protect you from all the things that make her like she is," he answered.

***

It was break time at Chetigré's cooking school. Hemmett was, as usual, the center of attention as various of the students plied him with their products of the morning session. He'd taken to running long distances and exercising like a demon, as the threatened weight gain had started to become a reality.

Chetigré was an excellent but strict instructor. She didn't allow a lot of chatter or clowning in her classes, but breaks were completely unrestricted. Students could eat as much as they wanted, talk uninhibitedly, flirt and socialize.

Katrin, Varnia and Eiren were glad to sit down and observe Hemmett's antics from a distance. The morning session had been absorbing but demanding. Some time off their feet would be most welcome. Eiren gave her right arm a rub – a well-beaten meringue had been part of the morning's work.

"I should learn to beat egg whites with my left arm as well – it would give the right one a rest," she smiled.

"I wish Cook could be here," Katrin said, rising and going behind Eiren, gently massaging her arm with a technique Doctor Franz had taught her when she went with him on calls.

"She might lecture Chetigré a bit," Varnia responded, a twinkle in her eyes.

"Chetigré would never permit that," Eiren laughed.

"Indeed, she would not!" Chetigré declared, approaching them. "I would have to quell her as I did that wicked Kaymar."

All three of them laughed quietly. Kaymar had, unexpectedly, decided to join the cooking class. He'd immediately taken Chetigré's measure and knew that she was very fond of men. He'd taken complete advantage of 4that. He'd clowned, teased, put his fingers in bowls and licked them, laughed when he was scolded and was finally driven from the room with an enormous whisk the size of Cook's particular spoon. Now, when he guarded Katrin on Hemmett's days off, Chetigré threatened to tie him to his chair to keep him away from the cooking tables. When he told her he wouldn't be able to protect everyone if bound, she informed him that she could do very well protecting everyone herself.

Katrin didn't doubt it. Chetigré was taller than Katrin, who was closer to six feet tall than she was to five. Chetigré also wielded a wicked knife after decades of cooking.

"Miss Emila, I'd like you to take a cup of tea with me," Chetigré invited, gesturing toward her parlor, adjacent to the large classroom. "If your mama and friend don't mind me taking you away from them."

Eiren smiled at Katrin and nodded.

"Not at all – I know she's be anxious to speak with you," she replied as Katrin rose and followed Chetigré into the parlor.

"Now then, a couple of lovely cups of tea." Chetigré busied herself at the funny little stove that warmed the room. "And we'll have that talk. Now, do you want plain tea, or will you trust me to brew up a spiced tea that you'll like?"

"Oh please, a spiced tea would be wonderful," Katrin answered, looking around the parlor with delight. She'd had glimpses of the interior, but now she could take a good long look.

As Chetigré busied herself, Katrin moved about, looking at the luxurious fabrics and carefully placed ornaments. The furniture invited her to sit and be comfortable. She had come to love Samorsan interior styles, which ran to overstuffed sofas and chairs, rich colorful rugs and profligate use of what Menders called "shelf doodads", little figurines and paintings.

Katrin's future had always been a blank to her. The Queen's permission was required for any venture she undertook. Menders had been flabbergasted when he received permission to take her abroad and out of Mordania for so long. With a mad Heiress to the Throne, the Queen had always made it clear that Katrin could be put in Aidelia's place at any time.

Menders had let Katrin know about the various plots and conspiracies that swirled around the Queen. It was a never ending torrent of desire for power, targeting a woman who, from all appearances, had never wanted to be Queen – as Katrin didn't.

Katrin was free to travel, but always accompanied and guarded. She could study anything she wanted – but what to do with it? She would not be permitted to take employment and make use of her learning. It was taken for granted that her residence was The Shadows – which she shared, at this point, with nearly one hundred people. Sometimes her childhood desire to be alone, to be able to walk about without being watched or protected, came back a thousand fold, like a crashing wave.

Katrin couldn't even imagine a home of her own, like other women, with a husband and children. She knew her friends dreamed about it, considered how they would furnish and decorate their domains, considered paint colors and curtain fabrics.

She liked this room. She liked the way Chetigré was independent and made her own world. Katrin knew her world was largely ordained for her by others and that any changes she could make were in the smallest details.

"Now, out of those dark thoughts!" Chetigré commanded, laying out teacups and saucers, then carrying over a teapot shaped like an adorable fat bird. "I don't ask you in here to have you become quiet and sad."

"I'm sorry," Katrin answered. "I was just wondering if I'd ever furnish a home of my own."

"A natural thought. Sit, my dear. We've been on our feet for hours, cooking away." Chetigré seated herself and adjusted the cups and other tea things. "To have so much of your life assigned to you – having a crown isn't what people think. It's a burden, though usually riches come with it, but what use riches if you can't make your own choices, eh?"

"When I was younger, I wanted to be a dancer, until I found out how small dancers had to be and what it did to their feet. I actually thought it was possible. Then I realized, I would never have been allowed to be a dancer, even if I'd been smaller than Borsen and born with wings on my ankles." Katrin gratefully accepted the cup of tea Chetigré prepared for her and sipped. It was tantalizing, sweet and creamy, strong dark tea laced with so many spices she couldn't sort them out.

"Good, eh? I thought that would suit you. I find the idea of royalty very disturbing, in truth," Chetigré mused. "We have a King here, of course, but we have a republic as well. Our King works from an office, not a palace and he helps with law making and policy. He is quite a funny man and likes my restaurant. His sons – some of them have asked to be left out of the Line of Succession, wanting to live a private life, and there has been no problem with that. I fear your country is nowhere near such a solution."

"No. That's a certainty," Katrin replied, setting her cup down.

"Now then, enough of what we cannot change," Chetigré announced. "You wish to know what I know of your mother."

"And my father. I have met my mother once and only answered her questions. My father died before I was born."

"Yes, poor man. They were a beautiful couple. Your mother was one of the most beautiful women I ever saw, Katrin. She was tall, like you, but fuller bodied, though she was some years older than you are now when I knew her. Her hair was a natural red-gold, not like that foolish wig she wears as Queen. Men drank toasts to her eyes. Like the clearest lagoon you've ever seen, a true aquamarine color." Chetigré sipped her tea for a moment.

"Your father – well. Many hearts fluttered over that man, I can tell you! You have his coloring, the intense blue eyes, the golden hair. You also have his height and length of limb, his way of moving and you have his kindness. It shows in your face as it showed in his.

"Your parents together were more as a couple than either of them standing alone. To the experienced, it was clear that your mother had been trodden down and harmed badly, but Bernhard Markha lifted her up, gave her a foundation from which she could be strong. Their love was a force that would not be denied."

"Was this before my sister Aidelia was born?" Katrin asked in confusion.

"No, my dear. Your mother had already had your sister before she began to travel. From what was told me, she had objected to the way the baby was going to be raised – but she was so trained to be obedient that she couldn't fight for long. Even though the toughening had rendered your mother weak, The Terrible was determined that your sister would be made strong by it. She ordered your mother away to travel."

Katrin was sitting upright, her cup in her hand.

"She tried to oppose Morghenna the Terrible?" she gasped.

Chetigré nodded gravely.

"She did, but she couldn't hold fast," she answered. "She was ordered away to do the Middle Continent Tour, to get her away from holding and loving the baby. There was no choice. She would have been sent by force or even executed if she persisted, since there was another Heiress available."

"Sometimes I hate my country," Katrin whispered. The cruelty of what Chetigré had just told her made her breath come short.

"It is due for change, that is a certainty," Chetigré agreed. "She and your father fell in love during that tour. She had a freedom while traveling that she'd never had. I think, with enough time with your father's support, she would have become a stronger woman."

"You must have known them very well."

"I did." Chetigré set her cup down and refilled it. She rose and went to a cupboard, coming back with a covered plate that was full of tiny cakes, each decorated with candied flowers.

"I'm sure your father, my old friend Menders, has told you he has a network of people all over the world, who provide him with information," she said, keeping her voice low.

"Yes, I know this – though I had no idea just how extensive it was until we started to travel," Katrin answered.

"Well, I am a part. I don't communicate directly to Menders, but through others, for safety. So do many, many people. Before Menders, to Thoren Bartan, the Court Assassin. Ah, I see you know him."

Katrin nodded. "He and his wife visit us and at the Palace, he helped us."

"At the time your parents were together, your father was forming a similar network. He wanted things to change in Mordania. He saw what toughening did to your mother and he saw how The Terrible fought to retain her control as the Queen. The Council was always plotting, always seeking to take away her power. He knew Mordania had to change and he was working from here to make that possible. I provided your parents with a safe place to communicate with other parts of his network, so the secret was kept."

The idea of her parents as rebels, working to change the backward elements of Mordania set Katrin's imagination on fire.

"Then your grandmother was struck down and your mother was ordered back to Mordania. I had no more direct contact with them. Then three years later I had word that your father had been in an accident and died. I think the rest you know."

"As much as anyone knows about the Queen," Katrin sighed. "She doesn't stay in contact with me. I've been with Menders ever since the night I was born and Eiren has been there since we arrived at The Shadows. They are my parents."

"They are indeed. Remember, though – there are those people who lust after power who will do anything to acquire it."

"Yes. We had a terrible man trying to kill us all two years ago," Katrin said softly. "There have been others as well, since I was tiny."

"You have a friend here, Katrin," Chetigré said, reaching out and taking her hand. "Samorsa is a big place. Remember that, if a bolt-hole is ever needed."

She sat up abruptly.

"Now, we will leave these dark things behind. Remember, your parents truly loved one another and wanted to make a better world. It was not always sadness and despair."

"No. No, it wasn't and I'm glad you told me," Katrin replied, setting her cup down so Chetigré could pour more of the aromatic tea. "I've wondered so often."

"Have a cake."

"I've had three!"

"Do you want another?"

"Well – yes, I do."

"So take! And you may have some to take to that dreadful Kaymar, who is so badly behaved!"

"I think you like Kaymar, Chetigré," Katrin laughed.

"Pah! He is a dreadful pest," Chetigré pronounced, taking out a prettily decorated box and packing several of the little cakes away in it for Katrin to take back to Kaymar.

PARITA, SAMORSA

21
COIL OF MEMORY

"Well, young lady, you're rambling around town on your own."
Varnia started and turned toward Ifor Trantz, who was smiling down at her.

"I didn't want to see the bullfights," she replied awkwardly. She'd begged off an excursion to the arena when asked by Hemmett and Borsen. Katrin and Kaymar had gone along, but Varnia hated the dust, noise and crowds. She had waited until the bullfight party departed and then dressed in her best, slipping out of the hotel to have a solitary look around Parita.

"Nor me," Ifor replied. "The bulls aren't harmed, and it isn't often that a fighter is, but it strikes me as a waste of time and effort, to say nothing of annoying and frightening an animal. So, would you care to join me for a ramble around beautiful Parita?"

Varnia tried to shield her expression, but could tell that she'd suddenly looked wary. Ifor seemed so courtly. She was fairly certain he was entirely nancy, unlike Kaymar who was attracted to both men and women and exuded sensuality – but could she be sure?

He'd caught that flash of unease and gave her a smile. His homely face lit up.

"You could not be safer with me, dear," he said gently. "I have no motive other than spending a little time with someone who would probably appreciate some of the same things I do."

He offered her his arm. She smiled suddenly and took it. Ifor squired her away, down a twisty little street full of shops.

They drifted along for some time without speaking, taking in what was displayed in the shop windows or looking at a peculiar or interesting building. Varnia's favorites were the ones Menders had told her were made of bricks and then plastered over with wet clay that was hardened by hot fires burned around the structure.

The Samorsans called this building style *ceramo*. It made corners into smooth curves and to Varnia's mind, the *ceramo* buildings looked like they had formed naturally from the ground, like enormous mushrooms that people lived in. They were always painted in cheerful and sometimes clashing colors that always seemed just right in the intense sunlight.

"Ah, now what I was wanting to see," Ifor announced suddenly. "Just a bit further along this way."

Varnia could hear splashing water and smiled to herself. So far Ifor's world tour had involved seeing famous fountains in many lands. Eiren had told her that Ifor an expert on all forms of artistic expression and had written several books about art under a pen name. Varnia suspected he was gathering notes for another one.

Suddenly they walked into a Samorsan road-courtyard, an open space around a fountain. They were fixtures in every Samorsan neighborhood, but this fountain was exquisite. It was made in a style similar to the *ceramo* buildings that ringed the courtyard, but of a lighter and finer clay. It soared to over fifteen feet, graceful curves sculpted like vines around a central trunk. Water poured from innumerable spouts, splashing into reservoirs, throwing up a fine mist that softened the dry air and glittered with reflected light.

"See, when they attempted this fountain, they had a lot of difficulty," Ifor said, pointing upward to the central trunk of the structure. "They built it and then fired it whole with a huge bonfire. This was not a good idea – but then, no-one had attempted such a thing before. It would have been better to fire it in separate pieces, assemble them and fire it again.

"The entire fountain crumbled on the first firing, but the builders didn't give up. You can see cracks and fissures that are repaired, but they did the repairs in such a way that they became part of the design. They patched it together, sculpted clay around the breaks and fired it again and again until it all held together. They ended up with this wonder – graceful, unique and incredibly strong."

It is a wonder, Varnia thought, looking at the stunning structure. What she liked most was that rather than simply decorating a space, this fountain was being used. People were coming for water, to take a drink, to rinse their hands. Children, hot and sweaty from playing, wet their faces or splashed each other. Horses drank from a trough fed by the fountain. Varnia liked useful things as well as beautiful things. This fountain hidden in a working class Samorsan neighborhood was both.

A little girl playfully flicked water at Ifor when he smiled at her and asked the name of her dolly, which she was giving a bath. He laughed and began singing back at her. Varnia's ear had become well developed during their time in Surelia. Though she didn't know much Samorsan, it was similar to Surelian and she was able to translate enough to know it was a comical children's song about a man who sold his cow to buy a calf, then went on to make a number of other poor trades until he ended up with a fly that proceeded to die.

She sat down on a nearby bench, amused, as Ifor entertained a growing crowd of children with his powerful bass voice. The bolder ones were singing the song with him and all were laughing as he mimed and gestured, telling the sad tale of the gormless bargain maker.

A woman sat beside Varnia, balancing a basket of wet laundry on her lap and sighing with relief. She smiled and then watched Ifor with appreciation.

"*Ello mariano vos?*" she asked. Varnia scrambled over the Samorsan words and realized she was being asked if Ifor was her husband. She smiled and shook her head.

"*Samorsona ve ne puarte, seronara,*" she replied, using her limited vocabulary to let the woman know that she truly didn't speak Samorsan. Her companion nodded and tried Surelian.

Varnia could bumble along in that language. She tried, but the woman went too fast, then switched suddenly to broken Mordanian. Varnia remembered how Menders had told her that Samorsa, because of its particular position on the continent it shared with Surelia, Fambré and Barambos, was a place where many languages were spoken and understood.

"So, Miss is Mordanian!" the woman cried in surprise. "You look Samorsan!"

Varnia nodded shyly. She had been told that many times since they'd come to Samorsa because of her black hair and gray eyes – and her hawkish nose.

"So, this singing gentleman, he is your husband?"

"No, only a friend," Varnia replied stiffly.

The woman shook her head and laughed.

"Best catch him, he would be a good one," she advised, sorting her wet laundry for a moment. "See how kind, how good to the little ones. Don't be long, someone will take him!" She rose, nodded politely and sauntered away with her basket balanced on her hip.

Varnia breathed a little sigh of relief. So many people in these foreign countries seemed determined to marry her off. One Surelian waiter had pestered her about marrying Hemmett until she'd been ready to cry and Hemmett paid him to go away. Even if she was interested in marriage, Ifor would be the last place she'd look, considering he'd been bonded to Kaymar for years and was utterly devoted to him.

She rose to cover her discomfiture and strolled over to the shops that ringed the fountain courtyard. Vendors spoke cheerfully but let her browse without pestering her. She finally stopped outside a hairdressing salon, intrigued by the hairstyle pictures in the window.

Varnia's hair was a trial to her. It had never been cut, as was the Mordanian custom. It nearly reached her feet, as Katrin's did. But Katrin's hair was something out of a fairytale – golden, curling and easy to control. Brushing made it gleam. When pinned up, it stayed in place until Katrin took it down.

Varnia's hair was midnight black, wavy, slippery in texture and almost impossible to tame. Once she was grown she'd always coiled and pinned it back severely, just to keep it out of her way. Then she had learned some looser hairstyles, but when wearing it so, it often got away from her. Worse, sometimes no matter what she did, she couldn't achieve a groomed appearance and had to run to Eiren or Katrin for help. Just lately, while riding on Borsen's little donkey, her hair decided to tumble down and got ensnared around the poor animal's legs. Only quick action on Borsen's part had kept the donkey from kicking in reflex and tearing Varnia's hair out by the roots.

Another aspect of her hair was more disturbing. Sometimes Varnia thought about it having been there all of her life. It had been through everything she had, a sort of silent witness that absorbed all her experiences. Sometimes when she wound it up and pinned it to the back of her head, she thought of it as a coil of memories – and Varnia's memories, until lately, had not been sweet ones.

The dashing and dramatic Samorsan hairstyles intrigued her. One in particular stayed in her mind, where the hair was cut to chin length and then sculpted in luxurious waves with a saucy curl pulled forward on each cheek. She could imagine the comfort of having such short hair in this hot land – right now sweat was trickling down her scalp and she wasn't even moving. She also had her habitual headache, spreading from the continual pull her coiled locks caused on the back of her head, her scalp irritated by dozens of hairpins.

She saw Ifor approaching her in the hair salon window and turned toward him. He raised his eyebrows for her permission to smoke, then took out a cigar and lit it.

"Interested in this one?" he asked, pointing with the cigar to the very picture of the wavy cut she admired the most. "That's the one for you, my dear."

Varnia looked up at him.

"I wouldn't dare," she said shyly. "I – what would everyone think?"

"They'd think you cut your hair," Ifor smiled back. "Don't let that keep you from doing something you want to do. Also, don't let me tempt you into doing something you don't want to do. You're the one who decides." He offered her his arm, as if to move along.

Varnia nearly took it, but hesitated, looking at the picture again. Light, cool, dashing and daring. Everything she was not.

Ifor leaned close and whispered something in her ear.

Varnia blinked. Then she smiled.

"Wait for me?" she asked.

Ifor winked and sauntered over to a bench, sitting and crossing his legs. He stretched an arm comfortably across the back of the bench and proceeded to relish his cigar.

Varnia went into the cool salon and within minutes was having her hair washed. The lady barber studied her tresses and then agreed that the style in the picture was exactly right and would be easy for her to maintain.

"So heavy, so hard to keep, all those pins!" she exclaimed, looking at the pile of hairpins that had been pulled from Varnia's hair. "We will help you."

Varnia didn't even flinch when the first lock of hair fell to the floor. Each cut lightened her head. Only then she realized that her neck ached from holding up that massive coil of hair.

Ifor blinked and jumped up from the bench when she came out of the salon. He bowed to her with a smile.

"I've hardly taken it in," Varnia said breathlessly, amazed at the coolness of her neck, the feeling of freedom when she turned her head and didn't feel the weight of that pinned up knob of hair. "They showed me in a mirror, but I was so excited I could barely look."

"That won't do," Ifor declared. He escorted her to a shop, took her inside and selected a beautiful ladies' hand mirror. He gave it to her and turned her toward the light from the window.

"That," he told her, "is a beautiful woman."

Varnia looked at her reflection and caught her breath.

Her hair framed her face, the cheek curls arranged to emphasize her suddenly very large and exotic eyes and her delicate chin. One of the assistants had put some lip rouge on her and showed her how to groom her eyebrows, saying she would never need more cosmetics with her striking features and good skin. Her nose, which she had always despised, now looked as elegant and regal as Borsen's.

She looked strong, independent and yes, beautiful. Not Katrin's pink, gold and blue prettiness or Eiren's tawny, redhaired loveliness, but something patrician and bold. Something far from a big-nosed scowling little girl or a big-nosed scowling woman.

"Now, don't cry," Ifor laughed. "I'll take you to lunch."

"A Samorsan woman advised me to marry you," Varnia laughed aloud, taking the handkerchief, he offered. Ifor laughed with her.

"We'd just conveniently move Kip into the linen closet," he answered. Then he turned around and bought the mirror for her, along with the matching brush and comb.

***

Varnia tried to take in all the reactions when she and Ifor walked through the door of the family's suite – but that proved impossible.

"Oh, you did it!" Katrin cried, jumping up from her chair and running over. "Look how it curls! Did they curl it? Oh, I wish I dared cut mine!"

"It's my natural curl," Varnia managed.

Eiren smiled and rose as well.

"It's lovely and very suited," she said. "Did you have a nice day?"

Varnia nodded and began to tell her about seeing the fountain, but then Hemmett came in from his room.

"Be upstanding for the lady!" he bellowed, saluting her in fine style. "Did Big Ifor give you a dare?"

"Give you a punch for that," Ifor muttered. Varnia realized how easily he spoke to her when they were alone and how unusual that was. He tended to mumble and mutter in company. "She had her own mind made up, just needed to hear some little, pertinent remark to put things in perspective."

Katrin was asking what the remark was, but all attention went to the main door, where Menders and Borsen were coming in to change for dinner.

Menders put his hat on the hall table and switched to his clear glasses – then he saw Varnia. He came to her and took her hands.

"My brave girl," he said softly. "I don't need to ask if you're happy."

"Doesn't she look like a lady revolutionary or heroine?" Katrin asked him delightedly.

"Indeed. Like a woman who knows her own mind and strength," Menders answered. He smiled at Varnia, released her hands and stepped aside – leaving her face to face with Borsen.

He looked at her solemnly and nodded.

"My beautiful, powerful big sister," he said so softly that no-one else could hear it. "Now you are found."

He came close and Varnia put her arm around his shoulders.

"And what was the remark you made to Varnia, Bear?" Kaymar asked from the sofa where he had been lounging, watching all the excitement.

"Simple enough," Ifor shrugged, taking off his jacket. "I just reminded her that it's hair – it grows back. Gave her all the perspective she needed."

Varnia thought of that when she sat before her mirror and used the brush Ifor had given her. Every time she moved her head, she heard the word 'freedom' in her mind. No hairpins, no long braid rubbing her shoulders or getting tangled around her neck during the night.

It was as if nearly seventeen years of incessant work, exhaustion, pain, hunger, despair and worse had been cut away – and Varnia was suddenly determined that they would haunt her no more.

She pushed up the waves, even though she was about to get into bed, smiled at herself, whispered "good night" and turned down the lamp.

PARITA AND SARONILLA, SAMORSA

22
HEMMETT'S TURN

"Of course," Menders said immediately. "You're more than due some leave, Hemmett. I'm surprised you haven't asked before now."

"Haven't come across a place I wanted to spend extra time in," Hemmett replied. "Like Borsen and Barambos – it speaks to me, as he says."

"I've always been fond of Samorsa myself," Menders smiled. "I like the modern government, the people, the freedom the women have. I prefer the climate further inland to here though, it's a bit hot for me in Parita."

"I can say the same. I actually want to go back to Saronilla. So, I'd like six weeks, if it's possible – if not, four would do."

"Six it is," Menders said firmly. "Here, let's stop off at the market and pick up dinner for everyone. Eiren wasn't feeling her best and I think an evening in with a simple meal might be just the thing. That way she doesn't have to dress and sit at a restaurant."

"I think Kaymar and Ifor were going out – Ifor's finally prevailed on him to go to the opera," Hemmett grinned. Menders snickered a bit.

"I'll prepare myself for Kaymar's recounting of the event tomorrow," he replied. Kaymar was not fond of opera but tolerated it frequently to accommodate Ifor's enthusiasm for it. "That makes things even easier then – dinner for seven, if you know whether Willem will be with us or going off on his own."

"He likes family meals, so he'll be there," Hemmett said. "There's some of the sunfruit Eiren loves so much. Let's get those." He gabbled his pidgin Samorsan to the stallholder and procured a large bag of the oval yellow fruit. "You know, I'm going to miss Will while we're in Artreya. He fits right into family life."

"He's a good man," Menders agreed, indicating to the butcher that he wanted eight roasted cockerels, a pan of baked ground Samorsan sausage and a box of meat rolls in crisp pastry. "He's been a tremendous help and a good companion guard for Varnia and Katrin. Kaymar is considering rotating him back to us while we're in Artreya, but wants him to train a bit with Menders' Men at The Shadows. We also need to get Borsen's donkey home before we leave Samorsa."

Hemmett laughed aloud. He was enormously amused by Boss and would miss him once he was shipped back to The Shadows. He had managed to teach the little donkey how to bow on cue. That and the dancing trick Borsen had introduced made the donkey a hit whenever "The Knot" went out as a group, taking Boss along to carry picnic baskets or extra wraps. Boss thought he was in heaven, never overloaded or ridden by anyone who chucked his mouth.

"I think Samorsa has been everyone's favorite stop so far – excepting Borsen, who was transported by Barambos," Menders said as he considered a display of freshly baked bread.

"Definitely mine. That situation in Fambré was unfortunate. Is Katrin still writing to the priest there?"

Menders nodded, indicating several different loaves to the stall owner, who began to wrap his purchase in brown paper.

"It's a nice correspondence for her and her first with someone who isn't connected with The Shadows. Of course, now she's writing to Chetigré as well. I'm sure she'll meet plenty of people in Artreya who will become pen friends. She wants to enroll at the University there."

Hemmett was looking over a vegetable cart.

"Varnia could make a salad from some of this," he said suggestively.

"You're a country boy, pick out some likely items," Menders answered, drifting toward a bakery specializing in desserts.

"A simple dinner," Hemmett muttered to himself in amusement, selecting several bunches of greens and then adding a number of other colorful vegetables for garnish. He caught up with Menders, who had already ordered a magnificent cake, a boxful of pastries, another of meringues and a platter of candied fruits.

"One other request," Hemmett said as he started to heft their parcels and bags. "Do not send anyone to shadow me as you did with Borsen."

"Of course not, and I mean that," Menders responded seriously. "You aren't a target. Katrin and Borsen are. You will be blissfully on your own, Captain Greinholz."

***

"Oh Bumpy, you mean you wouldn't travel into Artreya with us?" Katrin said in dismay. Hemmett had pulled her aside and told her about his leave.

"Now Willow, I've been two years without a real leave," he said patiently. "Don't put a spoiler on it for me by carrying on."

"No. I'm sorry," she said immediately, putting her hand on his arm. "It's just hard to think of going there without you."

"I'll be along in a few weeks. You can get settled and scout out the area. Then you'll be able to tell me all the best things to do when I catch up. I really want to see the Samorsan Games, Willow."

"I wish the university term started later, but we have to be there in three weeks," she sighed. Then he could tell she was determined to put a good face on it.

"And what else will you get up to while you're there?" she asked.

"For one thing, I will wallow in the bed until the sun is well up," he smiled, tucking her hand in the crook of his arm and walking her back into the suite. "I'll take afternoon naps, eat too much and if I feel like doing nothing, that is exactly what I'll do."

"And will you be on the watch for ladies?" Katrin teased.

"Very possibly. Now, let's help with this simple dinner which nearly broke my back to haul up here," he answered. "Menders was like a man gone wild, buying more and more. We have groceries for a week."

***

Hemmett sauntered down Market Street in Saronilla at a leisurely pace, reveling in not having to be vigilant. He enjoyed his work and he loved Katrin dearly, but the average person had no idea how tiring a heightened awareness of everything could be.

Truth to tell, he was still badly rattled by the situation that had arisen in Fambré and how he, Menders and Katrin's other security had miscalculated the temper of the place. If Katrin hadn't experienced that eerie premonition, or whatever it was, they would have all been just so many more dead bodies. Something like that couldn't happen again.

Menders had reminded Katrin's security, including the Menders' Men who stayed out of her sight, just how closely they had to watch for any sign of anti-Mordanian sentiment in Artreya. There had been some sabre rattling going on between the nations of late, not much more than the usual degree of disdain – but it was a different matter when a Princess of Mordania was traveling there anonymously.

Hemmett, if you got down to brass tacks, was not happy with the idea of the family traveling to and living in Artreya. To him, as to any Mordanian military man, Artreya was the enemy. Actually living in enemy territory struck him as a very bad idea.

But this sunny morning, he was putting that situation out of his head. He would deal with it when he joined the family in Artreya. For now, he was on leave, the Samorsan Games were beginning tomorrow and he was going to visit a certain market stall.

He could smell the mingled scents of spices before he saw the brilliant orange draperies over Luntigré's counter.

Luntigré looked up and put her hands on her hips, turning her head slightly, fighting a smile. Hemmett didn't know it, but the late morning sunlight was flooding the street behind him, turning his russet brown hair into a crown of light.

"Do you have any sweetbark for a wandering soldier?" Hemmett smiled as he reached her counter and leaned on it dashingly.

Without a word, Luntigré picked up a stick of sweetbark, broke it in two and shared it between them. She leaned on the counter, her face close to his as they savored the spicy treat.

***

"So, tell me about these 'tigré' names," Hemmett said as Luntigré ran her fingers through his hair, gently encouraging the curls he oiled into straightness every morning.

Luntigré laughed aloud.

"My mother's true name is not Chetigré," she explained. "She was born Julita Fortha and then married a man with the family name Bonno. He was a terrible man. He is not my father. She had me from another lover later. The marriage was arranged, you see. He wanted her to work all the time in the house and on the farm. There were other women and he flaunted that to her to make her cry.

"She left him and found she could not have the marriage dissolved, that she was, for all purposes, his property. No woman could have a marriage ended in Samorsa at that time, only a man. She refused to return to her husband and found work in Parita as a cook."

"She also discovered women who were forming a revolution, to make things better for all women in Samorsa. It's only recently that women have owned property and run businesses, only in the last twenty years."

"They've come a long way," Hemmett remarked, thinking of the independent Samorsan women he had met.

"Very much. They were brave and would not give up. All the women of the nation struck until they were given the same rights as men. My mother was in the vanguard of these women and won the name Chetigré, which means 'tiger woman' because she was so fierce and powerful."

"And so your name?" he prompted.

"Luntigré means 'moon tiger'. Both moons were full the night I was born and the first time my mother saw my face, the moonlight was on it. My elder sister is 'Montigré', which is 'mighty tiger'. Hers was a long birth and it took a great deal of strength for my mother to bear her. She held on tight!" Luntigré laughed aloud and Hemmett laughed along with her.

"And so what sort of tiger is your little girl?" he asked.

Luntigré shook her head.

"There are enough tigers in this family," she smiled. "Her name is Florina de Nizé, which is 'night flower'. It was high summer when I bore her. The smell of the flowers was so intense that night. When you meet her, you will see that it is the perfect name for her. We call her Flori."

"Where is she?" he asked. It was coming on to full dark now.

"She is with my sister and her cousins for a few days. They are all going to the Games. She is six years old," Luntigré said. "Do you like children, Hemmett?"

"Yes," he answered, sitting up against the headboard. "Eiren runs a school near The Shadows and there are always children around and about. I was also a tutor and instructor for the youngest boys at the Military Academy in my final year. When I'm back in Mordania I may do some more teaching there. I never grew up, you see."

"Very childish, oh yes," she remarked, sitting up as well. "So Eiren is an independent woman?"

"Very much, more than most Mordanian women. She attended teacher's college in Erdahn as a girl and then came back to

The Shadows, even though she'd had offers to teach at exclusive schools in Erdahn. She had a dream since she was small of having a school at The Shadows and improving the situation for the farm children. Now it's a well-known school."

"How wonderful! She is powerful."

"Very much so. I consider her my second mother. She's reserved but very brave."

"So, you appreciate women who are strong?" Luntigré's deep black eyes met his.

"I wouldn't be here if I didn't," Hemmett answered frankly, gathering her close. "I love my mother, but she won't do anything without asking my father if she can. That isn't the way he wants it, but it's how she was raised and how her first husband wanted things. I don't think she could change now. I saw how that stressed their marriage, how it burdened my father.

"I like to think any woman I choose to be with can make her own decisions and manage her own life. Of course, we would help one another, but I don't want to be asked permission if she wants to buy a yard of ribbon."

"Have no fear," Luntigré laughed. He smiled down into those lustrous eyes.

"Are you saying you'll have me?" he asked.

"Let us go on and enjoy being together and then consider it again before you have to leave," she replied.

Hemmett kissed her.

***

"What is behind your back?" Flori tried to see behind Hemmett, but as she was very small, and he was the opposite, she couldn't see what he held.

"It's a secret. I got it for a little girl I know," he teased.

"Let me see!" Flori cried, trying to run around him. He spun on his heel quickly, keeping himself between her and the child's cromar he was hiding.

Luntigré laughed from the kitchen, where she was cutting a sunfruit for the evening meal.

"Please let me see," Flori said, giving up.

"Now, that is better – far more respectful," Luntigré said approvingly. Hemmett knew when to take a cue.

"Here you are," he said, producing the brilliantly painted and decorated little musical instrument and holding it out to her.

"Oh, you got it for me!" she gasped. "Will it play like yours?"

"It will make the same sort of sound, but you'll need to learn to play before it sounds like mine does when I'm playing," Hemmett explained, taking a seat on a low stool so she didn't have to crane her head back to look up at him.

She was a pretty little girl, much lighter complected than her mother, with the same black, curling hair. Her father was a Fambrian fisherman. He and Luntigré were deeply in love when she was a young girl. They'd had five years together – then he'd been lost at sea when his boat was destroyed by a massive tidal wave when Flori was only two years old. Luntigré told Hemmett that only the child had kept her from complete despair.

Flori was delighted when Hemmett played his cromar for them and begged him to show her how. Her hands were far too small for his outsized instrument, frustrating her, so he sought out a child-sized version. He showed her how to hold it and then how to finger some simple chords. He already knew she was musical – she seemed to have perfect pitch and loved to sing.

"Let me work at it," she said intently. He took that as a signal to leave her alone and went to join her mother in the kitchen.

"You are a good teacher," Luntigré smiled, handing him a bowl of fruit salad to put on the table.

"She's a good student," Hemmett answered, listening as Flori worked a basic chord change diligently. She was picking it up quickly.

After dinner, Flori asked him to show her more chords. He did, but cautioned her that going too fast would prevent her from learning well. He gave her a command performance of a hornpipe he'd recently perfected and then reminded her that it was bedtime.

"School tomorrow, little one," he smiled. He inspected her chording hand and showed her how red the tips of her fingers were. "It takes time to build up calluses like mine. You don't want to overdo, or your fingers will blister."

She stretched up to kiss his cheek.

"Will you be here tomorrow?" she asked.

"I'll be here tomorrow and for another week. Then I'm going to Mordania to see my mother and father, remember?" She ritually asked him if he would be there tomorrow and his answer always contained the information that he would not be here forever. Though she'd been tiny when her father died, the loss had scarred her.

"And will you come back?"

"For a short time before I go to work in Artreya."

"Come now, Flori," Luntigré said, holding out her hand. "Your bed is waiting."

"I love you, Hemmett," Flori said, taking her mother's hand.

"And I love you," he smiled. "Good night. I'll see you in the morning."

He put the little cromar beside his, then rose and went to the window.

From this part of the world the constellation called The Weaver seemed to lie on its side. The three brightest stars shone dazzlingly. The stars seemed closer here in this mountainous part of Samorsa.

It had been a wonderful four weeks. He and Luntigré spent much of that time together, attending the Samorsan Games, enjoying restaurants, taking her daughter to parks, visiting her mother and sister. He'd even taken charge of the counter of the stall for short times so that she could have a break or walk her daughter home after school. It was a peaceful and happy life. He had yet to begin missing work – which he knew he would. For now, he was content.

"And she is asleep already," Luntigré said, carefully closing Flori's bedroom door behind her. "Stargazing?"

"Thinking. Let's have some wine out on the verandah," Hemmett replied.

They settled on a comfortable sofa Luntigré had covered with a brilliant orange and yellow fabric. It was the location of many an afternoon nap or evening conversation.

"So where are we, Luntigré?" Hemmett asked bluntly.

"It is time to decide, I think," she answered. "You must go to Mordania. It would be shameful to neglect your parents if you are on leave. I understand this."

"Do you love me?" he asked, taking her hand.

"Yes, I do. Very much. But it isn't a love like I had for Flori's father. I think that is a love that comes only once in a life, where you live and die for that person. But I do love you."

"Is there anyone else?" Hemmett asked. Luntigré shook her head. "You?" she asked.

"No-one," he answered. "It's been a while. I've been occupied with guarding Katrin since we left and there's been no opportunity for romance. There never has been anyone I've been serious about."

"So, you haven't found your great love," she prompted gently.

"I do love you – very much," he replied.

"I must ask you a question before we arrive at an answer," Luntigré said quietly.

"So ask me," he smiled. "I'm an easy man to talk to."

"I know that well. What are your feelings for Katrin? Is she the great love? Could she be?"

Hemmett stood and went to the verandah railing again. He looked at the stars for a moment, then turned to her.

"The truth? I don't know. In the past I've been so romantically in love with her that I could hardly bear it. Other times she's like my very dear sister. We've been together since I was three. I remember Menders showing her to me the day after she was born. I was sure he had a puppydog in that blanket and you could have knocked me over with a feather when I saw this little baby. I loved her at that moment.

"Sometimes she's like a very dear and close friend. Sometimes it's all three loves all mixed up."

Hemmett came back to the sofa, sat down and looked into Luntigré's eyes.

"I am not pining over Katrin. Even if she loved me romantically, which she doesn't, we could never marry. Even if she was removed from the Royal Succession, I still couldn't marry her. It would never be permitted because I'm common born.

"I'm a realist, Luntigré. No matter what, Katrin is as out of reach as those stars. If she is my great love, I've already lost it – just as you lost yours."

Luntigré nodded. Hemmett waited while she considered what she was going to say.

"If we decided to be together, I would not be with anyone else," she finally said.

"Neither would I. I've never been unfaithful when I've been with someone," he answered.

"The long separations? You would not be free to be here except for leaves. I could not leave my business for long, though I would love to see The Shadows, if I would be welcome there."

"Of course you would," Hemmett smiled. "I think we shouldn't fear the separations. I write a good letter."

"Then I think that we should be together," Luntigré smiled. "We'll have our own lives, but we also have each other. For as long as it gives us joy – and if the fire goes out, we'll still be true friends."

"For as long as it gives us joy," Hemmett smiled.

SIMERIDON, ARTREYA

22
ENEMY TERRITORY

Abbot Fahrin finally managed a few moments to sit down at his desk at the temple. He'd seen a letter arrive from Emila de Cosini, but had not been able to do anything more than anticipate reading it.

Now he settled in his chair and smiled as he saw that Emila had embedded a pressed flower in the wax seal holding the folded letter closed. He carefully slid his pocketknife blade beneath the seal and unfolded the letter.

She was growing up so very quickly, he thought as he scanned the lines of feminine but unusual handwriting. Her perceptions of the world were expanding all the time. Of course, he wasn't surprised after the determination and leadership she'd shown the night of the Failed Revolt. Amazing for such a young lady!

He read through descriptions of plants and places, a paragraph about how she missed her brother, who was taking a few more weeks in Samorsa before joining the family in Artreya. She included a funny story about the other brother bringing home a donkey from Barambos on the train. Excitement about arriving in Artreya and registering at the University, impressions of places and sights. All fresh and laced with her enthusiasm and vibrant sense of humor and sympathy.

He was smiling as he came to the end of the narrative.

Then he blinked.

Please let me know how Martine and her baby and everyone else are – and how you are, my dear friend.

Affectionately,

Katrin, Princess

Fahrin felt his heart lurch with disappointment and anger.

***

"Menders – I think I've made a terrible mistake," Katrin said quietly, standing in the doorway of Menders' and Eiren's room. She was holding a letter, her forehead tight with concern.

"What is it, Princess?" It was so seldom she was this distraught. Menders rose instantly and went to her.

She handed him the letter.

"Abbot Fahrin. I must have signed the last letter I sent with my real name and title. I was finishing it in a hurry so Kaymar could carry it with him last time he went to Fambré for you. I must have written 'Katrin, Princess' instead of 'Emila'."

Menders scanned the first lines of the letter.

Dear Emila or Princess Katrin,

I must tell you I was unpleasantly surprised to find you are not Emila de Cosini, whom I thought a very honest and forthright young lady. I was under the impression that our regard for one another was such that a deception as base as giving me a false name would not be possible…

Menders sighed and looked at her.

"My dear, this is a man who is hurt and angry lashing out. Look at the word he uses most."

She looked at the letter but then shook her head in confusion.

Menders pointed at multiple places in the letter.

"Look here – *I.* And again – *I.* And here – another *I.* It's all about him. This is written out of hurt, Katrin. That means there is hope to sort things out. It's when a man writes an angry letter full of *yous* to a woman that there isn't much hope left."

"How could I have told him my real name?" she asked, her voice shaking. "It could endanger everyone."

"Here, sit down. It's an understandable mistake. You've done nothing wrong."

He settled her on the sofa and then sat opposite her in an armchair.

"Now, let's talk about this and see where you are," he said firmly. "Do you love this man?"

Katrin shook her head.

"I hadn't known him very long. I like him very much. Maybe if things were different – but they're not," she replied.

"Consider the situation as if you were not a princess," Menders suggested.

Katrin looked grave.

"That's almost impossible for me," she finally said, looking at him with eyes that nearly broke his heart. "It's always been the great restriction, hasn't it? It's been there as long as I can remember. I like him. I enjoyed working with him and talking to him. But I can't imagine a situation where I would be free to love him or marry him."

They were silent for a moment. Menders was trying to tamp down the anger that always rose when he thought about how Katrin's life was constrained. Katrin was feeling hopeless and very unhappy about losing a friend.

"All right," Menders finally said, having managed to shove his fury back down below the surface. "I think you should recover from this letter for a bit. Don't keep reading it. Leave it here on my desk – and then, when the sting has eased, you should write to him. I will also write to him, to explain your situation and that you didn't mislead him out of any ill intent."

"Have you ever had anything like this happen?" she asked, her hands twisting around each other.

"Yes." Menders rose and went to the drinks cupboard, unlocked it and took out two small wineglasses and a particular fortified wine that was ethereally sweet and flavorful. "I have. I've never told you, but I was very much in love with Cahrin – yes, Cahrin who visits The Shadows with her husband, my friend Olner, and their children. When we were in our teens, we planned to marry. Then I was sent to Surelia.

"I wasn't able to communicate with her. Now, Cahrin is the daughter of an assassin and she knew, logically, that my not contacting her was part of my mission, but she became insecure and then angry as time went by. I realize now that my youthful brawling ways frightened her as well. With distance and not seeing one another, she began to be angry and chafed at how long it would be before I could be in contact again.

"I ended up with quite a letter full of *yous*. 'You do this, you do that, you don't do this.' In other words, Cahrin was falling out of love, felt hurt and was shocked at herself for both. So, she decided it was because of me."

"How horrible!" Katrin said as he handed her the little glass of wine.

"It happens all the time when people move away from the first flush of love," Menders smiled, reclaiming his seat. "There's a readjustment, where you lose your initial rosy view of the other person. If there's a desire to let the affair go – that's when the warts and failings of the loved one loom large."

Katrin sipped the wine and Menders was relieved to see she was becoming distracted from her own problem.

"Youthful brawling?" She looked up at him.

"I was a scuffler when I was at the Academy," he smiled. "People would jibe at me about my eyes, or because I was so small then. I was also angry about a lot of things. In no way was I ready to be married, so it's as well Cahrin had her tantrum. She's happy, so am I. It was all apologized for and forgiven long ago."

Katrin looked over at the letter on Menders' desk.

"Do you think this situation can be fixed?" she asked.

"I do. At this point, Abbot Fahrin is probably cringing that he sent that letter. Not only would it have hurt you, but he also showed his arse, as Kaymar would say. Give him a little time, give me a chance to write a letter to explain and then if you want to write back as well, we'll send them together."

She said nothing.

"Katrin – if the man didn't care about you, he would not have written that letter. He would have dropped you completely and you would never have heard from him again. He cares about your friendship. If he didn't, he wouldn't have been hurt."

"You think so?" she asked.

"I know so."

"How?"

"In case you haven't noticed, I'm a man. I know how he thinks. As Cook would say, he's had his rumpus and now he's probably sorry. Don't be tragic, little princess."

"No." She sat up and made herself smile. "I got so many good ideas to use at The Shadows from him. I think they would work very well to help the older tenants and when we have emergencies."

"Tell me about them," Menders urged.

She began to forget her grief as she outlined a number of strategies to give The Shadows' older retired tenants assistance. Katrin always warmed to the subject of helping others.

This is what she should do, Menders thought as he listened. She was born to help others.

He deliberately turned his mind from thoughts of prophecies.

***

Hemmett, as was his habit, was out on the train carriage steps before it came to a stop at the platform. He didn't expect to be met – he wasn't one for scenes at railway stations – so his eyebrows went up when he saw Borsen impatiently strutting up and down, gold watch chain and walking stick much in evidence.

"Inchworm!" Hemmett shouted to attract his attention.

Borsen turned, an unaccustomed scowl on his face. Hemmett felt a moment of fear, wondering if something was wrong. Then Borsen grinned and started toward him. With a sigh of relief, Hemmett swung himself and his duffel bag to the ground.

They gripped forearms briefly. Hemmett shouldered his bag and they started out of the station. To his surprise, Borsen walked over to the line forming at Customs.

"They'll dog you, so just keep a cool head," Borsen muttered as they entered the line.

"I already went through Customs when I came into port at Wenslas," Hemmett said in surprise.

"They hit you again here. Just give them your documents and don't let them rile you," Borsen muttered. Hemmett noticed him reaching into his inner coat pocket. He nudged his friend curiously, but Borsen kept his eyes straight ahead.

When they reached the customs agent, the man gave Hemmett a nasty look. His false documents identified him as Mordanian.

"Well then, here in Artreya for business or pleasure?" the agent asked snarkily.

"I'm joining my family here in Simeridon," Hemmett answered. Suddenly he felt Borsen stepping on his foot, gently.

"I didn't ask that. Business or pleasure?" The agent was smirking.

"Yes sir. Pleasure." Hemmett immediately shifted his face to a bland smile and his manner to earnestly wishing to please.

"Been sent to take a look at our military?" the agent queried.

"No, sir."

"And why not? There's a spectacular Changing of the Guard at the palace," the agent said, acting ruffled. He was not convincing. His performance was as stale as a children's puppet show.

"Is there? I didn't know. I'd like to see that," Hemmett smiled, picking up the cue.

"Might learn something of how a real military works," the agent taunted.

Again, Borsen's small foot pressed down on Hemmett's.

"I'm always interested in how other nations do things," Hemmett groveled.

"Well your sort can afford to learn." The agent gave him a look that dared him to be angry.

At that point, Borsen subtly slipped a large gold coin from his pocket onto the agent's counter. The man instantly leaned forward and put his elbow on it, trying to look as if he was lounging and having a nice chat with the traveling gentleman.

"All right, move on," he said abruptly.

Hemmett and Borsen followed his advice, ignoring him saying, "Scum" after them.

"Nice welcome," Hemmett said once they were in the street.

"That's far from all of it," Borsen responded gloomily. "Here, this tavern is friendly, run by a Samorsan. Let's have a drink. I need to talk to you."

Hemmett gladly sat at a table while Borsen went to the bar. He came back with a tankard of beer for Hemmett, whiskey for himself. As he sat down, he looked closely at Hemmett.

"Who's the lucky lady?" he asked, starting to grin.

"How the hell can you tell, you wily Thrun?" Hemmett laughed.

"Never seen you look so contented," Borsen shrugged. "Who?"

"Luntigré."

Borsen's elegant eyebrows went up in approbation.

"Just right. Heading for marriage?"

"No. For as long as the joy lasts, she in her place, me in mine," Hemmett answered.

"Endless joy to you both." Borsen shook Hemmett's hand and then sipped his drink.

"So, what's going on?"

"Oh, this place. The famous Artreyan sense of humor grates. It's not really humor, it's endless taunting and picking. At the University it never stops. Some of them never stop twitting about me being nancy."

"Oh, for Grahl's sake – what complete prats," Hemmett scowled.

"I'm used to it. There's always some idiot in the room who'll make remarks about sore knees or a sore backside. Not worth bothering with. What's really bad is that Katrin has fallen in with a group of rich little shits who are not the thing for her. Not at all."

"In six weeks?"

"They're the type who can smell money," Borsen said with distaste. "They sense that she's somebody important in Mordania and they're climbers. They included her right away, couldn't be more friendly. Katrin's never dealt with a truly manipulative or malicious person, Hem."

"Marvelous," Hemmett sighed.

"Then there was some stink from the priest in Fambré," Borsen continued. "Seems she automatically signed her real name to one of her letters and he got his nose out of joint. Wrote her a letter about how he didn't know who he was addressing. Full of betrayed rebuke."

"I don't think she loves him," Hemmett said after some thought.

"No, but there was potential for it. She was hurt. Their letters made her happy and she's afraid he won't write again. So, when she suddenly made all these new friends…"

Hemmett closed his eyes. He felt responsibility and duty settling over his shoulders.

"Poor girl," he sighed. "If she'd been raised like a commoner she'd have learned about false friends by now, but I can't remember one incident. She's so open and ready to love everyone. Well, let's see about getting her head turned back in the right direction."

Borsen nodded and indicated to the barkeeper that they'd have another round.

"One other problem," he said as their drinks were set before him.

"Kaymar threw a tantrum?" Hemmett wasn't willing to deal with more and resorted to making a heavy-handed joke.

"No. Wait until you see him. Ermand Godson."

"Sounds like a twit."

"Worse. He's rich, girls think he's handsome, he can spout authors and poets and philosophers, the big heartthrob at the

University. All the girls there think he's wonderful. He's got his eye on Katrin."

Hemmett groaned.

***

"You're going to take all your days off together?" Katrin asked in surprise. "Why, Bumpy?"

"So, I can go to Samorsa," Hemmett replied.

"Why?"

Hemmett crossed his legs and looked at her.

"Willow, I'll be spending as much time as I can with Luntigré and her daughter," he explained, taking out a cigar. "We're a couple now and part of our arrangement is that I'll spend my days off and leaves with them."

A smile of genuine happiness lit her face.

"Oh, how wonderful!" she said, sitting beside him on the sofa. "Are you getting married?"

Hemmett shook his head. "Not for now."

"Oh, they have to come visit us here! That would be so much fun."

Hemmett hesitated.

He'd been back with the family in Artreya for a week. He understood that his negative feelings about the country were influenced by Mordanian nationalism. He wanted to give it a fair chance for Katrin's and Eiren's sakes, as they were both wildly enthusiastic about the culture, landmarks and museums.

During that week, he had heard many nasty remarks directed at Borsen on the street. People didn't immediately identify him as Thrun because of his size, so the epithet heard most often was "Surytamian bastard".

How could he bring Luntigré and Flori here to be subjected to that, much as he missed them and wanted them to be with him? He'd heard threatening remarks leveled at a black-skinned Samorsan stevedore as well and Ifor had told him many of the taverns excluded dark people.

"Bumpy, you can tell me what's worrying you," Katrin said, taking his hand. He started. He must have been looking dire.

"We can think about it – maybe during the Lunar Festival," he said. Then he looked into her eyes and told her why he was concerned.

"I haven't heard anything like that!" she gasped. "Why wouldn't Borsen tell me about this?"

"I guess he doesn't want to spoil things for you," Hemmett answered bluntly.

"Should I hear anything like that, you'd better believe I won't just tolerate it, whether I like Artreya or not," she flared, her face going pink.

"What will you do, give them a whack on the karzi with your sunshade like Princess Dorlane trying to discipline Kaymar?" Hemmett burst out laughing at the image of Katrin taking on an Artreyan street tough with one of her frilled parasols.

"Absolutely!" She sprang up and grabbed one of her sunshades out of the rack, going on the offensive by assuming a fencing stance and poking at him.

"You meddle with a military man!" Hemmett roared, snatching another sunshade and defending himself.

She was a formidable opponent, as Menders had taught her the art of fencing just as he had the two boys in his care. She scored an immediate point with a sudden thrust at Hemmett's chest.

"Touched," he laughed. "Beware!" Having given the traditional warning, he went after her with every bit of skill he had. He was more in condition for the sport but Katrin was more ruthless. They trampled around the room, hooting and whooping, using the furniture as barricades. Pillows were hurled.

Menders opened the door in time to see Katrin disabling Hemmett with a swift jab from the tip of her sunshade to the back of his knee. Hemmett nearly fell and immediately retaliated with a broadsword swipe across her backside.

"Captain! Your Royal Highness!" Menders managed to sound stern.

Katrin flung one more pillow, directly impacting the back of Hemmett's head, knocking his hair wildly askew. He didn't dare another whack across her rear in front of Menders, but stood comically to attention, holding his sunshade like a rifle. He saluted.

"Good gods," Menders smiled, shaking his head. "It sounded like a groundquake."

"Her Highness was demonstrating how she would deal with anyone who makes remarks about those with darker skins, sir!" Hemmett barked.

"I'm just glad I was the only one home," Menders answered, picking up several pillows and putting them in place. "You'd have had Kaymar in here with his knives."

"I'm only thankful my sunshade didn't pop open during the duel, sir!" Hemmett replied. "Far too music hall for words, sir!"

"Where is everyone?" Katrin asked, wrenching the sunshade away from Hemmett and putting it back in the stand.

"Out and about. Varnia went to see the orphanage with Ifor. She's heard it's a model facility and wants to observe how they do things. Eiren has her literature class, Borsen went out somewhere. Same for Kaymar."

"I hope he'll be all right," Katrin said worriedly, looking at Hemmett.

"Kaymar?" Menders asked incredulously.

"No, Borsen. Hemmett has heard people saying some ugly things," she explained. "I wish Willem was here and could go around with him."

"He'll be fine," Hemmett said. "He told me he stays in the parts of town where that doesn't go on. It's only rough down around the docks and train station. I didn't mean to make it sound like Simeridon was a seething kettle of prejudice." He returned to his neglected cigar.

"Let me see – so you've told Katrin about Luntigré and Katrin suggested that she and the little one visit us here," Menders said.

"How you do that I will never know." Katrin went to the floor to ceiling windows opening onto the iron grillwork balcony that ran the length of the second floor of the house.

"I know the current topics, I knew he hadn't told you about Luntigré yet and I'm fairly certain that indignation about the remarks and prejudice Artreyans can show to people with dark skins led to your great fencing match," Menders explained. "Knowing you both very well helped too."

"Pah!" Katrin imitated Chetigré perfectly. "I'd rather believe you're able to read minds." He had often dazzled them with that particular trick when they were younger and at one time had them worried that he could tell what they were thinking at any time.

"Well, it did keep some of the mischief down to a reasonable level when you were small," Menders smiled. "Are you worried about bringing Luntigré and Flori here, Hemmett? I can guarantee them safe passage. That's what private train carriages are for. I can have Kaymar and Ifor accompany them if you don't."

"That makes sense!" Katrin added. "It would be wonderful to have the entire family together sometimes."

Hemmett felt a swift sting of tears and blinked as he stood and put his arms around her.

"Thank you," he whispered. Then he rapidly retrieved his cigar and went out onto the balcony to finish it and get control of his emotions.

***

Dear Abbot Fahrin,

I would like to explain what must be a very puzzling situation to you and see if a potential rift between you and the young lady you know as Emila de Cosini can be repaired.

In reality, Emila de Cosini is an assumed name, necessary to make it possible for Her Royal Highness, Princess Katrin Morghenna of Mordania, Second Heiress to the Ruby Throne to travel as a normal young person. Our entire party is traveling under aliases. I am Aylam Josirus Shvalz, Lord Stettan, Prince of Mordania, known as Menders, the Head of Household of Princess Katrin's estate. I have been Katrin's foster father and guardian since the night she was born. My wife is Eiren Spaltz, Headmistress of The Shadows Academy, housed on the estate.

Our three children are Katrin (Emila de Cosini); Hemmett Greinholz, Captain of Her Highness' Personal Guard (Rodrigo de Cosini); and Borsen Menders (Georgio de Cosini) who is my nephew and a High Chieftain of the Thrun.

During our Katrin's lifetime, there have been nearly one hundred plots against her life. Her mother, Queen Morghenna VIII of Mordania, consented that Katrin should take the Grand Tour of the Middle Continent when she came of age (sixteen in the Mordanian Royal House) only under the condition that she travel completely incognito. This arrangement has worked well until her unintentional error of using her true signature on the letter that upset you.

Katrin immediately shared your response with me, and I asked her permission to write to you directly.

Katrin is very concerned that not only did she inadvertently hurt you, but that she might have endangered the rest of the family as well. I have assured her of my confidence in your discretion and explained to her that your letter was the initial response of someone who feels as if he was deliberately betrayed. As a man, I am also aware that there is an element of anger and disappointment that a young lady for whom you have tender feelings is now irrevocably beyond your reach, and that she seemed to be toying with your affections while knowing such a thing would not be possible.

All I can say, Abbot Fahrin, is that Katrin is not that sort of young lady. In many ways she is very innocent, the result of being brought up far from the Mordanian Court. Her position places limitations on her activities and friendships and also limits her experience. She is not ignorant of matters between men and women, but her knowledge is entirely theoretical. She has no romantic experience whatsoever.

Katrin is a very honest and forthright person. She would like to write to you, but is reluctant to take the first step. She not only values your friendship and your interests in common, but also respects your expertise in managing charitable concerns. It is her wish to emulate some of your endeavors on her own estate.

If nothing else, I would like to encourage you to contact Katrin to let her know you understand she did not deliberately deceive you. She was under her mother's orders and mine. The name wasn't the truth, but everything else you learned about her during your association is. She is a decent, caring, loving young woman and was proud to call you her friend. In her position, true friends are very valuable and rare.

Should you have further questions about Katrin and her situation, please don't hesitate to contact me. I do hope that Katrin will hear from you soon.

Your servant,

Menders, Lord Stettan

My dear Menders,

Your letter of explanation was much appreciated. I acted rashly in writing to Katrin while angry. The letter had not been gone from here for ten minutes before I regretted sending it. I looked back on the time we had all spent together and realized there must be an explanation for the assumed name. I felt as if I had done something irrevocable and hurt a young lady we both care for greatly.

I have written to Katrin and asked that she also share the letter with you. Essentially, I have apologized and outlined my hopes that we will remain friends and collaborators in the future.

You are correct – I was developing romantic feelings for this lovely young lady, though I knew it would be a long time before any courtship would be appropriate. I regret the circumstances that make such a future impossible, but still wish to remain in contact with Katrin and the rest of your family.

If you should visit Fambré in the future, you will be most welcome at my home or mission. Thank you for your honesty and trust.

Galanth's Protection to you,

Abbot Fahrin

Dear Katrin,

As you doubtless know, I have heard from your foster father, Menders, about your situation and the reason you were using an assumed name during your visit to Fambré. I wanted to tender my apology to you, my dear little friend.

I reacted badly to the surprise of seeing your real name. I had barely sent the letter out when I regretted having done so. I nearly ran down the street to catch the letter carrier, but he had already moved along out of sight. What a spectacle that would have made, the priest of Galanth racing along, his skirts held up around his knees, shouting, "Wait! Wait!"

There, I hope that brought a smile. I hope you have no hard feelings. Please rest assured that I have none. I hope you will be content to continue corresponding with me. I take great pleasure in your letters.

All goes well at the feeding station. We are serving nearly two hundred people a day and half that many take advantage of the opportunity to bathe and wash their clothing. We are looking into the possibility of acquiring an inn that is closing down, so we may offer shelter more permanent than short periods of rest in the Temple itself.

Martine, the little mother you remember, is growing stronger and her baby is starting to thrive. We have found some tasks for Martine to do around the Temple and so far, she proves diligent and trustworthy. If only we could provide employment for all of these tragic people. It turns out she is the daughter of a cobbler, who lost his shop when the King chose to have one of the Palaces enlarged. The family was cast out on the streets and in time, disease claimed both her parents and her husband, who was the journeyman in the business, leaving her to beg with the baby. Her story is told a million times in this country, in one form or another. You can know that your concern and that of your family saved this little mother and her baby from the fire.

I would send you a wish that you might return to Fambré – but at this time, considering your position, that would be hazardous indeed. It is a tinderbox here and I fear it will be for a long while. Please write to me. I so look forward to your letters.

Your friend always,

Fahrin

Katrin watched closely as Menders read the letter from Fahrin. She smiled when he laughed over the image of Fahrin racing down the street after the letter carrier.

"Well, my little princess, it seems that has been smoothed over," he said when he was done, handing the letter back to her.

"Yes. The Dark Knight has made things right once again," Katrin said, taking the letter and folding it away in her writing desk.

"As you will remember, the Dark Knight didn't always sort things out," Menders told her. "In at least half the stories, the Princess solved the problem. Your favorite story was when the Princess tricked the evil wizard and freed the Dark Knight from a dungeon full of bones."

Katrin laughed aloud. "I did love that story. But I do appreciate you helping me with this, Papa. Do you really think Fahrin was in love with me?"

"I think he was on his way."

"I didn't realize it."

Menders smiled and helped her from her chair.

"My dear, don't rush your life," he said. "Be friends with him. Enjoy what's in front of you."

"What I want in front of me is a great big piece of cake. I'm ready to eat my shoes, as Willem would say." Katrin smiled at him.

"The Dark Knight can solve this problem," Menders smiled back. "I know the perfect pastry shop."

SIMERIDON, ARTREYA

23
NEW IDEAS, GOOD AND BAD

"Because I no longer want to go to that philosophy class," Borsen replied, keeping his voice even.

"But Borsen, you don't have to agree with all the philosophical theories," Katrin protested. "The point is to be exposed to different ideas."

"There are some ideas I don't care to be exposed to," Borsen answered.

Hemmett could sense one of Borsen and Katrin's arguments in the air and decided to intervene.

"Katrin, you have to admit that some of what was talked about in your class today was inflammatory," he said, keeping his voice gentle.

"Well, yes, it was," she admitted. "I don't agree with it. You know that! But the school of thought is out there. If we don't know what is being written and said, how can we possibly fight it?"

Borsen blinked in surprise.

"I hadn't thought of that, Cuz," he said softly.

They were sitting in the Three Elks Tavern, near the University of Simeridon, after Katrin and Borsen's philosophy class. The day's subject matter had rattled Borsen down to his pointed-toed, golden toe-capped, Samorsan shoes made from the skin of the viper he'd shot in the vineyard two years back.

The class had discussed Hardin's Philosophy of Racial Superiority. Borsen felt as if his chair was on fire as the students either avoided looking at him or stared at him as if he was growing a second head. By the time the issue of removing or exterminating "inferior races" to give "superior races" access to land and resources came up, he was ready to jump up and thump everyone in sight.

"But you didn't say anything against it in the discussion," Hemmett said to Katrin.

"I haven't read it. We were out late at the opera and I fell asleep over the book. Hardin is dull as well as horrible. They would have routed me – I need to know what they're talking about before just jumping into the discussion."

"I'm still not comfortable. It's not only the topic, it's the bastards we have to take classes with that I can't stand. Spoiled brats, the lot of them, nothing like the people we had classes with in Surelia," Borsen said.

"I have to agree there," Hemmett added.

"I haven't had any problem with them," Katrin protested.

"Try being tall and listening to their remarks about how thin the air I'm breathing is and how that affects my brain and makes me stupid. Oh, I'm laughing so hard over that one. See my smile," Hemmett replied.

"Well, it is an odd sense of humor and we aren't used to it," Katrin offered weakly.

"It isn't humor, it's rudeness being explained away as humor," Borsen snapped, cutting her off.

"You both came to Artreya prepared to hate it," Katrin's voice grated with exasperation.

"I haven't been disappointed," Hemmett answered.

"Same here," Borsen added.

"Well I think you're being very unappreciative of the opportunity that Menders has given you," Katrin burst out, glaring at Borsen.

For a moment there wasn't a sound. Borsen knocked back the remains of his drink. Then he slowly turned toward Katrin.

She was suddenly reminded of one of the few times she had displeased Tharak Karak, when she and his daughter, Thira, had gotten into some sort of mischief. When called to account, she tried to blame the entire incident on Thira. Now Borsen's eyes held the same cold brown fire that had bloomed in Tharak's. Katrin remembered how closely Tharak and Borsen were related.

"I am always completely aware of everything my uncle has done for me," he said, his voice quivering a bit with rage. "I am also completely aware of the fact that I have done a man's work at The Shadows, for a wage, since I was thirteen years old. That work includes making what you're wearing on your back this minute. Good day." With that, Borsen stood gracefully, picked up his marble topped walking stick, put on his hat and walked briskly out of the tavern.

Katrin turned to Hemmett, who was looking at her as if he found her very unattractive. She self-consciously ran her hand over the white furred cuff of her blue velvet jacket, which Borsen had made entirely by hand and given to her before they'd left for Surelia.

"Nice one," Hemmett said. "Why didn't you just call him the poor orphan boy who lives on your charity?"

"I didn't mean it that way!"

"Listen to me. You just pointed out to Borsen that he's not properly appreciative of all that is given to him – and you pointed that out to me as well, because you were addressing both of us. For your information, Borsen has paid his way on this trip. Didn't you know that? Well, there's a nice surprise for you. He's paid his passage himself, on every boat and train we've taken, to say nothing of his hotel rooms. Menders tried to get him to accept it all as a gift but Borsen said he wouldn't come if he couldn't pay his way. He pulls his own weight – more than pulls it. He works harder than anyone at The Shadows, with the exception of Menders."

"I know he does! It's the grousing about being here that I meant. It's a great opportunity to be here, for all three of us."

"Willow, we're only here because you want to be," Hemmett sighed. "Inchworm and I would have been more than glad to stay on in Samorsa for a while before going home, but you wanted to get here in time for the university term. So here we are, being insulted by a bunch of trumped up twits who think they're superior to every other nation on the planet. We don't need to be lectured like unappreciative boys who don't like their Winterfest presents."

"Oh, the two of you and Samorsa!" Katrin protested.

"I don't have a compelling reason to want to be in Samorsa?"

She couldn't answer, mingled embarrassment and anger choking her. She drained the last of her glass of wine.

Hemmett sighed. "Look, let's see if we can catch up to Borsen. You can make up to him and we'll go on somewhere else. This place is getting on my nerves."

"He's already run home to tattle to Menders, you can be sure of that," Katrin blurted. The faraway murmur was sounding in her head.

"This is pointless," Hemmett declared briskly. "Borsen does not tattle. That is truly small and not worthy of you. Come on, let's go."

Katrin heard the voices of the Queens growing louder, but she couldn't make out the words. She felt like a wire was tightening around her head and raised her hands to her temples.

"If I'm not mistaken it's the charming Miss Emila?" The cultured voice came from behind her. Katrin turned and caught her breath a little.

She was being addressed by Ermand Godson, the most handsome man in her philosophy classes.

He was the heartthrob of the university, with all the girls desperate to gain his attentions. Tall and lean with reddish hair, he boasted a mellifluous voice and was incredibly learned. Whenever he spoke, the philosophy students clustered around as he outlined brilliant theories about changing society for the better. His ideas were so exciting! The girls in her classes would be fuming if they saw him talking to her now.

The voices of the Queens faded to a distant hiss in her mind.

"Good afternoon," Katrin answered graciously, ignoring a soft farting noise Hemmett made with his mouth.

"I see your diminutive – friend – has abandoned you?" the tall youth said.

"He's my cousin," Katrin said.

Hemmett glared at her. She had always introduced Hemmett and Borsen as her brothers, but at the moment she didn't feel particularly sisterly toward Borsen. If Hemmett didn't like the fact that she'd told the truth, he could just live with it.

"Ah. How rude of him to simply walk away from you like that. Since his place is empty, may I take the liberty?"

"Greasy git," Hemmett whispered.

"Please," Katrin smiled. Ermand settled and signaled the waiter.

"May I get you something?" he asked, smiling at her.

"I'd like another glass of wine," Katrin smiled back.

Hemmett cleared his throat resoundingly. She knew he wanted to leave and didn't want her talking to Ermand.

"And this is?" Ermand asked, after he'd given the order, indicating Hemmett.

"My bodyguard," Katrin said evenly, ignoring the way Hemmett began to glower, not caring.

"Oh, a servant," Ermand responded, nodding dismissively.

Hemmett stood and moved deliberately to a table nearby, taking out his pistol and setting it in plain sight. His actions said to Katrin 'call me your bodyguard, and bodyguard I will be, for everyone to see.'

She ignored him.

***

Menders settled into his chair again and picked up the book he'd been trying to read for hours.

The afternoon had been fragmented, with Borsen coming in, pale to the lips, his spine as rigid as a flagpole. He'd asked for a glass of kirz.

Menders got it for him, poured one for himself and then got a story out of him that caused considerable concern.

Menders was aware Katrin had become involved in a crowd at the University that was not what he would consider ideal. He knew she was elated because people were making friends with her, not with her title and position – but she didn't have the experience to know these friends were not real ones. Traveling for so long was meant to give her experience she couldn't otherwise acquire. Sadly, experience couldn't always be entirely positive.

"Uncle, I'm really thinking of going back to The Shadows – and not just because of today," Borsen had said. "It isn't just what Katrin said. You know I'd never run home because of something like that. I really don't like Artreya and I want to get back to work. If I was accomplishing anything here, I wouldn't mind staying, but I feel as if I'm wasting my time."

It had taken some convincing and suggestions of ways Borsen could better occupy his time in Artreya to turn his mind from the hurt that Katrin had inflicted. Borsen agreed to give his options some thought and went to visit Kaymar, who had been confined to bed with a nasty case of bronchitis for two weeks. Unfortunately, Ifor was away at the deathbed of his mother. Since Ifor was a tempering influence on Kaymar and his incipient madness, the illness was taking a terrible toll on Menders' second. Any distraction was welcome. A visit from Borsen would be a benison.

Just as Menders was settling down with his book again, the door opened as only an angry Hemmett could open it, making as much noise as a door slam. Hemmett bowed exaggeratedly as he gestured for Katrin to proceed him. She flounced in and banged her pile of books down on the sideboard. Menders groaned and sat up again, putting his book aside.

"I wish you would stop it!" Katrin declared.

"Your *servant*, Your Highness," Hemmett growled.

"Hemmett, I wasn't the one who said that!"

"I didn't see you defending your humble *servant*, Your Highness."

"I didn't want to make a scene! You were doing more than enough of that."

"Your *servant* begs your pardon, Your Very Most Highness," Hemmett snapped, flinging his coat on the rack and smacking his hat down in a way that would have horrified Borsen.

"What the hells is going on?" Menders said wearily.

"Would you people be quiet! Kaymar just went to sleep!" Borsen hissed, coming in and glaring at them.

Katrin immediately looked guilty. Hemmett, his voice shaking with rage, said, "I have been identified as Katrin's bodyguard and servant to one of her Artreyan friends. It's five o'clock and I'm off duty, so this humble servant is going to his room."

"You didn't!" Borsen gasped, staring at Katrin.

"I said he was my bodyguard. I never said he was my servant," Katrin cried passionately.

"You certainly didn't correct him when he said that I was," Hemmett flung at her.

"Bitch," Borsen snarled, staring at Katrin with revulsion.

"All right," Menders interjected quietly, breaking the three-way standoff. "This isn't going any further. Hemmett, Borsen, please go and cool off for a while. Hemmett, let me apologize for anything insulting that was said to you by anyone. You are not, never have been and never will be a servant in this household, as everyone in this room knows. Borsen, I've already talked to you and everything I said remains in force. Go on now, my sons, please."

Borsen and Katrin were still glaring and bristling at each other. The stalemate was broken when Borsen suddenly and forcefully brushed one hand against the other, making the Thrun gesture indicating something or someone was worth no more than dust to be brushed away.

Katrin went pale. Borsen turned without a word and went down the hallway to his room. He was followed by Hemmett.

Menders waited. Silence would get Katrin talking. If he began firing angry questions, she would refuse to speak and nothing short of a beating would force words out of her – and he certainly was not about to administer a beating. As it was, he could see she was trembling over Borsen's silent appraisal.

"I notice you didn't say anything to Borsen about calling me a bitch," she finally burst out.

"Mainly because he voiced my own sentiments," Menders answered dryly. Katrin gasped, and stared at him.

"Can you think of a better way to describe someone who would deliberately allow Hemmett to be identified as a servant?" Menders continued. "Did you actually tell someone he is your bodyguard?"

Katrin couldn't answer. Menders shook his head.

"After all the things he's been to you," he said softly. "Brother, friend, playmate, confidant. On top of that, it's always been agreed that as part of your security, he would not be publicly identified as a guard, so you've been stupid and impulsive as well as rude and unappreciative of all Hemmett does for you. Though I will ask Borsen not to use such language to you again, I certainly understand why he said it. I am incredibly disappointed in you."

"I… I didn't mean what I said to Borsen to come out like it did," she sputtered. "And then I was so angry that when someone I knew came over to the table and asked who Hemmett was, I said he was my bodyguard."

"And you didn't correct this person when he identified Hemmett as a servant."

Katrin went stubbornly mute. Menders nodded.

"Then I entirely understand their anger," he said. "You've hurt them both very deeply."

"I'm not very happy with the way they keep on complaining about being here," Katrin mumbled.

"I understand that. I've already spoken to Borsen and I will speak to Hemmett. Borsen has promised to stop. Hemmett will do the same.

"Now, let me remind you, young woman, that when you take a slam at Borsen and Hemmett, they are unable to strike back because of your station. It is vastly unfair of you to do such things. It's time you learned to control that high-handedness of yours, Katrin, princess or not."

She stared at the floor.

"Now, you've put me in a quandary. Hemmett has done far more guard duty with you than he is rostered on for, and since Kaymar has become so ill, he has been taking care of all of your personal security. On a soldier's pay, this is a great deal of work for very little recompense. Of course, Hemmett does it because he cares for you and likes to be with you as a companion. He was right when he said he's off duty now. Because of this and because of his liaison with Luntigré and his responsibilities there, he should begin to take his off-duty time.

"This means, since Kaymar is ill and Ifor is in Mordania, that I'll have to take up whatever guard duty there is. I'm not willing to do a great deal of it, frankly. Eiren and I have a lot of plans and we've waited for years to have this time abroad together."

Katrin was looking at him as if he was announcing that he had decided to go and become a monk. Well, my dear one, Menders thought, I cannot bow to you forever. I've promised Eiren some time and she will have it. You can learn to wait at home when someone can't be there to watch out for you.

"I'm going to take Eiren to the lakes tomorrow, as the weather looks as if it is going to hold. Before you and Hemmett came in, I invited Borsen to come with us. Hemmett is leaving for Samorsa tomorrow, as his days off are due him. Kaymar is ill and can't possibly go around with you, so you will have to stay here tomorrow, where he is, so that you are guarded."

"But I have a class!" Katrin protested.

"You'll have to miss it," Menders said coolly.

"Can't I come along with you and Eiren?"

"Someone must stay here with Kaymar," Menders answered, struggling to keep his voice even. "Franz will be here, but he has a commitment in the middle of the day and Kaymar is too ill to be left alone. I invited Borsen to come along before I knew all that was going on. If I brought you as well, I'm sure everyone would end up miserable with the two of you sparring. Eiren has wanted to do this for months, Katrin."

He waited, knowing that if she bargained or protested one more time, he would lose his temper. She seemed to be struggling with herself.

"Katrin… remember everything Kaymar has done for you over the years and help us out gracefully," he finally said, sighing.

"Of course," she answered immediately, looking a little shamefaced. "And I am sorry about what happened today."

"I'm not the ones you need to apologize to," Menders said frankly. "Now, I have tried twice to take a look at this book and I'm going to ask to be left alone for ten minutes to do that."

Katrin trailed off to her room dejectedly. Menders settled back on the sofa with his book, hoping no-one else decided to have a crisis for a while.

He managed thirty minutes before Eiren came home. Her smile erased a lot of the upset and irritation of the afternoon.

"Hello, my darling," she said, bending to kiss his forehead. "Did you have a good rest?"

"Save me from our children," he moaned.

"Oh no. What happened?" Eiren took off her coat and hung it up and then sat where he made room for her on the sofa.

He went through the events of the day. Eiren groaned and put her hands over her face.

"I've seen it coming," she sighed. "Do you think Hemmett would like to come with us tomorrow too?"

"Not likely. Quiet contemplative activity is not exactly Hemmett's cup of tea," Menders answered. "He's leaving for Samorsa on the early train."

"Darling, there's a young man behind some of this friction – I just feel it in my bones," Eiren said quietly, looking up at him.

"Yes, I've divined that too. Katrin admires some of these people she's met a great deal and it's going to hurt her when they show their true colors. It's got the boys' hackles up. But I cannot protect her from everything, short of hiding her away forever at The Shadows. She's going to have to take some lumps when they come, just like today. I'm entirely in sympathy with the boys – and I must stop calling them boys."

"As must I. Today's incident is unfortunate but young women go through these things with attractions to friends who are not the best. Most go through it earlier than Katrin, but being sheltered as she has been, she's come late to it. She, Hemmett and Borsen are very passionate people, all three of them, and such things are to be expected from time to time."

Eiren kissed him and things started to look much, much better.

***

Katrin was shocked when Borsen took an easel at their art class that had been vacant through most of the term. They'd always stood together, passing the painting time talking or helping each other with their work. She had apologized to him and he'd accepted, but he was keeping his distance. He'd also dropped the philosophy classes they had together.

"Because they aren't talking about philosophy, they're talking about how great Artreya is," Borsen said briskly when she asked him about it. "If I want to hear that rubbish, I'll hang around the Three Elks when your friend Ermand Godson is around, holding forth. I don't like the philosophy classes, so why go? I can spend time at the museums or something, learning about what I'm interested in."

So Katrin now sat by herself in philosophy and she didn't care for it. Hemmett refused to sit with her, settling a couple of rows behind, his pistol on the desk before him. When she'd tried to apologize to him, he'd refused to listen to her. She'd complained about it to Eiren, as she knew what Menders would say to her – that she'd bit off more than she could chew and now would have to chew like the hells to manage.

"Darling, you denigrated both of them," Eiren replied after she'd vented her ire about the boys' reactions to her apologies. "You made it seem as if you don't value Hemmett's friendship and you also denigrated his work. He isn't a bodyguard. He's a Mordanian military officer and Captain of your Guard. Men identify with their work and Hemmett is very proud of what he does. He had to work very hard to achieve it and he did that because he's devoted to you and wanted to serve you. Why can't you understand how you hurt him and what a terrible insult you dished out to him?"

So Eiren had been no comfort. Katrin didn't know what Hemmett wanted. She couldn't crawl in front of him begging forgiveness and he refused to talk about it and sort it out.

When Hemmett wasn't on duty, he was elsewhere. When he was on duty and she went to the Three Elks with her new friends, Hemmett came along silently. He took a separate table. Once Katrin invited him to sit with the rest of them. He'd looked at her until she turned away.

Kaymar was still very sick and couldn't leave his bed. If Hemmett wasn't on duty, Menders had to come along with her to classes.

He too sat several rows behind her, looking bored. Sometimes when an idea was presented that Katrin thought was ridiculous, he would groan under his breath. And when Ermand Godson was speaking in class, Menders invariably made noise, either sighing loudly, shifting in his seat, or once snorting audibly in disgust.

"I'm sorry, sir, did you wish to respond to me?" Ermand had said, turning in his seat and looking back at Menders.

"I wouldn't dream of it," Menders replied sarcastically.

"If you have something to say, I certainly would welcome your comment," Ermand responded courteously.

"All right. You're a pretentious ass who is very fond of the sound of his own voice and your arguments are based on nothing at all."

The professor rapidly changed the subject, though Katrin saw Ermand look back at Menders again and flinch. She didn't have to look to know that Menders had taken his dark glasses off to look back at him.

As she was preparing to leave that lecture, Ermand came over to her.

"Emila, dear, who is that man with you today?" he asked very graciously. Katrin had learned her lesson.

"He's my father," she said quietly.

"Oh. Why do you think he was so rude?"

"He knows a great deal about philosophy. Definitely more than our professor. I am sorry, though, about what he said."

"Don't fret your very attractive head about it," Ermand smiled. "Sometimes we have to tolerate the older generation. Would you care to join us at the Three Elks?"

"Emila, it's time to leave," Menders said behind her, holding her coat for her. "Your mother and I have a dinner engagement."

"Good evening, sir," Ermand said elegantly, bowing slightly and then walking away.

Katrin hoped Kaymar could return to guard duty soon. The rift with Hemmett was wearing very badly indeed.

***

Menders shifted in the hard-seated chair and remembered how he'd always felt restive in lectures when he was in school. Listening to this drivel was agonizing. The professor was a puffed up idiot. Most of the students, or at least the ones who spoke out in class, were pampered brats who loved to listen to themselves speak.

"How would we apply this theory to the situation of – oh – the Artreyan Highlanders, or any other primitive race?" the professor asked the class.

The usual nest of hands rose and started wiggling and waving.

"Miss Farmore?"

"According to Hardin's theory, they would be forced to adapt to the culture of the superior race or be eliminated," a young woman answered.

"What if they resisted?" the professor prompted.

"It would be in their nature to resist, as they are less evolved," Ermand Godson replied without waiting to be called on. "It is impossible for such races to adapt to modern society, according to Hardin."

"And so?" the professor asked, beaming on Godson, whom he seemed to consider his protégé.

"They would have to be eliminated," Godson said dutifully, surrounded by so many nodding heads.

"Why?"

Menders smiled. The voice of reason was Katrin, who was sitting there quivering with indignation.

"I beg your pardon, Miss?" the professor said stiffly.

"Why would they have to be eliminated? What harm do they do?"

"The proposal we are discussing is that such primitive peoples may have possession of resources that would benefit the superior race," the professor explained smugly. "The theory argues the premise that since such people cannot make use of such resources, they should be removed from the resource rich areas."

"Removal would imply something less drastic than slaughtering them," Katrin said heatedly. "Why not trade with them for these resources, rather than eliminating groups of people?"

"It's impossible to trade with savages," one of the big talkers said.

"The Artreyan Highlanders are famous for trading!" Katrin cried. "It's the entire basis of their economic structure!"

"We are discussing the philosophical theory here, Miss," the professor smarmed, his voice oily. "It involves the ethical implications of the distribution of resources and postulates that resources should be the property of those who will use them."

"These people you call primitive use these resources, professor," Katrin said, obviously trying to keep calm.

"I am not aware of any primitive race that does," the professor bridled. "Perhaps you would give us an example?"

"Do you consider the Thrun a primitive race?"

"Oh, indeed."

"The Thrun make use of resources," Katrin snapped. There was a smattering of laughter.

"And pray, how do the Thrun use advanced resources?" The professor was now being openly sarcastic.

"Name an 'advanced resource' and I will. How can one resource be more advanced than another?"

"Lignus," was the professor' s reply.

"The Thrun use lignus for smelting metal."

"They don't know how to work metal. They live like animals," someone called.

"They work metal. I've seen them do it!" Katrin refuted the voice. "They do not live like animals. They have a very complex social structure. They don't live like us, but they are not primitive by any means."

"You are… familiar with these people?" Ermand Godson asked, turning in his seat and looking incredulously at Katrin.

"I am. They trade at my family estate every winter. They made this ring and this pendant. As you can see, they are as finely done as anything you would find in a jewelry shop." She passed the ring and pendant around. Menders could see there were some raised eyebrows as the Artreyan students saw the fine work resembling intertwined ropes.

"You could say they're a primitive race because they have no fixed abode," Ermand Godson said, looking at the ring.

"They migrate because of weather conditions," Katrin answered. "In the summers, they live on Thrun Island, to fish, hunt and make things to trade. In the winters, when the weather is severe on the island, they migrate over the ice bridge and travel about, trading. What's the difference between that and a rich man who shifts between a townhouse and a summer house in the country?"

"What products do they make, other than jewelry like this?" a girl asked.

"They trade hides, furs..."

"All in primitive, unworked form," the professor said smugly.

"Saddles, clothing, hats, boots, knives and faceted or polished gems," Katrin continued, as if she had not been interrupted. "The saddles and clothing are ornate and include embroidery, gemstone setting, leather tooling and tailoring. The results are far from primitive."

"They don't have any rules or laws or social structure," came another voice. "Those are the hallmarks of an advanced race."

"They have a very complex society and there are rules and laws," Katrin argued.

"The men sleep with any woman they want, they have no family structure," the voice argued back. "That's the very fabric of civilized society."

"The men do take multiple wives, but they are faithful to those wives," Katrin said, her voice rising in frustration.

"That's terrible!" a girl cried.

"It's a matter of adaptation," Katrin answered. "The Thrun have many more girls than boys, so this custom assures no woman is unsupported. The man doesn't co-habit with all the wives at once. When the first wife wishes to limit childbearing to preserve her life, she encourages him to take a second wife. He moves on to her as a marriage partner, though he continues to revere and support his first wife. The same thing occurs when the second wife wants no more children. Warriors are allowed three wives, though the chieftains can take up to seven. No man is allowed to take a wife if he can't adequately support her. There is no jealousy between the wives, as they consider each other sisters. They help each other. That help is needed because life is so hard. The women work all the time, as do the men. They have marriage ceremonies, there are rules for the provision for widows and orphans, there are laws that are very similar to ours."

There was a great deal of murmuring over Katrin's lecture on the marriage traditions of the Thrun. Menders looked down to hide a smile.

"They have no written language," Ermand Godson said.

"They do. It isn't a phonetic alphabet, it's symbolic," Katrin explained. "That pendant you're holding is one of the symbols."

He held it up. "Would you be so kind as to translate it?"

"Light Of The Winter Sun," Katrin answered. "Their language is multi-dimensional, and words have multiple meanings."

"How do you know what the hells they're talking about?" someone laughed.

"From the context. It isn't difficult – if you listen." Katrin's voice was pointed.

"Well, I for one would love to see a civilized Thrun," a young man smirked.

"You have. My brother, Georgio, is Thrun."

The room fell silent.

"That little fellow who goes about with you?" someone asked in the silence, the voice timorous.

"Yes. He's Thrun. Would you call him uncivilized or a member of a primitive race? Should he be slaughtered so some manufacturer can have more resources?"

"That boy has obviously been raised by advanced people…" the professor sputtered.

"Sir, you just said that people like the Thrun couldn't adapt to our society," Katrin fired back. "I personally know Tharak Karak, Highest Chieftain of the Thrun. He wasn't raised with what you call 'advanced people'. He speaks four languages, reads voraciously, can discuss any number of topics exhaustively. He owns hundreds of gowns and has excellent table manners. He bathes at least twice a day, more often if he undergoes exertion. It is not a matter of being raised by what you consider civilized people. What's civilized about believing you should kill people to take what's theirs?"

At that point a bell rang, and the class erupted into people gathering up possessions, standing, talking and moving about.

Menders went to Katrin, who was red faced and furious. Ermand Godson was handing her the pendant. She stood abruptly and gathered her books together while Menders held her coat for her.

"Miss Emila?" A quiet girl's voice came from behind them. Katrin turned to see a short, black haired girl holding out her ring.

"I kept it when they started getting rowdy," the girl said in a whispery little voice. "I've been studying it. It's truly beautiful. Do they do it as wire work that they heat, or is it cast? My father is a jeweler and he would love to see this."

"It's cast, isn't it Papa?" Katrin asked.

"Yes, in a fired clay mold," Menders told the girl, who smiled at him charmingly. "Some pieces are done in molds that are broken so the piece can be removed, others are replicated multiple times in the same mold. The Thrun's metalwork is very intricate and complex.

They not only make jewelry, but cutlery and hollow ware as well. Their knifemaking is unequalled on Eirdon."

The girl handed the ring to Katrin, who slid it onto her finger.

"Perhaps one day you would come to my father's shop and show him those pieces," the girl said with a smile.

"I would love to," Katrin said, smiling back.

"I'm Danica Forseth," the girl said. "I have to hurry, or I'll be late to my next class. Thank you for telling me about the jewelry." She bowed politely and walked away.

As Menders and Katrin turned to leave, they were surprised to see three other young people waiting for them.

"I wanted to take a look at that pendant, if you please, Miss," one boy said politely. "Once Godson got it in his claws, it didn't go any further. Could you explain the symbol and how the Thrun derived it?"

Katrin removed the pendant and handed it to Menders, who gave it to the boy. He explained the multiple symbolism in the piece, pointing out the pale gold used for the sun itself and the rays, the silver used for the ghosts of clouds around it and outlined the multiple meanings of the phrase. The young people seemed fascinated. It wasn't until the next class began filing in and the professor harrumphed for attention that they thanked him and Menders and Katrin were free to leave.

By that time, she had calmed down and looked less ready to bite the leg off a chair.

"Those are the young people who should be your friends," Menders said quietly as he escorted her from the room. "Not that other lot who think it's reasonable to slaughter people to take their land and resources."

"It made me sick. I know the theory, but it's just so absurd…"

"Yet many people in the world ascribe to just that. I was proud of how you stood up to them in there."

"Someone had to do something other than nodding like so many puppets. I wish I'd kept my mouth shut though."

"I'm glad you didn't. Come on, my dear, let's go home. I've had enough learning for one day."

SARONILLA, SAMORSA
SIMERIDON, ARTREYA

24
VARNIA'S TURN

"And so, you've seen it all," Gladdas Dalmanthea said, smiling at Varnia, who had just been toured through The Paralda School for Girls. She had traveled to Saronilla from Artreya at Gladdas' invitation, timing her visit so she could be escorted by Hemmett on his way to visit Luntigré and Flori. "I imagine a cup of tea would be in order."

"Very possibly a glass of beer too, Sweetheart," Hemmett agreed suggestively. Varnia shook her head at him, but couldn't resist a smile.

"Oh, we can manage," Gladdas laughed. She turned to a young woman who was walking their way and gave directions for tea and beer to be brought to her quarters. Then she linked arms with both of them and led them out into a courtyard garden, where both Varnia and Hemmett were grateful to settle on two conveniently adjacent benches.

"I was surprised to see you have male teachers," Hemmett said as Gladdas settled herself next to him and sighed in relief to be off her feet. Her walking stick was in evidence that day, so her knee must be acting up.

"There are men in the world, and our goal is to prepare the girls for the world," Gladdas replied. "We don't have the male teachers in residence, for their own comfort as well as the girls'. As you know, girls can develop crushes and it's best that the gentlemen don't live on campus. Doesn't Eiren have male teachers at The Shadows Academy?"

"You've got me there," Hemmett laughed. "I guess I was imagining an all-female institution."

"Now you can't believe all those rumors that I'm a man-hating old tommygirl," Gladdas guyed him. "I have nothing against the male sex – I couldn't work so closely with men in my network if that were the case. In fact, I wouldn't mind a teacher of tactics for my girls who are training for espionage, if you're interested."

Hemmett blinked.

"Tell me more," he said.

"I require them to learn about tactics, so they know what to look for and what to report on if they're assigned to a military matter," Gladdas explained. "I don't need to know that a general takes two sugars in his coffee, or goes to the privy every three hours. It's also valuable in teaching them how to make choices while they're in the field, how to weigh their prospects and actions. I hear you're a good man with tactics from more than one source, and that you're a good teacher as well. It isn't a class that is taught daily – I'd need you three to four times a year for several days. Does that fit in with your visits to your new family here?"

"Indeed, it does," Hemmett smiled. "I'm in."

"We'll work out a schedule and a syllabus," Gladdas replied. "And as for you, Varnia – I would like a teacher who would do the same thing for the girls who follow the housekeeping management curriculum – several days of class at intervals during the year."

Varnia gasped.

"Me?" she said, feeling foolish the moment she did it.

"Dear, I spent quite a lot of time at The Shadows and I oversaw the housekeeping staff often. I saw your organizational methods and your notes, your schedules and your paperwork. You attended Chetigré's cooking school and Cook assures me you're her equal or more in the kitchen. You're eminently qualified to come here as a special teacher for the girls who are working toward being professional managerial housekeepers – at hotels, hospitals, private homes."

"But – when I get back to The Shadows there's my job there," Varnia stammered, not knowing what to say.

"And mine is there too, but I will be coming to Samorsa regularly," Hemmett said, leaning forward and patting her hand. "Don't get flustered – and don't automatically turn down an opportunity."

"I'm not asking you to leave The Shadows," Gladdas added. "I know you're devoted to the family."

"When Borsen goes to Erdahn I'm going along to keep house for him," Varnia blurted, then covered her mouth with her hands and looked at Hemmett. He burst into a huge haw-haw.

"Varnia, you are the funniest girl," he gasped when he was finished. "If you don't think I don't know everything Borsen plans, you're mad! We're brothers, he tells me all. That's a couple of years down the road – we're not even at home yet! Don't borrow trouble, honey. I think you're going to need a beer too."

"Yes, let's go in, tea and beer should be ready," Gladdas smiled. Varnia was glad for the walk and by the time they reached Gladdas' quarters, she was calmer.

"I don't want to seem ungrateful," she said bluntly. "I'm thrilled by the idea. But how to get here on my own and – well, how would I teach? I've never done so."

"Hemmett, how will she get here?" Gladdas smiled.

"If you'll be willing to have us both here at the same time, she can travel with me. She knows I'm not going to make unwanted advances. Once she's familiar with how the connections are made, I would feel confident about her traveling within Samorsa alone, but I wouldn't like her to try it in Artreya. We're getting ahead of ourselves here and worrying about logistics."

"Kaymar and Ifor have both accepted similar positions," Gladdas said, handing a slice of cake to Varnia and another to Hemmett. "Those are other people you could travel with. Menders would be delighted to help you plan your travel and he's a master of logistics. As for never having taught – think of it this way – you will be showing young women what you already do very well. You may be as formal or as casual with your teaching as you wish."

Varnia started to smile – and then she did something none of The Shadows family had ever seen her do. She grinned.

"I'd say that's a big yes," Hemmett laughed. "Well, well, the two new teachers. That gives us some bragging rights, doesn't it, little sister?" He reached out and ruffled Varnia's hair.

***

My dear Menders,

This letter will be brief, as I am sending it back with Doctor Franz and he must catch the train within the hour.

Varnia's father is dead and the only creature to be credited for ridding the world of him is an old milch cow. He was found a week ago, gored and trampled near the gate leading to the pasture he usually couldn't be bothered to let the cattle into. At first, we suspected the sons, who are nowhere to be found, but eventually we located an old cow with dried blood on her horns. She had a small calf at her side that shows signs of being thrashed with a heavy stick. The herd apparently pushed through the gate after being without food for two days. In the process, they trampled his body.

We're assuming the sons found him dead and scarpered. Not knowing what was in the house, I can't say if they took anything of value or not – doubtful, considering the condition of the place. We've put word out through the grapevine that should they return to the district, they'll be dealt with as the cow dealt with the father.

So, the Polzen farm is no more. We have taken all the animals back to The Shadows, where they are being properly cared for. They are enjoying their new pasture with great relish. I decided to dry off all the cows that aren't nursing calves. Their condition is deplorable, but not irreversible. There are some chickens, sheep and geese as well, and two cowering but reclaimable dogs.

The Polzen buildings are in terrible repair. I have taken steps to have the property placed in Varnia's name under the provision that the sons have abandoned the farm and there are no other relatives. I am attaching a valuation of the farm for her information.

Franz is leaving now, so I must close.

In brotherhood,

Hake

Menders sat back in his chair, holding the letter.

He had spent a great deal of time in conversation with Varnia since the night she had run out of the house in her nightdress, fleeing the horrors that haunted her sleep. As she became more confident of her place in the family, she had begun to build a foundation of self-respect and dignity for herself. She was fiercely loyal and had a deep compassion for others, particularly children. Her quick temper and anger had receded to a reasonable level.

Her attachments among The Knot had grown deep. She and Katrin thoroughly enjoyed each other's company. Hemmett had gently and carefully provided non-threatening friendship and was almost moved to tears when Varnia spontaneously introduced him as her brother one day. Borsen was the darling of her life and she had a free and easy friendship with Willem Robbins.

It had taken her longer to be comfortable with the older men in the party, particularly Kaymar, who exuded sexuality despite trying to "behave" as he called it. Menders considered it a watershed moment when he walked into the lounge to find Varnia allowing Kaymar to assess her ankle, which she had twisted painfully and thought she might have broken. As Kaymar pronounced her ankle sprained but intact, she sighed with relief – and left her foot on his lap, chatting with him comfortably as he massaged the painful joint.

Menders dashed silently back to his room and whispered the news to Eiren. They had valtzed silently around, delighted the problem child was so well on her way to learning to trust and to take joy in her life.

Gladdas offering Varnia a teaching job had given her a degree of confidence that was the final polish. Menders felt that the news of her father's death would not set her back.

Varnia came in from a visit to the Simeridon orphanage where she spent several afternoons a week helping some of the children learn to read. Menders had seen her in action and often wished she had been there when he was trying to find a way to help Hemmett understand and remember the alphabet years ago. She had a wonderful affinity with children and the ability to see things as they did. She could pinpoint what was confusing a child and explain it in terms they understood.

"When you have a moment, I have something of importance for you to read," Menders said as she greeted him on her way to put her hat and wrap away in her room. "Don't be frightened, dear, I don't think you'll consider it bad news."

When he handed her the letter, she read it rapidly. She stood stock still for a moment, looking into space. Then Menders could see her shoulders relax, as if she had shrugged off a heavy backpack. She closed her eyes and took a deep, easy breath.

"I know the very cow," she said, as if she could see the animal before her. "Old Manya. I named the animals when I was younger, until so many of them died horribly – then I tried not to love them so much. She's an old darling, but very protective of her calves. She used to fight when they were taken away."

Menders put a hand on her shoulder and she opened her eyes.

"Sit down here and tell me about her," he invited.

Varnia sank down on the sofa and Menders perched on the ottoman before her.

"She was one for using her horns. She never hurt me with them, but if you were in her way she would hook one around your waist and nudge you aside. I never had any doubt that she would do much worse if she felt threatened. The old bull, Roysen – he was a mild creature too. I used to set my little brother on his back and Roysen would walk along as gentle as a pony. I hope he's still alive. I would love to see him again."

"I'll ask Hake to send you a list of the animals that were taken to The Shadows." Menders noted that it was the first time Varnia had mentioned her younger brother, the child who died when their father left him to "take his chance".

"That would be wonderful. If you're wondering if I'm feeling sorry about my father, I'm not."

"I didn't when mine met his end," Menders replied. "There is nothing wrong with that, Varnia, not in your situation."

"I didn't look at the second paper," she said, reaching for it.

Menders handed her the valuation for the Polzen farm. Her eyebrows went up as she saw the figure.

"Would it be worth this if all the buildings were burned or knocked down?" she asked, looking directly at Menders.

"Yes. That valuation is for the land. If anything, removing the derelict buildings would increase the value," Menders answered.

"Then I would have them knocked down and the cellars filled in," Varnia said. "I have no desire to farm it or live there – or to see the house and other buildings again. Could it become part of The Shadows?"

"I would be glad to buy it from you for The Shadows. It's excellent land with a great deal of potential," Menders told her. "The price would set you up, if well invested according to the Moneybags principles."

She smiled at him. Once she had jokingly called him Mister Moneybags when he was explaining investment possibilities to her and he enjoyed teasing her about it.

"Would it be a competency?" she asked, a little tentatively.

"More than that. You would be an independent young lady."

Varnia looked down at her hands while her eyes flooded with tears.

Her hands showed years of relentless toil on that ill-run farm. Some of her knuckles were still enlarged from chilblains, and though faithful application of lotions and creams had softened and improved her skin, it showed signs of exposure to the elements that would never be erased. Her hands were no longer cracked and raw, but if she wanted to remember endless hard work, all she had to do was glance at her knuckles.

"It would buy you a lot of gloves," Menders smiled. Varnia looked up at him. She collected gloves because of her hands, but she hadn't realized he'd noticed.

"All that is over, my dear," he told her, patting the scarred hands. "You need never work like that again."

"When we go home, I want to continue on as head of housekeeping," she protested. "The work at The Shadows is easy. It didn't do this damage, the farm did. I enjoy being the supervisor of housekeeping."

"And so you may. The Shadows will always be your home, Varnia, whether you wish to work there or not – but the money from your farm will give you a great deal of freedom. One day, you might want to leave The Shadows, if the circumstances are right. I want you to have the security to do whatever you wish. This is your opportunity to achieve that."

"Could you go ahead with the sale then?"

"Well, I can't act for both you and The Shadows – it would look very suspicious. Think of someone in Mordania who could represent you in the sale, and we'll go ahead with it. You'll get better than market price from The Shadows, I promise. Then I'll help you set up your money so it will grow and provide you a good living."

Varnia nodded, her face still very serious.

"May I ask that a portion of the farm be used for something?" she asked. "Can that be part of the conditions of the sale?"

"Indeed."

"Then I'd like to see some of it used for those animals – and other animals that are getting old or are hurt and are no longer of use. I know there is practicality in slaughtering them, but so many of them serve us for so long. Manya would be worthless as meat unless you threw it to the dogs, but she's provided years of milk and calves for market. Old Roysen as well – he probably couldn't serve a cow to save his life at this point, but I'd hate to see him slaughtered. Maybe I'm a fool, but I think that might be a decent thing to do."

"Miss Polzen's Animal Refuge," Menders said thoughtfully. "I like the idea. It couldn't be across the board or we'd have hundreds of chickens that don't produce eggs, but yes – it's something that would make sense in many cases. We have older boarhounds that deserve better than a bullet in the ear when they can no longer work – and I have some Menders' Men getting longish in the tooth who love animals and might be interested in such an endeavor.

"I tell you what," he continued, rising to his feet and offering her a hand up. "I believe this would be an excellent extension of The Shadows Academy. You know Eiren has always provided agricultural education as part of the school curriculum. What better practical application and way to keep the animals productive?"

"Yes! Oh – and Menders? How do I change my last name?"

Menders blinked and then smiled to himself. He had quite a history of young people wanting to change their last names, beginning with himself. He had used Menders, his mother's surname, since he was eleven years old. Borsen had asked him the same question years ago and chose to use Menders as his last name. Now this young lady was seeking the same thing – for good reason.

"There are legalities, not difficult to sort out. What name are you considering?"

"I thought of Menders, but then I thought I'd like to use my mother's name, Bayard," Varnia said. "I'd like to make it what she might have, if she'd had the opportunity. I loved her very much."

"I can ask Hake to have the papers drawn up in time for you to sign the sale on your farm as Varnia Bayard," Menders assured her.

"Oh – and I have a name for the new farm as well. It would go with the land."

Menders hid a smile and nodded.

"I'd like to call it Kindness Farm," Vania said firmly.

SIMERIDON, ARTREYA

25
FOOL'S GOLD

Finally, Kaymar was up and about again, and able to go back to his duties. Katrin had never been so grateful, because Hemmett had religiously stuck to his rostered duty times and would not accompany her after his regular hours. At every opportunity he left for several days in Samorsa.

Borsen had discovered a tailor who would take him on as an unpaid worker, and was happy as a lark between his art classes and learning the secrets of Artreyan tailoring. So Katrin was largely left alone. If it hadn't been for Kaymar's recovery, she would have spent very little time anywhere but at her classes. Now she could go with her new friends to the Three Elks, as she had when Hemmett would still go there after his regular hours. Kaymar made no attempt to join in the group, but sat nearby, thankfully without a gun in plain sight.

Without Menders escorting her, Ermand Godson was once again courting her. Kaymar didn't comment.

Ermand had come over to her as she sat with some of her other friends at the Three Elks and apologized for the scene in philosophy class on the day "inferior races" were discussed.

"I really felt badly about it, dear Miss Emila," he said very charmingly. "I could tell that you were very upset and trying to defend your friends. Unfortunately, people can be so intolerant."

"It was very upsetting, hearing that people really believe other people should be murdered."

"Yes, I know. Now, please tell me – how can it be that you have a brother who is a Thrun? I've seen the boy you've mentioned. He used to come to philosophy class with you. There is absolutely no resemblance."

"He's the son of my father's first wife," Katrin lied glibly. "His mother's side of the family was almost entirely Thrun, and our father is one-quarter."

"So that's where you get the exotic shape of your eyes," Ermand said, gazing at her intently. "Just a touch of Thrun? How delightful. May I sit down?"

She slid over on the bench. He settled himself next to her, and talked to her for a long time until he said he had another class to go to.

The next day, when Hemmett was acting as bodyguard, Ermand seemed distressed when he sat next to her at the tavern.

"May I ask who the man escorting you yesterday is?" he said rather peevishly.

"Who?"

"The very good-looking man you left class with, blond and blue, sharp dresser?"

"Oh! He's my cousin and he also acts as my bodyguard," Katrin said with relief. Ermand looked enormously relieved as well.

"Two bodyguards! Your Pappa must be enormously rich," he laughed.

"It's necessary," Katrin said and left it at that. Again, he sat next to her and was very charming and funny, keeping the entire table laughing while Hemmett sat at the next table looking bored, polishing his gun and rolling his eyes back in his head.

This became a pattern, and as time went by, Ermand began to escort her from one class to another. He always sat next to her at the Three Elks and in philosophy class as well. He defended her when she presented an argument in class.

Hemmett acted as if Ermand didn't exist. Katrin ignored him. He refused to join in whenever she was with her friends, even though she asked him to. From time to time he would say 'your servant' sarcastically. She'd apologized and was tired of it all.

After a few weeks, she was quite sure Ermand was in love with her. She got very giddy when he came up to her; her heart turned over when he smiled at her. He was so fascinating! He finally stole a kiss when Hemmett was looking the other way and she thought she was going to faint.

"Couldn't you just give him the slip some day and come and spend some time with me?" he would ask plaintively whenever Hemmett got up at the end of his duty shift, looking pointedly at his watch. Katrin would have to go with him and then would be stuck at home for all the evening hours, when she could have stayed with her friends.

She'd tried to get Menders to change Hemmett's shift, and Menders had compromised with two hours, which gave her a little more time. Hemmett had agreed to it, but refused to stay later, so she always had to leave just as things were getting to be fun.

One night she'd had enough. When Hemmett stood and looked at his watch, she went over to him.

"Please, can we stay a little longer?" she asked. "I really want to talk to some of these people."

"Can't do it," Hemmett answered coolly. "I'm finished for the day. Get Kaymar to bring you back."

"It's his off duty day. Please, Hemmett?"

"I'm sorry, no."

Katrin wanted to slap him. It was so unfair! He could go wherever he wanted and do whatever he wanted but she had to do what he said!

She stormed back to the table to say good-bye and to get her jacket, which was hanging on the back of her chair.

"Oh no! Can't he be reasonable?" Ermand protested, holding onto her wrist.

"I'm sorry, I have to go," Katrin sighed. Suddenly he looked wicked, leaned over and whispered something to the young man next to him. The young man nodded, got up and wandered around behind Hemmett, who was tapping his foot impatiently and looking around the tavern.

"When I say run, run," Ermand whispered. Just then his friend smashed his beer tankard on the floor behind Hemmett.

"Run!" Ermand yelled, as Hemmett wheeled, his pistol drawn. Ermand grabbed Katrin's wrist, she snatched her jacket, and they dashed out the side door nearby and down the alley while the tavern erupted into shouting and laughing behind them.

***

Two hours later, Katrin sat up in Ermand's bed, feeling ill. She was fighting tears, but refused to let them fall. After all, she'd made the decision to accept his offer to go to bed with him, after much fevered kissing and caressing, which had felt wonderful. So why had that stopped? Why had it all became so painful?

Worse, Ermand was treating her as if she'd done something wrong. She'd asked him was why she was feeling a lot of pain as he thumped away on top of her, not even looking at her, but at the wall behind the bed. She felt bruised and as if her insides had been damaged.

"It must be something wrong with you. No-one else has ever complained," he replied rudely, getting up and walking across the room to get a dressing gown, kicking the mess of papers and other trash on the floor out of his way as he went. She'd been shocked by the condition of his rooms, which were obviously never cleaned. The bed smelled sour. Suddenly all she wanted was to get out of it and away.

She wondered if her legs would hold her. She'd been so relieved when he'd finally finished thrashing on top of her. She moved her legs a few times, then slid over to the edge of the bed and stood up. She saw to her dismay that she'd left a streak of blood on the sour sheets.

"Oh, for the Gods' sake," Ermand said as he saw it. "Why didn't you just not do it if you were in the middle of a cycle?"

"I'm not," Katrin said heatedly. "It was the first time I've done this, you idiot!"

He looked at her, his jaw dropped. She rapidly gathered her undergarments and began to drag them on. She struggled with her corset and then asked him to help her.

"I don't know how the stupid thing works. Artreyan girls don't wear corsets like that because they aren't great frigid cows," Ermand replied meanly. "Too bad you don't have one of your bodyguards or your nancyboy Thrun brother here to take care of it."

Katrin tried not to sniffle, laced her corset in front and wrenched it around, then tried to pull it snug. She finally tied it as best she could and pulled her shift on over it, followed by her dress. She wanted desperately to wash. She could feel her blood and the mess he'd left soiling her drawers, but it didn't look like there was anything like a washstand in the place. She began pulling on her stockings, wrestling her dress out of the way. It was harder to put them on after the dress, but she hadn't wanted to be nude in front of him for another second.

"Aren't you getting dressed?" she asked. He was still standing around in the dressing gown, which made him look like a plucked chicken wearing a dress. For all his posturing and believing he was a very fine fellow, his body was soft and flabby. It was obvious he'd never done a tap of work in his life. She didn't expect everyone to be built like Hemmett, Menders or Kaymar, but there was something unwholesome about the way the flesh hung on Ermand Godson. Well look around, he couldn't even be bothered to clean up his own home. The most exercise he got was flapping his jaw.

"Why should I get dressed?" he sneered.

"I'll need someone to go with me. I don't know my way around this part of town," she said, horrified.

He shrugged. "I have an appointment later and I don't particularly feel like squiring you around. The problem with you is that you're spoiled. You have all those men constantly following you, like dogs, dancing to your every whim. Well, I'm not a gun for hire. Mordanians are so obnoxious!"

"So why did you want me to come here?" Katrin gasped, hands on hips.

"I thought with all that Thrun talk you might be good in bed, something different. If I'd known you didn't have any responses and were numb below the waist, I wouldn't have bothered."

"I've never even done this! I didn't know what to do!" Katrin protested.

"You're making me tired," he pretended to yawn. "Run along to Pappa now, I have things to do." He deliberately turned away.

Katrin thrust her feet into her shoes and pulled on her jacket before she got out of the messy rooms as fast as she could.

On the street she looked up and down frantically. They'd turned so many corners and gone down so many alleys that she had no idea where she was.

A woman with a basket of flowers came by.

"Have a pretty nosegay, young lady… why dearie, whatever is the matter?" The sharp faced flower seller looked closely at Katrin, who was wiping at her eyes with the backs of her hands.

"I don't know how to get home," Katrin said. "I don't know this area."

"Where do you need to go, love? Feller trouble, is it? Don't shed so many tears for 'im, 'e's not worth it."

Katrin told her the district the house was in.

"You're a ways from there," the woman mused, shaking her head. "Go down four blocks, take a right and then a left right after that. You'll be out on The Avenue then. You can ask directions from there. Be careful, love, this ain't the nicest neighborhood and it's darker'n a stack o' black cats tonight." The woman turned and went on, obviously deciding Katrin didn't need flowers.

Four blocks, then a right, then an immediate left, Katrin thought, rushing in the direction the woman had indicated, watching for the end of the block.

Someone reached out of an alley, grabbed her and dragged her off the street. A hand was over her mouth, so she couldn't scream. Another hand held both wrists, so she couldn't get her knife. She'd stopped carrying her gun some weeks ago, when Ermand had seen it and been shocked and disgusted that she would carry a weapon at all.

She struggled and kicked, but her captor was much larger. Her strength gave out quickly. She was already exhausted from struggling against Ermand's soulless lovemaking. She tried to catch her breath, hoping it would help her battle on.

"That's exactly what could have happened, and it wouldn't have been me!" Hemmett's furious voice hissed in her ear. He spun her to face him and then shook her in a frenzy of rage.

"You stupid, stupid girl!" he ranted. "You could have been killed! How dare you do something like this when I'm responsible and guarding you? How can you treat me this way, Katrin, after all those hours I've sat there watching while you waste your time with those stupid people? Am I just your servant now? I hope he was worth it, Katrin! I really hope he was worth risking your damn life for! You're going to have a hells of a time explaining this stunt to Menders!"

"'Ere! Calm yourself, young feller!"

Hemmett released her. Katrin looked round to see the silhouette of the flower seller at the entrance to the alley.

"It's all right," she gasped as the woman walked toward them. "He's not the one who hurt me. He's my brother."

"Looked like you was tryin' to rattle her bones, young sir. Bad way to be treating a little sister what's been hurt," the flower seller scolded. "Now, you walk along, get her to home. And hold your temper!"

Hemmett's breath rasped loudly and his hand was shaking as he grabbed Katrin's arm. He nodded curtly to the flower seller and started to walk along, fast, so Katrin had to struggle to keep up.

She finally gasped for him to stop and grabbed a lamp post, clutching at a painful stitch in her side.

"Please, Bumpy," she said when she could draw breath. Hemmett looked at her. It was obvious he was still beside himself. He whistled down a cab and put her in it unceremoniously, climbed in after her and gave the driver the address of the house.

"Wasn't he gentleman enough to take you home after rutting with you?" Hemmett growled, glaring out the window.

"Please," Katrin whispered. He fell silent, though she could see he was clenching his fists so hard his fingernails were cutting into his palms. When his face was illuminated by a street lamp, she could see traces of tears around his eyes.

They pulled up before the house. Hemmett lifted her down from the cab and pushed her before him into the house.

Menders jumped to his feet in the lounge and stood there looking at her. Incredible relief had crossed his face when they came in, but then he became expressionless.

"I found her wandering down one of the streets in the student quarter," Hemmett said, his voice harsh with rage.

"Katrin, did you go with this man willingly?" Menders asked, his voice quiet in the room.

"Yes," Katrin whispered.

"All right. Hemmett, track Kaymar and Ifor down, tell them that she's home and all right. I understand your anger and sympathize completely, but if you ever manhandle Katrin again, as I just saw you do, you'll answer to me."

Hemmett nodded crisply and went back through the door. Katrin sank down on a chair and shuddered with relief that he was gone.

"Uncle, I'll leave you now. I'm glad you're all right, Katrin." Borsen's soft voice made her look up in surprise. He'd been sitting with Menders but in her humiliation, she hadn't noticed him. "I'll let Auntie know she's back safe."

"Thank you, Borsen," Menders said, his eyes still on Katrin.

A few moments later Eiren rushed into the room, put her arms around Katrin for a moment and kissed her.

"Thank the gods, darling," she whispered, stroking Katrin's hair. "We were so worried." Then she was gone, stopping to kiss Menders on her way back to their room, leaving Katrin alone with him.

Katrin heard Menders walk across the room and back and then sigh. He was looking out the window.

"Hemmett is coming back with Kaymar and Ifor, so we'll wait for a few minutes," he said. "Would you like some water?"

Katrin nodded mutely. He fetched her a glass, giving it to her as the door opened and the three men came in. Katrin could tell they were all furious. They nodded briskly as they acknowledged her and Menders and then went to their respective rooms. Finally, she and Menders were alone.

"Now – are you all right?"

"Yes," Katrin whispered.

"Do you need to see Franz?" Katrin shook her head.

Menders settled into a chair and sighed.

"Katrin, Hemmett was terrified. He thought you'd been abducted. You and this man left absolutely no trace because of the way you went. No-one saw you go. It wasn't until he beat this Godson's address out of someone that he even began to get close. I have seen Hemmett in many moods but never terrified to the point of weeping. This behavior is so beneath you, my dear."

"It was… it was impulse, Menders, and I'm sorry that I did it. If I could relive it, I would never do it," Katrin said.

"I realize that. All I have to do is look at you to know you have not had a transcendent love experience," Menders said gently. "But Katrin… you treated Hemmett like a stray dog you were trying to get away from. He doesn't deserve that, no matter how strained things are between you."

"I… Menders, please believe me. It wasn't my idea and it wasn't intended to hurt Hemmett. I didn't want to leave to come home but I was getting ready to go. Ermand had a friend of his make a distraction and said 'run'… and I did. I didn't plan to do this, and I'll explain that to Hemmett."

"That's good enough for me. Just rest a few minutes now and then I can recommend a hot bath." He managed a smile, though she could tell he was still angry and had been very frightened.

She sat back and sipped the water, trying to clear her head, but there was far too much coursing through it. The bruised feeling was easing, but she was still very sore.

"Menders – is it supposed to hurt?" she asked in a very small voice.

He looked at her as he used to when she was small and hurt and there wasn't much he could do about it.

"It can," he said slowly, "for the woman, the first time, if care isn't taken. If the man is considerate, takes his time and makes sure the woman is responding, it shouldn't be painful at all."

"I know about that, but this is more like being bruised way up inside me."

"Ah. I'll bluntly tell you that's the handiwork of a man who is either an idiot or completely inconsiderate," Menders sighed. "I'm sorry, little princess, but it will pass. Now tell me, did he use a preventive?"

Katrin felt herself go pale and shook her head. She hadn't thought about that at all.

Menders sighed. "I will want you to let Franz have a look at you, but that doesn't have to be right away."

"I don't think we need to worry about a baby, my cycle is due," Katrin whispered.

"I'm not concerned about a baby, but about disease," Menders answered gently.

Oh gods, Katrin thought. I never even thought about it. I didn't think about anything! What a fool!

"Now, that's enough for one night. I'm infinitely glad that you're here and in one piece. You are not to fret yourself into melancholia over this," Menders said, rising to his feet and offering her a hand up. "The world won't end, little princess. Come here."

He put his arms around her and held her for a very long time. She wished that she could cry, but all the tears she'd been fighting back ever since leaving Ermand's rooms seemed bottled up behind her eyes and in her throat, stinging both. She clung to him while he rocked back and forth and stroked her hair.

"Now, a bath and bed," Menders said, making himself sound cheerful. "Does wonders."

Katrin managed an unsteady smile and went off to the bathroom to run the tub. The spouting tap triggered the tears, and she began to cry.

***

Borsen stood on the dark balcony outside the lounge, shamelessly eavesdropping on Menders' and Katrin's conversation. Normally he would never do such a thing but when Hemmett shoved Katrin through the door, her pallid face had alarmed him. He was determined to find out what had gone on and possibly skin Ermand Godson alive.

He heard a window slide up almost silently. In a moment Hemmett was beside him, a hand on his shoulder, signaling for silence. They stood there together as Katrin explained to Menders that she hadn't planned her defection, that it had been the device of Godson.

"Menders – is it supposed to hurt?" The question, asked in a tiny voice, made Borsen nearly bite through his tongue with rage. Hemmett's hand tightened on his shoulder so hard that it was almost painful.

They waited while Menders comforted her and then Katrin went off for a bath. Menders sank down on the sofa and put his head in his hands.

Borsen felt fury coursing through him. Yes, Katrin had been an idiot, but she hadn't done anything more than most girls did at some point. To think that puffed up twit had hurt her and given her no pleasure after obviously planning to get into bed with her!

Katrin started crying as the water ran. Menders got up and went toward his room.

They moved silently to the drainpipe. Hemmett simply climbed over the balcony banister, hung by his hands, then dropped the rest of the way. Borsen prepared to shinny down the drainpipe. Hemmett shook his head emphatically, holding out his arms. Borsen stepped over the banister and dropped into Hemmett's hands.

A moment later they were on the street and able to talk.

"I can manage a drainpipe shinny," Borsen said.

"And rip your hands apart like the last time you did?" Hemmett answered. "Save wear and tear."

They turned together to head toward the University and Student Quarter – and were face to face with Menders and Kaymar.

Menders was expressionless. Kaymar's eyes were like a snake's.

"You two go back inside," Menders said sternly. "You are not to be involved in this. No discussion."

***

Kaymar lit a cigar as he and Menders stalked down the Avenue toward the University. The night was young, and the end of the academic term was close. The students were definitely getting into a celebratory mood, with the taverns full to overflow and lots of drinking and carrying on in the street.

Kaymar stuck his head into the Three Elks Tavern and saw Ermand Godson holding forth with an admiring crowd around him. He had his arm around a girl, who was obviously agog.

"He's in there," Kaymar said, returning to Menders, who was waiting in the alley beside the building.

Menders nodded.

"Here, two florins to go and tell Ermand Godson that someone is waiting outside for him with a delivery," Kaymar said to a waiter lounging by the kitchen door. "And ten florins to go back to work before your break is over and five more for keeping the door shut."

"Your servant sir!" the man replied cheerily, pocketing the coins and going inside. Moments later, Kaymar could see him in the main room of the tavern, whispering something to Godson.

Menders receded into the shadows.

Godson sauntered out the side door, looking around. He finally spied Kaymar standing well back in near-darkness and walked over.

"It's the bodyguard cousin," Godson sighed. "Come to complain?"

"Oh, it's not that it at all," Kaymar answered, turning on the charm, making his accent suddenly very upper crust. He placed a hand against the tavern wall, leaning on it attractively. "Emila told me so much about your performance that I thought I would come and see if you'd be interested in me."

Godson obviously didn't know whether to say that Katrin hadn't been all that pleased or to preen himself. He was far too self-absorbed to admit he'd been less than scintillating in bed. He looked Kaymar up and down.

"I just might at that," he said unctuously.

Kaymar smiled. Godson stepped close. Very close.

Kaymar's knee introduced itself to Godson's testicles, dropping that particular young twit to the ground in a silent, agonized rush of involuntarily indrawn breath.

Next thing Godson knew, the toe of Kaymar's right foot was pressed against the spot where his testicles joined the rest of him. Kaymar was leaning over to smile in his face, his eyes glittering in the dim light.

"You hurt her," Kaymar said liltingly. "I don't like that. Maybe I should just kick a little bit and let you find out what it's like to be hurt right there."

Godson spluttered and gasped. Then he shrieked as the force that was Menders grabbed him by his shirt collar and ripped him up from the ground as if he was a rag doll.

Menders was known for his collar twisting technique, guaranteed to produce terror, temporary dimming of vision and devastating loss of bowel control. Kaymar was pleased to see Menders was in fine form tonight.

"You seem to have forgotten your privy training," Menders hissed, his white eyes staring into Godson's bulging orbs. "Such an educated gentleman too." Menders gave the collar one last twist and then gripped Godson by the hair as he started to sag toward the ground.

"Best stand on your own two feet," Menders said in a low, terrible voice. "Slumping around while I hold your hair could end up leaving you without a scalp."

"Now, I don't like rude little bastards who hurt young girls and leave them alone in strange neighborhoods at night. The young girl you hurt tonight is my daughter."

Menders shook Godson with all his strength before pulling him nose to nose again.

"You think I'm just a rich merchant, don't you? I can assure you, I excel at many things. Can you guess what I'm really good at? I'm very good at killing people."

Godson gurgled and then fainted.

Menders let the unconscious Godson fall into a pile of rubbish. He bent and sliced open Godson's trousers, laying him bare for the world to see, then backed away, gagging at the stench.

"Not much to write home to mother about. Poor Katrin, what a pathetic cretin she fell for," Kaymar gasped, drawing hard on his cigar to deaden his sense of smell. "Ah – this should wake him up."

There was a reeking bucket of kitchen slops outside the tavern side door. Kaymar flung it into Godson's face with pinpoint accuracy. The young man sputtered into consciousness to find Kaymar grinning into his face with all the warmth of an iceberg, his eyes bitterly cold, his knife held to Godson's crotch.

"Now, my very little man," Kaymar said, pressing hard with what was actually the blunt edge of the knife, "I am telling you what you're going to do for the next year or so. You're going to get up from here and go right back to your rooms, pack and run home to Mamma. You aren't going to tell her that the young lady's father and the bodyguard cousin taught you an important lesson tonight. You're going to say that you don't feel well and need a rest from university. You won't say a word about our girl, to anyone, ever. You won't come back here for over a year, or I'll be waiting here for you. Did you know that you can survive your old man being cut off? Oh yes, just bandage the area well."

Kaymar pressed up cruelly with the blunt edge of his knife while Godson fainted from horror a second time.

"Ugh," Kaymar said, turning away from the stink of Godson's fouled trousers immediately. "I have to get away from that reek or I'll have a damned fit."

Menders couldn't resist a well-placed kick in Godson's left buttock. The bruise would last for months and be a reminder of a certain night every time Godson sat down. The two of them walked calmly down the alley and started down the Avenue.

Kaymar lit a second cigar. His odd reaction to foul smells was probably close to making him faint. It had happened before.

"All right, Cousin?" Menders asked.

"I think I got away from it in time," Kaymar replied, blowing a smoke ring. "I wish we could stay around to see Godson's fawning friends discover him covered with fish heads with his shitty pants open and his pathetic old man hanging out."

"Just see it in your mind's eye. That's always far more amusing than the real thing. Such bastards, when they finally take a fall, don't really have the friends everyone thinks they do. Guaranteed half the people in that tavern like to do something similar." Menders was not looking nearly so grim as he had since Hemmett had burst into the house, frantic that he had lost Katrin.

"Ah, Father Wisdom has spoken," Kaymar laughed.

***

Varnia heard Katrin finish her bath and poured out a glass of warmed milk, dropping in a pinch of ramplane powder and sweetening it with honey. She carried it to Katrin's door and tapped, letting herself in.

Katrin looked better, hot water having done its job of cleaning away the relics of her experience and soothing her sore muscles. She managed a smile.

"Here, drink this. It'll take away the rest of the soreness and send you to sleep," Varnia said gently, sitting on the edge of the bed. Katrin took the glass and had two big gulps.

"Now, you'll need another hot bath in the morning," Varnia continued. "After that, go back to your regular bathing routine. No extra washing. You'll be tempted, but you have to fight the urge, or you'll be washing all the time."

Katrin looked startled, as if Varnia had stated exactly what was in her mind. She'd wanted to run another bath as soon as she got into bed.

Suddenly what Varnia must have experienced in the past became brutally clear to Katrin. Tears, already close, flooded to her eyes. Alone, the only female on that farm with those frightening half-brothers and an uncaring, callous father.

Varnia knew what she was thinking.

"You can get past this," she said, taking the empty glass from Katrin. "But that will happen only if you let it. Dwelling on something that can't be changed will poison your entire life. Menders taught me that. Sleep now, don't spend more time crying. You'll cry more in days to come, but not now. You need to rest and let your mind start moving on." She smiled and rose, seeing to it that Katrin was comfortably settled on the pillows.

Varnia went to the door, opening it to reveal Menders with his hand up, ready to knock. Varnia nodded to him and he smiled back, putting his hand on her shoulder for a moment before she went down the hall.

Menders took Varnia's place at the edge of Katrin's bed. He straightened her long golden braid on the pillow and took her hand. He sat there silently for a while, until her eyelids began to droop, and then stood and bent to kiss her forehead.

"Everything is all right – sleep well, little princess," he whispered.

"I'm so glad you said that," Katrin breathed, almost asleep. "I love it on the nights you say that before I go to sleep."

Menders smiled.

"I always say it. I've said it every night of your life, whether you are awake to hear me or not," he replied. "Sleep now. It will be much better in the morning."

She was asleep by the time he closed her door.

SIMERIDON, ARTREYA

26
KATRIN'S TURN

"If I have to be afraid for Flori's safety, no, I do not want to go," Luntigré decided, leaning back against Hemmett's chest. "I'm sorry for that, but I cannot take such a chance."

News of incidents of dark-skinned people being attacked and harassed in Simeridon had reached Samorsa. Other reports of people with dark skin being told not to visit Artreya during the annual Lunar Festival, a weeklong celebration of the spring conjunction of Eirdon's two moons were also in the newssheets.

"Sad as I am to say it, you would not be safe there – and you wouldn't enjoy it if you were constantly fearful," Hemmett sighed. He could have them travel in a private railway carriage and charter a boat to go over the sea to Artreya, but once in Artreya would they have to wear veils on the street to avoid harassment and worse?

He was disgusted by the entire situation and more than ready to leave Artreya. Once they were at The Shadows again, visits from Luntigré and Flori would be simple to arrange.

"Then that's settled. Have things between you and Katrin thawed?" She looked at him closely.

Hemmett didn't answer.

Things hadn't thawed. He didn't want them to. He was sorry Katrin had been hurt by Ermand Godson, but her actions leading up to the incident cut him to the bone. Running out with Godson was the last straw. She had to have known it would throw everyone into a panic.

Kaymar had charged out into the street without his shoes to go after them – no laughing matter in a town where the streets were absolutely filthy and paved with uneven cobblestones. Ifor went after him with his shoes and finally caught up with him but by then the damage was done. Kaymar's feet were still cut, bruised and battered and Doctor Franz was worried he'd picked up an infection.

Having to go back to the house to tell Menders that Katrin was gone with Godson had been one of the worst moments of Hemmett's' life. On first hearing the news, Hemmett thought Menders was going to pass out. He'd seen Menders in many moods and conditions during the last twenty years, but he'd never seen him terrified. It had lasted only a moment before Menders went into action, immediately organizing a search operation and keeping Varnia from racing out the door to wander around in the dark searching – but that moment had pierced Hemmett's heart.

It wasn't that he was punishing Katrin by not speaking to her. Quite simply, he was afraid he would fly into a rage if she started arguing or excusing what she'd done. She had to have known her family would think Godson had kidnapped her. Hemmett was very slow to anger, like his father, but when he was pushed far enough, he had difficulty controlling himself.

"Hemmett, she's your sister," Luntigré said softly.

"Yes. Haven't you ever been angry with your sister?"

"Of course. And at times we didn't speak. But for so long and when you are so close?"

Hemmett sighed.

"Darling, I'm afraid I'll hit her," he said bluntly. "If she starts to excuse what she did, I might just hit her. So, I don't talk to her."

Luntigré said nothing more.

***

Hemmett rose from his seat on the train from Wenslas to Simeridon, gathered up his duffel bag and went to the carriage door, sliding it open and stepping onto the small platform. He wanted to be away and getting through the customs line before the crowd was finished with collecting their luggage, engaging porters and slowing the lines down to a crawl.

He was tired and downhearted. His time with Luntigré had been short and the journey tiring. He'd hoped to reach some sort of peace with his situation during that week, but he was as conflicted as ever. He certainly wanted to see Borsen, Menders and the rest of the family but he dreaded seeing Katrin and speaking to her only when necessary. He also dreaded finding answers to certain correspondence he had initiated prior to leaving for Samorsa.

He had made inquiries about taking another posting, sending letters to several high placed officers and to Commandant Komroff at the Mordanian Military Academy. He was sure one of them would be answered in the affirmative and the letter would be waiting for him when he returned.

The train vented clouds of steam as the brakes squealed. Hemmett spotted Eiren standing by a pillar, her face solemn as the train pulled into the station. The similarity to Borsen meeting him on the same platform struck him – he was sure Eiren wasn't down here looking at the trains.

He swung down to as soon as it was safe and went to her. She returned his embrace warmly.

"And why are you down here meeting trains?" Hemmett asked, keeping his tone light.

"I want to speak with you, away from the house and the rest of the family," she said bluntly. A little crease was showing at the inner edge of her left eyebrow, an indication that she was concerned and possibly annoyed.

"I'll have to go through Customs," he reminded her.

"I'm patient," was her only response.

He got through Customs with the usual forbearance and bribe, then shouldered his duffel and offered Eiren his arm.

Seated in a nearby restaurant, coffee and pastries ordered, Eiren spoke directly.

"I want to know if you've come to a point where you can begin to treat Katrin properly."

Hemmett raised his eyebrows slightly.

"Are you saying I mistreat her?" he countered.

"You don't speak to her unless it's absolutely necessary. It has gone on for two months."

The sharpness of her tone startled him. It was easy to forget that although Eiren was reserved, soft spoken and gentle, she was born a farm girl and had spent her first thirteen years contending with all the difficulty, hard work and privation that could bring. He had never known her to shrink from a fight if she believed she was backing a worthy cause.

"Are you forgetting what led to that?" he asked.

"Of course not. I remonstrated with her myself after she insulted you and Borsen. I was terrified the night she ran away with that man. All I could think of was that the baby I helped raise, that the child I loved had been taken by someone who would do terrible things, who might even kill her. But I didn't withdraw my love from her."

Hemmett was silent as the waiter delivered their orders and then withdrew.

"Eiren, I love Katrin. But I'm afraid of my anger. I was the person who was betrayed in this. In all honesty, I don't know if I can trust her again."

Eiren pushed her plate aside, as if the idea of eating was suddenly nauseating.

"Hemmett, you've been having love affairs since you were sixteen," she said abruptly. "Some of them very trivial, some that were volatile, none of them truly serious until you met Luntigré. Yes, we knew about it – as your sponsor to the Military Academy, Menders was kept apprised of what you were doing.

"There's nothing wrong with you having that experience. The point I make is that Katrin never had that sort of opportunity to learn about matters between men and women. Her station makes it impossible."

"I know that."

"But you don't consider what it means," Eiren continued. "If she goes to a social occasion, she's escorted by Kaymar. If she dances, she usually confines herself to men in the family, just to avoid the men who are interested only in her station and money. She was never kissed by a man until this Godson turned up. She never even experienced puppy love, had a disappointment and learned how to judge romantic situations."

Hemmett looked away from her. He wrapped his hand around his coffee cup as if seeking warmth.

"She thought she was in love with him and that he loved her," Eiren said, lowering her voice. "He gave her every reason to think so. He manipulated that situation with nothing more than the intent of getting her into his bed.

"She was a fool, but not malicious. She didn't act to hurt you, Hemmett – but your behavior to her leading up to that night certainly pushed her toward what she did."

Hemmett thought of all the times Katrin tried to apologize for her insulting words on the day Ermand Godson called him a servant. He'd refused to listen, though she persisted, absorbing one rejection after another from him, then apologizing again.

"She also saw the letters you wrote inquiring about possible alternate postings." Eiren sugared her coffee and stirred it with more vigor than necessary.

A horrible shiver ran down Hemmett's spine.

"How?" he asked.

"You left them for Menders to countersign the morning you left for Samorsa. They were on his desk, not even folded. She's in and out of his study all the time, as you well know. She went in to get something and saw them. She didn't touch them, but you know how she takes in an entire page in a glance. She came out of that room dead white, Hemmett."

"I didn't leave them there to – oh gods!" He closed his eyes.

"We know you didn't. But the damage was done. She's been very quiet, and she's been crying at night. She's defeated and withdrawn. Katrin is my child, as she's Menders' child – we've raised her from the day she was born as if she was our own. I can't let this continue.

"If you're going to leave, you might as well do it now. Save all of us the discomfort of living in a house where you're refusing to speak to your sister, where every meal is uncomfortable. We've had two months of that. If the damage is so great that you can never forgive her, it's time to end it with no further torment for both of you."

"Did Menders send you to tell me this?" Hemmett's head went up and he looked directly at her.

"If we weren't in public, I'd slap your face," Eiren responded heatedly. "When does anyone, even Menders, act through me? I am speaking for myself."

Hemmett looked away from her again, his nostrils flaring slightly as he drew a deep breath, attempting to calm himself.

Eiren gathered her things rapidly.

"I remember a day when that monster, Madame Holz, was sent to The Shadows to be Katrin's nurse, so she could start toughening her," she said in a low tone. "Katrin was only six months old. Menders was keeping her away from that woman and went out into the vegetable garden where your father was hoeing beans and you were trying to make a pile of worms. You saw Menders and ran to him, demanding to see Katrin. When he knelt so you could, you patted her blanket and said, 'My baby!' You loved her so much and you were always gentle with her, as Menders taught you to be.

"Well even though you not laying a hand on her, you're harming her now." Eiren rose from her chair. "Maybe you should remember all the years where you and Katrin have been so close and try to forget the last couple of months where she was being a foolish, lovestruck young woman who was tragically taken advantage of."

She started to walk out of the restaurant but was startled when Hemmett reached out and caught a handful of her skirt, as he used to when he was a little boy, to get her attention.

"I need to think for a while, Mother," he said in a low tone. "But I should walk you to the house."

"I'm able to walk back by myself," she said, modulating her voice toward kindness. "I hope to see you later."

He nodded and released her.

***

Katrin stopped trying to read her book.

It was hard to concentrate. It was a glorious spring day. The school term was over, and it was a few days before the beginning of the big Lunar Festival, marked with a great deal of celebration in the form of street processions, people wearing costumes and much consumption of food and drink.

Katrin had not been sleeping well since she'd found Hemmett was inquiring about other postings. The finality of seeing those letters, the knowledge that lasting damage had been done to their friendship had stolen her energy and enthusiasm.

She tried to hide this. She feigned interest in the upcoming Festival. She had continued at the University after her dreadful night with Ermand Godson and during the time Hemmett refused to speak to her. That didn't mean she was happy about it.

Strangely, though she was unhappy, she felt peaceful. She knew she had done all she could from her side to make things right with Hemmett. She was thankful for all Menders and Eiren had done over the last two months, to say nothing of dear Doctor Franz, Kaymar and Ifor. They had all been kind and understanding once tempers cooled. Borsen had forgiven her right away and they were close again.

At first, she wanted to drop her University classes to avoid encountering Ermand. Menders kindly but steadfastly refused.

"My dear, if you should encounter him, behave as exactly what you are – a lady. Acknowledge him as any other acquaintance, and go about your business," Menders told her. "Don't let him know he's hurt you. His sort thrives on drama. You'll be all right, Katrin."

She'd looked dubious and he'd kissed her cheek.

"My girl who has faced so many things needn't be afraid of a walking puffer fish," he smiled. The image was so absurd that she had to laugh.

But at her next philosophy class, Ermand Godson was nowhere to be found. The philosophy professor announced that Mister Godson was called home on family matters and would not rejoin the class. Considerable snickering around the room puzzled Katrin. She was relieved that she didn't have to face him, though in a way she was almost disappointed in not having a chance to consider him a walking puffer fish to his face.

Now she felt very sure Hemmett was going to go away, that she would never see him again, that he would never speak to her or be her friend again – all because of her obsession with Godson. Trying to accept that and move past it was very, very hard.

She got off her bed and wandered out into the living room, pausing to kiss the top of Menders' head as she passed his chair, where he was intent on a book. He smiled, reaching up to touch her cheek. Then she let herself onto the balcony overlooking the street.

She couldn't help smiling as she heard Ifor snoring resoundingly in the room he shared with Kaymar. He was housed on the opposite end of the floor from all the other bedrooms for this very reason. Ifor had refined snoring to an art and he did it with vigor. Sometimes you could hear him two houses down as you walked up the street. The only person it didn't disturb was Kaymar, who was probably lying right next to him, napping or reading, while what sounded like a walrus crossed with a large fog horn roared, blatted and honked in his ear.

Katrin drifted from one end of the balcony to the other, idly watching the activity in the street below. Maybe not so idly – she knew Hemmett would be arriving today. The morning train from Wenslas should have come already, with plenty of time for Hemmett to walk to the house.

She tried to assure herself that he might have decided on a later train, but there was a sinking feeling around her heart.

The letter she had inadvertently seen on Menders' desk gave Luntigré's address as the most immediate way to reach Hemmett. If one of the people he had corresponded with about alternate postings replied immediately, he would have received the answer there.

If that was the case, it was likely he would go directly from Samorsa to his new posting. Katrin had tried to accustom herself to that possibility since she had seen the letter.

She leaned against one of the elaborate grillwork pillars supporting the balcony roof. Preparations were being made for the street processions that would begin three days from now. Colorful decorations were going up, elaborate lanterns were being hung from hooks along balcony railings and from posts along the streets. A street peddler pushed his cart of fruit along, calling out a singsong description of his wares. Katrin briefly considered lowering the basket on a rope attached to the railing to buy something from him, but decided against it. She didn't have much appetite lately.

After looking up and down the street several times, squinting against the morning sun, she sighed and sank down on one of the elegant wicker chairs ranged along the balcony. She crossed her arms on the railing, staring unseeingly at the house across the street, swallowing against a lump in her throat.

She had to get used to this. She had to.

Someone whistled piercingly down the block. With all the Lunar Festival decorating going on, there were a lot of men calling and whistling signals to each other. Katrin leaned her head on her arms and closed her eyes.

Another whistle, closer – long, almost painfully high-pitched and impossible to ignore.

"Willow! What are you doing hanging all over the street like a heartbroken grundar!" Roared at the top of a pair of huge lungs in a bold baritone. That voice.

Katrin bolted upright, staring down the street. The sun was growing brighter as the morning mist burned off. The pavement was still wet and glistened with reflected light. When that happened, she understood why people said Artreya had golden streets.

He was there. Bigger than life, looking up at her with that wicked, slightly crooked grin, standing on cobblestones the sun was turning into gold.

He threw his arms wide, holding them out to her.

Katrin flew through the living room, past Menders, who jumped from his chair, past Kaymar, who opened the door of his room, down the stairs, through the door and out into the street.

People dodged as she made a beeline toward him, never stopping or swerving until she was in his arms.

Hemmett spun her around and then held her close. She was crying but so was he.

"You came back! You came back!" Katrin sobbed.

"I did," Hemmett whispered. "I always will."

***

Katrin sat between Borsen and Hemmett in the Three Elks Tavern on an early autumn night. They were celebrating the end of exams with what had become their set, the merchants' and artisans' sons and daughters Menders had told her should be her friends at the University, not the spoiled wealthy brats who had clustered around Ermand Godson.

Without Godson functioning as a lodestone for the privileged students, Katrin and Borsen had found themselves to be very popular. Hemmett was included by their friends without a second thought.

Hemmett was singing an extremely bawdy sea chanty, accompanying himself with his cromar. Borsen joined in on the choruses, chiming in with a tenor descant to complement Hemmett's deep bass baritone. As always, young women clustered around Hemmett, hopefully eyeing his face and body and then dejectedly noticing Luntigré's ring on his wedding finger. They had not officially married, but were entirely exclusive.

Katrin caught the eye of Willem Robbins, eliciting a smile from that pleasant young man. They had been involved off and on since he had been rotated back to guard the family in Artreya some months back. The affair was not a particularly passionate one, but it was warm and comfortable. Willem was a kind, considerate man.

Katrin had been incredibly relieved to find she was capable of sexual fulfillment, but she couldn't passionately love Willem. As Luntigré would say, it wasn't the 'great love'.

Willem knew it too. It had hurt him at one point and caused a rift between them that they made up. It was nice to have a confidential friend and it was nice to have someone to sleep with. The problem was, Katrin wanted more. She wanted not only a friend and companion, but a lover and passion as well.

She'd mentioned it to Menders and he'd smiled a little ruefully.

"Just like me," he said. "Did I influence you so much, little one? I tried not to."

"You've never talked to me about it to any large degree," she'd responded, surprised.

"No, that's true, because I didn't want to influence you. Well, I can say this now – enjoy what you have and treat him gently. As a Kaymar's Man, he will be returning to The Shadows with us and I'll do all I can to keep him there, but eventually he will have to be rotated elsewhere."

Willem lifted his wineglass and raised an eyebrow, his way of asking if she'd like another glass. She shook her head, shuddering a bit.

She was very careful of her wine consumption after the night of the Lunar Festival. She, Hemmett and Borsen had gotten completely sozzled while they watched the processions from the balcony, with Menders and Eiren away with friends. Relief at being forgiven by Hemmett had led her to be incautious and she drank far more than she ever had.

The next day was terrible. She could only sit and stare fixedly at the wall. Hemmett insisted on drinking a bottle of cologne as an antidote for his hangover and sat around with his head wrapped in a wet towel, looking like something that had died. Only Borsen verged on normal, eating about half of his usual enormous breakfast and cleaning up the wreck they had made of the lounge and balcony during their debauch. He'd been holding that over their heads ever since. Menders was convinced Borsen had been weaned on kirz, because the amount he'd drunk that night should have killed him.

Willem laughed a little and went to get his own glass refilled.

The vacant seat at the table afforded Katrin a view of the room. It was full of students from the University as well as young soldiers and sailors from the Artreyan Military and Naval Academies. The night was young, and no-one was getting reckless or obstreperous yet.

Thank the gods it was cool, verging on cold tonight. Katrin had felt quite badly during the worst of the summer and spent a lot of time at the house, out of the sun. She'd also managed to pick up a mild eye infection that lingered. She'd resorted to continually wearing a pair of dark glasses, which she normally used only for bright sunlight. She was recovering, Doctor Franz said, but needed to be careful until she did. The light in the tavern was not particularly bright, but it hurt her eyes and she was grateful for the dark lenses.

With the late Artreyan autumn really setting in she felt much more energetic. Her lungs appreciated the crisp air and she was able to wear her beautiful blue jacket. She always felt happy when she had it on.

Suddenly Katrin was aware that someone was looking at her. A quick survey of the place revealed a young man on the far side of the tavern. He was staring at her fixedly. Seated next to a man in naval uniform, he was dark haired with a moustache, dark eyed and wearing a jacket that would make Borsen scream and run in horror. It was made of green velvet, looped extravagantly with black braid. The buttons were shaped like silver skulls.

She drew Borsen's attention to the man, who obviously wasn't sure if he'd made eye contact with her because of her glasses.

"Do you know who that is?" she asked Borsen after prodding him in the side three times, distracting him from alternately singing the descant to Hemmett's chanty and conversing with a girl who pursued him determinedly despite being told that Borsen was nancy.

"No, I've never seen… oh gods, that jacket! Must be one of the Artreyan assassins-in-training with those tasteful silver skull buttons. Pah!" Borsen turned away in disgust and returned to his conversation and singing

. Katrin tried to ask Hemmett, but he was too interested in his singing. No-one else was close enough or alert enough to see Katrin trying to catch their eye.

She looked back at the young man and saw he was similarly engaged, nudging the man in the uniform next to him and pointing toward her, obviously asking who she was. He looked back at her.

This time their eyes clicked and held, despite her dark glasses. Suddenly, Katrin knew what passion was. Her breath caught in her throat.

He was rising from his chair slowly, his eyes still on hers, a smile growing on his face. Katrin glanced over at Willem, who was talking to a girl near the bar – good. She didn't expect any trouble. At this point they were mainly friends but better to avoid misery, if it could be done.

"Children, I need to speak to you immediately," Menders said behind her, making her heart jolt in her chest. She looked over her shoulder and saw that he was pale and grim faced. Borsen and Hemmett rose immediately as Menders helped her from her seat.

Just then a group of young soldiers rushed in, talking loudly. They clustered around the bar, crowding the tavern. The young man with the dreadful jacket couldn't move and was shoving at people trying to get them out of his way.

They slipped out the side door into an alley, where Menders explained.

"War has been declared between Artreya and Mordania. A Mordanian patrol boat fired on an Artreyan fishing fleet. We have to get back to the house, pack and leave immediately. I have a boat ready to take us to Samorsa."

"Do I have time to let someone know I'm leaving?" Borsen asked.

"I'm sorry, son. This was so sudden that it may already be too late for us to get out," Menders replied, taking Katrin's arm, hurrying toward a carriage waiting at the end of the alley. Hemmett handed Katrin his cromar and ran ahead of them in his capacity as guard, Borsen at his heels. Willem joined them at the carriage.

Behind them, Katrin heard shouts of "War!" in the tavern, accompanied by cheering and singing. Borsen held the door of the carriage as she leapt in, followed by Menders, then swung up beside her while Hemmett climbed to the driver's seat, took the reins from Willem and shouted to the horses, urging them to a gallop.

26
ALL THE BIRDS FLY HOME

"I'm getting a sword!"

Flori's voice echoed through the entryway, staircase and hallways of The Shadows. Immediately, various of Menders' Men erupted from doorways to quell whatever might be endangering her.

Menders, laughing delightedly, waved them back as Flori snatched a sunshade from the umbrella stand and charged back toward the kitchen. From the sounds of things, mayhem had broken out amongst "The Knot", freshly home from their unexpected detour of some months in Samorsa while they waited for Mordania and Artreya to stop sinking each other's ships.

Luntigré and her daughter had come back with them for a visit and that had inspired Katrin to suggest a "Samorsan Night" dinner. All of "The Knot" had spent time at Chetigré's cooking school while they waited for the war to cool. Cook was wild to see the techniques they'd learned and Luntigré claimed some recipes she kept secret from her mother.

Menders followed Flori, who brandished her "sword" and took Hemmett on. He was using a whisk to fend off Katrin's feints with Cook's Second Particular Spoon.

"I'll help you, Aunty Katrin – he's a terrible old pirate!" Flori cried, thrusting the sunshade at Hemmett's aproned belly like a spear.

"Ho there, child, delete that adjective!" Hemmett ordered, disarming her before she did real damage.

"Yes, you should only call him an *old* pirate," Katrin told the child. "He isn't terrible, he's incorrigible."

"See if I beat any more egg whites for you then, Your Very Most Highest of the Highnesses," Hemmett retorted, giving her a light swat with the whisk. He raised his voice to a falsetto. "Oooh, Big Brother, please whip these egg whites for me, my poor twiggy little arms can't stand the strain." He turned back to the enormous bowl he'd been belaboring with the whisk.

Before Katrin knew what was happening, Flori, over-excited by the horseplay, grabbed Cook's New Particular Spoon and whacked Hemmett across the backside with it with all her might.

"Oh, well played!" Borsen laughed from where he, Varnia and Willem were grinding and measuring spices for Samorsan Seven Spice Soup.

Hemmett turned and gently took the spoon away from Flori. Looking for more weaponry, she picked up a double handful of shelled walnuts, giggling.

"No, my girl, no flinging of food in this kitchen!" Cook said briskly but kindly. "Never waste food."

Hemmett left his project and held a bowl for Flori to drop the nuts into. Then he picked her up and held her close, speaking to her softly, calming her.

Menders noticed all the women watching closely and then smiling at one another. That blow from the Spoon must have stung, would probably leave a mark and had startled Hemmett badly, yet he reacted calmly. It was the adults' rough play that had led to Flori's over-excitement, after all.

"He's learned the Samorsan way of gentle discipline for children," Luntigré said softly to Menders. She was compounding Samorsan rolls, her long-fingered hands almost a blur as she encased a sautéed savory filling in one finely rolled square of raw pastry after another.

"He's going to have a Spoon shaped bruise, I fear," Menders replied before he opened his mouth for the spoonful of filling she offered.

"He's a husky boy, he'll survive," Luntigré giggled. She and Hemmett exchanged a smile across the room.

"I just can't call it Seven Spice Soup when there are nine spices going into it!" Cook declared, looking over the little bowls that held the spices Willem and Borsen were grinding.

The entire "Knot" looked up and responded with Chetigré's battle cry.

"*Pah!* Salt and pepper are a *given!*"

Katrin had finished off the egg whites, which now mounded in the bowl like a captured cloud. She raised her eyebrows at Hemmett. He whispered to Flori and set her on a stool to watch as he began spooning the meringue into crisp pastry shells, telling her how they would be browned in the oven and then drizzled with melted chocolate. Luntigré joined them and Katrin walked over to Menders.

"Care to take a walk with me, Papa?" she asked.

"I would be most delighted, Very Most Highest of the Highnesses," Menders smiled.

They could hear Cook still arguing the Seven Spice Soup question as they strolled out into the Rose Garden. Katrin cupped a hand under one of Menders' cultivars, a glowing pink and gold rose named Princess Katrin.

"Your family are all blooming," she smiled, looking over the bed that was home to the roses he had named after each person close to him – Eiren, Captain Greinholz, Borsen and Princess Katrin were grouped together, flanked by Baronet Shvalz and Mister Trantz. From the bold and brassy orange Captain Greinholz to the elegant and small red Borsen, from tawny amber Eiren and the vibrant red hearted white Baronet Schvalz to the huge multi-petaled yellow Mister Trantz, each rose was an accurate summation of the person for whom it was named.

"I have some more roses to create," Menders smiled, rapidly deadheading some spent blooms. "I was thinking a single petaled copper for Flori, a yellow with an orange heart for our Moon Tiger while Willem Robbins will be a pink-hearted light yellow."

"How lovely. You're a poet."

Menders smiled, pitching the deadheaded blooms onto a nearby compost heap.

"Glad to be home?" he asked.

"So much. I had a wonderful time – most of it, but we've been away for a long time. When I saw the house, all shined up with new paint and the sun touching it, my heart leapt."

"Yours too," Menders said with satisfaction.

"While we were waiting in Samorsa, I spent a lot of time touring orphanages and schools – as you know," Katrin continued. "I also talked to Aunty Glad a great deal and exchanged a lot of letters with Fahrin.

"I don't want to drift any longer because I'm the Princess," she continued, standing straight and looking into his eyes. "I want to take a definite hand here at The Shadows – and I want to make some changes."

"I'm listening," Menders said, sitting on the Rose Garden bench and patting the place beside him. Katrin settled there.

"You and Aunty Glad told me that the orphanages in Mordania are terrible places," she began.

Menders nodded. "They are. Horribly overcrowded, little funding. Often the buildings are run down. A frail or sick child isn't likely to survive a stay in one."

"What happens to those who do survive?"

Menders shook his head.

"There are already many unemployed people in Mordania. They might be able to find low paying work, but I'm sure many of them end up on the streets. Prostitution, theft. Many of the nighthawks – paid thugs – in Erdahn are the products of orphanages."

Katrin nodded slowly before she spoke.

"There is a great deal of unused land on The Shadows. I would like to open an orphanage here, properly run, with training for older children so they can find a job when they leave. It's healthy out here in the country. Of course, there would be enough food and their medical needs would be met."

"How large a facility are you considering?" Menders asked.

"Aunty Glad says best to start small," Katrin answered. "I was thinking a group of ten to fifteen to begin."

Menders nodded in approval. "Good. I was hoping you weren't planning to bring a hundred needy children here at first, though in time that may be the population of our orphanage. I know you've taken many notes and have letters from Abbot Fahrin – we'll need to plan, of course. Shall we start tomorrow and have Varnia join us? She's gathered a great deal of information about orphanages as well."

"Yes! I'd also like to talk to Doctor about establishing a little hospital here. Whenever anyone is injured or sick and they're brought to the big house, there's this huge flurry while we're running around getting a room ready. Then they're trying to recover with a hundred people living under the same roof. What do you think?"

"Excellent. So far, you're impressing me," Menders laughed. "Franz will be delighted. Anything else?"

"My first idea, the one I had after being in Fambré when I wrote to Fahrin and he told me about the assistance they give to old people at the Temple. That old tenant farm house that no-one has taken in a while – it would need some refurbishment, but it's sound. I'd like to have a place where the retired tenant farmers and other elderly people could live if they wished. They would have help with meals or dressing and bathing. They wouldn't have to try to keep up a house, do repairs. No-one would have to go there, but if they wanted that type of support, they would be welcome."

Menders stood and looked down at her. He took her right hand and kissed it.

"It's wonderful to see you've found your way," he said softly.

"We start tomorrow," Katrin smiled.

***

Hemmett, excused from clean-up duty after Samorsan Night, sauntered out onto the wide front steps of The Shadows. Flori was running about on the lawn with several of the tenant farmers' children, their shadows long in the sunset light. It was now early autumn and there was a delicious tang of burning leaves in the air.

He sat on the middle step, his favorite perch, and lit one of the small, fragrant cigars Luntigré sold in her stall. They were rolled from tabak like regular cigars, but she included a number of herbs and spices, making them particularly flavorful.

Between puffs he began to whistle, a sweet little tune that had been in his head all day. He couldn't place it, but seeing the children holding hands and dancing in a circle on the lawn had brought it to his mind once more.

"I haven't thought of that song in years," Katrin said behind him.

"Willow, you're as silent as Menders," he laughed, craning his head backward to look at her.

"When you do that you look like an owl," she answered, sitting down next to him. "What brought that song to mind?"

Hemmett shrugged. "It's been in my head all day, but I can't remember where I learned it or the words to it," he answered.

"Don't you remember when we tried to play circle games with just the two of us?" She watched the children as they broke out of the circle they'd made and started playing a game of tag. "It's one of the songs we sang."

"That's it! What were the words… 'soldier, sailor'? Something about what we will be? I can't remember."

Katrin smiled and started to sing.

"Soldier, sailor, farmer, tailor

When I'm grown, which shall I be?
Teacher, lady, nursey, maidey,
When I'm grown, which shall I be?
And in time wedding bells will chime,
Husband, wife, forever be!
Father, mother, sister, brother,
I'll have little ones like me."

Hemmett grinned and gestured for her to repeat the song, chiming in immediately. Menders had taught both of them and Borsen to sing, as he was a fine singer himself. They could harmonize spontaneously and for most of their lives, having a singsong was one of their favorite evening pastimes. Now Hemmett's voice was a ringing bass baritone instead of a boyish contralto. It blended well with Katrin's soprano.

Borsen's tenor joined them halfway through, sliding a moment and then fitting into the harmony. He found a seat at Hemmett's feet. He was rapidly joined by Varnia – it was obvious the cleanup crew was finished and heading out to enjoy the evening.

It took Varnia a moment to find her confidence, but soon her alto was singing along with the tune and venturing into harmony. Rapidly Willem chimed in, settling behind Katrin and letting her lean back against him. They now had a choir singing the old Mordanian children's song.

"What songbirds!" Luntigré smiled as she sat beside Hemmett. Flori, tired and aware that the other children needed to start for home, trailed over and joined them, leaning against her mother's shoulder.

"One more round," Kaymar demanded, coming out the front door, immediately picking up the male falsetto line. Ifor could sense a singsong from miles away and was right behind him, his huge basso profundo suddenly adding a foundation to their chorus.

The children's song moved on to other favorites, with the chorus growing as people were drawn to the sound of singing and found themselves joining in. The sun was drawing down, the light going gold. It turned Eiren's hair to amber flame as she sat at Hemmett's feet and glinted on the frames of Menders' glasses as he settled beside her and added his baritone to the music.

Luntigré requested they sing Sweetheart, Kiss Me Tonight, which Hemmett had introduced to her. The old soldier's farewell drifted out across grounds.

Katrin looked up at the sky, where the three brightest stars were beginning to flicker through the twilight. She smiled.

BOOK TWO

OUT OF DARKNESS, INTO LIGHT

THE SHADOWS, MORDANIA

I
SPIDERWEB

Katrin looked up at the sound of Demon galloping toward the orphanage building site. It wasn't unusual for Menders to ride over during the day, but not at that pace.

As Demon grew closer, she could see Menders looked grim. She felt a twinge of anxiety and went to meet him.

He dismounted, settled Demon with a nosebag and then produced a letter with a very large seal.

"My dear, the Queen has commanded you to Court," he said, trying to keep his voice level.

Katrin groaned. Right in the middle of all the building and organizing!

He handed her the letter.

Lord Stettan,

You are commanded by Her Majesty, Morghenna VIII, to deliver the Princess Katrin Morghenna to the Palace by the fifteenth of this month to be presented to her mother. Failure to do so will result in the Queen's severe displeasure.

H.M. Morghenna VIII

"I wonder why now?" Katrin asked. "Curiosity, do you think?"

"It might well be," Menders answered. "It has been nine years since she saw you and she knew you were abroad. It would be reasonable to expect that she'd wish to see you again, now that you're grown."

"What a bother, things are so busy here. The fifteenth is tomorrow, we'll have to leave almost immediately," Katrin said with some annoyance.

Hemmett, who had gone to the construction site with her, meandered over, looking casual. Menders knew it was anything but – Hemmett had just delayed his arrival to give them some privacy.

"Bumpy, we'll need to go," Katrin said. "I have to go to the Palace."

Menders and Hemmett exchanged a glance behind her back.

***

At the house, Katrin went upstairs to get ready for the trip to Erdahn. Menders went to his study, where he had glimpsed Kaymar standing in the doorway as they came in. He'd been nosing around in Erdahn and must have set a speed record for getting back to The Shadows.

Kaymar was waiting, perched on the edge of Menders' desk. His blue eyes had a gleam to them that signified intense emotion of one sort or another. Menders closed the door.

"Bartan sent a letter," Kaymar said, handing him an envelope.

My dear Menders,

Katrin is being summoned to Court – my friend, do not fail to have her here or it will go badly for all of us. Aidelia has killed Lord Muran's eldest son in a fit of rage and the Queen is considering altering the Line of Succession to make Katrin her Heiress. Kaymar will tell you the rest. I cannot trust any more of this matter to paper, even carried by such as he.

In brotherhood,

Bartan

As soon as Menders was finished reading, Kaymar spoke rapidly.

"Aidelia snatched a halberd out of the hands of one of the Palace Guard," he said in a near whisper. "She hacked poor young Lauro Muran to death while the Guard stood there frozen – they didn't dare touch her. The poor fellow did nothing. She just started screaming and attacked him. He was only seventeen and just come to Court."

Menders sighed. He knew Lord Muran, had been at the Military Academy in the same class, though Muran had gone through regular military training while Menders was in Special Services. He'd been a good-natured, not overly bright youth. He had to be going through all the hells now.

"The Queen is sober, shocked into it by what happened. She has Aidelia under a continual watch."

Kaymar looked elated. Menders knew Kaymar had always hoped the Throne would come to Katrin. Many of Menders' Men did, but to Menders the very idea was laden with doom. Katrin did not wish to be Queen of Mordania – ever.

***

Menders rose and paced around the room again.

Katrin had been gone for hours. He had not been told where she was, only that she was with her mother, the Queen.

A Palace Guard was posted in the corridor or Menders would have gone looking for her hours ago. From time to time he could hear outbursts of revelry and hoped that was where Katrin was.

They had traveled to Erdahn with Katrin not knowing about Bartan's letter and the possibility of the succession being changed. Menders had eaten himself alive over having lied to her, but the Queen could fall back into her drinking and forget everything preceding her latest binge. It had happened many times. He had no wish to alarm Katrin only to arrive in Erdahn to find the plan had been abandoned.

So Katrin had been calm at their arrival. She was beautifully dressed and turned many a head as she, Menders, Hemmett and Kaymar were escorted into the Palace. Menders and Katrin were shown into a commodious room, while Hemmett was told to report to the Commander of the Guard. Kaymar went off on his own to talk to Bartan.

Menders was startled but not alarmed when he was summoned to speak to the Queen's Comptroller about The Shadows' operation and accounts. The messenger conveying the request assured him it was simply a formality requested by Her Majesty. Considering Katrin was surrounded by Palace Guards, who seemed most accommodating and even friendly, he'd gone without any show of resistance.

When he'd been returned to the room, Katrin was gone and a lone Guard was standing at the door.

"The Princess has been summoned to speak with and spend some time with her mother, Her Majesty the Queen," the Guard said evenly to Menders. "You are to wait here for her return."

Menders' apprehension had grown as more and more time slipped by. There was no sign of Kaymar, or Hemmett. There was no sign of Katrin returning. Menders even walked out into the hall a time or two to, but the Guard politely asked that he not stray any further, lest he not be there when Katrin returned.

Now it had been hours.

***

"Princess Katrin, the Queen bids you attend her."

Katrin was startled and looked up. She was alone. Menders and Hemmett had been called away and Kaymar was at Thoren Bartan's apartment.

The speaker was the Queen's Chamberlain. She recognized him from her visit to the Palace nine years before. He was an unusual looking man, obviously Surytamian.

"May I wait for my Head of Household to return so he may accompany me?" Katrin asked politely, not wanting to go anywhere in the Palace without Menders.

"It is imperative you attend Her Majesty immediately," the man said, his expression unchanging.

Katrin rose, squelching apprehension, knowing she had no choice but to obey. She was glad she hadn't eaten any of the food they'd brought along, remembering her mother's stench from the last time. An empty stomach would make it easier to hold her gorge.

She was shown into the room where she had been presented to the Queen when she was eleven. The Queen was there, looking eerily unchanged, wearing the massive armored, bejeweled gown and the hideous, false pointed teeth. Katrin curtseyed properly and was told to rise immediately. To her amazement, her mother walked over to her, obviously hampered by the weight of the gown.

The Queen looked Katrin up and down, then nodded curtly.

"I wished to see you alone," she hissed through the teeth. "Your guardian has seen to it that you've turned out… very well."

"Thank you, Your Majesty."

The Queen clanked away across the floor and then turned back to Katrin.

"I am changing the Line of Succession and will name you my Heiress," she said abruptly. "Your sister is not fit to inherit."

Katrin blinked and then felt a surge of icy horror. No. No!

"As a future Queen of Mordania, it is necessary for you to undergo the Ritual of Suspension," the Queen went on. "You may not refuse. You must not show fear or pain throughout the Ritual. It is painful, and you must bear it for as long as you can before asking to be released. I have been through it, as my mother was before me, as all Queens of Mordania have been since the time of Morghenna the Wise."

Katrin almost opened her mouth and refused – but she could not refuse. She was alone. They had her alone, without Menders or Hemmett. Even if she resisted, she could tell by the tone of her mother's voice that they would do this thing to her anyway.

"You will survive," her mother said more quietly. "Drink this. It will help deaden most of the pain."

She held out a vial. Katrin walked forward on trembling legs and took it. She removed the stopper and sniffed, fearful it might be poisoned, not willing to drink without checking, even if it had been given her by the Queen.

Ramplane. She knew the odor well.

Her mother smiled and Katrin saw that behind the teeth and the tragic ravages of years of drinking, it was a lovely smile.

"Smart girl," she said. "Trust no-one. I need an Heiress who is sane – and smart. Drink it, my daughter, and let us get this over with."

***

Katrin hung, suspended.

The ramplane had saved her the worst of the initial pain, but it was beginning to wear off.

She had been led to a room far from the Throne Room and told to remove her clothing. Two women had moved forward to assist her. She became aware that she was undressing for an audience – a group of people were standing in the shadows, apparently witnesses to whatever was about to happen. It was all she could do to let herself be stripped in front of them. Then as the ramplane took effect and buoyed her up, she began not to care.

She'd been told to lie on a table and obeyed, her limbs going numb, the usual effect of ramplane. Then her mother approached the table and stood beside her.

"Now begins the Trial by Suspension," she stated. She picked up an iron cuff and clamped it around Katrin's left wrist. It fit tightly, but not painfully so. Then there was a sharp jab of pain as Katrin realized her mother had closed the cuff by forcing a sharpened metal rod through the hasp, skewering her wrist from one side to another. Katrin could feel the metal scrape the bones of her arm as it passed between them and realized that it was hot, cauterizing as it passed through her flesh.

Even ramplane couldn't deaden all of the pain, but she showed no sign, using the Thrun discipline Menders had taught her years ago when her arm was badly broken. It didn't take pain away, but it allowed her not to mind it.

Her mother clamped two more cuffs on her left arm, below the elbow and between elbow and shoulder. The process was repeated on her right arm, and then on her legs. Then, to Katrin's horror, her mother shoved two curved metal rods under her collarbone. Katrin nearly cried out, only to have her mother's aqua eyes look quickly into hers, her expression a combination of desperation and severity. Katrin breathed in deeply and braced against the pain, trying to separate her mind from what was happening to her body.

There were more and more punctures, in her thighs, her belly, the soft flesh of her arms. A belt was wrapped around her waist and skewered into the flesh of her sides. Two more rods were shoved under her pectoral muscles. At this point, she was so exhausted that she lay limply and did not react at all. Each puncture was just one more pain to add to the totality of pain.

Oh Menders, she thought. You'll break your heart over this. This is madness. I don't want to be Queen! How does torturing someone make a Queen?

She'd been skewered thirty-two times when she saw her mother attaching the cuffs and metal rods to cables hanging from large, rusted iron hooks in the ceiling.

A leather strap was looped around her head. The pain became immense as someone operated a mechanism that lifted her free of the table by the cables. She was lifted high into the air, her limbs stretching agonizingly. The pull on her pectoral muscles was terrible. If the leather strap hadn't been around her head to keep it from lolling back helplessly, she would not have been able to breathe.

Katrin was ready to scream for them to let her down as the agony of clenching muscles and tormented flesh increased a thousand fold. If she could have thrashed in panic, she would have, but the insane apparatus she was suspended from had her drawn rigid. The only movement she could achieve consisted of rolling her eyes and breathing.

Suddenly she heard Menders' voice in her mind, teaching her how to control her body, to tense and relax different muscle groups if she was in a situation where she had to stand or kneel for long periods of time, preparing her for possible Court appearances.

"You can stay in one position and consistently rest one set of muscles after another, so you don't become exhausted," Menders had said, showing her the muscle groups he meant. "It's the same as when you're dancing. You only tense the muscles you need to use, not your entire body. Try relaxing one leg while letting the other take your weight, without shifting noticeably. Yes, that's it! Good, my little princess. Now keep changing the groups of muscles that hold you in position. You'll be able to stand for a very long time without much discomfort if you learn how to do this."

The intense memory made it possible for Katrin to think. She began to explore what would ease the stress on her pectoral muscles. She deliberately relaxed as much as she could, easing some of the pain, keeping her mind occupied.

She could bear this for a while. She could keep control. Soon this would end, and she could go home to The Shadows. Think of The Shadows. Breathe, relax, tense another set of muscles, relax others – think of The Shadows. Breathe, relax…

She lost track of time but knew she'd been suspended for quite a while. The witnesses were beginning to murmur to each other. There was movement in the room. Perhaps they were going to take her down now and she could go home to The Shadows.

"Mother… won't you have some wine?"

Katrin tensed and tried to turn her head to see the Queen. She knew that voice!

Aidelia.

"It's the best, Mother. After all, shouldn't you celebrate this occasion? One glass won't make a difference and you do allow yourself a bottle a day now that you've cut down so much. This glass can count against that bottle. No harm done." Aidelia's voice was honeyed and reasonable, but Katrin could hear the madness thrumming underneath the surface.

"No," she whispered. She wanted to shout it, but she couldn't. Her throat was swollen. "No."

"I have prepared a party for us all," Aidelia was saying. "There is more wine there, Mother. This is an auspicious day! You mustn't let it pass without celebration. Have some more. Here I'll pour it. Why you must be terribly thirsty to drink that fast, Mother! Come, you need to rest. I can arrange for Katrin to be taken down. Leave me the people who know how this thing works. Don't you want more wine? Yes, I thought you would. In the Great Hall, there's a table all spread there. Katrin and I will join you as soon as she's been taken down and given a chance to rest."

Katrin could hear people leaving the room. She tried desperately to see what was happening.

She felt herself being lowered, felt the blessed relief as the tension was released, as she reached the table and was no longer suspended. At least Aidelia wasn't alone with her. Other people were still there. It was over, thank the gods. She could go home to The Shadows now.

"Leave us!" Aidelia's voice rasped harshly and Katrin heard rapid footsteps. Then her vison was entirely filled by Aidelia's deathly pale face, framed by greasy red hair. Her breath was so foul that Katrin already weakened by the Ritual of Suspension, nearly fainted.

"You will never be Queen," Aidelia snarled viciously. "Our mother is weak, but I am strong! I can fool her! She's already fooled, out there drinking like a pig. You will be dead before this day is over and it will look as if it is her fault for going away and drinking, leaving you hanging from the ceiling like a spider."

"Please," Katrin whispered.

"Oh yes, beg, I like to hear it," Aidelia said companionably, taking up one of the long metal rods that hadn't been used. She contemplated it and then spat in her hand, wiped the spittle up and down the rod and then pushed it slowly through one of Katrin's breasts. "How was that? Going to cry?" She picked up another rod and spat on it, forcing it though the other breast. Katrin shuddered in agony, but refused to cry out and give this perverted woman any more pleasure than she was already garnering from her sadism.

Aidelia continued picking up the rods, spitting on them and forcing them through Katrin's flesh. Katrin bit her lips and tongue, but did not cry out. Aidelia looked at her closely, her expression a combination of arousal and insane glee.

"Think you're so strong, country cow?" she hissed. "Wait until you've been a spider a while longer, while I keep our stupid mother swilling down her beloved wine!"

Katrin spat in Aidelia's face.

"You'll be sorry for that," Aidelia growled. She ran to the suspension mechanism and hauled with all her strength, pulling Katrin higher than she was before. She fastened the rope off with a jerk that vibrated through Katrin in a spear of agony.

"Oh, I almost forgot," Aidelia said, coming back to her. "I forgot to take your halter off, cow!"

With that, she reached up and released the leather strap that supported Katrin's head. She ran from the room.

Katrin's head, unsupported, began to sag toward the floor, cutting off her breath.

***

Menders was going mad. It had been hours since he'd seen Katrin. It was obvious the Guard at the door was meant to keep him here. There was no sign of Hemmett or Kaymar.

Gods, where was she? No word had been left. He'd ransacked the room to see if she'd left a note or any indication, even a symbol scratched on the wall. There was nothing to indicate that Katrin had been there other than the book she'd been reading lying open on the bed.

Suddenly fast, light footsteps came unevenly toward the room, accompanied by gasping exhalations.

"Is the gentleman with the Princess here?" a woman's voice wheezed outside the door.

Menders was out of the room, face to face with a small, elderly woman dressed as a domestic servant. She was shivering with effort and breathing as if she was about to expire.

He felt the Guard step up behind him. A moment later the Guard realized Menders' knife was pressing against his throat.

"Sir! The Princess – they've hung her up! Hung her up and I hadn't the strength to get her down! She's breathing but very slow and her head falling back cuts it off. Hurry sir, please hurry!" The old woman had found her voice.

"Show me!" Menders saw the Guard was not going to do anything but walk slowly away, a wise man who was still alive.

The old woman grabbed Menders' arm and started down the hall. Menders rapidly outpaced her, hauling her along as she gasped out where to turn.

***

Wake! You must fight! Daughter of Mordania! Fight! You must survive! Wake! Wake!

The Queens spoke again. Katrin forced her head up once more. She could barely do it now. It had been an eternity. Sometimes she had been unconscious, but each time she was brought back by the voices of the Queens.

She had twisted and turned in the evil harness so that her head didn't loll back uncontrollably. Her pectoral muscles were being pulled through her skin because of her movements, as were muscles in her arms and legs, but at least she could change the amount of pressure on her windpipe because of the bit of mobility she had gained by maiming herself.

Keep moving! Fight! Breathe! You must endure, as we did! Struggle – don't give in! Do not let your sister win! Wake!

Katrin breathed as deeply as she could. If she lost consciousness again her head would fall back and Every time she'd been unable to draw breath, she had awakened with a start as the voices swelled and commanded – but the next time might be the time she didn't wake.

Someone had to come. Someone had to come soon – except that she knew that Aidelia was probably doing something to keep it from happening, keeping the Queen plied with drink, telling everyone she'd taken Katrin down and seen her to bed for a rest. People would be afraid of Aidelia. They wouldn't question her.

Menders, she thought. Please help me. Where are you?

You must fight! Eyes open! Breathe! Your sister must not win! Wake! Wake! WAKE!

Katrin's muscles were shaking. She fought, but couldn't keep them tensed any longer. Her head fell back, and everything went dark.

***

The old woman panted and wheezed beside Menders, who was practically carrying her along.

"Here, this corridor," she gasped. "The open door."

He released her and raced forward, his impetus driving him into the side of the open doorway, knocking the breath out of him. For a moment he couldn't see as the blood roared in his ears. Then his vision cleared.

"*No!*"

The scream he couldn't be his own, but he felt the agony in his throat. He coughed violently, blood splashing from his mouth.

Katrin, his perfect golden child, hanging from a spiderweb woven by demons from the hells, suspended from iron hooks in the ceiling, her head fallen back, unconscious, her beautiful hair hanging to the floor, draggled with blood. Naked, helpless, tortured, destroyed – dead.

"She's breathing sir!" the old woman moaned, pulling the door closed and bolting it.

He heard it, horrible rasping through a windpipe nearly crushed by the drag of gravity on her head.

He rapidly scanned the apparatus that held her, saw where it was moored to the wall, ran there and grabbed the rope.

"Catch her head!" he ordered, choking on the words. The old woman stumbled forward, holding her hands out. Menders lowered Katrin to the table rapidly, the old woman cradling her head and straightening her neck. Katrin's chest suddenly rose freely and rapidly as she struggled for air. Her eyes remained closed.

"Katrin! Katrin!" he shouted, his hands on her face, straightening her neck more, lifting her head slightly. She breathed more deeply, but did not respond. The old woman put her hands under Katrin's head as a pillow. Menders looked at her body and the foulness that had been done to it.

Madness descended.

He'd take a halberd from one of those toy soldiers and he was going to finish this insanity once and for all, butcher that drunkard Queen and her mad bitch of a daughter, kill every slavering sycophant in the place, have revenge for what they had done to his girl, his baby. They'd drown in their own blood and he would watch, and he would laugh!

"Sir, you must take her from here, before they come back!" the old woman cried, her voice full of terror.

The redness before Menders' eyes cleared. He saw the woman staring at him, her rheumy eyes wide with fear. He drew in a long sobbing breath, then another.

"That's a good boy," the old woman said shakily.

"Please – I know you are exhausted, but would you go to the rooms of Thoren Bartan, the Court Assassin, and tell him to send Kaymar Shvalz to me," Menders heard himself croaking. His voice was cracked and hoarse and he felt liquid in his throat. He coughed again. A spray of blood spattered his shirt.

He tore off his suit coat and flung it over Katrin, unable to bear another moment of her complete helplessness and the horror that had been done to her.

"Then, please, go to the Guardhouse and send Captain Greinholz to me," he croaked.

"The big lad came here with you?"

"Yes."

"Yes, sir," she said and went quickly.

Menders began unfastening the cables from the cuffs skewered to Katrin's limbs. He focused his mind only on that, on freeing her from the repulsive spiderweb dangling from the hooks in the ceiling.

"Only a few more, little princess," he choked, releasing one connection after another, not allowing himself to think of the metal rods being shoved into her, piercing her. "Then I'm going to take you home and you'll get well."

He unfastened the last cable and bent over her again, touching her face, stroking her hair, massaging her temples, willing her to waken.

"Katrin," he whispered. "Katrin, please. Oh gods, my little one, please."

She opened her eyes.

Blue eyes looking into his. She reached up, her arm weighted by the metal cuffs and grasped his hand. He clung to her hand, knowing her life depended on him keeping his sanity, on his staying in control.

"You are my little one," he whispered, as he had the night she was born.

Somehow, Katrin smiled. Her eyes closed.

Running footsteps. Kaymar exploded into the room, followed by Bartan. Kaymar stopped short, staring at Katrin. Bartan retched, then rapidly shook out a folded blanket he was carrying and flung it over her.

"We'll get her to my rooms," he said.

"Someone stop Hemmett before he gets here, tell him she's injured. I can't carry her safely, none of us can," Menders whispered hoarsely, his throat on fire. "He can't see her without being prepared. Kaymar, hurry, intercept him."

Kaymar fled. Bartan came to Menders and grasped his arm.

"When did they do it?" he asked. "They posted Guards on my damn quarters! Ten of them, because they knew Kaymar was there. They've been holding Hemmett as well. The old lady coming rattled them and they let us go."

"They took her hours ago – look." Menders drew back the blanket and his jacket so Bartan could see the muscles that had been stretched through Katrin's skin. "On her arms and legs too."

Menders grew faint. He bent over Katrin, resting his head against her so he wouldn't pass out. She needed him awake and able to function.

Bartan drew the blanket back over Katrin as Hemmett's running footsteps came down the corridor. Menders took a deep breath and stood upright, knowing he would have to steady the young man.

Hemmett appeared at the doorway. His face contorted in horror, then shifted to rage.

"Who did this?" he roared.

"Quiet," Menders rasped. "We have to get her out of here and you're the only one who can safely carry her. Pick her up and follow Bartan."

Hemmett automatically obeyed the order. He went to the table, tenderly gathering Katrin into his arms, flinching as the cuffs clanked against one another. Bartan rapidly led them away down the corridors, twisting and turning through back ways and disused passages so they wouldn't be seen. In his rooms, he directed Hemmett to put her on the bed as Bartan bolted the door behind them.

Hemmett knelt beside Katrin, whispering her name, touching her face, begging her to open her eyes.

"We'll need bandages, soap, water," Menders whispered and then coughed violently, spattering himself with more blood.

"Don't talk!" Bartan said roughly. "Sit down. I'll get what you need."

Menders went to Katrin, who had worked her eyes open again.

"Bumpy," she breathed and Hemmett sobbed with relief. Menders eased him out of the way, bending over her.

"Katrin, we're just waiting for some bandages and then we're going to take you home. Hemmett will carry you to the boat."

She smiled and closed her eyes.

A knock on the door heralded Kaymar, who had several bottles in hand.

"The Court Doctor doesn't have a bandage I'd put on a toad," he snarled. Bartan was already tearing up a clean sheet. Kaymar started on another.

"We have to go now," Menders gasped suddenly, feeling panic. "We don't have time to wait. Hemmett, pick her up. Bartan, get us out of here!"

Hemmett didn't hesitate, gathering Katrin up again. Just then, they heard the unmistakable sound of the Palace Guard searching, moving along a corridor nearby.

Bartan looked out and then led them at a near run to the passage he used to enter and exit the Palace without being observed. It let them out into the dark gardens, where a hidden path brought them to the street.

Kaymar dashed out into the traffic and stopped a cab, distracting the cabby while Hemmett dove through the open door with Katrin, followed by Menders. Kaymar climbed up with the driver, who whipped up his horse when he saw the fistful of florins Kaymar held out in exchange for illegal speed and recklessness.

***

Kaymar steadied himself against the bucking motion of the steam launch, knowing Ifor was up in the wheelhouse getting every last bit of speed he could against the choppy waves blown up by a storm passing over from the east. It would slow them down, making the journey between Erdahn and The Shadows twice as long.

They'd rushed Katrin from the cab into the boat with Ifor's help. In the cabin, they'd torn all the cushions from the seats and made a bed on the floor for her, while Ifor guided the boat away from the dock and opened the throttle all the way. While Hemmett tore the sheets, they'd brought with them into strips, Kaymar and Menders sat beside Katrin and began the grisly process of removing dozens of metal rods from her body.

Kaymar had seen some dreadful things in his time and was acquainted with some strange practices, but dragging metal rods from Katrin's body sickened and horrified him. He ground his teeth, he bit his lip, he chewed on his tongue – and he watched as Menders, face set and ghastly white, withdrew one rod after another, flinging them aside. He would wash the wounds tenderly, swab them with spirit and take a bandage from Hemmett, binding up the wound before going on to the next cuff. Kaymar did likewise across from him, trying not to think, trying not to imagine the pain.

Hemmett vomited when he saw the wounds on Katrin's chest, where the muscles were pulled through her skin. He stoically swabbed away the mess, washed his hands and began tearing more strips. Each time a rod was removed, Katrin bled, red patches appearing on the blanket. Menders bathed the distended, stretched muscles and then looked at Kaymar.

"I don't know whether to leave it for Franz or push them back into place," he whispered, for the first time appearing uncertain.

"Best to put them back," Kaymar replied, knowing the longer the muscles were exposed and distended, the greater Katrin's risk of infection and deformity would be.

He helped Menders massage and push the muscles into place, using bundles of the torn sheet as compresses when the blood flowed.

Suddenly Menders was shaking as if he was palsied. He had no control of his hands and sat back hard against the wall of the cabin. Kaymar leaned over and felt his forehead. It was icy.

"You've had enough, Menders," he said sternly. "Turn away."

To his surprise, Menders did as he was told, leaning against the wall, his eyes closed. Kaymar put a blanket around him.

Hemmett moved forward and began removing the remaining rods, his face set and fierce. Kaymar wanted to tell him to stop but didn't dare. Hemmett was not a force to be trifled with.

Finished with the cuffs that bound Katrin's right arm and leg, Kaymar gently turned the blanket down past the pectoral injuries he and Menders had cleaned and covered – and nearly vomited as Hemmett had. Hemmett's eyes opened wide. A horrifying expression distorted his face as he saw Katrin's skewered breasts.

"I'm sorry, Katrin," Kaymar whispered, forcing his hands steady as he began withdrawing the metal rod in her right breast. She moaned and woke, then cried out as he drew the spike free. Menders moaned and huddled against the wall, shivering. Kaymar rapidly mopped blood – and pus. His heart sank at the sign of infection.

"All right, Willow, I'm going to pull the other one," Hemmett said gently, his voice a wild contrast to the murderous expression on his face. Katrin gritted her teeth as Hemmett slowly and steadily withdrew the rod, releasing another gush of blood and pus. She cried out again. Menders turned, looked and began to retch.

"No Menders, do not look!" Kaymar said roughly. "I'll deal with this." Hemmett mopped away the fluids as Kaymar lowered the blanket more, revealing the belt skewered to Katrin's sides. He pulled the rods out as quickly and gently as he could, repeated the cleaning and bandaging process, watching as Hemmett began to bathe the wounds on Katrin's breasts carefully, his face so enraged that he looked as if he was wearing a mask.

"Aidelia spit on those rods." Katrin spoke, her voice barely audible over the slapping of the hull on the waves and the noise of the engine.

Kaymar knew she was aware her sister had probably killed her.

Later, Kaymar was resting against the cabin wall after turning the lamp low, his eyes closed in exhaustion. Hemmett was asleep on the floor. In the silence, Kaymar heard Menders crawling over to Katrin. He pillowed her head on his lap, leaning over her.

Menders began to speak softly, his voice no more than a whisper.

"Once upon a time, the Dark Knight found his beloved Princess injured and tangled in a terrible spiderweb. He cut the Princess free and removed the cruel needles that bound her to the trap. He cleaned her wounds with magical water and bound them up in clean linen."

Kaymar flinched. He was familiar with the fairy stories Menders had told Katrin from babyhood, about the Dark Knight and the Princess he had raised as a daughter. They were Menders' own inventions, based on their lives at The Shadows.

"I will take you back to the beautiful, safe place at the top of the world where I brought you up," said the Dark Knight, after the Princess' wounds were dressed. "I will take care of you until you are well and strong again."

"But the Dark Knight's heart was broken. He had failed the Princess and had not kept the sacred vow he'd made when she was given to him so many years before, that he would never let her come to harm…"

Kaymar sank his teeth into his lower lip, hearing Menders' voice shaking and then failing him. He knew Menders thought he was asleep and wouldn't hear. He fought to keep his breath even and steady, fought the sobs that rose in his throat.

"Oh, my baby," Menders gasped, the pain in his voice almost more than Kaymar could bear. "My baby." He said no more.

Kaymar was thankful the cabin was dark, so the tears running down his cheeks couldn't be seen.

THE SHADOWS, MORDANIA

2
THE RED BEAST CALLED RAGE

"The wounds themselves are largely superficial," Franz said. "No internal organs were pierced; no bones were broken. The problem is infection." He had just examined Katrin again, four days after their return from Erdahn.

Menders sat silently, exhausted. Eiren took his hand and he held on tightly. His guilt was endless and deep and though it had been days now, he could not break free of it.

Katrin – he hadn't kept her safe and this horrible thing had been done to her.

"I'm going to keep the infected sites open, so they can drain. She's strong and young, which is in her favor. She's never been seriously ill except for her bout with putrid fever. I'm wagering that she will survive, but it's going to be a struggle. I will do everything I know of to fight the infection."

Menders nodded. He knew about infection, far too well after the issues he'd had with his eyes. It could be beaten, yes, but he also knew that infection, even of relatively small wounds, killed people every day. Katrin's wounds were deep. At this point all thirty-eight of them were septic.

"I have sent a message to the Queen, to the effect that Katrin is seriously ill because of these injuries," Franz went on.

"Hemmett?" Menders asked wearily, his voice an agonized croak. The savage scream that erupted from him when he first saw Katrin hung like a slaughtered animal had torn one of his vocal cords

Franz shook his head.

"Very unstable. Furious, wants revenge. If we prevent him from seeing her, he'll get worse, but he becomes irrational when he does see her. It will take time."

Hemmett was tortured. He prowled constantly and could not sleep. He would rant to anyone who would listen that he was going to kill the Queen, he was going to kill Aidelia. Borsen and Villison were making sure he spoke only to them. The things he said would mean an instant death sentence, not only for him, but for the entire household as well. Franz had advised confining him, but Menders couldn't bring himself to do it.

Initially he'd hoped he could have Hemmett go to Luntigré in Samorsa, but as the depth of Hemmett's instability became clear it was obvious he couldn't be trusted not to try to get to the Palace instead.

"I've heard from Kaymar," Menders rasped. "The Queen is off the wine again, apparently trying to stay sober. Threw a fit that Katrin was gone."

"My letter will put an end to that," Franz said coldly.

"Franz, what else can we do?" Eiren asked.

"We need to continue constant nursing," Franz said. "You, of course. Borsen – he's very good with her and with nursing in general. He's able to stay in control of himself. Varnia, Zelia and Petra are good too. Katrin needs to see as much of people as she can bear, to keep her spirits up. This includes Hemmett, but he will have to be spoken to about his demeanor. He upset her the last time he visited her."

The room was silent. Franz continued.

"Katrin has begun to run a fever. We will have to watch to be sure it doesn't go too high. I have cut down my practice entirely, so I will be here at all times."

Menders leaned against Eiren, who put her arms around him.

He was exhausted. He'd barely slept since Katrin had been carried into the house and he spent most of his time by her side.

He had also brought together all of Hemmett's Guard, Kaymar's and Menders' Men, as well as the estate farmers and their families. He had given his orders.

They were on high alert, with extra watches and patrols. Every man on the place was doubly armed, with instructions to shoot first, ask questions later. Pairs of Menders' Men were patrolling the district on horseback, ready to raise the alarm if any sign of a force from the Palace was seen.

Menders fully expected a garrison to be sent after them. He had removed Katrin from the Palace without permission or notice. It would be considered an execution offense. He was sure it wasn't a matter of if a force was sent to The Shadows, but when.

He was done with obeying the Queen in any way. If soldiers came, they would be fought, down to the last man and woman on The Shadows. All the Men and all the estate farmers knew their Princess had been tortured and was near death. They were prepared to fight viciously to defend her against further harm.

An eerie stillness descended over the estate. Necessary summer work was going on, but the usual warm weather symphony of children playing, music being made, and laughter was silenced. Farm women were seen with gun belts buckled on over their aprons. The farmers carried rifles with them while they were in the fields. Everyone was watchful. Everyone waited for the next report on the Princess, who was confined to bed, shivering with fever and pale to the lips.

"I need to get back to her," Menders whispered, embracing Eiren briefly, then rising and leaving the room. He went up the stairs, cursing at his legs, which shook from weariness.

Borsen was sitting with Katrin, cooling her forehead with a cloth dipped in cold water. Katrin's fever was obviously rising.

"Uncle, please get some rest," Borsen said gently.

"I can't," Menders answered honestly, leaning over the bed. Katrin opened her eyes and somehow managed a smile.

"I'll get some more water," Borsen yielded the chair he'd been sitting in to Menders, who sank into it gratefully. Menders reached out, catching Borsen around the waist with one arm.

"Stay with me, my boy," Menders whispered, needing Borsen's calm presence.

Borsen leaned against him, an arm around his shoulders.

***

From Doctor Franz's files –

Captain Hemmett Greinholz

Patient continuing extremely mentally unstable, showing signs of obsession, possibly even delusion. No-one has seen him sleep and he barely takes enough food to sustain himself. He will speak in circles, going over and over plans he is making to kill the Queen and Princess Aidelia.

Having known Hemmett almost all of his life, I am aware of the underlying instability in his nature. He has a deep-seated sense of inferiority which evolved, I believe, from being raised with Katrin. His childhood difficulties with learning to read and write were in direct opposition to her abilities. Katrin has always learned with phenomenal ease while Hemmett, though as intelligent as she is, had a terrible time mastering academics.

Unfortunately, due to their closeness and isolation at The Shadows, where there were few other childhood companions available, Hemmett developed romantic feelings for Katrin early on, complicated by his early physical maturation. Though they were separated a good part of the time by his attendance at the Military Academy, the feeling on his side has never entirely been resolved. Katrin does not show the same attraction, though she loves him dearly and is, to a degree, rather dependent on him.

The trauma of the last few weeks has almost entirely unhinged this fine young man, and there is little I can do for him. I have remonstrated with Menders to confine him and possibly send him to the villa in Surelia for a while to get him away from the situation, to no avail. Menders is barely thinking rationally himself. Katrin is deathly ill and may yet sicken more and die.

It is at times like that that I realize how very useless much of medicine is. There are no answers. I can only put out the fires as they occur, to the best of my ability and do all I can to prevent two men who are dear to me destroying themselves through unfounded guilt.

Galanth, have mercy on us all.

***

Eiren bent over Katrin, feeling her forehead, thankful that she was sleeping soundly. It had become difficult for her to rest as her wounds swelled and became painful. The fever wasn't very high at the moment, though it would undoubtedly climb as the night went on. It invariably did.

Eiren turned toward Menders, who was asleep on the floor beside Katrin's bed.

She knelt, reached for a pillow and eased it under his head while whispering to him, so he wouldn't be startled and wake suddenly. At least he was asleep.

I must insist he have a mattress in here, Eiren thought, looking sadly at her adored husband, stroking his long silky hair. He'd tried sleeping in their bed but was so restive and had such terrible dreams that he'd given up. He would collapse beside Katrin's bed when he could sit up no longer. Perhaps if he slept more, his mind would swing more in the balance.

She stroked his cheek. A faint smile passed over his lips. She rose and left the room.

As she had expected, Hemmett was standing silently at the end of the lounge, silhouetted against the window. He watched from it constantly. Though Eiren could not be afraid of him, she was wary. He startled easily and when he did, it was a guessing game as to what emotion might be elicited.

He was looking at her, so she could approach him without fearing that she would come on him unawares.

"Hemmett, could you rest on the sofa for a while? Katrin's asleep and doing well."

"I'll sleep later, thanks," Hemmett replied, his voice emotionless. He looked back out the window, staring at the blooming moonlit orchard below.

"Can I get you something – water, something to eat?" Eiren asked, feeling desperate. Hemmett was growing gaunt. He barely ate, just as he barely slept.

"No thank you. I'll just stay here a while. Go ahead and get some rest," he answered.

Eiren touched his arm gently before going to her own room. She stretched out on her bed and closed her eyes wearily.

How was she going to help them? Menders, Hemmett – both in torment, torn by guilt and anguish. Poor Katrin, sick unto death, growing quieter and weaker every day as the infection coursed through her.

If she had any tears left, Eiren would have wept.

***

"He was coming up the road."

Kaymar kept his voice carefully controlled, standing behind the Royal Messenger he'd waylaid and brought to Menders. "He has a letter directed to you."

It was obvious the man was terrified. Menders kept telling himself the poor bastard had nothing to do with what had happened. He rubbed his eyes, which felt as if they'd been poured full of ground glass, and took the envelope the trembling messenger proffered.

"Get him off the place and wait to see he doesn't try to come back," Menders directed roughly, glaring at the messenger, who looked ready to faint. "There will be no answer to this message to be carried back by you. I'll use my own courier," he told the man. "Don't return here for any reason."

"No sir."

Kaymar accompanied the messenger out, closing the door of Menders' office behind them.

Menders put the envelope on his desk and steeled himself. He fully expected it to be an order to return Katrin to Court or to appear himself to face execution for removing her without permission.

If only he could take Katrin away, out of Mordania! They'd tried, very carefully bundling her up preparatory to transporting her to Surelia, but her suppurating wounds had opened when Hemmett and Ifor lifted her onto a stretcher. She'd bled so badly that Franz ordered them to abandon the plan. If she remained quiet in her own bed, she had a chance of surviving, albeit a slender one. Being moved would kill her.

If this is a summons to bring her, I'll go myself in secret and kill every one of them, Menders thought, picking up the envelope and breaking the seal.

Lord Stettan,

It is with regret that we have been informed Princess Katrin is so seriously ill. It is our hope she will improve with time and request that frequent reports of her condition and prognosis be forwarded to the Palace.

At present, until the Princess' condition is improved, the Succession will remain unchanged. We command you to do everything in your power to take care of her and keep her safe.

H.M. Morghenna VIII

Menders felt his mind collapse inwardly, spiraling down into darkness. His hand crushed the letter, the heavy wax seal shattering in his grip.

"I *was* taking care of her and keeping her safe!" he roared, flinging the letter from him, ripping his knife out of its sheath on his belt. "I've done it from the night she was born, you unnatural bitch! I always kept her safe until you butchered her!"

He felt his throat tearing again but didn't care, determined to go, now, get to Erdahn, get to the Queen, tear her throat out and then go on to her demented elder daughter and gut her like a fish!

Ifor burst into the office, followed by Franz. Ifor managed to catch the wrist of Menders' knife hand. Menders fought like a langhur to get away, roaring at the absent Morghenna VIII, pouring out his hatred for her and Aidelia. Franz had his other arm and was shouting over him, trying to make his words heard.

"Menders, stop! Katrin can hear you! Her room is right above us!"

"Give me the knife, Menders!" Ifor shouted, taking cuts on his hands and wrists as they grappled.

"That bitch is commanding me to keep Katrin safe!" Menders ranted. "I kept her safe! I kept her safe all her life until that drunken monster ordered her over there and tore her to pieces! I always kept her safe!"

"Yes, you did," Franz said, still fighting with him. "Stop, Menders, Katrin will hear you!"

Eiren ran in and stopped short, her eyes wide with horror. Menders felt blood gushing from his mouth, but didn't care. He didn't care about anything except killing Queen Morghenna VIII and Princess Aidelia. Ifor pounded on his wrist, trying to numb it so Menders would drop the knife. Ifor was finding out just what was involved in disarming the best assassin in the world.

"Let me go, you bastards!" Menders bellowed, madly twisting in their arms, pulling free of Franz and then struggling with all his strength against Ifor's grip.

There was a loud snap. Menders heard his knife fall to the floor an instant before the pain stopped him in his tracks. Ifor kicked the knife away and wrapped his arms around Menders, holding him fast.

"Be still now!" the big man commanded. Menders had no choice. His entire right shoulder and arm burned as if they were on fire.

Eiren stepped forward, swept up a framed picture from his desk and held it before his eyes.

"Menders!" she commanded. "Look!"

He did. It was the sketch he had made years ago, when Katrin was only three. He'd taken her for a ramble to the Giants and lifted her into the enormous stone hand that thrust up from the soil. Katrin laughed with delight and his pencil caught the moment. The sketch had been on his desk ever since, flanked with two other sketches, Hemmett and Borsen, both in the same stone hand.

Menders drew in a deep, rasping breath and stood completely still, Ifor's arms still around him.

"Your shoulder is dislocated," Franz said behind him. "I want you to sit down and let me put it back into joint. The sooner we do it, the easier it will be. Sit down, Menders. Your chair is right behind you. Sit down."

Eiren sank down into Katrin's chair across the desk from Menders, still holding the framed sketch. Ifor guided him down into his own chair. Then Franz had a hand under his arm while Ifor held him still. There was a steady, agonizing pull and a sickening sliding, crunching feeling as his arm went back into joint.

"Done," Franz said gently, suddenly removing the knife Menders wore in a sheath at the back of his trousers. "How many more of these do you have on you?"

"Please don't take my knives," Menders said, staring at the sketch.

"Menders, you are not in your right mind," Franz said very deliberately and firmly. "After what has just happened, I can't trust you with weapons. I'm sorry. I know you're the Head of Household here, but I'm your doctor. In this matter, I am overriding you. Ifor is going to take your knives for now. If you fight, I will put your arm back out of joint."

Menders looked at Eiren.

"Please – Eiren, don't let them do this," he whispered desperately.

"Leave them! You may as well cut pieces out of his flesh," she said sharply to Franz, standing abruptly. "He's all right now. He's back to himself. Please leave us."

Franz began protesting but the look Eiren leveled at him reduced him to silence. Ifor relaxed his grip on Menders' shoulders and stepped back.

"Leave us," Eiren said again, taking the knife from Franz. The two men obeyed her, though Menders could see Franz was reluctant to do so. Eiren closed the door behind them and shot the bolt before she bent and retrieved the knife Menders had dropped in his struggle with Ifor.

She came around the desk, secured the knife in the sheath at the back of his trousers, then replaced the knife he'd taken from his side sheath.

"There darling, there are your knives," she said gently, kneeling and putting her hands on his arms. "I won't let anyone take them."

Menders, ignoring the pain in his right shoulder, threw his arms around her and held onto her desperately. She held him close, her head nestling under his chin.

After a moment, the tears he'd held back since the night he brought Katrin home finally came, running down into Eiren's beautiful red hair.

***

"Menders, you need to get up to the battle room now," Villison said, coming into Menders' office abruptly and closing the door behind him.

Menders looked up wearily. "Why?" he asked.

"Hemmett's got the rest of Katrin's Guard up there, working out a plan to go to Erdahn to kill the Queen," Villison replied.

Menders rose immediately. "Come with me."

They went quietly up the three flights of stairs to the top floor, where Tomar and Borsen's workshop and the planning room, also privately known as the battle room, were. Menders saw the door of the tailor shop open. Borsen looked out, making signs to indicate that he'd wedged the battle room door shut from the outside.

Menders listened, able to hear Hemmett's voice, muffled but clear, through the door.

"There's a passageway not marked on this plan, right about here. It leads to Bartan's rooms. We'd be able to reach any part of the Palace from there. The Royal Apartments are here, not far. The Guard there is pathetic, toy soldiers, slackest bastards I've ever seen. We could do it in ten minutes, kill the Queen and Aidelia and be out again …"

Menders silently worked a pick in the lock. He could see from the light shining around the door that Hemmett did not have the bolt down, an absolute indication of his unhinged mental state. Exploding through the door was not the answer. Hemmett and half the men in the room would react instantly and kill him before they knew who he was.

He nudged the weighted chair Borsen had placed under the doorknob aside, making as much noise as he could. He twisted the doorknob slowly and stepped into the battle room.

The men surrounding Hemmett looked up as one, startled, with guilty faces. Hemmett stood at the end of the table, leaning on his hands. His eyes were hollow, and in their depths, mad. His face had grown skull-like in the two months of Katrin's illness. Even a man as large as Hemmett would eventually grow gaunt without sufficient food.

Menders reached through the cluster of men, snatching up the plans of the Palace in one fist and crumpling them into a ball, which he handed behind him to Villison.

"No." he said fiercely.

The soldiers stepped back a pace, avoiding his eyes. Hemmett began to stare him down.

"Hemmett, order your men out of this room," Menders directed.

Hemmett did not move. His eyes glittered in the lamplight.

"Don't make me give the order myself. This is your command," Menders continued after a long thrumming silence. "Tell them to go with Villison."

Hemmett continued glaring from beneath his brows, his breath noisy in the room.

"Command them now, my son, or I will," Menders stared back at Hemmett.

Hemmett blinked and then spoke defeatedly.

"Go with Villison, men. Stay there until further notice."

"Come on, lads," Villison added softly.

Hemmett's Guard filed silently from the room. Villison closed the door behind them, leaving Menders and Hemmett alone.

"Do you have any idea what you're doing?" Menders said, his voice like a diamond file.

"I'm going to kill them both," Hemmett responded, his voice cold.

"If you do that you will push this country into anarchy!" Menders answered fiercely. "Katrin would become Queen. Since she is unfit physically, there would be a scramble as to what cousin to put on the Throne! The next in line is only twelve years old, which would lead to her father being Regent. He wouldn't hesitate to eliminate Katrin, as she would have a stronger claim on the Throne. Carry out this plan and you kill Katrin. She will live if we're careful but if you carry through with this madness, she is certain to be murdered!"

Hemmett said nothing. He continued leaning on the table, his arms like tree trunks. Menders could feel hatred and madness radiating from the younger man. His own mind began moving toward the red fury that was Hemmett's.

Menders turned away and walked across the room.

"I have been mad with this too, Hemmett," he said softly, his throat still stiff and painful. "I want them dead. I want to have them helpless and terrified and kill them slowly. I want to enjoy every minute of inflicting every torment I can devise on them. Everything you are feeling, I have already felt and still feel now."

He turned back to the young man and saw that his expression had changed ever so slightly, away from the distorted face of rage.

"But like you, I have a sacred duty to something more precious than satisfying my desire to destroy them," he continued gently, as if he was explaining something to the little boy who had come to The Shadows with him. "Katrin. You and I, all her life, have been taking care of her. We must continue to do so. If you go to Erdahn and do this now, it will be the end of everything, your life, hers, everyone's here."

Hemmett began to sag, then collapsed on a chair. Menders walked slowly back toward him, until he stood beside him.

"You must let this desire to kill them go," he said softly. "It's understandable. It's even laudable, but you are a well-disciplined soldier. As your superior officer I am ordering you to let it go. You can put it out of your mind if you allow yourself to do so."

Hemmett shook his head but Menders saw it was the gesture of a stubborn child. Hemmett had been a very stubborn child and Menders had learned how to deal with him long ago.

"You must, for Katrin's sake. Franz expects her to live, though she will be very sick for a long time. We have to begin again, Hemmett. It's hard to do, but we can. I have done it before. Things will never be exactly the same but there is still a life with her so long as you sacrifice your desires to assure her safety."

Hemmett was determinedly keeping his face turned away. Menders could see the spasm in his jaw as he fought for control.

"Go ahead and cry," Menders said firmly. "I've seen men cry before. It doesn't frighten me. I've cried over what they've done to our girl."

Hemmett managed two more long, trembling breaths before the weight of the agony he carried became more than he could bear. Menders was relieved as the terrible sound of a big man weeping tore through the room. Hemmett slumped forward on the table and sobbed violently.

After a moment he twisted toward Menders, wrapping his arms around Menders' waist, hiding his face in Menders' shirt front. Menders put his hands on the big shoulders and let Hemmett cry, saying not a word.

Soon the words started jerking out of Hemmett. His confusing and conflicted love for Katrin. His guilt over feeling it while he also loved Luntigré. His rage with himself over his failure to protect Katrin from what had been done to her. The guilt for that failure that was eating away at his sanity.

He finally stopped speaking, but still held tight to Menders.

"I have always known you love Katrin beyond a brotherly affection," Menders said simply. He felt Hemmett flinch in surprise.

"You knew I love her?" he whispered.

"Since you were children," Menders answered, his voice soft.

"And you let me stay here?"

"You went to military school. That helped you, because you met other people and weren't always with her," Menders replied, reaching behind him and pulling over a chair. He settled in it, close to Hemmett, who leaned against him as if he had no strength left.

"I love Luntigré dearly," Hemmett said brokenly. "But she and I both acknowledge that it isn't the great love of our lives. I thought for a while that it had taken away my love for Katrin. I was wrong. I can't leave The Shadows and her or any of the rest of you, even though I thought I could when I was so angry with her in Artreya."

"I have always understood this, Hemmett. I've admired your self-control and wished that things could be otherwise," Menders responded gently, pulling two handkerchiefs from his pocket when Hemmett exhausted his own.

"I'm sorry – about all this," Hemmett finally said.

"No harm done, thank the gods. You have a good second in Vil, Hemmett. I've never said so, and that was wrong. Your judgement is good."

Hemmett, despite his severe emotional exhaustion, managed a look of pride. "Thank you," he said quietly.

"Now, as you know, I am assigned as your commanding officer," Menders said. "I've never observed that, of course. I consider your Guard your command and yours alone – but as your commanding officer and your foster father, I am ordering you to begin taking care of yourself. I'm ordering you to eat. I'm ordering you to sleep. Katrin asks for you every day. It would do her a world of good to have her closest friend with her. Can you do this for her?"

"Yes," Hemmett said, straightening up.

"Whenever the other thoughts come into your mind, put them away from you. Don't give them a chance to take over. It will be difficult at first, but it can be done."

"How do you know this?" Hemmett asked honestly.

"I have the same thoughts. I have had similar thoughts all my life, because of events in my past. You have a choice. You can let your anger eat you alive and destroy you, or you can put it aside and refuse it room in your mind. With your self-discipline, you can do this. I have every confidence in you."

"Franz thinks she'll live?" Hemmett said after a long silence.

"Yes, he told me so today. She's still septic, and will be for a long time. She's constantly running a high fever, but she is not getting worse. Some of the smaller wounds are trying to heal. Her body is fighting the infection. She needs rest, support and most of all, peace of mind. She is so close to you, Hemmett, that she can tell when you're angry and it upsets her. You must, for her sake, control your mind."

Hemmett nodded and looked resolute.

"I will," he said. "I'd rather march forty miles in the snow, but I will."

"I know it. I know my first boy very well," Menders said, managing a smile. "Now, do you want me to talk to your men?"

Hemmett shook his head and stood, seeming surprised to find himself unsteady on his feet.

"No, I'll explain to them. This will go no further," he replied. He straightened his great spine, drew in a deep breath, then another. He went to the door, properly upright, once again an officer.

"Thank you, Papa," he said very softly before he turned the knob and left the battle room. Menders could hear him walking down the corridor and starting down the stairs, on his way to the Guard Room.

Menders sat wearily at the table, spent. He'd been methodically forcing himself to eat and sleep. Eiren had insisted a mattress be put down in Katrin's room so he could sleep when he stayed by her at night, but his body was still run down.

A small sound let him know Borsen had come in. A moment later the small but strong hands were on his shoulders, easing his knotted muscles. Menders closed his eyes and let the young man minister to him.

"Thank you for wedging that door," he said after a while.

"I wasn't about to let him out to begin a bloody rampage," Borsen answered. "He would have had to go through me."

Menders smiled a little.

"You know, I don't believe he would have gotten past you," he said. People dismissed Borsen as a physical presence because of his small stature, but Menders knew his strength – and his indomitable spirit. If he'd been determined to stop Hemmett, stop him he would – by any means.

Menders sighed and prepared to rise. He found Borsen was holding him in the chair, pressing down on his shoulders.

"Stay a while, Uncle," the cadenced voice said softly behind him, the Thrun emphasis very heavy. "Just rest for a while. Rest."

Menders did.

***

Darling Luntigré,

I am so very sorry that I haven't written to you. Eiren told me she let you know what has happened, so I won't go through it all again.

I have been very ill in my mind, but I'm getting better now. Being so close to Katrin, seeing her like that was – I can't talk about that.

If I may, I would like to come and see you and Flori, if you will have me. I might not be the most fun fellow, but I love you both so much and I miss you.

Katrin is improving, everyone else is well and they all send love.

Hem

Dearest Hemmett,

You never need to ask. Come when you can, and I will be glad.

Luntigré

***

My dear Menders,

There is nothing I can say that will be of much comfort or use to you at this time, but I so wanted to let you know that my heart breaks for Katrin and the rest of you. If it would be a help and not a hindrance, I will come to The Shadows and lend a hand. Please let me know.

You must care for yourself, Aylam. I have seen Luntigré and she's told me of Hemmett's illness. Your children need you, my dear friend. You must find your strength again, for them.

Gladdy D.

SARONILLA, SAMORSA
THE SHADOWS, MORDANIA

3
WILLOW

Hemmett rose from the sofa in Luntigré's beautiful living room and paced again.

He wasn't even aware he was doing it, Luntigré thought. His mind was back at The Shadows, as it had been on all his visits to Samorsa since Katrin had been tortured.

Luntigré shuddered when she thought of it. She and Katrin had become close friends during the time the family waited in Samorsa until the latest dingdong between Mordania and Artreya was over. Luntigré loved Katrin's spirit and enthusiasm and she loved her devotion to Hemmett. Lovers might come and go from Hemmett's life, but he had a friend whose love would always ring true.

Hemmett turned away from the view outside, which he had already studied at least twenty times that evening and caught Luntigré looking at him. He ducked his head slightly in embarrassment and smiled.

"I'm sorry, darling," he said. "I'm a long way away."

"Does our love still bring you joy, Hemmett?" she asked. His eyes met hers, steady and true.

"It does," he answered.

"Then we go on," Luntigré smiled.

***

Katrin sat up against her pillows, slowly undoing her long braid. She was preparing to have her hair properly washed. She'd been getting by for months with Eiren brushing powder through it or only washing her scalp. She felt absolutely filthy. It would be wonderful to finally have her hair clean and gleaming again.

It was early spring. Almost a year had turned, the summer, autumn and winter since she was Suspended lost in a haze of illness, fever and pain. She had no recollection of days passing for much of that time, only of burning with fever, shivering with chills, crippled by pain and weakness.

It was only in the last week that she had not been continually feverish. She'd had to learn to be philosophical about fever. Franz told her it was the body's way of fighting infection, literally burning it away. She was still infected but some of her wounds were healing. Franz said she was getting better, but that is would be a very slow process.

The infections had turned inward, and Katrin had been low most of the autumn with infection in her lungs, only to have her womb become infected as soon as her lungs cleared. Franz believed the infection was traveling through her blood, affecting different organs. Katrin had taken so many blood cleansing medicines that she'd joked to Franz that she should just start eating some of the soap she'd made. He laughed heartily and told her if that was the cure, he'd have tried it long ago, that the only answer was to do everything she could to strengthen her body and let nature do the healing.

Nature was taking a long time and as for strengthening her body – it seemed impossible. She wasn't wasted, she was wizened. Her skin hung slackly from her arms and legs, wrinkled because she had lost so much weight. It was still difficult for her to eat and she could only manage small amounts at a time. Smooth soft foods were the most she could manage and not much of them. When she got out of bed she was very shaky, but got up as often as she could, so her flabby leg muscles would strengthen.

Eiren tapped at the door and came in, smiling brightly, several bottles in her hands and a basin under her arm.

"All ready?" she asked. "Do you want to commence operations there in bed or come over to the dressing table?"

"Oh, the table, too much trouble in the bed," Katrin replied, swinging around so she could use the bedstairs. Eiren swathed her in her warmest dressing gown and helped her sit at the dressing table. Katrin made a face at herself in the mirror.

"The face of ill health," she pronounced, making Eiren smile.

"Nonsense. You'll fatten up soon. And with your bones, your face will never be anything but lovely, at any weight," she replied, loosening the rest of Katrin's braid. "What this needs is a very good brush out before we wash it. Then you can move over to the window and let it dry in the sun. It's a beautiful day. It's warm early this year."

It had been an unusually warm winter, rain more than snow, even this far north. Katrin had been sorry, because the Thrun hadn't been able to come. Though she could never have attended the Thrun carnival outside, she would have been overjoyed to see Tharak and Thira. The early spring days were quite warm, and the trees were rushing to come into bloom.

Eiren picked up the hairbrush, taking the first long strand in her hand. Using short strokes to smooth any tangles, she worked her way up the five foot strand. Then she brushed down from Katrin's scalp with a full stroke. Katrin relaxed, glad they were finally started.

Eiren made a strange noise. Katrin looked at her in the mirror. Eiren's face was white and she was staring at the hairbrush. A long strand of Katrin's hair, at least a handful thick, hung from it.

Katrin's eyes flew to her own reflection. There was a large bald spot on the left side of her head, where Eiren had started brushing. She raised a hand to it curiously, pulling gently at the hair surrounding it. There was an odd sensation as the hair came away as easily as pulling a weed from wet soil.

Katrin felt very distant, as if she was standing across the room watching as she reached up to the other side of her head and gently tugged another handful of hair away.

"Katrin, don't!" Eiren cried. "Menders!"

Suddenly Menders was there. He looked at Eiren, who showed him the brush full of hair and then turned to Katrin, who was dreamily lifting more hair out of her scalp.

"Look, it just comes right out," she said, looking at the strands of golden hair in her hand.

"Don't!" Menders cried, catching her hands, keeping her from lifting them to her scalp again. "Get Franz," he said to Eiren, who dropped the hairbrush and rushed from the room.

Menders was saying something about this sometimes happening when fevers went on for a long time, but Katrin really didn't hear. She was studying the hairbrush, with so much of her hair ensnared in it.

"Ho there, Willow!" Hemmett spoke in the lounge of the suite. Then he was in the doorway of her room, come after his shift to visit with her, as he did every day. He smiled, and she smiled back dreamily in the mirror.

"My hair is all coming out," she said in a voice that sounded like a small child's. "See?" She plucked another strand from her head with slow precision, as Menders shuddered and reached to hold her hands still.

Hemmett covered his mouth with his hands and burst into howls of agony, staring at the fallen golden hair.

***

"I'd hoped to avoid this and thought we'd gotten away with it," Franz said wearily to Menders and Eiren. Katrin had been put to bed after a dose of ramplane, though she was eerily calm and kept on pulling her hair out until she fell asleep, making quiet remarks about how odd it was. She almost sounded cheerful.

"I had noticed her hair was shedding a bit," he continued. "That's not to be surprised at, considering how long she's had the high fevers. Many people tend to shed in the springtime anyway."

"I noticed the last time I helped her with it that she lost quite a bit, but I didn't worry. When hair is as long as hers, just a few strands coiling up in the brush looks like all the hair on her head is coming out," Eiren said. She was pale. "What frightens me is the way she's acting. If she'd cried or screamed, I would understand, but that little girl's voice and the way she just kept pulling it out …"

"Shock," Franz said simply. "Katrin's been through so much, and has been so ill and still is – she will slip back into shock very easily. It's almost a cushioning influence. It protects her from the import of what is happening. Her fairytale hair has always been a very large part of her identity. Having it suddenly come out is an incredible trauma. Her mind is shutting it off."

"What about her hair?" Menders asked, feeling cold and sick.

"It's all coming out," Franz said, his voice shaking for the first time. "Even if she doesn't pull at it, all the follicles have stopped producing hair because of the long fever. In most cases the hair grows back after a while – in almost all cases. It's the same as her recovery. We need to get her body as healthy as possible. That will give her the best chance of her hair growing back."

"She isn't even over the infection yet!" Menders exclaimed. Franz sighed.

"No, she isn't, and she won't be for a long time to come," he replied. "Menders, Katrin is very fortunate to be alive at all. She survived only because of the very healthy and active life she has led here. Anyone else would not have survived the first day, not after what happened to her."

Menders closed his eyes.

"I know. I'm sorry, my friend. It's just so painful, after everything else," he muttered.

"Yes, insult to injury."

"What about Hemmett?" Eiren asked.

"Sleeping. I knocked him out with some ramplane," Franz answered. "Look, we all know what has been going on with Hemmett about Katrin since they were children. He's always idealized her as a sort of fairytale princess, complete with the beautiful golden hair. The fact that she will always be out of his reach romantically complicates matters, because it only strengthens the idealization. That is what was behind his extended and extreme anger with her in Artreya. She turned out to be a normal girl after all, not the princess on the pedestal he's always considered her. Add his extreme guilt over not protecting her from being tortured, even though that would not have been possible, and you have the recipe for a breakdown."

Menders nodded. It was true. As a boy, Hemmett made excuses to touch Katrin's hair, sometimes would catch hold of a strand of it and simply hold it in his hand. Even the nickname he'd given her when they were tiny children, Willow, had to do with her hair. One day when they were small, he'd said she looked like a weeping willow tree in the autumn with the long golden strands flowing down around her.

"Good of you to put him in his old room in his parents' suite," Franz mused. "That way Menders' Men didn't hear him crying. It's bad enough that some of them consider him weak because of his madness after you brought her back from the Palace."

"They should be ashamed!" Eiren said fiercely. She stood abruptly. "He's been through hells, all of us have! Who are they to judge him as weak when it's because he loves her so much!"

"Shhh," Menders soothed her. "I'll speak with them."

"We must find a wigmaker right away, the best to be had," Eiren said, her voice still harsh and strained.

"Wouldn't it be better to wait and see if her hair comes back in? She could wear a scarf or cap…" Menders began. Eiren cut him off.

"No! She cannot be without hair, Menders. She's a young woman, not a man who can think nothing of shaving his head if it's hot in the summertime! I saved every bit that came out today. They'll be able to make a wig out of it, possibly two, because it was so long …" She shuddered and swallowed hard.

"I'll make inquiries first thing tomorrow," Menders put his arm around her waist. "You're right, my dear."

"I believe you are," Franz agreed. "Even if her hair comes in again right away, it will be a distraction. It would be far more cosmetic until she has a full head of hair again."

"How soon will we know about her hair?" Menders asked.

"When her condition improves," Franz answered.

Menders felt his heart sink. It would be a long time before Katrin's condition improved appreciably. There would be no miraculous rapid regrowth of Katrin's beautiful hair.

***

Darling Luntigré,

There is no easy way to put this, so I'll just bungle along in my usual way.

I've been thinking a great deal since Katrin's hair came out. I thought my mind had recovered after what happened to her at the Palace, but my reaction when her hair came out showed me that it has not. I'm sure you knew it, with me prowling and pacing around whenever I visited you.

You asked me once how things stood with Katrin and me and I told you the truth. I don't know if she's the great love, but I've always loved her.

I'm torn. I'm desperate to protect Katrin, to help her and take care of her. She's so sick. She needs my help. I want to take her far away where the Queen can never get to her again. I love her.

I love you. You make life beautiful and calm. I love Flori as my own daughter. When we're together, I'm so very happy.

I'm not asking you to decide for me, but I want to know your thoughts.

And yes, you bring me joy and I believe you always will. And Katrin does as well, but it's an entirely different and far more difficult joy.

Hem

Dearest Hemmett,

I have known for some time that you are torn between your life with your family and your life here with me. I also know that since Katrin was tortured, she needs you. She draws strength from you.

I do not know if Katrin is your great love, but I know that I am not. We have a wonderful love together, but I have had a great love and I know what it is.

If you find you have that great love with Katrin, I believe I would not disappear from your life. I know how you love Flori and I wouldn't want her to lose you. I would not want to lose you. But things would change. This might not be a bad thing, because I believe guilt – about Katrin and about me and about Flori – is adding to your illness of the mind.

Do not feel guilty over me. I have my life and my family here and I believe I will remain friends with your family whether we are lovers or friends. Is this not so?

You will not lose us if you decide things will change. You are always welcome here, darling Hemmett, as a lover or a friend. Never fear.

Your loving Luntigré

***

Katrin walked slowly across the Rose Garden and eased herself down on a bench, sighing a little as she took the weight off her shaky and unsteady legs.

A little farther each day, she thought. Two weeks ago, you couldn't have crawled out here, so don't get despondent and decide to give up.

Even though the sun was shining directly on her and it was a lovely warm summer day, she shivered a bit. She was thankful that her dress, made by Borsen to fit her much thinner figure, had long sleeves. Not only did they keep her warm now that her body seemed to be unable to, but they also covered the still-suppurating wounds on her arms – and kept her from smelling them as well.

She was drawn to anything fragrant – roses, lemon soap, scents that drowned the odor of her own infected body. Katrin had always kept very clean. Knowing her infected wounds smelled caused her more distress than almost anything – except for the nightmares of the sharp rods being driven deep into her body, of her hair coming out by the handful.

Her wounds were drained and washed innumerable times a day, but she still stank. There was no other word for it. It sickened her, and she knew others could smell it too. It was embarrassing and humiliating. Often when someone stopped by her room to visit, she pretended to be asleep, because she couldn't bear to see their determined cheerfulness in the face of the reek of pus and blood.

Franz kept assuring her that she was improving. Some of her wounds had finally healed completely, filling with healthy tissue. She didn't vomit very often now, and the fevers had dropped. There was no sign of her hair regrowing yet, but Franz said it could take quite a lot of time, not to be discouraged.

She had her wigs now. They looked natural because they were beautifully made, but she was always aware of them against her bare scalp. That was better than unexpectedly catching sight of her bald head in a mirror, or trying to hide the fact that she had no hair by having a scarf wrapped ineffectually around her head. She also didn't want to see how she had lost her looks, the gauntness, the shadowed eyes and pallid skin.

She was thankful she and Willem had finally called a halt to their on-again, off-again affair some time before she'd been ordered to the Palace. He was presently in Surytam, sniffing out some information for Kaymar. He wrote faithfully, but as a friend. She was glad he couldn't see her now and that she didn't have to try to be cheerful for him.

Enough, Katrin thought. This is being morbid and gloomy! That makes you worse and you know it. You're lucky to be alive and not crippled. Chances are once you get over this infection you'll look much better and your hair will grow back. All the doctors Franz has called in for consultation have said so. Don't concentrate on all that, concentrate on getting well.

She looked determinedly at the blooming roses. After a while, she felt the hunch go from her shoulders as her tense muscles relaxed. The sun was warm and Katrin breathed more easily. She closed her eyes and listened as Menders had taught her when she was small.

She began to hear the birds singing and in the distance, at Kindness Farm, cows lowing gently. Then she heard movement, someone walking across grass.

When she opened her eyes, she saw Hemmett coming toward her across the lawn, his face purposeful, his stride determined. She tried to get up, but knew she could never get back to the house in time.

It wasn't that she didn't want to see him. She didn't want to see him looking – and smelling – like this. Not after the weeks where he'd been desperate and half-mad about what had been done to her or how he'd howled in despair when her hair came out. He didn't need to see her sick and shaking. It was better if he visited her while she was in bed, with her skeletal body covered and her stinking wounds hidden.

It was too late, he was already there. He smiled, giving no indication that he could smell her. Maybe between the roses and the breeze he couldn't.

"Hello Willow," he said, bending and kissing her cheek. Then, to her amazement, he went down on one knee before her. She saw at that moment that he wasn't wearing Luntigré's ring.

No, she thought. No, please, don't do this. Don't do this to either of us. Don't do this to Luntigré.

"Katrin, there's no point in my pretending things are different any longer," he said, his words obviously chosen carefully. "I love you. I've tried for years to convince myself that it's all brotherly or between friends, but it is more. Marry me, Katrin. I'll take care of you. No-one will ever hurt you again." He reached out and took her hand, cradling it between his own. "Please Katrin."

For one mad moment, Katrin felt part of her mind urging her to accept him, to sink back in the softness of capitulation, to give her life over to him, to let him protect her forever and keep her safe. She closed her eyes.

They came. The Queens. An insistent whisper, not harsh, but intending to be heard.

"No. Not this man. This man is more than a lover, more than a brother. Other self. No. No. No!"

The voices came in overlapping surges, like waves on sand. Then harsh reality shrieked in Katrin's face.

She couldn't marry him, even if she wanted to. It would be certain death for him, gods knew what horror for her. Even if they ran away to another country, there would be the endless fear of pursuit, a price on their heads, no moment of peace for the rest of their lives.

And she didn't want to marry him. She didn't want to marry anyone. She loved Hemmett. He'd always been there, her friend and brother, someone she could confide in, someone she could laugh with. Even more – it was as if he was part of herself. He had been wonderful since he'd come to his senses after what had been done to her. He'd visited her every single day and kept her occupied and laughing in spite of the pain and illness.

But marriage and all it entailed? No. She couldn't do it, couldn't let him have her body, because she did not and could not ever love him that way. Making love to Hemmett was as impossible in her mind as making love to Menders would be – impossible, abominable. Even though Hemmett was beautiful and would be a considerate and sensitive lover, she could not even picture it in her mind.

And she was so sick now, constantly in pain from the internal infections caused by her wounds. The idea of letting a man, any man, make love to her was terrifying. She only wanted to be warm, to rest, to let her body heal. It had taken her a year to get this far. How long would it be before she would be able to be with a man again – if ever?

Above all, she knew her bald head repelled Hemmett. Every time he happened to see it, he blanched involuntarily. He tried to cover his dismay with big smiles and cheerfulness, but she could feel his revulsion. What if her hair never really grew back? How could she go through life married to someone who shuddered when he saw her bald head? It would be a continual reminder to Hemmett of what he believed was his failure to protect and care for her.

"We could go to Surelia," Hemmett continued, hope in his voice, as if he thought her silence meant she was tempted to accept him. "Or Samorsa, hells, even further if you want. We could inform the Palace that you died of your wounds and say you've already been buried. They won't look for you. You know Menders can arrange anything.

"Please, Willow, please marry me."

The tears Katrin was fighting began flowing. She was too weak to stop them. Hemmett's hands tensed around hers. He was not mistaking her weeping for tears of joy.

"I can't! I can't marry you because I can't love you that way!" she gasped. "We would never be safe or free. I could never be a wife to you, much as I love you, because you're my brother. I couldn't marry you any more than I could marry Menders because he's my father!"

All the tears Katrin had held back through the Ritual of Suspension, through the weeks of agony that followed, the months of illness and weakness, when her hair had come out that terrible afternoon – they were flowing now, running unchecked down her cheeks. She could no more have stopped them than she could have stopped the wind from blowing.

But Hemmett, his poor face white and bleak, his heart obviously breaking! And his mind, which had been made unstable by the shock of her ordeal and his guilt about it – what would this do to him?

Katrin almost took back the words, almost said she would marry him, almost asked him to forgive what she'd said and take her for his wife. Anything to make him happy and well in his mind again.

"No. No. No. You must not weaken. You must hold fast. He is your brother, your other self, No. No!"

The Queens' voices swelled again.

"I'm sorry. I'm so sorry my dear. I'm sorry Bumpy!" she gasped.

"No more," he whispered, patting her hands and putting them back in her lap. "I'm sorry too, Willow. I had thought… I was wrong." He rose quickly, walking away without another word, disappearing into the woods.

Katrin tried to stand, wanting to get back into the house, to her room, to her bed where she could sleep and rest and be warm. Her legs failed her. She sank back onto the bench again. She leaned forward with her head on her knees and wept.

***

Menders jumped in his chair as Villison burst into his office.

"You'd best get out into the Rose Garden to the Princess," he said abruptly, his breath coming short. He'd been on sentry duty on the roof and had obviously run all the way down.

"What is it? Why didn't you go to her yourself?" Menders barked, rising so quickly that his chair overturned.

"She's not hurt, not physical. Hemmett just went and asked her to marry him and she's refused him," Villison panted. "She's out there alone, he's gone off and she's beside herself crying. She don't need me, she needs you!"

Menders ran. As he burst out of the house, he saw Kaymar also racing into the Rose Garden and waved him back.

Katrin was on the bench furthest from the house. Seeing her huddled over her own knees, her dress growing wet from falling tears made Menders so angry that, at that moment, he could have killed Hemmett. Why now, when she was just starting to recover and was so weak and vulnerable? Why ask such a thing of her?

Katrin looked up as she heard him coming and had her arms out, as she would do when she was tiny and had some small hurt or fear. Menders was on the bench beside her, folding her in his arms, hoping that somehow, he could make this newest pain go away. She clung to him, her face buried against his shoulder.

"There now, little princess," he whispered, trying to keep his voice steady.

"I can't marry him!" she wailed.

"I know. If I had any idea he was going to do this, I would have kept him from it," Menders answered, rocking her slightly.

"I hurt him so!"

There it is, Menders sighed to himself. No wonder you're crying as if your heart was broken – because you've had to leave him with no hope. Oh, my little princess, sometimes I wish you were as hard as those women who can turn down sincere proposals and never lose a second's sleep over breaking a heart.

"Then that is the way it is," he said, knowing which horn of this dilemma to impale himself on, though his heart ached for Hemmett as well. "He will have to learn to live with that."

"So will I," Katrin whispered. "I almost said yes, just to make him happy, but I could have never slept with him, even if I wasn't ugly and bald and I didn't stink…"

And he thought you would take him because you need protection, Menders thought. Because at the end of it, Hemmett has never felt he was quite as good as everyone else, ever since that terrible struggle he had to learn to read and write. It doesn't matter that he's now stunningly handsome and desirable – he still sees himself as that awkward boy far too large for his age who made himself into a clown so that people would like him. The one who loved the fairytale princess with the long, golden hair. Oh, my poor children – both of you. You break each other's hearts and mine as well.

"All right then," he said, giving Katrin no indication of his inner musings. "It's over with for now."

"May I please go to bed?" she asked weakly. "I just want to rest."

"Of course," Menders answered, preparing to lift her. He had no problem doing so now because she had lost so much flesh.

"No, I'll walk. I need to walk out and back every day," Katrin quavered, starting to rise. He helped her up and kept an arm around her as she forced herself to take one step after another.

In the house Ifor was waiting at the foot of the stairs, and lifted Katrin to carry her up. She didn't protest, having expended every bit of energy she had.

***

"Nice job you just did, mate," Villison raged, bursting like a small swarthy whirlwind into the glade where Hemmett was sitting on the old swing he and Katrin used to play on, a cigar in his mouth.

Hemmett didn't react but Villison was spurred forward by his own fury.

"You've gone off and left her sitting there, sicker than a damn dog? What the hells is the matter with you, pestering her with something like this when she's so sick?"

Hemmett jumped up, his expression wildly startled. "Gods!" he cried, dropping his cigar into the leaves.

"A forest fire next? What other idiocy do you want to carry out today?" Villison roared, jumping on the smoldering cigar and stamping it out.

"Shut up, Vil!" Hemmett bellowed. The agony in his voice cut short Villison's tirade. He studied his friend closely and saw infinite pain.

"I'm sorry, Hem," he said. "Gods man, I'm sorry she wouldn't have you. Maybe when she's better…"

"No. It won't ever happen. It was better when I didn't allow myself to believe that it ever could," Hemmett answered. "I'd better get back there. Gods, I never thought I was leaving her there alone. I just had to get away."

"Menders went out to her, she's with him," Villison said.

"Doesn't matter. I've done the damage. I have to do what I can to mend it," Hemmett replied, hurrying away, leaving Villison to pick up the flattened cigar and shake his head.

***

Katrin reached up with the last of her strength and pulled off her wig. She couldn't bear it in bed yet, though the wigmaker had promised her scalp would toughen to it and she would be able to sleep in it. She handed it to Menders and drew the covers up high around her, hiding some of her baldness.

"Just rest now, little princess," Menders said gently, bending and kissing her cheek despite the covers. He set the wig on the stand. "Do you want me to stay?"

"No, I'm going to sleep," she answered, not wanting him to stay and see her cry more. Menders had been through so much since she was injured. He wasn't entirely well himself in either body or mind after all the months of being at her side every moment, consumed with guilt and rage.

"Best thing for you," he agreed with a fair attempt at heartiness. "I'll look in on you later." He went silently from the room.

Katrin turned her face into the pillows and let the tears flow.

***

Captain Hemmett Greinholz ran up the front steps of The Shadows and across the entryway to the stairs. When he reached the second story, he turned left, toward the suite where Katrin lived with Menders and Eiren.

Ifor was standing before the suite door and stepped in his way.

"No, Hemmett," he said. "Menders has just helped her to bed."

"This is not your business," Hemmett said fiercely.

"It is indeed. Katrin's had enough for one day," Ifor scowled.

"Stand aside, Lieutenant," Hemmett answered.

Ifor lasted for another thirty seconds, then sighed and turned away. Hemmett strode past him and knocked on the door of the suite before letting himself in.

Menders looked around from the window of the lounge.

"She's in bed," he said evenly.

"I would like to see her," Hemmett replied.

"No."

"This is between Katrin and me," Hemmett answered, holding his ground.

"Anything and everything concerning Katrin also concerns me." Menders held fast.

"Hemmett?" Katrin's voice called from the bedroom. Menders closed his eyes tiredly.

Hemmett went to her room and let himself in.

She was trying to reach for her wig, but he got to the bed before she could and took her hands in his. She had been crying and her face was wet.

"I'm sorry, Willow," he said. "I shouldn't have left you alone. That was very stupid of me."

"It's all right. I'm sorry too, that I can't be what you want," she said in a tiny voice, pulling a hand free and putting it on her bare head.

"Stop that," Hemmett said gently, "I've seen you without hair before, you know. I was alive before you was borned."

Katrin smiled at his repetition of his favorite childhood declaration, used whenever he wanted to boss her around. Suddenly Hemmett swooped her up from the bed, complete with her blankets, and held her close as if she was a child. He stepped over to her armchair and settled himself in it, refusing to contemplate the fact that he could lift her so easily now and how that had come to be.

He made her comfortable, cradling her on his lap and shoulder. He steeled himself to stroke her bald head, though even seeing it made him remember her lifting her hair out of her scalp, marveling in that strange soft voice about how easily it came away.

"I remember the very first time Menders trusted me enough to hold you," he said. "We'd been at The Shadows for about a week and I kept asking if I could hold you. He had me sit in an armchair like this and put you on my lap. Your head felt the same then, smooth and soft."

Suddenly her baldness wasn't so horrifying any more. He only felt regret that her beautiful hair was gone, not the revulsion that had gripped him whenever he'd caught a glimpse of her naked scalp.

He chatted to her about inconsequentials. Sometimes she would sleep for a few minutes, then wake and smile at him, content.

"I wanted to say yes," she finally ventured, as the light was growing low.

"I knew it. I felt it. I'm sorry you couldn't but you were right to tell me the truth," Hemmett responded, swallowing hard. He would not show her weakness again. He had done far too much of that since she was tortured. "We go on from here, Willow, just as Borsen always says. No point in trying to change what we can't."

"But what about Luntigré?" she asked.

"That's been sorted between Luntigré and me. I would never have done this without her consent. We understand each other and always will," Hemmett said with a touch of sternness. "Don't worry about us."

"I may not ever be able to be a wife to anyone," Katrin said, and she explained to him about the infection that had spread to her womb.

"I understand," he replied when she was finished. "But that wasn't why you said no."

"No. I don't love you that way, though I love you so very much. Even if I could sleep with you, I can't help feeling that it would be a terrible mistake," she sighed softly.

"Then there it is. Don't keep hashing it over, Willow. It hurts both of us. The sooner we put it away, the sooner we can go on."

"I do love you," Katrin said again.

"And I love you. Always have, always will, in whatever way you can accept. Now, enough."

"Aren't you getting tired holding me?"

"No. You aren't heavy. Do you want me to stop holding you?"

"No." She said it so emphatically that it made him laugh.

"Then don't make me think you do. Now, it's time for the flowers to start glowing, so stop worrying and watch with me." He helped her turn so she could see the orchard from the window, where the last of the light was dying, the long rays lighting the blooming trees so that each flower seemed to glow from within. They had watched for this effect when they were children and made up myths about the apparent lighting of the flowers being tiny creatures living inside them lighting their lamps for the night.

Katrin fell asleep once more. Hemmett gathered her closer, lowering his head to brush his lips against her forehead.

I'll always love you, he thought. I swear on everything I hold dear that I will always protect you, no matter what I have to do, no matter who I have to kill, no matter if I have to sacrifice my own life. I will never, ever, let you be unprotected or hurt again, Willow.

Never.

And I will help you get well. You're going to get well.

THE SHADOWS, MORDANIA

4
CAPTAIN GREINHOLZ'S REMEDY

Cook and Varnia were going over the week's menus when Hemmett breezed into the kitchen. At their request, he put on water for tea and while waiting for it to boil, made sandwiches and raided the cookie jars. An impromptu tea party assembled, he served the ladies and then sat down with them.

"Take a break from the menus and tell me what is in that food Franz is having Katrin eat," he invited.

"Not much to my way of thinking," Cook said defensively. "Mainly cereal, a little skimmed milk. Broth made from fish. It's supposed to keep her from feeling ill, but to my mind there's no nourishment to speak of." Cook lowered her voice conspiratorially. "I've been stirring an egg into the cereal while it's cooking and using cream instead of skimmed milk."

"Good for you," Hemmett said. "That doesn't sound very nourishing to me either."

Varnia shook her head.

"He showed us the recipes in a book about caring for invalids, but there's no provision for them recovering from being invalids," she said briskly.

Hemmett nodded. "I saw that same book. Just finished reading it. I think it's a crock of grundar turds."

"Language!" Cook said automatically, then flushed. "I'm sorry, Hemmett, I do forget you children are all grown now."

"Queen of the Kitchen, you may tell me to watch my language whenever you wish," Hemmett laughed. "This is your domain – and I'm going to ask if we can conduct an experiment here."

"Nothing that will explode," Cook said quickly, remembering various past events.

"Nothing that will explode. Something that I'm sure will make Katrin start getting well again."

"What?" Varnia asked, her eyes flashing as she looked at him.

"We're going to find a way to start giving her real food," Hemmett answered. "Starting with Seven Spice Soup. She's hardly eating anything because she has no appetite, but who would want to eat that invalid stuff? Better to use it to put wallpaper up."

"Have you talked to Doctor?" Cook asked as Hemmett rose and began dragging out the jars of spices.

"I have his blessing. Said if I can get Katrin to eat, he doesn't care if I carve Demon up and roast him," Hemmett answered.

Varnia strode from the room, headed to the chicken house to get one of the ingredients for the soup. Cook joined Hemmett in grinding and measuring the spices.

"Plenty of other things she can eat that would tempt her," she declared. "I know she has trouble swallowing because her throat was infected a while back, but we could put things through the colander there and press them through. That makes them very fine. Stews, soups."

"Just what I was thinking," Hemmett answered, giving her such a perfect example of his smile that Cook laughed a little and bent over her mortar and pestle full of sweetbark to hide her red cheeks.

***

"It's his, Luntigré's and the Princess' business and that's all!" Villison declared fiercely, glaring at several members of Menders' Men who had expressed indignation at Hemmett's proposal to Katrin.

"Don't tell us what to do, Villison," Haakel said with irritation. "We've known him much longer than you have."

"And there it is!" Villison shouted irascibly. "Menders' Men! All highly educated assassins and spies that can't be told anything by anyone else. Some of them haven't left The Shadows and carried out a mission in years, but that doesn't stop them knowing it all. Bloody bunch of killers for hire is all you are."

"Take care, toy soldier. You've got some stripes on your back for your kind of courage."

The nasty remark came from a new Menders' Man. He went only by the name Vartok.

The Men's Lounge went silent, even though a number of the "killers for hire" had been rising from their chairs in fury at Villison's detrimental remark.

"I had the guts to take those stripes so my men didn't get killed by an idiotic order to stand on an open beach shooting rifles at a boat firing mortar shells at them," Villison shot back. "Tell me about your courage, New Man, sitting in here with the rest of the old biddies, chucking gossip around about Hemmett and those two young ladies. It's none of your damned affair and you can call me whatever you want."

"All right, Vil, they're just upset because we all care for Katrin," Kaymar said, walking into the lounge from where he'd been smoking outside. His mouth was twitching with amusement at Villison calling Menders' Men 'old biddies'.

"If that's the case, they should be upset because they care for Hemmett too, since he's been hurt as well," the determined Villison countered. "What's wrong with him asking for what several of us have, a wife to love him? This matter is for him and the Princess alone – and for your information, he did it with Luntigré's knowledge and blessing."

Furious, the little man swung away from them and slammed out of the Men's Wing. A wave of indignant swearing swelled in his wake.

"He's absolutely right you know," Kaymar said quietly, stopping the conversation cold. "Menders would tell you the same. Don't think I don't know about the things that are said in here. Hemmett's life is none of your concern. Neither is Katrin's. I've heard that term 'toy soldier' far too many times since Katrin was hurt. I don't think any of you could have done what Hemmett did on the boat coming back from Erdahn with her nearly dead. He pulled steel spikes out of the body of the woman he loves until his mind broke under the strain. You are to put no further strain on him. Villison says this is not your business, and it isn't."

"All right, nancy," Vartok said sarcastically.

"Pack," Kaymar said. "Get off this place within the hour."

"Who do you think you are?" Vartok asked.

He found himself pinned against the wall by Kaymar, a knife held under his chin.

"I'm Menders' second and I'm still the best killer for hire in the world," Kaymar hissed. "You're finished here. Leave or you won't need to bother."

Kaymar released the man and gave him a shove that propelled him halfway to his room. Vartok hurried the rest of the way, shutting and locking the door behind him.

"Anyone else?" Kaymar asked very calmly and casually, turning back to the assembled Men.

Everyone rapidly found something important to do.

***

"Pa?" Hemmett looked up from the newssheet that he had been reading to his father. It was their evening activity whenever Hemmett was at The Shadows. Lucen dearly loved to be abreast of the news, but his reading was as slow and halting as Hemmett's had been in his boyhood.

"I hope that was the end of the article," Lucen joked.

"I would never cut short an article," Hemmett grinned back.

"I can tell when you start condensing, boy."

"Well Pa, some of them are very badly written. I'm actually sparing you," Hemmett said, laying the newssheet aside.

Lucen looked incredibly smug. "To think my son can tell when something is badly written and can write it off better in his head while he's reading aloud," he marveled. "Pretty damn good for a non-commissioned soldier and a peasant lass to have a son like that, eh Zee?"

Hemmett's mother, Zelia, looked up from the dress she was stitching for Flori. "Very good indeed," she replied. "You're a clever one, Hemmett."

"I need to be really clever, which I why I have a question for you, Pa," Hemmett smiled, winking at his mother, who hid a smile by looking down at the little dress. "I've been reading through that book of Franz's about caring for invalids and it seems to me that it keeps people invalids. You spent time nursing in Army hospitals. How did they build the soldiers back up after an injury?"

"That was an interesting thing," Lucen replied. "I've seen that pap that Cook has to make up for Katrin and it's got nothing much to it. We gave the soldiers beef if we could, pork if there wasn't beef to hand. Red meats. Broth, from the moment they came in. Milk if we could get it. They fussed over that, didn't like drinking milk – they wanted grog, of course. We gave them red wine. It's not that the meat and wine are red, but there's something in them that strengthens the body and helps make blood. So many of them were almost bloodless when they came in."

"What about eggs? Chicken?" Hemmett was listening intently.

"Oh yes. Eggs stirred into all sorts of things, because the men who were well enough didn't want them served as a meal. They wanted meat. Craved it. For the ones who were sick as Katrin is, broth with egg. Bring it to a boil, beat up an egg, whisk it in. Double goodness, you see. Milk too. Put it in everything. They'd fuss about a glass of milk, but make them a sweet custard and stand back. Men are fools for sweets."

"As I well know," Hemmett laughed, as he had just taken a chocolate from the box Zelia always had on hand. "Katrin is too, so the custard is a good idea, both milk and eggs. What else did they do to build injured men up?"

"As much fresh air as possible and we got them up and walking around as soon as we could," Lucen replied, warming to his subject and lighting his pipe. He offered one to Hemmett who brandished his case of small, fragrant cigars made for him by Luntigré. Lucen watched closely as he lit one of the few remaining.

"You'll need a refill of those," he observed.

"I'll be going to Samorsa before long," he assured his father. "Miss both my girls, need more cigars and Flori's birthday."

"Should bring her here for her birthday," Lucen rumbled.

"Perhaps you should come with me and explain that to Chetigré and Montigré and all her cousins," Hemmett replied. "They'd no more let her leave on that occasion than they would turn into a flock of birds and fly away. Luntigré and Flori would like to visit but Katrin is anxious about it."

"Now, why is that?" Zelia asked. "She likes Luntigré and Flori."

"Loves them both," Hemmett said, turning toward her. "She's sensitive about how her wounds smell."

"And they'll keep smelling if they're all wrapped up," Lucen added. "We used to keep wounds open to the air, try to get sunlight on them. Sunlight kills the infection. Wash them often, use ointment to keep them from stiffening. We had a doctor who swore by wrapping them up in garlic poultices. It drew out the infection."

"Considering how Katrin is about the smell now, I think we'll avoid the garlic," Hemmett laughed.

"It worked." Lucen took a moment to look at the window. "Why, it's our Kaymar," he grinned.

"Indeed, it is," Kaymar responded, stepping over the low windowsill and taking the seat Zelia indicated. He was a frequent evening visitor at the Greinholz's. He proffered a paper packet to Hemmett, who took it, opened it and saw it was full of a powdered substance.

"Will is just back from Surytam and brought me a double portion of it," Kaymar explained.

"I'm glad he's back!" Hemmett exclaimed. "He'll be a great help with Katrin."

"We didn't say anything, in case he didn't want to take another change of posting. He just went up now to poke his head in and tell her hello," Kaymar explained. "That's a medicine that the Surytamians use for deep infections like Katrin's. Put it in water or food. I use it all the time because I have some wounds that have never entirely cleared and healed. It keeps them from opening up again and causing trouble."

Hemmett raised his eyebrows, inhaling the pleasantly pungent scent of the powder. "Franz said I can change her diet and get her to exercise, but no medicines," he told Kaymar.

"So, don't tell him. Two small spoonfuls in her food or drink throughout the day – a little at a time. I can promise you it works well, but it certainly can't hurt her. It keeps that one crater on my back under control and that slice DeLarco put on me as well. That one's never healed properly."

Kaymar's back was a map of wounds, some of them deep enough for a man's hand to fit into. He never explained where he got them, though as Hemmett grew older and heard stories about Kaymar's youth from some of Menders' Men, he had a good idea. Kaymar had other wounds all over his body, largely from self-inflicted cuts or burns from his cigars. For some reason inflicting pain on himself helped him keep his madness under control. Infection was an ongoing concern for him, no matter how careful he was to clean the wounds afterward.

"Then we won't tell Franz," Hemmett agreed, closing and pocketing the packet. "Many thanks, Kay."

"Not to mention it. She's not getting better with what Franz is doing. I know it's the accepted medical method, but it just can't go on. Menders told me about what you're planning to do and gave his blessing for this medicine. Just don't let Sawbones know about it."

Kaymar grinned like a wicked schoolboy and lit one of his own cigars. "I left the window open for a reason, Zee."

"Yes, with the three of you, it would be most thick in here," she said, folding the little dress and setting it aside. "I'm weary tonight, so it's off to bed with me."

"I'll be shortly after you," Lucen said as she made her way from the room.

***

Menders watched Hemmett as he took over Katrin's eating and exercise regimens. His plan to cure Katrin was unusual and in opposition to everything modern medical science recommended – and it was working.

Hemmett put a stop to Katrin spending most of her time in bed, as had become her habit, insisting that being in the open air was what she needed. He helped her to walk each day, letting her move along alone as much as she could, then offering an arm so that she could go further. When she was tired and didn't feel up to walking, he carried her. He set up a sofa on the terrace and a chaise in the garden, and would walk or carry her to either. Then he would sit with her while she absorbed sunshine and fresh air.

He insisted, if the weather was warm, that she expose as many of her still-infected wounds to the sun as possible, helping her push up her sleeves or skirt, cradling her injured limbs with carefully placed pillows. If a wound became filled with pus, he would open it for her, so she didn't have to wait for Franz. He wiped away the evil smelling, ropey discharge as if he had neither sight nor sense of smell. He bathed the drained wounds thoroughly and had Katrin keep them in the sunlight as long as she could.

Katrin now drank several glasses of fresh milk a day as well as two glasses of red wine. Hemmett told her that wine would help her body make blood. He also coaxed her into eating a little more each day, persuading her to swallow eggs, cheese and meat. She protested at first that they were too coarse for her to swallow. Hemmett cut them up fine or whipped up batches of Lucen's broth with egg stirred in at the boiling point.

Soon Katrin was eating with appetite. Menders realized that the accepted medical practice of feeding her an invalid diet and his own reluctance to push her into anything she didn't want because of his own pain and guilt about her situation, had been in error. She needed to rebuild her destroyed body. Hemmett's ministrations were what she required to do just that.

Franz saw the improvement and ceremoniously burned a certain medical book about the care of invalids in his fireplace.

"It works. Bless the man, it works," he said. "Who am I to say it should be otherwise? Feed her as much as she can hold, keep her outside, help her exercise and I believe nature will do the rest. I've never been loath to admit when I'm wrong – and invalid food and rest were wrong."

He grinned out the window where Hemmett was hilariously serenading Katrin and Varnia with a naughty soldier's song, with Borsen and Willem joining in the choruses while performing an impromptu sailor's dance involving comical collisions. Katrin's laughter floated over the garden and through the window as Varnia slyly pelted the men with fallen flower petals.

"Unhealthy lungs can't laugh," Franz murmured. "Having The Knot all together again is helping too. Keeps her mind off of things."

"I was thinking a trip to the seashore at the warmest part of the summer," Menders said, joining him in watching the young people.

"Excellent suggestion, I'd love it," Franz teased back, and they grinned at each other. No-one had felt like joking for a long while. "It would be an excellent thing for her. Sea water will clean those wounds like nothing else and the warmth and sun would be a great help, as would a change of scene. We all could use a break, for that matter. It's been a hellish year."

***

THE SHADOWS, MORDANIA

5
VOICE OF THE PRINCESS

One afternoon when Hemmett was on perimeter duty and Borsen was contending with a backlog of mending, Varnia sat with Katrin as she rested on the chaise in the garden between walks around the rose beds. Varnia was reading to her. Katrin's eyes were bleary with a recent infection and her arms were still too weak to hold a book for long. She was becoming restless, so Varnia closed the book and put it down.

"Enough for one day?" she asked. Katrin nodded and smiled at her.

"Thank you for reading to me," she said softly.

"I love to read aloud," Varnia answered. "It's no chore."

"Bloody toy soldiers! Never one around when you need him!"

Katrin and Varnia looked around to see two Menders' Men walking down the hallway to the Rose Garden.

"What?" Katrin asked. "Toy soldiers? They can't mean real toy soldiers."

Varnia was silent. Katrin could see she was clenching her teeth.

"Tell me," Katrin urged.

"It's what Menders' Men have started to call Hemmett's Guard," Varnia burst out. "They ridicule them because some of them haven't seen action."

"What! Villison has, so have several of the others!" Katrin cried. "That's nonsense!"

"I think it's because Hemmett hasn't seen action," Varnia explained. "It's been very ugly since you were hurt. They think he's weak because his mind was ill after that day and because he cried when your hair… came out."

"Of all the stupid, cruel things!" Katrin was indignant. Her cheeks flared bright pink. "Hemmett helped get those metal rods out of me on the boat and he and Menders were afraid for weeks that the Queen would send troops here and take us all back to be executed.

No wonder his mind was deranged for a while! We're close, Varnia, we've been together since I was born!"

"Shhh now, don't upset yourself like this."

"It's good for me! I feel alive instead of half dead like an old root that's been dug up. I'll put a stop to this! How dare they!"

Varnia kept her from standing.

"Wait a moment. You need to know all of it before you fly off the handle and go ramming around," she said fiercely. "A lot of it is because he asked you to marry him and then went right back to Luntigré. They were angry that you were upset, especially when you're so ill. I think they believed he was being unfaithful to Luntigré and that going back to her meant he wasn't really serious about you."

Varnia suddenly looked relieved.

"You've known about this for a while, haven't you?" Katrin asked quietly. Varnia nodded.

"What a bunch of old women – Menders' Men indeed!" Katrin fumed, shaking her head. "What possible business of theirs – Hemmett was deadly serious when he asked me to marry him. So serious that just for a moment, I almost said 'yes'."

"I wouldn't blame you," Varnia replied. "He loves you like life – to say nothing that he's handsome as the morning, as Menders would say."

Katrin didn't voice the thought she'd often had – that Varnia and Hemmett would make a wonderful couple. Varnia was steadfast in saying that she would never marry and Katrin wouldn't tease her about that, no matter how lovingly.

"As for them poking their noses into Hemmett being with Luntigré, that is absolutely none of their affair," she fumed. "Hemmett and she have their understanding and it works well for them both. It's wonderful for Flori."

"That's what Vil said to them," Varnia nodded.

"Vil? Something else that went on?'

"He had a big set-to with a bunch of them in the Men's Lounge," Varnia explained. "They were cutting Hemmett down, ridiculing how he got so sick after you were hurt. Vil pitched right into them and then one of them, that nasty Vartok character, called him a toy soldier. Then Vartok got mouthy with Kaymar, who threw him off the place."

Katrin stood abruptly.

"Help me," she said succinctly. "I want to go into the dining room. Then I want to see all of Menders Men – actually, I want to see everyone in the entire damn house!"

"Wait, take my arm! We don't need you falling," Varnia gasped. "And how am I to get everyone in the house?"

"Ring the damn bell!"

***

There was a bell at The Shadows that was rung only under extreme circumstances. It summoned everyone within earshot to the Great Hall for instructions. In Katrin's lifetime, it had only been rung twice, once when an assassin was found on the grounds, when she was taken into the strongroom while the area was cleared, and once when there was a fire, which was rapidly extinguished by those who responded.

Now Katrin sat in the dining room, waiting. Varnia was ringing the bell with all her might. Katrin could hear the accumulating sound of many footsteps as people rushed to the Great Hall. There was a rising babble as they found only Varnia waiting there – at least until Hemmett's voice rang out, calling them to silence.

"All right, Varnia," Katrin said as loudly as she could.

She knew she looked terrible – her face gaunt, her wounds showing, as she'd had them open to the sun as she and Varnia sat in the Rose Garden.

Suddenly she pulled off her wig and set it aside. Let them see the truth.

Varnia came in, closely followed by Menders, Eiren and Hemmett, who rushed to her. Menders bent over her.

"What is it, my dear?" he asked gently.

"I'm going to dress some people down," she answered, squeezing his hand. "Not you."

"Darling, your wig?" Eiren asked, reaching out to help her with it.

"Let them see," Katrin responded, holding her bald head up proudly.

"Willow?" Hemmett looked down at her with concern.

"We're about to have a little talk about toy soldiers. Actually, I'm going to have the talk, people are going to listen." Her eyes met his.

Hemmett straightened up and saluted.

"Yes, Your Highness," he said proudly. Then he stood at attention beside her.

She looked at the gathering crowd and was annoyed to see some of Menders' Men were angry. Cook was giving one of them a stern look. Villison was watching them like a hawk. Kaymar and Ifor stood off to the side together, Kaymar looking amused, Ifor impervious.

"Hemmett?" she asked quietly. "Shut them up."

"Be upstanding for Her Royal Highness, Princess Katrin Morghenna of Mordania!" Hemmett bellowed.

The room fell silent. For the first time, people were looking toward Katrin rather than jabbering amongst themselves. They found that she was looking at them. Those who remembered Morghenna the Terrible found her gaze disconcertingly familiar. Others were stunned by her lack of hair – of course they knew about it, but she never appeared without one of her artfully made wigs. Even more were horrified by the lurid, seeping wounds that showed on her arms and at her collarbones.

"I have a few words to say about toy soldiers," she said, pushing as much breath into her voice as she could. "I also have a few words to say about gossip."

There was shuffling in the group before her. Some averted their eyes.

Katrin held out her hand toward Luntigré and Flori, who had come back with Hemmett after his latest trip to Samorsa. When they were beside her, she put an arm around Flori's shoulders and smiled up at Luntigré.

"Vil, Petra, come up, bring the children. Cook, beside me as well, please. Doctor dear, you too. Kaymar, Ifor, come up. Borsen, you took your time."

Borsen and Tomar had rushed in the door.

"Sewed my sleeve to a sheet when I heard the bell," he said, looking around in surprise. "Tomar had to cut me loose."

"Please, both of you, come stand with us," Katrin invited. "Lucen, Zelia, over here by Hemmett, please." Her eyes scanned the crowd of people and settled on one. "Willem – you too."

With people arranged to her purpose, Katrin began to speak to the people standing opposite.

"I overheard two Menders' Men calling Hemmett's Guard 'toy soldiers' only a few minutes ago. I've also learned that you ridicule the Captain of my Guard because he became ill after helping me escape from the Palace. This is not going to continue.

"Any one of you who does not wish to show Captain Greinholz full respect as a man and as the commanding officer of my official Guard can get out of my house and off my estate now."

She stared at the knot of Menders' Men, noticing how they stood together, away from Hemmett's Guard and the rest of the household. Disconcerting.

"Does any of you want to admit that you have been disrespectful enough to gossip about any of Hemmett's Guard?" she asked, looking from one Menders' Man to another. There was silence.

Haakel stepped forward.

"I have," he said bluntly. "I was very angry when he upset you so much a while back."

"You? Haakel, you spent years with us, you were our guard when we were children and split the job with Kaymar after he came. How could you say that? You know Hemmett better than most of the men in this room." Katrin looked steadily at him.

"I do and I'm going to be apologizing to him personally," Haakel answered, holding his head up. "And to Villison and the rest of the Guard. As well as to you, Tadpole."

Katrin very nearly smiled as she heard the old nickname he'd given her when she was three, but all she had to do was flex her wrist a little. The pain from her open wounds took away the urge.

"I'll talk to you later, Bullfrog," Haakel said directly to Hemmett, who nodded formally.

"Please come up and stand with us," Katrin said to him. He smiled with relief and walked over to stand by her.

"I know Haakel is not the only one," Katrin continued, not wanting everyone to start smiling and getting comfortable. "I will not have factions here, gentlemen. I will be speaking to Menders, the commanding officer for both Menders' Men and Hemmett's Guard, about a restructuring of how things are done. Let me assure you, we will not hesitate to transfer or even dismiss anyone who persists in this sort of divisive behavior."

Katrin reached over for Menders' and Eiren's hands.

"Now, I am going to explain, very clearly, my relationships to the people standing beside me and I hope that will help everyone here to understand why I do not consider family to be only a matter of blood tie," she said, looking at her household. "My family is large, and it is open to addition – if being added is earned.

"Menders and Eiren are my father and mother. They were there from the beginning, when the Queen placed me under Menders' care. Both of them have risked their lives for my sake and have loved and nurtured me as true parents."

Menders placed his hand on her shoulder. Eiren bent and kissed her cheek before they stepped back, as Katrin was reaching her hand out for Varnia.

"This is my sister," she said to the crowd. "My brave and bold sister who never fails to protect the helpless and weak. She would stand between a cannon's mouth and the ones she loves without flinching."

Her eyes met Borsen's and he went to her.

"This is my brother. He has nursed me and sat by me for hours during my illness, keeping me from despair. He is one of the most giving and hardworking members of this household and my most patient and understanding friend."

She gestured to Villison and Petra and their children. When Villison was close, she took his hand and then Petra's.

"These are my brother and sister – one of my newest friends and one of my oldest," she said, smiling at them. "They've been entrusted with knowledge that few have and that could endanger their lives. They've never flinched or swerved. Their little boy, Arden, is my beloved nephew."

Katrin reached out to the smiling toddler and held him close while he ran his hands wonderingly over her bald scalp.

"Soft!" he shouted. Petra gathered him up, kissing Katrin before she stepped back.

Katrin turned in her chair and gestured to Kaymar and Ifor.

"I have been privileged to have many fathers," she continued. "Kaymar and Ifor have been tireless guards, teachers and friends. Between them they stopped an assassin who was determined to kill me and my entire family by endangering their own lives.

"Hake is another father," she continued, smiling up at him and taking his hand. "He endured endless hours of tadpole hunting during the years he has been with me and is a steadfast friend – and he knows when to admit that he was wrong. All is forgiven, my dear."

Haakel's eyes smiled back at her as she released his hand.

"Lucen, Zelia, step up here. Not only do I have more than one father, like Lucen here, who was my first Guard – I also have more than one mother. Zelia is one. She's nursed me tirelessly during my illness, to say nothing of giving me more than twenty years of loving care and concern.

"Cook?" Katrin turned to Cook, who was shamelessly wiping away tears. She took Katrin's outstretched hand. "How many hours of care Cook has given me," she said, looking up at the stout woman. "Love, patience, discipline, reminders to watch my language and an endless supply of spice cookies. Her son, Tomar, I consider my brother – our patient tailor who came here when we were all but out of our clothing, who trained Borsen to become the youngest Guild Tailor on Eirdon."

Willem was next. They exchanged a smile.

"My brother and friend, Willem, proven to be brave, patient, forgiving and vigilant," Katrin said. "He's lightened my illness with many hours of companionship and has shown understanding and tolerance beyond anyone I've ever met."

She turned toward Luntigré, who was watching with glistening eyes. Their hands met.

"This is my beloved sister," Katrin said, her voice carrying across the room, though she spoke softly. "She has taught us a kinder, forgiving way of dealing with life. I am proud to be part of her family of tiger-women. Her little daughter, Flori, is my precious niece."

Flori embraced Katrin enthusiastically. Menders flinched, thinking of those wounds that ran under Katrin's collarbones. Katrin showed no sign of discomfort, though the pain must have been sharp.

"Help me up, darling," she said to the little girl. Flori braced herself so Katrin could use her shoulder for support.

Katrin rose slowly to her feet and then turned toward Hemmett, who had not faltered from his posture of attention. She reached out and took his hand.

"At ease," she said softly. Hemmett relaxed and looked into her eyes.

"This is my brother," she said, her voice suddenly ringing to the rafters. "From the day I was born, he has been my friend, my confidant, my protector and my other self. There is no knowledge, that I would not trust him with. His heart is pure and true, and it has been dedicated to being my Guard since he was a little boy helping me catch those tadpoles in the lake."

She turned away from Hemmett's eyes and looked at the crowd of Menders' Men, Hemmett's Guard and household members.

"I, Princess Katrin Morghenna Shvalz of the Royal House of Mordania place Captain Hemmett Greinholz under my protection as a Courtier and confer upon him the title of Baronet from this day forward – for all the things he has done and for all he will do to protect and love me."

The silence was overwhelming – then Hemmett saw Katrin starting to sway and put an arm around her, pulling her against his side, steadying her. Menders stepped over and supported her on the opposite side.

"Now we go forward together, my friends – as a family," Katrin said gently.

She looked over at Borsen. He smiled, and she nodded.

"We go on from here," he said loudly.

LEPTHAM, MORDANIA

6
FACE THE STORM

Katrin sat in the gentle surf on the beach at Leptham, watching Borsen walking out of the waves toward her.

They had been here a week and already she felt incredibly improved. She spent hours sitting in the surf every day, letting the sea water wash her wounds. The redness and swelling were diminishing, as was the terrible smell. Doctor Franz said it was the best thing she could do. Several of the injuries were healing cleanly now.

She loved the quiet and the endless gentle swish of the waves on the sand, the horizontal lines of sea and sky. It rested her. It helped her clear her mind of the nightmares, sleeping and waking, that had tormented her since she was Suspended.

"You'll get all wrinkled, Cuz, lying in the water like a crab," Borsen smiled. He settled beside her in the shallow waves, leaning against her companionably as he wiped his glasses dry on one of her towels.

"I am anyway," Katrin smiled.

"It's not so bad now that you're filling out again," Borsen assured her.

"Am I?"

"Oh yes. I'm a tailor, I notice these things."

"Well, I'm glad to hear it. I look like some dried up thing you find in an attic." Katrin sighed and lifted her arm free of the water. The flesh still hung on her bones and looked horribly unhealthy.

"It will come back. I heard Franz saying you're young enough that you'll make a very good recovery."

Katrin sighed. "Yes, but not a full one."

"No there's no way anyone would ever completely recover from something like that," Borsen said quietly. "You just go on with what you have left."

They sat together quietly for a while, watching Hemmett thrashing through the waves and standing on a sandbar many yards out in the water, diving off, resurfacing and climbing out to dive again.

Borsen scooped up a shell that came tumbling in on a wave and handed it to her.

"That's funny, usually you don't get good shells here like you do on the shore at Erdstrom, because of how shallow the water is. They get ground down to nothing on the sand bars. Must be a storm out there washing them up from the deeper water," he said.

Katrin shaded her eyes and peered out at the horizon. She shook her head. Her eyes were clearer now that her latest infection was abating, but her vision was still not perfect.

"It's hazy," Borsen said. "And the swell over that sandbar Hemmett keeps dancing on is getting bigger. I hope we have a storm. I want to see one come in over the ocean." He rolled over onto his stomach and looked up at her.

"Borsen, are you going to stay at The Shadows for a while?" Katrin asked.

"Looking to get rid of me?" he smiled.

"No, but your career… you've worked so hard toward it, and now you never talk about it anymore."

"I've been happy," he said, studying the little mussels that washed up with each wave and then burrowed down into the sand. "And I've been busy enough. I love being with you. I can't really do anything until I'm twenty-one anyway. Then I would be old enough to have some credibility as a tailor, so people don't think I'm a journeyman."

"Borsen, you're twenty now. Twenty and a half. You want a big establishment in Erdahn, you've always said so."

Borsen turned on his side in the waves, propping his head on his hand.

"Some things are more important, Cuz."

"Would you help me lie down like you? My backside is sore." He steadied her as she turned on her side and lay down eye to eye with him.

She appreciated his devotion. He had been a lifeline since she'd been brought home from Erdahn more than half-dead. He'd spent hours at her bedside, reading, talking, being there. He would sometimes bring projects down from the workshop and sit in her room, keeping her from being bored or lonely, stitching away nonstop.

But he'd worked toward having what he called "an establishment" for years with single minded intensity. Even the years they'd spent traveling hadn't damped his ardor. Now he was speaking as if he had stopped caring. She couldn't believe it. This was something to think about.

If she searched her soul, she desperately wanted Borsen to stay at The Shadows with her, but he was so talented and had so many plans that couldn't be carried out in a secluded country location. If he let them go for her…

A much larger wave, which they hadn't noticed in spite of Hemmett's shouting from the sand bar to warn them, hit them, causing Katrin to shriek and Borsen to jump to his feet and catch her before she tumbled along with it as it receded. They both laughed as he helped her up.

A cold wind raked them. The sky was rapidly growing black, clouds climbing high at the horizon. Hemmett, seeing that no-one was hurt or swept out to sea, dove from the sand bar and headed for shore. Katrin saw Menders was coming toward them along the beach, laughing at their scramble.

"We'd best get you back to the hotel, there's a storm coming," he said as he reached them, picking up the towels and bundling one around her.

"Oh, I want to see the storm!" she protested, resisting as he put his arm around her waist and prepared to help her walk back to the hotel. The wind was rising, and she felt exhilarated.

Hemmett coasted up on a wave and ran to them.

"That's going to be a big blow," he said. "Better get you inside right away, Willow."

"No! Let's wait for the storm," Katrin begged.

"Are you crazy? You'll get struck by lightning," Hemmett argued, pointing at the fiery bolts dancing from the bottom of the clouds out over the sea.

"We're going to compromise here," Menders said, indicating one of the hotel gazebos. He put an arm around Katrin's waist and helped her across the sand and into the shelter, while Hemmett and Borsen followed, having scooped up her towels and other paraphernalia, arguing about the wisdom of staying out in the storm.

"You can't protect us from everything!" Borsen yelled over the rising wind, answering Hemmett's continued scolding. He raced into the gazebo and stood by the railing facing the sea as the black clouds came rolling across the wild water. He started yowling like a maddened langur.

Menders, who had been trying to get Katrin to sit in a chair, burst out laughing. She eluded him and went to stand by Borsen. She hooted at the storm as well, laughing as an enormous thunderclap resounded across the ocean.

Hemmett stared at them for a moment as they stood there howling and laughing, then decided he may as well join the fraternity of the mad. He took his place beside them, roaring and pounding on his chest.

"You're all mad," Menders grinned, coming to stand next to them.

"Yell at it Menders, it's wonderful!" Katrin cried, cupping her hands around her mouth and yowling as gusts of wind shook the gazebo. Borsen rattled the railing with his fists, bellowing. The sea was rising in white capped waves and the lightning was coming closer. The wind grew stronger and colder. Katrin, feeling like a little girl again, whooped and yelled and wished she was strong enough to run along the shoreline fighting the wind and confronting the waves.

"Do your worst!" she shrieked. "I'm not afraid!" Thunder rolled across the ocean in answer and the wind caught up spray from the frothing waves and flung it at the gazebo.

"Look!" Hemmett yelled, roaring with laughter.

Kaymar and Ifor were running toward them along the beach, closed umbrellas in hand, obviously intent on a rescue. When Kaymar saw them standing there laughing and yowling defiance at the storm, he tossed the umbrella he held to Ifor. He ran gracefully along the wave line just as Katrin wanted to do, obviously as elated at nature's tantrum as the rest of them were. Finishing off his performance with three perfect cartwheels, he raced up to the gazebo, Ifor gasping with laughter behind him.

"Storm madness," was all Menders said before Borsen yelled, "Here it comes!"

Rain slanted under the roof of the gazebo and drenched them. Borsen, Katrin and Hemmett, already being wet, didn't care and stood right at the railing, laughing like children who had snuck out of the house and were playing in a rainstorm. Katrin was aware of Kaymar standing beside her, his shirt and hair drenched as he laughed too. With delight, she stretched her arms out and let the rain drum on them, washing her wounds, running down her face as she turned it up to the clouds, feeling light and clean again.

I'm alive, she thought. They didn't kill me. I'm going to live. With hair or without, sick or well, I'm going to live.

She let her hands fill with rain and brought them to her face, rinsing it with the soft water. Borsen was turning this way and that, allowing the rain to run all over him while Hemmett continued howling at the sky, alternating his roars with laughter as the rain drummed on his head and plastered down his hair. Menders stood next to Kaymar, his eyes closed, his expression truly peaceful for the first time in over a year as the rain ran down his face. Ifor stood with them, his hands on Kaymar's shoulders. He was laughing and calling them all mad, though he was getting drenched too.

THE SHADOWS, MORDANIA

7
STAND TALL, WORK HARD

Menders tapped on Katrin's door. She called for him to come in and smiled from the bed as he put a bowl of the soft custard she loved on the nightstand. He sat on the end of the bed against the bedpost, sighing wearily.

"Long day?" she smiled.

"Oh yes," Menders groaned. "Thank gods tomorrow is a rest day. I intend to stay in bed until the sybaritic hour of seven o'clock."

Katrin laughed a little. "Ah, such decadence."

"Maybe even until eight," Menders replied.

"The world will end if you do that, of course," Katrin smiled, picking up the dish of custard.

He waited while she ate, glad of the opportunity to relax. It had been a busy day, with the late harvest in full swing, several injuries and a number of dispatches from his network that required immediate attention and responses. What was more, he had let the accounts go lately and had spent several hours catching them back up. It had been a hard grind since before dawn.

Katrin finished her treat and put the bowl down on the nightstand again. She settled back against the pillows.

"Borsen," Menders said gently.

Instead of asking what he meant or looking surprised, she nodded.

"I know," she replied. "He thinks he needs to stay because of me."

"He's devoted to you," Menders agreed. "I've been very grateful for that, because he's a good companion for you now that the two of you don't spar with each other."

Katrin rolled her eyes and laughed a little in embarrassment.

"That all seems so silly, now that I've faced something really terrible," she said. "I'm glad we don't do it either, though you must admit that we didn't do it often."

"No, you didn't."

"Menders, I don't want other people to change their lives because I'm sick. Not that it isn't lovely for me having Borsen here. It is, because I can tell him all kinds of things. He has a way of listening and accepting that is very comforting. But I miss him talking about the things he wants to do. I'm going to be better one day and then what will he be?"

"He'll be one of those pathetic men who tells everyone about how they had a big dream once and were going to do great things," Menders said honestly. "I don't want to see that happen to him. His ambitions are enormous, but I believe he can achieve them, if he begins when he's young. There simply isn't the energy when one is older. Energy is what he's going to need to accomplish what he wants. He originally planned to leave here when he was twenty-one, and get started on his project, but he's almost twenty-one now with no firm plans in sight."

"So, which one of us talks to him?" Katrin asked.

"I would rather you did, if you can."

She nodded but he saw the glint of tears in her eyes.

"I will, tomorrow," she said.

"We'll try to fill in the best we can," Menders said. "I'll miss him terribly too, but he must have his chance – and I don't want him caught up in being part of the royal situation, if you know what I mean."

"I know very well," Katrin sighed. "Menders, is that why you've always encouraged Eiren to keep on with the school, even when she was away that year in Erdahn?"

He nodded.

"Absolutely. Eiren had great dreams too and she's made them come to pass. She needs her own projects and identity."

"And you gave her that," Katrin smiled. She shifted in the bed, settling down on her side. Menders could see she was sleepy.

"Menders – you regret not having children of your own, don't you?"

He sat stock still, wondering how she could have known.

"I've asked the wrong thing," Katrin said swiftly, sitting back up. "I'm sorry."

"Katrin – please never mention that to Eiren. It would break her heart," Menders answered.

"I wouldn't. You know that. But during the time we were abroad it occurred to me, when Varnia came along at the last moment and then Hemmett added Luntigré and Flori to the mix – you love us all as your children."

"Yes then – as time has gone by, I have regretted not having children of my own," Menders admitted, his voice soft. "I made some decisions when I was very young that I have realized were not necessary. It's one reason why I don't want to see Borsen making a decision he might later regret. It's also important to remember that it wasn't entirely my decision. Eiren was and is terrified of the idea of childbirth, for good reason. Though my feelings about having children have changed, hers have not – and since she would be the one taking the risk, I leave things as they are."

"I've hurt you," Katrin said, her voice very quiet.

"No. I'm awed that you realized it, my little princess. I have all of you who have come to be my children. I'm a lucky man. And there will be others, I think. Sometimes I see them when I'm falling asleep – children who will need me. Some aren't even born yet, but they will come to me when the time is right."

Suddenly Menders shook himself and looked sheepishly at Katrin. "Here I am waxing mystical and I don't have Tharak's presence to carry it off."

"Oh, you have plenty of presence." She smiled but he could see she was touched by his words. "I'll talk to Borsen tomorrow."

"Thank you, my daughter," Menders said, rising and then bending to kiss her cheek.

"Good night, Papa dear," she whispered with a smile.

***

"Let me see to the goats with you," Katrin said as she came upon Borsen scalding buckets in the kitchen, preparatory to milking their little herd. Borsen had been keeping their cheesemaking business going since she had been ill.

"It's chilly out there, Cuz," Borsen replied, looking at her with concern.

"I'll rug up. I can't stay inside the rest of my life." Katrin reached for the kettle to scald the last bucket. Borsen stopped her.

"That's heavy, I'll do it," he said.

She sighed and let him scald the final bucket, then followed him as he went for his coat. He helped her with hers, though she could tell that he was fretting over her going outside in the chill. She followed him into the gloomy autumn twilight.

Borsen lit the lantern that illuminated the barn where the house cows and goats were kept at night. He dragged a hay bale over for her to sit on.

"Your throne," he pronounced regally, bowing low.

"Thank you, knave," she laughed, seating herself. Borsen arranged the buckets by the milking stand and went to release the first goat from her pen.

The little doe knew Katrin and went to her immediately, leaning her head against Katrin's knee, then nuzzling up to her, trying to nip at her wig.

"You're such a pretty girl," Katrin said, stroking the fawn colored neck. She'd missed caring for the goats so much! She had always loved their odd yellow eyes with the horizontal slit pupils, their mealy noses and endlessly grinding jaws. Each one was a character, as unique as people. She'd missed the crop of kids being born this year, though Borsen would smuggle them into the house and put them on the bed when they were tiny and new.

"All right, silly girl," Borsen said to the goat, who jumped up on the stand and began to eat the measure of grain he'd put into the bowl there. Borsen sat and washed the goat's udder, then began to milk.

Katrin listened to the familiar sound of milk streaming into the pail and tried to remember the last time she'd milked – and couldn't. She was so out of things at The Shadows now! Cook had taken over the chickens for her, as Borsen had taken over the goats. Being an invalid had become her life. She was tired of it.

As Borsen was milking the last goat, Katrin stood up.

"Let me have a try, Cuz," she said, putting a hand on his shoulder. "You've milked her halfway. I can probably manage."

The goat was an easy milker but Borsen looked dubious.

"It's no trouble for me to finish," he said.

"Borsen, I know it isn't. I want to."

He hesitated, then yielded the milking stand to her.

Katrin settled in the familiar position, her shoulder against the goat's side, her fingers closing on the rubbery teats. It wasn't easy. The muscles in her arms and hands were slack and weak but the rhythm came back to her quickly. She was able to milk the goat out.

"You should do this every day!" Borsen said excitedly as he opened the pen for the goat and settled her for the night.

"I intend to, because I want you to go to Erdahn," Katrin answered. She didn't look at him, but occupied herself in putting the covers on the milk pails.

"Do you want me to go get something for you in Erdahn?" Borsen asked bewilderedly.

She held a hand out to him and had him sit next to her on the stand.

"No, I want you to go and find a place and get started on your establishment," she said.

She saw it, the smallest flicker of relief in his face, immediately crowded out by concern and hurt.

"It's the time you always planned to go. We're going to be twenty-one this winter," Katrin continued. "I know you're staying here because of me and I don't want that, Borsen. I want you to have your chance."

"It can wait a while, another year or two," Borsen argued.

"Or five? Or ten? Or never?" Yes, she saw fear, a flicker of it. He had thought of this, but he'd hidden it well.

"I thought I was helping you," he said, rising and walking over to the goat pens, where the does came to stand with their feet on the gate to be petted.

"You do help me, but I want you to go. You've worked so hard for this, Borsen. You shouldn't let it go now."

"I'm not letting it go!" He turned toward her, angry. "You can't tell me you don't want me to stay with you!"

Katrin closed her eyes. Borsen could make you think that he was easygoing, gentle, even a pushover, until you came up against that determination of his. Then he was a firebrand.

"Of course, I would…" she began.

"I don't want anyone sacrificing themselves for my sake," Borsen said fiercely. "I don't ever want that to happen again." His voice was so rough that the goats backed away fearfully. Contrite, he held out his hands to them and they came close, nibbling at his jacket cuffs and pushing their muzzles into his palms.

Katrin waited, wondering if he would explain, but he said no more.

"Borsen," she finally said in the stillness, broken only by the contented cudding of the goats, "I don't want people sacrificing themselves for my sake either, so you should understand. Menders is here because he was commanded to be. Hemmett has always wanted to be the Captain of my Guard and to be posted here. But your dreams take you to Erdahn. Though you are very dear to me and I'd hate to see you go, I think you should. I don't want you to be sucked into being a Royal House hanger-on, Borsen. It's hard enough that my life isn't entirely my own because I'm the Princess, without seeing you give up your life for my sake."

Borsen stubbornly kept his back to her and Katrin felt a flare of irritation. She squelched it immediately. She also had that deep determination which some people called stubbornness. She knew genuine caring and honesty could break it down.

"Borsen, you're the youngest Guild Tailor in the history of Mordania, possibly in the whole world," she said. "You've wanted to have your own establishment in Erdahn for as long as I've known you, even before you came to The Shadows. I am so grateful for what you've done. You've made my illness so much easier for me to bear than it would have been if you weren't here. You've put aside what you want out of the purest of motives – but I'm getting better now. Please, let me let you go, Borsen. I want so much to be able to walk into your establishment one day and say to myself, 'my brother did this because he's talented and took his opportunity when it came'."

Borsen propped a foot on the lower bar of the goats' pen and leaned his chin in his hands.

"Who would help you with the goats?" he said gruffly. "This has always been our project. There's no way you can milk them all out yet, especially not Old Cow. She's milking out over a gallon a day and her old tits are like trying to squeeze iron."

"Hemmett can help me."

"He milks like he's trying to ring a temple bell," Borsen grumbled. "It isn't good for the goats."

"Menders can help me then. He milks as well as either of us."

"He has a lot to do."

"I'll train Kaymar to do it then." Katrin waited.

Borsen couldn't resist laughing at the idea of elegant Kaymar milking goats. He turned to her. Despite the laughter, his eyes were wet. Katrin held her arms out to him. He sat with her and embraced her warmly.

"I'm torn," he said bluntly.

"Don't be. Go. Let Menders help you find a location for your establishment and a place to live. Take all the plans and patterns and drawings and suits you've made all these years and make yourself the grandest establishment in Mordania," Katrin said briskly, not wanting to cry herself.

She remembered the day Hemmett had gone away to military school, how Menders had stood on the steps and said goodbye, his words. She sat back and looked at Borsen.

"Make me proud," she said. "Stand tall, work hard."

ERDAHN, MORDANIA

8
TWO BIRDS FLY AWAY

Varnia stood in her room at The Shadows, looking from her packed suitcase to a folded sheaf of legal papers she had not yet been able to allow out of her sight.

She was going with Borsen to be his housekeeper in Erdahn. They had spent three months merrily traveling back and forth on The Shadows' steam launch, finding a townhouse that Borsen approved. Varnia had been stunned by its size and elegance and nearly fainted when he announced that a magnificent suite within it would be her apartment.

"What, you thought I would put you in a little hidey-hole off the kitchen?" he laughed as he nodded to the property agent. "My humble housekeeper in her little dark room? Think again, Sister!"

Menders had gone with them to be sure all was done properly, and they didn't get carried away and fall in love with a place in dire need of major repair.

Varnia had walked away into the glorious, sunny rooms that were to be hers, wanting to hide the tears in her eyes. She had been awed at her three rooms at The Shadows but this! It was a house in itself. There was a place that would be perfect for her plants and a little room that would be just right for sewing or painting, which Katrin was teaching her how to do.

"Happy with it?" Menders asked from the doorway. "He's about to sign the papers, so last call if you want to look further."

He smiled wickedly, knowing she was as in love with the house as Borsen was.

"It's wonderful," she said quietly, going to him. "I'm overwhelmed."

"It is well deserved," Menders answered, taking her hands. "I can't think of a better setting for you both. We'll be a few weeks having it brought up to snuff. Borsen is talking about a huge bathtub for one thing, but you should be right at home here within a couple of months."

Now the day had come. Furniture, including a massive bed Borsen found in the attics of The Shadows and claimed, had been shipped over, cleaned and arranged in the rooms. They hired a staff, including a cook's helper, maids and a laundress. Varnia had been astounded at this but Borsen insisted he didn't want her scrubbing clothes or floors.

"A housekeeper organizes the housekeeping, she doesn't scrub and dust," he said. "My sister, in particular, doesn't scrub and dust. If you truly want to do the cooking, that's fine. I can't think of anyone I would rather have cook for us. But having help doesn't hurt. I can manage this, Varnia."

"Varnia? Only half an hour before leaving." Kaymar said, tapping gently at her open door. "Is there anything I can take down for you?"

"The trunk, if you would," she smiled. He shouldered it easily, an amazing feat considering how many gifts and items had been wedged into it during the last few days. Katrin finally had to sit on it so they could get it to latch.

"I can take the case too," Kaymar offered.

"I'll bring it. I have something else to put in it," Varnia answered. He laughed and strode away down the hall with the trunk.

Varnia picked up the envelope containing the legal papers and drew them out once again. She unfolded them to look at her name next to Borsen's on the deed of the house.

When he first showed them to her, she had been speechless for several minutes. Then she had tried to protest that she had paid nothing toward the house.

"Varnia, you will more than earn your half of this home," Borsen said after she finally ran out of steam. "You already have. You've helped me since you first met me at Eiren's school. You brought me clothing because I was in rags. You shared what food you had for lunch with me. You tried to protect me against those toughs that beat me up and tripped me down the stairs. I'll never forget you ready to go after them the day Eiren's brother had to stop you. There are so many things you've done for me since – how can I possibly put a value in money on them?

"This is our home. We chose it together. We'll make it into a happy place. Don't argue and spoil it."

Varnia read the words making the house half hers, then rapidly kissed the paper, refolded it and placed it in the envelope. She tucked it into her case, closed and latched it, and went out the door.

***

"Are you sure?" Menders said dubiously, standing on The Promenade three blocks north of the Palace in Erdahn.

He and Borsen were looking up at the dingy façade of a three story building that had once been a mercantile. It had stood vacant for several years, with no tenant willing to take it on. If a building could have deliberately looked unprofitable, this was the one.

"It's sound, Uncle," Borsen replied, looking up with eyes that saw something Menders couldn't. "We've had it inspected. We've had it inspected twice. There's nothing wrong with it and it's in the perfect location."

Borsen, attired in a beautifully fitting black suit and matching top hat, was pacing up and down the sidewalk, looking up at the building, his gaze lovingly passing over rotting siding, desiccated lintels and grimy, small windows.

"I haven't found anything that would be better," Borsen went on. "It's across the street from the biggest investment banking firm in Mordania. What better walk by traffic could I have? This is the one, Uncle. I'm positive."

Menders turned to the real estate agent hovering some twenty feet away.

"Done," he said, seeing the man's face light up with relief. "Shall we return to your office to finalize the deal?"

Later, they relaxed over an early dinner at Malvar's, an elegant restaurant near the Palace. Menders had deliberately avoided looking at the hulking structure where the Queen resided, not wanting the red fury to rise in him again, not wanting to spoil his beloved nephew's happiness with any reference to that terrible day almost two years ago. This was Borsen's day, the beginning of realizing his dream. It should be free of the troubles of others.

"May I have the marble, Uncle?" Borsen asked after polishing off his second bowl of soup."

"Have whatever you want," Menders said firmly. "Don't hold back. The entire point of the exercise is to start you out in appropriate surroundings. The funds are available to you and as your business partner, I give you permission to use them however you see fit. You're no fool, Borsen."

Their main courses arrived while their conversation continued unabated. Borsen was brimming with ideas, ambitions and plans. Menders had come in on the deal with pleasure, not only because it supported the young man's dreams but because he was convinced it would be a profitable venture. The run down building was destined for great things. Menders would see to it, through investment of as much funding as was necessary, that Borsen would have sufficient workers and materials to bring it about.

"Three hundred workmen if you need them, just the way we built The Shadows Academy from the ground up in six months," Menders told Borsen as they plowed into second main courses, both of them ravenous. "As much marble as you please. Glass for a solarium on the roof. Do it all now, don't hold back. Even the letters for the sign over the door. The foreman believes you can be ready to begin in five months with a large enough work force. I'd rather you be in business and turning a profit in five months than have the work drag on for two years with no money being made."

Borsen's eyes were alight as he rapidly scribbled and sketched in his notebook, finalizing ideas, writing down lists of things he would require. Menders hadn't seen him looking so alive since Katrin had been hurt.

They strolled back down The Promenade to the townhouse Borsen had purchased as his home in Erdahn. They were greeted at the door by Borsen's boarhound, Magic, and by Varnia, who embraced Menders warmly before taking herself off to bed after another busy day of organizing and decorating the house.

"I must start back home," Menders said after he and Borsen had a drink together and talked over more plans for the building. "You'll be starting the refurbishment tomorrow, according to the foreman. Kaymar will be over often. Don't trust any letters to the mails. You know this, why am I nagging you?" Menders laughed a little.

"I'll be all right," Borsen said, coming to stand by him. "I couldn't be better provided for. I'll miss you terribly, but Katrin was right. It's time to do this, if I'm ever going to."

"Yes, that it is," Menders said. "And I know you're no fool, but please – be careful, my boy."

"I will, Papa. I'll write every week and I'll come home often."

Menders shook Borsen's hand and then couldn't bear it. He put his arms around the young man. Borsen hugged back with a will, holding on long enough to let Menders know he was not as confident as he seemed. This parting was painful.

Menders stood back and took Borsen's chin in his hand, looking into his eyes for a long moment before letting himself into the street. He didn't allow himself to look back. He heard Borsen close the door behind him almost immediately.

Menders walked rapidly down to the boat, untied the rope and tossed it to Ifor.

"Borsen all settled?" Ifor asked companionably, stowing the rope and making sure all was in readiness for the night trip back to The Shadows.

"Yes, all eager to begin," Menders answered before going to the prow. He stood there as the boat drew away from the dock and Ifor pointed it toward home, opening the throttle.

Standing there in the damp winter cold, Menders tried to squelch many emotions, determined to concentrate on Borsen's happiness, plans and the fact that Varnia was with him. But as was so often the case nowadays, since the peaceful world of The Shadows had been rocked to its foundations, darkness seeped in.

He wasn't entirely confident over Borsen being on his own, even with Varnia's companionship.

Borsen was brilliant and talented. He wasn't afraid of hard work, but Menders had been a tempering influence in his life from the time he was thirteen.

Borsen was Thrun – very much so. Since he'd been without the upbringing the Thrun gave their children, where they were lovingly taught strong self-control and mental discipline, he could be ruled by extremes – of emotion, effort and exertion. Menders had always seen this, and gently guided the boy and then the young man away from obsessive overwork, where he would forget to eat and rest.

Menders feared that given his head, with no guidance, Borsen would proceed to work himself to death. The potential was there. But it was time to let him go.

Katrin and Hemmett needed him most now, so that was where he must be, but part of his heart was back in Borsen's house in Erdahn.

"Let it be all right," he whispered to whatever might hear, wishing for the first time in his life that he was a religious man and could find comfort in prayer. Overhead the three brightest stars were misty blurs.

***

The door to Borsen's townhouse opened just enough to allow two shadowy figures to slip into the front garden. They moved silently to the street, where they were illuminated by the street lamp.

Borsen spoke softly to his dog and walked to The Promenade, where he turned south, toward the park where the statue of Glorantha, first Queen of Mordania was located. Magic paced gracefully alongside him, his sheer size and apparent fierceness more than enough deterrent for anyone who might consider accosting the young man.

At the park, Borsen released Magic's lead, bidding him to stay near. The clock tower struck three.

The dog romped across the unkempt park lawn, sniffing here and there, stopping frequently to ascertain his master's whereabouts before making further forays.

Borsen approached the statue of Glorantha silently, waiting for memory to return. He concentrated on senses other than sight, waiting for an impression that would let him know this was the place he sought.

He had not been able to sleep. The parting from Menders had been deeply painful; excitement and loneliness did the rest. He'd finally decided to seek out the statue he believed he remembered from a day when he was only four years old.

A dilapidated bench on one side of the statue drew him. In a moment, the smell of wet wood sparked the old memory. A heavy mist made the bench glisten in the light from the few working streetlamps and the pale crescent of Eto, Eirdon's larger moon.

Borsen reached out and touched the frieze around the base of the statue. A moment later, he knelt on the bench, pressing his face against the cold, wet marble.

"Mama," he whispered. Magic ran over and snuffled at his master before sighing in a great whoosh and settling on the ground beside the bench.

ERDAHN, MORDANIA

9
BORSEN'S

Borsen knelt next to an enormous, thin slab of facing marble as the work crew slowly slid another slab alongside. He was watching the pattern of green veins snaking richly across the crystalline surface of the white stone, waiting for a match.

"Just a little further, men," he said encouragingly. "I think … yes! Another match, that's it! Here, let's mark it." He pulled out his pencil and picked up the long measuring stick the stonemasons used, pushing it carefully across the polished surface of the marble where the foreman caught it and helped him straighten it. They drew the marking lines true with those on the slab they'd matched it to.

"Borsen, will you look at the waste on this one?" the foreman groaned.

"It won't be wasted," Borsen replied, sitting back and rubbing his knees. They ached, despite the cloth workman's knee pads he, like all the other men on the work team, were using. "Counters, walls where it doesn't have to match, steps, sidewalk out front. That's why I'm buying it by the slab, so we'll have plenty. It will be a saving in the long run. And I'm only matching the marble for the façade."

"You'll still have a lot of waste," the foreman said gloomily. "If you'd bought book-matched slabs, it would be a lot less."

"I don't like book-matched marble." Borsen grinned up at him. "I want it to look like one continuous slab."

The foreman gave up and laughed.

"There's no stopping you, is there? All right then, have at the marble, let's find another match."

"Food!" bellowed the man who had been sent for lunch. There was general approbation. Borsen allowed himself to be heaved up by the foreman, who had been responsible for the rapid building of Eiren's school. It was a relief to be up off the floor thick with marble dust. He hurried with the others to the stove in the corner where the chunky, heavy sandwiches favored by construction tradesmen were being doled out.

"And two for the boss," said the fellow with the bag of sandwiches, handing Borsen his usual double portion.

"Where do you put it all, boss?" one of the men teased, as someone did every day.

"Into my personality. It's larger than I am," Borsen answered, sitting down among them and tearing into the food, gratefully accepting the cup of hot coffee passed down the line to him.

There was the usual snickering, but he knew the men liked and respected him because he worked with them and he knew what he wanted. He hadn't handed them a bunch of wild plans, impossible to carry out, before snugging up in his townhouse, expecting them to work miracles. He was out here in the cold, crawling around the warehouse on his hands and knees.

When he wasn't here matching marble, he was at his building, lending a hand with the refurbishment. He even worked there on rest days, keeping things moving, doing the detailed finishing work he enjoyed the most. After eight years at The Shadows, he had plenty of carpentry experience. He had no problems with his work crew not respecting him, though he often had as many as three hundred men all working on the place at once.

They were matching the marble slabs that would be used on the building façade. It was tedious, frustrating, slow work. He knew the men hated it, but he found it oddly fascinating – but then, he loved marble. He had been delighted when his uncle told him to go ahead and have his building exactly the way he wanted it to be. That meant marble. Lots of marble.

He'd first seen marble when he was only four and his mother had been alive. On that day, his father was roaming up and down The Promenade in Erdahn, looking to shoplift or pickpocket while casing the neighborhood for possible housebreaking. His mother, who always refused to have anything to do with his father's thieving, took Borsen into the shelter of the marble plinth of Queen Glorantha's statue when a sudden rainstorm blew up.

Back then he hadn't been able to see much, but he was fascinated by the dark green veining in the white marble. He traced it with his skinny little hand while his mother recited a poem to him about the Giants under the ground, the life force of Eirdon that sometimes thrust up through the soil in the forms of great stone hands and faces.

"There are Giants in the ground,
There are Giants in the sky.
When clouds are thick and rolling,
You see them striding by.
When the snow drifts deeply,
There are giants far below.
Sleeping in the places,
Where all men's bones shall go."

She'd been able to keep her beautiful white eyes fully open because of the rainclouds dimming the sunlight. He could remember her sweet face and how she'd held her cape over him, so he would stay dry while he rubbed his hands over the smooth marble again and again.

"Always remember that you are Thrun, my little son," she'd whispered. "Remember you are from the first people of Eirdon."

All he had to do to hear his mother's voice in his mind was to run his hand over the polished surface of a statue or building façade. He'd decided that he would have marble in his establishment. So now he didn't care that he'd spent a total of thirty-five hours so far crawling around, matching the veining on the white and green marble that would be on the façade of his building. More would be inside – black marble in the foyer, yellow marble with gold veins in much of the rest of the building, with touches of pink, green and brown marble elsewhere, for contrast.

Borsen leaned back on his packing crate seat and tucked into his second huge sandwich. He was starving and exhausted. It would be a long afternoon, after which it would be all he could do to walk the three blocks home and crawl into the bathtub for a hot soak. He would do justice to whatever Varnia had made for dinner and then fall into bed. It was the pattern of his days now – and it was a pattern he was grateful for, because it kept him occupied all the time.

Borsen found Erdahn to be unsettling, even though as a child he had lived in it a time or two because of his father's endless migrations. He'd never been entirely on his own in a large city before and he'd had some experiences in the last couple of months that he was in no hurry to repeat.

He was extremely grateful for Kaymar's honest and frank advice when he was younger. Kaymar had made no bones about the fact that there were men who were going to find Borsen irresistible for a number of reasons, including his small stature, his youthfulness and his exotic features. He could be certain he would be approached by men who were interested in nothing more than his body. Indeed, it had already happened, more than once.

His first proposition in Erdahn came from a man who walked up to him on the street and offered him a knee trembler in a nearby alley, earning himself a close view of Borsen's largest knife and a brisk refusal. Borsen had been propositioned before, in Surelia and Artreya, but by men who were less crude and more philosophical about being refused.

There were also men on the work crew who were interested. At least they had been friendly and respectful. They treated him as a person they would like to know, not just a piece of meat they wanted to rut. Refusing them had been a matter of giving the impression he was already attached, something they assumed immediately once he graciously turned them down. He still felt at ease with them after disappointing them, but some of the streets in Erdahn were places he simply didn't go any longer. Better to stick to work and townhouse – and The Shadows, if he could get free to get over there. So far, he hadn't been able to go home. There was so much to do.

When Borsen wasn't at the building site, he was going through warehouses, looking for furnishings for his store, searching for stock, ordering fabrics, supplies, light fixtures, thread and a million other things that would be needed. He was also recruiting and hiring tailors, finishers, salesmen and cleaning staff, to begin work as soon as he had the store open.

"End of break, boss?" one of the men asked. Borsen looked up, a little startled. He took out his watch.

"Take some more time, fellows," he said. "It'll be a long, hard grind this afternoon. Let's rest our bones a while longer."

He could see by their smiles it was the right thing to say. Being stingy about a few minutes' rest would lose him much more than a little time.

***

Stevahn Rondheim was watching the activity at the building directly across from his family's bank on the Promenade in Erdahn. He had a bird's eye view from his third story office that fronted on the street.

The building had been vacant for over a year, attracting handbills and vagrants. The Promenade had gone downhill of late, as funding to municipal works dwindled during Mordania's most recent skirmish with Artreya. Businesses like his own paid cleanup crews to keep the sidewalks and adjacent road clean, but there were many stretches of The Promenade riddled with loose cobblestones, horse shit and trash. The empty building had become an eyesore. It was with considerable interest that he'd observed activity across the way, beginning some weeks ago.

Initially, the building was shown to potential buyers. Then a fine carriage pulled up and two men, accompanied by one of Erdahn's most prestigious property brokers, went over the building in minute detail. On successive days, they returned with various people, obviously carpenters and other tradesmen. Surveyors made measurements, plumbers came and went, glaziers stood out in the road and gazed up at the dingy and dark windows.

It was obvious the two men, who resembled each other and must be father and son, were coming from somewhere far enough away that they could not be in Erdahn daily. Then, after the rumor that the vacant building had indeed been sold went up and down The Promenade, the younger man was continually present, along with an army of workmen. Where most renovation projects might have a crew of ten, there were at least a hundred men all working on the building at once, sometimes many, many more.

Stevahn's secretary had news.

"The word is that it's going to be a tailor shop," she announced.

"That whole building for a tailor shop?" Stevahn asked in disbelief. "They're gutting the entire thing."

"They say he's a master tailor," she replied. "Goes by only one name, something beginning with a 'B'. The newssheet man told me, but I've forgotten. He's supposed to be very good. Perhaps he plans to rent the rest of it."

His secretary was a twitterhead, so he didn't give her announcement much credence. Anyway, he was far too occupied with watching the progress on the building from his office window.

The industry and effort expended was amazing. Cranes on the roof winched building materials from dray carts appearing at clockwork intervals in the street. Tons of lumber, carpeting, glass, mirrors and crated items were lifted from an endless procession of vehicles. The armies of workers were rapidly converting what had been a gloomy and dull mercantile into something quite other. It was intriguing – and the young man who was constantly on the site was even more so.

He'd been immaculately turned out in a black suit and matching topper when he appeared with the older man who resembled him so closely. He was still beautifully, if more casually dressed as he moved around the site all day long. He seemed at ease with the workmen and thought nothing of picking up a hammer or helping to move a heavy object. He sported dark, flowing, waist length hair that was usually clipped back out of his way. He wore spectacles and a dark jawline beard and moustache of a style not common in Erdahn. Small statured, he gave the impression of being a boy, but it was obvious he was full grown.

He was also fearless. More than once Stevahn watched agog as the young man hitched a ride from the ground to the building's roof on a load being winched up by a crane, holding the cable with one hand.

What was more, the young man stayed at the building after the workmen had gone home for the day. He could be heard hammering or sawing away into the evening. Sometimes when Stevahn stayed late at the bank, he could see lamplight within the darkened building across the street.

He was intrigued.

His secretary, who had been trying unsuccessfully for two years to seduce him, finally came up with some real information.

"His name is Borsen," she said excitedly, watching as the young man stepped off a second story windowsill onto a load of lumber being winched skyward. "He's the tailor. He bought the building outright. Paid in gold drammarks."

"What the hells is a tailor doing running around a construction site all day long?" Stevahn asked her, watching as the young man – Borsen – lightly stepped off the pile of lumber as it drew level with the roof.

"I don't know, but that's who it is," his secretary answered, sighing to herself.

"Incredible," Stevahn muttered, watching the slender figure silhouetted against the sky, hands on hips, looking across the rooftops of Erdahn. Borsen was standing on a narrow plank spanning a four-story drop. He stood there as confidently as if he was standing on a solid, granite floor.

"Are we going to finish this letter?" his secretary asked, her voice bleak.

Perhaps the poor thing has caught on, finally, Stevahn thought. I am not interested in her – or in any woman.

***

The next day, the marble started arriving.

The drays stretched back for blocks, drawn by eight horse teams, wheels creaking with the weight of slabs of marble of all colors – pink marble from Fambre, Baramban golden marble, the famous Portos green-veined white marble. The slabs were followed by pillars, stair risers and treads, floor tiles, mantlepieces.

Borsen was everywhere the marble was being installed, pointing out the joins, watching as the slabs for the exterior of the building were put into position, helping to inch them this way and that until the veining appeared to be unbroken. Someone has spent hours finding just where to join these sections, Stevahn thought in awe. I'll bet it was that fellow, kneeling on the floor of some warehouse, lining up marble slabs with the help of these men. And now he's out there, his sleeves rolled up, helping them swing those almighty huge chunks of rock around and making sure that all is perfect. What sort of man is that?

The glass began arriving next. In no time, a solarium was completed on the roof.

In five months' time, the project was finished. The last pile of refuse was carted away. A cleaning crew went in, scrubbing the place top to bottom. The sidewalk was replaced with marble slabs and a sign was installed over the massive mahogany doors:

BORSEN'S
PRACTICALITY – FUNCTIONALITY – EXQUISITE STYLE

"A bit pretentious for a tailor shop run by a boy," Stevahn's secretary said irritably.

"They say he's twenty-two or three," Stevahn answered, watching as drays unloaded hundreds of bolts of fabric and boxes full of what must be supplies. "Not a boy."

Suddenly Borsen himself ran out of the building and hefted a box, exchanging some cheery words with the drayman. He darted back into the building, only to return a moment later to heft another box. Stevahn forgot all about the report he was dictating, watching him.

***

Dear Katrin,

It's done. There is not one more bit of timber to sand, marble to polish, there are no more nails to bash with a hammer. The cleaning crews are going through one more time tomorrow and we will spend two weeks arranging and getting the displays put together – and then Borsen's will open for business.

I'd be a liar if I didn't say I was so tired I could scream, but screaming would take too much energy. This will not be a long letter, but Kaymar and Ifor are heading back tomorrow and I wanted to let you know it's all done and ready to be seen! I do hope you're well enough to come and see. I've thought of you and Hemmett so much and really look forward to showing you through the place and amazing you with my wood paneled elevator.

I never thought working at tailoring would be a vacation, but it will seem like it after the last five months. Remind me, should I ever decide to take up life anew as a carpenter, of just how all my bones ached today. It's going to be strange getting used to holding needles and pins again after all these months of hammers and crowbars!

I'm heading for the tub now. I hope to see you soon. Maybe you can come over next time Uncle comes. It's hard to believe. It happened so fast it almost seems like a dream.

Love,

B

***

"And how much of it did you do yourself?" Menders asked, looking Borsen up and down. He'd been taken on an exhaustive tour of inspection of Borsen's establishment. "You've lost weight you can't afford to, my boy."

"I have worked hard, Papa, but look at it!" Borsen answered excitedly. "I can eat anytime. I don't often get to put together my own establishment."

Menders laughed and put an arm around his shoulders.

"No, you don't. Enjoy it – you deserve it. Any interest?"

"Mobs. We already have appointments and we're not open for business until next week. Everyone is curious and there's a lot of gossip. The news sheet reporters were here asking questions. I'll send the articles your way as soon as they come out."

"We'll be glad to get them."

Borsen looked at him. "How is Katrin? I miss her."

"She's doing well, better all the time. Fewer nightmares and no waking dreams at all. She's back to making soap now, though she can't do much at a time. She's teaching music to the infant class again. She loves your letters, so please keep writing."

"I'd hoped she'd come with you."

Menders shook his head.

"She simply can't," he sighed. "It would be far too upsetting. She tried to come but when she got to the dock she began shaking so badly, I turned around and took her home. Borsen, it will take a long time for her to recover from what happened. Going within sight of the Palace is something she can't bear right now."

"Poor thing. It doesn't matter. She'll see it when she can. I'll draw pictures of it all and send them over," Borsen said. "Can you stay the night, Uncle?"

Menders shook his head. "I've never been away from Katrin overnight and now is not the time to begin," he replied gently. Borsen nodded and did a good job of not letting disappointment show. Menders sighed to himself, but there was nothing to be done about it. Katrin was far too fragile to leave for long.

"Now, let me take you to dinner, my young entrepreneur," Menders said more cheerfully. "I have to get back on the boat by eight, so we'd best hurry along."

Borsen caught up his hat and let them out the door of his shining, perfect building, not noticing the large-framed man loitering outside the bank opposite as he enthusiastically began telling his uncle about how all the display suits he'd made over the years were being put on mannequins, ready for opening day.

***

"It sounds so wonderful! I can't believe he's done it in such a short time," Katrin said after Menders had described Borsen's in extravagant detail and given her the sketches Borsen made of the building.

"He didn't do it alone, he had hundreds of workmen," Hemmett said, nudging her playfully.

"If you saw him, you'd think he'd done it alone," Menders said, shaking his head. "It'll be good for him to slow down and run the place. He's so thin you could shine a light through him."

Eiren frowned. "I don't like the sound of that, not considering the way Borsen eats and still stays so slender."

"Well, I took him to dinner tonight. He had two starters, two soups, two mains and two desserts," Menders smiled. "Once he's not working so hard physically, he'll bulk back up, my love. I did say something but he's so happy I couldn't dampen his spirits."

"No, I'm glad you didn't," Eiren agreed. "He's worked so very hard."

"So hard he hasn't managed to get home," Hemmett added a little grumpily.

"Oh Hemmett!" Katrin protested, sounding shocked. "He's been busy, and it's only been five months."

"Only takes a couple of hours to get here, a couple of hours to get back," Hemmett answered.

"He's going to try to get home very soon," Menders said firmly. "You can't have any idea just how hard he's been working unless you go and see the place, which I would recommend, Hemmett. Kaymar will be going over in a week to do some work for me. Why not go along with him? He'll be there overnight and he and Ifor always stay with Borsen and Varnia. You'll have a chance to see things firsthand."

Hemmett looked less grumpy. He stood and stretched.

"I just might do that," he said, sounding very interested. Then he yawned. "I'm going to turn in. It's late and I have early patrol in the morning."

"I'm going to bed too," Katrin said, rising and going to kiss Eiren and Menders. "Thank you for staying up and letting us know how it all looked. I do wish I could see it."

"You will. Borsen sends his love." Katrin smiled at Menders' encouraging reply and went off to her room.

Eiren waited until the door was closed.

"It took her quite a while to get back to normal," she told Menders in a low tone. "It's a shame. She was terribly disappointed, which is what put Hemmett in his current mood."

Menders sighed and shook his head.

"I'm afraid it's something only time can cure," he said. "It's absolutely understandable that she's frightened. Possibly curiosity will help her overcome the fear but I'm not about to push. She'll go when she's able. Borsen will be writing often and I'm sure he'll be putting tantalizing and interesting temptation in all his letters."

"Good," Eiren said, rising. "Come to bed, you've had a long day."

"My dear, farlins couldn't keep me from it," Menders grinned.

***

Stevahn had tried desperately to meet the now-famous Borsen in the last three months. He'd been sure to come out of his bank building at the same moment Borsen left his establishment a number of times. This was not an easy feat, considering Borsen worked longer hours than any of his employees and frequently stayed late at night. Stevahn had even strolled across the street on a pleasant summer evening, making sure that he reached Borsen as the young man was locking the door.

It was his first good, close look at the young man. He liked what he saw as Borsen locked the door, turned partially away from and unaware of Stevahn. He obviously tailored for himself. His suit was beyond perfection. It fit precisely, the color was an unusual grey with a golden undertone. Hat, shoes, waistcoat were all the goldish grey color, with the emphasis of a gold colored hatband and a rich, heavy gold watch chain. An elaborately carved walking stick with a marble knob was leaned against the door as Borsen turned the big key and then pocketed it. He reached out and touched the marble wall of the entryway for a moment, then picked up the walking stick with a flourish and turned, coming face to face with Stevahn.

Stevahn knew the word 'ravished' but had never considered it, particularly in reference to himself. Now he understood it completely, because he was looking at a face that would be burned into his mind until the day he died.

Borsen's eyes were large, brown and exotic, framed by rimless spectacles. His features were perfectly balanced - his nose high-bridged, definite and perfect, his lips full and sensuous. His face was defined by an elegant jawline beard and moustache. Diamond studs glittered in the young man's ears, but like everything about him, they were perfectly in proportion and not overdone. Though Borsen could not be more than five feet tall and dressed with style few men could carry off, there was nothing effeminate about him.

Obviously startled, Borsen had his hand in his jacket pocket in a flash, reaching for a weapon. Stevahn smiled apologetically and said, "Good evening."

"Good evening," Borsen answered guardedly, bowing slightly.

"Nice night," Stevahn said pleasantly.

"Indeed." Borsen nodded dismissively, stepped around Stevahn and walked away down The Promenade. Stevahn looked after him, intrigued by the unusual accent that flavored the three words he'd spoken. It was an inflection Stevahn had never heard before.

He sighed over Borsen's curt dismissal and began walking toward his own lodgings in the young man's wake, watching as Borsen occasionally gave his walking stick an absent minded twirl when the footpath was clear.

A beggar woman stepped out of an alley and caught at Borsen's arm. Borsen stopped and doffed his hat to her, bowing far lower than he had to Stevahn.

"I beg your pardon, Mister Borsen," the woman said frantically. "I hear that you gives jobs to people what can sew?"

"I do, though right now I'm looking for people who can make ladies' hats," Borsen answered, smiling at her.

"Oh sir! I was a milliner before I married," the woman gushed. "In Erdstrom and then here. I can make hats, straws, felts, bonnets. I can trim, set up patterns, anything you want. My husband's been killed in the latest fighting and I have three little ones I can't feed. Please, if you have any work, I can prove myself to you."

"Come to Borsen's first thing tomorrow, eight o'clock, and ask for me," Borsen replied immediately. He took out a money bag, and turned it out on his palm. He gave the coins to the woman, who stared at them as if he'd handed her a priceless jewel.

"How do you know I won't just go off with this?" she gasped.

"Because you asked that question, my dear," Borsen answered gently in that odd, cadenced accent. "I will see you tomorrow, bright and early and we'll get you started. Do you have care for your children?"

"Yes sir! I can leave them with my sister. Tomorrow, sir! Thank you, sir! Loving Galanth bless your sweet face!" The woman burst into tears. Borsen handed her a handkerchief, reached out and touched her hair and then went on his way.

"He gave me twenty florins!" the woman, overcome, said to Stevahn as he drew close. "Twenty florins! I haven't seen that many florins together in my whole life! My children will eat tonight, won't they!" She clutched the money close and ran down the alley, Borsen's handkerchief fluttering in her hand as she went.

Stevahn continued down the street but Borsen had gotten a good lead on him during the moments the woman was exclaiming to him about the money. He saw the young man turn off the footpath and vanish down one of the side streets turning off the Promenade.

Next morning Stevahn was in his office early, curious to see if the beggar woman actually turned up. It was obvious Borsen was already in the store building, as the lights were burning, though the doors were still locked.

At the stroke of eight, the woman came scrambling around the corner, along with several of Borsen's employees who arrived daily at that time. She'd made herself as presentable as extremely shabby clothing would allow. Borsen opened the door, gave his employees a friendly grin, then welcomed the woman and ushered her in.

"I'll be damned," Stevahn said to himself.

He had found to his delight that Borsen's personal workroom was directly opposite his office. Dictations to his secretary were enlivened by the ongoing pageantry there, as one gentleman after another was ushered in, shown various fabrics or given a large book to peruse. Whenever Borsen picked up the measuring tape always ready on his worktable, he would twitch the curtains closed, so that his customers would not be seen in a state of undress. The rest of the time the curtains were open to give the young tailor sufficient light for his exacting work. Stevahn saw a lot of him, bending over one suit or another, painstakingly stitching by hand or by machine.

Sometimes Borsen stood, easing his lower back with his hands and went to stand at the big window, looking down at the street. To Stevahn's complete frustration, Borsen never looked over at his own office, directly opposite.

***

Dear Katrin,

I can't believe it's been three months since Borsen's opened. I have so many orders! I don't know if I'll ever get caught up, so I just keep plugging along. More people than I ever expected have decided they want the full-on exclusive service, which means little Borsen has to stitch their suits by hand. But I'm getting ahead of myself here.

I finally settled on several levels of service when it comes to suits. There are ready-made suits you can buy off the rack, made by my tailors to my patterns. That's the lowest level of service. You try it on, you buy it, you leave. The next level is having one of the readymade suits altered to fit. After that, you can have a suit made to one of my patterns by one of my tailors, custom fit, the fabric you want. After that, you're looking at Exclusive Service. You get measured, a pattern made specifically for you, advice on fabric, the suit made entirely for you by the great man himself, namely me (feel free to bow down). There are even two levels of Exclusive Service, machine made suits and entirely handmade suits. Of course, the handstitched is the most expensive.

Well, I thought I would get a call for a handmade suit once a month or so. Silly little Borsen. I have over a hundred orders for entirely hand stitched suits now and there's a waiting list for people who want to be measured for the same! It's as bad as Tomar's workshop before we got the sewing machines. There I squat at my worktable, stitching madly away. I'm going to raise the prices of the damned things – not that I think it will ease the workload, but at least I'll die of overwork a rich man.

Never mind, I'm loving it all, but so stretched that I can barely find time to sleep. I wish I could come home and see you all, but there's no end in sight, and if I let things fall behind now and have people complaining about how they waited an eternity for Borsen to make them a suit … I simply shall not contemplate that. It can't happen.

Write me with all the news. My best to Petra and best wishes for her to have an easy pregnancy again this time. Punch old Vil on the arm from me. Love to Uncle and Auntie and Bumpy and most of all, for you.

B

Gods, it's what I was afraid of, Menders groaned inwardly as he read the letter from Borsen that Katrin had passed on to him. Borsen was an excellent tailor, phenomenally so. The clothing he made looked and fit so well that people would pay him any amount of money for it. Reading about his plan backfiring and how he had a massive workload of clothing to hand stitch was daunting. Menders knew Borsen was making it sound funny for Katrin's sake. Matters were probably much worse than he was letting on.

He set the letter down on the table and Eiren picked it up. She scanned it quickly and sighed.

"I'd better go over there," Menders said. "Want to come with me tomorrow for a day in Erdahn?"

"Of course," she accepted rapidly.

"We'll surprise him at home and keep him away from his workroom all day," Menders smiled, reaching out and pulling her down to sit on his lap. "I'll spoil both of you all day long."

"It's a deal, sir," Eiren laughed.

The next day, Menders rapped on Borsen's townhouse door at seven o'clock. He and Eiren were amazed when Varnia told them Borsen was at the store, working.

"Every rest day," she said irritably. "He's there late every night, then out of here at six the next morning."

"Is there anyone else there?" Menders asked.

"No. If you want to get his attention, you'll have to throw gravel up at his workroom window. I had to do that last week when Magic ate most of a book and then acted like he was dying."

Menders felt like an idiot standing in The Promenade, chucking bits of gravel up at Borsen's window while Eiren rollicked around, much amused by his discomfiture.

"I'm about to just break the glass – that should get his attention," Menders grumbled, flinging another small stone and adding a piercing whistle between his teeth. He was relieved when Borsen appeared, saw him and started laughing, then disappeared rapidly. A few moments later, he was at the door, opening it for them.

"If you'd told me you were coming, I would have been at home!" he grinned, hugging them both mightily. Menders groaned inwardly. He was thinner. When he saw the piled up table in Borsen's workroom, he wanted to scream.

"I'm snowed under," Borsen admitted. "We've had to push back all the measurement appointments and I now have to tell people their suit will take much longer, or I'd never get out of this room at all."

"I'm taking you out of it right now, for the entire day," Menders said briskly. "No, you're my business partner as well as my nephew and you are coming with me. You won't be of any use if you end up collapsing. If you don't come willingly, I will pick you up and carry you out, so get your coat and hat and let's go."

Borsen almost protested, then decided he'd rather not be carried out of his own establishment over Menders' shoulder. He got his coat and hat, and went.

ERDAHN, MORDANIA

10
WALDRUM THE DANCING BEAR FINDS LOVE

"If you want to meet him so badly, Mister Rondheim, why don't you go over there and order a suit?" Stevahn's secretary asked. "They say there's already a waiting list to have him make a suit personally."

I have become an idiot, Stevahn thought. I'm so intrigued by the little bastard, who is kind to beggar women but close to rude to men who say good evening that I've never thought of simply going over and ordering a suit from him!

He grabbed his hat, leaving his office without a word.

"Aren't you going to finish the letter – oh why do I even ask!" his secretary said waspishly to the empty room.

A smiling doorman swung the heavy red doors of Borsen's open for Stevahn and gestured for him to enter.

The foyer was incredible. It extended up into the second story and was entirely of black marble, with a brilliant chandelier hanging dead center. A man in a perfect suit was standing directly beneath the chandelier. He bowed as Stevahn approached.

"Good morning, sir," he said, his voice welcoming and very polite. "I am the Store Director. How may I help you today?"

"I'd like to see about having Borsen make me a suit," Stevahn answered, rather dumbstruck by the splendor of the place.

"Indeed, sir. That would be the third floor, accessible either by the stairs or by the elevator."

The marble stairs afforded a view of much of the store, so Stevahn opted for them. He stared around him as he saw most of Erdahn society engaged in buying clothing, from trying ready-made shoes to being measured for gloves. When he reached the specified floor, a man seated behind a counter rose and greeted him.

Stevahn repeated his desire to have a suit made by Borsen.

"Of course, sir. Would you be interested in ready-made, custom-fitted, or the exclusive service? If you wish to be attended by Borsen himself, there is an additional fee."

"Money is no object," Stevahn said. "I'll have the full exclusive service from Borsen."

"Very good sir." The man opened an appointment book, while Stevahn swore inwardly. The waiting list, of course. Oh gods, I'll never meet Borsen! Why don't I just go pound sand?

Just as the man was looking at dates three months away, to Stevahn's utter disappointment, a door opened to his left.

"Varens, has Menders turned up yet?" It was Borsen's voice.

"No," the man behind the counter said, far more casually than he'd spoken to Stevahn. "There's a west wind come up, so he's probably been delayed."

What does a west wind have to do with someone being delayed, Stevahn thought waspishly.

"Damn." Borsen's voice again.

"I have a gentleman here enquiring about the exclusive service," the counter man, obviously Varens, said, winking at Stevahn.

"Fine, I have time. Send him in. Here, before I forget again, that drawing for your son, fifth page in the book," Borsen said. A sketchbook sailed out toward the counter. Varens caught it neatly in mid-air.

"Please go in, sir," he said to Stevahn. "We're rather informal up here." He smiled, not knowing that Stevahn's returned smile was so warm because he now saw his wedding ring, knew he had a son and was not a special friend of Borsen's. You are pathetic, he scolded himself, going quickly toward the door before anything came up to stop him, possibly Menders, whoever he was, coming for his appointment.

He found himself in the workroom with which he was already familiar. Borsen was leaning over his table, writing something, which he finished almost immediately. He turned and smiled.

I'm dying, Stevahn thought. I've never been this bad, ever.

"Good morning," Borsen said. Then he looked curious. "Have we met?"

"Yes, outside your door a few months ago, right before you hired a beggar woman," Stevahn answered.

"Oh yes! You came very close to having a knife held at your throat, you startled me so badly," Borsen said lightly, with such humor that Stevahn couldn't be insulted. "I was a bit of a boor, I admit. I can be when I'm frightened. I'm glad it didn't keep you from coming to see me."

He just wants to sell a suit, don't get your hopes up, Stevahn muttered inwardly. He shook the hand Borsen held out.

"What sort of suit are you looking for?" Borsen asked.

Stevahn tried to think over his wardrobe rapidly so he didn't end up ordering something he already had.

"Blue… for winter, since it's coming," he said awkwardly.

"Dark blue?"

"Uh… yes."

"Wool? Silk and wool?"

"Uh… silk and wool, yes." He sounded like a rather foolish echo.

"I have some nice ones, but first let me take your measurements," Borsen suggested, picking up his tape measure.

I have to take my clothes off, Stevahn moaned inwardly. I never thought of it.

"There's a screen over there, if you wish," Borsen directed, taking his eyes off of Stevahn to draw the curtains. Stevahn looked out the window toward his office to see his secretary watching, her mouth open. He rapidly stuck out his tongue at her before Borsen twitched the drapes shut. Stevahn steeled himself and removed his jacket.

"If you could undress to your undergarments," Borsen said kindly, indicating the screen. Stevahn hurried behind it with relief, knowing he could never have stripped in front of the young man without having apoplexy.

He pulled off his clothes, bumping the screen several times. Each time Borsen asked him if he was all right. He laughed nervously each time, saying he was fine.

Then he knocked the screen down.

***

"And then he knocked the screen down," Borsen said as Varnia rocked back and forth in her chair, laughing.

"Oh, the poor man," she gasped, wiping her eyes.

"He was so nervous," Borsen replied. "I felt terrible, but nothing I could say or do seemed to help."

"Maybe he's never been custom fitted before." Varnia reached for her water glass and took several swallows, trying to catch her breath.

"I thought that, but the suit he wore was definitely custom tailored. Not well, mind you, but he's hard to fit. So, it isn't as if he's never been to a tailor before." Borsen shook his head and turned his attention to his plate.

"Why is he hard to fit?" Varnia asked when he reached a stopping point. He'd been eating ravenously between bouts of regaling her with the story of his nervous and funny client.

"Bottom heavy. Not fat but a heroic build, a large frame and thickset. Big thighs, big arse – one of those fellows where the tail of the suit jacket always gaps open. You have to cut the back of the jacket on the bias to get it to flow right and weight the tail, so it doesn't swing open. Most tailors don't bother or know that's what they need to do. They just cut the jacket bigger and it fits like a sack."

"Probably why he's nervous. He's embarrassed by it." Varnia got up to bring over the jug of milk. Borsen was drinking it as if he'd been crossing a desert. "Did you eat today?"

"I was busy, but yes, Uncle came and took me to lunch," he replied. "Just hungry. When am I not?"

"So, when does your bottom heavy man come back?" Varnia asked after a moment.

"Two days. I'd better get in early and get started on his pattern – and I'm doing it directly on muslin. I can't even imagine trying to fit a paper pattern on him. He'd manage to set it on fire."

Varnia laughed again, wiping at her eyes.

***

After three fittings, Stevahn gave up. He became utterly tongue tied in front of Borsen or said things that verged on the moronic. He also realized Borsen saw many people a day. Though he was invariably polite and pleasant, he was doing a job, just as Stevahn directed people's investments at his family's bank.

At his fourth fitting, the suit was nearly finished and Borsen said a fifth fitting wasn't even necessary. Stevahn asked if he could have a fifth fitting before taking it home, just to be sure.

An expression crossed Borsen's face for a split second that made Stevahn realize this was an error and that he had insulted the young man. He had no idea how to make it right. He decided to play stupid, which he was already excelling at.

At the fifth fitting he put on the completed suit and got a good look at himself in the mirror.

Stevahn didn't have an unattractive body when stripped, but he was difficult to fit. His suits, though carefully made, never quite became him because, as his last tailor had said, he had a "sway back and big arse". This suit, made entirely by hand and costing a fortune, fit as if it had grown on him. It made his sway back and big arse assets and pared pounds from his waistline. Best of all, Borsen had strategically weighted the hem of the jacket to prevent it riding up or swinging open awkwardly, as all Stevahn's other suit jackets did.

The suit was worth every pennig – except that he was no closer to being friendly with the little tailor than he had been when he walked into the place for the first time.

"It's wonderful," Stevahn said, gazing into the mirror where he could not only see his own greatly improved reflection, but Borsen's as well. Borsen smiled.

"I'm glad you like it," he answered, his voice even and neutral.

Stevahn made another appointment for another suit with the helpful Varens. When he turned up at Borsen's workroom for the initial fitting, Borsen appeared surprised.

"Unless you ate a great deal this week, we don't need new measurements," he said cheerily. "We won't need to do a pattern fitting either, unless you want to make changes in the style."

Stevahn had no idea what changes could be made, so opted for choosing another fabric, this time a dove grey. Borsen shook his head.

"It'll turn you bright red," he said, turning Stevahn to a mirror and holding the fabric up in front of him. Stevahn had the unpleasant experience of seeing himself suddenly looking on the verge of apoplexy. "It has a yellow tone to it. But this one, very close in intensity, but with a blue cast – look."

It was better, toning down Stevahn's naturally reddened cheeks. After the three fittings necessary for that suit, he was no closer to being friendly with Borsen.

He ordered another suit. Black. He managed to request a style change requiring additional fittings. Sometimes he succeeded in speaking lucidly about things without sounding like a fool or being unintentionally insulting. Borsen was professional, friendly in a businesslike way, as he would be with any customer – and that was all.

Stevahn ordered another suit, a grey pinstripe, remembering to choose a bluish grey. He'd heard stripes required additional fittings. They did. He made no headway during the extra fitting sessions, no matter how he tried to interest his patient but distant tailor.

He'd taken to browsing the other departments of Borsen's regularly, hoping that he would bump into him or just catch sight of him. He watched Borsen's workroom assiduously while dictating. His secretary had given up on him, to his relief, and was now engaged to a man who worked in Accounts.

Desperate after six months of buying suits, a year after having seen Borsen for the first time, Stevahn did the only thing possible.

He ordered another suit.

***

Dear Katrin,

I understand why you won't be coming to the store grand opening. It's all right, so dry your tears and know I love you always. One day you'll come in and be amazed at my grand place, which I will admit still amazes me. I can't believe I have all this and what is more, that I'm a success! I have the aching muscles and the weariness to remind me of how I became a success, but it's still very new and exciting to me.

I miss you very much and I keep trying to find a way to get over there, but I just can't do it. I'm so backed up with suits I have to make entirely by myself that I can't believe it.

Making matters worse, I have a customer who has now ordered six suits in total, one for every month since he's started coming in here! I had a free hour when he wandered in six months ago. I let him jump the queue, much to my regret, because he's taken up scads of my time ever since. He's now bought every possible color suit that he can without having one in a shade that will make him appear on the verge of a stroke. So possibly that will be the end of Mister Rondheim and I'll be able to get moving on some of these other things that are hanging over my head.

Do not fret any more. We do what we can, when we can. You have to listen to me and believe because I'm Thrun, which means I'm very wise. I may also be older than you, and therefore, your elder.

Love,

***

Borsen stepped out of the elevator at the top level of his store, the solarium, which was now open to waiting customers – and was presently empty.

It was late at night after the official grand opening of Borsen's. The event had been attended by everyone and anyone who counted in Erdahn and had been enormously enjoyed by all. Menders and Eiren had managed to stay until ten before having to leave to take the steam launch back to The Shadows.

Katrin couldn't come, of course. She wasn't emotionally able to be near the Palace, or the memories.

Borsen was alone in the building now, as he often was late at night. It was still amazing to him that his store was up and running, outstripping every other business in Erdahn. The work was crushing. At times he was so exhausted that he sank down on his bed or stretched out in his bathtub and cried like a baby.

Now he understood the stories people at The Shadows told about his uncle working like a peasant for the first five years he and Katrin had been there. People's lives literally depended on the amount of wood Menders and Lucen had been able to cut – Menders had cut wood for hours every day, to the point where he was continually physically exhausted.

Varnia was Borsen's lifeline, keeping the house running and freeing him from any domestic responsibilities. He was able to work the eighteen hours a day that were necessary and he could be sure of a hot meal and good company when he did get home.

He stood looking over the city, a small glass of wine in his hand, thinking of The Shadows. He must get over there. Katrin needed him. He missed her painfully. He missed The Shadows painfully as well, but he was so overwhelmed with work he couldn't see a way to go home any time soon.

***

Stevahn settled back in his chair while the waiter removed his soup plate. His sister, Stellia, smiled at him.

It was their tradition to have a bang-up lunch at Malvar's a couple of weeks prior to Winterfest. In recent years, their parents had opted to travel to the warmth of Surelia for a good part of the harsh Mordanian winter. This lunch meeting gave Stevahn and Stellia an opportunity to plan for the annual migration and do some catching up without the rest of their family present.

"You're beautifully turned out, Stev. You've found someone who can fit you properly, at last." Stellia nodded a thank-you to the waiter who bore away her soup setting.

With some pride, Stevahn displayed the monogrammed B on his suit jacket lining. Stellia's eyes widened.

"A Borsen suit? I've heard he's a wizard with cloth!" Stellia studied the details of the jacket. "I wonder if you could get me in to see him? I could use a new riding habit before the family leaves for Surelia"

"I can try. It was entirely by chance that I jumped the queue," Stevahn replied. "I went up there one day to make an appointment. He had an hour free and took my measurements and order. So ever since then, for the other suits, appointments haven't been a problem."

Stellia gave him a teasing look.

"Other suits. How many? You've never been a clotheshorse."

"Six. I'd be mad not to have a wardrobe made now that I've found someone who can fit my big arse."

"He should be able to fit your big sister for a riding habit if you've bought six entirely handmade suits," Stellia laughed.

Stevahn was glad their main courses arrived at that moment. He and Stellia had always been close and normally he would willingly disclose any romantic aspirations he had to her. Unfortunately, considering how his plans regarding Borsen had completely foundered, he was reluctant to discuss them with anyone. What's more, he wasn't entirely sure, after his latest anxious accident during a fitting, that he could ever bring himself to go back to Borsen's workroom, much less beg the favor of having Stellia jump the queue.

"I've been in Borsen's of course," Stellia said as they started their main courses. "It's absolutely amazing – and people say he's just a boy. You could get lost in the place for hours. Of course, he wasn't out on the shop floor serving customers. He probably sees people somewhere in the upper floors."

"Third floor, opposite my office," Stevahn said without thinking. He froze, then looked up and met Stellia's eyes.

"So, you gaze on him?" she laughed. "Of course, you've met him personally with all those suits. What's he like? I've heard he's brown as a Samorsan and has a foreign accent so thick you can cut it with a knife. Some people are saying he's a Hetzophian prince."

Stevahn's eyebrows went up.

"I hadn't considered – he looks like he might be Surytamian, but he's darker than they usually are," he ventured. "I would never ask, of course."

"I haven't seen you this uncomfortable since Selnor treated you so badly," Stellia said, putting her fork down and extending her hand to him across the table. "Whatever is the matter? Is it getting left behind here at Winterfest? You can tell me, Stev."

He took her hand, raised it to his lips and kissed it.

"My dear girl," he smiled. "No, I don't mind manning the bank for Winterfest – Pappa and Mamma need to go to Surelia after they were ill this autumn and they'll need you with them."

"Then what is bothering you? I thought we could always be frank with each other." Her eyebrows quirked a bit, as they always did when she was concerned over a loved one. "Stev, I know when something's wrong! Out with it, or I'll tell Pappa!"

He laughed aloud and relaxed.

"You'll tattle then, eh?" he played along.

"It you don't let me know, I shall," she said, truculently raising her chin as she did when they quarreled as children. Then she stopped teasing and went very serious.

"You're in love with Borsen," she said very softly.

"I never could hide anything from you," he said, just as softly.

"But that's wonderful!"

Stevahn shook his head wryly.

"My dear, he doesn't know it and considering what a fool I make of myself when I'm around him – I'm just as glad he doesn't know."

Stellia put her head on one side.

"Brother, dear – you are a very self-assured man, or you were until the end of your affair with Selnor – and thank the gods we've seen the last of that little felschat," she said intensely. "How could a man who tells entire nations how to handle their money make a fool of himself in front of a tailor?"

"Every single time I'm in his presence I say the most idiotic things, some of them insulting. It's like those stories where the princess is cursed to have toads jumping out of her mouth every time she speaks. And I shake the entire time I'm around him. He must think I have the palsy – and that I'm a rude, simpleminded fool."

"Good gods, what did you say to him?" Stellia asked.

"Oh, brilliancies like 'I want a winter suit because winter's coming' and 'it's a nice evening because the sun is going down'," Stevahn sighed.

Stellia tried to keep a straight face, but lapsed into a soft giggle, which Stevahn ignored.

"I knocked down the bloody screen you undress behind the first time I was there, with a great clatter and me standing there with my pants down around my knees."

Stellia gasped and ducked her face toward her plate, sputtering hilariously. Stevahn actually began to smile.

"Then, last time I was there, I let him give me a brandy and had a cigar when he suggested it, hoping it would calm me, and – Oh Stell, I put the damned cigar out in his own glass of some violently alcoholic stuff he calls kirz because I wasn't paying attention. There was this great flash of fire and the glass shattered…"

Stellia surrendered, dropping her napkin on the floor and sitting back to laugh. Her face reddened, making the waiter come over with a glass of water. She sputtered a few gulps down, managed to draw breath and looked wickedly at Stevahn, who was chuckling himself.

"Waldrum the Dancing Bear Goes to the Tailor," Stellia chortled, parroting the titles of the popular children's books about an inept bear who visited various shops. In every book, Waldrum awkwardly laid waste to whichever establishment he was patronizing, and everyone was angry with him – until he began to dance for them. His dancing was so dazzling that he was always forgiven his terrible clumsiness.

It was a chancy joke. Stellia knew Stevahn's most recent lover, Selnor, had ridiculed him by comparing Stevahn's bulky build to that of the fictional dancing bear. It had been the final blow of a vicious argument that led to the dissolution of the household Stevahn and Selnor had set up together.

From anyone else, Stevahn would have taken offense, but Stellia had never deliberately hurt anyone in her life – and he enjoyed her antic sense of humor, which was very like his own. He began to laugh as well.

"What did he do when you made his drink explode?" she gasped.

"He threw a length of fabric over it to put out the fire and he laughed. He kept laughing all through the fitting," Stevahn answered.

"Well, if he did that, all is not lost," Stellia began.

There was a flurry at the door of the restaurant. People began craning to see who was coming in. The headwaiter was bowing repeatedly like a bizarre clockwork and Malvar himself went bustling across the dining room from the kitchen, grinning like a demon.

A woman nearby whispered, "It's Borsen!" to her companion. Stellia's head went up and Stevahn could feel his face draining white. He put his knife and fork down carefully.

It was indeed Borsen, with two companions, men Stevahn had never seen before.

Borsen, as always, was dressed exquisitely in one of his signature suits, made of rich, dark teal green silk. A heavy teal silk scarf splashed with a repeating pattern of four arrows curving inward to a center point was tied in place as his cravat.

One of other men rivaled Borsen's splendor. He was blond with piercing blue eyes and a face that would be pretty on a girl. Decked out in what was obviously a Borsen suit of ice blue, he would have been eminently attractive to Stevahn if he hadn't been downright frightening. His movements and gait were snakelike in their sinister smoothness.

The third man shambled along in the wake of the brilliantly attired Borsen and his companion, intent on a copy of *Antiques and Antiquities*. He wore a well-fitted dark suit that had picked up dust from the street. His hair had obviously blown out of place and hung forward over his forehead in a black tousled shock. He towered over his companions by more than a foot and Stevahn couldn't help but wonder at the size of his feet as he clumped along behind the graceful younger men.

Stevahn felt a rush of jealousy as he saw how easily the blond man and Borsen got on. The damned blond snake talked and laughed as if he'd never said or done an awkward thing in his life. It was obvious they knew each other well.

They seemed oblivious to the murmuring and sensation swelling in their wake as Malvar himself guided them toward the private dining rooms. Borsen hadn't even seen Stevahn. His brown eyes were intent on the blond man's face.

Stevahn couldn't bear it. He found himself rising to his feet, heard his chair clatter to the floor behind him. He flinched but kept control of himself, willing Borsen to look his way.

Borsen and his party turned toward the racket. Recognition flashed across Borsen's face as he saw Stevahn with his overturned chair being uprighted by a waiter.

Stevahn bowed as elegantly as he could, a formal greeting between equals, giving just the right amount of flexion of the waist and inclination of the head. He was thankful doing so obscured his face for a moment. He drew a deep, shaking breath, hoping it would reduce the hot redness he could feel on his cheeks.

When he rose from the bow, he saw nothing but Borsen standing across the room, walking stick before him, his elegant hands resting on the marble knob. Then Borsen smiled, removed his hat in a sweeping gesture and bowed in return – the bow of a craftsman to a superior, more flexion, longer in duration, the hat held outswept to the side in an achingly graceful pose, one leg very slightly extended.

"Oh my," Stellia murmured appreciatively.

When Borsen stood upright the blond man asked him something, his face deliberately turned away from Stevahn, so his words wouldn't carry.

"One of my very best and most valued customers," Borsen replied, his voice soft.

Stevahn sank down into the chair the waiter shuffled under him, his heart pounding in his ears. Borsen and the two men were ushered into the private room, but not before the hulking third man looked directly back at Stevahn and raised his eyebrows inquisitively.

"What a pretty compliment!" Stellia said delightedly. "Both of you – Stev, you're a fool if you give up on him. He's just young. He probably has no idea why you're acting in such a silly way when you're being fitted."

"He's attached to that blond snake masquerading as a man," Stevahn said bitterly.

"Borsen doesn't wear a bonding ring. The other two men do. They're bonded, he's not." Stellia looked at him as if she dared him to refute her.

"How… how can you see things like that at a glance?" Stevahn asked, exasperated.

"I'm a woman and we look at details. If that young man didn't care about your feelings, he would never have bowed to you like that.

He's caring, and he has a sense of humor. What you need to do is show him who Stevahn Rondheim really is and stop bumbling around like Waldrum the Dancing Bear in a shop full of breakables."

"Oh yes, Mother – and what should I do to erase months of idiocy on my part?" Stevahn asked, a little snidely but with genuine curiosity as well. Stellia was no fool.

"I'd suggest, now that you've been clumsy and made a mess, that you begin dancing, Waldrum. It always makes people love you."

***

It was late. The Rondheim bank had been closed for two hours but Stevahn was lingering in the lobby, watching the building across the street.

He was hopelessly, pathetically, desperately in love and he had to do something about it, even if it meant an outright rejection from Borsen.

He had a plan. Borsen went through a nightly ritual when he left his store. He would gently stroke the marble in the entry of his building before turning and walking north along The Promenade. Stevahn had seen the routine night after night for months.

Tonight, he was going to intercept Borsen and invite him to dinner.

The light in Borsen's workroom went out and Stevahn went into action. He locked the bank doors and ducked across the street, positioning himself along Borsen's routine walk home. He waited.

Borsen emerged from the building, paused in the entryway and then turned south, as he had never done before. He began walking briskly toward the Palace end of the Promenade.

"Hells!" Stevahn raced after him, calling out. "Excuse me! Hello!"

Borsen whirled to face him in a slight crouch, hand flashing toward his coat pocket. Then he recognized Stevahn and let his hand fall by his side, waiting with a bemused and carefully patient expression. Stevahn managed not to slip on the icy pavement and came to a stop before him.

"Would you care to have dinner with me?" he blurted. To his horror, he sounded annoyed.

"Good evening," Borsen responded, sarcasm tingeing his voice. Stevahn swallowed and tried again.

"Would you have dinner with me?"

Borsen looked wary.

"Oh gods! This hasn't been about suits!" Stevahn yelled, grabbing his head in frustration, knocking his top hat into the snow.

Suddenly, Borsen smiled, a genuine smile, not a professional one. His eyes twinkled with mischief. He bent and picked up Stevahn's hat and handed it back.

"You simply cannot wear this – thing – with my suits," he said. "Come by tomorrow and order something decent from Petran. He's my men's hatmaker." He turned and started north along The Promenade again.

"Wait!" Stevahn heard the desperation in his voice and obviously Borsen did too, because he swung around and stared.

"What is it?" he asked quietly.

"Please – just dinner. Would you just have dinner with me? I do not want to eat alone one more damned time wishing that I was having dinner with you. Nothing more, just dinner. To get to know each other. To find out if we could be friends?"

Oh, my gods, I'm one step from kneeling in the slush and begging. What has happened to me, Stevahn thought, cringing inwardly. He thinks I'm insane. Waldrum knocks over another breakable.

Borsen smiled again.

"I thought you were coming with me. What are you waiting for?" he asked. "I'm starving."

***

Stevahn was basking in conversing with Borsen at an exquisitely appointed table at Malvar's. He found Borsen fascinating and an excellent companion. The young man listened intently, responding with humor or probity, depending on the trend of the conversation.

"How does a man your age become the owner of an establishment like Borsen's?" Stevahn asked.

"I could have set up the usual tailoring establishment, starting with a small shop and working my way up, but I have money," Borsen explained. "My uncle, who raised me from the age of thirteen, taught me to invest long ago. He's my business partner and he helped to set me up."

Borsen wiped his mouth and leaned back so the waiter could remove his soup plate. Stevahn noticed how Borsen thanked the man sincerely, something simply not done by most who dined in places like this. He noticed the look of gratification on the waiter's face. Something to remember, he thought.

"Not to say that having been set up to start out in such style means I'm some rich, spoiled brat who's playing at keeping shop," Borsen went on, replacing his napkin in his lap. "I've had to prove myself and work like the hells."

Something across the room caught Borsen's eye. He picked up his draftsman's pencil and sketched in a small book he'd placed on the table at the beginning of the meal. This had happened a number of times since they were seated.

"You see, failure is simply not an option," Borsen continued, looking up at Stevahn. "Not after the trust placed in me, and the effort put into me by my uncle and many other people. I know there is a rumor that I'm just playing around with this business. That is not the case. I'm only just starting."

"Starting! You're practically finished!" Stevahn exclaimed, making Borsen laugh.

"Not at all. What I have is a tiny baby compared to what I want. I eventually hope to trade in antiques, textiles, furnishings, art, anything else people want. Clothing and accessories - that's just the beginning, because it's my particular expertise."

Their main courses arrived. Borsen started on his as if he hadn't eaten for a week, though his manners were exquisite and flawless.

"How does one end up wanting to be a tailor all his life?" Stevahn asked. Borsen shrugged.

"Just as I could ask you why someone becomes a banker," he responded.

"It's my family business," Stevahn explained. "We all have money in the blood. Nothing makes the members of my family happier than making money from money, I'm afraid. To us it's fascinating – to most other people it seems dreary and dull."

"Money is never dull," Borsen grinned.

"Not to listen to my clients. They want me to handle it, so they don't have to deal with the dullness," Stevahn smiled.

"They need to spend a few years without money and then they'll find money – or what you can do with it – fascinating indeed," Borsen replied. Something caught his eye. He began sketching again.

His remark made Stevahn curious. It didn't fit the image of Borsen being set up in business with an enormous emporium.

"Well then, I could say that tailoring runs in my family, as banking runs in yours." Borsen picked up the thread of the conversation, having finished whatever he was sketching. "My mother was a talented seamstress. She made beautiful little suits for me from the time I was a baby."

"She must be very impressed with your success," Stevahn said.

Borsen shook his head.

"She died when I was six," he said quietly. "But she would have been thrilled."

"So Borsen is your father's family name?" Stevahn asked.

For the first time, Borsen's face clouded.

"No, it's my first name, given to me by my mother."

"I'm sorry."

"Why?" Borsen asked, his eyebrows going up.

"Obviously I've blundered onto something that hurt or offended you," Stevahn replied.

Borsen shook his head and smiled, but a bit stiffly.

"I took no offense. You didn't anger me at all, the memory of my father did. I don't use his name. I took my uncle's surname years ago for legal purposes, but otherwise – it's Borsen."

"Rapidly becoming a household word in Erdahn," Stevahn offered, hoping it would make Borsen smile. It did.

"Very likely," Borsen answered. He'd finished his main course and the hovering waiter appeared to remove his dish. "May I have the pork as well, sir?" Borsen asked, evoking a slight bow from the waiter, who bore the empty plate away.

Stevahn burst out laughing.

"I'm a bottomless pit. They're used to me here," Borsen grinned. "It seems to be a family trait. When Uncle and I come in here for dinner, they put on extra food in the kitchen. Last time we both had two soups, two starters, two main courses and I managed two desserts, while he opted for a cigar. I've been careful to be very dainty this evening but I'm still starving. If you want to go ahead to dessert, please do. I'll catch you up."

"I don't mind," Stevahn laughed. "It's novel, I'll grant, but I don't mind."

Halfway through his second main course Borsen sketched again and curiosity overcame Stevahn. He asked to see it, then wondered if he'd trespassed.

"But of course," Borsen said, blinking. "It's such a part of me that I don't even think about it. You must think me very rude." He handed the sketchbook over.

"Not at all," Stevahn answered, then fell silent as he began leafing through the book.

He was looking at a soul. Every drawing, even the smallest rough sketches, were infused with emotion. There were drawings of everything – The Promenade, Borsen's shopfront, the Rondheim Bank, views of the Harbor, the Palace. There were drawings of people, quick sketches of the clothing people wore, more fully realized sketches concentrating on form and face. As Stevahn turned page after page, his heart lifted. It was very obvious that Borsen was attracted to men. He worshipped the male figure. No wonder he was a magnificent tailor.

"Do you live alone?" Stevahn blurted, wanting to punch himself in the mouth the minute he'd said it.

"I live with my sister," Borsen replied quietly, seeming to find the question a reasonable one. "Varnia has been taking care of me since I was thirteen." He smiled at Stevahn.

"Thirteen – is she your younger sister?" Stevahn asked in confusion.

"No, some years older," Borsen said with a finality that Stevahn realized was setting a boundary.

"I'm sorry, I shouldn't pry," he apologized.

Borsen looked at the tabletop.

"Don't mind me," he replied suddenly. "I must be tired if I'm being short with nice fellows who ask me to dinner." He looked up.

Stevahn realized Borsen had let some of his courteous guard down, because for a moment, weariness showed plainly on his face.

"Anyone who works as much as you do deserves to be tired and testy," Stevahn told him.

"How do you know how hard I work?" Borsen's eyebrows went up.

Before he thought, relieved that the tense moment had dissipated, Stevahn gave himself away.

"My office is opposite your workroom. My family's bank is across the street. I can see you working away whenever I look out the window."

Borsen looked at Stevahn for so long that he felt like crawling under the table. It's over, he thought. You blockhead.

Suddenly Borsen smiled, then laughed aloud. Stevahn felt as if a great weight had fallen from his shoulders.

"So, you're the eyes I feel upon me," Borsen said. "I'd begun to think we had spooks in the building. I will have to look up once in a while and wave. So, you're that Rondheim."

Stevahn felt himself blushing, which only made Borsen laugh more. He wasn't entirely quelled until his dessert arrived.

To cover his discomfort, Stevahn took a cigar when they were offered and proffered the box to Borsen, who declined.

"I'll have another dessert though, the nut cake, thank you," he said to the waiter.

"What is your accent?" Stevahn asked bluntly, tired of being curious. Considering Borsen's obvious tolerance of faux pas, he felt the question wouldn't be considered an intrusion. "It's charming but I can't place it."

"Thrun," Borsen replied after swallowing a mouthful of nutcake.

"Pardon?" Stevahn felt as if he'd been smacked with a large fish. Thrun? City Thrun were invariably dirty and disheveled, usually creeping around up to no good. All the Thrun Stevahn had seen were very tall, massive people. How could Borsen possibly be Thrun?

"I'm three-quarters Thrun," Borsen affirmed. "Thrun was my first language and when my mother spoke Mordanian it was with a very strong Thrun accent. It's the singsong way of speaking and the drawing out of certain syllables that you're not familiar with. I'm not likely to lose it, I've been around Mordanians for ages, but it hangs on."

"Don't lose it," Stevahn said firmly.

"Not much chance. Now, before they come with a bill and there's a great to-do as to who will pay it, let me know the etiquette. I've never been to dinner with anyone who isn't family. Remember, I have added the equivalent of another person to this meal with my voracious eating habits." Borsen's eyes were twinkling again with inner amusement.

"You've never …"

"No. The family estate is quite remote, and I have not been to dinner with anyone who is not my family," Borsen repeated, looking down at his cake, obviously hiding a smile.

"I asked you. You're my guest," Stevahn replied, his mind whirling with the implication that Borsen truly was unattached. "Even with your extra courses. I'm sorry to seem surprised, but you've been so at ease, I just assumed you'd been out with a… friend before."

Borsen looked up from his plate slowly, his heavy eyelids moving in a manner that made Stevahn's heart skip a beat.

"There are many things I've not done," Borsen said, his voice dropping a bit, giving it a seductive husk that cut through Stevahn like one of the knives the young man had salted about his very attractive person.

THE SHADOWS, MORDANIA
ERDAHN, MORDANIA

II
THELAK CARVERS

Kaymar let himself into Borsen's workroom just as Borsen signed his name to a letter to Katrin detailing his evening with Stevahn Rondheim. Kaymar waited while Borsen put the letter into an envelope and made a distinct point of sealing it with a heavy blob of wax.

"Do not read that until Katrin's had a chance, Nosey," Borsen directed, handing the letter to his cousin.

"You cut me to the quick, youngster," Kaymar grinned.

"You'll survive. Could you check this name for me? Have Menders run it through the mill?" He handed Kaymar a card.

"Stevahn Rondheim? Banker, right over there," Kaymar said in surprise, pointing toward the building opposite.

"Don't gesture, for the gods' sakes, he'll see you!" Borsen pushed Kaymar's offending hand down.

"Borsen, what on earth are you up to? I can probably tell you anything you need to know." Kaymar sat on the edge of Borsen's worktable and observed him closely. Borsen, to his dismay, felt a red flush rising from his collar to his hairline.

Kaymar began to chortle.

"I see," he said with amusement. "Well, he's nancy, if that's what you're wondering."

"I've managed to figure that out, Father Wisdom," Borsen snapped.

"Oh, you've got it bad," Kaymar gloated. "Looking to give up your famous chastity?"

"Shut up! I never expected that kind of nastiness from you!" Borsen turned away, plunging his hands into his pockets.

Kaymar rose, closed the curtains so that Stevahn Rondheim wouldn't see this altercation and went to Borsen.

"I'm sorry," he said contritely. "I shouldn't have teased you. I can tell you that he's from a very wealthy banking family. They are very powerful in finance, very influential. He's the only son but surprisingly, they're not put off by him being nancy. Seems there's a sister who has a boychild who can carry the banking torch, so there's no pressure on Stevahn Rondheim to produce an heir. They're not nobility, so there's no nonsense about titles and heirs and convenient marriages. He seems a quite respectable fellow. No rumors of salacious doings. No attachments that I know of. I'll have Menders check more closely but I'm very sure you're safe to do as you like."

"You know this is about protecting Katrin, not me," Borsen snapped, still angry. "And how the hells do you know so much about him?"

"It's my business to know as much as possible about the powerful people in Mordania. Stevahn Rondheim and his family are some of them. My personal advice for you is to make him pursue you. Be sure he wants you as a person, not just a roll with a pretty young man who looks younger than he is. If he's only after the physical, he'll go his way to greener pastures. If he's looking for more, he'll be willing to put up with some unrequited passion to get to know you better. Then, be intimate only when you're sure he's what you want."

Borsen wasn't quite ready to lose his ire. "You know I don't want any danger coming to Katrin."

"Yes, I do, and I appreciate it more than you know," Kaymar replied, giving him a quick hug around the shoulders. He could feel Borsen taking a deep breath and saw that he was calmer. "Now, let's open this curtain so he doesn't think I'm seducing you. Gazes at you a bit, does he?"

Borsen nodded silently, returning to his work table.

"I'm going to the races with him tomorrow," he said suddenly.

"Wonderful. Have fun, and don't rush. I'll be back to you in a few days. Katrin's not going out yet, so I'm still redundant at The Shadows. Take care, Little Cuz," Kaymar said, letting himself out of the workroom.

Borsen sighed and bent over his table. Then he remembered, and looked up.

Stevahn was standing there at his window and looked startled when Borsen caught him at it. Borsen waved, and looked back at his work.

***

"Look at this!" Katrin said excitedly, handing the letter from Borsen to Menders. He took it, switched to his reading glasses and perused it, his eyebrows going almost to his hairline.

"I'll be damned," he said.

"Not only that, but he asked if you would run the man's name through the mill," Kaymar added, handing over the card Borsen had given him. Menders took it wonderingly.

"So, it's not all on the side of Mister Rondheim at all! Borsen is actually interested in someone!" Katrin looked extremely pleased.

"Very much so. He blushed like a bride when I asked why he wanted to know about the fellow," Kaymar grinned.

"Good! Maybe this man can keep him from working so hard," Katrin replied.

"I know who Stevahn Rondheim is but let's make the inquiries anyway," Menders said, picking up a flat grey dossier folder and handing it to Kaymar. "Not because I think he's anything other than an investment banker, but best not to take a chance."

"It's a pity Borsen has to do this," Katrin sighed.

"Yes, but he's sensible enough to know it must be done. I'm not worried about Stevahn Rondheim. He's not a threat, but someone could use him to get at Borsen – or at you," Menders explained. "We need to know if he's going to be impervious to manipulation. He's very bright. He has to be to do what he does. His father is impeccable, very astute and forward seeing. I doubt there would ever be a problem with them knowing about Borsen's connection to you. I'm sure Borsen will be able to go ahead with whatever he'd like to do, but I appreciate his caution and care."

Kaymar hesitated, looking torn over something. He shook his head a little and spoke.

"I was surprised Borsen didn't mention it in his letter – well, thinking about it, I'm not so surprised," he began. "He handled the matter himself, but I think you should know. Borsen's father turned up at the store a week or so ago. I wasn't there, but heard about it through the usual channels."

Menders and Katrin exchanged a startled glance. There had been no sign of Borsen's family from the time they had left him behind at The Shadows ten years earlier.

"I was afraid this might happen," Menders said quietly. "I need to know about it."

Kaymar perched on the corner of the desk, his hand resting on Katrin's shoulder.

"Seems he turned up one morning and asked for Borsen. From what I was told, the man is an enormous Thrun."

Menders nodded. Kaymar went on.

"He gave the store director a tragic tale of being Borsen's father, which I had warned him about when they opened. He rang the bell."

"What bell?" Katrin asked.

"There's an alarm bell at Borsen's. Many businesses have them," Menders explained. "It alerts the store security of a problem without frightening people who aren't involved. There's one on each floor of Borsen's, only the staff know about them." Katrin nodded and turned her attention back to Kaymar.

"Borsen heard it, of course. It's connected to his workroom as well as to the security room," Kaymar went on. "He came down in the elevator. When it opened in the lobby, he was face to face with his father.

"His father began the 'my long lost son' routine, but Borsen pulled out his sparkly little pistol and escorted him out without a word. On the street he told him never to come back around or he'd use the gun on him. Borsen then walked calmly back inside, thanked the director for his quick action and went back to his workroom as if nothing had happened."

Katrin sighed in disgust. "I'd hoped for something more dramatic than that," she said. Menders and Kaymar burst out laughing.

"And there is the difference between women and men," Kaymar grinned. "You want drama, we think Borsen is admirable for dealing with it without drama."

Katrin pinched him. He stood up and got out of range.

"It's time for my walk," Katrin announced, not wanting any more edification on the differences between women and men.

"I'll be right with you," Menders smiled. She went to get her coat.

"Is Borsen's father still in Erdahn?" Menders asked softly once he was sure she was out of earshot. Kaymar came close, so their voices wouldn't carry.

"I made some inquiries. He is. No sign of the woman he was with when he was in this area years back, no young people with him who would have been their children. He's either abandoned them or they've moved on or died. He looked very down and out, half crocked Varens told me. All ready to try to lean on Borsen for money, I'm sure."

"Eliminate him," Menders ordered quietly. "I don't want Borsen having to contend with this nonsense, and I don't want to risk his father getting his hands on him. Borsen will have his chance without worthless scum coming out of the woodwork to foul things up."

"Consider it done," Kaymar answered.

"And now to take Katrin for a stroll. Care to come with us?" Menders asked, as casually as if they'd been discussing the weather.

***

Thelak Carvers slumped in the corner of a cheap tavern that attracted City Thrun. He'd hoped to cadge a few drinks, but the crowd was very thin tonight and none of the Thrun he'd met since arriving in Erdahn were present.

He'd drunk his way through the coins he'd gotten for a pickpocketed watch and he had nothing else to pawn or spend. He huddled back into the dark corner and pretended to nurse his drink, though the glass was empty. If the barkeep noticed he was loitering and not drinking, he'd be out on the street. It was a stinking night, foggy and dank. Best to become invisible and spend more time in the muggy warmth of the tavern.

Erdahn was a mean town, hard to steal a living in. People tended to stay close to home, or traveled in cabs. They were wary of City Thrun and kept their hands on their money bags and watches whenever one was in sight.

Thelak was seven feet tall and couldn't blend into a crowd. He'd always depended on his woman for pickpocketing, but she'd dropped dead in Surelia from sickness last year. Their brats had long since gone their own ways, those that hadn't died along the way.

Women were not anxious to couple with him now, as years and drink had spoiled his face and body. He had nobody to help him and unless he could manage a housebreak, he was going to be a in a bad way. Housebreaks were hard to come by in this city of stay-at-homes.

In Surelia he'd heard stories of Borsen's, a great store in Erdahn run by a young Thrun man who was making a fortune as a fancy men's tailor. Thelak had been gob smacked. He was sure there couldn't be too many Thrun men named Borsen in Mordania. How his puny, nancy, eldest son could have managed such a trick was a mystery to Thelak. He caught a ferry to Erdahn, curious to see if this Borsen was actually Thara Borgela's priceless brat.

Thelak was dazzled by the imposing building. It was entirely covered in the white shiny stone the Surelians used for important buildings. More money than Thelak had seen in a lifetime was in the entryway alone, in those slabs of stone. It must have been some trick for Borsen, who was nearly blind and worthless at anything but being a coward, to become the owner of this place.

Thelak drifted into the store in the wake of a group of well-dressed people and was immediately struck by the elegance and costliness of the place. The stealing in here would be prime. Even if it turned out this Borsen was someone other than his son, he would be able to lightfinger enough out of this busy mercantile to get himself back to Surelia. And if Borsen was somehow the owner of this place, the right words would make a weakling sorry that his poor old papa was in a bad way. Thara Borgela had made the boy worthless with her prattling about the Way of Light. In Thelak's experience, people who were too pure were easy marks for a sad story. Thelak might end up getting some value from his oldest brat after all.

A dandified man approached Thelak and asked if he could help him. Thelak dropped into his most useful guise, the Thrun fresh from the country and down on his luck. It put people off the City Thrun wariness.

"Oh yes sir," he'd said humbly, intensifying his accent and holding his hat in front of him. "I did hear that the young man who owns this place is called Borsen and was wondering if he might be the little son I lost when his mother took him away long ago. I was worried about coming in such a fine place, so I could wait outside..."

"Just a moment, sir," the man said, going to a panel full of switches on the wall. He flicked one up and then down. "Borsen should be right along."

Thelak was aware of several men coming in his direction, but his attention was taken up by the ringing of the elevator bell and the door opening.

Being confronted by Thara Borgela's face on a tiny man who stared coldly at him through a pair of eyeglasses made Thelak catch his breath anxiously. It was his eldest son all right, a runt as always but dressed like a damned king, rings on every finger, diamond studs in his ears. How could that little bastard have managed this? He'd been worthless! Scared of his own shadow, always hiding in a corner and drawing pictures of men wearing fancy clothes!

Borsen was obviously not pleased to see him. Still he'd always been a shy brat. He might not recognize Thelak as his father, since he'd never been able to see past the end of his nose.

"My Little Man," Thelak said, making himself smile, feeling pleased that he remembered what Thara Borgela had called the little nancy. "It's Papa. I've looked for you for so long…"

"Shut up." Borsen reached into his pocket and took out a small golden pistol flashing with inset gems, only lifting it far enough for Thelak to see he had it. "Outside."

Thelak had seen the bore of the pistol. Though it looked like a toy, it was capable of putting a very large hole through him. He managed a sickly smile and went through the door with Borsen right behind him.

"Get away from here and don't come back. If you do, I'll use this gun," Borsen said abruptly. Four men came out of the store and stood behind him, also holding pistols discreetly but where Thelak could see them.

"But son, I want to make amends," Thelak tried desperately.

"That is impossible." Borsen stood there, his jewelry glittering in the bright sunlight, his hair shining. "If you come back here again, I will kill you."

Thelak fled down the Promenade toward the docks, not even daring to look back. When his heart stopped banging, he'd made enquiries among the City Thrun about Borsen and was enraged by the tale.

The little bastard was rich. He'd hove into town almost two years ago and set up that posh store, then made a name for himself making men's suits. He lived nearby. He had an enormous dog that went about with him, carried a walking stick with a lead-loaded stone handle, was armed with several knives and carried that improbable gun.

What Thelak hated, as he heard more and more about Borsen during the days after his visit to the store, was that the City Thrun were proud of him and spoke of him with a mixture of awe and enthusiasm. All of them claimed to know someone who worked for him, someone who otherwise would have no job, because only Borsen would hire Thrun as regular employees. He hired other poor folk as well, giving them a chance they otherwise would not have had. They all acted as if Borsen was something wonderful. They told about the charities he'd started and how anyone who wanted could go into Borsen's without fear of being chucked back onto the street, so long as they behaved and didn't try to steal. Borsen would order a discount on something if a customer was short of money or would give a voucher for a free meal in the store employee's restaurant if someone looked in need of a handout. Oh, but Thelak was turfed out straightaway by the little nancy!

Thelak watched Borsen over several days, peering from alleyways and shadows. The dog was no exaggeration. It was an enormous hairy thing, the size of a pony. Worse, Borsen met up with a big bruiser of a man from the bank opposite almost every evening and went off to a swank restaurant, the racecourse or the theatre. Noontimes were also devoted to the bank fellow. Probably the one who set Borsen up, though gods knew what the great people the brat had been left with in Old Mordania had done for him. That busybody white-eyed master of the estate who'd offered to take the brat for an apprentice had a bundle, that was certain.

Thelak gave up on the idea of approaching Borsen again and considered burgling his home, a townhouse on one of Erdahn's most exclusive streets. He found it was presided over by a housekeeper with the fiercest eyes Thelak had ever seen and a staff of servants. The house was never vacant.

At this point, Thelak was desperate for the fare to get back to Surelia, where the pickings were easy. He was reduced to scrounging behind restaurants for food and only lucked into the watch he'd pawned this morning when he found its owner unconscious in the gutter after a night of carousing, his moneybag already removed by another passerby who had left behind the almost worthless watch as not worth the bother of carrying.

He'd give anything for a fraction of the price of one of Borsen's pairs of earrings, the diamonds, the rich gold hoops, the blood sapphires or the grey stones that flashed with gold light. He'd settle for the cost of one of his shoes. Miserable nancy bastard.

Thelak lifted his empty glass and pretended to drink again, wondering how the hells he was going to get out of this mess, wishing Borsen dead like the mother who had turned him into a moral little ninny.

"Thelak Carvers?"

Thelak looked up in surprise. He didn't give his surname to the folk he knew here in Erdahn. Plenty of Thrun named Thelak. For safety, he used his first name only.

There was a man as well dressed as Borsen standing there. Definitely Old Mordanian with slanted blue eyes, blond hair, wearing a light blue suit and a top hat that rivaled Borsen's own. Not large at all, but strong. The voice was nancy, extremely so.

"Who wants him?" Thelak asked rudely.

"Borsen wishes to speak to you," the man replied, staring at him intently.

"He sent you?"

"Indeed. I'll take you to him."

It all comes clear, Thelak thought, perusing the man. Older than Borsen, obviously richer than most gods, nancy as they came. Likely the one who set him up in that palace of a store. Wonder if he knows about the fellow from the bank?

"How do I know you know him?" Thelak challenged.

"You'll know when we get there. He would like to give you some money to go away and not come back around," the blond man lisped.

That sounded likely to Thelak. He put down the empty glass and rose, unkinking his legs with a grunt of pain. Too many years sleeping in the elements had told on his joints. He'd love to get back to Surelia where the sun kept things warm. Borsen could just damn well pay for the fare if he wanted him gone.

The nancy turned, sauntering out of the tavern without a backward glance. Thelak followed. They walked along in the general direction of Borsen's townhouse. Thelak began to relax. He even smiled to himself. Trust priceless, weak Borsen to start thinking too much and decide it was worth it to give the old man some money.

They were passing a dark alley that ran down to the Harbor when someone reached out and flung a rock-hard arm around Thelak's neck, dragging him back into the shadows. Thelak struggled, but found all his assailant had to do was to tighten his elbow and things went very dark as his breath was entirely cut off. He was up against someone near his size and in much better condition. He stopped fighting and let himself be hauled down near the water, seeing that the nancy who had led him here was walking along with them.

Thelak could hear the Harbor water lapping against the seawall where the alley ended. There was reflected light from the houses and businesses along the Harbor Road. He could see the blond nancy who had lured him here.

"Now then," the man said, without a hint of a lisp, "before you go, I'd like you to know this is for leaving Thara Borgela to die and for starving and mistreating our boy. You'll never do anything to harm him again."

His arm swung in a vicious upward arc.

Thelak felt a burning in his belly, from pelvis to ribcage. Then a hot line grew from one side of his throat to another as a knife blade was drawn from ear to ear. He was dimly aware of a foot thrust hard against the small of his back and of tumbling toward the black water.

Kaymar Shvalz and Ifor Trantz leaned companionably on the railing of the seawall, watching as the water where Thelak Carvers had disappeared began to roil with the frenzied feeding of fish and crabs.

"Won't be enough of him left for anyone to recognize," Ifor said casually.

"No-one would bother. Just another Thrun dumped in the Harbor," Kaymar replied, his voice edged with disgust. "Effectively erased."

"Should we let Little Man know?" Ifor asked. Kaymar shook his head.

"He'll know without us telling him," he answered. "I don't want him troubled with this. Carvers gave him enough misery for a lifetime without Borsen having to know how we eliminated him."

"Good enough," Ifor assented. "What about some dinner, Kip?"

"Since I'm so beautifully dressed and stepped away from Mister Carvers at the right moment, you may treat me to Malvar's, Bear," Kaymar grinned.

THE SHADOWS, MORDANIA

12
UNDER THE HAMMER

Katrin waited anxiously while the specialist studied her scalp, using a magnifying glass. Franz was pacing at one side of the room. Menders exercised deliberate patience, leaning against his office window's frame, looking out at the wintry orchard.

"You've allowed the hair that is coming in to grow naturally?" the doctor asked, lifting one of the three thin wisps hanging from Katrin's scalp.

At first it had appeared that Katrin's hair was going to grow back in not long after it had fallen out. A fine baby fuzz sprouted all over her head, but it rubbed off almost immediately.

Those wisps were all that had grown back in spite of multitudinous treatments – lotions, creams, massage, sunlight, warm compresses, cold compresses, herbal concoctions spread on the scalp, herbal concoctions swallowed, special diet.

"Yes, I haven't done anything to it," Katrin answered.

"How much weight have you gained since you were ill?"

"About thirty pounds."

"You are still underweight," the doctor observed. "You may put your wig on."

Katrin did so, gratefully. She felt horribly vulnerable in front of this stranger without it. When she had it arranged, she sat back and looked at the specialist. To do him credit, he looked right back at her.

"I'm sorry," he said. "I can't tell you to hold out hope that it will grow back at this late date. In my experience, when hair loss caused by fever goes on for this long, it is permanent."

Katrin felt as if she'd been punched in the stomach. Those dangling wisps of hair had given her hope that more would come back in time. Permanent? To be bald – ugly, unfeminine, freakish – forever?

She looked wildly at Franz. His eyes were closed, a hopeless, frustrated expression on his face. She wheeled toward Menders, who looked stricken.

"Isn't there anything else I can try?" she asked, her voice small and pinched.

The specialist shook his head slowly. "I would be giving you false hope if I said there was," he replied, kindly but bluntly. "You have been without hair growth for well over a year. There is no sign of the follicles becoming activated again. Your fever must have been very high for a very long time. I wish I could give you better news but not being truthful would be cruel. Everything that might have worked has been tried. Doctor Franz has searched out every possible remedy."

The specialist looked as miserable as she felt, so she couldn't hate him – but she hated being bald! She hated her mother and her demented sister for having done this to her!

Katrin ran away down the hall and up the stairs to her room. She locked the door behind her and shoved a chair under the knob of the door adjoining her room to Menders'. Then she went to the mirror and pulled the wig roughly from her head.

Ghastly. A naked bald head with feathery bits of fluffy hair, almost white, hanging from it. Something from a ghost story. This is what she would look like without a wig for the rest of her life. What man would be able to bear that? It made people recoil. She knew it did. It made her recoil.

Scalding tears came. She flung herself on the bed, gave up trying to control herself and cried like a baby.

Menders climbed the stairs, his heart heavy. Katrin had looked so stricken. She'd tried so hard to be hopeful about her hair. He'd begun to dread just what the doctor had told her today, but he'd been unable to speak with her about it. He couldn't bring himself to add another blow to what she'd already endured.

"Katrin?" he said softly, tapping at her door. He could hear her crying so desperately that she was making herself retch. He leaned his head against the door, grinding his teeth.

"Katrin, please open the door," he called gently when he heard her trying to draw in a breath. There was no answer, just more abject sobbing.

"What the hells is it?" Hemmett's voice startled Menders terribly. He turned, short of breath. He'd been so intent on trying to get Katrin to open the door that he'd never heard Hemmett coming down the hallway.

"Gods," Menders gasped, sagging back against the door.

"What is it?" Hemmett repeated, beginning to look angry.

"Hemmett, this isn't a good time…"

"What the hells is it!" Hemmett shouted, a raw edge to his voice that let Menders know he was on the brink of rage.

"Hemmett, keep control of yourself," Menders said briskly. "It's bad enough that she's this upset. She's just been told there is no chance of her hair growing back."

He wished he'd cut out his tongue. Hemmett said nothing. He turned from Menders and walked away down the corridor, until he came to his apartment. He opened the door and let himself in, the silence he left behind him broken only by Katrin's heartrending sobs.

***

Eiren walked in the front door to find Franz pacing, waiting for her. He told her what the specialist had said, then put his hands on her shoulders.

"All three of them are in a state," he said quietly. "Menders has been trying for two hours to get Katrin to open the door of her room. She's hysterical, won't answer and he won't just break the door in. Hemmett's completely broken down, so he must know. I can't get through to any of them, though I've tried."

Eiren patted Franz's arm and started up the stairs. He followed her into the suite. Menders was leaning against Katrin's door. Eiren could hear Katrin weeping.

"For the gods' sakes, Katrin, please open the door," Menders was pleading, his voice shaking with exhaustion.

"Darling, just pick the lock," Eiren said gently, but firmly, putting her hand on his arm.

"I don't want to force her to open the door or open it myself against her will," he said wearily.

"Menders, when a woman is crying like that, she's beyond any sort of reason," Eiren answered. "She's not even hearing you. Pick the lock."

After a moment, he took his lockpick from his pocket and, worked the lock open.

"I'll go in to Katrin," Eiren said gently, looking up at him. "Hemmett is in a bad way, Franz says. Would you go see to him?"

"Katrin…" Menders began.

"Let me deal with her," Eiren answered. "Right now, she needs a mother."

Menders blinked in surprise. Franz stepped up and put a hand on his shoulder.

"Let's go see to the young man," he suggested heartily, steering Menders away down the hall. Eiren let herself into Katrin's room.

Katrin was collapsed on the bed, her wig flung on the floor, her face buried in the pillows.

Eiren went to her.

"My poor darling," she whispered, climbing up next to Katrin, putting her arms around her. Katrin started and then buried her face in Eiren's lap. Eiren stroked her bald head gently.

"Go ahead and cry," she said softly. "Cry it all out. Then Hemmett needs you, because he's gone to pieces."

Eiren waited. As she expected, Katrin's sobbing lessened almost immediately now she'd been distracted by the mention of Hemmett.

"I'm sorry," Katrin sobbed. "I heard Menders out there, but I couldn't get up and open the door. I didn't want him to see me. I don't want anyone to see me."

"It is a terrible loss," Eiren answered, crying herself. "Menders can't really understand and would have said all the wrong things, because he can't ever know what a Mordanian woman's hair means to her."

"I know everyone still loves me, hair or not, but I want my hair back!" Katrin said gruffly. "I don't want to be bald!"

"Of course you don't. You don't have to be brave and cheerful in front of me, darling," Eiren answered, her voice gentle.

Katrin wept again, but this time the tears were healing and didn't last long. She sat up and let Eiren wipe her eyes.

"Would you help me clip off these straggling bits of hair?" Katrin asked. "I'd rather be completely bald than go through life looking like a plucked duck."

"I will, but let's do it later," Eiren decided. "We need your help. Could you come and see Hemmett? I think seeing you collected and ready to go on with things will help him immensely."

Katrin sat up on the edge of the bed.

"Yes," she replied, retrieving the wig, going to the dressing table and giving it a brush before putting it on. Eiren observed that she avoided looking in the mirror until she had the wig in place, then left the hair loose, as she'd often worn it as a child. She went to the washstand and bathed her eyes, gave her nose a determined blow and nodded.

Franz and Menders were standing outside Hemmett's apartment, accompanied by Zelia, who looked stricken, and Lucen, frustration showing on his usually placid face.

"Why are you just standing there?" Katrin asked, making them turn. Then she heard Hemmett.

Even as a little boy, she couldn't remember hearing or seeing him cry outright. He might sniffle a bit or have tears in his eyes, but sobbing aloud where other people could hear him? Never.

He was doing that now.

Katrin shook her head, took the lockpick from Menders' pocket and opened the door.

"Katrin, it might not be a good idea," Franz said quickly. "I don't know how stable…"

"Nonsense. This is between Hemmett and me," Katrin said briskly, her face still ravaged by her own storm of emotion. She stepped into the room and closed the door in their faces.

Menders, Franz and Eiren exchanged a glance. Lucen and Zelia looked dumbfounded.

"Now my dear, what's all this about?" they heard Katrin saying tenderly.

Hemmett's sobbing went muffled. Katrin spoke in a low tone that made words indecipherable. After a while, Hemmett was still.

"I think we should leave them alone," Eiren prompted, turning Menders and Franz away. "They can help each other best. They've always worked things out between them." She ushered them away.

***

Hemmett stirred the batch of spiced tea he'd brewed up on the small spirit stove Katrin had given him for his Military Academy rooms when he became an upperclassman. Then he simultaneously poured from the tea pot and a carafe of warmed milk, filling two large teacups with the fragrant liquid.

"Here you are, my dear," he smiled, handing one to Katrin, who was snugged up in his armchair. "You're right, we could both use a hot drink." He leaned against his bureau, holding his own cup.

He looked devastated, as Katrin knew she did. Her eyes were aching and Hemmett's were red. Neither of them were ones for crying. When they did, they ended up with stuffed up noses and headaches.

"You know, Willow – I know people are going to say it's only hair, but I know something about how you feel when you lose a part of your body," Hemmett said almost brusquely. He tapped his right foot emphatically, reminding her of the broken toe that had been amputated during his first year at the Military Academy.

"You didn't seem to mind much," Katrin said in surprise. "You joked about it."

"Bravado. It rattled me and sometimes still does. I almost forget about it, then look down when I'm barefoot. This nasty shock runs down my spine when I see the gap in my toes. It feels like someone tapped my backbone with a hammer."

"That's what all this has been like. One damned hammer blow after another," Katrin sighed.

"We've had it easy," Hemmett replied after taking a draught that nearly drained his cup. "I do say, I think that's the perfect brew and I'm unchallenged as the master Samorsan tea maker."

"Oh yes, pat your own back," Katrin teased. "What do you mean, we've had it easy?"

"Willow, you know we had loving and protected childhoods here. So now when things have become so difficult, it's as if we're taking one blow after another. While you were sick, Borsen left me in awe. Here he is, this tiny little man – he was a tower of strength. Nothing shook or rattled him. He dealt with me going off my head, Menders being scary, you at death's door. He, Eiren and Varnia held things together for quite a while, along with Doctor Franz.

"Well, I've thought about it. All of them were under the hammer when they were children. Eiren's childhood was damned gritty before we came to The Shadows. None of the estate farms were prosperous and then her mother nearly bled to death during that childbirth with only Eiren home with her, all of thirteen years old. Varnia doesn't talk but we can guess what her life was like and then she lost the little brother she loved so much. Borsen – hells, his father and stepmother abused and starved him. He should be seven feet tall, like his old man, but he's been stunted from starvation. Imagine being that hungry for so long – to say nothing of bullying and beatings and losing his mother so young."

"And Doctor Franz has always been blunt about being a Court Physician," Katrin added, seeing where Hemmett was going. "He said it made him able to endure anything, after learning to contend with some of what he saw there."

Hemmett went to his dresser and took out a wrapped bundle. He opened it before her.

"Vil brought this back from Surelia, but it was made in Surytam," he told Katrin, revealing an exquisitely made knife with a brilliant green handle carved from stone. "He gave it to me while you were ill and told me I could learn a lesson from it."

"Cheeky fellow," Katrin frowned, taking the knife.

"Not at all. Wise fellow," Hemmett replied. "Look at the blade."

The blade sported many alternating, light and dark wavy lines that shimmered slightly with iridescence. Katrin had seen tempered blades before and understood how tempering was done, but she'd never seen anything like this.

"In Surytam the men who make these knives heat the metal, pound it out thin, fold it, pound it again," Hemmett said, pointing to the wavy lines undulating along the length of the blade. "It takes thousands of hammer strokes, but these are the strongest and most durable blades on Eirdon."

Katrin took the knife, surprised by how light it was. The blade shimmered and seemed to vibrate slightly.

"That's what we need to become, Willow. Each hammer blow needs to make us stronger."

"Easy to say," Katrin said, turning the knife to see the iridescent colors shifting in the light.

"I never said it's going to be easy," Hemmett told her gently. "But it's a decision we need to make. We can't go on like this."

Then he looked right into her eyes.

"I want to tell you something else – something I realized when you came here to me earlier. You could have been frightened and rightly so, because I was losing control of my mind again. But you came right in, sat here and took me in your arms – and I was suddenly whole.

"That day you dressed down Menders' Men, you called me 'your other self'. I never said so, but on that day, I finally understood the way I love you, Willow."

Katrin almost flinched and looked away, but there was an assurance to his voice that let her know this wasn't a lover's plea.

"I never could understand how I could love you so deeply while the physical aspects of a romantic love weren't truly part of it. I've always felt incomplete when I wasn't with you, even though I went through the years away at the Military Academy and I can go and stay in Samorsa with Luntigré and Flori and be very happy – but that's because I know you're here in the world with me. I came apart when it was likely I would lose you, when you were so sick after they hurt you at The Palace.

"That day you fussed at Menders' Men made it clear. I even went through a pile of Menders' philosophy books trying to find whatever name they put on that sort of love – but there isn't anything. It's closer than sister and brother. It's closer than a lover. I don't know if it's closer than Luntigré's 'great love', but I think it may be, in a very singular way."

He knelt in front of her, putting his hands over hers as she held the tempered knife.

"I never want to be without you, Willow," he whispered. "I'm not asking for physical love – that would ruin what we have, and it isn't part of what we have. You're my other self – the other part of me. We need to help each other to be stronger, so we don't collapse under the hammer when it falls."

Katrin felt an enormous surge of emotion – relief, joy, love. They were free of trying to be sister and brother or lovers or old childhood friends.

They were one. They had always been one.

She leaned forward and put her cheek next to his.

"Yes," she whispered. "It has come clear. My other self – the other part of me."

After a moment, Hemmett sat back on his heels and took his handkerchief from his pocket. He pressed it to the tears on her cheeks and then against his own streaming eyes before he stood.

Katrin looked down at the knife in her lap, at the beautiful blade formed by the torment of metal heated and pounded thousands of times.

"Would you take me to the orphanage site tomorrow?" she asked. "I think it's time to get our construction crew back. I don't want that project to fade away. I want to get back to it."

"I shall indeed – and I also request leave to go and see my little family in Samorsa before much longer," Hemmett grinned. "I don't want that project to fade away either."

Katrin rewrapped the knife and held it out to him. He shook his head.

"It's yours. One day you may need to look at it and remember," he smiled. "Care for some more tea?"

ERDAHN, MORDANIA

13
BONDING

...I want you to know that your continuing success is a great comfort to us all, particularly to me. There have been some very dark days where knowing that you are so successful is a great comfort.

I've just realized this letter will reach you on your birthday and mine, and that you will be twenty-three. I will send my gift to you with Kaymar, as Eiren, Katrin and Hemmett are doing the same. May I say that the last ten years of my life have been infinitely enriched by your presence, my dear son.

Your loving father,

M

Borsen finished reading Menders' letter giving him the news about Katrin's hair loss being permanent. He set it down with infinite care on his worktable.

Then he threw a pattern weight across the room as hard as he could before he rested his head in his hands and tried to stay in control of himself.

***

At the end of a month of being in Borsen's company, Stevahn was going mad. The only good thing he could say was that he had contact with Borsen while going mad, where before, he'd been going mad with absolutely no satisfaction at all.

He'd been out with Borsen almost every day since they'd been to dinner together, sometimes just for a stroll, sometimes to dinner or lunch or the theatre, sometimes to the races. He felt no closer to knowing much about Borsen than he had been at that first dinner.

Borsen was companionable, amusing, touching. He was also, on occasion, distant, grumpy, infuriating and downright irritating. He seemed to have no sexual urges. In a month of steady romancing and no end of opportunity, he had not so much as offered a kiss.

Several times Stevahn told himself that nothing was going to come of this non-existent affair, that perhaps Borsen only considered him a friend. He would tell himself to accept what there was and try to be at peace about it.

Then he would wait with his breath held at his office window each morning until he saw Borsen coming up the street to open his store. Borsen would look up, smile and wave. Stevahn's heart would melt and he'd be anxious for the next time they were together.

On the morning of the shortest day of the year, Stevahn was startled by the announcement that Mister Heldstrom was waiting to see him. Heldstrom specialized in information and worked for Stevahn's family. Because of their position in finance, they had to know what was going on in Mordania and abroad.

"Hello there, Stevahn," Heldstrom said, taking the chair offered. "I'm short on time this morning but wanted you to know someone has been making inquiries about you. Not what I would expect in financial circles either. About your personal habits."

"What?" Stevahn frowned.

"We can trace it back to someone known as Menders, also deals in information, has for years," Heldstrom said. "Ring any bells?"

Stevahn shook his head.

"Well, that's the most we know of it. I thought you should be informed."

After Heldstrom left, Stevahn sat there, puzzling over it.

It wasn't rare for inquiries to be made when one was in the banking business. After all, investors weren't about to belly up to the counter and lay down millions of florins without being confident of the solvency of an investment bank. There was also a great deal of corporate espionage involved in all facets of business. But inquiries of that sort were about stocks and bonds, holdings and assets, to say nothing of debts. They weren't about one's personal life.

Stevahn had arranged to meet Borsen for lunch and was still puzzling over the situation as he met him by the statue of Queen Glorantha. He was late because of Heldstrom's unexpected visit. He could see Borsen wasn't happy about it. Borsen's eyes looked shadowed, as they had of late. He had complained a time or two about not having slept well. His mood had degenerated in concert with his looks.

Stevahn hurried to the bench where Borsen was sitting with all the ease of someone lounging nude on an ice floe.

"I'm sorry," he said quickly, sitting next to him. "I couldn't get away."

"It doesn't leave us much time to eat. I have an early afternoon appointment," Borsen replied wearily, with a bit of snap.

"Poor boy," Stevahn said, getting a good look at him up close. He looked terrible, as if he was ill.

The words acted on Borsen like a lit fuse would act on a bomb. He stood abruptly and whistled piercingly at a passing cab.

"I'm not a boy," he said viciously, stepping into the cab and giving the driver the address of his store, leaving Stevahn sitting there staring after him.

When Stevahn returned to his office, a note was waiting for him, from Heldstrom.

Stevahn,

Happened on information about the Menders name. Seems it's attached to Borsen's, being both the name used by Borsen himself when he signs a legal document. It's also that of a partner in the business, a relative of some kind. If the same Menders as the one who deals in information, these are very powerful people. If you owe Borsen for a suit, you might need to pay up!

Heldstrom

Stevahn's secretary nearly fell out of her chair as he stormed past her and banged out of his office, leaving his coat and hat behind, though it was snowing outside.

Stevahn crossed the street furiously, strode past the store director of Borsen's, tromped resoundingly up the stairs and banged into Borsen's workroom. He'd seen from his own office that there was no client there. Borsen had not been working, but was sitting rather limply in an armchair, looking as if he had a headache.

Now he found himself facing an entirely different Borsen, one who was on his feet in a half crouch, holding a very large knife in his hand. It stopped Stevahn's forward momentum but not his fury.

"Oh, for the gods' sakes!" Borsen cried, tossing the knife on his table in disgust and straightening up. "Can't you just send in your card, knock, something?"

Stevahn held out Heldstrom's note. Borsen took it, scanned it, then turned pale.

"If I call you 'boy', it's a term of endearment, you ass, not an insult. I'm in love with you. Do you know enough now?" Stevahn snarled.

He didn't wait until Borsen answered, but backtracked while he still had enough rage seething through his veins to get him back across the street and up to his office.

He was sulking and calling himself every name in the book an hour later, sure he'd finished his friendship with Borsen forever. His secretary skulked in, trying to be invisible, and delivered a note without a word. He groaned and opened it.

My dear Stevahn,

I have hurt you a great deal because I'm trying to protect someone else. The people making the inquiries that upset you have been more inquisitive about certain matters than they should have been.

I would like to talk to you about this personally. I cannot trust certain information to a written note. If you are still interested in knowing me, please come to my home at six o'clock tonight. I will explain whatever you want to know then.

I also apologize for being so rude at lunchtime today. I just had bad news. The shortest day of the year is also a difficult one for me. I acted like a bastard and you are justified in being angry with me. It is not the way I usually am, Stevahn. I have been under a great deal of pressure lately. No excuse, I know.

Borsen

***

Stevahn stretched enormously and opened his eyes, launching himself directly into the experience of waking in an unfamiliar place. For a moment, his eyes roved the room and then came to rest on Borsen, who was sound asleep beside him, snugged against his side.

Stevahn smiled and reached over to stroke a stray lock of the young man's hair away from his eyes. Then the door opened, silently but suddenly. A hawk-faced but attractive woman stuck her head around it.

She looked Stevahn over rapidly, her face remaining impassive. Then she looked at Borsen and raised an inquisitive eyebrow as she looked back at Stevahn again.

"Asleep," Stevahn mouthed. She nodded and mouthed back "Breakfast or lunch?"

Stevahn looked at the clock and then whispered, "Lunch," with a sheepish smile. The woman withdrew, pulling the door shut silently.

So that's Varnia, Stevahn thought, thankful that he hadn't been out of bed and stretching. That would have given her an eyeful. He had to admire her aplomb, because he knew she'd never looked in on this situation before.

He'd kept Borsen from getting up at the crack of dawn and heading out to work on a rest day, then had drifted in and out of sleep since then, cradling Borsen close and basking in the joy of loving and being loved – because after the night just past, he had absolutely no doubt in his mind that Borsen loved him, intensely and deeply.

He'd accepted Borsen's dinner invitation despite his anger. Initially things had been tense, but Borsen had explained the reason for enquiries being made – as well as many other things.

By the end of the evening, through dinner and conversation afterward, he knew a great deal about Borsen's life, from his relationship to Princess Katrin to his own personal circumstances. Particularly vivid was the moment after Borsen told him about his mother's tragic death by starvation and exposure after a desperate struggle to keep them alive through whatever means possible, leaving him to the mercies of his vicious father at the age of six.

"My dear boy," Stevahn had said softly. "I... I don't know what to say."

"That's the part I was afraid to tell you out of the way," Borsen replied, looking relieved that Stevahn hadn't reacted with repulsion or dismay.

"Why would you be afraid to tell me this?" Stevahn asked, taken aback.

"Perhaps you wouldn't wish to know the bastard son of a thief and a street whore," Borsen replied levelly.

After many months of inadvertently saying the wrong thing, Stevahn finally found his voice in the wake of Borsen's confidences.

"I'd like to kill your father. I wish I could have saved your mother and I want to know you," Stevahn answered. "Borsen, it doesn't matter. I judge people by their actions, not by the circumstances of their birth. I love you for who you are – and I do love you."

After that, there were no more barriers – and this morning, Stevahn knew what he wanted. No need to wait.

He slid his favorite ring, a large diamond clasped in fine gold which he'd bought in celebration of finishing college, from his little finger.

"I'm not good at the loverly talk," he murmured to Borsen, who slumbered on. "I'm going to put this on your finger and see if you'd like to keep it forever. A little surprise for you when you wake up. I do hope you'll want it – and me."

He slid it carefully onto Borsen's wedding finger, pleased to see it fit perfectly.

Then he stretched again, rose and decided a bath before his dear one woke would be a very good idea.

***

Borsen woke for the second time, sighed luxuriously and had an enormous stretch before thumping his pillows into a more comfortable conformation and snuggling into them. Stevahn was not in the bed, but splashing and what sounded like an enormous bee humming in his opulent bathroom let Borsen know that he was not far away.

The alarm clock had gone off resoundingly at six that morning. Borsen struggled to turn it off, failing several times before he silenced the strident jangling. He'd only had a couple of hours' sleep after spending the night with Stevahn. He'd managed to force himself to sit up on the side of the bed and groped for his glasses. He was shaking his head groggily when a big hand closed around his arm and pulled him back down onto the pillows. His glasses were removed with a by-your-leave and returned to the night table.

"No," Stevahn said firmly. "It is a rest day. Your store is not even open. You do not need to start running around after almost no sleep. Why on Eirdon are you getting up?"

"I have a lot of things to do at work," Borsen protested, struggling against him, unable to resist laughing.

"No. You're pushing yourself far too much, I can see that. No wonder your eyes are like pissholes in the snow."

"Last night you said my eyes were beautiful," Borsen replied.

"You should look in the mirror. Two hours' sleep makes even you look like death warmed over."

"Let me get up and I'll go look in the mirror."

"No, little Mister Clever, you won't trick me that way. Come here." Stevahn pulled the covers up over them both and wrapped his arms around Borsen. "Go back to sleep. We both need it."

Borsen had nodded off again, held against Stevahn's broad chest, feeling more secure than he had in a very long time.

Now he heard Stevahn getting out of the tub. He put his glasses on, looked at the clock and groaned.

"Twelve o'clock!" He hadn't slept this late in the morning in his life, but then he'd never spent almost all the night hours with a lover before either. Truthfully, he really didn't want to go to the store by himself and make patterns today. He wanted to be with Stevahn. It was a rest day, after all. He'd done precious little resting lately.

"Oh, the hells with it," he muttered, turning on his side, preparing to slide his left hand under the pillow. He stopped and stared at his fingers as if he'd never seen them before.

"I have managed not to get water all over your beautiful bathroom," Stevahn said cheerily. Borsen looked up to see him standing there, festooned in only a towel, using another on his hair.

"I seem to have acquired a new piece of jewelry," Borsen replied, his voice thick with emotion, holding up his left hand where a gold and diamond ring he'd seen many times on Stevahn's little finger was now on his wedding finger.

The equivalent of marriage, what nancyboys called 'bonding', a ring given and accepted as a token of lifetime devotion and fidelity. He felt breathless.

"If you'd like to have it, leave it there," Stevahn smiled, toweling once again all over and then stretching out on the bed to be eye to eye with Borsen.

"You're not getting it back, that's for certain," Borsen said, grinning. "Thank you."

"Good. It comes with all my love." Stevahn reached out, took both Borsen's hands in his and said, "I promise to stay with you all my life."

The bonding words. Borsen felt his hands trembling. He had almost lost his ability to speak Mordanian. He sat up against the pillows, swallowed twice and responded.

"I promise to stay with you all my life."

They were both smiling and fighting happy tears when Borsen's stomach growled – thunderously.

Stevahn burst out laughing. "Let's get you fed. A formidable lady looked in here about half an hour ago and mouthed 'breakfast or lunch?' I told her lunch."

Borsen laughed aloud, sitting up. "That's Varnia and I'm sure her curiosity finally got the best of her after seeing your coat and hat in the closet when she got home, long after we'd gone to bed. Hungry as I am though, I would like a bath."

"I left the tub running, your bath is assured," Stevahn grinned. "So thoughtful of you to have a tub big enough for the likes of me. I was amazed beyond words when I saw it. You should install a diving board." He bent and started sorting out the tangle of his clothing on the floor beside the bed. Stevahn's suit trousers were a rumpled mess, his shirt missing two buttons from his haste to get free of the garment.

"Charming," he said, examining the shirt. "I shan't sit down at the table with you and your sister in this. While you're in the tub, I'll nip over to my place and get into some clean clothes."

"Why do you live in lodgings?" Borsen asked, reclining against the piled pillows and looking at his new diamond ring with smug satisfaction.

"After my last romantic disaster, I didn't feel like setting up in a new place. They're nice lodgings, don't sound like I'm living in a single room warming up day old soup over a spirit lamp." Stevahn stood and started fastening his trousers.

"Maybe you'd like to bring the suits I made for you and your other things over," Borsen said tantalizingly. "There's a lot of room in the closet. And in the bed, as you know. I – I would very much like it if you were here."

"So I shall," Stevahn smiled over his shoulder.

"Let me tell Varnia you'll be coming back in, so she doesn't think you're a brigand. She's a darling but she can be very protective of me." Borsen got up and went for his dressing gown.

***

"Oh!" Varnia cried delightedly as Borsen displayed his bonding ring before her wide eyes. "Oh, I'm so happy! He looks like a lovely man."

"He is," Borsen assured her. "He'll be moving in here over the next few days."

"Of course. Will he move furniture in?"

Borsen laughed. She was all ready to organize.

"I don't know, dearie," he smiled. "We've put the cart before the horse a little – he came for dinner and some explanations and he's walking out of here a bonded man. We'll find out over lunch. He went back to his lodgings for a change of clothes. He'll be knocking, so please let him back in."

"Won't you want to eat together without a chaperone?" Varnia asked.

"No. I'm sure Stevahn and I will have many meals alone together, but I want him to be part of the household right away. That means you eating with us just as you've eaten with me, as a family. Now I want to get a bath quickly before he gets back."

Borsen submerged himself in his marble bathtub, a copy of the enormous one Menders had installed at The Shadows. Requiring extensive reinforcement of the house structure to hold it up, it was large enough to float around in with plenty of room to spare.

His thoughts drifted to the letter he'd had from his uncle the day before and how it had led to the barriers between Stevahn and himself coming down. The letter had made him long for home.

The hells with it, I am going home at some point over Winterfest, he decided. It gets slower than a tortoise in Erdahn once the solstice is past. So many people leave town for the holidays. I'm going home. Katrin needs me. And maybe Stevahn would want to come, which would be wonderful. I'd love showing him The Shadows.

He felt light and happy and started raucously singing a ridiculous and very vulgar lyric Kaymar had coined years back to the effect of being glad to be a nancyboy. Years of Menders' careful training had given Borsen a good strong tenor voice, so he opened up the pipes and was caroling the third ribald verse, simultaneously sending great splashes of water ceilingward with his feet, when he heard cackling laughter from the bathroom doorway.

"This is the distant, chaste and remote young man I have been pursuing for over a year?" Stevahn gasped, holding onto the doorframe for support, having obviously returned from his lodgings. "Floating around in a tub you could dock a tugboat in, flinging water about and yowling a positively obscene song? I have died and gone to the halls of the gods!"

"Wait until you hear the fourth verse," Borsen smirked and immediately launched into it, while his bonded howled with laughter and finally slid down the wall to the floor, helpless.

***

Kaymar breezed into Borsen's workroom.

"I got your message," he said airily, preparing to stretch himself out on Borsen's sofa. "Something you want me to carry over to Menders?"

"A letter. I'm almost finished with it," Borsen replied from his desk. He reached with his left hand for blotting paper.

Kaymar closed his own hand around Borsen's left wrist. Borsen looked up to see Kaymar gaping at the glittering diamond ring Stevahn had bonded him with.

"Child, what have you done?" Kaymar asked, his face horrified.

Borsen wrenched free and stood up slowly.

"Would you like to retract that?" he asked. His voice was ice.

Kaymar stepped back, for once devoid of his usual self-assurance.

"I'm sorry," he apologized. "That was… Borsen, I thought I told you to wait a while."

Borsen drew a deep breath.

"Kaymar, I followed your advice and almost lost him. Not entirely because of what you told me – I added plenty of fuel to the fire, but Stevahn was very uncertain as to my feelings because I was being so hard to get."

"It's just that you don't have any experience…" Kaymar began, looking sheepish.

"I know! I didn't know how to act with him! I nearly lost him. Thank the gods he has patience and accepted my offer to explain everything to him. And thank the gods he still wanted me after he heard what I came from."

Borsen turned away from Kaymar and strode across the room to the window, snapping the curtains closed lest Stevahn look over from his office and see this scene.

He was startled when Kaymar grasped his shoulders and turned him around roughly.

"Don't ever say that," Kaymar commanded. "Don't believe it. I didn't help raise you to think that someone is doing you a favor by loving you. He's a fortunate man to have you."

Kaymar released him just as suddenly as he'd taken hold of him and turned away for a moment. Both men were breathing quickly, tempers ready to flare.

Borsen squeezed his eyes shut. This was not the reaction he'd expected from Kaymar.

He heard his cousin turn around. He opened his eyes, knowing resentment showed on his face. To his surprise, Kaymar looked contrite.

"Borsen – I'm sorry," the older man said bluntly. "It's not that I'm unhappy you've found someone. It's just that you're so young. It startled me."

"How old were you when you bonded with Ifor?" Borsen snapped.

Kaymar shook his head. "Younger than you – but my situation was entirely different, Borsen. There's no comparison. I'd been bonded twice before and widowed tragically each time. Gods knew I had enough experience for ten young men. I just thought that some more time on your own would be a good idea."

"I love him!" Borsen burst out. "I want him!" He clenched his fists, hard, hearing his blood roaring in his ears.

Kaymar groaned in frustration. He walked over to Borsen.

"I must accept the fact that you're grown up," he said, putting his hands on either side of Borsen's face, resisting Borsen's attempts to pull away. "I'm sorry I've hurt you and sounded like I don't approve of what you've done. I would like for you to have gotten to know Stevahn Rondheim better before taking this step, but he's a good man and he'll be good to you. Please forgive me for being an old hen and tell me about it. Come on, try to forget me being an idiot."

Borsen let himself be pulled down to sit on the sofa. A moment later he was given a glass of kirz and Kaymar settled opposite him with a drink of his own. Kaymar leaned forward and took Borsen's left hand, turning the ring to the light.

"It's beautiful," he said simply. "Tell me about it."

"He – he put it on my hand when I was sleeping. I saw it as soon as I put my glasses on in the morning," Borsen said stiffly. "It means a lot to him. He bought it for himself when he finished college, it isn't just a ring he went out and bought that day."

"After you first slept together?" Kaymar asked gently.

Borsen nodded. "I – we had a scene that afternoon because I was upset over the news about Katrin's hair never growing back. He was upset because he found out he'd been investigated and that it came from me. I asked him over to explain. We talked and sorted out that we want the same thing – someone to be with forever. I didn't want to wait, to seem to be testing him. That would show lack of trust. I trust him, Kaymar."

"You see, I had hoped that you'd be on your own for a couple of years before bonding – mainly because I think that would have been the best thing for me when I was a boy, rather than living the way I did. I liked the thought of you being busy and happy and free of serious attachments for a little while, a protracted innocence of sorts. But that's not what you wanted, is it?" Kaymar mused. "I can't try to force you to be what I should have been. Are you happy?"

"Very much," Borsen said, his voice shaking. "I'm so glad to go home and have him there."

"Then I'm happy too," Kaymar said firmly. "Truly I am. You know that I'm not entirely stable. Sometimes my mouth runs away with me. Now, there's something my dear father said to me many years ago, when I was much younger than you. It pertains here. No matter what happens, no matter what you do, Kaymar loves you always, Borsen."

Borsen felt his anger ebbing away, along with it the terrible cold fear and doubt that Kaymar's reaction had stirred within him. He felt comfortable again. The joy about his bonding was back. He sighed with relief and Kaymar laughed aloud.

"Now, will you introduce me to your man? I have some time free before going back to The Shadows," Kaymar said, taking out his cigar case.

"I'd love to," Borsen replied.

THE SHADOWS, MORDANIA

14
WINTERFEST

My dear Borsen,

Please come home as soon as you can and Stevahn is completely welcome. As I'm sure you guessed, the news is already out here. Everyone is very happy that you are no longer alone. I look forward to meeting Stevahn and welcoming him to our family.

I applaud your decision to close Borsen's for a short time. I doubt there will be much harm done to business, but continuing at the pace you have been keeping will cause harm to you and your enterprise. A rest will be excellent for you, and give you a chance to think about how you will carry out your next year of business. You are also in a position to pay your employees for the unexpected break and I applaud your decision to do so.

I am very proud of you, my boy, in so many ways.

Your loving Papa

Dearest Stevahn,

Mama and Papa are letting me write in response to your letter to all of us, since I knew about your being in love with Borsen. They have scolded me roundly for not telling them about it, but I know when to keep my mouth shut about such things. After all, that is what older sisters are for!

I'm so glad you caught your elusive fish! I will now admit to you that I used your name as a reference to have myself measured for a riding habit by your Borsen, just to get a look at the young man who so caught your imagination. He's a darling and I know you'll forgive me for the subterfuge, little brother. As you said in your letter, that exterior of brisk businessman is a blind for something far more vulnerable and sweet.

We're so happy that you are confident and content. We're curious to know about Princess Katrin and this place called The Shadows – and as you know, no-one would ever say or do anything to endanger her.

Mother and Father have asked that you bring Borsen out to meet them the rest days after you get back from Old Mordania. Versen warns that you rug up while there and wear plenty of long underfugs to keep from being frostbitten (he's being very naughty and hanging over my shoulder cackling at his wit. I will not write down his exact words), as there is a sort of cold there in that part of the country that we never experience in Erdahn.

We are all well here in Surelia, enjoying the summerlike weather. I'm so glad you will not be alone over the holidays. I know that's one of the drawbacks of being in business, but it makes for lonely times.

Many hugs and kisses to you and to Borsen.

Your loving sister,

Stellia

Stellia dear,

Writing this in haste, as an unexpected business matter has made it necessary to send another messenger to Father, but I did want to respond to your letter to accept the invitation to bring Borsen to meet you all - also to let you know your words touched me and made me smile.

Because you and I have always been confidants, I will say I am deliriously happy and I know that this will last. Since you've met Borsen, you know he is something rare and fine. I will admit that when I finally realized I had won his heart, I was suddenly terrified, as if someone had handed me a little jeweled grasshopper, something so delicate, exotic and precious that any rough handling could destroy it.

Though Borsen appears physically strong, he is bird-boned and fragile, only five feet tall and so light I can pick him up with ease. Despite this, he has indomitable strength and determination. He can and has moved mountains to get what he wants. I marvel at him, and that I have him, every day.

Have a wonderful Winterfest, my dear. I so look forward to having you all meet Borsen in the new year.

Little brotherling,

Stev

***

Stevahn had expected a busy Winterfest holiday, but the whirl of activity he was presented with at The Shadows couldn't have been anticipated.

From their arrival, life had gone by at a joyful pace. No sooner had the force of nature that was Hemmett driven Stevahn, Borsen and Varnia up to the front steps of The Shadows, but a little copper skinned girl dashed out of the house without a coat.

"Which one is the bride?" she cried, looking from Borsen to Stevahn. "Is it you, Uncle Borsen?"

Hemmett laughed, swung out of the sledge and crouched down to her eye level.

"Flori, when two men have decided to spend their life together, there is no bride," he explained quietly. "A bride is always a lady."

"I hoped to see a bride. I've never seen one yet and I'm almost nine years old." Flori looked very disappointed.

"You're seeing a bonded," Stevahn smiled at her, having stepped out of the sledge himself before he helped Varnia down and gave Borsen an arm to lean on. No point in risking a fall with Borsen's bones. "Actually, Borsen is my bonded and I'm his bonded. It means we're bound together forever. I'm Stevahn."

"Then you're my Uncle Stevahn," she smiled, crunching over the snow and reaching up to him.

Stevahn was used to his sister's boy and swung her up in his arms.

"So my first hug and kiss here at The Shadows come from the Night Flower," he laughed as she placed an enthusiastic kiss on his cheek.

"How do you know my name is Night Flower?"

"I'm a wizard. Now, shall we go inside?"

"Yes, likely you can't bear the cold here, you're a city boy," she replied. Hemmett rolled his eyes skyward, trying not to guffaw aloud. Borsen had already run up the steps and was in the arms of the man Stevahn had seen over a year ago, standing with Borsen in front of the building that had become his splendid store.

"That's Menders. I call him Grampy," Flori whispered helpfully in his ear.

"Here, Miss Mischief, into the house with you, give Stevahn and Menders a chance to say hello," Hemmett said, taking Flori into his own arms and dashing up the steps with her, snorting and neighing like a horse as they went through the door.

Stevahn mounted the steps more sedately, giving Borsen a few more moments with his uncle, looking around at the snow carpeted gardens with wonder. The place looked like something out of a legend. It was magical.

"Uncle, this is Stevahn," Borsen said. Stevahn turned to be given the warmest, strongest handshake he'd ever known, as Menders looked at him over his dark glasses. Borsen had prepared him for Menders' unusual eyes. Stevahn looked into them, wanting more than anything for this man to trust and accept him from the first.

"Yes," Menders said after a moment. He nodded and smiled. "I'm very glad you're here, Stevahn."

"Thank you for having me," Stevahn replied sincerely.

"No need. You're part of this family now – just brace yourself, because I'm informed by this beautiful lady that we're overwhelming, at least at first." Menders grinned suddenly, transforming his very serious mien to one of fun as he indicated a stunning, very dark Samorsan woman who had appeared at the door – Luntigré.

"Please come in," she invited. "They forget the cold and that Katrin cannot come out into it." She took his hands briefly, kissing his cheek, then reached out for Varnia and embraced her before ushering them in. "I will leave you outside, Papa, if you don't come along and then we'll have no choice but to put you out with the ice animals on display," she teased Menders, who was loitering with Borsen.

And so Stevahn met Katrin, who was waiting near the fire.

The signs of illness were there, gaunt hollows in her cheeks, shadowed eyes and an air of fragility. She had golden hair, a wig, but a very good one. Her eyes were the most intense blue he had ever seen – and her smile was the most beautiful.

"And you're Stevahn, of course," she said, putting her arms around his neck and kissing his cheek. He gathered her close, understanding now why Borsen had been so distraught over her being unwell. She was obviously frail and Borsen had said that she'd recovered enormously, so the poor girl must have been near death for ages after that demented torture she'd been subjected to. He restrained a shudder, thinking of the horror that Borsen had finally described to him in full.

"You will be my brother," Katrin whispered. "I'm so very glad you found Borsen."

"Thank you, little sister," he whispered back, kissing her forehead as she stood back and smiled up at him, putting her hands in his.

Things had only escalated from there, with an enormous dinner with fifty-six people at the table, two days of nonstop preparation for Winterfest Eve, impromptu sledding parties and snowball fights. Stevahn saw a menagerie of animals being built from snow and cut saplings which were then showered with buckets of water to convert them into enormous ice sculptures. Borsen explained that what had started out as a birthday surprise for Katrin years ago was now a local contest, which drew people from the estate and nearby villages to compete or to goggle at the beauty of the display.

On Winterfest Eve, Menders and Hemmett asked if Stevahn would like to accompany them as they walked a perimeter patrol. It was their habit to do so on holidays to give Menders' Men and Hemmett's Guard a break. He accepted readily and was gratified by beautiful views of the estate and the quiet companionship the two men offered away from the ongoing activity at the house. They confided that this tradition had begun out of necessity but continued because it gave them a chance to stop hanging greenery or helping in the kitchen, enjoy their cigars and consider changes to be made on the estate in the coming year.

Winterfest Day passed in a flurry, quieting toward nightfall as everyone began feeling the increased activity, to say nothing of the feast that made the tables groan. Cook and her staff had outdone themselves, offering an amazing array of temptation.

Borsen, yawning mightily after helping clear Winterfest dinner, suggested an early bedtime and Stevahn was glad to comply. As they put on the thick nightshirts that were the only way to stay comfortable in this frigid part of Mordania, Borsen told Stevahn that Menders was quite sure the Thrun would be there within the next few days.

"Coming over the ice bridge so early would be a real risk, but Tharak got word of Katrin still being ill and sent word back that he was determined to get here this year. The last two winters were so mild that they couldn't get across from their Island to the mainland at all. Tharak hates it when he doesn't get a chance to see Light Of The Winter Sun every year." Borsen finished braiding his hair back for the night and climbed the bedstairs, flopping down on his pillows with a sigh.

"What? Light of the Winter Sun?"

"That's Katrin's Thrun name. There's so much to help you catch up with!" Borsen said. "I have it from Thira, Tharak's daughter, that there is a Thrun prophecy about great changes in the world that are going to come in the near future. Apparently Katrin, Hemmett and I are supposed to have major roles in making this come about. Our Thrun names are reflective of this, but I don't know just what it is that they're supposed to mean, and no-one will tell us. Katrin is Light Of The Winter Sun, Hemmett is Light Brighter Than The Sun and I'm Reflection Of My Friend. And now you know all I know. Uncle doesn't want us knowing about it at all, because he says that when people know about prophecies, they automatically try to make them come to be."

"Your uncle is a wise man," Stevahn said, shivering a little. Something about those names disturbed him, though he couldn't say why. He flapped across the room in his own blanketlike nightshirt, provided by Katrin after he nearly froze his first night at The Shadows. He climbed into bed beside Borsen.

He jerked awake in the middle of the night, every hair on his head prickling with fear. Magic was awake and alert, his great shaggy head silhouetted by the fire, his lips drawn back as he growled gently.

Stevahn looked around the room. He'd already been startled one night by Menders coming in silently to make sure the fire was burning high enough, as a cold snap had caused the temperature to plummet. Menders whispered Stevahn's name the moment he woke, explaining that he made the rounds of "the children's" rooms before going to bed on cold nights to be sure the fires were well fueled, and the rooms were warm. Borsen was prone to nightmares if he got cold, Menders said. Stevahn stored that morsel of information away in his memory.

He could see there was no-one in the room and knew the dog would not be growling at Menders. He wondered what had sparked such a visceral reaction in himself and Magic.

A wolf raised a moaning howl, right outside the window. It was so close it sounded like it was in the room.

Borsen didn't wake but sighed in his sleep and turned onto his back, obviously accustomed to such winter night serenades. With every fiber in his body vibrating with panic, there was no way Stevahn could possibly lie there, not after that paralyzing sound.

A snuffling at the shuttered window finished him. He got out of the bed, fast, wondering if he should grab Borsen and flee. Then he heard claws clicking away over the verandah floor outside.

He flung on his dressing gown and stepped into his slippers, double checking the bolt on the window shutter and getting his pistol before letting himself into the hallway, telling Magic to stay with Borsen. If a wolf was that close to the house, it would be a good idea to let Menders know.

He strode out to the entryway to find that Menders already knew, as he was coming down the stairs similarly attired, pistol in hand.

"Some of our winter friends woke you?" Menders asked cheerfully.

"One howled right outside our window," Stevahn said, glad his voice wasn't shaking like his knees.

"Raises your hackles a bit when that happens," Menders said. "Borsen didn't wake?"

"Wolves' howling is just a winter lullaby to Little Man, he's been hearing them all his life," came Kaymar's voice. Stevahn turned to see him walking toward them, also armed. "That bastard yowled outside my window too. He even cut through Ifor's snoring. Sounds like there are more than one nosing around."

"It was snuffling at the window," Stevahn said.

"Probably smelled Magic," Kaymar remarked, looking out one of the narrow panes on either side of the door. "I don't see any here, Menders."

"They're over near the Rose Garden, I saw them from upstairs," Menders answered. "They don't seem hungry. They're just sniffing around, so I suspect they've followed our friend Tharak down and we can expect to see him tomorrow. Sorry, Stevahn, I forget this is all new to you. Old Mordanian wolves tend to follow Thrun clans when they're on the march because they always cook meat. The scraps and bones are left for the wolves – having wolves around encampments is a way the Thrun adapted long ago. Not many people would risk the wolves to get at the Thrun. These wolves are likely circling around Tharak's band, so they're close enough to march in here tomorrow. How good a shot are you?"

"I'm a crack shot," Stevahn replied honestly. Firearms and hunting were two passions his father had passed on to him.

"Well then, I think between the three of us we can risk opening the winter shutters at the end of this hall to have a look at these gentlemen," Menders said, leading the way toward the shuttered glass door at the end of the corridor. "Be ready to fire. If he does decide to come through the glass you won't have time to cock your weapons."

Menders unbolted and slowly opened the shutters of the large door at the end of the wing.

"Hello," Menders said softly, pointing at an enormous wolf standing with his nose pressed to the other side of the glass. They stepped back, pistols ready. The huge animal looked at them impassively.

Now Stevahn understood what people meant when they said the Old Mordanian wolf was nothing like the Southern Mordanian wolf, which was basically a large, shaggy dog. This creature was like no dog that Stevahn had ever seen. It had a high, humped back, the knobby elongated head carried low on massive shoulders ridged with great slabs of muscle. The legs were as thick as young tree trunks, the front pair significantly longer than the rear, making the ridged back slope abruptly downward at the hindquarters. Three-toed feet culminated in foot long claws, which matched the glistening fangs protruding from the creature's mouth.

He stands chest height to me and I'm over six feet tall, Stevahn thought. The wolf's eyes were light yellow and devoid of fear. It tipped its head to one side, never taking its eyes from them.

"They have to be with the Thrun, they're used to people," Kaymar whispered.

"Very much so – not always a good thing. As big as he is, yes, he's from much farther north and east," Menders said. "He is a beauty, gentlemen." Then he sniffed the air subtly. "Borsen is here," he said, so they wouldn't be startled with their guns armed. Just then Borsen said, "It's me coming down the hall." Stevahn looked away from the wolf to see that he too had a pistol, the elegant jeweled pocket weapon he habitually carried.

"Look at the nancy gun," Kaymar teased.

"Let's say I try shooting you in the knee with it, Kaymar, and you can tell me if it works all right," Borsen teased in return, edging between Menders and Stevahn so he could see the wolf. "I think he's the biggest fellow we've seen here."

The wolf gave them one last impassive stare, then turned and trotted away across the terrace, through the garden and into the trees. A moment later they heard several wolves howl.

"That's what scared him off! You're in luck tonight, Stevahn, take a look at that big bastard," Kaymar exclaimed, pointing.

"You mean that huge rock with the tree growing out of it?" Stevahn asked, trying to remember what he could of the layout of the garden.

"No, I mean that big grundar buck that you think is a huge rock with a tree growing out of it. Step closer, our wolf friends will have gone on now that this fellow's here."

"Don't wolves eat them?" Stevahn asked, gazing in amazement at the enormous elk, which was easily three times his height and standing not ten feet away, pawing the ground with a foot the size of a wagon wheel.

"Not a full-grown buck like that," Menders answered. "There wouldn't be enough wolves in any pack to pull him down, he's fifteen feet at the shoulder. He would kill them. Kaymar, can you see his points well enough to count them?"

"Looks to be over fifty," Kaymar said. "No wolf that wasn't mad would take that on. It would be trampled and gored into jelly."

The enormous grundar threw back his head and began to bellow, the massive neck bulging at every bugling roar. Stevahn saw Kaymar releasing the hammer on his gun, and did likewise. The wolf pack howled again, but much farther away.

"He's chased them off," Borsen said, leaning against Stevahn.

"My father is an avid hunter, but I don't think he could bring himself to kill something like that," Stevahn said.

"You should bring him up in the autumn. The Men put on a huge boar hunt," Menders said, smiling at Stevahn over Borsen's head. Stevahn felt a grin spreading across his face at the implied acceptance not only of himself but with the acceptance extending to his family.

"I don't know about the rest of you, but I'm for making a kitchen raid," Kaymar said suggestively.

There was a rapid diaspora.

THE SHADOWS, MORDANIA

15
BALANCING MAN

Stevahn was just pulling on his trousers next morning when a horrific, vibrating, shattering crash nearly made him jump out of them again. He could hear icicles crashing to the ground outside.

"Uncle was right," Borsen said, rising from where he'd been lounging on the bed and scrambling for his clothes. He rapidly donned long undergarments, trousers and a thick knitted sweater, looking nothing like the picture of elegance he was in Erdahn. He fought on two pairs of thick socks followed by boots and then dashed for the door, Magic leaping around him. He hadn't even brushed out his hair.

"What the hells was that noise?" Stevahn asked, his head still ringing.

"The big gong. Hurry, you'll miss it!" Borsen was jigging around at the door. A low droning sound began to vibrate the house.

Stevahn hurried, dressing similarly to Borsen and then following him down the stairs. There was a general convergence of people thrashing to get out the door, trying to put on coats and the like and getting in each other's way. Borsen hauled on Stevahn's arm.

"We won't freeze, hurry!" he demanded, rushing out the door and down the front steps, then racing away down the drive. Stevahn could see that Hemmett was ahead of them and that he had a laughing Katrin flung inelegantly over his shoulder.

After a headlong race the four of them skidded to a halt. Hemmett lowered Katrin to her feet with care, pulling the shawl flung over her shoulders closely around her. Stevahn was shocked to see that she was out in the bitter cold with no warmer wrap. Just as he was about to protest, Borsen touched his arm and gestured for him to remain silent, pointing down the drive.

At least three hundred people were moving toward them while blowing various horns, banging gongs and shaking strings of bells. Under it all was the stomach-churning low drone note that shook the very ground.

The column of people moving forward in a ceremonial strutting swagger was broken by huge carts drawn by great hairy cow like animals, and by strings of farlins, which were rearing, snorting and kicking, snaking their long, sinuous necks around to snap at and bite each other.

A man led the massive column toward the house. Stevahn knew this had to be Tharak Karak a'a' Thrun.

He was dressed in an opulent ankle-length gown of red, embroidered with gold and studded with gems, an enormous horned hat on his head, weapons and bells hanging from his thick leather belt that had a buckle the size of Stevahn's hand. His boots, upturned at the toes, were red leather with gold embroidery, thickly furred at the cuff. His hair was loose, as Borsen and Menders usually wore theirs, but his hung to below his knees.

"Gods," Stevahn breathed as Tharak Karak drew closer. Stevahn was a big man, well over six feet and solidly built, but the Thrun chieftain towered over him and he was two of Stevahn in volume. His dark eyes traveled from Hemmett to Katrin to Borsen and then lingered on Stevahn. He stopped. The column behind him stopped as well. Tharak held up a hand for silence.

He went to Katrin and tipped her face up to his.

"Little one," he said softly and drew her close. Then, the embrace finished, he grinned at her. Katrin nodded.

To Stevahn's astonishment, Tharak Karak caught her up off the ground and flung her up in the air like a man would toss a child, while Katrin whooped. He caught her as if she weighed nothing, held her high and turned toward the people behind him, bellowing in his own language.

"Light Of The Winter Sun," Borsen translated in a whisper. Stevahn was nearly knocked down by the noise of the Thrun cheering, honking their horns and banging on their gongs.

A snap of Tharak's fingers brought several Thrun running with armloads of white furs, which he gently wrapped around Katrin, crowning her with an exquisite hat to match.

The big Thrun engulfed Hemmett in a huge embrace, giving his hair a rub that left it rampantly ruffled. Another snap of the fingers saw Hemmett wrapped in deep brown furs.

Tharak turned to Borsen.

"Here I go," Borsen said just as Tharak roared, "Little Man, Tharkul a' Thrunar, Reflection Of My Friend!" The chieftain snatched him up off the ground as if he was made of feathers, holding him high for a minute and grinning up at him. Then he lowered him to the ground and pulled him close before releasing him and having him bundled in a black fur coat.

It was obvious to Stevahn that this reunion differed from previous ones. Katrin was fragile, Hemmett had suffered as she did and Borsen was burdened by their troubles. There were tears close for everyone.

"You are all here, my little ones," Tharak said. "You've all come through the trial. This is what matters. And now," Tharak continued, looking at Stevahn, "who is this?"

Borsen moved to Stevahn and took his arm.

"Mine," he replied in a way that told Stevahn it meant much more than a simple word.

Stevahn found himself experiencing scrutiny from Tharak Karak. Though he was thirty-one and far from sheltered, he found the experience simultaneously unnerving and in some way soothing, as if he could look into those exotic, dark eyes for hours without wanting to do anything else. Then the Thrun Highest Chieftain nodded and grinned.

"Yes, he is the one," he said to Borsen. "Thetan a' Thrun – Balancing Man. A blessing on you both." He reached out both hands and shook Stevahn's firmly, then turned because Menders had reached them.

"Magic In The Eyes!" Tharak bellowed as he and Menders grasped one another's forearms and then embraced. Again, Stevahn got the impression that the embrace was longer than the usual. Tharak said something in a low tone and hugged Menders a second time before releasing him.

"And now, my friends, we will show you hospitality!" he announced. He grabbed Borsen off the ground and set him on one enormous shoulder, despite Borsen protesting that he was a grown man now. Then he put an arm around Katrin's shoulders and beckoned to Hemmett to join them. The music began again as he strode on toward the house. Borsen looked back at Stevahn, shrugged, grinned and waved.

Menders walked over to Stevahn.

"And it begins," he said. "You're as bad as the rest of them, out here without a coat."

"Menders… what is Thetan a' Thrun?"

A brief flash of surprise crossed Menders' face.

"It's a complex name," he replied slowly. "A force that brings balance to the world – literally, 'Balancing Man'. He called you that, did he?"

Stevahn nodded.

Menders was silent for a moment.

"Tharak rejoices in the mystical," he finally said. "Sometimes it's best not to think about his pronouncements a great deal."

"I know about the prophecy, as much as Borsen knows," Stevahn said.

Menders sighed. "Yes, and Borsen would know more than Katrin or Hemmett because Borsen would think to ask a Thrun, being Thrun himself," he said slowly. "Stevahn, I don't know the entire prophecy and I've made it a point not to know. I believe that you understand, without a lot of explanation, why this is the best thing to do. I will say one thing – you will keep Borsen from burning himself out with his own fire. You have already done a great deal to settle him and you will continue to do so. You are the only person who has ever been able to."

"He's a very motivated young man," Stevahn said.

"It goes beyond that," Menders replied, linking arms with him and following in the wake of the Thrun. "Borsen is a driven man, as he was a driven boy. Ever since I met him, he has always pushed himself to and beyond his limits, determined to be the best at everything he attempted. With much patience and care I've managed to deflect some of that. Because he is devoted to me, he has taken my advice. I saw him go to Erdahn with trepidation, though I encouraged it, because he was becoming determined to give up his dreams, so he could stay here with Katrin after she was injured."

"What?" Stevahn was stunned. "Borsen was going to give up opening his store?" Stevahn could hardly imagine it.

"Yes, he was." They had reached the house, where Stevahn gratefully retrieved his heavy fur coat from the rack. He pulled it on as they walked back out onto the steps.

"I asked Katrin to encourage him to go to Erdahn," Menders continued. "Borsen doesn't know this. It was difficult for her, as they are very close. He was a rock for her during the first year of her illness. Like me, she realized Borsen was about to destroy himself to help her. But I also feared the possibility that he would push himself far too much once he was on his own in Erdahn."

Menders was silent for a moment, his hands in his pockets.

"One cannot follow one's children around all their lives," he went on, his voice lower. "At some point it's necessary to step back, and this is the time for me to step back from Borsen. He accomplished the impossible getting Borsen's open so quickly and he's already two years ahead of his plan for the place."

Menders drew Stevahn's attention to where Tharak was standing, shouting directions, Borsen still perched on his shoulder. Then he continued speaking.

"I had begun to despair, to be truthful. I saw in my mind's eye the possibility of Borsen working himself to death before the age of thirty. I can't leave Katrin for long, because she has been so desperately ill. I simply could not be a continual tempering influence in Borsen's life because of the distance involved.

"That was a terrible decision for me to make, because my late-arriving boy is incredibly dear to me. I had to let him go and hope what I have given him would carry him through. At times it appeared it might not be enough. I was infinitely relieved when we received his letter about your bonding."

"Thank you," Stevahn said softly. "I have managed to keep him from overworking and driving himself so hard. He's begun to listen – and you were right, he was on the way to working himself into ill health, at the least. Hells, I've physically prevented him from going off to work alone at the store on rest days, which was more than a minor tussle. By now he's getting used to the idea and last week he even groused at me when I got up at eight on a rest day and woke him by dropping something in the bathroom."

Menders smiled. "You have no idea what good news that is to me," he said. "Let that be your answer for the meaning of your Thrun name, Thetan a' Thrun. You balance this young man. You must have noticed how infinitely precious he is to all of us."

"I certainly have noticed. I've never seen anyone more loved," Stevahn replied, watching as Tharak finally crouched and let Borsen off his shoulder.

"Borsen was a very lovable and endearing child," Menders said. "He caught your heart and held it – and he desperately needed love. It was easy to forget how driven he was because he was so adorable. Then it surfaced with a vengeance as he got older. I recognized it, of course, because being driven is also a trait of mine.

I'm glad he's finding that he needn't pour every ounce of his energy into his ambition."

Menders put his hands in his pockets and looked out over the spectacle of the Thrun rapidly converting an empty lawn into a town of circular tents. He seemed to stand taller suddenly, tension leaving his body.

"I had meant to speak to you of this at some time during your visit," Menders continued quietly. "I hadn't intended to do it in the freezing cold or standing on the steps but there you are. Sometimes the opportunity arises, and you have to take it. Now – my family is here and there will be five days of contests, trading, races, eating and drinking far too much. Tharak will once again try to trade me an enormous pile of saddles, jewelry, knives and furs for Eiren to become his seventh wife. Let the worries go, Stevahn and let's go join the carnival."

***

"He's gone completely Thrun," Borsen said with some amusement, watching Stevahn try to lift a small block of wood from the ground from the back of a running farlin. It was his fifth attempt. This time, instead of tumbling to the ground, he grazed the block with his fingers and managed to haul himself erect on the farlin's back.

Katrin, who was strolling toward the Thrun carnival, her arm linked with Borsen's, laughed.

"He's entranced with it," she agreed. "I can just remember how I was the first time the Thrun came here and he's the same way. I was so thrilled when Menders and I spent a night in Tharak's tent! Stevahn's having the time of his life out there, though he'll be black and blue when the bruises come up."

Stevahn took another run at the wooden block. He managed to snatch it, then swung himself upright on the farlin's back.

"Well done!" Borsen shouted excitedly. It was no easy feat, particularly for a large man. Stevahn was an excellent rider but no matter how skilled, any stunt from horseback was made more difficult with every pound of body weight.

"How much plunder has he traded for?" Katrin smiled.

"It's good we're going home on the launch and not by train, because the train wouldn't be able to pull it all. As it is, the launch will ride much lower in the water," Borsen replied. "Being a banker, he's driving good bargains too. I know he has designs on putting most of it, gems and jewelry, into his vault at the bank. He also has five jugs of kirz stashed under the bed, to take back to the fleshpots of Erdahn."

Katrin burst out laughing. Borsen was glad to see some color in her cheeks. It had been good for her to get outside, despite the cold. The distraction of the Thrun carnival was working on her like a tonic.

"Before he's done he'll have a horned hat and a gown," she said.

"He has the gown already," Borsen laughed. "Of course, it's beautiful and now I don't have to hide mine away, so he won't find them and think I'm a nancy. Try not to laugh yourself to death, my lovely sister and Princess. Now, what would you like me to trade for as a gift for you? We'll have to do it fast, before Stevahn gets everything."

"Oh, a dress, I think," Katrin said. Borsen raised an eyebrow. It had been a long time since she'd shown much interest in clothing, and he'd expected her to ask for a saddle or bridle for her farlin, Trouble. As far as he was concerned, it was a good step forward.

Stevahn had returned the farlin to its owner and was walking over to them.

"Ah, the Thrun city boy," Borsen said as Stevahn reached them.

"My two favorite country bumpkins," Stevahn responded, unfussed.

"I beg your pardon, sirrah, you are in the presence of royalty," Katrin said regally. "We're going to go and trade for a dress for me, if you wish to come and see true business acumen."

"Indeed, fair lady, I would love to be tutored in the ways of finance by one who can so crush my pride," Stevahn answered, turning with them and keeping pace.

"Borsen, you'll need to trade for a gown for yourself, for the Last Night celebration," Katrin said suddenly. "Unless you brought yours with you." Borsen was so delighted to see her eyes sparkling with mischief, that he decided not to kill her on the spot.

"I'll look around," he replied casually, but Stevahn was already gloating.

"So, Reflection Of My Friend has a Thrun gown?" he asked, grinning. "After all that jeering I was given after trading for mine?"

"He has four, actually," Katrin said very innocently. "Or is it five now, Borsen?"

"All right, yes, I have five."

"He didn't want you to know, so he's hidden them," Katrin said confidingly to Stevahn, who was squiring her along in a courtly way. "He says he was afraid if you knew, you'd think he was nancy."

"Why would I ever think such a thing?" Stevahn responded, managing somehow to keep a straight face.

"Katrin, I think I might not get you that dress," Borsen teased. "Where's Thira? Her mother always has the best gowns and dresses, and yes, evil ones, I am going to get myself a gown for Last Night now that the secret of my nanciness is out."

"Gods, I love you both," Stevahn laughed. "I haven't found a staid boring person around this place yet!"

"We have them all locked up down cellar," Katrin said blandly, making him hoot some more. "There's Thira's tent."

Thira, a tall and attractive young Thrun woman, looked up and saw them coming her way. She smiled, shooing her two children away to play. She put her arms around Katrin and kissed her cheek.

"I haven't seen enough of you," Thira said in careful Mordanian.

"I know! It's been so busy, but we've two days left. Come to the house tonight and we'll have a good talk," Katrin smiled. "I also need a pretty dress for Last Night."

"I have a beautiful blue and gold, embroidered with snowflowers," Thira answered.

"It's obvious the ladies want to talk," Stevahn murmured to Borsen. "May I speak with you for a moment?"

"Let me just signal Hemmett," Borsen replied. He looked around and caught Hemmett's eye, motioning with his head toward Katrin. Hemmett nodded and took Flori's hand, moving closer to Thira's stall.

"Of course, Katrin is entirely safe with the Thrun here, but I want someone near in case she feels ill or needs to get into the house," Borsen explained as he walked beside Stevahn.

"I wanted to ask you about Katrin's charity – the orphanage. I'd like your opinion about something."

***

"You hadn't mentioned to me that Borsen's finger was broken," Tharak said, taking another glass of kirz from Menders and settling back in one of the deep upholstered armchairs in Menders' office. Menders poured himself a measure and settled in the other armchair. He clenched his jaw for a moment, then looked at his friend.

"It was, before we went to the Middle Continent. That's how we found that his bones are brittle. It was a minor mishap and shouldn't have done more than smart a bit. Instead – well, it healed, but it's crooked. He says it works as well as ever." He sipped from his glass, knowing what was coming.

"So, all three of the chosen children have had their maiming injuries," Tharak said, looking steadily at him.

"I'm sure you noticed that Katrin's had far more than that," Menders snapped.

"Aylam – the Suspension Ritual was prophesied as well," Tharak said calmly. "You say that you don't remember the Prophecy Saga, but I know you. Your mind is not that weak."

Menders counted to ten – twice.

"I thought we were going to talk about the Thrun Kingdom," he finally said.

"Indeed. The Prophecy affects it as well as the rest of Eirdon."

Menders stood abruptly and went to the window behind his desk. He could just see the eastern end of the Thrun camp beyond the leafless orchard. Hemmett was leading a farlin with Katrin and Flori on its back.

"When I look at them and know what they've been through, I don't give a damn about the rest of Eirdon," he said vehemently. "Yes, I remember that Saga. I hate every word of it and I can't believe that it dictates the lives of those three young people! I know how it spins out! I know what is supposed to happen to them! Do you think I want that to happen to my children, Tharak?"

"There are those who wish to exterminate all Thrun as they would rats," Tharak's voice replied by his ear. Menders nearly jumped out of his skin. He had never heard his friend move. "They come with larger and larger guns. They mow us down like stalks of grass. Do you think I want that to happen to my people? We have waited hundreds of years for the Circle to turn."

Menders closed his eyes.

They had arrived at stalemate and stood there silently. After a few tense moments, Tharak put his hand on Menders' shoulder. Menders reached up and covered Tharak's hand with his own.

***

"Of course, it's frustrating to have to wait for the winter to pass before we can begin construction again, but I'm happy to see the delay in going ahead hasn't affected the construction that was completed," Katrin said, leaning on Stevahn's arm as they surveyed the site for the orphanage. Hemmett and Menders were checking the covers that had been put over the incomplete building.

"No, it's been well protected," he replied. He'd been on a tour of the proposed hospital site and the functioning home for elderly tenants as well as looking over the half-built orphanage.

"In spring we're going to use the same method that got The Shadows Academy built in five months and Borsen's renovated in six," Katrin smiled. "No more delays."

"Excellent. Now, we've been out in the cold for two hours – why don't we get back to The Shadows? I have a few ideas that might be of interest to you."

After their brisk sledge drive back, they were grateful to find a good fire going in Menders' office, as well as coffee and sandwiches. Borsen was waiting for them, with Tharak and Eiren.

"Now," Stevahn said once everyone had chatted and warmed themselves with the coffee and food, "you know me as Borsen's bonded, the man who took more than a year to bring about a runaway match with him."

As the laughter died, he went on.

"In my professional life, I'm known to be far more decisive and directed. I'm an investment banker, yes – but another thing I do as part of my work is the direction and management of the business affairs of a number of charities."

Katrin looked directly at him.

"Your ideas are wonderful," he told her. "They're feasible and they provide for definite needs. You have the wherewithal to make them reality. All this we look for when we are considering whether we wish to take on a charity's account management at the bank – or for that matter, when we are deciding whether we want to back the charity financially ourselves."

He saw Katrin's eyes kindling and she smiled.

"Yes, my dear – I feel entirely confident in offering the assistance and support of The Rondheim Bank," he said.

"The Rondheim Bank!" Katrin gasped. Stevahn burst out laughing.

"Surely you know my last name is Rondheim," he grinned. "Did you think I ran some little loan service down near the docks in Erdahn?"

"I didn't make the connection," Katrin gasped, still laughing at her own naiveté. "My life has become very insular of late."

"And that is what I wanted to explain to you," Stevahn said, masterfully keeping the conversation focused. "If you have management for your charity, should something happen where you can't cope with it – like this terrible injury and illness you're recovering from – your charity will continue to run effectively. You're walking into a similar situation to Borsen's, biting off far more than you can chew. If an issue comes up that makes it impossible for you to chew, everything comes to a grinding halt. If people are dependent on your charity and it stops functioning, people suffer."

"What about the possibility of abuses?" Menders asked. "I'm sure you know that there are those who will find employment at charitable institutions who are seeking to exploit something."

"Very well," Stevahn replied, leaning comfortably against the edge of Menders' desk. "It's something we seek to avoid and over the years we've found ways to be certain things are run as they should be. I will bring you a great deal of information the next time I'm here and of course, you may come and see me at any time. Our little institution is easy to find. It's right across the street from that newfangled store some young Hetzophian prince started up."

He and Borsen exchanged an amused glance, but Stevahn was dealing with business – and that was his métier.

"In reality, I'm proposing that you will need more financial backing than you should try to provide yourselves – and you will need continuing support. Building an institution isn't like building a monument, a single expenditure and then it's done.

"I suggest keeping your charities private, to avoid the issue of having a board of directors and all the power struggles and slowdowns that creates – and having the backing of The Rondheim Bank and the very lucrative Borsen's."

The joy on Katrin's face gave him his answer.

"I've felt so terrible all this time," she finally managed. "I thought of children who needed somewhere to go where they would be cared for and here that building sits, half-finished for two years while I've been sick. The hospital as well. I'm grateful we used a building we already had for the old tenants, because this winter has been colder than usual. Thank you, Stevahn."

"One provision," he said, suddenly looking steely. "You must learn how everything we are going to do works. You can't expect anyone else to learn it and give you the salient points. We – the bank employees and myself – will teach you. It's vital that you understand the entire process and make good business decisions."

Katrin nodded while Menders managed to hide a smile. Stevahn must be a formidable banker, he thought. He comes off as soft spoken and even a bit vague, but it was obvious he was a shrewd observer of people and unafraid to speak his mind when necessary.

"You told him about the chickens," Katrin said suddenly, looking right at Borsen.

"Of course. He knows all your wickedness," Borsen replied.

Tharak burst out laughing, then rose to his feet when Stevahn nodded to him.

"I would like to request that you consider Thrun children for your orphanage, as well as others," he said to Katrin. "The numbers of abandoned and orphaned City Thrun boys and girls in Erdahn are staggering now. You shouldn't take them exclusively – they should live with children of other races so that they can all learn that we are one people. I also offer that any such children, if they wish, may return to the Thrun and be welcomed into good families which will cherish them – as any City Thrun would be."

"You know I would never turn down a Thrun child," Katrin replied.

"Indeed, I do. And I vouch for Balancing Man – after all, I have money in his bank," Tharak pronounced.

"My little project is suddenly growing some amazing legs," Katrin said as Stevahn convened the business meeting and began to pour more coffee for everyone.

"And so it shall. Let Pappa and me work through it, and when we come back in the spring, I'll bring along a proposal and other information for you to consider," he replied.

"In the spring! How wonderful!" Katrin turned to Borsen. "Will you be able to take the time?"

"He just let my surprise out," he said, giving Stevahn an amused look. "We will be coming to visit at least once every season. I will make the time."

"Life is coming back," Katrin smiled.

***

Stevahn lay face down in the wonderfully soft pillows of the bed, finding out for the first time just what a kirz hangover meant. He'd been mildly drunk on the stuff a couple of times since the Thrun had appeared, but reined himself in so he hadn't suffered to speak of the morning after. He could hold his liquor well, but Last Night, the final celebrations of the Thrun carnival had tempted him beyond caution.

He'd been astounded by the Thrun finery that abounded among The Shadows' population – until he saw what the Thrun themselves considered Last Night adornment. All were dressed to the teeth in beautifully embroidered gowns or dresses, elaborate hats and gallons of jewelry. There had been endless food and drink, wonderful dancing and performances. To Stevahn's amazement, Borsen was called forward to sing. He had given a stunning rendition of a Thrun story, partially spoken, partially sung, partially danced.

Tharak had come to sit by Stevahn, looking as if he had been made out of gold and then showered with jewels. His gown was magnificent and must have weighed fifty pounds. He translated the tale Borsen was singing as the hunt of a Thrun chieftain for a particular spirit bird that knew an ancient secret of how people had come to Eirdon on a falling star.

"How did he learn to do this?" Stevahn asked in wonder, watching as his firelit bonded performed as if he was a seasoned actor-singer.

"He visits much with Tharan-T'ul, whenever we are here. Tharan-T'ul passes on our legends and the way of telling them to him. Tharkul a' Thunar is a high chieftain of our people, Thetan a' Thrun," Tharak smiled, never taking his eyes from Borsen's graceful movements. "He has learned his heritage well."

The night became wilder as it became late and Stevahn had a vague recollection of being helped to bed by Borsen.

Now he felt every single drop of the stuff he'd swallowed, and thought he might be going to die.

"It's time to get up," Borsen said from somewhere in the room.

"Unh."

"Come on, it's better if you start moving around. The Thrun are leaving, and we have to say good-bye to them."

"Unh."

"Come on, Stevahn, if you have something to eat you'll feel better."

The very idea was agony. He felt Borsen sit on the edge of the bed, pushing him, turning him over.

"You have to come and say goodbye," he said insistently. "You're one of them now, don't you realize that?"

"Borsen, I'm dead."

"I give it to you on good authority that you are breathing. House rules are that anyone who gets drunk on kirz is not allowed to complain about the hangover," Borsen smiled, looking fragile himself.

"How come you're not hungover?"

"I haven't been to sleep yet."

"What?"

"You fell asleep, I went back to the camp and sang for them some more. They always leave early. Get up."

Borsen rose and horrified Stevahn by pouring out a quarter measure of kirz and carrying it over to him.

"Here – hair of the dog. Drink it. If you don't drink it, I'll hold your nose and pour it down your throat."

Stevahn gave up, somehow managed to hoist himself into a sitting position and poured the drink down his throat. He was amazed when he began to feel better within a few minutes.

"All right, Brother Persistence, I'll go say good-bye," he said. "You are a cruel man."

"It's important, Stevahn," Borsen answered, all seriousness. "I wouldn't have wakened you otherwise."

The Thrun were making their camp disappear as rapidly as it had been assembled. Tharak Karak, with several of his children following in his wake, was striding this way and that despite obvious signs of having had too much kirz. He saw them and walked over.

"Ah, good, you are the first out," he said, grinning gingerly. "You like our kirz, Balancing Man."

"Not this morning," Stevahn replied. Tharak laughed resoundingly.

"An hour's walk and I will be young again," the huge man said. "Take care of Borsen, my friend. He is precious."

He turned to Borsen.

"And you, Reflection Of My Friend, remember that Balancing Man is the most important thing in your life. Nothing comes before the two of you."

Tharak pulled Borsen close, then clapped Stevahn on the shoulder so hard he thought he was going to collapse. Then Tharak looked beyond them and smiled. Stevahn turned to see Menders approaching with Katrin, Eiren and Hemmett.

After all parting words had been said, Tharak strode away to the front of the newly-formed column of Thrun, wagons and animals.

The enormous gong was struck, icicles cascaded off the house. The big horns droned, bells and small gongs were struck, and the Thrun rapidly walked away. Tharak stepped out to the side and let the column pass until only he was silhouetted against the sky.

He turned toward The Shadows, holding his arms out, palms toward the sky, at shoulder level. Then he raised his arms into a circle, his fingertips meeting over his head.

"Until The Circle Turns Again," Borsen whispered to Stevahn. "The Thrun have no word for good-bye."

ERDAHN, MORDANIA

16
TOWARD LIGHT

"A letter from Surelia addressed to Waldrum the Dancing Bear?" Varnia said in confusion as she sorted through the envelopes that had just been delivered.

"Oh, that would be for me, dear," Stevahn said with a smile, holding out his hand. Varnia and Borsen exchanged a look as he broke the seal and took out the letter. They watched as Stevahn read it, smiled broadly and then began to put it in his jacket breast pocket.

"You're enjoying this, aren't you?" Borsen said.

"Hmm? Oh, it's from my sister, Stellia." Stevahn looked very innocent. "Just letting me know how things are in Surelia."

He handed the letter to Borsen, who exchanged another puzzled glance with Varnia and then held it so they could both read it.

Darling Stev,

Only a short note this morning, as Pappa is anxious to go for his walk. He and Mamma are very much improved and are eager to return home, so they may meet your Borsen. It will be difficult to get them to stay the time the doctor prescribed. You know Pappa once he has an idea in his head. They say you are very naughty for not letting them know you were bonded in time for them to send Borsen a Winterfest present!

How are you and your little jeweled grasshopper faring? How was your visit to The Shadows? I hope you enjoyed every moment! Our Winterfest was very pleasant, but I missed the winter cold and snow that is such a part of the holiday.

I must close now, Pappa is pacing up and down the hallway. But I must know – did you show everyone how very beautifully you can dance, Waldrum?

Your loving sister,

Stell

Borsen looked over at Stevahn, who had picked up a financial newssheet and was showing great interest in it.

"Why does she call you Waldrum?"

"Hmm?" Stevahn didn't look up from his paper.

"Breakfast is about to burn, you get it out of him," Varnia murmured to Borsen. She shook her head as she walked away, chuckling.

"Stevahn! What the hells is this about?" Borsen persisted.

"Oh, the letter?"

"Of course, the letter!"

"Have you ever heard of the Waldrum The Dancing Bear books?"

Borsen nodded. "Of course – I read them after I got my first pair of glasses, trying to improve my reading. Before then I could barely read at all. There was Waldrum the Dancing Bear Goes on the Train, Waldrum the Dancing Bear Goes to Town, Waldrum the Dancing Bear Catches a Social Disease," he answered.

"Well, I told Stellia about the time I made your glass of kirz explode and she said it sounded like Waldrum the Dancing Bear Goes to the Tailor," Stevahn explained. "She said if I just started dancing instead of knocking things about and making them blow up, I would get the sort of attention I wanted from you. She'll be very smug when it turns out she was right."

"Knocking your hat off in the gutter was dancing?" Borsen laughed.

"After that. Gods, you were impressed by me knocking my hat off?" Stevahn teased. "Then you must have been mesmerized by me knocking your screen over."

"Oh, overcome with passion," Borsen snorted, looking at the letter again.

Suddenly Stevahn reached out and tried to take it. Borsen held it away from him.

"Give me my letter back," Stevahn ordered.

"Pah! I'm reading, leave me alone… who is your little jeweled grasshopper?"

"Give me my letter back!" Stevahn stood and took a swipe at it. Borsen eluded him easily, jumped up and put his chair between them.

"Remember, my uncle taught me how to elude and how to fight," he grinned. "Grasshopper? That's what you think of me? Bug eyes, skinny legs, knobbly knees?"

Stevahn snorted in exasperation, knowing that if Borsen worked at it, he could never catch him.

"I called you that in a letter to Stellia – my little jeweled grasshopper, because of your size and looks. Not some grasshopper out in a field, but a gold one covered with jewels, something rare and singular," Stevahn sputtered in embarrassment.

Borsen looked up at him, his almond eyes rounded with surprise.

"That – that's beautiful," he said softly. "I thank you, my dear."

Then he grinned wickedly.

"I'm going to write to your sister and let her know how beautifully you've been dancing," he announced, going toward his desk. "She should get to know her very attractive and adorable brother-in-law."

"Give me back my letter, you felschat!" Stevahn couldn't help smiling. Being called Waldrum by the likes of his onetime lover, Selnor, no longer mattered a damn.

"Here you are. I can remember the address."

In the kitchen, Varnia shook her head and laughed out loud.

***

"Will you look at this trash!" Alahno Beregovia spat furiously as Borsen walked into his workroom at Borsen's. He picked up a handful of gemstones and let them run through his fingers like sand. "Every piece a chunk of swarf! That Surytamian bastard switched the stones I chose for this useless garbage!"

Borsen put a hand on his new jeweler's shoulder and looked closely at the pile of stones. They were indeed trash, flawed, some cracked, others dull or partly occluded. It was an old trick some suppliers tried, switching out the quality goods they'd shown for lesser merchandise – but it never worked more than once when they tried it with Borsen's.

"That'll be the end of him then," Borsen said, stirring the glittery pile, shaking his head at the cracked and damaged stones.

"What they think they gain by doing it, I don't know, but I have quite a few crates of similar trash."

'They gain the damned five hundred florins I paid them! I paid them, from my own pocket!" Alahno snarled.

"Just think of all the florins they lost," Borsen answered abstractedly, picking up a stone and holding it up to the light. He drew a chair over, settling in it and perusing the stone. "We'll never trade with them again."

"My friend, I'm glad you can be calm, but it was my pocket this came out of, not Borsen's," Alahno said, frustration ringing in his voice. He picked up a flawed gem and then flung it down in disgust. "It won't bankrupt me, but it will cut deep into my profits for a good long while."

"What if I find a way for you to recoup your loss and more with these stones?" Borsen asked, his voice preoccupied as he picked up one gem after another and held them to the light. He reached out abstractedly and picked up Alahno's loupe, holding it near the stones rather than against his eye, a concession to his corrected vision.

"As what, a doorstop? They're nothing but trash, Borsen!"

Borsen looked sideways at the irate Samorsan.

"I'm an old trash-picker from way back," he said with a glint of humor, but Alahno wasn't amused, too distraught over the loss to his brand-new business.

"Pah, what did you ever pick through trash for?" he snapped, glaring at Borsen.

"Something to eat, usually," Borsen said in the distant voice that indicated he was completely absorbed, peering intently at a gem that should have been a uniform gold, but was instead half-gold, half matte black.

Alahno began to retort and then stopped. He and Borsen had met when Borsen's family toured the Middle Continent. They gravitated toward each other in an art class where they were the only nancy men present. They had no attraction to each other, but became friends easily. Alahno's traditional Samorsan family disowned him after he refused to join their family jewelry business, preferring instead to strike out on his own. Upon hearing this, Borsen rapidly invited him to join his growing army of craftsmen, who were given free shop space within the enormous store in exchange for a percentage of their profits.

Borsen had told Alahno he had been poor as a boy. Now Alahno knew more about Mordanian City Thrun than he had at the time he'd met his new friend. He knew Borsen had been destitute, one of the desperate Thrun who lived hand to mouth in the most literal sense.

"Here, now, could you do something like this in gold, Alahno?" Borsen asked, shaking off his abstracted daze and picking up a pencil. Within seconds he slashed out a drawing of a pendant, with space for a dagger-shaped stone – like the flawed piece he held in his hand. Some rapid shading and crosshatchings finished, he placed the stone on the paper, as if it was being put into the sketched setting.

The worthless stone was now part of a soaring, heart-lightening piece of jewelry – or would be as soon as Alahno could get his hands on his tools.

"Gods, Borsen, we could sell this for – well, more than that entire shipment of trash cost me," he said with glee.

Borsen picked the stone up again and held it close to his eyes.

"From Darkness Into Light," he murmured. "No, you don't get to sell this one. I want it for a gift. But I'll do the same for a number of those stones. You'll make a pretty profit by the time we're done. So, soothe your nerves and get to work, because I need this first pendant before Spring Festival."

***

"Menders, could you show me some exercises and ways to build myself up?" Katrin asked once Borsen and Stevahn had left. She was already feeling their absence, and was loath to become depressed over it. She loved being with Borsen and had rapidly come to love Stevahn. But they would be back in the spring and there were always letters. Hopefully this year she would manage to go to Erdahn and see Borsen's.

"Of course," Menders smiled, looking up at her across the partner's desk in his study. "I think that's an excellent idea. Franz can help us with that too."

"May I use the Men's gym?"

"I don't see why not. That would help you build up very quickly, now that you're good and steady on your feet and able to walk so much."

Franz was called in on the matter and gave it his blessing. Katrin insisted that her exercising in the Men's gym be done at a certain time, so that they would know she was there. This was not because she wanted them to keep out, but so they would not be embarrassed by walking in nearly stripped down, as some of them were prone to do.

For a while Katrin carried out her exercising alone or with Kaymar, who helped her learn to use the equipment and pace herself, but in time, the Men became used to her being there. Many of them would come in and exercise alongside, though she would never be able to go through the contortions some of them did. Kaymar, in particular, kept his body in a condition that was awe inspiring.

Every day she could feel improvement. She moved more easily, she weighed more. She could walk farther, her skin looked tighter. It kept her going back, even though she sometimes felt more exhausted by the exercise than otherwise.

When Borsen and Stevahn came back in the spring, Borsen took one look at her and applauded.

"Yes!" he said, giving her a kiss. "Now you're starting to look like my Katrin again!"

"You look different yourself," she laughed. He did, far less haggard, with much of the weight he'd lost regained

"Ah, because of a very clever thing I was coerced into doing," he grinned, obviously teasing Stevahn, who just looked at the ceiling and hummed The Smile I Love.

"Which was?" Menders asked, coming up behind them.

"I only hand stitch thirty suits a year now, no more," Borsen answered as Menders put an arm around his shoulders. "They're numbered and if you miss out, you have to wait or settle for machine stitched."

"Good for you!" Katrin said to Stevahn. "However did you get him to do that?"

"He flung me down on the floor, sat on me and crabbed at me until I gave in," Borsen said sunnily.

"I took him in my arms and lowered him onto the floor after he tried to thump my head and threatened to beat me up when tried to reason with him," Stevahn said calmly to the ceiling.

Menders burst out laughing along with Katrin.

"Good thing too. I never got out of my workroom. I may as well have been running a little tailor shop somewhere because I never got to design anything but suits. Now I'm almost through the backlog and people have been told it will be a while, whether they like it or not. I've had a chance to get my hands on a few other things I was interested in. So, I'm glad the big grundar wouldn't let me get up off the floor until I agreed to limit the hand stitched work."

"I'd think it would make the hand stitched suits much more in demand," Katrin said.

"Oh, it has. I have three years' worth of orders already in line, but I will not make more than thirty a year. And now that my hand stitched suits are much more difficult to get, people are ponying up fifteen thousand florins for one." Borsen delivered this bombshell and stood there, grinning at Menders' and Katrin's goggling at him in amazement.

"Fifteen thousand," Menders said reverently.

"I told him to go to twenty thousand, but he got shy about it," Stevahn said. "I'll get him to twenty thousand yet. And now he has time to design other things. If you don't give her that present, Borsen, I'll take it and give it to her myself."

"All right, Brother Impatience, don't hurl me to the floor again," Borsen smiled. He reached into his pocket, took out a jewelry box and handed it to Katrin. She was surprised, because he would have been likely to snap at that sort of prodding when he and Stevahn were there during the winter.

She opened the box and gasped.

"It's my first jewelry design," Borsen said, putting an arm around her waist.

It was a necklace of beaten gold, set with a stone that shaded from a deep black to sparkling gold. It was crowned with three brilliant diamonds.

"Alahno was furious when he saw that stone. A gemstone trader did the bait and switch on him. He was ready to fling it on the scrap heap, but I told him I could design a piece for it and make it worth a great deal. And I did so," Borsen smiled, taking the necklace from the box and fastening it around Katrin's neck. "When I looked at how that stone moved from flat darkness to all that dazzling light, I thought of you – and designed this." He kissed her.

"It's absolutely stunning," Menders said quietly. "Scrap heap?"

"It's typical of Alahno. He expects perfection in stones and dismisses the ones that aren't," Borsen smiled. "But I find the less perfect ones far more interesting and worth thinking over. I'll be doing a lot more of this. Of course, he has the difficult part because he's the one who has to work out how to make my design up, but he enjoyed it and was mournful when I wouldn't put this one in the showcase to sell, and wouldn't let him duplicate it."

"You must duplicate it!" Katrin gasped.

"There's only one stone like that on all of Eirdon, and it's yours," Borsen laughed. "I have plenty of other inspiration."

In her room, Katrin looked at the necklace in the mirror, and then focused on her own reflection. She was pleasantly surprised.

She'd formed a habit of not looking at herself, only checking her clothing to be sure it was neat, or her wig to be sure it was straight and arranged properly. She'd avoided looking at the reflection of her face because it had been hollow-eyed and sallow for so long.

Now she had a trace of pink in her cheeks and the gauntness was gone. The necklace complimented her face and drew out her eyes. Borsen was so clever! No wonder people flocked to pay him fifteen thousand florins to make them a suit!

She took out a gold colored dress she'd worn for festive dinners before she was hurt. It had been a particular favorite of Hemmett's. Though it was not quite as form fitting as it had been, it looked well once she drew the sash tight and used a couple of pins to take up a bit of slack. She switched her simply styled wig for one she had done in a more elaborate style, settled it into place and added a pair of gold earrings. A splash of perfume – and Katrin smiled at herself in the mirror.

She wasn't as good as new, but she certainly wasn't a pallid invalid either.

Katrin walked out of her room with a light heart, coming face to face with Hemmett, who was there to take her down to dinner. When he saw her, his face lit up.

"Now there's my Princess," he said, bowing and then taking her hands. "Look at you! Is that the sparkly Borsen had made? He wrote me about it, all in darkest secrecy of course. Isn't it something! Out of Darkness Into Light was what he told me, and he was right. Clever little bastard!"

"Hemmett!"

"All true. He's clever, he's little and he's a bastard and you know I love him like life, so don't lecture, schoolteacher," Hemmett laughed. "And now, take my arm and I will escort you in all dignity and pomp down to table."

"Let us descend to the dining room, Baronet Bumpy," Katrin laughed, taking his arm.

"By the way, there's a new Menders' Man tonight too. The poor fellows always seem to turn up on family dinner night and undergo the trial by fire," Hemmett said as he squired her down the hallway.

"I didn't know Menders had hired another one," Katrin mused.

"Kaymar recruited him to replace the fellow who went off to Surelia. Menders is always glad to get someone good. There, we're just on time."

Eiren looked up from where she was showing the new Menders' Man his place. Eiren smiled as she saw Katrin, excused herself to the Man and came around the table.

"You look so beautiful," Eiren said, kissing her cheek. "That necklace is perfect!"

Other people were complimenting Katrin too. She felt her cheeks flushing pinker with happiness. It had been a long time since she'd had a compliment that wasn't forced or a comparison of how she looked less ill than she had looked formerly.

Menders came in, obviously rushed, but stopped when he saw Katrin. Like Hemmett, his face lit up.

"My dear little princess," was all he whispered as he took his place at the head of the table, but she could see his eyes behind his dark glasses and knew he was very pleased.

Borsen gave her a wink from his place next to Eiren, and she touched the necklace in response and mouthed "It's magic" toward him.

"No Cuz, you're the magic," he replied aloud, causing some laughter from the people around.

Hemmett seated Katrin and dinner began, the usual companionable and somewhat noisy meal that resulted from over fifty people sitting down and eating at once.

Katrin felt someone looking at her and casually glanced around to see who it was. She was startled when she saw it was the new Menders' Man. He was seated halfway down the table next to Haakel, who was holding forth at length. The new Man wasn't paying much attention, but was watching her instead. He was embarrassed to be caught out and turned his attention to Haakel, giving Katrin a chance to observe him.

He'd been quite tall when he'd been standing with Eiren, so he would be a spy, not an assassin. Assassins were usually quite small statured – their work required it. He was red-haired and quite handsome, probably a little older than she was.

Suddenly he looked over at her again, starting when he caught her perusing him. Then he smiled.

Katrin thought that it was very nice to be looked at by a man in that way again.

***

"Want company?" Borsen asked from the door of the gymnasium, as Katrin slowly worked her arms with one of the weight machines.

"Of course," she smiled. He came in, stripped off his shirt, and immediately jumped up on the most horrifying equipment in the place, a device that allowed one to hang from the ankles and do the equivalent of sit-ups. Borsen delighted in the contraption and threatened to get one for his house in Erdahn, to Stevahn's dismay.

"How you can do that I don't know," Katrin said, continuing with her own exercise.

"If I don't do it, I lose my nice small waist," Borsen grinned, easing himself off the platform used to buckle into the thing and swinging from his ankles. "And I lose my strength, which I have to really work to keep up. Being starved didn't do me any favors. I have to work to keep my muscles." He began to flex into a sitting position while hanging upside down, more easily than most people would sit up while lying on a floor.

"Now you're successful, perhaps you could do with a bit of a paunch," Katrin teased.

"Oh, ha! I happen to like my wasp waist and pretty body, thank you," Borsen grinned.

"Just watching you makes me hurt," Katrin said.

"Avert your gaze then. Build your arms up and don't mind me. I'll be finished here in a minute and then I'll do something less daunting."

"Why don't you work up to doing that instead of always doing it first?"

"Swallow a felschat first thing in the morning and nothing worse is likely to happen to you all day," Borsen replied. The exercise was telling on his steely stomach muscles and he was grunting with exertion. "I must get something like this at home, I can hardly manage," he groused.

"Stevahn would never let you."

"He'd not like it if I got fat and round," Borsen groaned, forcing himself into yet another flexion. "He's convinced I'll hurt myself, as if I haven't been working my body since I was thirteen. I tried to get him to hold my legs while I did sit-ups off the side of the bed. He got all panicky and let go and I fell on my head."

Katrin laughed, and stopped working her arms.

"What did you do?" she asked.

"Oh, acted like I was all injured, so he would spoil me," Borsen said wickedly, hauling himself back onto the platform and releasing his ankles. He lay there panting.

"Naughty. And I'm fairly confident that he would like you just fine if you got fat and round."

"Yes, of course he would but I wouldn't," Borsen agreed. "I wouldn't want him if he wouldn't love me whatever way I might be, just as I would love him no matter how he might look. But I like to look my best. I have to stay strong too."

"Why?"

"Cuz, small men are targets. Small nancy men are bigger targets. Wealthy, small, nancy men are enormous targets. Why do you think Kaymar stays so fit? It's your only hope in a fight with someone bigger." Borsen sat up, lowered himself down from the platform carefully and came over to her.

"That's good sense," Katrin agreed. "I'm going to work legs now."

"Good, I'll use the arm machine then," Borsen smiled as she got up.

She was halfway through her leg strengthening exercise when Borsen spoke.

"So, what do you think of the new Menders' Man?" he asked. Katrin felt herself flushing and was glad he was turned away from her.

"I haven't talked to him much. He's been busy getting to know the place. You know how they have extra patrols at first to get to know where everything is," she obfuscated.

"I was just wondering. He seemed quite taken with you at dinner the other night."

"Maybe he was interested in the necklace," Katrin replied, making Borsen giggle to himself.

"All right, we'll leave it then," he said, hauling away at the arm machine, much faster than she had. "I just thought he seemed very interested."

In the silence that followed, Katrin concentrated very hard on her leg exercise, until she looked to see Borsen grinning over at her like a monkey.

"Do be quiet!" she ordered.

"Why Your Highest of the Highnesses, this poor boy didn't say a word," Borsen laughed.

***

"I never intended for him to fall for Katrin," Menders said with considerable irritation to Franz and Eiren. They were sitting around the table in Eiren's room after a late lunch. Katrin was at the school and was going to go along to the village, escorted by Kaymar, to deliver some of her rose soap after giving her infant school class their music lesson.

"He's a nice enough fellow," Franz said calmly. "She seems to like him too. She is twenty-three, Menders. If things were otherwise, it's very likely she would have been married by now. I consider her interest in this likely and pleasant young man a very healthy sign after what she's been through."

Menders sighed. He knew it. He was tormented by an urgent compulsion to keep Katrin safe, to keep her from ever being hurt again.

"I just don't want her to be – disappointed," he said.

"You can't protect her from everything," Franz replied.

"As far as I know, nothing serious has happened," Eiren added, putting a hand on Menders' arm. He smiled and patted it.

"Yes, it's probably all a tempest in a teacup," he answered, trying to put it away from him. "And if it isn't, Franz is right. She's all grown up. I only wish the Queen would allow her to marry or arrange a marriage for her. I'd feel she was safer if she was married and I think she would be happier. What I don't want is the Queen naming her the Heiress."

"She won't, not with the reports I keep sending," Franz said. "I still say Katrin's an invalid. That's keeping the interest in naming her the Heiress to a minimum. I'm surprised the Queen has succeeded in trying to stay somewhat sober for so long."

Menders said nothing He could hardly mention the Queen without becoming furious, remembering how her drunkenness had nearly destroyed Katrin.

"Perhaps if something comes of this interest in Karlen Grevchev, she would be given permission to marry him, since he's nobility," Eiren said softly. "If the Queen continues to think she's an invalid and she has no value as the Heiress, what matter who she marries?"

Menders sat there silently.

"It might not be a bad thing at that, if anything develops," he finally said. "I would truly be happy to see her safe. Being married and removed from the Line of Succession would give her added security from being ordered to Court."

Franz looked at Menders, his expression troubled.

"You weren't concerned by her involvement with Willem – that was off and on for almost two years," he said.

"That was before her sister nearly succeeded in killing her," he said. "I can't feel easy about anything that might draw attention to Katrin."

***

Dear Borsen,

I have made seventeen florins this month selling our famous cheese and was wondering if you wish me to send your portion of this profit along. I know your desperate need for this money is great and wish to keep you from utter poverty.

How are you, Stev and Varnia? It's hard to believe you were only here a few weeks ago. Wouldn't it be wonderful if there was some fast way to get from here to Erdahn, so that you could all live at The Shadows and travel back and forth to work?

That's selfish of me, isn't it? I know you love your house and you so deserve it. I've gotten very insulated here, I think. I'm trying to work up the courage to come to see everything you've done. I've talked to Menders about it several times. Though he's understandably nervous about my being that close to the Palace, he thinks it would be good for me. I believe it would be good for him as well. He's still blaming himself for what happened. That's ridiculous, as there is nothing he could have done to prevent it.

I'm feeling better all the time. I ride for quite a while each day and go out with Menders or Kaymar. I've also started to resurrect my garden, which Lucen kept going for me. He has no idea of growing herbs and keeps them cut into square shapes, as if they are a hedge! He's so very sweet. I save any work harder than pulling a few weeds for when he's taking his nap, so he won't come and take the shovel or rake away and insist on doing it himself.

You put some Thrun spell on Karlen Grevchev, my dear. He is indeed interested – and I can admit in a letter that only you and I shall see (and Stevahn too, I'm sure, but I don't mind) that I am interested too. I'm feeling much more myself now and the attention is welcome. Before I was so exhausted and ill that the most handsome man in the world could have cast himself down at my feet bearing gifts of jewels and chocolate and I would have only wished he would go away.

It's nice to be living again. Perhaps during the warmer weather I'll look out those old widow's weeds you made for me to sneak into Bumpy's graduation, and turn up at Borsen's to be dazzled by the marble and all the other glory.

Willem has written from Surytam. As soon as his letter has made the rounds here, I'll send it on. Seems there is a certain Surytamian miss who goes by the nickname of Four and wedding bells are about to ring! What's more, Kaymar knew her when she was just a little thing – her parents worked for Mikail, the man he was bonded to when he first came to The Shadows. They're now quite prominent people there, very powerful. Good for Will!

Everyone is well and they all miss you, especially Bumpy.

Love,

Katrin

Dear Cuz,

I will allow you to keep and invest my portion of the seventeen florins. I expect a full financial report quarterly, as well as a dividend of half of all interest derived thereof. This will give you good practice when Stevahn quizzes you about your orphanage account.

Doesn't that sound official? Since I'm the bonded of a banker (that sounds like one of those awful novels we thought were so naughty and passed around between us when we were younger) I've become very knowledgeable of such things and can sound very impressive. I impress myself most of all.

All is well here. Stevahn tripped over Magic the other day and pitched headfirst into a small table. He managed by some miraculous luck to be uninjured, except for his dignity, which was lightly bruised. This was not helped by Magic's determination to kiss him all better as he lay there in the wreckage of spindly table legs and porcelain shards. Secretly, I thank him because I didn't like the table at all once I got it home and was too proud to send it back. That has nicely solved a little problem that irked me every time I passed it.

It would be wonderful if you came to visit. Perhaps you could bring Uncle, Auntie and Bumpy with you and stay with us for a while. There is plenty of room. Though Erdahn is run down in many ways, there are compensations. I really miss the times we had when we were in Samorsa and Surelia, going to restaurants and generally bashing around. It would be so much fun showing you Borsen's.

I put no spell on that very handsome young man, my dear, you did it yourself. I hope all goes well and that you've found something of value. I didn't get to see much of him during our last visit, but he seemed very nice. Of course, a Menders' Man is never a slouch mentally. Let me know if anything develops, if you aren't too shy and maidenly.

So, Will is going to the altar! Kaymar said something about Miss Four, but his memory of her is a three-year-old baby who tried to take care of him when he was very ill with wounds infected much like yours were. He seems a little dazzled when I explain, kindly and slowly (he gets SO mad!) that Miss Four is now a young lady of twenty-two and more than old enough to marry Will. Let's decide on a decadently extravagant gift from Borsen's, though from what I know of her family through Stevahn, it probably wouldn't equal what they have.

Must stop now, I'm afraid, as I must do a fitting. The fellow is a great fat man, but very jolly and pleasant. It's been fun working with him and making his suit turn out so he looks stately. He makes me laugh so much when he's here that my stomach aches.

Love,

B

Dear Borsen,

First the sad news – my darling Dara died in her sleep the other night. Bumpy went to whistle her up and found that she was long gone. I've cried of course, but I can't really be too sad because she was beginning to suffer from being so achingly old. Of course, that is because she had the best care and lived better than many humans – but there are drawbacks to such old age and poor Dara was becoming so infirm that I dreaded having to have Franz dose her with ramplane. Thankfully, nature took its course and Dara, after having a good dinner and a lovely time playing a bit with Menders and me before she went to bed, has drifted away to the place where all good dogs go.

I miss her, of course and find myself whistling for her or snapping my fingers. She has been with me since I was six – imagine. Bumpy keeps talking about me choosing another boarhound puppy, but I want to wait a while. You can't replace someone like Dara.

As for good news, we are all well. I've gained another ten pounds and Franz has declared me to be quite well. My clothes fit right again.

Every day I think about coming to see you and it's easier each time. Now that summer is just about here, I think I'll be able to make definite plans. The orphanage, as I'm sure Stev has told you, is going to be ready for children in the autumn, which will be good, as so many are in need as winter sets in. I still feel a little panicky when I think about being around the Palace, but I just tell myself that I'm not going there, and it fades. So, I hope to be there with you soon!

As for Karlen – yes, something is developing but I'm taking my time. Since Karlen is posted here with Menders' Men, there's no sense in rushing and he knows I've been sick for a long time. He's very sweet and kind, dances divinely and is interested in all the things I am. So far, it's wonderful and I'm glad he was there when Dara left me.

How did your fat man's suit work out? I've been dying to know. And yes, the Mordanian silver set would be best – no point in sending Will and Four Surytamian porcelain!

Love,

K (I can do that too)

Dear K,

I am so sorry to hear about Dara, though it was obvious it would be soon the last time I was there. One of the disadvantages of being away is that I can see the changes in everyone when I come back. Sometimes this is a joyful thing, like being pleasantly surprised at how you've improved. It can also be painful, like the last time I saw dear old Dara. I'm glad it was easy and quick. I understand why you aren't rushing to try to replace her. You never could, and it wouldn't be fair to a new dog to expect it to take her place.

I'm thrilled to hear you're still considering coming to visit! I think once you've come and nothing bad happens to you, you will be much easier in your mind.

I'm so glad to hear that your clothes fit right again too. Having your clothes not right is bothersome, because you can't be comfortable in them. When you come here, I'll measure you up for some new things and you'll have a new wardrobe for your regained health.

As for my fat man, his suit turned out beautifully. He looked majestic, and was very happy with it, as he's spent a lifetime looking like a sack of potatoes tied in the middle. To my astonishment, he also gave me the nancyboy version of a marriage proposal (he is not observant as my bonding ring is always much in evidence). He was disappointed when I told him I am already bonded and pointed out Stevahn across the street, who happened to be standing at his window watching the fat man's final fitting. Thankfully, Stevahn, unaware that I was being mildly romanced by the rotund one, smiled and waved graciously.

Mister Evanov was quite philosophical after my refusal, told me I have beautiful eyes and ordered another suit. I was concerned that he might continue romancing me, but he's only been friendly. He desperately needs some clothing that fits him properly! I felt badly for him at first, but he's now got his eye on Petran, a very nice young fellow and my men's hatmaker. Petran seems interested, so Mister Evanov might indeed find love at Borsen's. I can then advertise that not only do I make the most exquisite clothing on the planet, but that I make love matches as well!

An amusing side note to my fat man's abortive romance with me was a brief jealous spell on the part of Stevahn. It lasted for only about five minutes, but was most gratifying. Sometimes he's almost too calm and collected. He's very reassured now that I was not at all tempted by Mister Evanov and his great belly – and he laughed very heartily at his flirtation with Dame Jealousy when I began to giggle over the thought.

I'm glad you're finding Karlen likeminded and rewarding company. In the long run (quoth he from his vast eight months' experience as a bonded man) companionship is most important. All the other things, romance, passion, sex, are very important too, but if you aren't good companions, all else would fade, I think. If something happened to Stevahn that made him unable to make love to me, I would still want to be with him. I know he feels the same way if something happened to me. We work well together, if you know what I mean. At least I hope you do.

I'm late for a meeting, hells!

Love,

B

Dear Matchmaker,

I think I have what you do. At least it seems so and Karlen has already made noise about marrying, which I would be very happy about. The news from Menders' network is that the Queen is considering having me drummed out of the Succession altogether in favor of my poor little cousin, Glorantha. Doctor Franz keeps sending reports that I'm still an invalid and unfit to take on the "duties" of the Heiress. I do so hope she removes me from the Throne line, because then I can get permission to marry and have a life free of the endless worry over the Royal Family! They can have the country and all that goes with it.

About visiting - we've pretty much settled on a plan, so long as it works for you. We'd like to come there for a week right before the two weeks you and Stevahn had planned to spend here. That way we could all travel back together for your holiday. Would this be all right with you? If it isn't, don't hesitate to let me know, because we can alter this very easily from our end. I will have to be disguised, of course, since I'm supposed to be an invalid and can't come walking up The Promenade all hale and hearty, but we'll come up with something.

Sometimes I think I would like to travel again, this time not as a youngster, but as an adult. If I got removed from the Succession, I would even consider going alone – or with Karlen, if things work out. I love The Shadows. We all do, but life is static for me here, as you know. Since it's my property and not a Crown holding, it would remain with me and would always be home, but I would like to own other properties elsewhere. Bolt holes in a way, but also places to help grow and prosper, like Menders built The Shadows from an abandoned old house and a few tenant farmers.

In other news, the orphanage is progressing quickly. I've been contacting various Temples of Galanth as sources of children in need. Abbot Fahrin has been a great help – I'm so glad Menders wouldn't let that friendship die and calmed him after my blunder in signing my real name! That seems so long ago.

Let me know if our plans are going to work out. We all miss you both so much!

Love,

Katrin

THE SHADOWS, MORDANIA
ERDAHN, MORDANIA

17
WE GO ON FROM HERE

"Princess? Katrin? What is it?"

Menders moved quickly, catching up with Katrin, who was rushing down the corridor from the Men's Wing. One glance told him she was disheveled and extremely upset.

"What is it, my dear?" he asked, keeping his voice calm. It was obvious. Her clothing wasn't even completely buttoned.

"I'm all right, Papa," she said shortly, though she had tears in her eyes. "I'd like to go on to my room now."

"I'd like to know what has happened," Menders responded, keeping his voice very even.

"I wasn't attacked or forced," Katrin said, suddenly looking him in the eye. "My damned wig came off. I had never told him I wear a wig. My stupid mistake. I could see in his eyes he was horrified and repulsed. So that's over. Now, I am going to my room to make myself presentable."

She turned and rushed away.

Menders clenched his fists and then turned toward Karlen Grenchev's suite.

***

"The hells you are!" Kaymar roared. "The hells you're going to kick a man I recruited and trained out on the fucking street!"

"He is not staying here!" Menders retorted. "Not after treating Katrin badly!"

"He didn't treat her badly. Her hair came off her head in his hand when he was stroking it. That would tend to startle anyone!"

"The word she used was 'repulsed'," Menders growled.

"Why don't you mind your own damned business!" Kaymar stepped within arm's reach of Menders – a direct challenge. "They're of age. Katrin is twenty-three, Karlen is twenty-six. She can take care of herself and so can he!"

"She has been sick unto death for two years! Now this little bastard has broken her heart and I'm supposed to act as though nothing happened?"

"You said she was angry, not sobbing! I've broken a woman's heart or two in the past. Broken hearted women don't get angry, they go to pieces. I think they've both discovered that it isn't the great love of the ages and it's a damned good thing too, before they did something permanent."

Hemmett rushed in, drawn by the shouting. He immediately stepped between them.

"Let's calm down, gentlemen," he began.

Kaymar slapped him right across the face.

***

"Didn't anyone send so much as a note?" Borsen asked.

"There are four notes, but I wanted you to know what was happening first." Kaymar took out four envelopes, handing them to Borsen. He had just brought the news that after the incident between Katrin and Karlen Grevchev at The Shadows, Menders had decided against the family the next day coming for the planned week-long visit.

Borsen surprised himself by opening the note from Eiren first, setting the one from Menders aside.

Darling,

As I'm sure Kaymar has explained, all has gone to madness over here, with Katrin disappointed in love, Menders getting his back up and arguments between them, between Menders and Kaymar and with Hemmett getting in the middle of it and being slapped.

It is not a good idea for us to come there at the moment, though I know this will be a bitter disappointment for you. It's really for the best that we put off, and I hope you and Stevahn will come to The Shadows as planned. We can make future plans then.

Sometimes, Borsen, it all gets very disheartening. I'm so sorry that you're hurt, and hope we can make it up to you. I'm very proud of you, darling.

All my love,

Auntie

"What's going on?" Stevahn asked, letting himself in, having seen Kaymar and Borsen talking heatedly from his office across the street. Borsen set Eiren's note aside and let Kaymar do the explaining, tearing open the note from Katrin.

Dear Borsen,

I am so mad right now I could bite the leg off a chair! Once again everyone has decided to jump into my personal business. I'm ready to swim across the damned ocean to see you. I've had a horrible fight with Menders that had us both in tears, and now my stupid body has decided to get into the act and I'm feverish again. I'm not fit to be around. Kaymar said he would explain, as I don't want to go into it.

I'm so sorry Menders has decided to postpone. Please don't get mad. Come when you expected to, and we'll make new arrangements. I'm hoping we'll go back with you to spend that week – after all, I don't have a lot of reason to linger behind now. I just wish I'd shown Karlen my head to begin with. I will never sleep with a man again without showing him. If he can't deal with it, I'll end everything there.

I have to stop. Kaymar is ready to leave and he's so mad I know he won't wait long. I will get there, I promise. Please don't be angry.

Love,

Katrin

Borsen surprised himself by laughing aloud, and opened the note from Hemmett, while handing the other two to Stevahn, who was sitting on the edge of Borsen's desk now, a hand on Borsen's arm, while Kaymar leaned on Stevahn's shoulder.

Dear Inchworm,

Well, we're all so happy here at Misery House. Katrin and Karlen have had a bad scene and ended their affair. Menders got righteously wrathful. Katrin did too and argued him down. Menders and Kaymar started circling and yowling at each other and I decided to be a good fellow and intervene. Then Kaymar smacked me in the face. It didn't half hurt either. Of course, it hit me as funny a minute or two later and I had to flee so I wouldn't start haw-hawing during all the drama.

Now poor Katrin's sick again with a fever, so we're not going to bring all this joy to you.

Sometimes I think I just want to resign my commission and go live with Luntigré and Flori and forget about all this – but I could never abandon Katrin, particularly not now.

Hopefully everyone will cheer up by the time you and Stevahn get here. Please don't fly into one of your snits and refuse to come. I need to spend some time with my good mate. See if that man of yours would consider a trip to Sarmorsa sometime and we'll arrange it – we could soak up some sport, food and joy.

Your friend forever and brother,

Bump the Grump

Borsen passed this along with a grin and then hesitated briefly before opening the envelope addressed in Menders' hand.

My dear son,

I'm in the process of hurting you and I can never apologize enough for doing it. I know Kaymar is going to give you a more balanced version of what has gone on than I possibly could, so I will let his explanation stand. I do feel, however, as Kaymar does not, that Katrin shouldn't come to Erdahn right now, for reasons physical and mental. This isn't just my imagination – she is running a fever and I want to avoid a relapse.

I am hoping that we'll return with you and Stevahn after your two weeks here, or failing that, a little later in the summer.

Please find some forgiveness for me, Borsen. So often I must choose one over the other. I had hoped it would never come to you. I've managed to keep you apart from this sort of dilemma until now. Please know I am incredibly proud of you, and always remain

Your loving father,

Papa

Borsen handed the letter on to Stevahn and used a finger to wipe at his eyes under his glasses. He did the same several times before he had control of himself. Stevahn put an arm around his shoulders.

He turned away to his desk, picked up his pen and wrote.

Dear Everybody,

All forgiven and love to everyone. We can't change what has happened – we go on from here. Don't fret. We will see you in a week.

Love,

B

Then he drew another sheet of paper over, and wrote swiftly.

Dear Papa,

Yes, it hurt but I understand. We'll just manage it another time. Please don't feel you need to apologize – not to me. Not ever to me.
I love you.

Your son,

Borsen

"This one goes to Uncle only," Borsen said, folding and sealing it before handing it to Kaymar, who tucked it away with the other in his jacket pocket. "Do not read it."

To his own horror, Borsen suddenly found himself shaking uncontrollably, his eyes burning with an unwelcome rush of tears. A hitching, childish sob burst out of his throat. He clapped his hands over his mouth before he could humiliate himself further.

He turned toward Stevahn, burying his face in his shirt front, but even that couldn't muffle the fact that he was crying, like he had in the cold dark as his mother lay dying, when he was only six years old.

***

Stevahn sat in a comfortable armchair at home.

He knew he had led a charmed life. Tragedy had only touched his family once, the death of his younger brother from putrid fever. All other family crises had been run of the mill – tiffs between his parents, Stellia staying out too late with suitors and causing a flurry of concern and scolding, poor school marks on his part that got him a severe talking-to.

Stevahn's family was blessedly normal. They had given him the ultimate security of unconditional love and acceptance. He had wanted for nothing, yet had been handled with enough discipline not to be spoiled.

He'd never thought of being from placid, even dull people as a blessing before – until he had met Borsen.

Between Borsen himself, Menders, Katrin and Kaymar, Stevahn now knew the entire tragic story of Borsen's childhood and had surmised other things as well from his knowledge of history and a few facts Borsen let drop about the town he'd lived in at the time of his mother's death. He knew Borsen had been subjected to the worst sorts of neglect, privation and abuse. He fully understood his bonded's intense loyalty and devotion to Menders, who had replaced Borsen's hateful father as an almost godlike figure.

It all made for Borsen being a person of intense emotional extremes. No-one could laugh and enjoy a joke as Borsen could. Unfortunately, the negative side of the emotional spectrum took a bitter toll on the young man. Stevahn was shaken by the depth of hurt Borsen had displayed that morning. He had never seen anyone cry like that, not even his mother when his brother had died. No matter how hard Borsen tried, the tears kept flowing down while the anguished sobs, seeming to have a life of their own, jerked from his throat.

Then, after ten minutes, Borsen drew on something deep within and gained control of himself. He rose to his feet, took handkerchiefs proffered by both Stevahn and Kaymar, wiped his face and faced them both.

"What the hells we're going to do with enough plucked chickens to feed an army, I don't know. I'm going home early. Coming with me, gentlemen?"

Once home, Borsen excused himself and then retreated to the big bathtub, leaving Stevahn and Kaymar downstairs.

Kaymar paced back and forth across the room.

"I'm fed up with this, I'm asking for another posting," he muttered furiously. "Why? Why hurt this boy, cousin?"

Stevahn realized Kaymar was giving way to his own emotional difficulties and decided to cut the monologue short. Borsen had told him that at times Kaymar began to talk to himself and could become entirely caught up in it.

"I could do with a drink," Stevahn said. "Why not pour out for both of us?"

Kaymar blinked and then shook his head.

"Don't mind me raving, it's a rotten habit," he said. "What's your poison – whisky?"

When Kaymar returned with the drinks, Stevahn remained seated. Kaymar continued prowling around the room.

"Gods, I wish I had made up some lie," Kaymar sighed, taking a sip. "If I'd known he'd fall apart like that, I would have held a gun on Menders and made him come. I never thought it would mean so much to him."

"It does. You're all his family. He'll come around, Kaymar. I find it's best to let Borsen work things out. Eventually he'll talk it out with you or me, or with Varnia. His wounds are deep and they're never going to heal completely. I accepted that before I bonded with him and I accept it now. However, I don't feel that what I call 'the royal situation' is good for Borsen and I'm glad he's at a remove from it," Stevahn explained.

Kaymar's blue gaze was startled as it turned on him.

"It isn't good for anyone, my friend," Kaymar answered. "Not since the Queen got hold of Katrin and strung her up. Menders – Stevahn, Menders is my cousin and closer to me than a brother, but he has his failings. When those dear to him are threatened, even if it's only in his mind, he wants to go to ground. He's like a chicken, thinking that if he hovers over his brood, the hawk will never know they're there. It's an obsession and I don't know how to begin to help him break it. He didn't get the nickname Papa Hen for nothing."

Kaymar took another swallow of whisky.

"But I never thought he would hurt Borsen," he continued quietly. "Menders worships him, Stevahn. Borsen is the son he denied himself and he adores him. I never thought if it came to a choice, that Menders would hurt Borsen – but he has."

"The reaction you saw isn't only about that, Kaymar," Stevahn replied. "That goes back to Borsen's mother dying in Linzt. This was the second time an adored parent has, in a manner of speaking, abandoned him – his mother by dying, Menders by hurting him today. I can't say it's entirely a bad thing. Borsen would have to know, sooner or later, that Menders has his flaws and faults."

Stevahn took a sip of his drink and then realized Kaymar had gone the color of clay. He sprang to his feet and steadied the smaller man, lowering him into an armchair.

"Your heart?" he asked bluntly. Kaymar shook his head and reached for the glass Stevahn had taken from him. After a deep draught of whisky, he began to regain his normal coloring.

"Linzt? He told you he was at Linzt?"

"When speaking of his mother's death, yes," Stevahn answered quietly, taking his seat again.

"I had no idea. He's never said – he's told me how his mother died and that his father took him but…" Kaymar choked slightly and took another deep pull at his glass. "It had to be that winter…"

"It was. Linzt was burned to the ground in the spring. Borsen remembers the fire."

Kaymar put his head in his hands.

"Aylam," he whispered. "Please say he doesn't know. It would break him."

"You don't give Menders enough credit. He knows. He listened to Borsen speak of it on the nights he woke up screaming as a boy. Borsen told me himself."

Kaymar rose and poured himself another stiff drink. He waved the decanter at Stevahn, who shook his head.

"I was going to tear Menders' skin off and hand it to him when I take that note from Borsen back," Kaymar said. "Now – he's had more than enough pain. That little boy… that poor little boy… Stev, if you'd seen Borsen when he came to us, like a starveling bird, afraid of his own shadow… he was at Linzt!"

"That young man is the bravest person I have ever met," Stevahn said firmly, his voice drawing Kaymar back from an invisible precipice.

They were silent then, having referenced the name of a town so synonymous with horror that its surviving inhabitants had burned it to the ground after a winter spoken of only in hushed tones.

***

"I'll tell you what we're going to do with all those chickens," Varnia said firmly, looking at Kaymar, Stevahn and Borsen. "We're going to cook them tomorrow, just as we planned, and take them over to the orphans, who will have a wonderful dinner and be very happy."

Borsen smiled suddenly.

"I love you," he said, putting his arms around her.

"You got carried away," she responded, holding him close. "It's a disappointment but no harm done if Katrin doesn't sicken. It's the upset giving her that fever. We'll all go at the end of the week and spend a happy vacation at The Shadows and then if she's well, they'll come back here."

Borsen laughed and turned toward Stevahn and Kaymar.

"This is the person who always puts things to rights," he said.

"You have a right to cry – these two years and more have been terrible for everyone and at this point, no-one is reacting sensibly," Varnia said. "Now, I have a pot of Seven Spice Soup ready, fresh bread, cheese, meat, coffee and a pot of wicked hot mustard for Kaymar. Be seated, gentlemen."

"Marry me?" Kaymar smiled, giving her a melting look.

"Don't rattle me or you'll get your soup in your lap," Varnia said, completely unfussed. She let Borsen seat her and began taking their bowls to fill with soup.

***

Kaymar walked into Menders' office and handed him the sealed note from Borsen. Menders unfolded and read it.

"I need to talk to you," Kaymar said quietly.

"Of course."

"First, how is Katrin?"

"Franz had her to go to bed. It's a precaution but she is feverish," Menders replied evenly. "We'll postpone for now, but I intend to take her to Erdahn when Borsen and Stevahn return there."

Kaymar nodded and deliberately sat opposite Menders.

"Borsen broke down and cried after he wrote the note," he began. Menders' face went cold.

"No, Aylam, I'm not blaming you for that," Kaymar rushed to continue. "It sparked some memories of his mother's death. He had his cry, went home to a hot bath and then ate an enormous dinner. He's a powerful man and he's bonded to another. He's fine – but it worries me. I think you need to see him – alone. As it turns out, you did the right thing, but it hurt him deeply. There are scars from his past, Aylam. Stevahn says they'll never heal and I believe him."

Menders drew a deep breath.

"I had Katrin send Borsen to Erdahn," he said, his voice still soft and full of pain. "He was going to give up his business plans to stay with her. I asked her to intercede. She did, even though it meant she was giving up her closest confidant. I sent him away at the time when I most wanted him here, with me. I do not make the decisions I do out of selfishness or favoritism, Kaymar. I am exhausted and heartbroken over this entire sorry affair and I made the best decision I could."

"I know."

Menders looked at his cousin for the first time since he'd come into the office. Kaymar managed a smile.

"Go see him, Cuz. I'm your second. I can make sure the place doesn't burn down, that wolves don't get in, that Menders' Men don't decide to go on strike. Ifor can take you there and back in one day, so you're not away overnight. I think it's important for you to take your eyes off The Shadows for a few hours – and I know it's important for you to see Borsen alone."

Menders hesitated.

"Be as good to yourself as you are to the rest of us," Kaymar said with a touch of snap, rising from his chair.

***

Menders stopped short as he walked up the Promenade from the docks, where he had just come ashore from The Shadows' steam launch. He had taken Kaymar's advice, setting out for Erdahn with little planning.

He'd expected to find Borsen at the store. He hadn't expected to see the young man leaning on his walking stick, surveying an array of crates and chatting companionably with a drayman. He had not yet seen Menders.

The city sophistication Borsen had acquired during his time in Erdahn was impressive. He'd always dressed well from the time he learned to sew and began making his own suits, but now he combined taste with daring, wearing clothing both unique and striking. His suit, conservative enough in cut, was made from a rich, dark bronze wool.

His hat was made to match, his jewelry was heavy gold. No wonder the rumors about Borsen being a Hetzophian prince proliferated so readily.

Menders might have stood there watching for some time, but the drayman looked up and caught him at it. He said something to Borsen, who turned, blinked in surprise and then smiled broadly.

With a parting word to the drayman, Borsen walked rapidly to Menders, looking up at him through his glasses with an expression of delight.

"Papa! I didn't expect to find you lurking around on this end of the Promenade," the young man said, shaking Menders' extended hand and then tucking his own hand in the crook of Menders' arm as they started to walk up the Promenade.

"I wanted come and see you," Menders said, deciding the direct approach would be best. "Kaymar told me how upset you were. I wanted to see how you are."

"Kaymar needs to mind his business," Borsen sighed.

"He is. His business is to look out for me and mine. He was right too. Do you have time to stop for some lunch?" Menders asked.

"Very much so. Stevahn is at the bank and since I had already arranged to be away from the store this week, I'm taking advantage of that," Borsen answered. "I know of a good Samorsan place, Papa, very private, if that would suit."

The restaurant menu was enticing, and Menders was glad to feel a twinge of appetite. He'd been almost nauseated since the blow-up at The Shadows.

"Now, why the tears?" Menders asked, after their orders had been taken.

"I've thought about it," Borsen said slowly. "I'm not entirely sure. It meant a great deal to me that you and Auntie and Katrin would come and stay at my home – and that Katrin would see the store. But something made me remember Mama's death."

He looked up at Menders and suddenly, all the self-assurance he displayed was stripped away.

"I was six years old again, blind and alone," he said softly. "Just for a little while."

Menders picked up his water glass and swallowed determinedly. The look in Borsen's eyes…

He was amazed as Borsen suddenly became the confident young businessman as the waiter set his starter in front of him. As always, he thanked the man sincerely and then launched into the food as if he hadn't eaten in a week – highly unlikely with Varnia taking care of him.

"Son," he said abruptly, startling Borsen. Menders drew a deep breath.

"I had to make a decision when I saw the state Katrin was in – and as it turned out, it was the right one. She's been sick and needed the time to rest and get over a bout of fever. But now I see that another of my children needs me to make a decision."

Borsen put his fork down, his dark almond shaped eyes never leaving Menders' face.

"I asked Katrin to persuade you to leave The Shadows and get started here in Erdahn," Menders said after a moment. Borsen's eyes widened in surprise. "I didn't want you to become entangled in her situation, as Hemmett has. Though I really wanted the comfort of having you at home, I knew if I didn't let you go, you would become captive to Katrin's title like the rest of us."

The waiter was approaching their table again, but saw a serious conversation going on and turned away quickly, much to Menders' relief.

"On the day Kaymar reminded me that Katrin had come of age, I realized I was no longer bound by the orders of the Queen. For one moment, I thought of leaving The Shadows. I thought of taking Eiren and you, and going to live somewhere else, as a normal family, free of the Royal Family and everything that goes with it."

Borsen seemed to have stopped breathing, hanging on every word.

"Of course, I wouldn't do that," Menders went on quietly. "Katrin was young for her years and had nowhere to go but to Court, which is the last place a decently raised young girl should be. She is my child and I love her with all my heart. I wouldn't abandon her. Of the three of you, she is the least able to choose her own destiny and forge her own way, simply because of who she is. You are capable of making your own life. Hemmett has the connections and training to make his way anywhere in Mordania. But Katrin – what can she be but a Princess of the Royal House? The accident of her birth has blighted her opportunities, Borsen. She needs me more than you or Hemmett do."

Borsen nodded, slowly and silently.

"What I want you to know is this," Menders went on relentlessly, though it cost him to voice the thought he had held close to his heart for ten years. "I have had three children come to me and become my own. Katrin was sent to me by her mother, for reasons I have never been able to discover. She is my beloved daughter, my first child, my golden girl I'd defend with my life.

"Hemmett was lent to me, because he has living parents who love him dearly, but were simply not equal to the task of raising him – so I took a hand and he became as dear to me as he is to them.

"But the child I never expected, the stray bird that fell into my hands, was meant to be mine – the child of the sister I never knew, blood from my blood, body from my body, my son. You, Borsen. I love you most of all. I have never told anyone this. I've hardly admitted it to myself. But that is the truth – and it must stay between us."

Borsen swallowed hard, then yanked a handkerchief from his pocket, briefly covering his face with it. He collected himself almost immediately, put the handkerchief away and took a deep breath.

"Thank you, Papa," he said softly. "That is wonderful to know. We go on from here."

The waiter bore down on them with their mains, doing a rapid shuffle as he removed the starter plates and set down the next course.

BOOK THREE

WHEN THE TIME OF TRIAL SPINS OUT

THE SHADOWS, MORDANIA

I

DEATH, REVELATION, DECISION

Menders dashed to the front door of The Shadows. Kaymar was riding up like a lunatic in the teeth of a violent thunderstorm, through lashing rain with lightning bolts piercing all around him. He leapt off his mare and sent her toward the stable with a slap to the rump, then raced up the steps, wet as the day he was born and panting from exertion.

"You came across in this?" Menders asked, peeling Kaymar's drenched jacket off him.

"Your office," Kaymar wheezed, staggering in that direction, giving vent to the ragged cough that began when his heart had been strained. Menders snatched up a sofa rug and tossed it to Kaymar, who wrapped it around himself, shivering. Menders closed the office door.

"The Queen is dead," Kaymar said immediately. "Officially from heart failure; in reality, of poison. Aidelia did it, of course. Aidelia has been proclaimed Queen."

Menders collapsed back against the door, his head reeling. All possible ramifications of the news hit him at once.

"A Royal Messenger is on his way, will probably get here before nightfall but I know what he's carrying," Kaymar continued, rubbing his streaming hair ineffectually with the rug. "Aidelia's commanding Katrin to stay here, not to come near Erdahn for the funeral or coronation. She's been declared Aidelia's Heiress."

Menders closed his eyes. All they'd begun to hope for, that Katrin was going to be removed from the Royal Succession, was gone, and a madwoman who'd tried to kill her was on the Throne.

Kaymar coughed again and Menders opened his eyes. He could see his cousin's heart pounding through his sodden shirt.

"Hurry, go get in a hot bath," he said. "No-one's been at the hot water today, so there'll be plenty. Is there anything else?"

Kaymar shook his head, still coughing from deep in his chest.

"Go on," Menders said, accompanying him from the office. "I'll tell Katrin."

Kaymar went coughing up the stairs. Menders collected himself for a moment before listening to find where Katrin was.

Hemmett laughed suddenly, Borsen laughed immediately afterward, then Katrin said something indistinguishable. They were in the Great Hall, probably fooling about with the spinets. Stevahn's deep voice chimed in, evoking more laughter. He and Borsen had arrived two days before with Varnia for their two-week visit.

Menders wished he could delay this conversation forever. He went to the door of the enormous room, and saw indeed that Katrin was seated at one spinet, Stevahn at the other. A brisk argument over tempo was being waged.

"Katrin, may I speak to you for a moment?"

She turned to Menders. Her face went white.

"What is it?" she cried. He realized he probably looked ghastly.

"No, don't be frightened," Menders said, going to her quickly. "I'm sorry my dear – hells, I can tell you all at once. The Queen is dead. The official story is by heart failure. Kaymar says that Aidelia poisoned her."

Katrin looked shocked and pensive. Stevahn and Borsen looked thoughtful, realizing that their businesses would be affected. Menders saw a fleeting expression of satisfaction pass over Hemmett's face that was frightening. It was immediately replaced by concern as he turned his eyes toward Katrin.

"There's more," Menders said, sitting beside Katrin on the spinet bench.

"I was afraid of that," she replied, looking directly at him.

"We'll leave you," Borsen said, rising from where he'd been perched beside Stevahn.

"No… stay, please. We're all in this together," Katrin said, never taking her eyes off Menders'.

"Aidelia has commanded that you not leave The Shadows," Menders said quietly.

Katrin groaned. Hemmett put his hands on her shoulders.

"Menders – is there anything we can do?" he asked.

"Yes, there would be several options," Menders said. "I'd like to think a bit first before we talk about them. At the moment, you're in no danger, as you've been declared Aidelia's Heiress. We needn't rush into anything."

Katrin groaned again. Menders could have groaned himself.

"I should have swum," she said suddenly, looking at Borsen.

"Don't worry yourself about that now," he answered. "It's not important – not now."

"Yes, it is," Katrin said quietly, bitterly. "Yes, it is."

***

"You could ask to be removed from the Line of Succession," Menders explained, sitting at the battle room table with Katrin, Eiren, Franz, Borsen, Stevahn, Kaymar, Ifor and Hemmett. "This would be the easiest for you. We could make the excuse of ill health – but it's very unlikely that Aidelia would allow it."

"I thought that," Katrin said.

"You could contest Aidelia's claim to the Throne on the grounds of her madness," Menders went on. "That would have to be done sooner rather than later, while her claim is very new. The drawback to this is that she wields absolute power and would be able to control the military. She doesn't have the brains to do it, but those around her do."

Katrin was silent, waiting.

"You might have a good chance at deposing her, because she's mad as a spoon," Menders went on. "It would be easily demonstrated. This would make you Queen. You could always abdicate after deposing Aidelia, but that would make your second cousin, Glorantha, Queen. She's still a child. Her father would become Regent. He is one of the people who are determined to eliminate the Thrun."

Katrin rubbed her eyes tiredly.

"You could leave the country. There has been no sign of Aidelia sending a force to keep guard over you. It's believed that you're an invalid. This would remove you from immediate danger, but it would put a bounty on you and a death sentence for anyone who helped you, possibly even for yourself. How motivated Aidelia would be in finding you I don't know. If she decided to leave you alone and remove you from the succession, then her Heiress, unless she produced one herself, would be Glorantha."

"Back to that," Borsen muttered.

Menders got up, went to the door and looked out into the hallway. Then he bolted the door, came back and sat at the table again.

"Aidelia could be eliminated," he said very softly. "It would not be difficult with Bartan still at the Palace. Some of her Court would have to be removed as well. This would make you Queen."

Katrin nodded, keeping her eyes on him.

"You could die," Menders said, beginning to sound weary. "Franz could claim you died of your illness and you could leave the country. That would …"

"Leave my cousin with the father who wants to kill all the Thrun," Katrin said just as wearily.

"Yes, and the sticking point would be that they would probably demand to see your body."

"And if I stay here as Aidelia commands?"

Menders turned his hands palm up.

"Katrin, I don't know. I have people placed who send me information about her, but there is no way to predict what a madwoman is going to do. She might have such a good time as Queen that she won't worry about you. You could wait and see what happens, but if she commanded you to Court suddenly, you would have very little choice. Your only option would be to flee the country if that occurred, and all that entails, including Glorantha becoming the Heiress."

The silence around the table was stifling.

"What should I do?" Katrin asked Menders.

"I can't tell you that," he answered. "It will have to be your decision. I can advise you as to what course of action … no, I can't."

"Why not?" Katrin cried.

"Because you would do whatever I consider the best course of action. I can't let you do that," Menders said quietly. "You must think about all of it and decide what you're going to do."

"Can't you help me?"

"I have. I've told you what options I believe you have. Perhaps someone else here can come up with another possibility, but these are the most reasonable and likely to succeed."

"What would you do, Kaymar?" Katrin asked desperately, turning toward the end of the table where he sat. Her voice died away as she saw the infuriated expression on his face.

"I would eliminate Aidelia. Menders would tell you the same," he replied, his voice rough with anger.

"But that would make me Queen and if I abdicated my cousin's father would go after the Thrun!"

"Yes, it would make you Queen. So?"

"But, I don't want to be Queen! I've never wanted to be!" Katrin exclaimed in horror.

"I can't help that. Your choices are limited and none of them will give you exactly what you want. So, you deal with the choices you have," Kaymar replied. "You don't want to be Queen? I didn't always want to spend years of my life guarding a little girl either. Did you think it was interesting work? Hours sitting behind doors, up in trees, around corners? I did it because I cared about you and because I considered you the best hope for Mordania, if it came to you becoming Queen." He met her gaze intently.

"You want me to have my sister killed?"

"She tried to kill you, didn't she?" he shot back. "Surely you aren't so foolish to believe she won't try again if she begins to believe you're a threat. I've been at the Court almost every week for years. The woman is demented. She's now the Queen of this country – and she has absolute power."

"Kaymar, it has to be Katrin's decision," Menders said, his voice steely.

"You know what she's going to decide!" Kaymar burst out. "She's going to take the path of least resistance and stay here hoping Aidelia forgets she exists! Do you think you're going to become invisible, Katrin? Do you really think that mad bitch is going to forget that you're alive and a potential threat to her ability to play her mad games for the rest of her life?"

"I don't want to be Queen!" Katrin said. "Not if I have to be a murderer!"

Kaymar stood abruptly and leaned across the table. He thrust his hands out right in front of her face.

"How many times do you think I've killed with these hands so you would be safe?" he asked in a terrible voice. "Far more than once, I assure you. Do you think I like it? Do you think I don't consider the lives I've taken before I fall asleep at night? That's a burden I shouldered willingly for your sake.

"Do you think he hasn't killed for your sake?" Kaymar pointed to Menders. "Eiren risked her life and damned near killed someone who was a threat to you. Borsen risks his safety by having several of the back rooms at his store turned over to Menders' Men so information from Erdahn and beyond can be gathered and transferred here. He could be tortured to death for what he does. Stevahn knows about it – he could lose his head for that! Franz has spent twenty-three years knowing about things he could lose his head for. Hemmett knows about all of it and has helped. He could end up on the roasting spit. You don't want to be Queen? None of us wanted our particular burdens either, but we've taken them on willingly for your sake!"

Katrin looked from one to the next and saw that his words were true.

"That's enough, Kaymar," Menders said, his voice gentle. "She didn't know about most of this."

"Is it enough? This is what happens when you protect someone too much," Kaymar retorted bitterly. "She has a chance to do something for this country, to change things. She's hesitating and trying to find a way to avoid that responsibility, because she doesn't want to do it."

"Nothing is going to be decided tonight," Menders replied levelly, rising. "Katrin must think about it and come to her own decision, or everything we've done all these years is for nothing, because she would be our puppet. That can't happen."

"And if she makes the wrong decision?" Kaymar said, still staring at Katrin.

"We'll have to abide by it," Menders said, his voice firm. "It is her life, Kaymar."

"Her life affects all of our lives!" Kaymar stormed out.

Katrin looked around the table, from one to the next.

"Borsen?" she whispered.

"Yes, I'm a Menders' Man – a spy," he answered. "I gather information myself, other information is collected at Borsen's. People talk to tailors, just as they talk to barbers, bartenders and hairdressers."

"Me too," Stevahn added softly. "Financiers hear lots of things. I contribute financial information that isn't public knowledge as well."

Katrin looked at Eiren.

"It was during the year I was at teacher's college in Erdahn, when you were fifteen," she answered. "The man who sent all those assassins after the family was trying to use me as a source of information about The Shadows. Kaymar, Ifor and I tried to kill him."

Katrin turned toward Franz.

"Of course I know everything that goes on, I'm the damn house doctor," he said gruffly. "I'm a dead man if it all comes to light. I was in on the formation of Menders' Men, which is an illegal military unit. I know who's killed who, who's spying. I patch up those who have been injured in action. I have my personal roasting spit all picked out."

Hemmett met her eyes. "Yes, I know everything, and I've helped with everything," he said. "They'll have a hells of a fight if they try to kill me."

She finally looked at Menders.

"Why haven't I been told all this?" she asked incredulously.

"Because you've been ill. Because at times you were too young. Because I've protected you far too well," he answered. "In hindsight, the wrong thing to do, but I made the best decisions I could. Now only you can make the decision as to what you will do."

"How can you expect me to?"

"I have never thought for you!" Menders snapped, his voice like the crack of a whip. "Don't begin to imply that I have when I've stood aside and forced myself to accept decisions and actions of yours that I knew weren't the best. Stop being emotional. Think over your options and decide what you're going to do! Then do it – as everyone here and Kaymar have always done what they must – without flinching."

He got up and left the room.

***

Katrin looked up to see Kaymar coming toward her across the garden. It was an early autumn day and she had left the over-quiet atmosphere of the house because every nerve in her body was crawling.

Borsen and Stevahn went back to Erdahn according to plan, anxious to see what was happening to financial markets and other business matters since the death of the Queen. They'd said nothing more about Katrin's situation, though she knew they were both troubled and concerned for her. Borsen held her close for a long time before leaving.

It was the same with everyone else involved in that meeting. No-one brought up the issue. Sometimes the silence was deafening while Katrin felt abandoned and at sea. Discourse was the staff of life at The Shadows; people talked all the time. Sometimes they argued and had shouting matches. For people to refuse to talk because they feared she would base her decision on what they said was alien to her.

She knew they were right, but this decision was one she didn't want to make.

The only person who showed outward anger was Kaymar and he wasn't keeping silent.

"Kaymar, I really don't want to talk to you," she said warningly.

"I don't care," he retorted, standing where she would have to go past him to escape. "Every day Aidelia is on the Throne lessens your chances if you're going to challenge her or have her eliminated. You've decided to do nothing, haven't you?"

"I'm not finished thinking about it."

"That's absurd. You've already wasted the time where we could have acted the most easily. Just be honest with me – you're going to be a good girl, do as your mad sister says and stay here as a sitting duck, endangering everyone around you. Isn't that right?"

Katrin stood and glared at him.

"What do you mean?" she snapped.

"Katrin, have you thought of the danger everyone else will be in if you continue to live here, with all the covert operations going on in Menders' network? Do you have any idea how many people are involved, Katrin?"

"There are fifty-five Menders' Men," she said angrily.

"There are over three hundred Menders' Men in the world, with more than one hundred of them here in Mordania and at risk! Yes, that's right. All the Men in Mordania will be at risk, including Borsen, as long as you sit here and do nothing!"

"Kaymar, please stop blaming me for things I was never told about!" Katrin shouted. "I am not a mind reader! This has all been kept secret from me and I don't appreciate that – or being taken to task for things I had no knowledge of!"

He pressed his lips together for a moment. It was obvious he was trying to calm himself.

"Yes, that isn't fair," he said more quietly. "But Katrin, Menders is making an error by not speaking with you about this, because when you're faced with something you don't want to do, your tendency is to do nothing. I've known you and been with you almost every day since you were four years old. You know this is the truth."

Katrin looked down at her feet.

It was true. If she didn't care for something she needed to read, she tended to put it aside. Chores she disliked led her to procrastinate, putting them off until someone else did them. Borsen held The Shadow's record for killing chickens for dinner because if it was left to her, the roosters would still be crowing in the poultry yard when the dinner bell rang. It was a bad habit and she knew it – but still, she did it.

"Kaymar, please try to understand," she pleaded. "I don't want to be Queen. I don't even know how. I'm terrified of the Palace. What if we failed? You're asking me to sacrifice everything to take a terrible risk."

"The Queen of Mordania has absolute power, Katrin! You can be any kind of Queen you want!" Kaymar nearly shouted, his temper gone. "You don't have to be like your mother was. You're better than that. Oh gods, after all the care and love and effort that has been put into you, are you going to do nothing when you have the opportunity to make things better for the entire country?"

Katrin sank down on the bench she'd vacated and closed her eyes.

"How long do you think Borsen, with his sparrow's bones, would last on the rack?" Kaymar whispered directly into her ear. "If they catch him, that's what will happen to him. What do you think they would do to Menders? He's committed treason so many times for your sake. Katrin…"

She was cold all over and felt as if she was going to vomit. But there was so much fear. The Shadows was safe, and she'd been commanded to stay there.

Suddenly Kaymar's hand was under her chin, as it had been so many times before, turning her face up to his. The anger was gone from his eyes. He looked tired and, suddenly, old.

"They took it from you," he said sadly. "That fire you had. I can't blame you, Katrin. I know you're afraid – but please. Please, consider what I've said. So many of us have sacrificed so much for your sake. We would help you. You wouldn't be alone. Now, I'm going to go and stay in Erdahn for a while, because… Good-bye, Katrin."

He walked rapidly away, letting himself into the Men's Wing through the double glass door.

A memory came to Katrin suddenly – a dreary winter afternoon at The Shadows when she was only five years old. Hemmett was refusing to play with her, in one of his 'no girls!' moods. Menders was called away to one of the tenant farms and Eiren was teaching at her school.

Katrin rambled around the nursery, moving from one plaything to another. Nothing held her interest. She wanted to go outside, but she didn't want it to be winter. She wanted to go on the swing, but the snow was too deep to get there and it was so cold. It had been sleeting all day and everything was crusted with ice.

She threw the doll she'd been holding and sat down hard on the nursery floor. She covered her face with her hands and then drummed her heels on the floor for a moment out of sheer frustration.

"Well now, I have a little girl here who isn't at all happy."

She was startled, having forgotten Kaymar was watching her that afternoon. He'd been snugged away in the corner, behind an old screen. He didn't play with her often as Haakel did, but read a book or wrote a letter on his funny little portable desk.

Now he was sitting beside her on the nursery floor.

"What's put you into a tantrum?" he asked, his blue eyes looking right at her.

She threw her arms around his neck suddenly and wept.

"I want to go on the swing!"

The minute she said it, she was sorry, because she didn't sound at all like a big girl.

"I imagine you do," he replied, patting her back and holding her close, like Menders would have if he'd been there. "It's a dreary day and more to come."

"Hemmett won't let me play with him. He's a toad!"

"Yes, he gets his grumpiness out in other ways, while you throw your dolly and hammer your feet into the floor," Kaymar laughed. "Now then – you know we can't get out to the swing. So, what should we do?"

"Don't laugh!" Katrin cried harder.

"Ah – yes, Cousin Kaymar won't be able to jolly you out of this, will he?" Kaymar replied. He was quiet for a moment and Katrin could feel that he was looking around the room.

"I know how you can swing," he said suddenly. He propped her up on her feet and rose in one motion from the floor. "Now, you go pick up your dolly and apologize for throwing her around while I do a little prospecting."

He went out of the nursery and through the door that went into the lower attics, leaving it open so she could see him. Katrin wasn't allowed in the attics, but she went with her doll to stand at the door.

Kaymar looked at many things, shuffling objects around and finally made several trips to the nursery from the attic with rope, boards and a lot of old paintings. With the help of a ladder and a hand drill, he assembled and hung a swing from the wooden beam high against the nursery ceiling. Then he lined up the paintings, all of flowers, against the wall.

"Now, you have a swing and you have spring," he laughed, setting her on the seat. "I can't provide sunshine on a miserable day like today, but look at those flowers while you swing and it will do."

"You swing too!" Katrin said excitedly. She laughed when he sat beside her. He'd made the seat big enough for two, he said in case Hemmett decided to stop being a toad sometime. He pushed them off and soon it seemed as if they were swinging high enough to touch the sky.

He is your protector. He can help you. He made spring in the middle of winter for you. Do not let him go, foolish girl! Go, keep him with you!

The voices – the Queens. She had not heard them since she was Suspended.

She wouldn't listen. She would stay here, where it was safe.

***

Menders looked up as Kaymar came into his office and shut the door.

"Post me in Erdahn," he said abruptly.

"What?"

"I want to leave The Shadows. I just hectored Katrin and I won't be able to keep from doing it again. I need to be away from her. Post me elsewhere, please, or I will have to resign."

"Is she all right?" Menders started to rise.

"Of course she's all right! I didn't beat her. Sit down, stop running after her like she's a sickly baby! She needed to hear some of the things I said."

"I don't appreciate that, Kaymar," Menders growled.

"Stop it! Give over, Menders! Katrin is recovered. She's strong and she's twenty-three years old! I swear you have gone mad with this overprotecting and it is killing you and damaging her!"

Menders sat back in his chair and looked at his cousin.

"Kaymar, sit down, please," he sighed. "This tension is telling on us all."

"There's no tension for me now," Kaymar replied, sinking into the chair across the partners' desk from Menders. "I know what she's going to decide to do – nothing. I can see it in her eyes. I wouldn't be able to resist keeping after her and that's not fair. I need time away, Cuz, please. Post Ifor and me in Erdahn. Assign us to keep an eye on Borsen. He's in danger now, as you know. I can get information from Bartan for you. I don't dare go into the Palace now, even covertly. Aidelia's got the place bristling with Guards and they aren't the toy soldiers who used to be there. I can't take the chance of being caught and leading anyone back here."

Menders sighed, pulling his keyring out of his pocket.

"Here's the key to the house in Erdahn," he said quietly, handing it across his desk. "You and Ifor are welcome to stay there, or you could stay with Borsen and Stevahn if you'd rather, if you think it's safer for them."

"Thank you." Kaymar reached out and took the key. "I'll get information back to you as often as possible and make sure Borsen is guarded."

Menders nodded, not looking at him.

"Aylam, I don't blame you for what's going to happen," Kaymar said after a moment. "So many things have gone into the soup. Almost all of it was beyond your control. If this had happened before The Queen and Aidelia got hold of Katrin, she would have had the will and fire to do what she needs to do. I can't blame her for not being able to act now. I don't blame you for it either. Don't waste time blaming yourself."

Kaymar stood and held his hand out across the desk. After a moment, Menders took it and held it hard, looking up into his cousin's eyes.

"Be careful, Kaymar – take care of my boy," Menders said gruffly.

"You know I will." Kaymar squeezed Menders' hand in return.

THE SHADOWS, MORDANIA
THE PALACE, ERDAHN, MORDANIA

2
COMMANDED INTO NIGHTMARE

Katrin woke earlier than usual. For the first time in a long while, she felt very peaceful and lighthearted.

It was spring, her favorite season at The Shadows. A long, wet autumn had been followed by an unusually warm but stormy winter, that made up in dreariness for what it lacked in cold. The Thrun had been unable to visit. Life at The Shadows was subdued during the long dark season. No further communication came from the Palace and if Kaymar and Ifor were reporting to Menders, Katrin knew nothing of it.

Borsen and Stevahn came over for a week in the autumn and again for a week during Winterfest. They were uncharacteristically silent when it came to news about Erdahn. They only said they were glad of a chance to rest, spending a considerable amount of time together in their room. Katrin had knocked a few times, received no reply and peeked in to see they were sound asleep, cradled in each other's arms in the middle of the day – something unheard of for Borsen, who was endlessly active.

Katrin never made the decision Kaymar tried to push her to. She abided by her sister's command, feeling it was the safest course for everyone. So far it was as if she'd vanished from the face of Eirdon. Likely Aidelia considered her no threat and was so busy being Queen that she had not a thought to spare for Katrin.

Katrin's main sorrow was the necessity of postponing the orphanage project once more. Arranging to have children brought to The Shadows would draw far too much attention to her. The last thing Katrin needed was Adelia's scrutiny.

Menders was quieter than usual and spent many hours with Haakel, going through piles of notes and dossiers regularly brought by Ifor, sometimes by Kaymar. Katrin deliberately avoided the office when she could hear Kaymar speaking. He and Ifor had stayed in Erdahn during Winterfest rather than joining the gathering at The

Shadows. This was unprecedented and many of The Shadows' residents expressed regret, but in all honesty, Katrin had been relieved not to face Kaymar.

She had considered talking to Menders about the vastness of his network and the information it continually fed him, but then let it slide. Since mid-winter a lassitude had plagued her. Sometimes she had to chivvy herself to get out of bed. Menders had always managed his information network and he'd never shared it with her, so why start pushing now? If something was important enough for her to know, he would tell her.

But now the dreary winter was over and spring was in full bloom outside. Katrin could see the orchard trees from her window and sat up in bed to look out at them. She could even smell them, though the window was closed – a pity, considering what a beautiful day it was going to be!

Katrin got up and cast off her heavy nightgown, going to her wardrobe for something to put on to go out into the garden while the day was fresh and new. She found a light, spring dress she'd worn last year to make soap, and pulled it over her head, not bothering with her corset or bloomers. No-one would see her. Everyone was still asleep. The garden was calling.

She ran downstairs and out into the garden barefoot, reflexively looking up toward the sentry on the roof. To her relief it was Hemmett, who grinned down at her, playfully shaking a chastising finger at her lack of proper clothing.

Katrin put her tongue out at him and ran over to take a look at how many daffodils had opened since yesterday. They were overhung with fragrant white garberia blossoms, dripping from vines that twined through the trees. She stepped closer to the tree line to inhale their scent.

"Stand there, Your Highness," a male voice said.

Suddenly Katrin saw an enormous squad of uniformed men hidden in the forest, stepping out from behind trees and bushes.

"Her Majesty the Queen commands you be brought to Court."

Katrin wheeled to run back to the house, as the emergency bell began clanging raucously.

"We are ordered to shoot you if you resist," the voice said behind her. Katrin stood still, feeling cold sweat break out all over her body.

"Katrin! Katrin!" Menders was shouting for her in the house. Katrin looked up and saw Hemmett, rifle on his shoulder, aiming behind her. She waved her arms.

"Don't – there are too many of them! They're armed and aiming right at you!" she shouted. Hemmett hesitated.

Menders exploded through the side door of the house and raced toward her.

"Stand where you are, Lord Stettan!" barked the same voice, bringing Menders up short. Katrin could see the defeat in his face. Hemmett's Men had come out all over the house, rifles raised.

"Hold your fire!" Menders shouted at the top of his voice. "They have Katrin!"

***

Katrin read the decree the Commander of the Queen's Guard handed her, then passed it to Menders. He took it, running his eyes over it quickly.

It was a Royal Command that Katrin go to the Palace immediately. She could be accompanied only by a maidservant – which Katrin didn't have.

"We live simply here," Katrin said to the Commander, sounding calm though Menders could see her shivering in that ridiculous light dress which she had obviously thrown on over nothing else. "I have no maidservant."

"I have my orders, Your Highness," the Commander replied, his voice devoid of expression. "You may not bring your Head of Household or anyone but your personal maidservant."

"Then I will have to go alone," Katrin managed.

"Then you will have to," the commander responded. "Please come along."

"Officer, I have no shoes on, nor am I properly dressed," Katrin protested. "I need a few moments to change and pack some essentials."

"My orders are to bring you immediately and to have you shot if you do not comply," the man replied in that same, flat tone.

Menders could hear Hemmett and his Men and the farmers who had rushed to the estate house moving, tightening their hands on their weapons. The Queen's Guard raised their rifles immediately. Menders caught Hemmett's eye and shook his head slightly.

"I am not wearing shoes," Katrin countered. "Do you wish to explain to my sister why you refused to let me put my shoes on before taking me a day's journey from home?"

The Commander flinched very slightly, his eyes wavering away from Katrin for a moment. Menders watched as he underwent a mental crisis and then turned toward the women, who had been herded together.

"You – get a pair of shoes for the Princess and bring them here to me," he said to Cook, who was the closest. She gave Katrin a stricken look and scurried away up the stairs, returning very shortly with a soft pair of low shoes. She held them out to the Commander, stepping back as he inspected them closely.

He dropped them to the floor at Katrin's feet. Katrin stepped into them.

"Follow me please, Your Highness," the Commander said, turning toward the door. The soldiers began filing out.

Menders tore Katrin's medal, worn by all members of her household, from his jacket. It had long ago been converted to a dirk brooch. He reached over her shoulder swiftly, pushing it out of sight into her cleavage. It wasn't much, but it was a weapon. Katrin didn't acknowledge the sudden contact in any way, walking after the soldiers.

Menders went down on one knee in a formal Court bow, removing his dark glasses at the same time. There was a rustling as the rest of the household and the tenant farmers who had come to the sound of the bell followed suit.

Katrin turned back and looked into Menders' eyes.

He looked at her steadily, trying to give her courage, trying to let her know without words that he would help her, that she would not be alone. He could see Hemmett in the same posture at his side and Eiren, curtseyed low to the floor, her eyes on Katrin also.

Katrin smiled. How she could do so when he could see she was shaking with terror he couldn't imagine.

"Thank you. Thank you all," she said, looking from Eiren, to Hemmett, to him – with a smile. Her eyes looked into his again and for a moment, there was nothing else in the world.

"Come with me now, Your Highness," the Commander said sharply.

Katrin turned and was immediately surrounded by the soldiers. They took her through the front door to the drive, where she was lifted onto a horse that had been brought up from the woods. She was flanked by dozens of mounted guards before they rode away down the drive.

"Search the grounds!" Hemmett shouted. "Make sure they're gone! Go!" His Guard and many of Menders' Men scattered for the doors, as Villison sprinted up the stairs to the roof.

"Hemmett, get to the boat – go through the stable tunnel!" Menders yelled, racing up the stairs behind Villison, followed by Eiren. "Get steam up and be ready to go the minute I get there!"

Hemmett bolted for the strongroom, followed by the rest of Menders' Men. Menders could hear the trapdoor being hauled up.

"I'll get a food parcel together!" Cook shouted, hurrying away.

Menders leaned over the rail.

"Bertel, Klausen, I want you with me. Get dressed and armed. The rest of you, spread out, check for stragglers of that lot. Haakel, I need documents. Anything you can think of, Royal Orders, passport – you know!"

He ran to his room where Eiren had already emptied several drawers onto the bed, so he could find what he needed quickly. He tore off his clothing and began dressing from the skin out in an assassin's gear, pulling on the lightweight silk underwear that moved like a second skin, then strapping one knife after another to various parts of his body, followed by the black garments that allowed him to fade invisibly into shadows. Over these he pulled his normal clothing. Eiren was in Katrin's room, bundling together necessities, nightgown, brush and comb, toothbrush.

"Wrap everything as flat as a can, to fit into my pockets," Menders called to her, packing more clothing and weapons into a bag. Outside he could hear Hemmett's Men searching, probably desperate to find anyone they could tear to pieces. Villison was shouting directions from the roof – evidence that Katrin and the men who had taken her were out of earshot. He heard a train whistle at the halt.

"The bastards had the train down the line!" one of Hemmett's Men said in the doorway. "They just pulled it up here. They must have stopped far down the line last night and marched up here after dark, then filtered into the woods between patrols."

"How many are there?" Menders asked.

"At least two hundred. We could never take them," the man replied.

The train whistle sounded again. A moment later Menders could hear Villison's light footsteps racing down the roof stairs and along the corridor.

"They're going," he said swiftly. "They didn't treat her badly, handed her up nicely enough, no sign of abuse. Train's already pulled out. It's a special, of course."

"Thank you," Menders said shortly. "You're in command of Hemmett's Guard. Hemmett is coming along with me. If you find any of them here, which I doubt, don't kill them. Keep them here and get word to me. I can be reached at Borsen's home."

Eiren rushed in with the parcels for Katrin. Menders pushed them into his pockets.

"What else do you need?" she asked, her voice calm, belying her shaking hands.

"I'll get it in the kitchen – I'll need food to take and flasks for clean water." Menders rapidly threw the last few things he needed into the bag and turned to her.

"My darling, don't come down with me. I'm going to stop at the kitchen and then I'm on my way," he said, forcing himself to sound calm. "I will send word back as quickly as I can."

Eiren flung her arms around his neck.

"Take care of her," she whispered, clinging to him with all her strength. "Stay alive. Please stay alive!"

"I will, Little Bird," he whispered. "I love you." He kissed her and then moved swiftly toward the door.

"Menders!"

He turned. His heart broke at the sight of her stricken face.

"I will come back to you," he said, his voice fierce with love.

***

"I'd rather you stayed home," Stevahn said to Borsen, looking critically at him across the dining table at breakfast.

"I must admit I feel like it," Borsen sighed. He had not slept well for months. Neither had Stevahn. They were both on edge and had been since the coronation of Queen Morghenna IX – Aidelia.

Aidelia's reign was already characterized by bizarre royal decrees and sudden disappearances of people. The rumor was that death by torture had become a favorite entertainment of the demented Queen of Mordania.

To make matters worse, Aidelia had been ordering arrests of nancy men on "morals violations". Several of Borsen and Stevahn's acquaintances had been arrested on trumped up charges and taken to the Palace dungeon. Their families were unable to get permission to visit or write to them. One was an employee at Borsen's, young Petran Borghel, the hat designer who had caught the eye and heart of Mister Evanov, Borsen's fat man.

The best sleep Borsen and Stevahn had during the nine months of Aidelia's reign had been during their visits to The Shadows or to the home of Stevahn's parents. There they spent far more time in their rooms, sound asleep, than would be considered polite behavior for guests.

Complicating matters, Borsen contracted a severe cold during the winter. It lodged in his lungs and lingered well into spring. He was finally free of it, but all illnesses hit him hard. This latest siege had been lengthened due to the strain of Petran's arrest and the ongoing threat to himself and Stevahn. He looked ghastly, his attractiveness lost in shadowed eyes and haggard lines.

"Please do," Stevahn said, shaking his head. "You look dreadful. If you stay home, I promise to come home for lunch and pamper you."

"You do look dreadful, little brother," Varnia added, coming in from the kitchen with a fresh pot of coffee. She sat opposite Borsen and poured out a cup for him.

"I'll forgive you both for saying I look dreadful if you come home to pamper me and if you keep plying me with coffee," Borsen joked, looking from Stevahn to Varnia before leaning back in his chair and closing his eyes.

"Did you sleep at all last night?" Varnia asked.

"Yes, but the dreams won't leave me alone," Borsen sighed. It was so unlike him not to fight the idea of staying home that Stevahn was truly concerned. Inspiration dawned.

"Why don't we all go to Surelia for a while?" he suggested. "We could stay at my family's house there. Pappa would be glad to take over for me at the bank and it would be a relief for everyone to know we're out of Aidelia's reach.

"I'm backlogged at the store," Borsen replied. "I can't say that it isn't a tempting idea. I would welcome some sleep without nightmares. Let me think on how I could manage."

"Why not take what you need with us, do your stitching there and we'll post it all back?" Stevahn suggested.

"You are a brilliant man," Borsen replied, rubbing his eyes wearily.

"Eat something, dear," Varnia urged softly, marveling that she had to urge Borsen to eat.

Rapid hoofbeats outside the front door brought them to their feet. Borsen's hand went to his pistol and Varnia drew hers. Stevahn stepped over to a cabinet and extracted a shotgun hidden behind it.

Magic snarled, barked and jumped at the front door. Then he began burbling and yodeling happily as someone knocked resoundingly.

Stevahn ran to the door and pulled it open, revealing Menders, Hemmett and two of Menders' Men.

"Papa!" Borsen cried in amazement as the men came in swiftly. Stevahn closed the door, locked and double-bolted it.

"Aidelia's had Katrin arrested," Menders said, dropping the bag he carried. "She's on her way to Erdahn on a train with over two hundred Mordanian soldiers."

"No," Borsen breathed. Stevahn went to him, putting an arm around his shoulders.

"You all look done in," he said firmly. "Sit down, breakfast's just been laid on. We'll talk about this while you eat."

"I need a base of operations," Menders continued, taking a seat at the table. Bertel and Klausen did the same, falling on the food as if they were starving. Borsen went to the kitchen but found that Varnia had anticipated him and Hemmett had joined her. More food was already in the pan and Hemmett was carving rashers of bacon. Borsen then exchanged a look with Stevahn from behind Menders' back. Stevahn read it immediately, and nodded slightly. Borsen indicated for him to speak.

"Our home is yours," Stevahn said with finality. "What can we do to help you?"

Menders began explaining how he needed a place where he could get food and water for Katrin, as she could not safely eat or drink anything offered at the Palace. Suddenly he stopped and looked around.

Borsen had moved out of his line of sight, knowing his darkly shadowed eyes and the weight he'd lost during months of illness were something Menders hadn't noticed in his initial rush into the house.

But Menders was faster than he was. He turned rapidly in his chair, getting a good look at Borsen as he started to duck into the kitchen. He was up in an instant, following in Borsen's wake.

"My boy," he said softly, catching Borsen's shoulder and turning him. "Good gods, what is wrong?"

"It's not serious. I'm just not sleeping well," Borsen said. "That cold knocked me down for a while. You know how it is with me."

"I'm endangering you both," Menders said. "We won't stay, we'll go to my safe house."

"No. That's all the way across town. You need to be closer to the Palace," Borsen said firmly. "We're already endangered – if it gets too bad, we'll go to Surelia and leave you the use of the house. Let us help you, Uncle."

Menders held him at arms' length, scrutinizing him.

"You should have let us know you were so ill," he said softly, then put his arms around Borsen and held him close. Borsen could feel the fear in him and hugged back with all his might.

"Now, tell us what you need us to do," Borsen said when Menders released him, leading him back to where the others were.

***

During the train journey, Katrin showed no sign of the terror she was feeling, the fear of what she was walking into, how at a loss she felt without Menders. She gave an outward appearance of looking at the scenery during the long ride and then taking interest in the part of the city they rode through to reach the Palace. Inside, she was a wailing, sobbing child, terrified at the sight of the enormous building.

At the Palace, she was left for a long time in a windowless anteroom. Certain no-one was watching, she delved into the depths of her cleavage for the object Menders had pushed there during her abrupt departure from The Shadows. Her fingers found it and she knew it instantly, before drawing it into the light.

It was the small medal Menders always wore over his heart, her personal badge, the Mordanian coat of arms with a superimposed K, issued to her household when she came of age. The design was embossed on a heart shaped piece of metal that could be attached to a garment with a pin. But in this case Menders had altered the medal, so it was held in place with a thin triangular blade rather than the usual brooch pin. It was intended to be used as a weapon in a pinch. It wasn't a deadly weapon, but thrust into an eye or temple, it would definitely dissuade an attacker.

Katrin smiled, looking at the little heart, then slipped it back into her bodice. No sooner had she done so but a Palace Guard appeared, and she was taken to Aidelia.

Katrin's half-sister was surrounded by her court of sycophants who were nearly as mad as she was. Katrin could feel their eyes roving over her, taking in the casual hairstyle of her wig, the lightweight and childishly simple old dress she'd thrown on, the soft basic slippers Cook had fetched for her because she would be able to step into them quickly. Katrin made a full formal curtsy, sweeping down onto one knee and staying there – ultimate respect, waiting for the Queen to allow her to rise.

"Well, well, well, milk and honey from the country," Aidelia smiled.

Katrin saw with horror that Aidelia's teeth had been filed into the sharp points that were part of the official appearance of the Queen of Mordania, but which all Queens since their great-grandmother's reign had created by wearing false teeth. Her hair was plucked back to create the traditional skull-like shape of the forehead.

Aidelia was seated on the Ruby Throne, wearing the great bejeweled and armored gown Katrin had seen their mother wear. All around Aidelia's eyes the whites were visible. Her eyes continually roved the room, never resting on anything. It was exhausting to watch them rotating.

"Isn't she sweet?" Aidelia went on, rising stiffly and clattering toward Katrin in the stiff gown. "Straight from milking the cows, eh little sister?"

It was etiquette to answer any direct question, so Katrin, maintaining the strained posture of the curtsey at its deepest point, spoke.

"When I received your order I came straightaway, even though I was not properly attired, Your Majesty. Please forgive my appearance."

Aidelia raised her pale eyebrows, causing creases in the thickly applied makeup that rendered her pale complexion a corpselike white.

"Your appearance, as always, is that of a fat country pig," she said brightly, as if she'd given the greatest of compliments. "You're fatter than you were the last time I saw you. I was greatly hurt, sister, that you did not attend my coronation."

"I felt the coronation should be for you, and you alone, Your Majesty. I did not want to be a distraction at the occasion," Katrin said contritely, wanting to shout that it was Aidelia herself who had ordered her to stay away.

Aidelia considered this. Katrin could hear soft murmurs among the gathered Court. She kept her eyes on the ground, a picture of sweet humility.

"Well done," Aidelia said in a way Katrin knew she thought sounded truly queenly. "You may rise."

Grateful for every hour she'd ever spent in exercise, Katrin rose gracefully, feeling the ache in her thighs and buttocks as they were finally released from the tension of her curtsy. Another whisper rippled through the Court as she faced her sister.

Gods, she reeks, Katrin thought. Their mother's proclivity for uncleanliness was obviously passed on to Aidelia. The filed teeth had punctured her lips in several places, the scabs painted over with lip rouge. Her breath was vile, a combination of sour wine and decaying food caught between those shark like teeth.

Katrin looked as if she was smelling the most delicate perfume and smiled as if she had never been so glad to see someone in her life.

"I would have you always near me," Aidelia said, reaching out and putting a hand on Katrin's arm, squeezing with something that felt like an iron clamp, some device she had hidden in the palm of her hand. Katrin showed no sign, but inclined her head as if accepting a wonderful blessing.

"After all, little girls living in the countryside can get into all sorts of mischief at your age. You will attend me. Proper clothing will be provided for you, but today I want you to stand behind me, so I know my dear sister is close."

Katrin stood behind the Throne for hours. She made miniscule shifts of weight from one foot to another throughout that long afternoon and evening. Her feet would swell, of course. One couldn't combat all the ill effects of hours on one's feet, but the soft shoes would expand.

Katrin acted as if she didn't see the glances raked over her by the members of Aidelia's court, ranging from scorn to lewdness, depending on who was looking. Two meals were eaten without anything being offered, but a tightening of her back muscles countered any dizziness she felt. As the tedious day went by, Katrin thought continuously of The Shadows, of Menders, of Hemmett, her horse Taffy, the garden. She found an odd island of peace as she stood at her sister's command.

Finally, Aidelia seemed tired of forcing her to stand and dismissed her abruptly.

"You won't need any dinner, considering your size," she said nastily. "We shall keep you on a diet until you're a more fashionable shape." She reached out and pinched Katrin's left breast, sending a spasm of pain down to Katrin's toes. "And don't appear before me in such ridiculous garments again. You will wear what is given you. You will be taken to your room now."

A sniggering maidservant was summoned. Katrin followed the girl through endless corridors until she was shown the door of a very small room. The maidservant told her contemptuously that there was a change of clothing in the wardrobe, and stood there with a smug smirk on her face, offering no assistance.

"You may go," Katrin said to the girl. "Do not forget that I am the Princess and Her Majesty's Heiress, or I shall tell my sister, the Queen, how you fail to show respect."

The girl seemed slightly intimidated and sketched the merest curtsy before flouncing out of the room, closing the door behind her.

The door had no bolt. Katrin groaned in frustration at the thought that anyone could enter. Then, exhausted, she sank down in the lone wooden chair that stood beside a crude table. She lit the single candle there. It guttered and burned low. At least she wasn't sitting in darkness.

Clasping her hands together, Katrin used her thumb knuckles to rub the tension between her eyebrows away.

Then she felt it – a presence.

Menders, dressed all in black, stepped out of the shadows.

Katrin was so startled that she began to cry out. He moved forward quickly, putting a hand over her mouth, shaking his head. Then he knelt beside her. She threw her arms around his neck while he held her and then pressed a fervent kiss on her forehead. She tried to whisper, but once again Menders shook his head. Releasing her, he produced a piece of paper and a pencil.

You must not speak, he wrote rapidly. *They cannot see into this room, but they can hear, and it is certain someone is listening.* He handed her the pencil.

How? she wrote. He shook his head, but she gestured toward the word, and he took the pencil and wrote quickly, *On the boat of course.*

Katrin couldn't help smiling. You had to get up early in the morning to get around Menders. She was so glad to see him that she wanted to cry, but wasn't going to give any listening spies the satisfaction of hearing her in tears.

He wrote again.

You're in great danger. You will have to behave as if nothing is wrong, that you are happy to be here and that you are stupid. Eat nothing that is given to you, and do not eat anything the Queen eats alone and offers to you.

Because she might have taken an antidote to poison in the food, Katrin thought, nodding. Then she took the pencil.

I've eaten nothing at all today, she scribbled.

Menders smiled and immediately removed a packet from his shirt, putting it on the table. Katrin folded back the cloth and started on the food ravenously, recognizing a typical Borsen-made sandwich – heavy on the meat and cheese, sparing of mustard. Two apples and several homemade cookies like the ones Cook kept in abundance at The Shadows completed the meal. There was a little drawing beneath the sandwich, a tiny heart drawn on a scrap of paper in Borsen's unmistakable style. Katrin smiled, wolfing down the food.

Menders rose and padded across the room to the water pitcher. He poured the contents slowly and silently into the privy, then replaced it on the washstand. He produced a flask of water from a pocket and handed it to Katrin. She drained it and sighed in relief. It had been a long, dry day.

Menders motioned for her to open the wardrobe. It contained a set of underwear, including a fashionable straight fronted corset, a black gown, stockings and a pair of shoes three sizes too small. Everything was made of cheap, coarse material. No nightgown, no hairbrush or toothbrush, no soap or washcloth.

No wonder Aidelia stinks so, Katrin thought ruefully. She probably doesn't even know what a bath is. She turned away from the wardrobe to see Menders extracting more tightly wrapped bundles from his clothing and opening them.

He'd brought one of her nightgowns, her hair and tooth brushes, adhesive to secure her wig, the lemon soap she made at The Shadows and two towels. She sighed in relief.

Both the corset and dress fasten in the back, she wrote quickly. *I can't get into or out of them on my own.*

Order the maidservant to help you, he wrote in return. *If I do, short of you growing arms that can fasten your own clothing from the back, I'll be given away.*

Katrin nodded and watched as he produced other flasks of water and then turned his back. She stripped and washed rapidly at the stand, inhaling the delicate scent of the soap, letting it bring The Shadows to her mind. When she slid her nightgown over her head Menders turned back to her and wrote on the paper.

I will have to take everything away each morning, in case they search your room. Don't try to wear those shoes tomorrow. Come up with an excuse. She'll keep you standing again and if you wear them, you'll be crippled. I will have duplicates in the proper size made at Borsen's.

Katrin was about to scribble a question as to how he knew she'd been standing all day, but then she looked down at her feet.

They were unrecognizable, swollen into disgusting sausage shapes. They were beyond pain – they were numb.

Menders set the stool used for climbing into the high bed in place and handed her up, then gently massaged her feet until some feeling returned. Katrin's eyelids drooped. She was exhausted.

Menders drew the covers up over her, then removed all evidence of her dinner and water having been brought in. She watched him in the feeble light of the single candle on the table. He could be at home, at The Shadows, seeing to it that she was provided for. She turned on her side, finding sparse comfort in the coarse sheets and scanty pillow, enormously thankful to have him with her.

Katrin came to wakefulness moments later when she realized Menders was bedding down on the floor. Clearing her throat to catch his attention, she gestured for the paper and pencil.

My father does not sleep on the floor, she wrote emphatically, moving over against the wall. Menders smiled and sat on the edge of the bed, taking the paper and pencil back and writing just as emphatically. He handed the paper to her, holding the candle so she could see the penciled words.

Everything is all right – sleep well, little princess.

Menders took back the paper, placed it in a pocket, smiled back at her and blew out the candle. Just before she slept, she felt him settling himself beside her on the bed. She smiled. It had been a long time since she'd had a visitation of the blue frogmouth, the nighttime terror of her childhood imagination, and run to climb into bed with Menders.

His presence comforted her as she fell into sleep.

***

Menders let himself into Borsen's house to find Kaymar and Ifor sitting in the lounge. Borsen was stretched out on the sofa, asleep. Kaymar rose silently, following Menders into the kitchen, where their voices would be muffled.

"Stevahn slipped him something at breakfast," Kaymar said quietly, putting a skillet on the stove and rummaging in the cool box. "He's absolutely tormented about Petran being arrested and no word of whether he's alive or dead. He hasn't slept well in months."

"I wish you'd let me know," Menders said, wearily removing the water flasks from his pockets and rinsing them at the sink before refilling them.

"Cuz, you've had enough grief. If I thought he was in danger, I would have informed you. Stevahn had talked him around to going to Surelia for a while just when this all blew up. If this goes on much longer, it might be a good idea to make him go." Kaymar slung a steak in the hot pan. Menders saw that a pan of mashed tarmon root and another of gravy sat on the back of the range, keeping warm.

"It might indeed. I was horrified when I saw him," Menders answered, sinking down in a chair at the kitchen table. "Where's Varnia?"

"Out at the market. Stevahn's coming home around noon to check on Borsen and see if there's anything we need. How do you want this steak?"

"Cut off its horns, wipe its arse and put it on a plate," Menders replied, his stomach growling audibly. Kaymar snickered and turned the meat over.

"How's Katrin?" he asked.

"Remarkably calm, though terrified," Menders sighed. "Right now, Aidelia's entertained by making her stand for hours and taunting her. Katrin can hold her at bay for a while but there is no guarantee of how long Aidelia will remain interested."

Kaymar forked the steak onto a plate and added two generous dollops of tarmon root and gravy before he handed the plate to Menders.

"Aidelia tires of entertainment rapidly," he said, taking a chair at the table as Menders tore into the food. "She's always looking for something new. It's always sadistic."

"I'd guessed," Menders grunted.

"She's stupid though," Kaymar continued. "Katrin can probably stay ahead of her but if Aidelia goes into a tantrum, anything can happen. Katrin has to be warned about that."

Menders nodded, shoveling food nonstop. He'd been ready to faint from hunger and was furious with himself for not having provided enough for Katrin to have breakfast.

"Any ideas as to who is manipulating Aidelia?" he asked once the ache in his stomach had diminished.

"There are a couple of them, as far as Bartan can tell," Kaymar answered. "He says one fellow has been around for a while. Big, dark hair, hangs right on Aidelia. Bartan says he's sleeping with her. He has his own Court that's formed around him."

"I can't risk poking around myself," Menders said, scraping up gravy with a piece of bread Kaymar cut from the loaf for him.

"No – you mustn't," Kaymar agreed. "Right now, it's imperative to keep Katrin safe."

"Let me finish this and then we'll sort out plans for different contingencies," Menders said. "I also have to find …"

Borsen cried out in the lounge. Ifor spoke immediately, calming him.

"It's all right, Borsen. You're at home. Menders is here, having something to eat. Can you go back to sleep? No? Well, sit up then."

Menders closed his eyes.

"Let us see to him," Kaymar said quietly. "It's been going on for months and he's holding up all right. You have to concentrate on Katrin. She's in immediate danger, Borsen isn't. No-one is going to get to him so long as we're here. Even if they got past us, they'd never get past Stevahn, who's a bulldog when it comes to protecting him and is a better marksman than any of us, yourself included. He's got a shotgun behind the cabinet that would cut a platoon in half."

Menders did not reply.

"Menders, you have to focus," Kaymar said abruptly. "Get your heart out of it or you're going to make a mistake that can't be salvaged."

Menders drew a deep breath, and then another. Then he nodded and continued to eat.

***

You will have to stay ahead of her, Menders wrote, as Katrin sat wearily at the table in her miserable room at the Palace. *She can turn deadly if she goes into a tantrum, so you must avoid this.*

Katrin nodded. She'd eaten, but it had done little to revive her. Aidelia had kept her kneeling for hours. Every muscle in her body ached.

Menders had rigged a way to keep the room door closed from within, a device that wrapped around the doorknob and then around the doorframe. It gave Katrin a feeling of security to know the door couldn't be flung open.

Menders nudged her and pushed the paper, on which he had been writing again, under her nose.

Katrin, I need you to be alert. I know you're tired and afraid, but right now you're the person who can get the information I need.

"What information?" she mouthed silently.

Who is around Aidelia. Their names, who seems to be manipulating or influencing her. Physical descriptions. Observe the times they're here, see if there is a pattern of absence and presence. What clothes they wear. Try to hear what they're talking about and remember it, so you can let me know.

Katrin felt a spark of interest. She had been mentally exhausted by the tedium of the day, where she'd knelt or stood for hours without food or water. This would be something to occupy her mind.

Now, why don't you get ready for bed and get some rest, Menders wrote.

It was the best thing she'd heard all day. She hurried to bathe and change while Menders gathered the papers they had written on and the scraps from her dinner. He'd brought enough food this time so she could have breakfast in the morning. That would help. It had been a long, hungry and thirsty day.

Suddenly she thought of something, pulled her nightgown over her head and turned to him, getting his attention.

"What about you? Have you had dinner?" she mouthed.

He smiled and nodded. "Don't worry about me," he mouthed back.

"How is Borsen?" she mouthed. Menders tried to hide it, but concern showed on his face. He took out paper and pencil again.

Strained, he wrote. *One of his employees has been arrested and he's very upset about that – and he and Stevahn are under threat, as you know. He's holding up well for now, but it's hard on him.*

Katrin sighed and nodded. She had not known that people had been arrested on little or no charge during the time since Aidelia had been crowned, but it had become painfully obvious to her now from what she had overheard during her hours in the Throne Room.

Suddenly she felt mortally tired.

THE PALACE, ERDAHN, MORDANIA

3
THINK OF THE SHADOWS...

Dearest Eiren, my darling Little Bird,

Please forgive me writing in haste, but I need contact with you after this week past. We're all well, so be at ease about that. For the moment, Katrin is holding her own against Aidelia and seems to be safe. Bartan keeps an eye on her during the day. I would like to send Kaymar in, but it is too risky for him. I stay with Katrin at night and have devised a way to secure her door. I bring food in to her, so she doesn't risk eating anything provided at the Palace.

Borsen looks terrible. There has been no word about young Petran, his men's hatmaker, who was arrested suddenly a while back. As you know, Borsen is far from a disinterested employer, and the young man in question is not much more than a boy. He is the only child of a widowed mother and the bonded of Hermann Evanov (Borsen's fat man). Even Bartan has not been able to get information about him. Many nancy men are being arrested on trumped up charges or no charges at all.

Stevahn had arranged to go to Surelia, out of harm's way (he is far more frightened for Borsen than he is for himself, so like him), but his father has become seriously ill. His life is not in danger, but he will not be able to take over at the bank for some time. Stevahn is unable to leave and Borsen refuses to leave him here alone.

So far, we're playing a waiting game, trying to find out who is manipulating Aidelia. Katrin is feeding us a lot of information and we're working on a plan to end this situation once and for all.

Please write immediately, as Kaymar will be returning here after delivering this to you and picking up some things Katrin and I need. Tell me some wholesome and pleasant gossip, whose baby has just said "howgah", how the garden looks, what you are reading. In this vile atmosphere, I desperately need to know there are places where life is otherwise.

I love you,

M

Darling man!

It was such a relief to see your handwriting! I knew you were all right – Kaymar has been keeping us informed very regularly, but still, knowing you wrote that letter has worked like a tonic on me.

I am sending as many things as I think Katrin can use, including some additions to the list you sent. I am also sending some more things for you, including some black clothing Tomar ran up quickly, so you'll have a change. I'm including a few of your favorite books. I know you don't have a lot of time to read, but perhaps they'd help.

I only wish poor Katrin was out of that place and safe! I can hardly bear to think about the poor young man from Borsen's who has been arrested. No wonder Borsen is suffering so – he cares so much about the people who work for him. I wish he and Stevahn could come to The Shadows for a while, but with Stevahn's father unwell, I imagine that would be impossible.

Here all are well. My mother has been a bit under the weather, but it doesn't seem to be anything serious. Planting is over. The gardens are particularly beautiful this spring, with all that rain we had over the winter. The lanar tree blossoms are stunning and their fragrance is delectable.

Vil and Petra's little girl is the next to say "howgah", though she hasn't quite managed it yet. She's very bright and alert and I keep her for Petra while she's working, when I'm not at the school. It helps to have such a little bit of innocence around, chortling and clamoring to be picked up.

I miss you so. I hope you find a way to help Katrin soon, so you can both come home.

Your loving wife,

Eiren

***

Hemmett sat at Stevahn's desk at the Rondheim Bank. He and Stevahn had just arranged for his will, a sensible precaution in his current situation. The bulk of his possessions and investments would go to Luntigré and Flori, his military death benefits and pension would help to support his parents and specific mementoes to everyone else.

He was a practical man and years of military training had made him realistic about death. He hoped the weeks to come wouldn't see him dead, but it was best to be prepared.

Right now, he was stealing a few private moments to write a couple of letters in what had become an endless routine of surveillance, running errands back and forth between Erdahn and The Shadows and attending endless planning meetings.

My darling Luntigré

A note today to let you know everyone is still as well as can be. Endless stalemate here, with Katrin still held at The Palace, Menders there all night and most of the day as well. Borsen looks like he's being drained by a vampire and I wish Stevahn would just spank him soundly and drag him off to Surelia.

That's rotten of me. My temper is quite short these days. I hate seeing Borsen so frightened, yet staying where he's in danger. They can't go at the moment anyway – Stev's pa is still very sickly so Stev is stuck at the bank.

I'm sure you've guessed, but I must give you the bad news that I cannot be there for Flori's tenth birthday. Things are very critical, with Katrin under the current Queen's control. Much is afoot, and I am deeply involved. Can say no more, my lovely lady. You know.

I am sending Flori's birthday gift and a letter for her along with this upside-down letter where I haven't been courteous enough to ask how you are and what you are doing. Let me know and please forgive my being so gamfoozled, sweetheart. I wish I could be there. I do much better in person.

When this is over I will come there and take you and Flori somewhere wonderful. I always keep my promises.

I love you and the joy you bring,

Hem

A happy birthday to my darling daughter, Flori,

I'm sure Mama has explained that I cannot be with you for your celebration this year. There is a serious situation here that requires me to stay – otherwise, even Demon couldn't keep me away. I have sent your present along as well, but you cannot have it until the big day! No begging Mama for it early, now. Yes, I know all about you!

Sometimes, Flori, soldiers have to make hard choices and obey orders that keep them away from the people they love. This is where we are now. Auntie Katrin and Grampy need me here to help them. You are old enough to understand that sometimes countries are not run by the best of people. Mama can help you to understand what is going on here far better than I can in a letter.

On your birthday, I want you to have a wonderful time and eat an extra piece of pastry for me. Write back to me to let me know if the present I've sent is what you wanted. Give Mama an extra hug and kiss from me too.

Above all, little girl, I want you to know how very proud I am that you chose to make me your Papa all those years ago. I am very, very proud of such a lovely and clever daughter.

So much love,

Papa

A tap at the door heralded Heldstrom, the Rondheim's trusted eyes and ears.

"Sorry to interrupt you, Captain," he said, taking off his hat respectfully. "I'll need your messages now – I don't have much of a margin to catch the ferry to Samorsa."

"Just finished, Heldstrom," Hemmett said cheerfully, as he squelched down the regret and worry that writing the notes had touched off. "I have a parcel as well – a birthday present for my daughter, Flori. Don't give it directly to her or she'll have it open too early."

Heldstrom laughed.

"That little one is a caution," he said. "Last time she was here, she had Stev and old Mister Rondheim sliding around on the polished floors in the lobby in their stocking feet, pretending they were skating."

Hemmett laughed aloud.

"That sounds about right," he said.

Heldstrom opened the office door, looked out into the hallway and then closed it again, locking and bolting it. Hemmett stood and went close.

"Borsen and Stev need to get out soon," Heldstrom whispered rapidly. "The Mad One has been asking questions about Borsen. I've already let Stev and Mister Rondheim know."

"Thank you," Hemmett whispered. "I'll talk to Menders, see if we can get Borsen to The Shadows at least."

"All right then, I'm off. Shame you have to miss the little girl's birthday party."

"Soldier's life," Hemmett managed jauntily, seeing Heldstrom out.

***

For two weeks, Aidelia delighted in toying with Katrin, alternately humiliating and tormenting her. Katrin's daily regimen might consist of standing humbly behind Aidelia's chair or kneeling abjectly at her feet. She might be forced to sit with the rest of the court to watch a boar-baiting, dogfight or cockfight, these being among Aidelia's favorite entertainments. Several times Aidelia became very lascivious and would circle Katrin, touching her and rubbing against her, giggling dementedly the entire time.

At other times, Aidelia would pinch, gouge, slap or scratch her. She had grown her nails very long and filed them sharp to match her repulsive teeth. The lacerations she left when she scratched festered, no matter how carefully Katrin bathed them as soon as she was in her room. Katrin was in constant terror that the infection she'd battled for so long would return because of the new injuries.

During it all, Katrin behaved as though she was honored and grateful to attend her sister's court. She accepted all punishment as if it was richly deserved. She pretended to watch the cruel boar-baiting or cockfighting while concentrating on memories – The Shadows, playing on the swing with Hemmett when they were children, riding with Menders, teaching the little ones at Eiren's school, the time the family had spent traveling through the Middle Continent.

Having achieved this level of detachment from the debauchery of Aidelia's court, Katrin was confident she could stand anything that was thrown her way. Then, at the beginning of her third week of captivity, Aidelia and her perverted hangers-on gathered in a room to watch a torture session. Katrin was horrified as several of the Palace Guard dragged a young man in and strapped him to a table. Aidelia and her freakish Court were already agitated, madly kissing and rubbing against each other even before the torture began.

Suddenly, one of Aidelia's courtiers sat down beside Katrin. She was trying desperately to make herself blind and deaf, desperately calling up her memories as the torturer went to work and the young man began screaming.

"What bothers you so, pretty little sister?" the man asked, leaning against her. He was heavily perfumed, to cover up the stench of an unwashed body. Katrin nearly gagged and was grateful for the distraction. Working not to vomit made her less aware of what was going on right in front of her.

She said nothing. She was terrified of the man, who was Aidelia's favorite and called himself Prince Talbreth. Anything she said would go straight back to Aidelia.

"You find this entertainment too sophisticated for you?" he asked, as the screaming grew louder.

The poor boy was crying for his mother! Katrin thought she was going to go mad and looked around, unbelieving, at the freakish band who were thoroughly enjoying the spectacle. Two of them were rutting in a corner already. Aidelia was cackling and rocking in her chair, her blackened, pointed teeth like the maw of something horrible that lived deep in the sea.

Katrin suddenly simpered at the man, taking a good look at him. It was the closest she'd been to him and she wanted to be able to give a good description to Menders.

"It's very new to me," she whispered coyly. She took in his greasy black hair hanging to his shoulders. Several golden teeth gleamed in his scummy mouth as he grinned at her and started to run his hands up and down her body.

She wanted to pull away, but a brainstorm had come to her.

If she could distract Aidelia's attention this way, perhaps her sister would lose interest in the torture session and focus on her. She knew by now that Aidelia was extremely possessive of this slimy courtier, with his false title and vile smell. It might cut the torture short before the young man was dead.

Katrin tried to look as if she was being aroused by the man's groping, fetching up a stupid, vacuous giggle.

"At first watching such a display can be unnerving, but given time, one becomes inured to the fuss made by the victims and can begin to concentrate on the subtle pleasure of seeing the pain inflicted," Prince Talbreth murmured unctuously. "It's best, when one feels pangs of conscience to say, 'what care I?' and let such inconvenient thoughts fall from your mind."

Katrin managed to act as if she was being given pearls of wisdom.

"It must take a great deal of experience to have such control over unwanted thoughts," she cooed.

"Indeed, my pretty one. Experience I would gladly share with you." He leaned toward her mouth and she wondered if she could endure him kissing her without being ill.

"Enough!" Aidelia shouted. Katrin started and the slimy courtier snapped away from her. Katrin saw Aidelia glaring in their direction. The torturer stood as if frozen and the screams from the young man died away to moans. At least he was still alive!

Prince Talbreth rose and went immediately to Aidelia, simpering over her and stroking her grease-matted hair. It worked. She didn't go into a tantrum, but took his arm. They walked from the room, the Court following in their wake. Aidelia gave Katrin a furious look over her shoulder before she went through the door.

Katrin waited until the room was almost clear and then addressed the torturer, who was unstrapping the barely conscious young man from the table.

"What of this one?" she asked arrogantly.

"He'll live to entertain you another day, my lady," the torturer said obsequiously, heaving the young man into a sitting position.

Katrin wanted to fling herself at the torturer. She wanted to gouge his eyes out, slash his throat and somehow get that young man and herself out of this horrible place!

She kept her face haughty and bored, nodded magisterially, and followed the rest of the Court.

***

Menders faded into the deep shadow beside the wardrobe in Katrin's room. She was coming down the corridor with the rude maidservant. He waited while they came in and Katrin allowed the girl to loosen the fastenings of her dress and corset before going out and thumping the door closed.

He stepped out of the darkness as Katrin sank down on the wooden chair and put her face in her hands. She began shaking uncontrollably.

Menders placed the paper and pencil before her.

Torture, she wrote. *A young man, barely more than a boy. They said he committed treason. They were all rubbing and kissing each other. I tried not to see, but tonight I couldn't do it. He was screaming for his mother.*" She retched violently.

He took the pencil from her.

You must put it from your mind.

"I can't," she mouthed.

"You can," he mouthed back. Then he wrote, *you must – or you will be destroyed by it.*

Katrin shuddered, staring bleakly at the wall. She retched again. Menders cast desperately about in his mind, trying to think of anything that would help drive the horror from her mind.

Remember The Shadows, he wrote rapidly, pushing the paper under her nose. He knelt and put his arms around her.

Katrin sighed and leaned into his embrace. He rocked her gently, stroking her hair. After a moment or two, he could tell she was gaining control of herself.

Can you describe the young man? Menders wrote. Katrin closed her eyes for a moment and then took the pencil.

Very young and blond. Blue eyes. Medium frame, she wrote. *I tried not to look. I'm sorry. Why do you want to know?*

Understandable, Menders wrote back. *I was wondering if he might be Petran, Borsen's hatmaker. It sounds like him.*

"Gods," Katrin whispered, closing her eyes again. Menders squeezed her shoulder and then set a food packet in front of her. She shook her head, but he gave her a little shake. She had to keep her strength up.

She sat up, determinedly opened the packet and then drew the paper over to her.

I think the courtier who is influencing Aidelia the most is the one who calls himself Prince Talbreth, she wrote. *He sat next to me during the torture and tried to kiss me, gave me a bunch of sickening nonsense about being able to enjoy watching that poor boy being tortured if I was sophisticated enough. I tried to draw him on, hoping Aidelia would see and get angry and go away before the boy was killed. It worked. She did see and stopped the torture. I asked the torturer if he was alive and he said he'd live to be tortured another day.*

She shoved the paper away from her in disgust. Menders picked it up.

"He's alive?" he mouthed rapidly when he was finished, staring at her. Katrin nodded, wearily.

Menders took her shoulders again, then put his mouth by her ear and cupped a hand around.

"You must never do anything like that again," he whispered, a mere breath she could barely hear. "You cannot risk your safety. Aidelia has killed people in her tantrums."

"It stopped the torture," Katrin mouthed.

Menders shook his head at her and then indicated for her to finish eating. Once she had, he put his mouth to her ear again.

"Watch this Prince Talbreth," he whispered. "Don't let Aidelia see, but let me know everything he does."

Katrin nodded.

***

Katrin dreaded a repeat of the torture session the next day, and was surprised when word went round the Court that dozens of fighting cocks had been delivered to the Palace that morning. Several nights were taken up in watching the resulting cockfights, until all the birds were dead. Menders kept asking her about them, until she realized he was behind the anonymous delivery.

The morning after the pathetic birds had all expired, fighting dogs were delivered, wild, fierce beasts that frightened even Katrin, who had been around enormous dogs all her life.

Katrin found that Prince Talbreth was taking credit for the gifts of fighting cocks and dogs. She reported this back to Menders, who said nothing. When the dogs were gone, several large boars for boar-baiting were delivered, providing more of Aidelia's favorite sort of entertainment.

Katrin knew the deliveries of the doomed animals were an attempt to divert Aidelia's attention from the young man who had been tortured and from herself as well. Menders' fears were realized – Aidelia was jealous after seeing Prince Talbreth snuggling up to Katrin. It was a dangerous position to be in.

Five weeks from the day Katrin had been arrested, Aidelia demanded to see her alone.

"You bore me, Sister," Aidelia said sulkily. "You seem to be very limited."

"It grieves me to disappoint you," Katrin said. You disgusting idiot, Katrin thought.

Aidelia was lounging on the Ruby Throne, where she spent most of her time.

"I had thought to find you more entertaining, but the sophisticated pleasures of the Court seem to be beyond you. It is a pity. I had hoped to share all this with you, but most of the time you seem to be uncomprehending. You're stupid, as well as fat and countrified."

"I do appreciate the opportunity to be here," Katrin said humbly.

"Well, you won't burden my staff any longer with your endless demands," Aidelia snapped. Katrin nearly fell down – could she be sending her home?

"Though you're deadly dull, you have tried to behave yourself, and deserve some reward," Aidelia went on. "You will be moved to a suite and your staff from the country will come here. They can take care of you in the manner to which you're accustomed – but remember, when you're summoned to me, you will appear appropriately. Otherwise, live quietly and draw no attention to yourself, until such time as I find use for you. Most of all, stay away from the other members of my Court. You are not to speak to any of them!"

Aidelia got up and clanked down the steps from the Throne. She began circling Katrin, looking her up and down.

"Yes, perhaps I can think of a way that you can be entertaining. I remember you being entertaining once, very entertaining, when you hung from the ceiling like a spider. If you were entertaining, you would be of some use."

Please, Katrin thought, please, please don't let her start panting and drooling. I don't think I can bear it.

Aidelia was requiring more and more extreme spectacles to achieve the level of excitement and arousal she craved. The debauch of cockfighting, dogfighting and boar-baiting that the anonymous gifts of animals had provided was palling. Now Aidelia was craving something stronger.

"Maybe it's time a consort was found for you," Aidelia ranted on. "That would be a lovely spectacle."

Katrin managed a stupid smile while screaming inwardly at the images Aidelia's words were causing to incarnate in her mind. Aidelia's chosen "consort" would probably rape and torture her while Aidelia's Court looked on, giggling, panting and rubbing against each other, with Aidelia herself rolling her eyes and drooling from an excess of arousal.

"But then, you might have a child and that would be a threat to my throne," Aidelia continued, coming around Katrin from behind. "Country girls with big teats fall pregnant very easily. I'm surprised you haven't been so yet for all the years you lived out there snugged up with your minder. They say he's had his way with you all your life, you know."

Katrin allowed herself to look mildly surprised.

"I don't understand, Sister," she said in the soft, innocent voice that sometimes caught Aidelia off guard.

"No, you're far too stupid," Aidelia said, seeming satisfied at her summation. "I have no use for you today. Go to your room and prepare to be moved to a suite tomorrow."

Katrin sank into a deep curtsy and backed away, leaving her sister alone. Then she flew down the corridors as fast as she could, not stopping until she reached the wretched room she'd tenanted for weeks.

Menders was there, though he often wasn't during the day. She secured the door and gestured for the paper and pencil, but Menders spoke.

"No-one is listening. Keep your voice low."

"They're moving me and they're sending for you and the others at The Shadows," she replied.

"I know," he whispered.

"How do you know?" she began, but he shook his head. He would tell her nothing.

"This isn't a reprieve," he told her.

"At least you won't have to sneak in and out," she answered.

"No, but you must be careful – more than careful, Princess. Now she's tiring of you, so you are in more danger than you were when she was enjoying tormenting you."

Katrin said nothing, and Menders finally said, "Tell me."

She repeated Aidelia's words about a "consort" and then the reneging, where Aidelia mentioned that Katrin might fall pregnant. She left out Aidelia's repulsive intimation about Menders. She couldn't bring herself to tell him that.

Menders remained impassive.

"There is nothing we can do about this today, but you must be very much on your guard. You must be of interest to Aidelia. So long as she feels that you're entertaining, she won't begin thinking of getting rid of you."

Katrin said nothing. She would have to stop being a stupid little girl from the country.

***

Stevahn was just on the edge of sleep when he heard it – footsteps, loud ones, downstairs. He jerked into wakefulness, looked rapidly at Borsen, who still slept but turned and murmured restlessly.

After a moment, Stevahn could breathe again. It wasn't an intruder. It was Hemmett, pacing. Again. Wearing his boots.

Stevahn hoisted himself from the bed, feeling every weary bone in his body. He pulled on his dressing gown and hurried out, wanting to stop the racket before Borsen woke. It had taken ages to get him calm enough to sleep after an attempt to bribe the Palace jailer to release young Petran Borghel failed.

Borsen's fragile health was shattering. Any sleep he managed was light and restless. Desperate, Stevahn had resorted to slipping a sleeping potion into a glass of water that he pressed on Borsen. He'd then held him close until he heard the slow, steady breathing that signified deep sleep.

Stevahn went to the ground floor of the townhouse and spoke to Hemmett, who was engaging in his new habit of pacing and wringing his hands.

"Hemmett, please, Borsen just went to sleep," Stevahn said, trying not to sound annoyed.

Hemmett turned and instantly flushed red.

"Gods, I'm sorry," he apologized, using his toes as bootjacks, prying his boots off. He set the enormous offending footwear against the wall. "I don't even realize I'm doing it."

"Not to worry, he didn't wake," Stevahn replied, mightily tempted to swallow the same sleeping potion himself. He hadn't been sleeping any more than Borsen lately, between worry about his father's health, worry about Katrin, the danger of being in Erdahn at all with Aidelia on the throne, and of course and most of all, worry about Borsen.

"Hemmett, I desperately need to get some rest myself. If I take something, could you stay on guard for me?"

"Guard is my middle name," Hemmett grinned. He looked haggard and worn too. He wasn't sleeping much either – to be expected, with Katrin in such danger.

"Thank you," Stevahn said gratefully, going toward the kitchen to dose himself.

The front door opened quickly, and Menders rushed in.

"Hemmett, we have to get back to The Shadows," he said briskly. "Aidelia is having Katrin moved to a suite and her household sent for. The messenger just went out by train. We need to get to the boat so we're there when he arrives."

Hemmett began pulling on his boots.

"This means less danger?" Stevahn asked anxiously.

Menders shook his head.

"So long as Aidelia is alive, Katrin's in grave danger," he replied. "This means we'll be able to be with her openly. Hemmett and I will be staying in the suite with her. It will make access to the Palace and Aidelia much easier. We'll be more aware of what is going on and better able to protect Katrin. Hopefully I will be able to get a look at this Prince Talbreth character and I might be able to do something for Petran Borghel."

Kaymar let himself in.

"I heard," he said, cutting off the beginnings of explanations. "If you don't need me to go with you, I'll stay here. Stevahn and Borsen shouldn't be alone. Ifor's already down at the boat, getting up steam."

"We'd best hurry," Menders said. "With this sudden shift, the gods only know what Aidelia is going to do. Bartan has Bertel and Klausen at the Palace now, so Katrin is as well guarded as she can be.

"Stevahn, it's best we get all this out of your house – safest for you. I'd like to say good-bye to Borsen and let him know what's happening." Menders was rapidly gathering up dossiers from the table and handing them to Hemmett.

"I'm sorry, I dosed him. He's sound asleep and I doubt you could wake him," Stevahn explained.

"Good. I'm glad he's asleep," Menders nodded, though Stevahn could see regret in his face. "I'll talk to him when I get back." He went to Stevahn and put a hand on his arm.

"Take care of him," he said very softly, then turned and went out into the street, Hemmett behind him.

Stevahn turned to Kaymar.

"So, what does this mean?" he asked.

Kaymar leaned against the kitchen table.

"Katrin made Aidelia jealous to distract her from the Borghel boy being tortured," he said quietly. "Apparently Aidelia's swain was trying to snuggle up to Katrin. Aidelia must have been stewing over it and has decided to get Katrin out of the way. Unfortunately, this means that Menders and Hemmett will be within Aidelia's reach, but at least they'll have some freedom of movement. Menders isn't likely to let Eiren come here. The danger is too great. You can be sure most of Menders' Men will come back with him. The more people they can get around Katrin, the better."

Stevahn felt himself becoming stupefied by exhaustion, by the need to lie down and let go and sleep for a few hours.

"What are they going to do, Kaymar?" he asked suddenly. "This can't go on forever."

"There's only one thing to do," Kaymar answered. "I don't want to spell it out right now and you look ready to drop. Take whatever you gave Borsen and go to bed. I had a full night's sleep down on the boat. I'll keep watch here."

Stevahn was too weary to consider what Kaymar thought was the only thing to do. He poured out a dose of ramplane, knocked it back and climbed the stairs to the bedroom. He climbed back into bed and snuggled up to Borsen's back, looping an arm over him. He smiled as Borsen pressed back against him in his sleep and mumbled something in Thrun that sounded loving.

***

Eiren was trying read student essays, but it was impossible. It had been several days since anyone from Erdahn had been to The Shadows. She was sick with worry over Katrin and Menders and was concerned about her mother as well, as she was failing to pick up after a recent bout of illness.

Suddenly she heard Menders' voice downstairs. She stood so quickly that her chair clattered over onto the floor. She fled out of their suite and down the stairs, throwing herself on Menders where he was standing in the entry, talking to Haakel.

"Ah, there's my girl!" Menders said, trying to sound hearty, catching her in an embrace so strong she thought she would never breathe again.

"I'll get right on it," Haakel said, kindly leaving them alone.

"What's happened?" Eiren asked when Menders finally put her down and smiled at her. His face was hard, though he was trying to hide it.

He explained about Katrin's household being sent for. Eiren was elated.

"Good! I can pack in no time…"

"No," Menders interrupted. "You must not come with us."

"What?"

"Let's go upstairs," he said, taking her arm.

Once in their suite, Menders sat on the edge of the bed and looked at her.

"Desperately as I want you with me, my darling, I can't let you come along," he said. "It's incredibly dangerous. Aidelia could order us all put to death the moment we get there. Worse, she could get hold of you and use you to get at me – or the person who is controlling her could."

"What if I came in very quietly, dressed as one of the Men?" Eiren asked desperately. She had not seen Menders for weeks. To think of him turning around in a couple of hours and going again, without her, was unbearable.

"Eiren, they started to torture a young man to death the other day, as entertainment. It's bad enough that Katrin's in danger of that. I can't take you into such a situation. I wish I didn't have to take Hemmett and the Men, but I need them."

"Oh, my gods," Eiren whispered.

"Yes – if they got hold of you…" Menders' voice shook, but he rapidly gained control of himself. "You're safer here, though not entirely. It might be necessary for you to go back to your father's house. I'll send word if that's the case but I'm hoping it won't have to be." He unbuttoned his shirt and shrugged it off.

"What are you going to do?" Eiren asked, knowing he wouldn't answer.

"I can't tell you. Hopefully it will be soon," Menders replied, looking up at her. Then he held out his arms. "We have a few hours. Help me think of anything but mad Queens and boys being tortured to death."

THE PALACE, ERDAHN, MORDANIA

4
"IT HAS COME. THERE IS NO STOPPING IT"

Living in a suite with Menders and Hemmett was a great relief to Katrin. Menders had brought along all the assassins who were part of Menders' Men, dressed as servants. Katrin was never alone and Aidelia's lack of interest was evident, as there was no question about why Katrin's household servants were all male.

Katrin's senses and emotions seemed blunted. Being surrounded by so much madness, chaos and filth was taking a terrible toll on her ability to concentrate. Menders seemed distant a good part of the time. He kept Hemmett busy running errands and wandering around the Palace. Menders told Katrin nothing of what might be planned or what they might be working on, only asking that she give him all the information she could on the rare occasions where Aidelia sent for her. He always reminded her to keep Aidelia interested.

Katrin no longer pretended to be a country bumpkin and was relieved when she saw renewed curiosity in Aidelia's eyes. She began providing answers to Aidelia's tirades that were more than gentle and humble acquiescence. Sometimes she imitated Aidelia's eye rolling and other mannerisms, as if she admired and wanted to emulate her half-sister.

She even deliberately drew Aidelia to be angry with her, watching as she grew excited with the heat of rage. Then Katrin would become cringing and abject, begging Aidelia to forgive her while her half-sister rained slaps and kicks on her like a three-year-old in a tantrum. It kept Aidelia occupied. So far Katrin had been able to defuse the rage before Aidelia screamed for her to be taken to the dungeon.

It was a deadly and terrifying game. Katrin, upon returning to her rooms, would frequently fall directly into bed and huddle there, hoping Aidelia would forget about her for a while and leave her alone, let her be with those who loved her. Her longing for The Shadows was palpable.

***

Menders perused the information spread before him on the table of his safe house in Erdahn, one where he'd never lived but which was used as a nexus for Menders' Men. Then he looked around the Men who were with him – Hemmett, Bertel, Klausen, six others. There were more at the Palace with Katrin, who was asleep after another exhausting day. Aidelia had returned to forcing her to stand and kneel for hours at a time. Katrin was also keeping Aidelia's interest by deliberately provoking her. It was a difficult line to walk, straining Katrin's inner resources to the limit.

Menders had deliberately kept Katrin out of the planning he and Menders' Men had done. He knew she felt he was being distant. It was better that she know as little as possible, not only for her own peace of mind, but in case she was pressed for information. He hated doing it, but ignorance might be her only hope, should the worst come to the worst.

For Menders, that had already happened. He had a document in front of him, intercepted by Bertel just that day. It was a warrant for Borsen's arrest. There was no more time to gather information or plan – action must be taken now. Someone in Aidelia's Court knew of Borsen's relationship to Katrin.

The warrant having gone astray would give Borsen enough time to disappear into Surelia. Menders had seen him onto a ferry that afternoon. Stevahn and Varnia were going on the night boat with Magic, after arranging for an absence from their townhouse. At least Borsen wouldn't be alone, though he would be cut off from knowing what was happening to Katrin and the rest of them.

"All right," Menders said. "We're out of time. Tomorrow afternoon, Katrin is removed from the Palace and brought here. We move tomorrow night."

He looked around the table. It was pointless to go through the plan again.

"If we fail, get out of there. We'll get Katrin out on the boat, and evacuate as much of The Shadows as we can, because if we fail, The Shadows will be attacked. Everyone there is aware and ready to move on the signal."

They all looked back at him, not one face showing fear or doubt.

"We can't afford to fail, gentlemen," Menders said.

***

Katrin started when she was abruptly summoned to attend Aidelia in her private rooms. When Hemmett tried to follow her, he was prevented by the Palace Guards who had come with the message.

"Don't worry, I'm well looked after, Captain," Katrin said with false cheer, forcing a smile. Her eyes met Hemmett's for a moment. She left with her two grim escorts.

It was a hot day. Katrin closed her mind to the stench of Aidelia's rooms, trying to ignore the mingled odors of smoke, spilled and vomited wine, the musty stink of the bed, which hadn't been changed in gods knew when. Aidelia, for once not wearing the bejeweled formal gown, was lounging about alone, her inner circle of perverts apparently elsewhere, probably trying to escape the heat. Her face was a mass of pimples and sores from her continual use of thick white makeup. Her lips were suppurating from the festering wounds inflicted by her sharpened teeth.

"I've planned some surprises for you, Sister," Aidelia said lazily. "I've sent for some people you know, to come to Court to entertain us."

Katrin kept a smooth façade while a volcano erupted inside her. Aidelia's idea of entertainment was well known to her.

Aidelia was slobbering on.

"You never told me we had acquired a little cousin," she drawled. "When I was given that information, I was very interested indeed. I've sent a little invitation to him, so I can get to know him. I'm sure it will be very entertaining."

Aidelia was staring at Katrin, licking her cracked lips hungrily.

"To think he's been living right in the same town with me, and I was never informed that he was a relative," she slurred through a grotesque smile. "I feel very hurt about that. After all, we're such a small family now that our dear Mamma is gone. I think you meant to keep your little Borsen all to yourself, greedy little sister. He grew up with you out at your farm, I hear."

Aidelia gave Katrin a look to let her know an answer was expected.

"Borsen has always wanted to make his own way, Sister," she replied, keeping her voice low. "He didn't wish to take advantage of his close relationship to us, but sought success his own way. He never wished to impose, particularly once you became Queen."

"I understand he lives nearby too. So rude, never to visit family," Aidelia went on as if Katrin hadn't said a word. "He lives with another man. Is our cousin a nancyboy, Sister? You know how I feel about them. I should have them both here for a visit, don't you think? You'd like to see them, I'm sure."

Katrin's head spun. She tried to think of anything she could say to help Borsen.

"Once I heard about this cousin, I began to understand why you're so soft and weak," Aidelia continued. "If your minder, that freak who raised you, surrounded you with such people it's no wonder your mind is so feeble. He will have to be called to account for failing to produce a proper Heiress for the throne of Mordania.

"I've seen enough to make up my mind. Your minder is a traitor for failing to follow a Royal Command. You know what that means. He will be executed by torture – and the rest of your household as well. Perhaps even the people out on your farm."

Katrin tried to speak but when she opened her mouth, no sound came out.

"You don't like that, do you Sister?" Aidelia whispered.

She heaved herself up from the sofa and started to circle Katrin. Suddenly, without the formal gown, Katrin saw that Aidelia was pregnant, at least in the sixth month.

"That's right, Sister – I'm expecting my Heiress," Aidelia sniggered. "You won't be the Heiress much longer. You'll be only a stupid country cow with no purpose. Once this bundle arrives, you will be – removed. Permanently."

Suddenly inspired, Katrin said "May I congratulate you on your pregnancy," with a gleeful smile.

Aidelia looked startled and then preened a little. Katrin could see that she was drunk and having trouble concentrating. She'd already been diverted from talking about executions. Katrin could see Aidelia was trying to recall her train of thought, so she helped derail it further.

"It's terribly hot, Sister," she cooed. "Can I get you something to drink?"

"I want wine," Aidelia said. "Be my maidservant, Sister. Fetch me wine." She turned back to her sofa, her pregnant body awkward and bulky.

Katrin went to the table where her half-sister's ever-present wine was stored – right near the brimful chamber pot. Her mind was racing. She must get away quickly, to find Menders and let him know what Aidelia was planning. If she could get Aidelia to send her for more wine – perhaps it was sour? But no, Aidelia would drink almost anything. It would have to be absolutely foul for her to reject it.

Katrin looked around. Her eyes fell on the chamber pot.

She could see Aidelia reflected in the glass of the decanter. She was lying on the sofa again, her eyes closed. A half-snore let Katrin know she was not paying attention.

Katrin rapidly dipped the rim of the wineglass into the chamber pot, scooping up a portion of the contents. She filled the glass with wine and carried it, a picture of sweet sisterly caring, across the floor to Aidelia.

Aidelia woke from her drowse with a snort as Katrin proffered the wine.

"I fear it smells off, dear," Katrin said in a honeyed tone.

"I like it sour," Aidelia slurred, taking the glass and sipping. Her lip curled.

"It's foul," she snapped, flinging the glass across the room. "Go get some that is better."

"Should I fetch the steward?" Katrin asked abjectly. From the smell on Aidelia's breath, she'd been drinking for hours. She was having trouble staying awake.

"No, fetch it yourself. You are to serve me from now on. Without your household, you will need to earn your keep here as part of mine, for as long as I let you live. Get me some fresh wine and bring it back quickly."

Katrin curtseyed deeply and left the room. The two Guards who had accompanied her from her suite were not there. The corridors were practically deserted, with only a drowsy looking page here and there. The Palace echoed with silence.

She raced down the halls toward her own suite, her mind whirling.

The mad bitch meant to kill Menders, Borsen, Hemmett, everyone at The Shadows as well – and she was pregnant. Gods knew what sort of monster she would bear and create, raising it at Court the way she had been. Aidelia had spoken of killing everyone Katrin loved in that final tone that meant this was something she would not forget, as she forgot so much else. She was wandering in her mind now because of the wine she'd drunk, but she would remember and give the order.

Katrin found her suite empty. Her heart plummeted. She ran from room to room, but Menders, Hemmett, Menders' Men were nowhere to be found. Aidelia had gotten to them already! They'd been arrested while she'd been playing cat and mouse with Katrin. How to help them?

Suddenly, Katrin remembered walking on the beach at Leptham with Menders – she had been fifteen years old, and learned that if she became Queen of Mordania, she could change the way things were.

If she was Queen of Mordania, she could free Aidelia's prisoners. She could free Menders and the rest of the people she loved. She did not want to be Queen, she had never wanted it, but if it would save them … how to become Queen?

Katrin bit back gushing tears and grabbed a decanter of wine from a tabletop, knowing she had to get back before Aidelia became impatient. Then she slowed and stopped, still as a statue.

Then they came, the voices. The Queens.

It is the time of sacrifice! Show your strength, daughter of Mordania! You must tip the scales. Act! Now! If you fail, Mordania will run red with blood! Self must die! You must sacrifice yourself! Now! Now! Now, my daughter, now! Show your mettle, girl! Now, my beloved daughter!

Katrin was not a country girl for nothing. She knew the uses, good and bad, of many garden plants. She knew the plant growing outside the windows in great profusion. She knew it well. Ramplane.

Given in small quantities, it brought on sleep, relieved pain and fever. Given in large enough quantities, it would kill a grundar.

Not allowing herself to flinch, she went to the window, reached low to remove the fleshy leaves from a place where it would not show and then crushed them against the lip of the decanter, watching as the thick, gooey sap ran down and mingled with the wine. When there was half again as much sap as wine, she shoved the mangled leaves into her pocket.

Katrin turned to the honey pot used at meals, drizzling the golden sweetness into the mixture in the decanter. She clapped the stopper into the neck and shook the entire concoction viciously before running back toward Aidelia's rooms, the image of servility, eager to please, hurrying as quickly as she could with what her sister had demanded.

Aidelia was groggy but groped eagerly for the wineglass Katrin proffered.

Katrin felt her breath come short as her sister gulped down the entire glassful without drawing breath and gestured for more.

"It's excellent," she slurred as Katrin poured more wine for her. "You must give me a few bottles."

"Gladly," Katrin smiled.

Aidelia finished the second glass before her head drooped onto her chest. Katrin caught the glass and set on the floor. Aidelia slid down onto the sofa in a deep sleep, her breathing unnaturally slow and shallow.

Then the breathing stopped.

Katrin waited several minutes, then felt for a pulse. There was none.

She took the decanter with her, leaving the room quietly, calling over her shoulder for her sister to sleep well while easing the door shut. She walked decorously back to her suite. Once she was unobserved, she raced to empty the decanter out a window, then washed it out carefully. She refilled it with wine and replaced it on the table.

Then she sat down, exhausted, shattered.

Menders and the others were safe.

She was the Queen.

She was a murderer.

***

Menders never hesitated to take advantage of a situation. When he found most of the Court were absent, attempting to escape the heavy, wet heat of the day by traveling away from the city, he sent Hemmett and Menders' Men in to capture and lock up those Palace Guards who were on duty, as well as the Palace torturer and the Queen's Chamberlain, whom Aidelia had inherited from her mother.

Hemmett told him that Katrin had been sent to Aidelia. Once Menders was sure there were no Palace Guards they had not secured, he went to Aidelia's apartments to fetch Katrin and take her to the safehouse he'd arranged. Aidelia could do her worst. If she confronted him, it would only speed matters, as this was going to be the last day of her life.

He listened briefly at the doors of Aidelia's rooms, then eased them open an inch and listened again.

Not a sound – not so much as breathing. He was sure Aidelia had been left behind by her favorite and her Court. He'd seen them leave in a train of carriages that morning, bound for someone's country house. Aidelia, who of late had been drinking and sleeping through the long summer days, had not been with them. They were not expected to return until night, when the temperature would drop rapidly.

He opened the door and went in.

Menders had seen death many times and needed to make no examination of Aidelia to know her condition. He was shocked to see that she had been pregnant. Even his intense information gathering had not given him that tidbit.

Suddenly he remembered his long illness when Katrin was just a baby, which had spread from infected eyes – and the medicine he'd been unable to take to lower the fever and ease the pain, ramplane. He cast about for a reason why this memory had cropped up – then he knew.

He could smell it. Ramplane. Faintly, but definitely. It was stronger near Aidelia. There was an empty wineglass on the floor near her. He picked it up and sniffed.

Yes, someone had already killed the mad bitch. But the Palace was practically deserted. Whoever it was had taken away the ramplane and wine mixture, but neglected to take the glass or rinse it. Definitely an amateur.

Menders stood there, the glass in his hand, a horrible knowledge dawning within him.

***

Katrin sat limply in her deserted suite, in what seemed to be a deserted Palace. She hadn't heard a sound since leaving Aidelia's rooms, not so much as a word or footstep.

She knew that sooner or later they would come and say, 'long live the Queen'. She didn't know if she could stand that.

She would have to. Her first Royal Command would be for them to release Menders and the others. Until they came, she would sit here, as she had been sitting for the hour since she'd killed her sister, desperately trying to will herself to move.

Just then she heard rapid footsteps. The door of the suite banged open and then shut and the bolt was shot. Then Menders was in the doorway.

He pulled off his glasses so she could see his eyes, staring at her with such an expression of anguish that she jumped to her feet.

"What in the name of the gods have you done?" he said in a tone she'd never heard from him before. He crossed the room and grabbed her by the shoulders, shaking her slightly. His eyes were streaming tears from the light. "Child, what have you done!"

"I've done what was necessary," she heard herself saying.

"That was not for you to do," he answered, his voice shaking with emotion. "You were not intended to have blood on your hands. I never intended you to have blood on your hands or the guilt in your heart. It was for me to do murder, never for you."

Katrin stared at him, seeing the horror and despair in his eyes.

"She was going to kill you," she cried. "She had sent for Borsen to be arrested and she said she was going to have you and Hemmett and everyone else executed by torture! I managed to get away from her to come and warn you, but when I came back here you were all gone! I thought she'd already had you arrested!"

She dropped into the chair, unable to stay on her feet. "There was no time. I did what I had to do! I made the sacrifice!

"Don't look at me like that, Menders!" Katrin heard her voice going high. Tears were close, but she couldn't stop staring at him.

"I knew about her planning that!" he replied. "Borsen and Stevahn are already in Surelia, they're safe. I was coming to get you and take you out of here."

Katrin felt herself being destroyed by the look of desperation and despair on his face.

"I didn't know you knew about it – I didn't know, Menders! You never told me anything and I was alone!" she gasped.

He turned away, unable to meet her gaze any longer.

"I will never forgive myself," he groaned, his voice deep with grief.

Katrin clung to the sides of her chair with her hands, dizzy with horror.

"It didn't hurt her," she said in a very small voice. "She just went to sleep. She wasn't afraid. She didn't even realize what was happening."

He didn't answer, standing with his back to her. Katrin held onto her chair and shook with shock and misery. The tears she'd refused to shed during all the weeks she'd been in the Palace were spilling out now. She could no longer hold them back.

"I don't want to be Queen," she finally gasped. "You know that. I never did. I want to live at The Shadows with you and Eiren and Hemmett and everyone else. I killed her to save you, not because I want to be Queen."

He kept his back to her. She could see him clenching his fists.

"Menders, I can't bear if it you don't love me anymore!" she finally wailed.

He turned to her and she understood why he wouldn't turn around before – he, too, was in tears. It wasn't because he despised her. He came to her, knelt before her, and took her hands.

"You have my eternal love, my little princess," he said huskily. "I never intended for you to bear the murder of your sister. You've once again precipitated me."

"Do you think I'm as bad as she was?" Katrin asked, staring at him, her breath coming short.

"You killed her for the purest and most unselfish of reasons. She killed for pleasure. Answer your own question, Katrin."

His answer, his slightly sharp tone, made her tears slow. It made her think.

"And you still love me?" she asked.

"You know it. I grieve for your loss of innocence and I love you." He kissed her hands. "Can you forgive me?"

She could only answer, "Can you forgive me?"

They both smiled at the same time.

"Now hurry, there might still be time to get you away," he said, rising to his feet. "You don't want them to declare you Queen, not now, and they can't if you're not here…"

Just then there were shouts from the direction of Aidelia's room. Menders went to the door and looked out, replacing his glasses on his nose.

"The Council!" he gasped. "Why would they be up here?"

"They come up when they need a signature. She never goes – went to the meetings," Katrin said weakly.

She knew it was too late to run.

Destiny, one she did not want, had drawn even with her. No matter what she did, it would not be denied. She had chosen her sacrifice out of love. The thing she had most feared all her life would come to pass.

"Hurry!" Menders cried, grabbing her hand and pulling. "We can still get to Bartan's rooms…"

Katrin looked up and met his eyes.

"It has come," she said softly. "There is no stopping it."

Menders had his mouth open to protest but then drew a deep breath and nodded.

"Yes, I know," he answered, just as softly. "I am so sorry, my little princess. My little golden girl." He looked at her, his expression full of regret and love.

Then Menders went slowly down on one knee, arms extended out to his sides, head inclined in the most formal Court bow.

"You have my unswervable fealty, Your Majesty," he said quietly.

Katrin shuddered at the words Your Majesty. Then she stood and gave him her hand as a signal that he could rise. His fingers tightened on hers and he drew her into a strong embrace. She threw her arms around him and held tightly to him.

Thundering, floor-shaking footsteps rushed down the corridor toward the suite, an inexorable tide. The Council was hastening to make obeisance to the new Queen.

Menders put her away from him as the pounding on the door began.

"We must let them in, Katrin," he said.

Katrin drew herself up. She knew she looked dreadful, tear streaked and red-eyed. They would think she was mourning the death of her sister, the news brought to her by her retainer. That would be the official story.

Menders had taught her well. She straightened her spine, held her shoulders back, and took a deep breath.

Queen. Queen and sacrifice.

"Open the door," she said.

THE PALACE, ERDAHN, MORDANIA

5
"THAT'S THERBALT!"

"Katrin, stay here in the suite," Menders said. "No matter what you may hear."

He looked significantly at Eiren and Franz, who had been sent for as soon as Katrin was declared Queen. They had just arrived by the steam launch. Not long after them the Court had returned in the late summer twilight. Menders' Men and Hemmett's Guard met the courtiers and sent them directly to their quarters.

"I'll see to Petran," Katrin answered, trying to smile.

Smiling didn't come easily. It had been a terrible afternoon and early evening. She had ended up roaring orders to release all prisoners to a Council obviously unaccustomed to obeying Queens. Then poor, young Petran Borghel had been brought to her rooms by her command, while Aidelia's other prisoners were released to go to their homes.

The young man's condition was dreadful, though Franz said he would live with good care. Petran kept grabbing and kissing Katrin's hands anytime she was near and would become disconsolate if he couldn't see her.

Katrin knew what Menders was going to do. She wasn't going to think about it. She didn't want to know.

***

Hemmett stood in the doorway of a room he had seen only once before.

His brown eyes roamed over the hooks and wires from which Katrin had been suspended. They fell to rest on the bloodstains on the floor, which hadn't been cleaned in the years since she was tortured here.

He felt fury, pure and hot, surging inside, reaching all the dark places in his mind, cleaning them with the intensity of flame.

His sword rang in the silence as he pulled it from its scabbard and turned to go join the others.

***

Menders looked at his assembled soldiers – all of his Men brought over from The Shadows the day before, all of Hemmett's Guard. With them were Bartan and two of the Palace Guard who had been at the Military Academy with Hemmett and had proved themselves loyal during the past weeks, doing much to ease operations and to keep Katrin safe, at great risk to themselves.

They'd been busy through the long afternoon and evening, meeting the returning Court members and escorting them to their rooms, locking them in. Bartan had let Menders know which ones were in Aidelia's group of confidential courtiers. They were given extra guards. No-one was permitted to leave the Palace.

"You know who to target," Menders said. "All the freaks Aidelia kept around her. I want Prince Talbreth in particular. Bring him to me alive, if at all possible. He's not back yet, so Villison is going to watch for him. Deal cleanly and quickly with the rest of them."

They dispersed rapidly, in pairs. Menders was left alone and then set out for his own destinations.

He let himself into the chamber of the Palace Guard Commander who had arrested Katrin and refused to let her dress properly or bring anything with her. The man had been held in his rooms that afternoon by none other than Corporal Villison and a very large gun. Now he sat sullenly, glaring at Menders.

"Now," Menders said, in a very quiet and reasonable voice, "You have one minute to explain why you didn't allow a young woman to dress properly when you arrested her."

"I have no need to answer to you," the man replied firmly.

Menders drew a long knife from its sheath and made sure it flashed in the light. He had the pleasure of seeing the soldier swallow nervously.

"Imagine how that girl felt, in that thin dress and nothing else, being taken by you and your men," he said companionably. "You didn't show her the least bit of mercy. No-one would have known if you'd waited for ten minutes to let her dress herself and put on proper shoes, but you refused to allow her that much decency. Now that young woman is Queen. What do you think of that?"

The man went pale and started to speak.

"No, no, no, you're out of time," Menders said kindly. He swung the knife in a rapid arc, neatly slicing through the bull neck of the Commander as if he'd cut through a flower stem. He left him, still spouting blood, and went to visit the Palace torturer. Then he would be paying a social call on the Queen's Chamberlain.

***

For an hour, there were muffled cries and screams and the occasional gunshot as the members of Aidelia's inner circle were removed, along with others Menders knew would be a threat to Katrin later. Menders' Men and Hemmett's Guard moved with speed and precision, eliminating one courtier after another, including many who had at one time or another been involved in plots against Katrin's life.

There was no sign of the courtier who called himself Prince Talbreth. Menders had begun to suspect he'd gotten wind of the day's happenings when there was a clatter of hoofbeats in the Courtyard. Then Villison ordered someone out of their carriage.

There were sounds of a scuffle, then a shot and a cry – Villison's.

Hemmett was already halfway to the door when the courtier known as Prince Talbreth raced into the Palace, contrary to anything anyone could expect. He made a sharp right turn and fled toward the stairs leading to the dungeons.

Kaymar bellowed, "That's Therbalt!" He grabbed a halberd from a rack of weapons and raced after him.

"It's just me arm, Hem, get him!" Villison roared in the courtyard. "Right in me Watch the Lady arm! Bastard!"

"I want him alive!" Menders shouted, running after the tide of Men who were pursuing the large man.

Talbreth plunged into the stairwell and could be heard leaping from one flight to another over the bannisters. Kaymar, unable to move that quickly with the halberd, dropped it with a clang that echoed up through the staircase over the thunder of dozens of men's feet on stone steps.

The pursuit ended in a hall that was a dead end. There was no sign of Talbreth by the time Menders got there. Kaymar and Ifor, along with half a dozen of the other men, were desperately pushing and shoving at the wall.

"It's a damned hidden door he's gone through!" Kaymar groaned.

"It'll lead down to the ocean from here, go, go!" Menders roared to the rest of them, who went full tilt for the staircase again. He tried along with Kaymar and Ifor to find the hidden apparatus that would cause the nearly invisible door at the end of the hall to open, but had no luck.

"That bastard is the one who was after Eiren years ago," Kaymar panted, finally giving up and leaning against the wall. "The one who set DeLarco on us. Therbalt."

"Shit!" Menders hissed, studying the door again. It would take hours to sort it out, and likely Therbalt or Talbreth or whoever was long gone down a hidden passage or stairwell.

"Best go see to Vil," Ifor reminded them in his deep slow tones. Kaymar and Menders started guiltily and moved for the stairs, hurrying back upwards and out into the Courtyard, where Doctor Franz was crouched beside the little corporal, who was more angry than anything else.

"Hells, it's hardly in there, Franz, just squeeze the bastard good and stand back, the bullet will pop right out," he was griping. Hemmett crouched on the other side of Villison's wiry body, looking exhausted. There was blood on his uniform. Not all of it was from Villison.

"We'll take you inside and do things right," Franz said with some amusement.

"Bastard came out of that carriage shooting and then ran right over me, put his damn big foot right in me shoulder," Villison raved.

Hemmett looked up at Menders, who shook his head.

"We lost him, some damned secret stairway," he sighed. "Turns out he was an old friend. Therbalt."

Hemmett groaned and stood up.

"All right," Franz said. "Hemmett, could you carry Vil in for me, please, take him back to Katrin's suite? I need to see if I can get that bullet out of him."

"'Ere, let me sit up first, I don't fancy bein' lifted like a fairy princess in a dead faint," Villison groused, heaving himself up from the ground. Hemmett hoisted him easily and went off into the Palace.

Menders looked at the carriage in disgust. The driver had obviously fled during the chaos. The horses were frightened, showing the whites of their eyes.

"Ifor, can you see to these horses?" Menders asked. "Kaymar, the bodies in The Palace have to be removed and disposed of. I don't want any of them found. It's as if they never existed. Has everything been done?"

"Yes," Kaymar answered quietly. "The Men are filtering back. They aren't going to catch him. I'll get them started on the rest of it."

"Thank you." Menders turned and walked into the Palace to see to Villison.

6

WHEN WE'RE GROWN, WHAT SHALL WE BE?

Borsen sat at the table overlooking the vineyards of Menders' house in Surelia, watching the sun set.

He'd been here for five days with no word from Erdahn. Despite his worry over everyone involved, he had finally been able to sleep decently. He felt much less fragile and shaky. Though still worried about what was happening at home, being away from the continual fear and strain was a blessing. He could draw a breath without feeling his tense muscles creak.

Stevahn walked out on the verandah and came over, putting down a plate of cheese, butter and bread provided by the new housekeeper, who bent over backwards to do everything she could to make them feel welcome. She was quite a contrast to Madame Spinta.

Borsen had to smile, remembering how Katrin had drawn herself up in majesty and confronted that particular she-dragon. The smile faded, as he wondered what was happening in Erdahn and if she was all right.

Stevahn sat down.

"It's hot, but it's peaceful," he sighed, reaching for the bottle of wine on the table. "I've just talked to Karlen and Varnia, who walked down to town. No word of Mordania in the newssheets."

Borsen sighed, but not with contentment. He wished he knew something – anything. The not knowing was the reason why he had resisted coming here for so long, though he had to admit seeing his name on a death warrant was enough to make wings grow on his feet.

"I have to assume that something has happened, because I know Uncle was going to make a move," Borsen said. "Just what, I'm not sure. I've been half expecting he and Katrin will drive up at any time. I know there was a plan to get her out of Mordania altogether."

Stevahn shook his head.

"I haven't expected it," he said. "I was privy to more than you were, I'm afraid. The plan was to eliminate Aidelia but with Katrin where she couldn't be declared Queen."

"I guessed that," Borsen said. "That opens another can of worms with a Regent determined to eliminate the Thrun and Katrin too, since she would be a threat. I just wish we knew something."

"Me too." Stevahn sipped his wine and looked over at Borsen.

"You aren't sitting there feeling guilty because you're out of it, are you, light of my life?" he asked.

"You know I am," Borsen answered, looking directly into his eyes.

"Don't. You did all you could, to great detriment to yourself. You proved yourself a very brave man," Stevahn said. "I didn't say anything at the time, as you had enough weighing on you, but I was incredibly proud of how you stood up to it all."

"And here I thought I was a fainting violet through the entire crisis." Borsen couldn't help smiling.

"Because you showed the strain? We all did. Last time I saw Menders, he looked like Grim Death himself. Borsen, you don't have the constitution the rest of us do, despite your ability to walk on your hands and shoot the eye out of a fly at a hundred paces. Pressure is always going to affect you. You gave your home over to operations that, if they were found out, would have resulted in you being tortured to death. You risked everything you have. Day after day of not knowing if each minute wasn't going to be your last – that wasn't an easy thing to bear, and you bore it well. Pappa was bragging about you just the other day, when I went to tell him we were going. Said he'd never known anyone so gutsy. His very own words."

"Dear Pappa," Borsen laughed. "He just thinks I can fly because I'm so nice to you."

"Courage isn't always charging up the Promenade with a sword and hacking off heads," Stevahn laughed. He fell silent as Borsen sat up straight and sniffed.

"What?" Stevahn whispered. He'd learned to trust Borsen's senses.

"I think we're about to be invited to play a game of Watch the Lady," Borsen said, smiling and slumping back in his seat in relief. At the same moment, Stevahn smelled what Borsen had moments before, a peculiar cigar smoke.

"Evening, gents," Villison said as he sauntered around the corner of the house and came up the verandah steps, one of his favored cigars, a rare and expensive brand, in his mouth. His right arm was in a sling and he looked a bit pale, but was obviously in good form otherwise. He pulled up a chair and sat as Stevahn reached to the sideboard for another wineglass.

"Come on, Vil!" Borsen said impatiently.

"All are well," Villison said. "Katrin's declared Queen."

"What? Uncle was going to get her away so that wouldn't happen!" Borsen cried.

"Yeah, I know it, but Katrin bolluxed everything. She panicked and killed Aidelia herself, poisoned her with ramplane," Villison said.

"Grahl's Teeth!" Stevahn muttered. Borsen stared.

"Aidelia threatened to kill Menders, you, Hemmett and everyone else and then sent Katrin back to her suite for wine. When Katrin found the suite empty, she thought everyone had been rounded up and put in the dungeons. Knew there was no way out but to put Aidelia down, so she did.

"The Council was in a meeting and needed Aidelia's signature, went up and found her growing cold, ran down the hall and declared poor Katrin Queen. Of course, some of that is Menders' fault, as he kept her in the dark about the plans, hoping it would protect her. Hells, there's no way to know the best way to do these things. What would've happened if Katrin didn't become Queen – it would still be just as dangerous and as big a mess, with her in danger as well as everyone else."

Borsen groaned with frustration, but knew Villison was right. There was no happily-ever-after answer to the situation, no matter how you looked at it.

Arden, Villison's little boy, ran out onto the patio.

"Uncle Borsen!" he bellowed, throwing himself on Borsen's lap. Borsen was one of his favorite people.

"You're getting so big," Borsen laughed. "Brought the whole family?" he grinned at Villison.

"Got meself wounded in the cleanup operations," Villison grinned back, brandishing his arm. "Turns out that Prince Talbreth was an old friend. Same fellow called himself Therbalt, the charming gentleman who sent DeLarco after the lot of you, as well as those two women who tried to kill Eiren and Katrin. I tried to get him out of his coach and he shot me in the arm, then ran over me – with his feet, not the coach. His boots did more damage than the bullet, cracked me collarbone. So, I'm sicked out. Ere, son, don't grab at the food like that, you've been raised better!"

Villison snapped the fingers of his good hand resoundingly. Arden immediately stopped shoveling cheese into his mouth and smiled winningly at his father, who shook his head, trying to suppress a smile.

"So Petra and the baby are here with you as well?" Stevahn laughed, reaching for a small plate and arranging a snack for the young fellow, who kept admonishing him to pile on more.

"All of us, taking a bit of a family holiday until things are more settled and I'm of use again," Villison replied. "They don't need me with all the Guards and Menders' Men crawling around the Palace. I'm glad for the rest. Even minor gunshot wounds aren't pleasant and cracked collarbones let you know you're in pain every time you breathe. Ol' Vil's more than ready for a rest cure."

"I've missed you, Uncle Borsen," Arden declared, between mouthfuls of cheese and bread. "You haven't been to see me in a long time."

"I'll have to make up for that," Borsen answered.

"I want you to make me a coat," Arden said. "A red one, with the big gold B on the inside."

"I'm sure I can manage this," Borsen grinned, resting his chin on the top of Arden's curly head, winking at Villison, who rolled his eyes. Arden had no idea that what he was demanding would cost anyone who was not "family" a small fortune – but Borsen would deliver the little coat gladly and free of charge, complete with the monogrammed B on the lining that identified it as his own hand work.

"Good. I'll need to be measured. I've been growing again, though I shall probably stop for a while so I can be sure to wear the red coat a lot," Arden said, holding out his plate to Stevahn to be filled again. He was firmly convinced that he could start and stop his growth at will.

"All right, me boy, that's enough from you," Villison laughed

"We'll go ahead and plan to go back," Borsen said, but was surprised when Villison looked pensive.

"Fellows, listen to Ol' Vil here a bit," he said after a moment. "I stopped in both your places of business before coming on over. I have messages for both of you, but your seconds assured me that all is well and they can hold the fort for a while. Katrin is refusing to have a coronation, so there isn't going to be any sudden rush for clothes at your place, Borsen. Your Pappa is up and around and able to stop into the bank for a while every day, Stevahn, so you're covered there if the markets start to go wild, which it doesn't look like is going to happen. Take a week. Let the dust settle."

Borsen raised an eyebrow and waited. It was obvious that there was more, but you didn't rush Villison.

"My meaning is this," Villison said after he'd puffed on his cigar a few times. "Menders has his hands full with what's going on. Katrin isn't happy, but she's giving it a good try. Give her a little while with just herself and Menders working on the situation. It's a mess, as you can imagine. Having too much family around right now – not good. It would distract her, and she needs to adjust. The less distraction, to my way of thinking, the faster she'll get over being upset about everything, and get on with business.

"Oh, hells, I nearly forgot, that youngster works for you, Petran? He's alive and going to be all right."

"Thank the gods!" Borsen burst out.

"That was right in my ear, Uncle Borsen," Arden groused. Borsen hugged him in apology, feeling ashamed that he'd forgotten to ask about his employee.

"Yeah, sorry I didn't mention it. Katrin had him released, all the prisoners that Aidelia had taken too. He's hurt, but nothing that won't heal in time. He's back home with his Mamma now and your fat man, Mister Evanov. Looked very perky when I checked on him on me way to the boat."

"So you see," Villison went on, "I think a bit more time to recover wouldn't be bad. And not to be rude, but you're far from your usual bloomin' image, Borsen. You've had a rough time. Be good to yourself."

"Yes, and you could shoot a snake for me, so I could have some snake shoes too," Arden added. He had been well tutored in the saga of Borsen and the viper.

"'Ere, don't you be worrying about the snakes here, they're not like the little friendly fellows we've got back home," Villison laughed.

"I'm full, let me go see Mama," Arden demanded, clambering down and running away into the house.

"So, what'll it be, gents? Gonna take Brother Vil's advice?"

Borsen and Stevahn exchanged a look. After a moment, Stevahn nodded.

"I don't think we need to be involved in what's going on at the Palace right now," he said slowly. "We've always been a step away, having lives separate from The Shadows and now the Palace. I'd like to keep it that way."

"It's best," Villison said. "That's why I always stayed a step back too. I love all those folks like life, don't get me wrong. I think the world of Menders and I'm devoted to the service of my Princess, but it's not a good thing to be sucked in and become a royal hanger-on. You've got a nice life. Keep it that way. You can see plenty of them, but you don't have to be inside it."

"A little time away sounds good enough to me," Borsen said.

He was gratified to see Stevahn smile to himself and relax.

***

"You asked me not to keep things from you," Menders said levelly, looking at Katrin, who was seated at the head of the table, surrounded by himself, Kaymar and Ifor, Hemmett and various of Menders' Men. "I'm doing as you asked. Your cousin Glorantha's father is a very real threat to you – to your life and to your throne. It is a situation that must be dealt with. We sent a man into his home to see what is going on. It's not good at all. Kaymar?"

"I had young Marius go in as a manservant," Kaymar said to Katrin. "The girl is twelve years old, as we know. She's been raised in the good old Mordanian way, including toughening. She seems fairly bright but very beaten down. She always wears red dresses cut to look like the Queen's formal gown. Her father constantly talks about Mordania needing a real Queen and has pushed the poor child toward that all her life. There's even a little red throne that he has her sit on when they have guests."

Hemmett grimaced in disgust.

"We've been over all this before. If Glorantha came to the throne now, not being of age, her father would act as Regent," Menders said, picking up the thread of conversation. "He is known to be one of the main proponents of exterminating the Thrun. It is also very likely he would not tolerate an abdicated Queen, no matter how sincerely you tried to convince him that you don't want anything to do with the Throne. He's one of the biggest war profiteers in Mordania and has been a major supporter of all the wars in recent history."

"He has been known to talk about eliminating Aidelia, and before her, your mother," Ifor said quietly. "It's inevitable that he will consider eliminating you. Since Glorantha is your Heiress, he will be more motivated than he was in the past. He has the money and the power to support an assassination. So far, he's biding his time. We're watching him and his connections."

Katrin looked around the table.

"What suggestions do you have?" she asked.

"The easiest and most certain route would be to have Glorantha come to Court as your Heiress, thus removing her from her father's influence. Then, eliminate him," Menders replied coolly.

"No! No-one else will die because I'm Queen," Katrin snapped. Menders sighed and ground his teeth.

"Katrin, unfortunately this sort of thing is a fact of life in royal circles," Kaymar said tiredly.

"No-one else is going to die. I won't order it and I don't want you men going behind my back to do it," Katrin declared. "What else do you have to offer?"

"You could get your own Heiress," Menders said, the coldness of his voice making her look at him fearfully.

"What do you mean?" she asked, the snap gone from her voice.

There had been a nasty confrontation between them two days previous that ended in Katrin blaming him for her situation. It had been painful for both of them. For once, Menders didn't feel particularly forgiving. He readily admitted keeping her out of his plans had been an error, but when she'd ignored his apology out of frustration and anger at being in the situation she'd never wanted, he'd gone cold and distant.

Making matters worse, Eiren and Franz had been abruptly recalled to The Shadows. Bad news had come back. Eiren's mother was seriously ill with one of the internal rots that killed its victims slowly and painfully. Franz predicted that it might take two to three years before the disease killed Marjana Spaltz. Most of her remaining time would be a pathetic torment of pain, illness and increasing debility.

Menders was deeply grieved by the news and understandably wanted to be with Eiren, helping her through the coming ordeal – but he was bound to stay with and help Katrin as well.

Katrin suddenly turning on him had angered him deeply. He was in no mood for more of the self-pity and blaming of others that she had been engaging in since the shock of her ascension to the Throne wore off.

"I mean that you can have a child who will be your Heiress," he explained quietly. "Then Glorantha will be bumped out of that position. Of course, that would mean her father would have designs on your child, but you don't want him eliminated, though it would be an excellent thing for Mordania if he was."

"I – I might not be able to have a child," Katrin replied in a small voice.

Menders knew it. Her cycles had never returned to any sort of regularity after her long illness. Franz had expressed doubts as to her being able to bear children after the long infection of her womb. But she had asked for her options and he was going to give them to her. She was convinced that he had erred by protecting her from some of the harsh realities that went along with being a royal person, and he would err no more.

"You wouldn't know unless you tried," he said neutrally. "If you had an Heiress, your line would be secured."

"Can't I name one?"

"Yes, you can name someone who is not born of your body," Menders answered. "This has never held up historically, however – and it would be more reason for Glorantha's father to get rid of you, depose the Heiress you name, mostly likely by killing her, and then put Glorantha on the Throne so he could rule in her name. You know the rest."

"I can abdicate," Katrin challenged him, going mulish.

"Yes, you can. You would still be a target and the country would be handed over to Glorantha's father. Those are your options, Katrin."

He looked down at the open dossier on the table in front of him, desperate to control his temper.

Katrin had tried, he would give her that much. She had truly tried to take up the reins of governing.

She discovered, to her own and Menders' dismay, that the country had long since slipped completely out of the control of the Queen, between Katrin's grandmother's long final illness, the weak reign of her mother and Aidelia's short time on the throne. The Council ruled, and they considered the Queen a figurehead, someone to sign the documents they drew up.

When Katrin attended her first Council meeting, the Council members greeted her coolly, then completely ignored her. She asked for explanations a few times, tried to interject some comments and met with a stone wall of indifference. The members of her Council had no need of her and no interest in her opinions. They made this abundantly clear. It was even suggested that she not trouble with the meetings at all.

Worse, Menders found both the Council and upper Palace staff approached him, rather than Katrin, on official business, cutting her out of the equation with an attitude of "we men can deal with this and not bother the little Queen about such things". Despite Menders' insistence that they deal directly with Katrin, he met the same stone wall. The Queen was not a player at Court, had not been for decades and was not going to be again if the Council or staff had anything to do about it.

Menders had expected this to anger Katrin, with the usual result of her getting results through definitive action. Instead, it seemed to drive her into herself. She was deeply traumatized by the way she had come to the Throne and riddled with guilt over Aidelia's death and those of Aidelia's courtiers. Katrin didn't want to be Queen and she was dealing with the situation through withdrawal and inertia.

Menders realized his presence was intensifying the problem. So long as the Council and staff saw him as the dominant member of Katrin's household, they would never accept her authority. He would have to adopt a different bearing and appearance, for a number of reasons. He must appear harmless and innocuous, so he could undertake the covert work necessary to keep Katrin safe.

He had, after some thought and discussion with Kaymar and a few of the Men, cut off his long hair and cropped it close, shaved his beard and talked Borsen into making him several suits designed to make him look round shouldered, thin and twenty years older.

Borsen made no secret about being angry as hells over the project, but delivered what Menders asked for. Like all his work, it was very good. Menders didn't recognize himself in the dry, fussy, thin old clerk in an old-fashioned, high collared suit looking back at him from the mirror. A sagging of the spine and knees, a slackening of the upper back as well as a daily powdering of his hair completed the illusion that the Queen's Royal Advisor was a doddery old retainer who trotted after her like an elderly lapdog. In fact, the rumor went around that Katrin's childhood guardian had left the Court in disgust and been replaced with an older relative.

Menders didn't like his new appearance, to say the least. He hated the restriction of the tight padded jacket. But short of openly becoming the power behind the Throne with Katrin seen as nothing more than a puppet of her minder, he had little choice, other than leaving Katrin on her own. Considering her present state of mind, that would be a disaster.

Poor Eiren had been horribly rattled by the alteration in his appearance, though he'd warned her beforehand and explained all the reasons for it. Hair and beards could be grown back. It was a temporary measure to deflect attention to Katrin, where it belonged.

Pre-occupied with her mother's illness and the care of her father's household, Eiren hid her dismay over Menders' transformation as best she could and put a good face on it. Everyone was putting a good face on the miserable situation – except for Katrin.

The silence around the table was growing very heavy. Menders looked up to see that all the men seated there were glowering in Katrin's direction, while she was glowering at him.

"Those are your options," he said again with emphasis.

"I don't care for any of them. There must be another way," Katrin said.

"I can come up with nothing else," Menders said, meeting her eyes.

"You'll have to. These options are not acceptable. I am not going to have anyone else killed." She was dug in now, and would continue with the equivalent of yelling "isn't" every time he said "is". Further conversation would be pointless.

Something in Menders gave way. He stood abruptly.

"Of course there are other options!" he shouted. "You can go up on the damned Tower and jump off – there's one! Leave in the night and disappear, there's another! Go down and work as a prostitute on the docks, there's another! There are endless options, of course, all of them unacceptable. I've given you what I think would work.

"You want me to do the impossible, Katrin, which is to turn back the clock. If I could, I would, at least to the point when you had a chance to work through this in a reasonable way. When your sister poisoned your mother, I told you the best choice would be to eliminate her and then work out a way to abdicate without turning this country and the Thrun into a bloodbath! You chose to do then what you're doing now. You're refusing to take any sort of action and waiting for me to do something. Well, I am not the damned Queen, you are! I can't do what is necessary, only you can!

"Nobody in this country gives a damn who the Queen is, except the people in this room. Only you can make people care that you're Queen. You are not going to do that if you sit around being a spoiled child who didn't get the biggest piece of cake while we go around and around the same damned argument we've been having for months!"

Katrin was on her feet too, glaring at him.

"I didn't want this!" she cried. "I never wanted it! I've had my entire life taken away from me and I want it back!"

The silence after her words was crushing.

"I had my life taken away from me too, twenty-four years ago," Menders said into the stillness following her outburst. "Everything I worked for, everything I wanted, my chance to have a life of my own was taken away. I thought it was the end of my world – but I took what I was given and I made another life out of it. It took accepting the pain and disappointment and doing what needed to be done. It is pointless going on like this."

With that, he turned and walked out of the room, leaving Katrin with her mouth hanging open and tears welling into her eyes.

One by one, the men around the table stood and filed out. Only Hemmett remained where he was, arms crossed, looking at her. When the room was empty, he spoke.

"I was there, you know. I'm the only person here who was there," he said coldly. "A little boy can go places most people don't think to. I saw what Menders went through those first years at The Shadows, when it was a big, cold, dirty, empty house where the loudest sound was the big clock ticking. There was a place on the back stairway where he would go sometimes when he'd been chopping wood for hours. He would sit there in the dark, where no-one could see or hear him. Sometimes he would cry - not because he didn't get his own way but because he was bone tired and frustrated and lonely and had nothing in front of him but more tiredness and frustration and loneliness.

"After he'd sit a while, he would always get up, go upstairs to the nursery and pick you up. I could see that he felt better and stronger after he did. Even though he didn't want you when they gave you to him, he loved you. He was so in love with you. He was six years younger than I am now, commanded to be a nursemaid for the rest of his youth and he was still able to love the child whose care took his life away from him."

Hemmett stood.

"He's been what I've wanted to be, my entire life," he continued. "He's strong and he's good. Yes, he has his failings. He protected you too much. He can't read the future or do any of the other impossible things you seem to want him to do. He's just a man, not a god – but he's the greatest man I know. If you can't see that and appreciate every moment he's devoted to you at his own expense, then you should be ashamed, Willow.

"Now, I'm going to go down and pretend to guard this huge Palace where nobody ever comes. I'll do my job because I've sworn to do it. I learned how to persevere during those years at The Shadows, even when my only outlook is tiredness, frustration and loneliness. I learned that from our father. Obviously, in spite of you being the one of us who was so smart and who learned so quickly, you didn't learn that."

Hemmett walked from the room, his head held high.

Katrin looked after him for a moment, then wiped her eyes with her hand and gathered up the dossiers the men had left behind. It wouldn't do to leave them out for anyone to find.

***

"Reassign me, Menders."

Menders sighed and sat back in his chair, looking up at Kaymar.

"I understand why you want to go," he began.

"I'm not going to stay," Kaymar interrupted. "I don't want to leave off working with you, but I am absolutely useless here. I'm Katrin's official escort and bodyguard, but she never goes anywhere. Sixteen feet of stone wall is bodyguard enough. If she ever does decide to so much as go down the street to Borsen's, she has more than enough protection from the Palace Guard and Menders' Men. Now, I'm asking you to reassign me where I can do something other than standing around being useless, or I'll have to leave. I can't stand to watch what is happening, Menders. Let me do something useful."

Menders sat quietly for a moment, closing his eyes.

"I'm going to need a great deal of information," he finally said. "I can definitely use you to get it for me – both you and Ifor, so you won't be separated. I'd be very interested in expansion of our network in Surytam, building on what Willem has done so far."

"Thank you." Kaymar went to the door, then turned back.

"I'm sorry," he said.

"No need to apologize, cousin," Menders answered, his voice soft and tired.

***

"Menders?"

A sigh. "Yes, Katrin?"

She hesitated. Menders was sitting at his desk in his Palace office, his chair turned so he could look out the window. It was the first time she could remember him not sounding pleased that she was there.

He swiveled the chair around and looked at her over his glasses.

"What is it, my dear?" he asked, his voice more kind.

"I… I wanted to apologize for what happened today," she said.

"Thank you," Menders answered. Katrin sat tentatively in the chair opposite him.

"I was thinking. Maybe I would be able to get somewhere with the Council if I wore the formal gown," she ventured. "When you changed the way you look, it worked. Maybe they don't take me seriously because I haven't been wearing the proper clothing."

"It's a thought," Menders said after a moment. "Unfortunately, people accept what they see, and the formal gown is what the Queen is expected to wear."

"Can it be – cleaned?" Katrin ventured. "I can't stand to think of putting it on after Aidelia or my mother."

"I'm sure it can be arranged," Menders answered. "But Katrin, just wearing a dress is not going to change things. It's going to take bearing and attitude and determination. It's very hard to change things that have become entrenched. Mordania has not had an effective Queen in decades. Nothing is going to change overnight."

Katrin nodded. Then she shuddered.

"What about the teeth?" she asked. Menders grimaced.

"I would hope that wouldn't be necessary," he said. "You want to get their attention, but the dress should do that. In time, once you've gained authority, you could probably stop wearing the dress."

"I'd like to give it a try," Katrin said.

"I'll arrange to have the dress cleaned very thoroughly," Menders said. "Now, tomorrow I'm going to The Shadows. It's been three weeks."

"Oh," Katrin said in a small voice, feeling a cold shudder go over her. "How long will you stay?"

"I'll be back tomorrow night. I've never left you overnight, Katrin," Menders said, sounding surprised. "You can come along with me, if you'd like – then we could stay for a few days. I'm sure Grandmother would be glad to see you. There won't be many more opportunities as time goes on."

"I'll think about it," Katrin said, feeling panic rising in her throat. She stood up. "I'll think about it." She could hear her voice rising in panic.

"What is it?" Menders asked, rising as well. He looked concerned.

"Just – I'm just feeling jumpy," Katrin said, trying to smile. "I think I'm going to go rest for a while."

"Yes, it's been a difficult day," Menders said, watching her closely but managing to smile back. "I'll look in on you later."

Katrin hurried toward her room in their suite. She stopped in the lounge and poured herself a glass of wine, which she drank quickly. She followed it with another glass. She didn't care much for wine, but it made the rapid fluttering of her heart stop.

***

Katrin woke early the next morning, feeling energy she hadn't felt in months.

I'll get up and get dressed and go with Menders to The Shadows, she thought, turning over in bed and looking at the window. The sky was dark of course. It was winter, though the days were longer now that Winterfest was past.

She could hear Menders moving around in the suite, and caught a whiff of hot cloth. Apparently, he'd resorted to ironing a shirt for himself again. The Palace staff was so slack! She would have to do something about that, give orders that they start to do their jobs properly or be dismissed. It was ridiculous for the Royal Advisor to be ironing his own shirt before dawn! She'd give the orders as soon as they got back from The Shadows.

She sat up against the pillows and began to think about what to wear. She would just get up now and go to the wardrobe and see what to wear. It would need to be something warm, of course. It would be very cold out on the water and on the way to the boat. Too bad they would be going so early, because they might have stopped at Borsen's. She still hadn't gotten around to going there, though he came up the street three times a week to see her. She'd just been so tired…

She would just get up now and check the wardrobe for something to wear. It wouldn't be hard, just a few steps across the room and choosing an outfit. She had dozens though and it would take some time to get dressed, so she'd better get moving. Just a few steps across the room but how would she ever decide on what to wear? She would just need to get out of bed, and then it would be a few steps…

She was beginning to feel tired. Well, it was very early in the morning and it was so cold out. She hadn't really planned on going and it would take such a while to get dressed and have breakfast, and Menders was probably ready to go. She wouldn't hold him up this time. She'd sleep a little more and then she'd deal with the staff for being so slack – but without Menders there, who would send for them? She'd have to wait until he got back, so there wasn't much point in getting up right now. A little more sleep would do it. She'd feel more lively then.

Katrin snuggled down in the bed and was asleep again before Menders looked in to see if she was coming with him. He sighed and went on by himself.

***

"Yes, it's been troubling me for some time," Franz said, looking across his desk at The Shadows at Menders. "I'm fairly sure it's melancholia. Unfortunately, that is something we don't know much about. We don't know what causes it or how to treat it. There are some herbs that work in mild cases, and believe me, I've dosed Katrin with those already with no effect. It's a derangement of the mind, but it affects the whole body. In some people, it can be set off by a particular event, as it has been in Katrin. In other people, it seems to start for no reason at all."

"I know killing Aidelia was contrary to her entire moral code…" Menders began.

"It began before that,' Franz broke in. "After the Suspension Ritual and during her illness. It was mild then and I hoped it would disappear with returning health. To a degree it did, though she never recovered entirely."

"That was to be expected," Menders said. "Getting over injuries and an infection like that can take years. I didn't feel entirely myself for a couple of years after the infection I had when we first came to The Shadows."

"That's correct. Given time and support, Katrin should have made a full recovery, but the trauma of being arrested and held by Aidelia, and then killing Aidelia has triggered a major melancholia."

"What do we do?" Menders asked.

"Change of scene is recommended. Sometimes it works," Franz said. "I've tried every medicine I know of. I did it without her knowing, so she wouldn't try to please me and say that she felt better. You know she does that, of course."

Menders nodded. He knew.

"For some people, new challenges or interests help," Franz went on. "Being Queen could provide that, but it's a challenge she doesn't want and that she truly wasn't ready for."

"She won't leave the Palace," Menders said suddenly, surprising himself.

Franz stared at him.

"What do you mean?" he asked, his voice tense.

"She seems to be afraid. It isn't because she loves the place," Menders tried to explain. "She hates it there, but she won't leave. She hasn't even gone down the street to see Borsen's. She won't go riding in the grounds or go to the stable see her horse. She stays in the suite most of the time."

"What does she do while she's there?" Franz asked.

"Reads. Paints. She'll play DeGratz with me. Talks with Hemmett. Borsen comes trudging up the street three times a week to visit. Varnia comes a couple of times on her way to and from her various charities. Katrin looks forward to their visits. But any time I suggest she go out, even in a closed carriage, she seems interested initially, but then finds a reason not to go. It's too cold, it's going to be dark soon, she's tired, she feels a fever coming on."

"Does she have fever?"

"Not that I can tell. She gets frightened, starts to breathe quickly. I can see her heart pounding. She can't make decisions either – everything from what to wear to whether to abdicate or not."

"It's worse than I thought," Franz said. "She needs to get away from there right now. I wouldn't even suggest her coming here. She needs to go someplace entirely new. Coming here will re-ignite a lot of other memories and could make her even worse."

"How am I going to get her out of there if she won't go?" Menders asked in frustration. "I can't drag the Queen out of the Palace kicking and screaming!"

Franz said nothing, just lit a cigar.

"She did come to me yesterday and said that she wanted to wear the formal gown, hoping that would help get the attention of the Council," Menders said after a moment. "It's the first genuine interest she's shown in anything for a while."

"The vampire Queen gown? Menders, that could make things even worse, particularly for a young woman with Katrin's cosmetic sense."

"I know." Menders closed his eyes. "I'll try to see if I can get her to leave for a while. Possibly she'd consider going to Leptham or to visit Dorlane at Moresby."

"That's a thought. Only happy memories there," Franz said.

"What about Marjana?" Menders asked after a moment. He had been to see Eiren's mother and was shocked and saddened by her rapid decline over only a few weeks.

Franz puffed on his cigar.

"It's going to be a long, hard road," he said. "Any woman who has survived eight childbirths and years of farm work is strong. It's going to take a long time to kill her. I give her two more years at least, and most of it's going to be ugly. I've supplied her with a fatal dose of ramplane, but right now she's frightened and clinging to life. Resignation doesn't come until later, if it does at all. She's very dependent on Eiren and Sana, now that the other children have all married and gone to homes of their own. There are still some good days and she's making the most of them."

Menders said nothing. He was trying to calm his mind, which was roiling with resentment and sorrow and a desperate desire to be free of all of it, to be somewhere or someone else.

"Eiren's holding up well," Franz went on. "I've convinced her not to live at her parents' house just yet. The later she becomes an integral part of the situation, the better. I've also insisted the other children do part of it. Some of them were claiming to be busy with family responsibilities and the like, but I put an end to that. If need be, I'll insist that Eiren go back to you in Erdahn."

"It isn't much better there," Menders sighed.

"I know. Is Katrin drinking?"

Menders looked at Franz, startled.

"Wine with dinner occasionally, yes. I haven't noticed her drinking more than that," he answered.

"Start looking for signs that she's drinking and hiding it," Franz said, stubbing out his cigar. "She's going to start doing something to feel better, especially if she's panicked or frightened. She must not start drinking. You're going to have to force her into a routine. Otherwise, she's going to start sleeping all day and staying up all night to avoid coping with life. The more you can keep her on an even keel, the better. The sooner her situation is resolved, the better. The fact is that she shouldn't be Queen. If there's any way for that to stop, it would be best."

"I've always known that," Menders said tiredly. "The problem is that she is Queen, and grown, and I can't just tell her what to do any more."

***

Menders and Katrin looked at the formal gown of the Queen of Mordania, the only garment the Queen ever appeared in. It had been handed down over centuries. The core of it was supposedly the same dress worn by Morghenna the Wise when she and the first Lord Stettan led a people's revolution against the Surelian Occupation. The first Lord Stettan had specifically chosen the color red for the dress so that their army could easily see the young Queen on the battlefield and rally to her quickly. It had been added to ever since – leather and metal armor plates, padding, jewels.

It was atrocious.

It hung from a large, iron stand. It weighed almost a hundred pounds.

Menders ordered it thoroughly cleaned, with soap and then with steam. Katrin had been infinitely relieved to find that it required a stiff corset to be worn underneath, which would keep it from directly touching most of her skin. She'd refused to consider the corset Aidelia and her mother had worn, remembering how filthy both women were. She had Borsen make a duplicate, which he had done under violent protest. It was reinforced with steel. When Katrin crushed her body into it, flattening her breasts and squeezing her hips and bottom, it was painful.

"All right," Katrin said wearily, casting off the dressing gown she wore, revealing that she was already in the corset, with a shift underneath to prevent the steel stays from pressing too painfully on her skin, "Let's put the damned thing on."

The dress opened at the back. Katrin stepped into it. Menders began closing the buckles and tabs on the back, each one clicking noisily into place in the silence. When the final fastener was secure, Katrin felt as if she could barely breathe.

The weight of the thing was incredible and she hadn't even tried to step off the stand.

"You'll need the shoes," Menders said quietly, setting the elevated pattens in place before her, so she could step into them. Otherwise, the hem of the weighty dress would drag the ground and trip her.

Katrin stepped into the shoes. Menders buckled them on for her. Then he steadied her as she stepped off the platform of the dress stand.

"Oh gods!" she gasped, as the weight of the dress, no longer supported by the stand, hung from her body. "Oh gods!"

No wonder her mother had been such a sad, drunken woman, with this terrible weight burdening her! Why would anyone put a woman in such a terrible thing?

Menders was deliberately not looking at her. She knew he couldn't bear it.

She took a step and then another, the dress clanking around her, the armor plates moving like so much sheet metal. At least the skirt was a stiff cone shape, held out by a cagelike farthingale, so it didn't tangle around her legs. The clanking sound made her feel sick, bringing back memories of Aidelia wearing this wretched garment.

"I'll be in big trouble if I need a piss," Katrin said suddenly, feeling a surge of humor, grinning at Menders. He looked at her in surprise. She didn't swear often.

"I believe there was a special pot," he replied, smiling back at her.

"Please, don't get it. Don't bring it to me. Should I need to visit the privy, you'll just have to get me out of this thing. I certainly don't intend to wear it often," Katrin answered, feeling for a moment like her old self. "Let's hope it gets the attention of those puffed up twits."

"It will do that," Menders said, looking at the horrible dress. "There's a king's ransom set in it."

"Don't I know it. I feel every ounce," Katrin sighed, walking forward again. "What a wretched, stupid thing – like everything else about being Queen."

THE PALACE, ERDAHN, MORDANIA

6
STAGNANT

Dearest Little Bird,

I just had to spend some time with you, even if it's only through a letter. I miss you so much.

It's been a wretched week here. Katrin tried wearing that cursed dress to a Council meeting for the third time. She can barely move in it. The dress has a terrible effect on her emotions. To make matters worse, the damned Council continues to ignore her. She has refused to sign their documents a time or two. That does get their attention. It always results in a yelling match which exhausts and upsets her. She gives in to them after she's hurt and furious enough. I can't blame her. In all honesty, I think I would too.

She has made some headway with the staff by wearing the dress, which evokes terror in them. The place is cleaner, and I'm not having to press my own suits and iron my own shirts, as if I didn't have enough to cope with. It goes against Katrin's grain to do all this shouting and fit-throwing, which is apparently the only way things get done around here. We've decided to start bringing in new staff and rotating them out after a few months to the other royal estates. New brooms sweep clean, as you know.

Otherwise, Katrin continues as usual, melancholic and afraid to leave the Palace. I've suggested going to The Shadows, going to Leptham, visiting Dorlane, touring the other Royal estates to see what they are like, going to Surelia, going with Hemmett to visit Luntigré and Flori – nothing. She finds excuses.

Enough of that. Tell me about how things are going. I am hoping to come at the end of the week, but Bertel stopped by and offered to carry a letter back, so I jumped at the opportunity.

I have decided to acquire a Rollig device at the Palace. The military has had them for some years, but I would like a faster means of communicating with the Men and The Shadows, not having to depend on hand carried letters.

I hope our Mama is continuing comfortable. Kiss her from me and tell her I will be there, probably in two days. Hemmett will be coming with me. We're hoping Katrin might be willing to venture out with both of us escorting her.

Hemmett wants to see his parents. He's been very worried since he was sent word of Lucen's illness.

I think of you so much. I wish… never mind.

I love you,

M

Hello darling!

What a wonderful surprise to get your letter– and then Ifor and Kaymar turned up. They're going to be taking the boat right back to Erdahn, so I have a chance to get a letter out to you.

Mama is still continuing comfortable. There isn't much pain and what there is can be controlled with ramplane. We took her to see the ice animals the other day, which she's always loved. Then she had a good time seeing the boys out sledding. We're taking each day as it comes. So far there have been more good days than bad.

I'm so sorry to hear about Katrin and all the troubles. I was shocked the last time I saw her. She's so diminished looking. I have read all I could find on melancholia. It seems to be a terrible mystery. I hope she will come along with you and Hemmett.

Having a Rollig device would be so wonderful! To be able to be in touch with you right away would be a mercy, even if it was just a message saying good night or good morning. Haakel loves the idea, though he rumpuses that it should be for official use only. It would save much writing and letter carrying.

I can't wait until you're here, my love. Kaymar is stalking around the hallway, so I'd better close.

Loving you always,

Your Eiren

Dearest Little Bird,

I have sorted it out with Katrin that I will be going to The Shadows at least twice a week and more if possible, so do not trouble yourself about this anymore. I am sorry about Katrin's condition and I'm doing all I can to find a doctor who will be able to help her, but she simply cannot keep me from going to help you.

It is nothing personal directed at you, as you know. She is deathly afraid of being alone, of going out, of me being away from her, etc. We've worked it out so that Hemmett and I are not gone at the same time. That seems to have settled things for her. She became terrified when we were both at The Shadows a few weeks ago. Villison ended up having to sit with her all day and put her through endless games of Watch the Lady. He sent down to Borsen, who came with Varnia. They stayed with her that night until we got back.

I have talked to her at great length about abdication and have tried to work a way it can be done to her satisfaction – in other words, without killing anyone. It might be possible to set up a Regent Council for Glorantha rather than allowing her father to become Regent. There would always be the danger of skullduggery on his part to gain power, however.

Katrin is digging in her heels. She is determined that wearing that damned dress is getting her somewhere and, gods help me, she's now asking me for the teeth and wig! She's convinced that they frighten people. They do, particularly me because of the way she gets when she's wearing the damned things. There is much bravado while she's wearing them, but then she gets very upset and cries.

I've tried to get her to go elsewhere for a change of scene. If I bring it up she panics. It's very genuine and terrible to see. Terrible for her too, because it makes her physically ill. She has nightmares afterward. Even suggesting Leptham had the same effect. And of course, I can't drag her from the Palace or render her unconscious and cart her out.

Enough of this. It's the same old story, but I have secured our bit of time together. I was also going to suggest that you try to come here during this time while your mother is still fairly well. You will not have much opportunity later.

I am so sorry about all this Eiren, but I don't see any other way, at least for now. I want so much to be with you. Please forgive me.

Your loving husband,

M

Darling Menders,

Please don't apologize for things you and Katrin can't help! I fully understand she is suffering from an illness. She is the Queen. She does have responsibilities and she's trying, as best she can in her state, to carry them out. I am furious with the Council for treating her as they do, and furious as well with the foolish women who came before her and caused this situation. It's hard to believe that in the past there was a Queen called "The Wise" and another called "Clearheart" – the latest crop of Queens should have been called "The Drunkard" and "The Mad". Of course, we had "The Terrible", didn't we?

Don't mind me, I'm feeling snipey today. Mama has been feeling sorry for herself and though I certainly can't blame her, it wears on the nerves. Thankfully, Sana is taking over for me here for a week so I can come to you. Perhaps I can talk to Katrin and help her understand that she really is ill and needs to try a change of scene. Let the dratted Council go to her if they need a signature!

I can't wait to see you! I warn you, I intend to go to Borsen's and try to make you a poor man. I was looking at my things the other day and they are sadly worn. This will not do for the wife of the Royal Advisor!

Bertie's champing at the bit to get back to Erdahn in daylight, so I will stop now. Try to stay cheerful, my love, and I will see you in a few days.

Your Eiren

***

Menders met Eiren at the dock. She leapt off the boat almost before it stopped moving and was in his arms. Though he had been making a point of getting back to The Shadows often, it was always only for a day at a time. He knew she was delirious at the idea of spending a week together.

He, on the other hand, was worried about her seeing Katrin for the first time in a year. Katrin was enormously changed for the worse. It would be a shock.

It was indeed. He saw Eiren go pale and was glad he had arranged things so that she would see Katrin before Katrin saw her.

Katrin, not taking part in the usual walking and riding that had been her regular forms of exercise, had gained weight. It did not look bad on her, but combined with a face puffy from too much sleep and too much drink, to Menders' dismay and anger, she had aged noticeably.

Katrin was indeed drinking, as Franz had suspected. After enough vociferous arguments about it, Menders had given up. Otherwise, Katrin became upset and drank even more after the arguments. She wasn't drinking until she was drunk all the time, as her mother had, but she was drinking to get herself to sleep, and then drinking to counteract the hangover the next morning. It did not sit well on her. When she did get drunk, she was morose.

Eiren stepped back out of sight with an almost silent gasp of dismay. Menders rapidly walked her away so that Katrin couldn't possibly hear her.

"Gods!" she said, tears coming to her eyes. "I wouldn't have recognized her. Oh gods, Menders!"

"I know. It shocks me every time I'm away for the day. Borsen goes pale every time he walks in. Stevahn came with him one night and I thought he was going to need a drink himself to get over it. Hemmett, on the other hand, never shows a thing but then goes and takes it out on a training dummy with a bayonet. We've gone through quite a few training dummies."

"Can't you get rid of the drink? Just get all the drink out of the Palace?" Eiren asked desperately.

"If I did, she could send for more and she would. She's the Queen, my darling. I can't tell her what to do. Sometimes I manage to convince her of something for her own good. Because she loves me, she'll do it, but I can't move her on the drinking. She says it's just a little to calm her nerves – and then she finishes off a bottle of wine before bedtime. I can't even get her to paint or play the spinet any more. She's gotten on a hobby horse of building a new suite up in the Tower and since it's the only thing she shows interest in, I encourage it. Anything she shows interest in…"

Eiren, hearing the frustration and pain in his voice, put her arms around his neck and kissed him.

"Now, I have myself collected, so let's go in," she said firmly, smiling up at him. Then she rubbed a hand over his short-cropped hair. "Mister Bristles," she teased, making him smile broadly for the first time in a long while.

***

Darling,

I'm back home and in one piece. The Rollig device is being set up as I write. Haakel is beside himself, as you can well imagine. Keeps trying to send messages even though it isn't entirely installed. He's driving the poor military fellows mad. Kaymar is here and he's wild to have a go at it as well. I just stay away and enjoy listening to the arguments and general rumpusing.

It was so wonderful to be with you, to sleep with you all night and wake up with you in the morning. You are right. For as long as it's possible, I am coming to Erdahn for at least a week per month, possibly more. It was also good to see how Katrin perked up a bit with me there and didn't drink much. We can see if having me around helps her, and adjust schedules accordingly. Like you, I'm willing to do anything if it would help her, even if it means dancing around naked as a newborn babe while painted green.

Mama weathered my absence well and is enthusiastic about me going again. She feels a great deal of guilt about us being separated. Thankfully she still continues comfortable.

There is great shouting down the hall, I think the Rollig might just be fixed up. I shall saunter down and see.

It is! Instant communication! Haakel is being very stern about it being used only for official purposes, during which lecture Kaymar went behind his back and tapped out a love note to Ifor, which will doubtless amaze some poor person receiving it there at the Palace. I could tell it was rather naughty from his expression. A very interesting initial communication from The Shadows!

I shall close now, and see if there is a way I can send you a kiss by the wire!

Your loving Eiren

TO: MENDERS
FROM: MISTRESS MENDERS

KISS!

TO: MISTRESS MENDERS
FROM: MENDERS

THREE KISSES. FIVE HUGS. I WILL BE THERE DAY AFTER TOMORROW TO RECEIVE KISS IN PERSON. DANCING NAKED AS NEWBORN BABE PAINTED GREEN REQUESTED. LOVE LOVE LOVE!

TO: MENDERS
FROM: HAAKEL

UNAUTHORISED USE OF ROLLIG IS PUNISHABLE BY FINE. KINDLY RESERVE ROLLIG COMMUNICATION FOR OFFICIAL BUSINESS. THANK YOU.

TO: HAAKEL
FROM: YOUR SUPERIOR OFFICER

SHUT UP YOU OLD GRANNY.

***

Katrin took a long look around the new suite she'd had built in the Tower. Since she'd become Queen, she, Menders and Hemmett had made do with a temporary refurbishment of the suite she'd been assigned by Aidelia. She'd wanted something permanent, something of her own, a sanctuary that no other Queen of Mordania had lived in. Something like The Shadows, restful and pleasant in the Samorsan style she'd fallen in love with when she'd toured the Middle Continent.

The Palace itself was incredibly outmoded, drafty, parts of it ancient. There was no indoor plumbing. Katrin, after years of living with no indoor plumbing at The Shadows until Menders had it modernized, was one of Eirdon's greatest proponents of the flush water closet. When she'd found some of the rooms on the upper floors of the Palace actually had drop privies, she'd nearly fainted. She insisted that the new suite be modern, with the help of a water tank on the roof. It rained very frequently in Erdahn, so keeping a supply of fresh water was not difficult.

The Palace was made largely of stone and had never been intended for comfort. The walls were sixteen feet thick, making it cave like in many places. There was little natural light and it felt dank and cold at the best of times. The furniture was minimal and what there was seemed to be extremely antique or made of stone.

Upon becoming Queen, Katrin insisted the Palace be completely cleaned and aired, particularly the quarters Aidelia had used, which she had ordered cleared and scrubbed. She would never be able to bear to live in them, Royal Suite or no. That's when she gave orders that a new suite would be built.

Now the suite was finished, with quarters for Menders and Hemmett as well as for herself, with additional rooms for guests. It accessed the roof of the Tower, where a garden would be laid out. The ocean shore could be reached by a private hidden staircase. The rooms were large, modern and comfortable and were easy to heat with stoves and efficient fireplaces. Katrin had decorated her rooms with beautiful silken fabric from Surelia, draping off the private part of her bedroom with an exquisite curtain. This was to prevent interruptions on the part of the Palace staff at the times when she was not wearing her vampire Queen guise.

Katrin had found the traditional appearance of the Queen of Mordania a useful thing. The costume fed the rumors that the Queen was a two-hundred-year-old vampire, thanks to the teeth and the fact that all Queens within living memory had presented the same face to the world, always using the same name, Morghenna. Her appearance kept the Palace staff and the Council at a distance.

At this point, Katrin didn't care much about matters of policy. She'd struggled for over two years to make headway with the Council members. Essentially, the Council did as the Council wanted to do and even if they told her one thing when she signed a document and then did exactly the opposite, they seemed to have no fear of her. Menders told her this constituted treason and that she would be within the law to have those who deceived her summarily executed, but Katrin did not want any more deaths on her hands. She gave up and decided the Council could be buggered.

She went through the motions of attending meetings – sometimes. Other times, she signed what they sent her and didn't bother to get into the heavy dress and clip the disgusting teeth into her mouth. It didn't make a difference. She'd found when she refused to sign something, her signature turned up on it anyway. She left the day to day running of the staff and the Council to Menders, who excelled at it. It kept him busy and it kept him from nagging at her.

She was tired of being chastised for having a drink to calm her nerves. Menders kept after her about it for months before she finally told him to leave her alone.

"Who cares?" she asked him. "It isn't as if I have to go and do anything, so why can't I have a drink of an evening?"

"Because drinking a bottle or two of wine every night is not having a drink of an evening," Menders countered.

"Leave me alone about it," Katrin answered. That was the end of it. She was twenty-seven now and certainly didn't need to be told what to do. It was bad enough there was no way out of being Queen without endangering Tharak Karak and the Thrun. If she had to be

Queen, at least she could have a few drinks once in a while to ease the tedium.

The first two years had been worst. There had been endless fights with Menders, the Council, Kaymar, sometimes even Hemmett. To her relief, Kaymar had gone haring off on a bunch of missions for Menders, taking Ifor with him. That had eased things considerably. Hemmett gave up early and readjusted to the way life was now. He went to see Luntigré and Flori regularly.

Menders had held on the longest and said the sharpest things. He tried to force her into regular risings and bedtimes, as if she was a child. He also tried to keep her from having wine with dinner and he'd thrown a fit when she'd tried some Samorsan black hargweed, which she'd read about and sent for.

"It helps me feel calm!" she'd snapped when Menders caught her with a pipeful. "Maybe you should try it."

"I've never needed anything to calm me. I'm capable of self-discipline," Menders snapped in return.

"Try being Queen for a few days," she'd returned.

"As if you do anything? Who do you think is having to be Queen?" Menders shot back. Then he saw that he'd hurt her and regret showed in his face.

"Princess – my little princess, you can be any kind of Queen you want," he'd said, sitting opposite her, his nose pinched in distaste at the smell of the hargweed. "You don't have to stay in the Palace. You can rule from anywhere, from The Shadows if you want. You could go to the old Winter Palace in Erdstrom, or build a Palace elsewhere. I can't believe it's good for you to be here. You don't exercise. You don't seem happy. Poor Taffy is getting absolutely fat, and I can't give her enough exercise. Why don't you try riding again?"

"Who cares? If I wanted to go riding, I would," Katrin answered.

"What about Taffy?" Menders asked in astonishment. "She needs your care."

"Sell her. I don't give a damn," Katrin returned levelly.

Menders looked stunned, got up and went away, which was what Katrin had wanted.

Now he seldom protested, though he wouldn't bring her any wine and certainly would never have so much as handed her the pouch of hargweed. That wasn't a problem, because the Palace had plenty of staff who would bring wine up. She could manage the hargweed herself.

Katrin moved into the suite and spent most of her time there. She and Menders came to a sort of truce. She managed not to blame him openly for her predicament and he didn't nag at her about her habits. If she told him to drop a subject, he did. He no longer chivvied and nagged her if she decided to stay in bed all day. After all, what difference did it make if she didn't get up? He no longer nagged her to read over the documents sent up by the Council before signing them. He spent a lot of time with the Menders' Men who were posted at the Palace, doing gods knew what – as if it mattered.

A lot of the time, Katrin felt as if she lived inside a glass room. She could see everyone else going around, enjoying themselves and living full lives, while she was muted and at a distance. Things didn't upset her or sadden her any more – they didn't make her happy either. It was a bit like being underwater. That had its advantages, because she was free of the extremes of sadness and fear that had plagued the first two years of her reign. Being numb was nice, in a way.

And after all, who cared? She certainly didn't.

THE SHADOWS, MORDANIA
THE PALACE, ERDAHN, MORDANIA

7
DESCENT

Eiren opened a drawer of Menders' desk at The Shadows, in search of a pamphlet, and saw the pistol.

She had seen it hundreds of times of course. It had been there since Katrin and Hemmett were old enough to be trusted not to take it out and play with it. Menders always had plenty of weaponry on his person, so this pistol was strictly backup, but it was loaded and ready to fire.

It beckoned to her.

Her mother was suffering horribly. Ramplane couldn't help much now, unless it was given in near-lethal quantities. The pain was always there and the most her mother could manage in the way of sleep was a near-stupor, induced by ramplane. The rest of the time she tossed, chewed what remained of her lips, moaned, screamed and writhed.

She was unrecognizable, her hair gone, her lips largely chewed away, her face like a skull. Her abdomen was bloated by the rot slowly eating her internal organs. Her skin was yellow and spotted with dark lesions. She could not eat, could barely drink and her body reeked between her loss of bowel and bladder control and the stench of the illness itself.

She barely registered the presence of anyone at her bedside. If she did, she continually begged them to help her. Franz was keeping her dosed into a near coma most of the time, and said there was no way to predict how much longer this could go on, as her body was remarkably strong.

Worst yet, the rot had reached Marjana Spaltz's brain and she was now mad. She said terrible things during her lucid spells, things Eiren knew were not true. Nonetheless, it hurt to be cursed or vilified by the mother she was giving up so much to nurse and care for.

Marjana's madness completely demoralized Eiren's father, who had been a rock until the first time his wife hissed that she hated him and always had. He'd shrunk back in horror and had been a shell of himself ever since, despite Franz's reassurances that the desperately ill woman did not mean what she said and wasn't even aware of what she was saying.

Marjana's illness was rapidly eating away a lifetime of happy memories just as it was eating away at her body. Eiren was terrified that if it went on much longer, she would have no recollection of her loving and happy mother and all the years they had spent together in harmony.

Now the pistol was there, under her hand.

I could end this all now, Eiren thought. I could put pillows around her head to muffle the shot and hold in any blood or brains. She would never know I'd done it. I could burn the bloody pillows and put a nightcap on her to cover the bullet hole. It would release her. It would release all of us. She would be out of pain. Papa would be free of seeing her turning into this hateful demon who accuses him of things he would never have thought of.

Why aren't you here, Menders, she fumed waspishly. Why is your gun here when you aren't? Why are you so determined to stay with Katrin when it's obvious she's never going to do anything, that she's determined to be as ineffectual as her mother was? Why must I always come second to someone set on destroying herself? I don't care what you swore when you were no more than a boy. I need you here. My mother is rotting away and I'm all alone and I'm calmly thinking about shooting her to end it all. Why aren't you here?

"Come, my dear, I think you need to sit down," Franz said quietly. Eiren started. She'd never heard him come in, but there he was, right in front of her. "Let's close that drawer now. We'll go to my office and have a cup of coffee and a talk." He reached over the desk top and closed the drawer, then took her hand and drew her around the desk, out of Menders' office and down the hallway to his own. He left her there long enough to get some coffee, then came back and closed the door behind him.

"Now, you have that," he directed. "Drink it and rest for a moment. Then we'll talk."

Eiren was grateful for the hot cup in her hand, which warmed her fingers. She realized they were as cold as ice. He'd made the coffee double strength – Thrun style. After a few sips, she began to feel more like herself.

Franz waited until they were both finished, then took the cup from her.

"Now," he said bluntly, "That is not a decision for you to make. That decision is for me to make, and me only. I'm the doctor. Don't you fret about it anymore."

"She's in such agony! She can't make a decision," Eiren protested weakly. "Poor Papa is destroyed – he could never decide to end this. What is the point of keeping her alive, Franz!"

"I know. You leave this to me," Franz said implacably. "I've sent word for Menders to come and he just wired back that he's on his way. He'll have to go back tonight, but he will come every day until this is over.

"Oh yes, he'll go back every night," Eiren snapped. The she was shocked at the bitterness in her voice.

"He doesn't have a choice – not with the condition Katrin is in," Franz said quietly. "We don't want a second death on our hands, Eiren. I know you feel abandoned and I certainly understand why, but there is grave danger to Katrin too."

Eiren stared at him. Katrin had stagnated for four years now.

"She doesn't seem particularly desperate," Eiren said.

"She's stopped fighting the melancholia. That's a very dangerous time," Franz said. "When she was going through times of being angry or sad, when she cared enough to argue with people or cry, I felt easier. This indifference – that's when people simply don't care to live any more. When they're like that, ending their lives seems the only way out. If Katrin should have a spell of being more energetic, she could very well take her own life. She should not be left alone, particularly overnight."

Eiren closed her eyes.

"So, though Menders should be here with you during all this, he can't be, but he's going to do the best he can," Franz went on. "I don't agree with some of the choices he's made in his life, but we don't have the benefit of hindsight when we make our choices. He'll be here soon, dear."

"Thank the gods," Eiren wept. "These are terrible days, Franz."

"I know, my dear. It will be over soon."

Later, when Eiren went back to Menders' office and looked in the desk drawer for the forgotten pamphlet, the gun was gone.

***

TO: KATRIN
FROM: MENDERS

MY DEAR PLEASE COME TO THE SHADOWS. GRANDMOTHER HAS JUST DIED. GRANDDAD IS BEREFT AND WOULD LIKE TO SEE YOU. BORSEN AND STEVAHN JUST SENT WORD THAT THEY WILL BE GLAD TO COME BY FOR YOU. KAYMAR IS BRINGING THE BOAT AND WILL PROVIDE SECURITY. PLEASE KATRIN. DO THIS FOR EIREN'S SAKE.

TO: MENDERS
FROM: KATRIN

I'M SORRY, I CAN'T. PLEASE TELL EIREN AND GRANDDAD I'M SORRY.

Menders looked at the Rollig message Haakel handed him and felt his face flush with rage.

"Thank you," he said quietly, moving quickly toward the door, seeking refuge in his office.

Once there, he crumpled the paper and flung it into the fire.

***

Katrin heard Menders coming slowly up the stairs well after midnight. She crept to the door of her room and opened it.

He looked terrible, weary and angry.

"I'm sorry, Menders," she said in a tiny voice.

He nodded and went into his room without a word.

***

Katrin heard Menders moving about early next morning. She got out of bed quickly, pulling on her wig and a dressing gown. She would go with him. It was terrible of her not to go to see Eiren, who'd been nursing her mother for so long only to have it end so sadly. She loved Granddad. She had to go.

She began dressing quickly, knowing from the familiar sounds that Menders was hurrying. She pulled on her underwear and began struggling with her corset, lacing it rapidly in front and then twisting it around and pulling the laces tight. She grabbed a dress and dropped it over her head.

It was too tight. She hadn't bothered to dress for some time now, living in her dressing gown. She'd gained enough weight that she couldn't get the dress buttoned. She tried another. It was the same.

A desperate hunt through the wardrobe let her know that most of her clothing didn't fit any more. She tried pulling her corset strings tighter, but it didn't make much difference. She couldn't button most of her clothing.

You fat, disgusting mess, she thought, finally finding a loose-fitting dress that would fasten. You've got to stop just sitting around. This is the end! You're going to start exercising and doing something about yourself.

She looked up at the mirror and froze.

A frowsy mess of a woman, overweight, wearing a dress that draped so it made her look larger was reflected there. Katrin saw that her face was swollen. She looked older than she was! Her wig wasn't well groomed. It would take hours to get herself together.

She pulled the dress off and got back into her dressing gown, just in time for Menders to knock rapidly and come in.

"I'm going back to The Shadows," he said briskly. "I will need to go every day for a while, because Granddad is not well and Eiren needs me. I will come back at night, but it will probably be late."

"What time?" Katrin heard herself ask. She went cold as Menders glared at her.

"I will be back when I get back! Damn it, Katrin! I have a heartbroken wife who has struggled along for three years without much help from me. Now her father is destroyed because his wife of forty-eight years has just died horribly! I should be staying there with them, but I'm trying to do the best I can for all concerned. I will not leave you alone, but I am going to be away a lot of the time. Hemmett is going for the funeral today but there are plenty of the Men here, as well as Villison and the Guard."

"I'm afraid!" Katrin cried.

Menders closed his eyes and she saw he was struggling.

Yes, she was afraid. She wanted him to stay with her. She was frightened whenever he left. Some nights she lay in bed, pretending to be asleep, waiting for him to come in and make sure all was well, just to hear him whisper that everything was all right, to sleep well – as he had every night of her life.

"Go," she said suddenly. "Please. I'm sorry. I got up and tried to come with you this morning, but none of my clothes fit. I can't button anything. Go and tell Eiren I'm sorry. I'll write her a letter. And one to Granddad. Please go."

Menders opened his eyes and looked at her. There was so much love and sorrow in their pale depths that it nearly made her burst out crying.

He came to her and kissed her cheek.

"I'll be back around midnight," he said gently. "We'll talk then."

He turned quickly and went out of her room, while she collapsed in her chair, weeping.

***

They didn't talk when Menders came back. He found Katrin sound asleep, reeking of wine, three empty bottles bearing witness to how she had spent the day.

Exhausted by emotion, by the grief of the people he had tried to support and help all day long, he turned away, went to his room, pulled off his clothes and fell into bed, only to find that he couldn't sleep.

He tossed and turned for a couple of hours, desperate. He was to leave again early in the morning and had to get some rest.

Finally, he knew what was wrong, why he couldn't sleep.

He rose, threw on his dressing gown and went back to where Katrin was unconscious, sprawled across her bed.

He put a log on the fire, so it would burn until morning. He pulled the covers up over her and set her wig, which had come unmoored from her scalp, on its stand.

"Everything is all right," he finally whispered. "Sleep well, little princess."

He doused the light, and stood there for a long time in the darkness, telling himself that tears on his cheeks didn't mean he was crying.

THE PALACE, ERDAHN, MORDANIA

8
WHO CARES?

Borsen wrapped his tape measure around Katrin's waist. "Yes, a couple of inches more, but you're hardly ready to run away to join a pack of walruses," he smiled. He showed the figure to Varnia, who wrote it on the elaborate chart Borsen used for fittings.

"I should just try to lose the weight," Katrin said glumly.

"You need clothes, Cuz. Let's dress the body you have now. If you lose weight, we'll dress the body you have then," he smiled, ignoring her tone.

"Oh, why bother! Who cares?"

"Don't say 'who cares' to me again or I'll throttle you with my tape measure," Borsen answered cheerfully. "You can't just lie around up here all the time, wearing a dressing gown that needs a wash – badly." He wrinkled his nose.

"Why not?"

"Because it's disgusting. Don't fence with me, Katrin. I can come back at you all day long. When it comes to being nasty, you're a downright amateur," Borsen replied, taking her hip measurement. "This is three inches more. Nothing that drastic. Now the measuring is done. Let's talk about colors."

"I don't care, just make anything."

Varnia sighed audibly.

"All right, I'll make everything in puce," Borsen responded, coiling the tape measure and slipping it into his pocket.

"Fine. Who cares?"

Suddenly Borsen snatched a handful of Katrin's dressing gown collar in his fist. It was difficult for her to breathe. It was easy to forget just how strong Borsen was.

"I care," Borsen said brightly. "You can lie around here looking like a wet week and being as appealing as a wet fart for the rest of your days if you want, but you aren't ever going to say 'who cares' to me again, do you hear? I've seen real misery, Katrin. Did you know my mother starved to death so that I wouldn't? Imagine being in a tiny, dirty, icy room in the middle of winter out on the Sea Of Grass. Imagine weather that makes winter at The Shadows look like springtime. Imagine watching your beautiful, loving mother dying because she hasn't had any food in weeks and the room is freezing. Imagine being six years old, practically blind, helpless, watching that. When you've imagined it for a while, get back to me about whether you want to keep saying 'who cares' to me."

He released her collar and picked up his hat. Varnia stood and folded the chart neatly, her face impervious.

"Now, I will come and visit you anytime I damn well please, because I want to," Borsen continued, sounding very cheerful. "On the day I don't turn up, you will know that I've ceased to care. Before I come back day after tomorrow, I suggest you give some thought to colors and fabrics. Don't wear that reeking dressing gown again when I have to smell it, or I'll rip it off you. Good evening."

He put his hat on, cocked it rakishly and offered his arm to Varnia. They walked over to Menders, who had frozen in the doorway at the tableau of Borsen throttling Katrin with her collar.

"I'll see you in a couple of days, Uncle," Borsen said as they went off down the hall.

"Did you see that?" Katrin gasped.

"Yes. I'm starting to think it's not a bad idea," Menders replied, setting down a dinner tray. "Time to eat."

"I'm not hungry."

"Go without. It will set the stage for what Borsen told you to imagine," Menders retorted sharply, following in his nephew's wake.

***

"Darling, I will come to Erdahn to see you, but I am not going to stay with you at the Palace again," Eiren said emphatically. "I'm afraid I will strike her if I'm around her much more. If she says 'who cares' one more time, I will. I know I will. I'll stay with Borsen and Stevahn, or at your house across town, but I absolutely will not be around that any longer."

"I can't blame you," Menders sighed. They were at Malvar's, having dinner away from the Palace and the long streak of misery and misanthropy Katrin had become. He hated to think of the night without Eiren, now that she was free to come to Erdahn more often.

He'd so looked forward to it, sleeping with her in his arms, waking beside her to see her smile at him.

"I'll come to The Shadows more often," Menders said, wondering just how the hells he was going to manage it. More and more was falling on him. His network of spies and informants was enormous now and spread over every country in the world, apart from the closed nation, Chetkinkev. The information his operatives gathered poured in at an incredible pace now that Rollig devices had been installed in so many places. It all had to be collated and filed after it had been read and cross-referenced with other incoming dispatches.

He was also doing what Katrin's job should have been, governing the country, at least as much as the Council would permit. For all Menders had done to avoid being the power behind the Throne, he had become just that.

It had come home to him one morning when he found himself forging Katrin's signature on a document to be put into effect that day. Katrin had been unconscious after the previous night's binge.

"Did I make her weak?" he said aloud.

"No, you didn't," Eiren answered fiercely. "Her heritage did. What a family of weak women."

"But her grandmother wasn't weak," Menders said. "'The Terrible'? She was far from weak. At the end she was ineffectual due to ill health, but she certainly wasn't weak. Katrin's mother was a weakling, I'll give you that. Aidelia wasn't weak, just stupid and mad."

"No-one could have been a better father," Eiren replied defensively, looking at him with eyes full of anguish and love.

"No, but perhaps I should have been a better drill sergeant," he answered.

"How do you deal with her behavior now?" Eiren asked, catching him by surprise.

"Largely, I tolerate it. It's better than constantly arguing with her or having her in tears. She can't help a lot of what she does, Eiren."

"Can she? How does she behave around Borsen, now that he's laid down the law?" Eiren responded.

"Quite well," Menders answered slowly. "She dresses in something clean and she doesn't say 'who cares' or spar with him. Of course, our boy seems very gentle, but he can be downright frightening if he chooses to be."

"Perhaps you should take an example from him," Eiren replied. "It's tragic that she has melancholia, but if she can control her behavior around Borsen, she can control it around you. Perhaps she can learn to live with melancholia, as some people live with chronic illness or a leg missing – or how Kaymar lives with his madness."

Menders raised his eyebrows, pondering.

***

Several weeks later, Katrin pushed Menders to a crisis point.

He'd been coping with multiple disasters, governmental, in his own network, domestically and with her. Katrin was in a horrific mood, was drinking more heavily than ever, tried to pick a fight with Hemmett and hadn't been near her bathtub in days.

Menders was worn thin. He was lonely now that Eiren was back at The Shadows and he was tired of contending with behavior he would expect from an early adolescent.

Katrin had sighed 'who cares' to almost everything he'd said that morning, as he tried to make her understand what was happening in the government.

"Oh, leave me alone," she finally hissed at him.

"Katrin, it's imperative…" he began

"Who cares!"

Menders rose suddenly and raised a hand, ready to slap her across the face. He barely stopped himself.

"Don't you ever say 'who cares' anywhere I can hear you again," he said in a low, terrible voice. "If you ever do, I will no longer be able to control myself. You are very close to having me walk out of here and never come back, young lady. I stay with you because I love you and want to help you. You will not ever treat me like so much rubbish again."

Katrin was staring at him, her mouth and eyes like three circles.

"Now, you read those damned documents, and be ready to talk to me about them when I get back here. I'm going down to Borsen's to see if he and Stevahn want to have lunch with me." Menders turned on his heel and stamped out of the room, slamming the door behind him.

Suddenly he threw the door open again, went to the dressing table and picked up the bottles of wine she had lined up there. He took them to the window and flung them out. There was a yell from Hemmett below as they smashed into the courtyard.

"Curb your damned drinking too," Menders added, slamming out again.

***

When he returned, Katrin was wearing one of the new dresses Borsen had made. She still looked dreadful. Over imbibing had done considerable damage to her looks. She was clean, however, and looked alert.

"I've read the documents," she said quietly. "I need you to explain the situation more, because I don't have enough background to fully understand it."

"I'll be glad to," Menders replied. He sat down and went through the information, explained several issues at length and then answered the few feeble questions she could come up with.

"Should I sign anything?" Katrin finally asked in a small voice.

"No. There is nothing to sign in this matter, but it's something you must be informed about," Menders answered briskly, rising. "I have a lot to do this afternoon, so I will see you later."

"What will I do?" Katrin asked, sounding lost.

Menders turned to her.

"You live in incredible luxury here in this Palace," he answered. "There's the entire city of Erdahn right outside. Borsen has a superb business establishment three blocks away which you've yet to see. There are shops, museums and galleries all over the place. You aren't a prisoner here. You can go anywhere you like. The prison is in your mind, Katrin. I gave you accomplishments you can use to amuse yourself. I spent years teaching you music and dancing. I spent years teaching you to read and write. Why in the name of all the gods, now that I'm having to do your job as well as my own, do you expect me to entertain a grown woman of twenty-seven?"

Katrin looked at the floor and nodded. Menders turned away and went to his work.

SARONILLA, SAMORSA

9
PREPARING TO LEAVE

Hemmett swung his duffel bag onto his shoulder to give his arm a break. He'd been gripping the handle too tightly and now his entire arm ached. The boat trip from Mordania to Samorsa had been rough, a storm blowing up from the south. The train journey from the coast seemed to take forever. He would be very glad to stop moving for a while. The street where Luntigré and Flori lived was a welcome sight.

Luntigré's balcony was a riot of yellow and orange flowers. They twined around all the fancy ironwork and hung almost to the street. The scent of them was reaching him, sparking many happy memories of Flori fashioning crowns from the rambling vine and placing them on the head of anyone who would let her. He'd always let her.

Luntigré had written to Hemmett, asking him to come to her as soon as he could – and he had been glad to comply. After the gloom and silence of The Palace and the dreary days of pointless drill and guarding, this dizzyingly colorful, sunlit street was just what he needed. Samorsan warmth was what his body craved and the peace and joy of Luntigré's home would satisfy his soul.

He ran lightly up the stairs to the apartment, gave the door a quick rap with his knuckles and then let himself in.

He knew the moment he saw her. The light that always seemed to emanate from her was diminished, almost quenched. She was thinner, her motions were slower – but her eyes were still lustrous and dancing with love and mischief as she turned toward him.

Hemmett dumped the duffel and took her into his arms, burying his face in her magnificent curling hair.

"Is there still joy?" she whispered, knowing that he knew.

"There will always be joy," he answered.

***

"It's in my blood," Luntigré explained, lying in Hemmett's arms in her breezy bedroom. "Doctor Franz came last week and took me to several doctors. There are things I can take to support my health for a time but there is no cure for the illness."

Hemmett was silent, thinking of the recent painful death of Eiren's mother, who had acted as his grandmother since the day he had arrived at The Shadows.

With that odd prescience she had, Luntigré said, "There will not be pain, my darling. Only increasing weariness and loss of energy until I pass to spirit."

"I'm glad for that," he said honestly. Though he had once seen Doctor Franz as a figure of fun when growing up around the jolly man at The Shadows, Hemmett knew now that he was one of the foremost physicians on Eirdon. If he took Luntigré to other doctors, they were as learned and skilled. When Franz said there was nothing to be done, that was the case. Protesting and insisting that more doctors be consulted would only cause pain for everyone.

"How are your family?" he asked, shifting to sit against the headboard. Luntigré reclined with her head on his belly.

"Sad, of course. Samorsans look at death differently, Hem. They understand I'm going to leave and they are happy that I feel peaceful. Of course it is a hard thing for us all, but we face it together."

Hemmett stroked her hair back from her forehead.

"Flori?" he asked softly.

"She's well. She was the first to notice that I was ill," Luntigré answered. "We have talked many times about important things. She would rather have her mother stay with her, of course, but she understands that I will still watch over her and love her."

"And will you watch over me and love me?" Hemmett smiled.

"I don't know. Such a wicked man," she laughed. Then she reached up and pulled him down to her for a kiss.

"Always," she whispered. "I will always watch over you and love you, my bold young man who flirts so outrageously."

He smiled, remembering leaning on the counter of her stall and blatantly asking her if she liked what she saw. Thank all that might be thanked, that she had.

"Hemmett – Flori has said she would like to live with you when I go," Luntigré said.

"Of course," he answered instantly. He saw the relief in her eyes and sat her up beside him.

"We have never engaged in nonsense or guessing games," he said, holding her hands in his. "If Flori wishes to live with me, she will live with me. I've been her father for eight years. I've been thinking about buying the townhouse between Vil's and Kaymar's. I wouldn't want to take Flori to The Palace the way things are now."

"Poor Katrin," Luntigré sighed.

"Poor all of us. Flori doesn't need that. Is there any reason why she doesn't want to stay here?"

"She's closer to you than to any of the family. You have so much more in common – your music, your frankness, your silliness. Also, Flori does not wish to join the family business. She doesn't care much for cooking. She wishes to design ladies' clothing and to continue studying music."

Hemmett's eyebrows went up.

"She couldn't find better place to do both than Erdahn," he responded. "So long as your family is not hurt…"

"It is Flori's future. My mother and sister understand. They also know you would be sure that she visited. There would be no jealousy, no hard feelings. Montigré has four children and they all love the restaurant business. Flori is fourteen – almost fifteen. She knows who she is and what she wants. I could think of no-one I would rather have her with."

"You make me proud, my lovely," Hemmett whispered.

***

"I will need to go there often, and when she becomes too weak to manage, I'll stay with her until the end," Hemmett explained, standing before Menders and Katrin. "I know my being here when Menders isn't helps you, Willow, but Luntigré is dying. I want the time."

"I wouldn't ask you to stay away from her, Bumpy," Katrin answered softly. Her eyes were full of tears.

"Thank you," he replied.

Menders blinked and cleared his throat.

"How can I – how can we help you and Luntigré?' he asked.

"For one thing, I need to buy a house," Hemmett replied. "I'll also need a housekeeper, because I don't want Flori rattling around by herself. She's quite the young lady now, but not quite ready to be entirely on her own while I'm on duty."

"She's coming to live here?" Katrin asked, a touch of eagerness in her voice. Hemmett saw Menders look at her in surprise.

"I'm her father," Hemmett smiled. "She wants to live here with me. I will need help from all of you once she's here. She'll need to adjust to living in Erdahn as well as to the loss of her mother."

"Of course," Katrin said. "I wonder if Varnia could help us find a housekeeper – or is there someone at The Shadows who would suit, Menders?"

"I believe that there might be, since Petra's mother is widowed now and doesn't want to stay as a tenant farmer. I'll make some inquiries if you'd like, Hemmett."

"I would. Thank you both – and now I have to talk to Vil and see what we're going to do about scheduling." He nodded and walked away toward the stairs.

Katrin turned toward Menders and was shocked to see that he had tears in his eyes. She felt awkward – at one time she would have gone to him and put her arms around him, but they were distanced from each other now. There had been too many arguments, too many tense moments.

"It's all right, princess," he said, taking out his handkerchief. "That beautiful woman... Hemmett... the child… Please excuse me, my dear." He walked away into his bedroom and shut the door.

Katrin went to the window and looked out at the skyline of the city through her own tears, thinking about losing Luntigré – thinking about Flori coming to Erdahn and how she could help her.

***

Hemmett sat beside Luntigré's bed, holding her left hand in both of his. Flori was on the bed beside her, while Chetigré gently massaged Luntigré's feet and legs at the foot of the bed.

Luntigré's remaining time had gone quickly and peacefully. There had been happy times during the three months when Luntigré had enough energy to go about. They had revisited favorite spots and explored a few places she had always wanted to see. There were family gatherings and quiet times with only Luntigré, Hemmett and Flori.

Then Luntigré began to fail and was often too tired to rise from her bed. Hemmett let Menders know the end was coming and stayed in Luntigré's apartment, taking over the day to day running of their lives. Flori left school and spent all her time with her mother, reading to her, helping her bathe or dress, bringing small gifts of flowers or loving letters she had written.

Each day was a gift to Hemmett. The four years of Katrin's reign had been marked by heartbreak, frustration, anger and stagnation. He had often forgotten what it was to feel at peace. Here he was seeing his brave lady facing her death like a warrior, showing no fear, accepting what would be. There were tears, of course, and regrets that she could not stay longer, but they passed easily because she didn't try to hold them back.

Then a greater peace came into the room that had become their world. During the last two weeks, Luntigré had become serene as she waited to drift into the world of spirit.

The sun was setting when Luntigré woke from the sleep that claimed her most of the time now. She looked at Chetigré, who rose and bent over her daughter. The big woman stroked Luntigré's hair and kissed her, smiling into her eyes. There were no words. Then Chetigré sat at the end of the bed and placed her hands on Luntigré's feet again.

Luntigré looked toward Hemmett. She smiled to see his hair, unoiled and curling, backlit by the sun, as it had been when he'd come to see if she would have him. Words were beyond her now – she hadn't the strength to speak. Hemmett didn't need words. He knew.

"I'll take care of her," he whispered, leaning forward and kissing her cheek. "You can go without worry, my darling girl." Their eyes met, and he felt her joy flowing into him. He smiled, then turned Luntigré's head so that she could see Flori.

"I'll listen for you on the wind, Mama," Flori whispered. "I'll know when you are near. I love you. Thank you for being my mother."

Flori gazed into her mother's eyes until they closed, slowly, gently. Then she rested her head on Luntigré's breast and sighed.

Eirdon's moons were new and setting in the lingering sunset light when Hemmett felt an infinitesimal movement of Luntigré's hand, as if she had pressed his fingers in farewell. Her last breath was no more than a gentle whisper, her eyes closed, her face smooth, the slightest smile on her lips.

Chetigré felt her daughter pass and pressed her lips to her oiled, perfumed feet, as she had so often done when Luntigré was a baby. She lowered her head to rest on them, trysting with memory.

Flori heard her mother's heart beat slowly down to silence. Her tears flowed down without pain.

SARONILLA, SAMORSA
ERDAHN, MORDANIA

10
TRANSPLANTING

Hemmett waited while Flori walked slowly around the apartment that had been her home for almost fifteen years. Most of the furniture and decorations were being shipped to Erdahn so Flori would have them for her rooms in the townhouse Hemmett had purchased.

Flori seemed to be impressing the place on her mind. Her movements were unhurried as she moved from room to room.

"Flori?" Hemmett waited until she looked at him.

"Do you not want to go, sweetheart?" he asked gently. "Don't be afraid to tell me if you've changed your mind."

"Oh, I want to go, Papa," she said, coming over to him. "I was just looking at how the light comes into the apartment. I always thought it was so beautiful. But it's time to leave, because everything that was home is already on the boat to Erdahn."

"Very good," Hemmett smiled, picking up her valise. He let her go down the stairs ahead of him. On the street, he offered her his arm.

"Do we have time for a stop?" Flori asked as they started down the street toward the docks.

"More than enough, unless you want to be fitted for handmade shoes," Hemmett answered. "What's your pleasure? Hungry?"

"We just ate, Sir Stomach," she laughed, easily using the funny nickname her mother had given his appetite. "I would like to have my hair cut, like a modern Samorsan woman. It's for my new life."

He looked down at her.

She was going to be a stunning woman, like her mother. She'd inherited her mother's black curls. She'd always worn her hair long – but now was a time of changes.

"We certainly do," he assured her. "Let's find a lady barber."

They were both pleased with the result. The shorter locks framed her exotic face and brought out the symmetry of her features. Her eyes were devastating, as dark as her mother's and just as lustrous, long lashed and almond shaped. Her mouth was sensual and naturally pink, contrasting dramatically with her copper skin.

"I believe I'm going to have the loveliest daughter in Erdahn," Hemmett smiled as he paid the barber. "Any other stops you'd like to make? Grandmama and Auntie and the cousins will be seeing us off."

"No more stops. We're on our way." She took his arm and they began their journey.

***

Borsen turned the pages of Flori's sketchbook slowly, taking his time over each fashion design. Flori waited, seemingly calm – if you didn't see her right foot twisting back and forth, back and forth, Hemmett thought. He exchanged a glance and slight smile with Menders, who could also see that foot in its elegant shoe, twisting a swirl into Borsen's carpet.

"I can tell from your drawings that you can sew," Borsen said, looking over the book at Flori. "How well?"

She almost said something modest but then remembered who she was talking to. Borsen hated false modesty and she wanted very much for him to be her future employer.

"I sew very well, Uncle Borsen," she answered. "Mama taught me, and she was a wonderful seamstress."

"Yes, she was indeed," he said, going back to the book. Flori's foot picked up the tempo.

"How long until you turn fifteen? I'm bad about dates," Borsen asked abstractedly.

"Three weeks."

Borsen nodded. He reached the last sketch and carefully closed the little sketchbook, putting it down on the desk blotter before him.

"Are you wondering how I knew you could sew from your sketches?" he asked.

"Yes, a little bit," Flori admitted.

"You don't design anything that is impossible to sew," he explained. "You know the limitations of the craft and materials and work within them. There are no absurd, impossible to sew designs in your book. At not quite fifteen – I am impressed, Flori."

"And impressing him isn't easy," Hemmett added.

"Quiet, proud papa," Borsen said, the corners of his mouth quirking upward in amusement. "This is a job interview."

Hemmett snorted comically and crossed his arms.

"Flori, I would definitely like to have you here as an apprentice designer," Borsen said, looking directly at her. "But I think we need to come to agreement on a few conditions."

"He just doesn't want anyone here who's prettier than he is," Hemmett murmured.

"Hemmett, would you like me to call in a big man to escort you out of my office?" Borsen asked with mock patience.

"That would have to be a very big man," Hemmett muttered toward the ceiling.

"We will ignore his misbehavior," Borsen said to Flori. "My concern is your education, Flori. Fourteen – let's say fifteen since it is so close – is very young to leave off formal schooling altogether. I would like to see you put in some more years of study."

"I don't care for school," Flori ventured, her voice tinged with disappointment.

"Borsen didn't either," Menders said. Flori turned to him in surprise. "That doesn't mean he didn't continue to learn. Eiren and I set up a curriculum for him and she did most of his tutoring. He still writes out lists of spelling words every night because he had a great deal of trouble with that subject."

"That's true," Borsen said as Flori looked at him in amazement. "I have a terrible time with spelling, so I memorize a list of twenty words every evening. Would you consider working with a tutor for a couple of hours a day and whatever independent study that would involve?"

Flori nodded.

"Good enough. One other condition. If you should find you no longer wish to be a designer – if you work at it for a while and realize it is not for you – I want you to tell me. Don't be afraid, or convince yourself that since I've spent time training you it would be ungrateful to tell me the truth. I'm not capable of lying, Flori and I expect honesty from the people who work for me. Can you promise me that? If things change, you need to let me know."

"I will, Uncle Borsen."

"Then you are my apprentice. Surprised? That isn't because you're my niece – it's because you're that talented. We'll have to find our way, because I've never had an apprentice before. I think half days to begin with. You need time for study and to get used to living here. Pay is fifty florins a week. Is that acceptable?"

Flori nodded, delight on her face.

"Well then, I say we have lunch," Borsen smiled, rising to his feet and checking his watch. "The restaurant here does an excellent Seven Spice Soup, which is what I'm starting with. Why not go ahead with your grandfather? Papa and I will catch you up after we're done with the legal matters."

Hemmett and Borsen could hear Flori burst into excited chatter the moment she and Menders cleared the doorway of Borsen's office. They laughed into their hands until she was out of earshot.

"Poor darling, she pawed a great divot in your carpet," Hemmett said, scuffing the spot to get all the nap going in the same direction.

"That is exactly how I would have interviewed any young person with the same abilities," Borsen explained. "Don't worry about that, the cleaning crew will sort it. Now, you're her legal guardian?"

"Yes, that's all settled."

"Excellent – I'll ask Varens to have the paperwork drawn up and we can get her working as soon as you think best. If she's anything like you and me, she's wanting to get to work."

"Well, Luntigré always remarked on how much she was like me, so there we are," Hemmett grinned. "She needs projects and goals, that's certain. Never happy when she's at loose ends."

"Well, I'll keep her busy. She could have quite a distinguished career as a designer – she might even become a great designer," Borsen said seriously. "The potential is there. How are you both weathering Luntigré's death?"

Hemmett put his hands in his pockets.

"We have our crying spells – together and separately. We talk about her a lot. But Luntigré made sure we were prepared, and she was so calm and peaceful that it wasn't a terrible experience. We miss her, but there was no fear or horror at her death – not like what poor Eiren and her family went through."

Borsen flinched.

"Yes, that was ghastly. I want you to know I don't believe in making apprentices do pointless or dirty jobs, just as Tomar didn't with me. Flori will actually be working on designs, she won't be sweeping the floor or running errands."

"I didn't think she would. Are you ready to eat? I'm about to chew off my own shoes."

"To the restaurant then," Borsen laughed.

***

"Flori being Samorsan will simplify arranging security for her," Hemmett said. "Acceptance of reality is a large part of Samorsan culture. If she understands the reasons for it, she'll adapt to it readily. She'll fight like a langhur against anything she considers unjust or unfair but something necessary and sensible is another matter."

"It needs to be as unobtrusive as possible," Kaymar added. "I wouldn't feel confident about any girl her age going around Erdahn on her own – and much as I hate to say it, Hem, her association with you could make her a target."

"I'm well aware of that, no need to apologize," Hemmett replied philosophically, taking out a cigar.

"May I join you gentlemen?"

Cigars went down, chairs scraped back, and five astonished men were upstanding for the Queen of Mordania.

Katrin had braved a flight of stairs to walk into this meeting. She had not ventured below her own floor in the Tower in two years. Hemmett could see her pulse pounding at the side of her throat. He immediately led her to his chair at the head of the table.

Menders filled a glass with water at the sideboard. Fear had brought Katrin out in a sweat and it was obvious from the way she swallowed repeatedly that her mouth and throat were dry. He bent over her as he put the glass in her hand.

"Well done," he whispered, placing two clean handkerchiefs in her lap. Katrin smiled weakly.

"Please go ahead," she whispered, sipping water desperately. Her tongue felt glued to the roof of her mouth. "I'd like to help with Flori's security, if I can."

"I'd be most pleased, Willow," Hemmett smiled.

Kaymar looked stricken. He had not seen Katrin up close since he had asked Menders to reassign him. He and Ifor had spent the years gathering information in Surytam as well as acting as ambassadors to the Hetzophian court. He had written to Katrin a few times, but she never responded. Menders told him that she wrote to no-one.

Seeing her now, overweight, haggard, the ravages of melancholia and drink destroying her uniquely beautiful face made his heart go slightly out of rhythm, sending a jab of pain down his right arm.

Ifor sensed it and reached over, filling another glass from the pitcher. Kaymar surreptitiously slipped a small tin from his pocket and palmed a tablet into his mouth, following it with a hefty swig from the glass.

"Let me catch you up with the discussion," Menders said, as if Katrin attended meetings every day. "Hemmett's townhouse is positioned between Kaymar's and Villison's, so that provides a great deal of built-in security that won't be obvious or intrusive. Cook and Varnia found that Petra's mother would love to be housekeeper for Hemmett and Flori now that she's widowed, so she will be arriving next week. I can't think of a scrappier, more powerful woman to preside. It gives her a chance to be near Petra and the grandchildren. She's also a good shot and a wonderful cook."

"She larruped my backside with a razor strop once," Hemmett said comically, looking downcast.

"That was when you nearly got Petra and Artur drowned down at the stream when we were little, playing pirates," Katrin said, managing a slight smile.

Menders looked from one of them to the other.

"Debriefing on the unreported near drowning will commence later, Captain Greinholz, Your Majesty," he said sternly.

Katrin laughed.

The men froze again. They had not heard that sound in a very, very long time.

"Please go on with your meeting," Katrin said gently.

"The question today is how much bodyguard coverage to give Flori," Menders said after clearing his throat several times. "As you know, being continually watched is not an easy thing."

Katrin nodded agreement, feeling her heart fluttering with panic.

"Deep breaths, Cuz," Kaymar said suddenly. "Push your diaphragm right down."

Automatically, she obeyed him. The fluttering stopped as she drew in big draughts of air.

"Don't mind me," she said. "Go on."

"I'll be back on duty in two more weeks," Hemmett said, taking the attention off Katrin's struggles. "We need someone in place by then to escort her to Borsen's and back or anywhere else she'd like to go. As her father and considering her age, I would like to avoid a handsome, young male bodyguard. Flori needs time to adjust to the changes she's been through – we don't need romantic complications at this time."

Katrin leaned toward Menders and murmured something. He nodded agreement.

"Why don't we see if Gladdas has a young lady who could do the job?" Menders said to the table at large.

"Shame on me, I never thought of it," Kaymar burst out. "That would work. It also wouldn't be as obvious as having a fifteen-year-old girl going back and forth to Borsen's with a man every day."

"It's something we've never had to consider," Menders replied. "Katrin's situation was very different, as she was surrounded by security all the time and had you as an unobtrusive and vigilant bodyguard. But if Flori wants to shop for clothing or perfume, it would be awkward to have a man following her about. I know for a fact that Glad trains a wickedly good security ma… woman."

"I like the idea," Hemmett agreed. "Good call, Katrin. Any other ideas?" He smiled at her.

"How do you feel about owning a boarhound?" she said softly.

"Fine. I never had one at The Shadows because Ma didn't want one in the suite," he replied. "I'm taking Flori over to The Shadows in the next couple of weeks. There are several boarhounds ready to go to new homes, so we'll pick out a brace of them."

Katrin smiled again. Each time it was easier. She drew in a deep breath to control her fluttering heart.

"Should I bring one back for you, my other self?" Hemmett asked, looking right into her eyes.

"I'm not sure…" she whispered, looking down at the table top.

Then she looked up at him.

"Yes," she said firmly.

Hemmett smiled.

***

Flori stood at the bottom of the massive Tower Stairwell and clapped her hands once. The sound carried upward in a bright spiral, resonating against the stone walls.

"Papa, what a wonderful little concert hall this would make!" she cried enthusiastically. "The acoustics are perfect! You couldn't squeeze a full orchestra in, but it would be lovely for chamber concerts."

Hemmett had given in to Flori's repeated requests to see The Palace. The ancient building was far from inviting, other than Katrin's suite and some of the galleries on the main floor. He hadn't pressed for an invitation to visit from Katrin yet. He knew she cared about Flori and would ask her when she was able to provide a pleasant time.

Flori, however, was fascinated by the great building. She would look at a room and then talk about how she would make it beautiful, describing draperies, furniture, carpets. Hemmett had always considered the place a ghastly mausoleum himself, but she sparked his imagination with her enthusiasm. She had already done wonders at their townhouse and she hadn't been in Mordania for two weeks.

"You would have room to put chairs in for a small audience," he said, surveying the area with interest. "A food table could go over there."

"Oh Papa, your stomach! Imagine a flute concert or a choral group. A rug on the floor would make it a little less live, but otherwise, it would be just right."

"Just right for two cromars?" Hemmett said, looking at her out of the corners of his eyes.

Flori smiled back. "I'll beat you to the house!" she said, darting back out into the Courtyard. Hemmett was quite a runner, but it took some effort to keep up with her.

Within fifteen minutes they were back, setting up two chairs and tuning their instruments. Flori preferred a small soprano cromar, similar to the child's instrument Hemmett had given her when she was six. Hemmett cherished his huge, baritone cromar, which had traveled with him everywhere since he was ten years old. They had played together for years and could proudly boast an admirable degree of excellence as a musical duo.

Hemmett counted off silently and they launched into their "bring down the house" piece, an arrangement of Samorsan dance tunes that required lightning fast runs and melody playing from Flori and precise rasgueado strumming and bass line picking from Hemmett.

Their music soared up the Tower stairwell and echoed down the halls of the silent Palace. They were intent on their playing and did not see Menders, Kaymar and Ifor coming down one of the long hallways to listen. Menders covertly peered up the stairwell and then nodded to his companions.

"A song, Papa!" Flori laughed as soon as the dance suite was done. They were off again, singing a complex Fambrian duet, switching off the melody lines, their fingers drawing a complex counterpoint from their instruments. They were so delighted with their performance that they laughed aloud after the final chorus.

"And now, your Mama's favorite, to finish," Hemmett directed, launching into the accompaniment to Sweetheart, Kiss Me Tonight. "You sing it, daughter. I'll cry if I do."

"Sweetheart, kiss me tonight,
While the dew falls soft on the rose.
Hold me close in your arms, dear
While evening sunset light glows.
Sweetheart, swear to be true,
Though I must roam far from your side,
Sweetheart, kiss me -
And tell me you'll miss me –
Sweetheart, kiss me tonight.

Oh love, I swear to be true,
Though the war horn calls me away
To shores uncharted and lonely
Where Death's battalion holds sway.
If from this life I am called
I will still be there at your side.
Oh Sweetheart! Kiss me –
And tell me you'll miss me –
Sweetheart, kiss me tonight."

Flori's voice echoed up the stairwell, making the old soldier's song into something sublime. She finished the performance with a climbing run to the highest notes of her cromar and then smiled at her father. He reached out and cupped her chin in his hand, nodding.

Menders, Kaymar and Ifor were just about to applaud when they heard clapping high above them. Menders looked upward again and saw Katrin standing on the landing below her floor, smiling down at Hemmett and Flori as she applauded.

"Flori, would you like to come up for a visit?" Katrin invited. "Bring your Papa – I can't manage coming all the way down there."

Menders closed his eyes and allowed himself to feel hope for the first time in years.

BOOK FOUR

LIGHT OF THE WINTER SUN

THE PALACE, ERDAHN, MORDANIA

I
SUNNY

Hemmett was true to his word and brought back a huge boarhound from The Shadows for Katrin, a golden male a bit older than the more rambunctious pups he had acquired for himself and Flori. Katrin instantly named him Sunrise because of his color – he was Sunny by the end of his first day at The Palace. The dog immediately sensed Katrin's illness and was gently protective, never any further than an arm's length from her side.

The morning after Sunny's arrival, Menders heard him whining somewhere in the Stairwell. The tone of alarm in the big dog's voice made Menders rush upward.

Katrin was cowering on the stairs between the fifth and fourth floors, the boarhound alternately licking her hands and whining.

"Did you fall?" Menders asked, kneeling beside her.

She was panting desperately, her eyes wide, streaming with tears. She couldn't speak, but managed to shake her head. That was when he saw the leash in her hand, attached to Sunny's collar.

She had been trying to go down the stairs to take the dog outside. After four years of being unable to go more than one floor down from her Tower suite, she had come down three flights to try to care for her dog before she collapsed out of sheer terror.

"I'm sorry," Katrin finally gasped, desperately fighting for breath. "He needs to go out. I forgot all about that when I asked for him. I tried to take him down to the Courtyard – but I couldn't! I couldn't! I can't go down those stairs!"

Swift light footsteps climbed toward them and Villison appeared around the curve of the stairway.

"Here, Katrin, I was just coming to take the perambulating carpet out," he said, sounding chipper, as if he found her panicking on the stairs every day. "Let me have the big grundar. You let Menders help you back up to your suite. We'll be up shortly once all business is properly attended to." He whistled softly for Sunny's attention and then trotted down the stairwell with the big dog pacing alongside.

"Come along, my dear," Menders urged gently, getting an arm around her and encouraging her to rise. "Let's get you back upstairs. A facewash and cup of coffee will be just what you need."

Katrin shuddered and shivered but climbed the stairs with minimal assistance. She went to her washstand and bathed her face and streaming eyes, then sat at her table where Menders had poured out cups of coffee for them both. A neatly appointed kitchen was part of the suite, which saved endless trips up and down the stairwell.

"I'm so sorry," Katrin shuddered.

"I'm proud of you," Menders countered. "Here, have some of this coffee and let me fetch some food over. Have you eaten this morning?"

"Not yet. I didn't order breakfast last night – didn't think of it, I was so excited over Sunny," she replied, her teeth chattering.

Menders went through the kitchen, pleased to see there was bread, butter, fruit and cheese available. It was evident that Katrin had been preparing snacks and meals for herself of late. He rapidly piled food on a platter, scrabbled up plates and cutlery and went back to the table, not wanting to lose the moment.

Katrin's breathing was less frantic and ragged. She picked up a slice of bread. Her hands shook so violently that Menders took it and buttered it before handing it back to her.

Once she began to swallow, the rapid breathing and shivering started to abate. They ate and drank coffee without speaking.

"That was a brave move on your part," Menders finally said, when he saw that Katrin had calmed enough to pour out a second cup for herself. "It's also a hopeful sign that you will be able to recover."

"I just wanted to take care of my dog," she said softly.

"The best of motivations," Menders replied. "I have an idea. The rooftop garden here – we've not done much with it, but we could arrange a spot where Sunny can relieve himself when there is no-one available to take him outside. You'd have to clean up after him regularly, but that way you can take full care of him. The rooftop garden could use some work as well."

She smiled slightly and looked interested.

"Would you like to go and see, once you're finished eating?" he asked very gently.

"I'll try," she replied. "It's all I can do, but I will try."

"That's good enough for me," Menders answered.

It was an early winter morning, but the sun was bright and still held some warmth. Katrin wrapped up warmly and then stood for several minutes in the doorway to the roof garden – part of the original design for her suite.

"One step," Menders said.

Before she knew it, she closed her eyes and took a step past the doorway. Then another.

"No further without opening your eyes, Katrin. We don't need you falling," Menders urged.

She obeyed him automatically. She was so frightened she could barely see. She stood motionless, concentrating on Menders' voice as he strode around, explaining how they could situate Sunny's privy near a rain drain for cleanliness, keep water handy to wash his urine away and in the spring, provide a grassy area for him to use.

"This will be an excellent solution to the problem, until you're able to come downstairs again," he said with a smile, turning toward her.

Suddenly a rush of memories of The Shadows hit Katrin. Menders looked younger and happier than he had in years, occupied with solving a problem. She saw him as a young man, tossing her in the air and then catching her close for a hug, calling her by her baby nickname, Snowflower. She remembered talking to him, reading with him, riding…

Katrin grimaced in sorrow and covered her face.

"What is it, little princess?" Menders asked, moving rapidly to stand with her.

"Taffy!" she gasped. "I told you to sell her. Oh, how could I do that? How could I have sold her?"

"Now, now. That's enough. Come right over here," he said, pulling her toward the wall that surrounded the garden. She could see down into the Courtyard, where Hemmett was talking to Villison while Sunny sniffed the bushes, deciding just where he was going to do his business.

Menders whistled to get their attention. They both looked up and gaped as they saw Katrin next to Menders, who gestured toward the stables. Then Hemmett grinned.

"Want to see your other beast, oh Highest of Highnesses?" he shouted up impudently. He dashed away and within moments came back with Taffy, sleek and shining, prancing a bit at his side. She whickered at Sunny, who nosed curiously around her feet.

"Can you call to her?" Menders urged. Katrin tried, but couldn't manage. Menders whistled to make Taffy look up at them.

"I've been exercising her and Borsen takes her out as well. A couple of Menders' Men ride her too. She's well, fat and sassy, Katrin. She'll be very glad when you can come down and visit her. Now, let's get you back inside. It's not that warm."

Katrin was seated at the table again when Villison brought Sunny in. The big dog trotted right over to her and put his enormous head in her lap. Menders brought over a pan of warmed milk and poured it into a fresh cup, not wanting more coffee to give her the jitters.

"Now then, my little princess, I have work I must get to," he said after he was sure she was calm enough to be left alone. "If you need anything, I'll be in my office."

Katrin smiled and nodded, then poured out a portion of milk in a saucer for Sunny.

"We can go outside any time now," he heard her saying softly to the big dog. "We have a lovely garden right outside the door there. You can widdle as much as you like and then when it's spring, we might be able to manage the stairs."

Villison had been shamelessly eavesdropping at the suite door. He and Menders engaged in a wildly enthusiastic handshake, though Menders whispered, "Don't spread the word, Vil. Let's see what happens. I need to speak with Franz right away."

***

From Doctor Franz's files:

The recent improvement in Katrin's condition has remained stable for several months now. Her empathy and concern for others, always the strongest aspects of her personality, are coming to the forefront, helping her in coping with her long term melancholia.

This is encouraging, but Katrin still suffers greatly. I have been administering a medication brought by Kaymar from Surytam which has been very effective in lessening his own mental symptoms. This is being done without Katrin's knowledge, so she won't try to please by reporting improvement that isn't there. Beginning the use of this medication coincided with Hemmett returning from

Samorsa with Flori and the gift he made to Katrin of her new boarhound. It's possible that it will never be clear what led to her improvement.

Menders has suggested approaching her about the orphanage project that had to be abandoned during Aidelia's reign. This might be an ongoing impetus for her. I feel it is absolutely necessary to prevent her backsliding. It is obvious that being able to help others goes a long way toward lightening her situation.

***

The next two years moved along more peacefully. Katrin remained a recluse in the Tower, but she tried to improve her condition. She kept herself clean, made herself presentable and curbed her drinking.

Even on days when she was obviously melancholic, she never said "who cares". To Menders, after the many months where she had fired that phrase off to everything and anything that was said, this was an incredible relief.

Damage had been done to the bond between them. There was a rift, and he mourned it. He made a point of being as gentle and loving toward her as he could – not always easy on the bad days when she couldn't seem to control herself, drank and would avoid everyone.

Eiren came to visit often and Menders went to The Shadows, sometimes as frequently as four times a week. He desperately wanted Eiren to come live with him in Erdahn, but she had been caught up in more family trouble. Her father suffered a severe bout of melancholia after the death of his wife. To make matters worse, one of Eiren's sisters had been widowed by the most recent scrap with Artreya. She moved back to the Spaltz farm with her four children, very much at a loss as to what to do and how to live. Eiren had been dragged back into being a caretaker and the situation was such that she simply couldn't pull up stakes and leave.

Katrin spontaneously spent time playing her spinet or painting. She devoted a lot of effort to plans for The Shadows Orphanage. Stevahn visited weekly in a business capacity, going over the operations of the facility. Varnia came along with him to give her weekly progress reports of the ten children who had been placed as the Orphanage's first residents. Katrin took a lively interest in the children and made up clothing and toys for them.

She looked forward to Borsen's visits and was openly happy when Flori came to see her. She spent time talking to Hemmett and sometimes could be heard laughing at Villison's nonsense.

Sunny was always at Katrin's side and even on her bad days, she never failed to care for him. She might be so burdened with sadness that she couldn't speak, but she rose, prepared his food, took him out to get sun and fresh air in the Tower garden.

One autumn day Menders found her planting spring bulbs in one of the huge raised garden beds that had been installed at her request. He watched as she spoke to Sunny, telling him that there would be flowers there in the spring – snowflowers, the blossoms that often pushed their way through the winter snow.

"Menders used to call me Snowflower when I was a tiny girl," she told the loving dog. "Maybe this spring we can go down the stairs and look for snowflowers outside. But if we can't, we'll have snowflowers here."

Katrin was slowly climbing out of the darkness she had lived in for so long.

ERDAHN, MORDANIA

2
"I'VE BEEN WITH THE GHOSTS OF VOICES SINGING"

Stevahn finished putting the studs in his formal dress shirt and began working on his cufflinks. He and Borsen had found long ago that they could not shave or dress in the same room at the same time. Collisions led to bellows of frustration, which led to shouting matches neither of them enjoyed. They now dressed separately, particularly for formal occasions.

He could see Borsen in his workroom down the hall, sitting at his drafting table in his impeccable evening dress, whiling away the time it took Stevahn to dress by sketching.

Suddenly Borsen sat upright and shook his head, then rubbed the back of his neck.

"What's the matter?" Stevahn called.

"Just dizzy for a second. It's gone now," Borsen answered, bending over his work again. Stevahn worked his second cufflink into place, shrugged on his jacket and checked his reflection in the mirror. Good enough, but Borsen would fuss around him, twitching his tie into place, tweaking his clothing here and there, making him look even better.

"I'm ready to go," he announced. Borsen nodded, stood and shook his head again.

"How long since you've eaten?" Stevahn asked, watching him obviously trying to banish another dizzy spell.

"Too long, obviously. There, it's better now." Borsen walked toward Stevahn with a smile. "Are you wearing that? Your tie is under one ear."

He collapsed in an unconscious heap at Stevahn's feet.

Stevahn was kneeling beside him in an instant, rolling him onto his back and supporting his head in his hands. Borsen's eyelids fluttered. Stevahn felt his forehead. Fever – burning fever.

"No!" he whispered, knowing what had struck Borsen down. Borsen blinked and then their eyes met. Stevahn could see that he knew too.

"Have you had it?" Borsen asked, his voice suddenly weak.

"Yes, years ago," Stevahn answered, not adding that the same illness had killed his younger brother.

"Send for Doctor Franz – and Papa," Borsen whispered. "Right away."

"Let me get you to bed first."

"I can't fall farther than the floor," Borsen managed to smile. "Time is of the essence, my dear."

Stevahn ran to the landing and shouted for Varnia. She hurried to the foot of the stairs and looked up at him.

"Varnia, have you had putrid fever?" Stevahn asked rapidly.

"Years ago," she answered, looking puzzled – then realization dawned. She swayed, clinging to the newel post for a moment. He could see her rallying her strength.

"We need Doctor Franz and Menders," Stevahn said, trying to keep his voice calm and even. "Please, dear – I can't leave him."

She rushed away. Stevahn ran back to Borsen. He was shivering violently, still stretched out on the floor.

"All right, here we go," Stevahn said with careful cheerfulness. He lifted Borsen easily and put him on the bed, then rummaged out a heavy nightshirt for him and began to strip off his formal attire. Within a few minutes, Stevahn had him bundled up in bed, a heated brick at his feet and extra blankets tucked around him.

"I might not have long to be lucid," Borsen said rapidly. "I'm going to have Papa make a couple of amendments to my will. It isn't up to date. Everything goes to you and Varnia except for some personal items."

"Borsen, don't do this," Stevahn whispered, despite knowing putrid fever was invariably fatal in adults.

"Please – I won't have a lot of time where I can talk and understand," Borsen continued firmly. "I saw it kill people many times when I was small. I always assumed I'd had it as a child, though I couldn't remember it. We were always living in places where it was rampant."

Suddenly he gripped Stevahn's hand with both of his, hard. His eyes went wide with fear.

"Stay with me. Please stay with me so long as I know you're there. Please," he choked.

"I'll stay with you," Stevahn answered firmly, bending and putting his arms around Borsen. "I promised to stay with you all your life."

Borsen sighed with relief. He wrapped his arms around Stevahn's neck and held on.

***

"Has he been down by the docks?" Doctor Franz asked Stevahn. They were standing in the hallway as Menders talked to Borsen.

"I don't… yes! He had to go and see about a shipment three days ago."

"It's rife down there. The outbreak is brand new, so he wouldn't have heard about it," Franz sighed. "I know he's always avoided it, because we had no idea what he'd had and what he hadn't."

"What do we do?" Stevahn asked, his heart feeling as if it was encased in ice.

"Careful nursing, keep the fever down," Franz said, obviously keeping his voice unemotional.

"My brother died of it," Stevahn said quietly.

"The mortality rate among adults is… total," Franz responded, his eyes finally meeting Stevahn's. "You must brace yourself, Stevahn."

"How can I do that?" Stevahn answered bleakly.

Franz put a hand on his arm.

***

"There is a painting, a small one, of Snowflake," Borsen told Menders, who sat on the edge of the bed holding his hands. "I want Katrin to have that. There's only one, so there'll be no mistake."

Menders nodded.

"I want Hemmett to have the belt and money bag I had made from that snakeskin," Borsen continued. "He'll like the joke. He could never wear the shoes. Save them for Vil's boy, he's always coveted them."

Menders nodded again.

"I'm the one who took Cook's Particular Spoon," Borsen went on. "It's hidden in the strongroom, behind the shelf. Give it back to her. I never got around to it." He managed a grin, between violent chills. Menders couldn't help smiling.

"And here I blamed Hemmett for that all these years," Menders replied.

"I enjoyed keeping the mystery going," Borsen smiled. I want Doctor Franz to have my painting of him."

"Done," Menders said.

"There's a piece of jewelry – a ring – that I designed for you, for Winterfest," Borsen said, his voice a little fainter. "Alahno, the jeweler at the store is working on it. Don't forget about it. I mean you to have it, Papa. You'll understand when you see it."

Menders felt a burning behind his eyes, but remained calm. Borsen was managing, so he could do the same. Borsen deserved to have someone hear his last requests.

"I have a book of sketches of you. I want Auntie to have that," Borsen continued. "It's on my worktable at the store."

Menders nodded.

"Please, keep Stevahn part of the family. Don't let him fall by the wayside."

"We never would, son."

"One last thing." Borsen gripped Menders' hand tightly and looked at him intently. "If I live through this, but as an idiot, I want you to kill me."

Menders froze. Borsen kept his brown eyes on him, despite the rapidly rising fever – the fever that wasted bodies and destroyed brains.

"I don't want to live as an idiot," Borsen continued intensely. "I don't want to be a burden to Stevahn, Varnia or to you. If I survive, but I'm an idiot from the fever, I want you to promise you will end it for me. I won't be able to do it for myself."

Menders looked at him – his late arriving boy, his beloved son.

"I will," he said roughly.

"Thank you."

Borsen held up his arms and Menders gathered him close. He found he was rocking the small body, horrified as he felt how hot it was growing.

"Thank you for everything you've done for me," Borsen whispered in his ear. "I love you, Papa."

"Thank you for coming to me," Menders answered. "I love you, my son."

Cherish this moment, he told himself fiercely. It is going to be very ugly soon. Cherish this. Remember everything, his voice, his arms around you, his hair against your cheek. Oh, my boy.

"Now, we'd best have Franz and Stevahn back," Menders said when Borsen began shuddering from a chill, settling him back against the pillows and making sure he was covered. He wiped Borsen's eyes for him. Then he rose and went to the door, letting Stevahn and Franz back into the room.

They began to fight what they knew would be a losing battle.

***

Katrin ran to the head of the stairs as soon as she heard Menders coming, looking down at him as he walked up as slowly and tiredly as an old, old man would.

She couldn't speak. She waited.

Menders looked up and saw her there. He closed his eyes for a moment and then finished his climb up the final steps.

"It's putrid fever," he said softly, touching her cheek.

Katrin stared at him, her hands over her mouth.

"No," she whispered. "No!"

Menders put his arms around her. She flung hers around him and held on with all her strength.

***

TO: EIREN
FROM: MENDERS

BORSEN ILL WITH PUTRID FEVER. PLEASE COME AS QUICKLY AS POSSIBLE TO SAY GOODBYE.

FROM: EIREN
TO: MENDERS

LEAVING IMMEDIATELY. WILL TAKE CAB FROM DOCKS. DO NOT LEAVE HIM TO COME FOR ME.

***

Stevahn rose stiffly, slowly straightening his kinked back and legs. Borsen was asleep at last, after another bout of high fever that nothing would bring down. Doctor Franz managed to give him a dose of ramplane, giving Borsen some relief from the massive muscle spasms that racked sufferers of this terrible disease.

"Best get something to eat now," Franz said wearily to Stevahn, washing his hands thoroughly. "He'll need you with him when he wakes. It won't be long. I don't dare give him a large dose of ramplane."

"How long until the bowel involvement begins?" Stevahn asked, filled with dread.

"Another twelve to twenty hours," Franz answered.

Stevahn made his way down to the kitchen and forced himself to swallow food methodically. Varnia, her eyes painfully red, poured coffee for him and rested her hand on his shoulder for a moment before gathering up fresh towels and linen and starting upstairs with them.

"Stretch out beside him for a while," Franz said when Stevahn returned to Borsen's bedside. "You look done in. You're going to need every bit of strength you have later."

Stevahn took his advice, lying close to Borsen, putting an arm over him, pressing his face against Borsen's long silky hair.

***

Hemmett rushed into his townhouse, startling Flori and their housekeeper, Alisa Gunter. The women were sitting by the front room fire chatting and laughing about some event of the day.

"Flori, have you had putrid fever?" Hemmett asked, hurriedly taking off his uniform overcoat.

"When I was five, right before you met Mama," she answered. Her eyes widened in fear. "Who has it?"

Hemmett felt a surge of relief. Flori worked with Borsen daily and would be sure to contract putrid fever if she had never been exposed before. She was old enough that it would be extremely dangerous, if not fatal.

He sat beside her and took her hand.

"It's Borsen, sweetheart," he said. "I have to go there now to help them."

"I'll get some things for you to take along," Alisa said, rising quickly and hurrying into the kitchen.

"Oh Papa! He seemed fine this afternoon," Flori protested, her forehead creased with anxiety.

"It moves very quickly. He was well one minute and fainted the next," Hemmett replied. "You can help us a great deal if you will make a list of everyone you can remember being around Borsen's workroom in the last three days. Can you do that?"

"Of course. Should I bring it up to Borsen's house?"

"No – Vil will come by for it in about half an hour. Flori, I very seldom forbid you anything, but I am very serious. I do not want you going to Borsen's house. There are enough people there to take care of things. I don't need to be worried that you'll try to go up there on your own at night."

Flori's face quivered for a moment. In the two years she'd been working with Borsen, she'd grown very close to him.

"I know," Hemmett said. "He's my little brother. He wouldn't want you to see what is going on now. If you can make up that list so we can locate the people who were in contact with him, we might be able to prevent an epidemic. It's very important that you do this – and it will give him peace of mind."

She nodded. Hemmett held her close.

***

"For the gods' sakes, give him more ramplane!" Menders growled at Franz.

"I can't! Not for a couple of hours or it will kill him outright," Franz answered. "He's not like you or me, Menders! This is a delicate constitution we're dealing with. His heart slowed so much after the last dose, I thought I'd killed him. If I give him enough to lower the fever, he comes close to dying, never mind giving him enough to kill the pain completely."

Menders turned away, his fists clenched.

"If you think it doesn't torment me to see him in such pain, you're mad," Franz snapped, stomping away down the stairs.

"Shh, it's all right," Stevahn whispered in the bedroom, where he was holding Borsen upright in his arms. He constantly massaged

Borsen's arms and legs, which rippled with agonizing muscle spasms. Borsen groaned involuntarily and shuddered with pain. Eiren sat on the other side of the bed, sponging his burning forehead.

"Where's Papa?" Borsen asked during an apparent lull.

"Right here, son," Menders said, going rapidly into the room.

"I need to see Katrin," Borsen said rapidly. "I need to tell her something. Could you ask her to come?"

"Yes, I will, right away," Menders replied, rushing to the door. He shuddered as he heard Borsen's soft groans and cries of pain as another muscle spasm began, then dashed down the stairs.

Menders managed to snag a passing cab outside and made good time to the Palace. He raced up all the stairs into the Tower.

Katrin was drunk. It was obvious she'd been drinking for hours.

"Damn it!" Menders said, going to her. "Borsen is asking for you!"

"I'm sorry."

"Get up. Come with me, please," Menders pleaded.

"I can't. I can't go out there," Katrin answered.

"Katrin, he's dying! There is not going to be another chance," Menders said, his voice rising with anger. "It's a last request. I'll help you get down the stairs. Please!"

Katrin turned away from him, her head hung low.

Menders wheeled away from her, going out of the suite as quickly as he had come in.

When he got back to the sickroom, Borsen was worse.

***

Later that night Katrin awoke to the sound of Menders' footsteps nearing her bedroom door. He crashed in and wrenched aside the hanging blocking the private part of her room.

"Borsen is asking for you – still," he said bitterly. "There is something he wants to tell you. He can't rest because he wants to talk to you. Would you please have the decency to get up and go to see him?"

Katrin shrank away from him, shaking her head. Sunny moved protectively closer to her.

"Katrin!" Menders sprang forward and grabbed her by the shoulders. He shook her viciously. Sunny growled but a look from Menders made him slink off the bed onto the floor.

"Borsen is going to die and he knows it! It's in his bowels now! It's eating him alive! He's a wreck and he won't be conscious much longer. He's asked for you all night long. He cries when you don't come. He's dying a horrible, painful death! How can you just lie around here when this is happening?"

Katrin began to cry, still shaking her head.

Menders stood upright and stared at her, the expression on his face horrifying.

"All right," he said coldly. "I am going to leave in five minutes to go back down there. It's six blocks away. I have a cab waiting. We can carry you down the stairs if you can't manage on your own. You don't have to walk down the street. There's a cab right outside in the Courtyard.

"After everything Borsen has been to you... no, I'm not going to beg. If you aren't ready to go in five minutes, I will go without you. I don't think there is anything you can do that will ever mend things between us if you fail Borsen now."

Katrin heard him go.

She leapt from the bed suddenly, dragging a dress on over her gown, pulling her wig on, not even bothering to look in the mirror.

Menders descended to the ground floor, where Villison was waiting, pacing frantically.

"She didn't come?" Villison blurted in dismay.

"I've given her five minutes," Menders said furiously. "I'm not going to lose another minute with him because of her." He took out his watch and held it in his hand. Villison groaned and paced back and forth.

Rapid footsteps started down the stairs above them – Katrin. Menders and Villison dashed upward to meet her.

The footsteps stopped in mid-flight. After a pause, they began to climb upwards, slowly. They could hear Katrin's panicked breathing rasping through the entire Stairwell. The door to her suite closed and the lock was turned.

"I won't lose another minute," Menders said coldly, turning and racing back to the cab.

***

Menders sat at the side of Borsen's bed. Stevahn was stretched out beside Borsen, his arms around him, his mouth against his ear. Eiren had nearly collapsed from exhaustion. Menders tucked her into bed in one of the spare rooms, sitting with her until she slept.

Hemmett was asleep in a chair in the corner of the room, years of being a soldier making him capable of sleeping anywhere, anytime. Franz was asleep on the floor beside the bed. Years of being a doctor made him capable of sleeping anywhere, anytime.

Varnia was expending her sorrow by scrubbing out the soiled linens from the bed. Menders could hear her rapidly turning the handle of the wringer in the laundry downstairs.

Stevahn whispered from time to time. At this point, the big man didn't care who heard, snatching any moment when Borsen was conscious to talk to him. Borsen must have moved or opened his eyes, because Stevahn was speaking to him again.

"I'm here, light of my life," he said. "Everyone else is asleep except Varnia, who's downstairs, and Menders. He's here sitting by the bed. It's very late.

"I've been remembering all those months when I was a fool and stood in my office window watching you while your building was being renovated," Stevahn went on. "I used to marvel at you. I still marvel at you, every day. I only wish I'd had the sense to tell you how I felt sooner, so we would have had more time. All that time wasted when we could have been together. Nothing else matters now."

Stevahn stroked Borsen's hair, which was matted with sweat. Eiren had braided it back carefully when it became impossible for him to sit up, so it could be brushed and cared for. He'd thanked her very quietly and somehow she'd managed to maintain her composure.

"I know we promised never to leave each other, until death," Stevahn said after a few moments of silence. "I just never thought you would have to go so soon. Please stay with me. Please stay with me."

The room was quiet again as they waited. Menders reached out and put a hand on Borsen. Life was still there, but far away and ebbing.

***

Katrin stood at the top of the Tower Staircase, fully dressed and wearing her winter coat. She gripped the handrail, drew a deep ragged breath and began to run down the stairs as fast as she could.

She managed three flights before she tripped and rolled on the landing. She shuddered as she tried to pull herself upright.

Her ankle buckled under her and she fell again. She couldn't stand on it. She must have injured it when she fell.

The Stairwell was dim here. Katrin sat up, pulling her skirts back from her ankle. She could feel it swelling already. Her breath was starting to come short. There wouldn't be time for her to get to the bottom of the stairs before the fear came!

She began sliding down the next flight of stairs on her backside, like a little child. The fear was growing now. She could feel her heart pounding. It banged in her ears.

At the next landing she tried to stand and wrenched her injured ankle. She cried out and bent over it. The lantern over the landing had gone out. She was in the dark, alone.

Terror leapt out at her. She huddled there, shivering and moaning softly. Far above, she could hear Sunny yelping and scrabbling wildly at the door she had closed between them.

An hour later, Villison was walking his patrol, which included the Tower Staircase. He braced himself for the climb and started upward.

Harsh, ragged breathing reached him as he climbed to the fourth floor. To his horror, Katrin was lying on the landing, curled into a ball, sobbing and gasping for breath.

"Here, sweetheart!" He dashed up to her and knelt beside her. "Tell me you didn't fall all that way, please!"

"Going to Borsen," she choked, barely able to breathe.

Villison was going over her arms and legs, fearful of finding broken bones. When he felt over her right ankle, she cried out.

"Katrin, this is sprained or broken," he said. "We either have to get you down to the Guardroom or back up to your suite. It has to be iced and bound up – I'd go for Doctor Franz, but he's got his hands full with Borsen. I could find another doctor…"

"Upstairs," Katrin gasped. "I can't be out here! I can't! Get me back upstairs!"

He got a shoulder under her right arm and they started up the stairs together.

"I tried!" she burst out. "If I hadn't fallen, I would have gotten to the bottom. I tried, Vil!"

"I'll make sure Menders knows, Katrin," Villison said, stepping up yet another tread. "We're almost there. Just a few more steps, dear."

***

Stevahn dreamed of a groundquake and woke to find the bed shaking. Franz and Menders were on their feet, their hands on Borsen's shoulders. Hemmett was kneeling on the mattress, holding Borsen's legs down as a massive convulsion contorted his body.

"His tongue's going back," Menders said almost calmly. Stevahn saw him slide a finger into Borsen's mouth, holding it there despite the massive clenching of Borsen's jaw muscles until Franz could get a wrapped tongue depressor between Borsen's teeth.

Stevahn rolled over, wrapping his arms around Borsen's waist. Borsen's skin was so hot it should have been flaming. Stevahn could feel it through the nightshirt and sheet. He could see Varnia at the foot of the bed, doggedly wrapping steaming towels around Borsen's feet.

Eiren squeezed in beside him, a dripping towel loaded with ice in her hands. She held it to Borsen's head.

The convulsion seemed to go on forever as they struggled with Borsen's thrashing body. Eiren determinedly held the cold pack in place, while Franz did the same with cold compresses on Borsen's wrists. Finally, the seizure slowed and then stopped. Franz didn't bother with his stethoscope, pressing his ear to Borsen's chest.

"Still with us," he gasped with relief, stripping back the blanket and sheet so that they could start cleaning up the mess once again. At this point the bed was heavily padded against involuntary loss of bowels and bladder, so it was easier to keep Borsen clean and dry.

"Could we try a tub of ice water?" Stevahn asked hoarsely, cutting away Borsen's fouled nightshirt with his pocketknife, not wanting to disturb him more than necessary.

"I'm afraid to try it," Franz answered. "With another patient I would, but it could put him into shock or stop his heart. He's too frail. We'll leave the nightshirts off now. The covers should be enough to keep him warm. We'll have to continually sponge him to try to – Hemmett, grab him, he's going again!"

They rode out another convulsion. Stevahn watched with horror as the clean pad under Borsen turned red with blood.

***

Menders walked wearily toward the Palace, needing to change into clean clothing before returning to Borsen's house. His exhaustion was so complete that he was barely aware of his body.

He finally reached the Tower suite and staggered through the door.

Katrin was sitting up. It was obvious that she'd been drinking. He could smell it in the room, but she was upright and lucid. She looked up at him fearfully.

"Is he still asking for me?" she whispered.

"He's having convulsions. He can't ask for anyone," Menders answered, his voice flat and expressionless. "The time to talk to him is gone. You had a chance, and now it's gone. So why don't you just pour some more wine down your throat? Then it won't matter a bit when my boy dies."

She tried to speak, gesturing toward her right foot, but he turned away. He couldn't bear any more.

He went to his room and changed his filthy clothing, stuffing the soiled garments into the fire. Then he sank down on the edge of the bed for a moment, desperate to stop moving.

At the window, Eirdon's twin moons were full, high in the sky – supposedly a portent of great things. The wind was rising, howling around the Tower, the true winter wind the Thrun called The Ghosts Of Voices Singing.

Suddenly Menders heard the voice of Tharan-Tul, shaman of the Tailors Clan, the man who had taught him to endure hardship and grief when he was a battered and exploited little boy.

"There will be a time when three arise:
Light Of The Winter Sun from the Royal House –
Light Brighter Than The Sun from the warrior caste –
Reflection Of My Friend from Thrun.

They will find Weaving Man,
Who holds the three strands:
Weaving them into one –
Teaching them to love –
Training them in sacrifice –
Leading them by his own life.

When the time of trial spins out
The chosen children shall rise to their tasks:
Light Of The Winter Sun shall rise from the way of death to rule with peace –
Reflection Of My Friend shall cherish the key that opens the lock of Truth –
Light Brighter Than The Sun shall become living love and sacrifice.

He had heard Tharan-Tul chant the Prophecy Saga when he was very young. He had not thought of it again until Tharak gave Katrin, Hemmett and Borsen their Thrun names and began calling Menders 'Weaving Man', replacing the Thrun name, Magic In The Eyes, which he'd been given by Tharan-Tul as a child. The Saga had haunted him since that time and he tried to tell himself he didn't believe it. But now…

Borsen, Tharkul a' Thrunar – *Reflection Of My Friend shall cherish the key that opens the lock of Truth.*

Suddenly alert, Menders rose and went to the window, looking away from the moons toward the constellation called The Weaver – the grouping of stars the Thrun called Weaving Man.

Nothing in The Weaver had changed. The three brightest stars glowed in a triangle at The Weaver's heart, the same positions they had held since the night Katrin was born and the third star rose unexpectedly, baffling the scientific men of Eirdon.

Menders ran from his room, past Katrin, who cried his name in astonishment, down the many flights of stairs and into the street.

He raced the five blocks to Borsen's house and burst in the front door.

Stevahn was collapsed on the sofa, broken down in agony at last. Menders grabbed his arm, pulling him upright.

"He is not going to die!" he cried, feeling wild exhilaration.

Stevahn stared at him as if he'd gone mad.

"He's not going to die – there's something he must do first!

"For the Gods' sake, Menders!" Stevahn shouted, his voice breaking with pain, his face distorted with misery. "He's been convulsing since you left! No-one survives putrid fever once convulsions set in!"

"He will! Go back to him, he'll need you!" Menders shouted exultingly.

A light of hope sparked deep in Stevahn's blue eyes. He stood slowly and started up the stairs.

Menders sank down on the sofa, the feeling of elation and joy completely gone. He tried to remember the words of the Saga that had come to him, but they were gone as well.

If he'd given Stevahn false hope, he wouldn't be able to live with himself.

***

Borsen was aware of there being no more pain, of being lighter than he ever had been, even when he was a starveling child. He rose rapidly from his body, as if impelled by a force he couldn't see.

He was lifted high above Erdahn. He could see the Harbor and farther, the world turning beneath him as he was blown along by a windstorm toward The Light At The Top Of The World.

Suddenly he was caught in loving arms and pulled away from the power that had torn him from his body. He wondered if it was Stevahn holding him – but these arms were softer. He knew them.

"Mama!" he whispered, looking up into beautiful white eyes.

"It is not yet time for you to join us, my little son" she answered. "This illness is the work of forces that seek to destroy. There is work for you to do in the world for many years to come."

"Mama, I want to stay with you," he pleaded.

"I am always with you." Her voice was magnified as if there were hundreds of her, all speaking at once in a melodious whisper.

"Why must I go back?"

"You must sacrifice part of yourself for the benefit of many, as I sacrificed myself so that you would live," she smiled. 'You must love your Balancing Man. There is more as well, much more. You have much yet to do, my little man. There is much joy and much suffering to know. Come, I will take you home."

They spun back across the sky, The Light At The Top Of The World growing distant behind them. The Ghosts Of Voices Singing wrapped round them, singing of life, joy, love and sacrifice.

The pain in Borsen's body grew as they spiraled down toward Erdahn – across the great city, past the Palace, down to his house, through the window, to the bed and the gaunt, broken frame he had been pulled from.

His mother bent, gently settling him back into his body.

"Always remember that you are Thrun, my little son," she whispered. "Remember that you are from the first people of Eirdon."

"Stay with me!" he begged, clinging to her.

"We are always with you," she smiled. "If you listen, you will hear us – and wherever the shining stone you love is, there am I, my little man. Time to wake up now. Time to live."

She rose away from him.

Borsen opened his eyes.

***

Hemmett jumped as a wild gust of wind blew the east window of Borsen's room open with a bang.

Doctor Franz started, then continued sponging Borsen's unresponsive body. Eiren held a steaming towel to Borsen's feet, trying to draw the fever away from his head.

Hemmett wrestled the window closed just as Stevahn walked into the room, an odd light in his eyes.

Franz jumped back suddenly, then bent back over Borsen.

"Look who's here," Franz said, his voice shaking.

Hemmett looked around and saw that Borsen's eyes were open and moving from one face to another, squinting as he tried to focus.

Stevahn took Borsen's glasses from the nightstand and slid them into place. Borsen smiled at him.

"Borsen, who am I?" Franz asked. Stevahn sank down on the side of the bed and put his hands on either side of Borsen's face, gazing into his eyes.

"I've been talking to my mother," Borsen said to Stevahn in the slightest whisper. "I was being taken to The Light At The Top Of The World by something bad, but she stopped it and brought me home."

"Say something that makes sense," Franz snapped.

"All right. That's the ugliest shirt you own. It makes you look as yellow as a Surytamian and when I'm able, I'm going to burn it in the middle of the Promenade – Doctor Rainer Franz," Borsen whispered, turning his eyes toward Franz.

Hemmett burst out laughing. Eiren sank down on the floor at the end of the bed and began to laugh and cry at once.

Menders came rushing up the stairs and stood in the doorway, holding onto the frame. Varnia ran up behind him, then shoved him aside to get to Borsen's bedside.

"He's just criticized my shirt," Franz said, his voice shaking. He stood upright and looked at Menders. "I'd say he's going to stay with us. I don't know how. It defies everything that's happened up until now, but unless we're all hallucinating, I have a man who was ready to be nailed into his coffin who now shows every indication that he's going to live."

Menders went to the bed, looking down at his nephew, taking Borsen's withered hand in his own. Borsen was wasted and barely recognizable, but his brown eyes burned with life.

"I've been with the Ghosts Of Voices Singing," Borsen whispered, looking up at him. Menders nodded, not trusting his voice.

THE SHADOWS, MORDANIA

12
CAPTAIN GREINHOLZ'S GREAT LOVE

"All on the mend," Villison said in answer to Menders' query about his children, Arden and Koral. They had come down with the childhood form of putrid fever during the brief flare of the disease in Erdahn that had infected Borsen. At the height of the upset over Borsen's illness, Villison had been called home during the middle of the night shift because of the children's sudden illness and had been there ever since.

"Did Katrin tell you how she hurt that ankle trying to get down the stairs to go to Borsen that night he was so sick?" Villison asked as they turned to walk into the Guardroom off the Palace Courtyard. "I promised her I'd let you know but got called home before I had a chance to see you. Been pretty preoccupied ever since. Arden had a mild case but little Koral was bad for a couple of days. Slipped my mind. Menders? Here, sit down!"

Menders was aware of the hard seat of a wooden chair beneath him and a cup of scalding coffee being pushed into his hand.

"She told me she turned her ankle taking the dog into the garden," he said, his eyes meeting Villison's.

"What! Menders, I found her up there on the fourth landing in a blind panic that night Borsen nearly died. Said she was trying to run down the stairs fast enough not to get scared, that she was trying to go to him. It wasn't barely any time after I got the Guard's doctor up there to see to that ankle that the message came from Petra that my kiddies were down sick, and I had to race off. Why would she lie like that?"

Menders couldn't answer, remembering his cruel words to her when he came back that night that Borsen had – died. And come back to life.

"The time to talk to him is gone. You had a chance, and now it's gone. So why don't you just pour some more wine down your throat? Then it won't matter a bit when my boy dies."

He finally shook his head a little and took a gulp of the bitter coffee.

"She lied to spare me," he said raggedly.

Then he rose and began scaling the Staircase to Katrin's Tower suite, to apologize.

***

Dearest Little Bird,

I was glad to hear you got back safely and that all is as well as it can be. I hope our father continues to improve. This has been such a difficult time for everyone. It was good to hear the news of Borsen's recovery cheered him so much. He always loved his Little Man!

Things are not good here at the Palace and I am in the process of making some difficult decisions. Katrin has begun drinking heavily again and there has been a return to lying in bed all day, not dressing, not bathing. Even though Borsen is recovering, Katrin can't bring herself to go and see him. Once again, she does nothing but lie around, sleeping all day, wandering all night.

She still cares for Sunny, but she has lost interest in the activities she had taken up before Borsen was ill. She cries a great deal. I have apologized for my behavior during that time and she has forgiven me, but great harm was done. If only Vil had a chance to let me know she'd injured herself trying to get down those damned stairs to go to Borsen! If I had known she'd made that effort I wouldn't have lost my temper and been so cruel to her.

This is no life for either of us. I have spent the last two weeks thinking a great deal and have come to

"Menders?"

Menders looked up from his letter to see Hemmett, pale to the lips, standing in his office doorway, holding a Rollig message.

"I was in the Rollig room when this came in for you," he mumbled. Menders jumped up and went to him, pushing him down into a chair. He looked ready to faint.

TO: MENDERS
FROM: FRANZ

LUCEN AND ZELIA DIED SUDDENLY LAST NIGHT FROM WHAT LOOKS LIKE THE SUDDEN ONSET OF PNEUMONIA. PLEASE INFORM HEMMETT. THE BURIALS WILL NEED TO BE AS SOON AS POSSIBLE AS THE GROUND IS STARTING TO FREEZE.

"My gods!" Menders gasped, crouching beside Hemmett, who was blinking as if he'd been suddenly awakened. "Oh, my boy, I'm so sorry! That damned fool never thought you might be the one to take the message!"

"It's all right," Hemmett replied quietly. "I've – I hate to say it, Menders, but I've been expecting it. Papa was well over eighty, Mama was seventy-five. Last time I was there I could see they were frail, that anything might carry them off. It was just getting the news the way I did."

"I'll arrange to leave immediately," Menders said. "Let me tell Katrin."

He went up to the suite, where Katrin was stretched out on her bed, staring at the ceiling.

"Katrin – Hemmett's parents died very suddenly last night," he said quietly.

She sat up slowly and stared at him.

"How?" she asked.

"Franz thinks pneumonia," Menders replied. "We're going to leave immediately, of course. Please come with us. We'll help you."

Katrin swung around so she was sitting on the edge of the bed and Menders felt his heart leap – it looked as though she was going to get up and come with them.

"No," she said flatly. "I can't."

Menders felt rage welling inside him, but he couldn't afford to let it show. Hemmett would need him calm and supportive.

"Not even for Hemmett? Not after all these years?" Menders heard himself asking.

Katrin silently shook her head.

Menders sighed. He turned and walked away.

***

Menders felt enormous admiration for the way Hemmett coped with the deaths of both parents and all the preparation and ritual that went along with death. He carried off the funeral formalities beautifully, wearing his dress uniform and looking properly solemn but welcoming as he accepted condolences from many mourners, Flori standing at his side.

Menders was suddenly reminded that Hemmett was thirty-three and that it had been six years since Katrin had become Queen. Hemmett was no longer a youth. His youth had passed in service to Katrin.

Stevahn had come along with them, as had Villison. Borsen was still in bed and would be for some weeks yet. His body was severely damaged by the putrid fever. Menders and Hemmett stopped to see him when they picked up Stevahn.

Hemmett surprised Menders by lifting Borsen right out of bed and holding him close. Borsen surprised Menders even more by not protesting at being treated like a child.

"I'm coming with you," Borsen said forcefully while Hemmett hugged him. "Hang Franz anyway, he's an old lady!"

"If I took you over there against his orders, he'd hang me," Hemmett burst out laughing. "You stay snugged up here and we'll be back in a couple of days. I'll bring you some of Cook's special delights."

"I can't eat real food yet, I'm still on baby pap," Borsen groused as Hemmett put him back on the bed and then proceeded, against vociferous protests from the invalid, to tuck him in like a baby.

Hemmett and Flori hosted a reception after the burial, in keeping with the Samorsan custom, wanting to avoid the traditional Mordanian wake. It was an excellent choice. People from the area congregated at The Shadows the evening after the funeral. The ambience of the Great Hall combined with Hemmett's bonhomie and Flori's graciousness converted a solemn stand-around into a quiet, homelike party.

Conversations ranged through the room. People enjoyed one another and reminisced about Lucen and Zelia. The gathering became a celebration of their lives rather than a welter of unhappiness over their deaths.

Hemmett, true to form, hunted up Lucen's old helmet, which Lucen had converted to a flowerpot for his enormous, cherished, red geranium plant. Hemmett placed it in the middle of the food table as a centerpiece. It was a fitting touch and tribute to Lucen, soldier-turned-gardener, and his wife. Menders was glad Hemmett had thought of it.

Eiren gave Menders a smile from across the table, where she was laying out a platter of cold meat. He smiled back wearily, thankful that he had her.

Menders had been utterly determined to stay at The Shadows the night before the funeral, but by ten o'clock he was so anxious that Eiren asked when he was going back to Erdahn. He'd pulled her close and kissed her gratefully. Then he collared Ifor, who was always happy to pilot the steam launch, and left, promising to be back in the morning.

Menders reached the Palace after midnight to find Katrin sitting up silently, staring at the wall, much as he'd left her except that she was in a chair and in her dressing gown, with Sunny lying at her feet. He gave her a few details of the funeral, who was there, told her how people had asked after her.

"I imagine they hate me as much as I hate myself for not being there," she said abruptly.

"No-one hates you, Katrin," Menders said.

"Of course they do – and I don't blame them," she answered.

Menders sighed. He was too tired and emotionally drained to argue or do anything but bid her a quiet good-night and go to his room. He found that he was unable to sleep and finally rose to check on the fire in Katrin's room, as he had every night since she was born.

She was deeply asleep, assisted by most of a bottle of wine, After he put a log on the fire, he looked at her for a long time.

I must find a way out of this, he thought wearily. It can't go on, for either of us.

"I hope everything will be all right," he whispered. "Sleep well, little princess."

Menders shook off his memory, bringing himself back to the present. Motion across the Great Hall drew his attention.

Hemmett, who was standing very quietly to one side while people helped themselves to food and drink, had noticed something or someone. He raised his head suddenly, like a prowling langhur.

Curious, Menders followed Hemmett's line of sight and felt a smile cross his face.

His longtime friend from a neighboring estate, Reisa Spartz, had just come into the room with her daughter, Lorein. They had been unable to attend the burial but sent word that they would come to the reception to express their condolences.

Hemmett was looking at Lorein as if he'd never seen her before. He'd known her since childhood, but Lorein was seven years his junior. To him she had always been a little girl in pinafores and pigtails.

Lorein was now twenty-six and had spent three years at a boarding school in Surelia before her mother sent her on a grand tour of the Middle Continent, including time at finishing school. Lorein's and Hemmett's paths hadn't crossed in years.

Lorein was as beautiful as her mother had been at the same age. She was a tall, distinguished, white-blonde with a ravishing figure. Menders knew Reisa was puzzled that her daughter had turned down many marriage proposals. Lorein was lively, accomplished, wickedly intelligent and would be a wonderful catch for any man.

Lorein must have felt the gaze Hemmett was directing at her. He stood stock still, looking across the room as if there was nothing else he could do. She turned away from her mother's conversation with another lady and saw Hemmett.

Their eyes locked. Menders swore he could smell lightning.

It wasn't until Reisa saw Lorein and Hemmett gazing into each other's eyes across the room, with people taking notice, that the charged moment ended. Reisa touched Lorein's arm gently, speaking to her. Hemmett blinked when Lorein looked away.

When she and her mother spoke formally to Hemmett, Lorein's demeanor and etiquette were perfect – but she looked at Hemmett in such a way that Menders knew exactly why the eligible young lady was still unmarried at twenty-six. Hemmett responded in kind and Menders noted that his eyes strayed to Lorein many times during the rest of the evening, though they didn't talk together again.

***

Hemmett tapped lightly on the door of the room Flori used when she was at The Shadows. She looked up from her sketchpad and smiled invitingly.

"You don't have to knock, Papa," she said, removing a pile of papers from the easy chair close to hers. "Please sit down."

"What are you working on?" he asked, getting settled.

"Some designs for when Borsen can come back to work," she replied. "He'll be terribly behind, and I thought having some ideas on paper would help."

"These are grand," Hemmett said, looking over the book she handed him. "The men's outfits in particular. In fact, the third one? I'm ordering it."

"Flatterer!" She laughed.

"No Flori – the moment I saw it, I wanted it. That's how Borsen's sketches used to strike people – they'd take one look and drool to have the clothing he'd drawn. If you can do that, my darling daughter, you have learned a great deal from your apprenticeship."

"Borsen calls me his assistant now," Flori smiled, making a checkmark by the desired outfit. "Once we're back in Erdahn, we'll go through fabrics and you'll have a new suit."

Hemmett smiled, watching her put away her drawing things.

"Flori, I wanted to ask you how you'd feel if I stayed on at The Shadows for a few days," he said as she closed her box of pencils and sat back in her chair.

She frowned a little.

"Papa, I don't mind, of course – and I understand that you would like to stay for a while. The thing is, I must get back. I've been helping Varens keep things running up on our floor and I don't want to be away for too long."

"Would you be happy to go back with Menders? I wouldn't stay too long. I have some things of my parents' I want to pack up and bring back – and I have something else I want to talk to you about."

Flori nodded and waited.

"You know how your mother used to speak of a great love?" Hemmett began.

"Very well," Flori smiled. "Is it Lorein Spartz?"

Hemmett laughed and crossed his legs, sitting back in the chair and shaking his head.

"Well, Papa's carefully considered speech flies out the window," he snorted. "Yes, I'm in love with Lorein Spartz."

"Have you talked to her?" Flori asked.

"Only at the reception the other day. But I know. She loves me too. Your mother always said I would know if my great love came along. So, I would like to have a chance to talk to Lorein and ask her to marry me – but I want to be sure you would be happy with that."

Flori rose and went to the teapot keeping warm on the woodstove in the corner of the room.

"I would be entirely happy with that," she said, carefully taking out two delicate teacups and pouring spiced, fragrant tea for them both. "I spoke with her at the reception while you were buttonholed by the mayor of Artrim. She's lovely and had so many questions about how you were, how I liked Erdahn, how Borsen was. She kept glancing at you and I could tell – like I could tell with Mama. You brought Mama peace. Even when you couldn't be with us, the idea that you were there in the world made her happy and peaceful. I felt that same peace in Lorein."

Hemmett accepted the cup she offered, wrapping his hand around it rather than trying to manipulate his large finger and thumb into the graceful but small handle.

"I remember as a kiddie she used to love to hang around me," he smiled. "I called her Firefly, because her hair caught any light and glowed. But I was seven years older and when you're a boy and then a wild young man, that's an enormous age gap. She was just a funny little girl."

"Not now," Flori laughed. "She's one of the most beautiful women I've ever seen."

"Then we're well matched," Hemmett grinned.

"I will not rise to the invitation to flatter you," Flori said, sipping her tea. "You are already well aware that you are a very handsome and well-built and vain man."

"Oh, well played!"

"As well as Mama could have done it," Flori agreed.

Hemmett nodded and swallowed some tea.

"I love your mother very much – and I say it in present tense because I will always love her," he said gently. Flori kept her large brown eyes riveted to his. "She gave me so much – including you. I want you to remember that, always. My loving Lorein doesn't supplant your mother."

"Big man, big heart. Plenty of room," Flori smiled. "I know, Papa."

Hemmett finished his tea and carefully set the cup down.

"One more thing you've probably anticipated but that I would like to bring up anyway," he said. "If Lorein should accept me…"

"As if she wouldn't," Flori smiled into her tea.

"I feel that confident too, but hear me out, my daughter," he continued. "If she accepts me and we marry, I would like us all to live together. I don't want you to feel that you have to go out on your own. I don't believe you're old enough for that yet. You're the delight of my house and it is always your home."

"Thank you, Papa. I have no wish to leave."

They exchanged a smile and Flori rose to get him another cup of tea.

***

Later Hemmett undressed in his boyhood room, put on a dressing gown and spent a few moments neatly sorting away his clothing. Years of military discipline had made him very orderly in his habits – funny, considering the pit his boyhood room had always been.

Everything settled, he turned the lamp down and shucked off his dressing gown, standing in the dark with his eyes closed.

Are you there, he thought. Darling girl, Luntigré? Can you hear me? Do we really go on when we pass into spirit, as you used to say?

He waited.

There was a shifting in the air, almost as if the lightest summer breeze had come into a wintertime bedchamber at The Shadows. A sense of peace settled over him like a loving rain shower.

I've found my great love, my darling, Hemmett thought. I knew it the moment I saw her again, after so many years. I knew then she'd always been in love with me – I saw it in her eyes. We spoke without saying a word. Was that how it was with you and Flori's father? As if it was all settled without a word being said?

Joy surrounded him, wrapped around him, curled into his heart.

I'll always love you, my beautiful moon tiger. I know now that never dies. I will be taking off your ring but my love for you will always be a part of me.

And yes, you still bring me joy – and you always will.

Filled with joy, wrapped in peace, Hemmett opened his eyes. By the light of the moonlit snow outside his window, he slid Luntigré's ring from his wedding finger and placed it in the velvet case it had come in so many years before. He nestled it in a box of other small treasures, then lay down on his boyhood bed and fell into a deep, cleansing sleep.

***

Hemmett rode through the winter woods toward the Dower House of the Spartz estate. It was not truly cold yet – at least to someone who had lived most of his life in Old Mordania. There was a pleasant bite to the air that made him feel clean and alive after years of living at the Palace.

He was glad he'd sent a Rollig message to Menders for another week of leave. Being away from the rift between Katrin and Menders was a relief.

He hated to admit that to himself, but it was true. He understood all that had led to Menders' anger with her the night Borsen had, apparently, died and then returned to life. Menders had endured years of watching Katrin disintegrate. Desperation over Borsen's approaching death had driven him beyond being able to control his temper. That didn't mean Hemmett wanted to be around the aftermath.

Hemmett loved Katrin and always would. His love for her was unconditional. He hated her bad days and her recent relapse into severe melancholia, but she was his other self. They were one. Nothing would change that.

Some time ago, he had forced himself to read a great deal of information about melancholia that he requested from Franz. It had sickened him, because he was a practical man who wanted answers and solutions for problems. Apparently, there were none for melancholia. It was a horrible, insidious disease. It stole people away and made them into something pathetic and detestable.

Hemmett reined the horse in for a breather. The snow was already getting deep in this part of the woods It would be better to take the road. After the horse had caught its breath, Hemmett guided it in that direction. Once they were moving along more easily in a well-travelled rut, Hemmett let his mind wander again.

He'd done a lot of thinking since Luntigré's death and returning to Erdahn with Flori. By the time Katrin had been Queen for three years, Hemmett knew pretending to guard the Palace was going to drive him mad with boredom. He'd gone to see Commandant Komroff at the Mordanian Military Academy, where that excellent and patient man was still overseeing the education of Mordanian boys.

Hemmett had been pleased when the Commandant offered him a teaching position there three mornings a week.

Hemmett found teaching the boys a great deal of fun. He truly enjoyed being with them and seeing them progress. The Commandant had recently told him if he ever wanted to teach at the Academy full time, the position would be his. It was nice to know he had an alternative if things changed.

Hemmett had known Menders for thirty years. They didn't need to spell things out to each other. Menders was tired of being separated from Eiren and heartbroken by seeing Katrin a complete wreck. Things were going to start changing, soon. Hemmett approved. Anything would be better than the endless stagnation they were all suffering under.

It had come as a complete surprise when Hemmett saw Lorein Spartz at the reception following his parents' funeral. He had not seen Lorein in years, as the time they'd all spent abroad and then Katrin's becoming Queen had kept him away from The Shadows.

Lorein was now a stunning woman, tall, distinguished and achingly beautiful. After five minutes of talking to her, Hemmett knew her soul and spirit matched her looks. After ten minutes of talking to her, Hemmett was helplessly in love. Lorein made no secret of the fact that she felt the same way, though she was elegant and reserved, as became a lady attending a funeral reception.

The next day the invitation came, welcoming him to visit her at the Dower House on her mother's estate, which was now her home. Having returned from her long tour, she'd developed a taste for being on her own and had no desire to return to her girlhood room and hang about her parents' house all day being a little ray of sunshine.

Lorein taught at Eiren's school and helped her mother with the estate business. She went on sick calls with Doctor Franz when he was in residence at The Shadows and gave music lessons to several talented children on her mother's estate, as well as to the orphans at The Shadows' Home for Children. On the rare occasions when she wasn't at the Dower House, she was at her parents' townhouse in Erdahn, where she had a circle of friends and enjoyed what cultural benefits Erdahn had to offer.

Hemmett had been gob smacked when he'd realized that he was alone with Lorein in the Dower House, without a chaperone. She was calm and collected and made it clear that she was her own person and quite grown up. Within minutes she'd set him completely at ease.

Within an hour they were talking about spending the rest of their lives together.

Lorein did admit that if he hadn't turned up at The Shadows when he had, she would have been forced to start calling on him in Erdahn. Hemmett laughed uproariously at the idea of Lorein, behatted and wearing an immaculate suit, knocking genteelly on the huge iron gates of The Palace and asking to see Hemmett Greinholz, passing a calling card between the bars. Lorein joined in and he'd held his arms out to her – and she'd gone into them.

He'd stayed the night and had the pleasure of helping her cook breakfast and of lingering over innumerable cups of coffee as they talked.

They talked about Katrin and Luntigré – and about Flori. Hemmett described her calm and joyous reaction to the news that he'd found his great love.

"She's a lovely girl," Lorein said firmly. "I had heard you had a daughter and I was so bowled over when I spoke with her at the reception – she's so bright and full of life. I'm glad she wants to stay with us and that I will have a readymade daughter. Have no fear of a wicked stepmother spoiling your lives."

Hemmett smiled at her. He couldn't imagine it.

"Well then, all secrets are out, you don't mind living with me in Erdahn or if I end up a teacher at the Military Academy. Do you love me, my Firefly?"

"Completely. Home is where you are, Hemmett. Now, what would you like to have first, a boy or a girl?" Lorein poured another cup of coffee for him.

"Ah, you've found a way to guarantee one or the other?" Hemmett laughed.

"Just curious, since we've decided to go ahead with the project," Lorein grinned back.

"Not that it really matters – but a boy first, I think. I'd like a girl too. One of each," Hemmett said, as if he was giving an order in a restaurant. He stroked back a lock of her incredible white-blonde hair, marveling at the fineness of it.

"Good, I want a little boy too," Lorein smiled.

"When shall we get married?" Hemmett asked. There had been no proposal, just a mutual admission that they wanted to be together.

"Why not today?"

He blinked. "Where?" he asked.

"The Temple of Galanth in Artrim will do weddings at no notice – they make out the licenses and all."

"Checked up on that, did you?" Hemmett asked, looking at her out of the corners of his eyes, a smile playing around his mouth.

"Of course. Any objections?"

"Not at all. But – would there be any problem for your parents?" Hemmett asked, suddenly feeling cold. He hadn't given it a thought because Lorein was so independent, but he was common born. Her parents, though they were wonderful people, might just kick.

"My mother will jump up and click her heels with glee that I've finally gotten you," Lorein chortled. "She's lived with my unrequited love for the dashing Captain Greinholz since I was tiny!"

"I wasn't a Captain then!" Hemmett howled, a vision of Reisa Spartz hitching up her elegant satin skirts, jumping and clicking her heels hitting him right on his funny bone. "I was a boy too big for his age with a head shaped like a potato!"

"Lovemaking brings out the nitpicking side of you," Lorein laughed. Then she sobered.

"What about your people?" she asked. "Katrin and Menders, and everyone else?"

"Everyone will be pleased. And I just remembered something. I'm a Baronet – Katrin made me one years back when she was angry about Menders' Men thinking I was a weakling. So, I am worthy to be marrying you, m'lady."

Lorein stood up, laughing delightedly and curtsied to him in her dressing gown. It gave him ample opportunity to get hold of her and sit her on his knee.

So, they were married that day, after buying him a fresh shirt that was a bit too short in the arms and wedding rings for them both.

Now Hemmett saw the lights of the Dower House ahead of him. The horse tossed his head a bit, knowing he was nearing his stable. Hemmett had borrowed him to ride over to The Shadows to send a Rollig message to Menders that he would return the following week. He had included nothing about his marriage. A second message went to Flori, letting her know about the runaway match with an admonition that it was secret for now.

Lorein's parents were delighted with their daughter's choice and had been truly welcoming, raining blessings on them joyfully and excitedly discussing possible wedding gifts. With the final worry that they might object to his common birth set aside, Hemmett had a peaceful feeling of all being well.

Lorein's stepfather popped out of the stable door ahead and waved, so Hemmett dismounted in front of the Dower House. He gave the horse a gentle slap on the rump, which sent it toward its owner, eager to have its oats and to be bedded down for the night. Hemmett waved at his father-in-law and opened the door of the Dower House to the smell of dinner cooking and the warm glow of firelight in the lounge.

Home.

Home is where you are, Lorein.

Hemmett stepped over the doorsill and closed the door behind him.

THE PALACE, ERDAHN, MORDANIA

13
A TERRIBLE HIGH-PITCHED WHINE

Dearest Little Bird,

As I feared, there has been no change for the better in Katrin. I believe that there is a great deal of self-loathing because of her failure to come to Lucen and Zelia's funeral and for failing to go to Borsen when he was sick. As usual, she is trying to avoid thinking about it by drinking. She is not bathing or changing and spends her days sleeping and her nights up wandering around and drinking. All the progress that was made over the last two years seems to be lost.

I have received information about a new weapon developed by the military. Of course, they are trying to keep it secret, but my sources have let me know it is an explosive of unparalleled power and intensity. This is of great concern, because war with Artreya is once again threatening. If this weapon works upon testing, the war-mad lunatics in the military will use it, regardless of the consequences.

There is to be a test of this bomb in a few days. It is my intention to force Katrin to go and see it, dragging her if need be. I hope the gravity of the situation will become clear to her and perhaps push her toward taking responsibility for herself and her position.

Should she remain indifferent, I am going to resign. I'll dismantle my espionage network and come home. I will do my best to get Katrin to abdicate if this is the case, and get her to come home with me. Even if she refuses, I am going to hold fast. It is pointless going on like this.

The damage done to my relationship with Katrin is immense, as is the damage she's done to herself. That things would ever come to such a pass is heartbreaking for me to contemplate.

I looked in on Borsen on my way back. He is better, making gains every day. Very impatient to be able to eat regular food again, but Franz says there is no rushing the healing process, that he must stay on a soft diet because of the damage the putrid fever did to his gut. For the most part, he is cheerful enough, snugged up in bed with his sketchbooks and pencils. Stevahn is overjoyed, of course, and comes dashing down the street from the bank several times a day to look in on him. I'm glad they have each other. I only hope that one day, Katrin might find such devotion. Hemmett as well.

I will write to you after getting Katrin out to see the test. I will manage it if I have to drag her by her feet.

Loving you,

M

***

Katrin woke to insistent shaking. She worked her eyes open, wincing at the light from the bedside lamp.

It was Menders shaking her.

"It's time to get up," he said heartily. "You have to go and see something today."

Katrin stared at him as if he'd gone mad.

"I'm not going anywhere," she answered slowly.

"Yes, you are. There's a test of a new weapon today. The Queen is to attend," Menders countered.

Katrin dragged the covers up over her head. Menders dragged them back down.

"We can do this easily or the hard way," he said quietly, looking at her over his glasses. "You are going to go to see this demonstration. You can walk out of here decorously or I can drag you every inch of the way. You don't have a choice. You've shown that you're incapable of making choices, so I'm taking choice out of it. Now, get out of that bed, have some breakfast and I'll help you get into the dress."

"Menders!"

"Don't make me resort to dragging you around," he said firmly. "I am going to stop at nothing to make you go, my dear. It would be so much easier for both of us if you would come along without forcing me into any drama."

Shaking all over, Katrin got out of bed. She felt ill and told Menders so.

"Probably the wine you drank last night," he answered. "Eat something. It will help." He pointed to the table, where a breakfast tray was waiting. He was already dressed and ready for the day.

Katrin managed to gnaw some toast and swallow a cup of coffee. Then she shivered and shuddered while getting into the horrible formal gown and putting on the severe red wig, grotesque makeup and false vampire teeth. Menders proffered her furs and helped her into them.

At the doorway to her suite, she balked. Sunny whined, having been told to stay in the suite.

"Don't make me drag you," Menders said evenly. "I will. I'll think nothing of making the spectacle of the Queen of Mordania being forced into a carriage. Now come along."

Katrin found herself going down the stairs. She tried twice to turn around and retreat, but Menders held onto her arm and hauled her steadily downward.

At the fourth-floor landing, she stopped. This was the place where the fear always caught her, paralyzing her into utter helplessness.

Menders pulled her downwards, but she held tight to the handrail, staring at the stairs descending before her. Her breathing became ragged and tight. Her vision darkened.

Menders whipped off his glasses and looked up at her, standing frozen on the step above him, sweat bubbling up through her makeup and pouring down her face.

"Think, and tell me what is frightening you!" he commanded, his white eyes glowing in the gloom of the Stairwell.

"I don't know!" she moaned. "I don't know, but I can't go down from here. I can't! I can't!"

"Katrin! Listen to me. Breathe, as Kaymar taught you. Do as I say!"

She forced her diaphragm down, stopping the shuddering under her ribcage.

"Now, look around. What is it that frightens you? There has to be a reason for this," Menders said, his voice even and forceful.

She gasped and looked around, seeing nothing, blinded by fear.

"Focus, Katrin. I know you can. Remember the day I took you to the fair. Remember it!"

The images came to her instantly – the day of the fair, a high point in her childhood, where she and Menders had dressed as tenant farmers and gone incognito to a tawdry little roadside fair. To a little girl who had never traveled from The Shadows, it had been glamorous and exciting.

She saw herself riding the carousel with Kaymar standing beside her bobbing wooden horse. She saw Menders buying her every taffy apple, fried pie and sausage in a bun she asked for. She saw Doctor Franz escorting not one, but two pretty ladies – she remembered the piles and piles of cheap, gaudy jewelry and toys that the fifteen Menders' Men who had been there in disguise had won at the various games and given to her. They had become her pirate treasure, a prop for many happy hours of playing with Hemmett.

She smiled, drew a deep breath and looked up. She saw what she had never consciously seen before.

Her hand, almost of its own volition, rose slowly and pointed.

A hook – ancient, its blackened surface scabbed with rust. A hook with a cruel, curling point.

A hook like the ones she had been Suspended from. The morning sun came through the fogged windows and touched it.

Menders followed her pointing finger. She could hear him gasp.

"All right. Good, Katrin. Now, I'll show you what we'll do with that. Hold the handrail. No, don't go back up – watch. Watch me, Katrin."

To her amazement, he boosted himself to stand on the handrail, clinging to the carved masonry decorating the edge of the ceiling with his left hand.

He reached out with his right hand and got a grip on the hook. The muscles of his arm bulged as he wrestled with it, looking as if they were going to tear through the tight fitting, padded coat Borsen had made for him, to make him look like a dried up old clerk.

He wrenched the hook back and forth, as crumbling plaster and stone dust rained down.

"Damn it!" Menders twisted the hook relentlessly, eroding its moorings – then, with a final vicious twist, it was free, clutched in his bleeding hand.

He dropped from the handrail with a dancer's grace and flexed his right shoulder. Then he held out his hand before Katrin's eyes, the hook held tightly in it.

"Now, this is what we're going to do with it," he said. He drew back his arm and hurled it with all his might through the window on the landing above.

Katrin stared at him, her mouth open. Then she smiled, ever so slightly.

"Glass is cheap," she said.

He used a handkerchief to staunch the abrasions on his palm. Then he looked up at her again as he settled his dark glasses back on his nose.

"Now you can walk down the stairs with me – like a Queen. I know you're afraid, that removing that hook didn't fix everything. This is something that must happen, Katrin. Now, one stair at a time."

He held his bandaged hand out to her. She took it.

She took one step. Then another.

***

"Where's Hemmett?" Katrin asked as Villison and several other of the Guard joined them on the ground floor.

"He's at The Shadows. He asked for several more days' leave," Menders answered. "The carriage is waiting outside the door. We have to hurry, or we'll miss the train."

"Train! You didn't say anything about going on a train!" Katrin cried.

Menders shook his head and she knew he wasn't going to give in to her fear.

She walked beside him. It was only a short distance from the front door of the Palace and the carriage. Once in the conveyance, she pulled down the shades, but Menders simply put them up again.

"This is the end of all that," he said firmly, though his tone was kind. "Don't pull them down again."

Katrin sat silently all the way to the station, looking straight ahead of her, avoiding the windows. Menders wrote in his notebook, changing his handkerchief bandage once. When they arrived at the station, she saw that her Council ministers were already there, as were several military men.

She sat firmly where she was. She couldn't go out there!

"There is no time for this, Katrin," Menders said, taking her arm in a strong grip. He began pulling her out of the carriage. She tried to pull away, but he was stronger. She was being dragged inexorably from the vehicle.

"Do you really want me to drag you all the way?" Menders asked when she was halfway out. That made her step down under her own steam.

The Council members looked amazed. They all sketched bows before Menders showed her to the Royal Carriage at the end of the train. She struggled up the steps in the heavy clanking gown, then huddled in a seat, seeing and hearing nothing because she was so frightened.

"All right, my dear," Menders said after rebandaging his hand again. He settled himself and opened a case he'd been carrying, "I need to tell you something about this device we're going to see. This information hasn't been given to the Crown. It's come to me through Menders' Men."

"Why did you change the bandage again?" Katrin whispered.

"Pulling you along opened the wound," he answered. "Are you ready to listen to me?"

Katrin managed a tiny nod.

"Could you do with a drink of water?" Menders asked. She nodded again. He fetched a glass for her from the fountain at the end of the carriage, then reseated himself, picking up a sheaf of papers.

"Now, the bomb is made from a substance called Thermaline, which is refined from Therminus, a raw mineral that was recently discovered. It's found, at least so far, only in the Stormvern Mountains, which as you know, is the large mountain range in the far eastern part of Mordania."

"Yes, I know," Katrin breathed, determinedly looking at him, and avoiding the windows. The train lurched forward suddenly with a great hissing of steam. She gasped.

"That engine driver should be flogged. He's burning the rails," Menders remarked companionably. "Now, apparently the process of refining Therminus into Thermaline is very risky. A number of people have blown themselves up trying it. At this point, there is only a small amount of refined Thermaline available. It can be used to generate enormous amounts of power and would be very useful in providing electric power for lights and to operate machines without using coal fuel to create steam pressure. Unfortunately, our military and scientists are far more interested in seeing just how big an explosion it can produce. They have used it to manufacture bombs."

Despite her fear, Katrin felt interest and concern. The specter of war was always with Mordania because of the centuries-long hostility with Artreya. The military forces of both nations were always looking for new ways to kill people.

"This test is the first official one," Menders went on. "There have been others with small bombs that were done in secret."

"Why haven't we been informed?" Katrin asked. Menders looked at her, and said nothing. She knew, of course – the Queen was not a player.

"This test is being carried out a hundred miles from Erdahn," Menders went on. "We should be there in a couple of hours." He reached over and placed the sheaf of papers beside her on the seat. She could see that much of the handwriting on the pages was Kaymar's.

After about fifteen minutes Katrin picked up the papers and tried to look through them. She found she couldn't concentrate, as had been the case whenever she tried to read lately. She would want to read, but a terrible weariness kept her from maintaining enough enthusiasm or interest to finish anything.

She finally put the papers down. She sat. In the dress it was almost impossible to do anything else. She could hardly move about in it, and she was so frightened that she couldn't budge from her seat.

Suddenly she spoke.

"Menders? I'm sorry pulling me opened that wound on your hand. You won't have to pull me again – but I might take a while to do things. I'm so frightened. But I'll do them. I don't want you to be hurt."

She went back to looking at the far wall of the carriage.

***

Menders maintained the guise of being absorbed in writing in his notebook while covertly watching Katrin and feeling his heart sink.

As Hemmett had said in the worst of his grief after Katrin had been tortured, she was broken. Body, mind and spirit. She'd begun to come back to a semblance of herself after the Suspension Ritual, but then Aidelia had summoned her to Court. Since then he hardly even recognized her. It was hard to believe that six years of her life and his had passed while the Katrin he knew disappeared, leaving in her place this pale, puffy stranger mired in lassitude.

He'd watched her trying to read the papers he'd put beside her. She did try, but it was obvious that it wasn't so much a case of wouldn't, but couldn't. She couldn't focus her mind. Katrin, who as a girl had to be hauled away from a project or book she was interested in, couldn't focus her mind long enough to read through a sheaf of fifteen pages.

Time for it to stop. He'd been running like a mad thing for thirty years, trying to do more than one person ever could. Katrin was destroyed, despite thirty years of continual vigilance and protection. It was not her fault, poor darling. She didn't deserve what had happened, what was happening. It had to end, before the love he felt for her was as destroyed as she was.

He was going to force her to abdicate, kill Glorantha's father so that he would not be Regent and disband Menders' Men. Then he would take Katrin and Eiren and go someplace where no-one had to be Queen or the power behind the throne. Let Katrin walk in the sun and try to regain something of herself. Give Eiren the time that had been stolen from her for so many years. Have a quiet life free of intrigue, espionage and endless, ceaseless vigilance.

It was decided then. No more.

***

Katrin clung to the railing of the Royal Carriage steps as she tried to negotiate them in the enormous, heavy dress. No matter how she tried to manage, the weight pulled downward so badly that she had to step back onto the small platform outside the carriage door.

"If Hemmett was here, he could just lift me down," she quavered, terrified that she would fall.

"Let's not begrudge him a few days off. He did just lose both his parents," Menders responded quietly. "I'm not nearly as large as he is but I can manage to help you down. Give me your hand and don't worry about leaning on me. Come on, Katrin." He looked up at her and smiled suddenly. It had been so long since she'd seen him really smile.

"It's all right. Let me take the weight. Now, step down and shift your weight to that foot. Good! Now bring the other foot down to that step. Take both my hands and lean against me. That's it. Two more steps and we're there. Gods, this dress is heavy!"

"I hate it," Katrin said faintly.

"I don't blame you, my little princess," Menders answered, and she felt a slight lifting of the terrible weight on her heart. It had been a long time since he'd called her that. She'd missed it.

Then she was standing beside him in the snow. Menders wrapped her furs around her and she was grateful for them. As heavy and cumbersome as the dress was, it was far from warm. It was bitterly cold here, in an arid part of Mordania west and inland of Erdahn. The milder winters of Erdahn had spoiled her. She used to bear cold greater than this at The Shadows with ease.

The Council, military officers and scientists were milling around near the train engine. They paid no attention to her or to Menders. There was nowhere to sit, no building nearby. Villison and the rest of her Guard were standing around looking rather furtive.

She looked around the bleak landscape. It was treeless. Barren rock and soil showed through patches of snow. In the distance, there was a small metal shed and a rickety looking tower. Katrin wondered briefly what they could be.

About a mile from the tower, she could just see a dreary looking village. She thought about asking Menders for his binoculars – he always had a pair with him – but didn't really want to bother all that much.

"Just sit here on the lowest step," Menders said after a while. "Corporal Villison, could you attend the Queen please? I need to have a word with these… gentlemen."

Katrin actually smiled when Villison sniggered and winked at her. Only Menders could so effectively make the word 'gentlemen' sound as if he'd said 'bastards'.

"Mornin', Your Majesty," Villison said softly. "Care to sell me that dress? I'll give you eighty florins for it."

"If I wouldn't freeze to death, it would be yours," Katrin said just as softly.

"I think it would make an elegant cover for a boiler meself," Villison quipped. Katrin bared her vampire teeth at him. They'd been brought along and she'd clipped them on before leaving the carriage.

"Oh charmin'! A smile I'd fall on me sword to avoid," Villison sniggered and Katrin was astonished to feel a small chortle of laughter in the depths of her belly.

Villison, not to be outdone, proceeded to whistle "The Smile I Love" between his teeth while they watched Menders speaking forcefully to the little knot of men near the engine and then come stalking back to them.

"They'll proceed shortly, I'm told," he announced darkly. He drew off his gloves and handed them to Katrin, who pulled them on gratefully, while Menders stuck his hands in his pockets. She hadn't even thought of gloves. It had been so long since she'd been outside at all, except for visits to the Tower Garden. How long had it been?

There was a flurry among the men at the engine end of the train, a brief conclave. Then one came toward them reluctantly. Katrin rose from the step.

"The test is about to commence, Your Majesty," he said from a distance of about twenty feet. Then he remembered to bow. Then, still bent over, he turned and began to retreat rapidly, gradually rising to an upright position.

"Well of all the absurdities," Katrin muttered. Menders shook his head in disgust.

"Truly polished, ain't he?" Villison grinned. "Nice view of his backside walkin' away."

The men near the engine roiled around a bit more and then lined up, facing the metal shed and tower.

"They tell me it will be set off electrically…" Menders began.

He was interrupted by a terrible, high-pitched whine that made them clench their teeth. Katrin saw a couple of the Guard covering their ears. She did the same.

There was a brilliant bright light. Menders cried out in pain and covered his eyes. Katrin felt as if her eyeballs were being pushed back into her head. The contraction of her pupils was agonizing. She closed her eyes in panic.

Sound forced her eyes open again – a roar so loud that the ground jolted beneath her feet. She knew she was shrieking in pain from the onslaught on her eardrums, even through her hands, but she couldn't hear herself. She couldn't see, still blinded from the incredible, bright light.

Then a mighty wind hit her, so powerful that it blew her, massive dress and all, onto the steps of the Royal Carriage. It was hot, in this cold place! She could feel the carriage rocking on the track and wondered briefly if it would tip over and crush her.

Suddenly she felt a hand close over hers. She gripped it. She was hauled upright against the wind. Strong arms helped her away from the railroad carriage, then went around her and held her securely.

Menders. She put her arms around him and held on with all her strength until the wind died and she began to be able to see a bit around the edges of her vision. Her ears felt as if they'd been stuffed with wool. She felt, rather than heard, Menders speak to someone. Then she felt his hands on her face and he was speaking to her.

"Katrin, can you hear me?" he asked. She could, as if he was very far away, underwater.

"Barely," she said.

"What do you see?"

"It's coming back. It's still black in the middle, but more coming around the edges," she replied, knowing it didn't make much sense. She was unable to put words together more effectively. Her head was spinning.

"Let's get you into the carriage," Menders said, his words fuzzy and faint. Someone took her left hand and he held onto her right. She started to climb the steps of the carriage.

"It's gone!" Villison must be shouting. She could hear him more clearly than she could hear Menders.

She turned and tried to focus.

"What's gone?" she asked, wondering how loudly she was speaking. Her ears were roaring now, as if she was hearing a miniature version of the terrible blast of the Thermaline bomb.

"The village! It's flattened!" Villison answered.

***

Menders slammed open the door of the saloon car, where the military and Council were celebrating the successful detonation of their horrible device. His violent entrance made them all fall silent. The only sound was his rapid breathing.

"Why wasn't the Queen warned about the light and the noise?" he said in a low tone that carried to every square inch of the carriage.

There was much exchanging of glances and shuffling of feet. Apparently, none of these men were suffering the after effects of near-blindness and near-deafness that were affecting Katrin and several of the Guard.

Menders was fearful there might be permanent damage done. He'd closed his eyes in reflex quickly enough that his vision was only slightly affected and was clearing rapidly, but his ears felt as if there was water in them.

"We… ah… we seem to have underestimated the strength of the blast," one of the scientists ventured. "It's unfortunate that the Queen suffered some ill effects, but they should be temporary."

"I notice no-one here is suffering such ill effects," Menders replied coldly.

More shuffling and averted eyes.

"What has happened to the people in that village?" Menders continued. "The Queen wishes to know how many people were hurt so help can be sent to them."

"Ah… we haven't gotten a figure… we didn't realize that the blast would affect the village."

"Liar." Menders wasn't going to listen to more. "Why haven't you sent someone to see to the injured?"

"We will be going there in a few moments, sir," Reinhart, the Minister of Defense answered. "There is a siding there and a turntable for the engine. We will appraise the situation then."

"You are to report casualty figures to the Queen immediately upon your 'appraisal' of the situation," Menders ordered, removing his glasses and raking them all with his eyes. He couldn't see them clearly, of course, but they didn't know that.

His white eyes had their usual effect. The carriage was silent, and the people within it were very uncomfortable indeed.

Menders slammed back out.

***

Katrin looked out the window of the Royal Carriage as the train pulled up to what had once been a village full of little houses, with a small train station. The platform was still there, but the office was gone, as was most of the village. There were only a few walls standing. There was no sign of life.

Katrin rubbed her eyes. They felt sandy, but her vision was clearing now, and she could see fairly well. The train was passing the platform and moving onto a siding. She could see into what was left of the village. She squinted, trying to see if anyone was moving about.

A harsh intake of breath from Menders made her start. She followed his gaze to a shattered stone wall that was still standing.

There were dark shapes on it. Paint? Then they drew nearer, and Katrin could focus her bleared vision.

It was as if someone had painted silhouettes on the wall – people. Frozen forever as dark smears of ash against the stone, seared into shadows by the Thermaline bomb.

***

The train ground its way back to Erdahn. Once there, Katrin fled to the carriage and horses, accompanied by Menders and the Guard. They were all quiet, sickened.

They had been able to hear the cries of amazement and jubilation from the Council, scientists and military officers as they walked through the destroyed village. Menders jumped down from the carriage and followed them, but had returned within minutes.

"There is no-one alive," he said, his voice shaking. "Not even bodies. All burned completely away." He flung himself down in a seat and said no more. Katrin couldn't speak. She felt cold and weak, and huddled close to the small lignus heater in the center of the carriage.

Finally back in her suite, she held still for Menders to get her out of the formal gown of the Queen of Mordania and then went to her wardrobe and took out her warmest dressing gown before she removed the ugly red wig and makeup, transforming herself back into – who? She wasn't too sure of who she was any more.

Instead of collapsing on the bed, she made her way into the lounge of the suite, sinking shakily down on the edge of a chair. Sunny sat down beside her, licking her hand in an attempt to comfort her.

Menders also appeared in a dressing gown and settled on the sofa. Once or twice he tried to speak, but couldn't seem to summon the energy. His face looked haunted, his eyes hollow behind his clear indoor glasses. She wondered if she looked the same.

"Having something like this…" Katrin managed once, then fell silent again, shivering, though the fire was roaring merrily.

The room grew darker. The year was well into the long nights now. Neither of them had the energy to light a lamp, but sat silently as the light dimmed.

"I wish I was a little girl again," Katrin heard herself say abruptly. "Then I would still be small enough to climb into your arms, so you could hold me and make it all right."

Menders looked directly at her – then held out his arms.

In a moment, he was holding her close.

"My little princess," he whispered.

"Why would anyone make a thing like that?" Katrin asked after a while.

He didn't answer.

***

Menders stood at the window of his office in the Palace, looking down on The Promenade below. It was the day after the test of the Thermaline bomb. He was still shaky and felt as if his ears were stuffed with wool.

He'd been trying to write another letter to Eiren, but couldn't manage it. He hadn't been able to do anything, not since seeing that hellish device detonated and the horrifying, greasy black shadows that had been people and animals.

Katrin was still in shock, very quiet and withdrawn. She wasn't drinking, to his surprise. She'd clung to him last night until he'd fallen asleep. He'd wakened in the morning to find he'd been stretched out on the sofa and covered, a pillow placed under his head. Katrin had been asleep in her bed.

Once she'd risen, they'd been very gentle and kind to each other. She'd spent a lot of time looking out the suite window that overlooked the same view he was gazing at now.

The moment he'd seen what had happened to that village, he'd known his plans to end everything, make Katrin abdicate, disband the Men, go away somewhere and live a normal life, were over. He could never do it now, not with things like that bomb in the world, controlled by the kind of men who could run around an annihilated village, celebrating how effective their firecracker was. Not with nations in the world like Mordania and Artreya, which were more than fond of playing at war every few years.

Mordania had this terrible weapon – how long before Artreya had it too? There was a brisk trade in contraband, including military weapons and supplies. Thermaline was still a secret, but for how long? Somehow, the madness would have to be controlled.

He would not have a quiet, private life – ever. The chance for that was gone. He was trapped, forever – and so was Katrin.

THE PALACE, MORDANIA

14
IT IS TIME TO RISE

Katrin was in a small glass room, looking out at the world passing by. Inside was silence. Inside was stale air breathed many times. Inside was heat, thick and oppressive.

She could see people outside the glass room. They laughed and walked, they talked to each other. She saw Hemmett stroll by with Flori. Borsen and Stevahn rode by on their horses. Menders and Eiren, Kaymar with Ifor, Petra with her children, Cook, all moved along, talking, smiling. She couldn't hear their words, but she could see that they were living and breathing, while she sat in the silence of her glass cube.

Suddenly she heard a high-pitched whine and tried to cover her ears. Her hands refused to move. She was frozen in place in her tiny glass world. She called out to everyone, to warn them to run, to take cover, but her voice wouldn't reach beyond the glass.

There was a brilliant bright light.

There was a roar of sound so loud it made the ground tremble.

When the mighty, hot wind came, it struck the glass wall of Katrin's cube. She saw the glass shatter. The fragments flowed down like water.

She heard screams and the sound of flames. The smell of burned flesh reached her and her stomach turned.

Then there was silence. The wind was gone. The world was black and sere.

She was alone.

Then they came – the voices of the Queens, which had been silent for all the years since she had not stopped Kaymar as he went to be reassigned.

There is no time! You must throw off the shackles! It is time to rise, child! Rise my daughter! Show your heritage, daughter of Mordania! Queen of Mordania! Queen!

Katrin sat upright in her bed, her breath coming in loud, noisy wheezes. She was in her room at The Palace. It was still dark, but a rim of light was showing at the horizon.

She felt her heart racing. The roaring sound in her ears from the bomb had almost subsided, and she could hear a few sounds out on the street, despite the closed windows, carts moving, hoofbeats.

The air felt clean. She was breathing deeply.

It was cold in the suite. The fire was guttering low.

She was shivering a little. The streak of light at the edge of the world was an incredible, cold green, color so intense that it nearly made a sound. She felt the beauty of it in her heart.

It could all be destroyed, if the men who loved that horrible bomb had their way. All of it, as black and dead as the world in her dream.

She had to do something!

She was the Queen!

***

Menders jerked upright in bed and lunged for the knives always kept on his bedside table. He rose to his knees, tangled in the covers, the knives held ready in both hands to use on whoever had slammed his door open with a resounding crash.

"Menders! Get up! Get up! Hurry, we have to do something about Thermaline!"

It was Katrin, standing at the foot of his bed in her nightgown. She grabbed his bedcovers and flapped them violently. Menders dropped the knives and snatched up his glasses, collapsing off his knees with a hand against his heart. It felt as if it was going to jump out of his chest.

"Katrin…"

"Hurry! We have to do something! You need to teach me about this horrible Thermaline! Get the Council! I'll give a command to stop making these bombs! Why are you still lying there?"

Menders managed to sit up against his pillows, dragging up the bedclothes so he wasn't stark naked in front of her. He tried to collect his wits, which she had effectively scattered.

She's finally gone mad, he thought, as she continued to berate him for lying around while the world was ending. Then he began to really hear her words.

Not mad.

Not mad at all.

"Hurry! I'm going to get dressed! What do you want for breakfast? I'm starving! How do we get the Council here? Why are you just staring at me like you've never seen me before?"

Katrin apparently had no idea of the spectacle she made in her long nightgown, bald as a newborn baby, her eyes blazing with the fire he hadn't seen in so long. Sunny, excited by all the shouting and gesturing, gamboled around her, his wagging tail a happy blur.

Menders began to laugh.

Katrin put her hands on her hips.

"It isn't funny! We have to stop them before they make more bombs! I want to see if we can bring charges against them for killing those people in that village. Stop laughing! I'm the damn Queen! I have to stop this!"

Menders laughed some more and then managed to speak.

"Yes, little princess, I'll get dressed."

"Good! Hurry! If you didn't sleep naked, you'd be able to get out of bed when someone needs you instead of sitting there like a stone image! Gods, I hope my clothes fit. I'm so fat I'm jiggly. And let your hair grow back in, you look terrible! Hurry up!"

She disappeared from his doorway.

Menders lay back in his pillows and laughed as he listened to her yelling out further instructions, observations and admonishments as she rifled her wardrobe for something to wear. Then he heard crashing in the courtyard below and knew she was throwing bottles of wine, conveniently kept on her dressing table, out the window.

His Princess was back.

***

Dearest Little Bird,

I don't even know just how to begin to explain what has happened except to say that Katrin has made sudden, incredible strides toward recovery. I had given up hope altogether and was going to force her to abdicate. Seeing that horrific bomb set off did something to her. She appeared in my doorway at dawn two days later, shouting at me to get up and help her do something to stop it all.

She also scolded me for sleeping naked and told me to let my hair grow back in. I'm sure you'll be pleased with the latter and also to know that I have no intention of beginning to wear a nightie, despite the Royal Command, unless the weather is cold enough.

Of course, I finally pulled her back down to ground level. She ate an enormous breakfast and then I spoke with her calmly about the realities of the situation. Though she is an absolute ruler, it is not possible for her to simply command that no more of these bombs be made. Mordania has been without an effective Queen for so long that many factions have a finger in the pie. If she did such a thing, which would put a considerable kink in the plans of many men who profit from war, she would be placing herself in considerable danger.

Katrin fought me on this at first. As you know, she always tends to go for simple, if brilliant, solutions to problems. It took some explaining and unpleasant revelations to make her understand that such a solution cannot be used here. It seems perfectly reasonable that, as Queen, she should command the construction and use of Thermaline in bombs be stopped – but that would result in many plots to remove her through assassination, with the object of setting up a more tractable Queen. So far Katrin has been quite safe because she's been so ineffectual and uninvolved. For her to suddenly stride forward issuing unpopular commands would be catastrophic.

I had to reveal to her just how many plots there have been against her life in the past. She was dismayed and exhibited considerable anger that she hadn't been told about them. This led to me having to point out that many of these were when she was a child, when it would have been utterly inappropriate for her to be informed of plots against her life. Also, if she had been told about every amateur plot that we've uncovered over the years, she would never have known a moment's peace.

All in all, there have been over a hundred plots against her life since the day she was born. Most of them came to nothing – and the rest were thwarted through one means and another. The fact that such things do happen made her understand that she cannot change things abruptly – at least not until she can be sure of popular support.

So, we are working on a feasible plan for Katrin to begin taking back the Queen's power, as is her right. It will take time, but I think some devious doings can make it nearly impossible for the armaments manufacturers to procure Thermaline. In time, she will be able to issue commands to put an end these weapons. They are truly terrible things, my darling. Seeing the effects of the one was blood chilling. Seeing the jubilation on the parts of the men who intend to use these things against other people was much worse than that.

There has been a great deal of damage done between Katrin and me, as you know. Things are strained and I find her altered from how she was before the melancholia. Some of it is her own bewilderment at what she calls "waking up".

Now that Katrin can talk to me at length about her condition, it seems she was experiencing things like reduced sensation and altered vision – colors were muted, her sense of touch and perception of pain were somewhat deadened. She wasn't even aware of the passage of time in any realistic sense, and is somewhat startled to realize that she is about to be thirty years old. This is understandable – I'm about to be fifty. I find that hard to believe and I haven't been suffering from melancholia.

I must close. Katrin is determined to go and see Borsen this afternoon, and since she's been terrified of the idea of going outside for so long, I don't want to squelch the project. She is frightened to go out even now (she is far from completely over her illness, and may always suffer from it to a degree, Franz tells me) but she is utterly determined. Since it is only three blocks and we'll go in a carriage, I think it's a good idea.

Please let me know if you will be able to come here anytime soon. I miss you so very much, and I don't want to turn fifty without you!

Loving you,

M

***

"Is that Borsen's?"

Katrin was staring out the window of the plain carriage she'd requested for her trip down the Promenade. Menders tapped on the roof of the carriage. The Guard who was driving slowed and pulled over before the huge, marble fronted building.

"It is indeed," Menders replied, looking out his own window.

A fresh snowfall, not yet dirtied by city traffic, added to the glamour of the store's matched marble façade. Pillars, steps, walls all glistened as brightly as the snow. The huge red double doors stood out invitingly under the sign and motto that was now famous.

BORSEN'S
PRACTICALITY – FUNCTIONALITY – EXQUISITE STYLE

"Menders! Oh!" Katrin craned her neck around, gazing at one part of the building after another. "Look at that dress! Oh, can I get out and look?"

She pushed the door open and had one foot out on the steps, while the members of the Guard who were riding on the roof jumped down in surprise. Then she hesitated, backed up and closed the door.

"No – not until Borsen can be there," she said firmly, still looking at an exquisite, sea-blue dress in the store window. The Guards exchanged looks and clambered back onto the roof.

Menders pursed his lips, trying not to laugh out loud – not only at the funny spectacle that had just taken place, but just for the sheer joy of seeing Katrin noticing something and reacting.

She caught him at it.

"What's so funny?" she demanded.

"Cured of melancholia by pretty clothes," he teased. "If I'd known that would be your reaction, I'd have bought out the entire store and hauled it all up the Tower."

"I probably wouldn't have so much as noticed," she smiled ruefully as the carriage started forward again. "Borsen made that incredible place!"

"It is incredible. I'd love to be there when you go to see it."

"Of course you'll be there. Oh, look at that open gig! It's like my gig at The Shadows. Can we have that brought over here, Menders?"

He was about to say something about security and driving in open gigs, but stopped himself. If nothing else, she could drive it on the Palace grounds – they were enormous.

"We'll work that out," he replied. Katrin's smiled response was worth the considerable headache arranging security would cause. "This Stevahn and Borsen's street."

When they pulled up, Katrin alighted from the carriage and dashed to the front door of Borsen's townhouse. She felt uncomfortable on the street, out in the open. She knocked quickly, before she lost her nerve.

She felt a hot rush of shame as she looked at the gracious house and the small but exquisite front garden that Borsen had designed and planted with Stevahn. Despite living in Erdahn for six years, she had never been here, just as she'd never gone to Borsen's. All those years and she'd never set foot in the places that were important to her beloved brother.

"I'll get it, dear, don't get up." She could hear Stevahn speaking beyond the door. The knob turned, and the door swung open.

Stevahn blinked when he saw Katrin there, grinned as he hugged her warmly, then passed her on to Varnia, who disobeyed him and sprang up, her arms outstretched, her face joyful.

"I didn't let you know we were coming in case I just couldn't get all the way here, so please forgive us bursting in," Katrin gasped, her breath coming short.

"You come anytime. Breathe. Katrin, breathe in deeply," Varnia said, looking closely at her face.

"Katrin? Is Katrin down there?" Borsen was shouting somewhere in the house.

"Baby's awake," Stevahn laughed. He pointed toward the stairs.

Katrin ran. Stevahn followed, not wanting to miss anything.

Borsen was confined to bed and looked far from his best, having lost many pounds during his illness. He was weak, tired easily and slept quite a bit, but having heard Katrin's voice coming toward him, he was wide awake and up on his knees in the bed, trying to see down the stairs leading to the first floor.

Katrin flew into the room and flung herself at him, catching him in an enormous hug. He returned it with a vengeance.

"Oh, look at you!" he laughed when she finally released him and he settled back against his pillows, rather out of breath from the squeezing she'd subjected him to.

"I had to come as soon as I could. I'm sorry about not giving you warning," Katrin smiled.

"I can't think of a better surprise," Borsen grinned back, straightening his glasses, which had been knocked askew. He studied her with satisfaction.

"Don't. I know I look dreadful," Katrin protested. "And the dress is too tight as well. I gained even more weight lying around like a doorstop."

"You gained it in the right places," Borsen appraised. "You're all right, once you get some things made to fit. Hello, Papa!" Borsen turned to accept a swift hug from Menders.

"I was just about to bring some late lunch up to this youngster," Stevahn grinned. "Could you do with something?"

"Maybe not," Katrin said, looking down at her now very dramatic curves.

"Nonsense," Borsen said briskly. "You can't expect the same body at twenty-nine that you had at nineteen. Even I haven't managed that. If you're determined to suffer, you can have some of my finely mashed baby food while I have a steak sandwich – a steak between two steaks."

"I'll give Stevahn a hand," Menders said with a smile, shaking his head a little as he left them.

Katrin sat on the side of the bed.

"I am so sorry I didn't come when you were ill," she said awkwardly. "I'm ashamed of myself for that."

"You aren't allowed to belabor it," Borsen replied autocratically. "You were ill yourself. Whatever happened to you, Katrin? What caused the change?"

She told him about the Thermaline bomb. When she was done, he looked grim.

"Yes, people like those military officers and Council ministers would think nothing of people who live in bleak little villages full of little houses," he said darkly. "You can be sure that was no accident. They wanted to see how effectively their horror kills."

"That's what Menders says. I keep hoping it was an accident," Katrin said.

Borsen looked at her.

"You grew up among decent people," he said quietly. "You were privileged but you were never allowed to treat people who weren't as fortunate as if they were inferior to you. You'll find that many of the privileged people in the world treat poor people like objects. How do you think my mother came into being? She was Uncle's half-sister. Have you ever considered how that happened?"

Katrin was shocked to realize she'd never thought about it. Menders had told her his father had an illegitimate daughter and left it at that.

"I… I just assumed Menders' father had a Thrun woman as a lover after Menders' mother died," she finally said. Borsen shook his head.

"No – my mother was born first. Papa's father used the people on his estate as objects, including little serving girls. He had many bastards, none of whom he ever bothered to acknowledge or support. I've been one of those poor people, Katrin. I know what it's like to have a carriage driver try to run me down on purpose because his wealthy master considers it a good thing to eliminate 'vermin' and will give his driver a bonus for each City Thrun he runs over. I can remember a well-dressed man kicking my mother in the shins and telling her to move along when we were sitting in a public park, because she was City Thrun. Those are the sorts of people who killed the poor souls in that village. They'd think no more of it than they would think of stepping on an ant hill."

Katrin was struggling with tears.

"Every one of those little houses had someone living in it," Borsen continued, taking her hand. "Katrin, if you're really going to be Queen now, promise me one of the things you do will be helping those of us who were born poor. I was lucky. There are millions just like me who will never get the chance I did."

Katrin wiped her tears and looked at him, feeling a determined resolve forming in her mind.

"I will," she said firmly. "All my people will be given chances, just as we did at The Shadows. There are going to be schools and decent places to live. First, I have to stop this Thermaline madness, but then things will change."

They smiled at each other, hands tightly clasped.

"Now, before lunch arrives, what did you want to tell me when you were sick?" Katrin asked.

"I don't remember," Borsen answered quietly.

"Please," Katrin pleaded. "I wish I had come, but I was so ill. I just couldn't. I tried. Twice. I even tried to run down the Staircase so I'd get to the bottom before the fear began."

"No, I'm not keeping it from you, Katrin. I really can't remember," Borsen explained. "I remember I wanted to see you very badly and I had something I wanted to say, but it's gone. There are some… gaps. I can't remember some things, particularly when I was sick. I also can't remember some things from the days right before it all started. The fevers were so high they cooked my brain a bit. Franz says that it's to be expected. I simply can't remember what I wanted to tell you." He smiled sheepishly and shrugged a little.

"Poor thing," Katrin smiled back. "Maybe it will come back."

"Perhaps," Borsen answered, stretching a bit. "I am remembering some things about being sick, including some things I'd rather not. So, it might come back. And I do remember the important things, like wanting to see you and seeing my mother."

Katrin stared at him in amazement.

"I did. You needn't gawp at me as if I'm going into a fever again," Borsen said briskly. "I died. Adults don't survive putrid fever. If they ever do, they end up dribbling idiots. I died. I was taken out of my body and pulled toward The Light At The Top Of The World, but my mother stopped me and brought me back. There's something I'm supposed to do yet, so I couldn't die then."

"A dream?" Katrin ventured. Borsen shook his head.

"No dream. It was real. I saw The Ghosts Of Voices Singing. I saw The Light At The Top Of The World – and it was a wonderful and incredible thing." He smiled at her. He was gaunt and ill, but Katrin saw something different in him. She cast about in her mind for the answer – and it came to her.

The longing that was an integral part of Borsen was gone. It had always been there, even when he was laughing or playing – a deep, gnawing need that sounded through his soul like a drone note sounded through music.

Now he was truly content, as if he'd found the answer to a question that had always eluded him.

"Have you told anyone else about this?" she asked.

"Stevahn and Uncle of course. I would never tell Franz. He'd just say I hallucinated it. As it was, he rumpussed when I opened my eyes and said I'd been with my mother."

"Do Stevahn and Menders believe it?" Katrin asked doubtfully.

"Stevahn does, without question, but then he knows me better than anyone," Borsen grinned. "Papa too, though he's keeping his counsel."

"I can't see Menders believing it," Katrin said quietly.

"He does. He's far more mystical than he lets on," Borsen refuted. "He tries to be logical but if you really think about it, you'll see that much of his thinking is based on intuition. What is intuition but mysticism?"

"And Stevahn believes it?"

"Didn't I just say so?"

"I just can't see it," Katrin said, shaking her head bewilderedly.

Borsen started rearranging his pillows.

"If I saw a blue monkey playing a cromar on the windowsill and told Stevahn, he would believe me," he said. "He knows I don't lie, Katrin, and he knows I have enough sense not to imagine things. I did see my mother. I am not mistaken. It wasn't a dream. I know what a dream is like. It was real."

The smile on his face couldn't be denied. Katrin finally understood what it was Borsen had longed for so desperately – his mother. Now he had her again, be it through fever dream, hallucination or… reality.

"I'm glad for you," she said, smiling back at him.

"Thank you. It's nice to know where she is," Borsen answered. "Now, do I get the job of dressing the new Queen Katrin the First once I'm back on my feet and can show you my wonderful establishment?"

"Morghenna the Tenth," she corrected him. "And once you're back on your feet, you're definitely going to give me that long overdue tour of Borsen's."

"We've had too many Morghennas," Borsen said, curling his upper lip. "I think you should be Katrin I. A new Queen, a new era. No more monster dresses and fake teeth."

Katrin blinked. She'd never thought of it. The dress had been useful in getting people to do her bidding, but she despised wearing it. She really hated the teeth and that wretched red wig.

The appearance was useful, but once she had power again, real power, why not leave off the masquerade? Make a Court that wasn't an absurd throwback to more primitive times – like she'd made the suite in the Tower?

"Food," Stevahn announced from the doorway, Varnia and Menders behind him, all carrying trays.

"Hurrah!" Borsen pulled himself fully upright. His appetite won out over any bodily infirmity. Once they were all settled with their lunches, Katrin turned to Menders.

"Borsen was asking if he could dress the new Queen," she said. "What do you think of banishing the 'vampire Queen' persona? Not right away but when the time is right?"

Menders' eyebrows went up and he raised a hand, his signal that he wanted time to consider his answer.

"Once you've stopped this new weapon insanity," Borsen added. "That's the most important. You said this Thermaline can be used as a fuel, yes?"

"Yes, a very efficient one," Menders answered. "As I understand it, the refinement process to make it explosive is completely different than the process making it into a fuel," Menders was continuing. "So as a fuel, it's not dangerous."

"Think what could be done with a fuel like that," Stevahn said, rapidly writing something in a notebook he'd picked up from his own bedside table. Doubtless he would be looking into Thermaline as an investment as soon as Menders gave him the go-ahead.

"Something wonderful could be done with a fuel like that," Borsen said, his cup of soup halfway to his lips. "Imagine all the things that it could make easier. No more soot from wood and lignus fires, no more smoke in the cities on still days, no more endless woodcutting or scavenging for fuel for poor people. That's something wonderful."

Katrin's eyes glowed as she thought about it. Not just to stop the destructive use of Thermaline, but to find a way to make something wonderful come of it.

***

Hemmett climbed the last flight of stairs to the Royal Suite. He was a bit puffed, despite being in good physical condition. It was a pity Katrin had been so determined to have her new suite in the Tower, far up and away from everything. Possibly Menders would consider installing an elevator.

He dreaded going into the suite, for fear of seeing Katrin disheveled and drunk, or stretched out on her bed in the sodden unconsciousness she considered sleep. Hemmett had enjoyed four happy days with Lorein, despite their proximity to the funeral of his parents. He hated the idea of his memories of Lorein and their marriage being completely drowned by the tide of Katrin's misery.

Hemmett reached the landing, caught his breath and then swung the door open, calling out to announce himself so Menders didn't come leaping out with a knife.

Instead, someone ran at him full tilt, so fast he didn't really see who it was. Hemmet found himself enveloped in an enormous hug. He looked down at golden hair in confusion. Then he realized that Katrin was jabbering away while fixed fast around him. She began to jump up and down, still holding onto his waist.

"What is it, you big old crazy girl?" he asked bewilderedly. He had to jump along with her in self-defense, or he would have been jostled into nausea.

"I'm so glad you're back!" Katrin cried, grinning up at him, still jigging up and down. "We have so much to do! Menders and I are making all sorts of plans because there are people making bombs that have to be stopped and then I'm going to build schools and good housing and burn that stupid dress in the Courtyard! I'll have all sorts of cultured people come and live at Court and make all kinds of scholarships so that people can be educated and bring Mordania out of being backwards! Come and sit down and I'll show it all to you – oh!"

The rush of words stopped and Katrin looked horrified.

"I'm so sorry about your parents, Bumpy. So sorry that I couldn't come to their funeral." Her expression shifted to one of chagrin and she covered her mouth with her hands. Her eyes filled.

Hemmett looked down at her for another moment, keeping his face immobile.

Then he started to laugh. It began with a mild chuckle, but within seconds had grown into the enormous haw-haw that had so often gotten him into trouble. He rocked back on his heels with his hands on his hips and laughed, while Menders appeared in a doorway further into the suite and looked amused. Katrin stared at him.

He stopped laughing when his stomach was sore and his throat felt raw.

"Hello Willow," he said to Katrin. "Still not doing things by halves, I see."

"I am sorry," she said. "I should have come with you… but I couldn't. It's a terrible thing, melancholia. One thing I want to do is find a cure for it, because when you have it, you're dead. Worse than dead, because you know that the rest of the world is going on without you."

Hemmett put one hand under her chin and another one over her mouth.

"Now then," he grinned. "Let me get a word in edgewise. It's good to see you, my darling other self. May I go and put my uniform bag away before I get drawn into the plan for a new Mordania?"

Katrin nipped at his fingers to make him let her go and he haw-hawed a bit more.

"Menders, I like the sound of that. 'A New Mordania'. Put your bag away, Bumpy and then hurry, we have to make plans about how I can go out and around and be guarded. I'm still afraid to go out but I went to Borsen's house yesterday and did all right, and I expect I'll get used to going around before long, but I'll need an official way to do it. And I want to know how everyone is out at The Shadows! How can it take you so long to put your bag away? Borsen's house is magnificent! I'm going to steal all kinds of ideas from him to make this Palace habitable. I've taken a look around it and most of it isn't fit to house a horse. Whoever came up with the idea of stone chairs?"

Katrin's chatter followed Hemmett to his room, used to store extra uniforms since he acquired his townhouse.

Hemmett flung his bag on the bed, going against military training that told him to unpack immediately and put everything tidily away. He could do that later. It wasn't often that he married his great love and had his other self come back to life in the same week.

"Come on, old toad, hurry up!" Katrin was shouting.

"On my way, your Royalness," he said, shucking off his coat and tossing it on the bed.

"That's Majesty to you, subject," Katrin called.

Hemmett went to her, laughing.

***

"Letter from Eiren for you," Hemmett said, handing an envelope to Menders. "I would have given it to you before, but the wild woman drove it all right out of my head."

They were in the Tower roof garden, having fled the plans for a New Mordania after two hours to let Hemmett have a smoke.

"I can't bring myself to rein her in much," Menders answered. "It's to be expected for her to be elated now with the melancholia lifted. Franz says it will probably settle down – and we have to be braced in case she swings back into melancholia again."

Hemmett grunted, lighting his cigar. "I'll place my bets on Katrin," he said once he had it glowing.

"To be honest, so will I," Menders agreed, running a finger under the seal on his letter. "Good leave?"

"Yes, very," Hemmett answered, leaning on the parapet and looking down at The Promenade.

It was obvious that confidences would not be forthcoming at this time, so Menders gave his attention to his letter.

Darling!

What wonderful news about Katrin! Everyone here is overjoyed and hoping the improvement will continue. Katrin has always been so concerned for others that her lack of interest in the people at The Shadows during her illness has been very disconcerting for all concerned. It was as if a stranger had come to live in her body – as you know.

It's fully understandable that you and Katrin will find your relationship is strained. The last six years have not been kind to either of you and because of your forced proximity to her, damage was inevitable. It's not possible to see your child become completely lost and not suffer as a result – and of course, you were in dread that she would end up like her mother. Add to that very understandable anger and frustration on your part and the fact that she did deliberately antagonize you at times because of her illness – and the damage is done. I do believe it can be undone.

I must admit that I feel very much as if I had abandoned you, though I certainly could not have avoided staying here as I did, between Mama's final illness and Papa's collapse. I felt terribly torn – and then would be so frustrated when there was nothing I could do to help Katrin. I hope you can forgive any failings of mine.

I had a funny little note from Borsen yesterday, complete with a sketch he's calling "the new Katrin". He says she now has the figure of a goddess, and that he can't wait to design some things for her to wear. He mentions that she wants to get rid of that red horror she wears in public. I must say I fully concur with such a plan. Wearing that wretched dress and knowing who wore it ahead of her cannot have helped her.

It is truly tragic that our Queens have been regimented into such madness. I know we've always accepted it, but when you know the woman who must force her body into that horrible heavy dress, it comes home to you what the others have suffered – and why? We're no longer primitive people who need a Queen who frightens potential conquerors away, yet we cling to this foolish tradition that degrades and debases our Queens.

Of course, I will be with you when you turn fifty! As if I would ever let you celebrate a birthday alone. It's still a couple of months away and I'm afraid I'm very much tied down here for some weeks yet. Sana is under the weather and I am doing double duty at Shadows Academy. Once this term has ended, I will arrange it so that I am no longer over-committed. Come what may, I will be with you on the shortest day of the year.

Give my love to Katrin. I will write to her directly, but not for a day or so – things are that frenetic. Perhaps you and she could arrange to come to The Shadows now that she's so much better. I know Hemmett, in particular, would love a reason to be back here. I am otherwise sworn to secrecy and must say no more, lest I brave his wrath.

And now the bell is ringing (yes, the headmistress is spending her work hours writing letters to her man) and I must be off. I miss you so very much.

Your Eiren

P.S. I am in complete agreement with Katrin about your hair. Now that she's broken the ice, I will join in the chorus – bring my handsome man's hair back! It is most unpleasant consorting with a bristly manquar!

Menders laughed aloud and folded the letter into his pocket, giving his short-cropped hair a self-conscious rub.

"She's leaving out something," Hemmett said seriously, turning toward him. "Her sister isn't doing well. Seems melancholia is the order of the day, but not like Katrin and Granddad had it. In fact, I think it comes up at convenient times, so Eiren will take over and look after children, housework and the like."

"Damn!" Menders looked out over The Promenade. "I wish she'd told me."

"She'll sort it out," Hemmett replied. "She's beginning to understand how to balance her responsibilities to her family. She's fallen into being the one who provides all the care and who is expected to sacrifice herself the most, mainly because she hasn't had children. It happens to Sana too, but she's less likely to tolerate being taken advantage of. You know how Eiren tends to put herself last."

"I do indeed," Menders sighed. "It hasn't served her well, considering the life I've had to lead."

"Granddad feels that way too. He already blames himself for Eiren staying there so long when she could be here with you. Even if she wanted to stay on at the school full time, which I doubt, she could get over here more often if she didn't have one after another getting some illness or another."

"Hopefully this will all change now," Menders said, smiling to himself.

"Looks that way. Do you really think Katrin can implement all the changes she's planning?" Hemmett asked, leaning back against the balustrade.

"Yes, in time. Being Katrin, she wants to do it all at once. That's understandable in this first rush of energy. She'll pace herself as she gets accustomed to being well again. You know how she is."

"Oh yes," Hemmett grinned. "How is Borsen? I thought of stopping by on my way up from the boat but decided to wait until evening so Stevahn would be home."

"Doing well, coming back day by day. Still angry that he's having to eat all that soft stuff, but Franz will take him off that soon, he says. He seems very peaceful otherwise. He stays in bed with his sketchbooks and pencils. He's wild to design new clothing for Katrin and is probably madly drawing away at that."

"Good for him. Tough little mate," Hemmett said, blowing a smoke ring.

"Indeed, he is," Menders smiled. He wasn't about to voice it, but his joy over having Borsen still with them was sometimes overwhelming. The circle of his acquired family was not broken – thank the gods, should there be any.

"Best get back to the New Mordania," Hemmett said, dropping his cigar end and grinding it out with his heel. "Sounds like it'll be a nice place."

"It does indeed," Menders agreed.

***

Dearest Lorein, my lovely wife,

Katrin's better. I'm completely gamfoozled over it, but apparently something she saw shocked her out of the melancholia. Came running to the door when I came in, jumping all around, yakking on about how she's going to change Mordania and make all kinds of things better.

Menders is fearful that it won't last, and she'll be back to the melancholia in a day or two, but in many ways I know Katrin better than he does. She's back. She's changed a bit. There's no way anyone could go through what she has and still be the same, but she's not going to be sick again. She's far too busy, and has some wonderful ideas.

I've kept quiet about our marriage because I'm enjoying having it to myself. I'm happy about Katrin, of course, but there's that deeper happiness of knowing about us. I'm not willing to share it round yet. When you're here in a few days we can tell everyone together.

Katrin says she wants to gather a Court. The Palace has been practically empty since she came here and we got rid of those freaks that hung around Aidelia. Katrin says she wants intelligent, cultured and forward-seeing people. That reminded me of a certain lady I know. I wondered if she would be interested?

Would you be? You're exactly the sort of person Katrin wants. She'd be likely to make you a lady in waiting, though she does for herself and would continue to do so. You wouldn't have to dress her or any of that nonsense, but be a friend and companion. You wouldn't live at The Palace. I've been in our townhouse since I came home with Flori. I still have a room in Katrin's suite if I need to stay overnight for a guard shift, and I keep extra uniforms in there in case Vil spills coffee on me, but home is down the street.

I know we talked about all kinds of possibilities before I left, and I never expected to come back and find Katrin well again. So, I'm not dismissing the possibility of resigning my posting and teaching at the Military Academy fulltime. I just wanted to let you know what is going on, and say that if you would like to try, I could remain here, and you could be part of the new Court. Either way is fine with me, so long as we're together.

Write to me soon. I'm missing you so very much.

Love you, my darling,

Hemmett

Darling Hemmett,

I was so happy to have your letter this morning! I was also very glad to hear of Katrin's recovery. It was tragic even thinking about her being so unlike her old self and knowing she was so unhappy.

Hemmett, I will be delighted to live in Erdahn with such new ideas coming into being. It's exciting to consider and so much what this nation needs. What I would love most would be living with you, wherever you are.

I understand how devoted you are to Katrin and that you would like to stay at Court now the situation has changed so much for the better. I could not be more pleased. I am not a jealous sort – except back in the day when my friend Rivka and I used to pull each other's pigtails when we argued over who would marry you! I must seek her out and strut in front of her – actually, she married a pudgy merchant some years back, has three babies and has probably forgotten all about beautiful Captain Hemmett and our great rivalry over him.

You know Mamma and Pappa were thrilled with our runaway match and their dashing and handsome son-in-law – and they have managed not to look utterly relieved about not having to plan a great do involving a dress that looks interesting from the back. As a wedding gift, Pappa has given us the money he would have spent on a big wedding, to do as we like with. They have always been such comfortable parents! They're anxious to have Flori come and visit them.

Mamma was enchanted with her at the funeral reception and already talks on about her granddaughter! I'm so very happy things are turning out so well!

Hemmett, there is truly no way that I can really tell yet, but I am very sure our child is already on the way. I feel changed in an essential way and it isn't only from knowing that we're going to be together forever. My body feels different, more alive. I asked Mamma about it, but she couldn't say for sure, it's so early. She said if I am pregnant, I will feel a lot less alive when the morning sickness starts! But this morning when I was dressing, a necklace I wore two weeks ago was far too tight. I said something about it to our cook, who said that's one of the first signs – something about increased circulation and the veins in the neck! Another couple of weeks and we'll see!

I miss you so much. I will be with you at the end of the week! Kaymar has been having all my doodads and fandidingles (see, I'm learning to speak Hemmett and will gamfoozle you with my expertise!) hauled over to the steam launch so I can bob across the briny in your direction.

All my love,

Lorein

TO: EIREN
FROM: BRISTLY MANQUAR

HAVE CANVASSED ALL AVAILABLE PARTIES HERE AND THE CONSENSUS IS THAT I AM BY NO MEANS A HANDSOME MAN. SUGGEST YOU STOP BY OCULIST TO HAVE EYES EXAMINED. AM NOT YET GROWING HAIR OUT BUT HOPE TO DIMINISH BRISTLINESS IN NEAR FUTURE ONCE NEED FOR BRISTLY APPEARANCE IS GONE. KATIN HOPES WE CAN COME OUT TO THE SHADOWS IN ANOTHER WEEK TO TWO WEEKS AFTER SOME OFFICIAL BUSINESS IS DONE HERE. SHE CAN'T WAIT TO SEE YOU AND NEITHER CAN I.

TO: MISTER MANQUAR
FROM: MISTRESS MANQUAR

DESPITE CANVASS I DECLARE YOU A VERY HANDSOME MAN AND SUGGEST THAT THOSE IN ERDAHN HAVE BECOME JADED WITH CITY LIVING IF THEY CAN'T SEE

IT. YOUTH IS ALWAYS BLIND. LET US KNOW WHENEVER IT IS POSSIBLE FOR YOU TO COME AND IF MY SCHEDULE CLEARS I WILL POP OVER EVEN IF ONLY FOR THE DAY. KISSES TO KATRIN, HEMMETT AND BORSEN AND SAVE SOME FOR YOURSELF.

THE PALACE, ERDAHN, MORDANIA

15
LIGHT OF THE WINTER SUN

"We have to be very careful, Katrin," Menders said, looking at her across the table. "I know it seems most logical to have you command that the production of Thermaline bombs be stopped. In a sane world, you would do that, and the problem would be solved."

"Unfortunately, it's not a sane world," Hemmett added. "These men – and the people behind them – would not take kindly to such a command. We don't know everyone who was behind Aidelia killing your mother, but it's possible these war profiteers were involved. They would think nothing of having you killed."

Katrin looked pensive and ground her teeth for a moment.

"I understand," she said, finally. "Along with that, the fact that I've been docile for so long has set a precedent with them. They expect no trouble from me."

"In many ways that's to your advantage," Kaymar responded.

It was the first time he'd spoken since the meeting began. Menders had asked him, along with Ifor, Hemmett, Villison and several of Menders' Men to sit down and discuss options for stopping the production of Thermaline weapons. Katrin hadn't seen him in a very long while, and then only at a distance. He and Ifor had been spending long periods of time abroad, doing surveillance work, gathering information and acting as diplomats for Mordania.

"Tell me how," Katrin invited. "This is all new to me."

Kaymar nodded and smiled slightly.

"They're used to you not being involved," he replied. "They know they will have their way whether you like it or not. At this point, essentially, you don't exist. If you play your cards right – if you don't rush off half-cocked and tip your hand, suddenly seizing command could work to your benefit, because they would never see you coming."

Katrin looked at Menders, who kept his face impassive.

"You would have to have sufficient protection and support," Ifor added, smiling at Katrin. "You can't just stride in there as the bold girl and demand that they stop doing something that makes them very, very rich."

"No, that would spell disaster." Kaymar took up the thread. "Doing just that got your mother killed. After years of being completely ineffectual, she ran into a situation where she felt she had to take command. She tried to replace Aidelia with you – and she tried to have a character who called himself Prince Talbreth eliminated, because he had complete power over Aidelia, to say nothing of much of the Council."

"I remember him! He was a disgusting man!" Katrin gasped.

"Very much so. Years before, under the name of Therbalt, he sent all those assassins after the family, including DeLarco the Surelian." Kaymar looked levelly at her across the table.

Katrin knit her brows for a moment and then looked disgusted.

"His clever alias is switching the letters of his name around?" she said with a snort.

"It works. He manages to change his appearance effectively – and he makes sure that he is never seen or known by everyone he's manipulating. We've been after him for ages now, ever since we realized he's the same man behind your mother's murder. He's gone to ground and no amount of digging around has stirred him up. He did that before, after we missed him with bombs we planted in his Surelian townhouse right after DeLarco nearly killed me. He seems a fool – but he isn't. That's the most dangerous sort to combat. It's easy to become lulled into thinking it will be a simple matter to eliminate him."

"It's a matter of gathering as much information as we can, mustering support and being very careful in how we proceed," Menders chimed in. "It's the hard part of ruling, Katrin."

"What can I do now?" she asked.

"Consider what we've talked about. Read the information we will be passing on to you. If any ideas occur to you, let us know," Menders replied.

"Concentrate on getting well," Kaymar added, looking directly at her. "You aren't, not by a long shot. Take it from one who knows."

"All right then, unless someone wishes to add to the discussion, we've covered everything we're here for today," Menders said. There was a general rustling and movement as the members of the meeting put their papers and notes together, chatting freely with each other.

Katrin made her way around the table to where Kaymar and Ifor were talking in low tones. She waited for them to finish.

Kaymar looked around and noticed her. Ifor turned, smiled and hugged her close.

"So glad to see you doing so well," he rumbled.

When he released her, Kaymar offered a hand, then leaned forward and gave her a swift kiss on the cheek.

"You hearken to what I said," he murmured, his voice warm though his face was impassive. "Lots of rest and sleep, good food and plenty of exercise. Keep your mind occupied and stay off the grog."

"I wanted to ask you – I'm afraid of the melancholia coming back," Katrin began.

"It might. If it does, fight. If you start feeling numb or listless, fight it, don't just sit there. You can't always turn it around, but sometimes it helps. If you get into that trap where you can sit there for hours thinking about how you're going to walk across the room, you're in trouble."

"Thank you – I'm having dinner in my suite for the family, those who can come. Hemmett and Flori, Vil, Petra, Varnia and Menders, of course. Please come join us," Katrin asked.

"I'm sorry, my dear, but we're on our way right now to catch the evening ship to Artreya," Kaymar said smoothly. "Going over there to keep an eye on the situation now that this Thermaline bomb has been tested."

"Is there danger?"

"Always, with Artreya, but no imminent danger, so rest easy," Ifor said. "Can we be asked to dinner another time?"

"Of course!" Katrin smiled.

She watched as they began to leave – then stepped forward.

"Kaymar!"

Both of them turned, Ifor looking troubled, Kaymar showing no emotion, his face a smooth, still mask.

"I'm sorry, I must speak to you for a moment," she said apologetically.

"I'll go ahead," Ifor said. "I'll hold the boat if necessary. But hurry, Kip." He strode over to Menders, speaking with him briefly before going out the door.

"Can it go in a letter?" Kaymar asked.

"No – please."

"What is it?" He stepped close, pulling her back toward a niche that held a bust of one of Mordania's Queens.

"Kaymar – if the melancholia begins to come back, would cutting myself as you do keep it away?" she asked bluntly.

He blinked. Then his face grew less impervious.

"No, Katrin. I use that for the other side of my madness, which I don't believe you have. The side where I can't sleep for days on end, where the voices in my head are giving me no peace and where I'm consumed with fear or anger and feel the only solution to everything is to… let's just say commit mayhem. Do you have any of that?"

"No. Only the terrible sadness and inability to do anything."

"I've never used cutting myself for melancholia – well, I tried once and all it did was make me even sadder and made a mess of the carpet. I'm like a seesaw – melancholia on one end, what Franz calls mania on the other. My main problem comes from the mania – I don't dip into melancholia very often. I do the things I just advised you to do – stay as busy as I can, believe strongly in things. I can't say it's a panacea, but it works for me."

"Why are you being so distant? Is that part of it?"

Kaymar looked down at the floor, avoiding her eyes. He seemed to be having an inward argument.

"Katrin – it's self-preservation, and it's something that would serve you well," he finally said. "Think back on the times you've been in trouble, when you've ended up in a situation that is hurtful or harmful to others. Everything from running away from your guards when you were a child to getting involved with a man who was the last thing you needed. You're a very emotional person – I'm another. It's something you must control or being impulsive and emotional could destroy everything you care about – while at the same time, your strong emotions are one of your greatest assets.

"At this time, I need to keep myself distant so that I can concentrate on what I have to do. You need to learn when to hold yourself separate, Katrin."

"Is there more going on than I know about?" she asked.

"No – not at the moment. But Katrin, a secret is only a secret when one person knows it. How many people saw that bomb go off?"

He looked at her, his bright blue eyes, so like hers, serious.

She nodded.

"Rest assured news of this bomb has reached Artreya," he went on. "Menders would have been telling you this sooner or later, but as usual, you've precipitated him. Bear and I are going there to see how things stand. At this point, there is no more than the usual danger from Artreya. Leave it at that and trust us to let you know when that changes. That's also important to a Queen – knowing who and when to trust. And no cutting yourself – you can't risk infection. If it wasn't the only way I stay out of an asylum, I wouldn't do it."

Katrin was silent, stunned by his blunt revelation. They had only spoken of his injuring himself once before in all the years they'd known each other. It had always been part of him, just as the scars it left behind were.

Kaymar seemed to be arguing with himself again.

"I'm going to tell you something that my father told me when I was fourteen, and that I've told Borsen since. I want you to remember it and keep it by you. No matter what happens, no matter what you do, Kaymar loves you. Now, I must go. Have your party, my dear and don't fret. This is what we do – all of us, Menders' Men. We won't fail you. And we'll be at your next celebration."

He turned away, went to Menders and spoke softly to him for a moment, then picked up his hat from the table and went to the door.

Before he went through it, he looked around at Katrin, nodded and winked.

***

Menders looked over the simmering pots and pans in Katrin's kitchen. She had insisted on preparing the dinner party entirely by herself. From the wonderful aromas, she had done a very good job.

"You have outdone yourself," he smiled, very tempted to do some tasting. Katrin, however, had already driven Hemmett from the suite with the broom when he daringly sampled the appetizers despite her forbidding it.

"Would you be a dear and pick some bottles of wine that would go well with this?" Katrin asked, collecting silverware to finish setting the table.

Menders froze for a moment, looking at her – feeling his heart sink.

"Couldn't that cause a problem?" he ventured.

"No, I don't really like wine and I'm not having melancholia," she answered, busily putting out the silverware. "I'm not going to have any, but other people might like a glass or two."

"Of course. I'm sorry, Katrin."

"Don't be. I understand," she smiled.

Menders returned with the wine in time to intercept Varnia, who was puffing up the Tower Staircase with a basket of bread. He relieved her of it as well and put an arm around her to help her with the final flight. Katrin heard them coming and had the door open for them.

"About your stairs," Varnia gasped.

"The elevator construction begins next week," Katrin answered, taking the bread basket from Menders and guiding Varnia to a chair.

"Here, hold the door, Menders!" Villison's voice floated up the Staircase and then he and Petra came into view as they came around the last curve of the great spiral and began scaling the final flight. No sooner had they gotten into the suite but Stevahn came climbing up in their wake.

Varnia looked around in alarm, but Stevahn anticipated her reaction.

"Now dear, His Majesty himself sent me," he explained. "Germaine is there with him for the evening, more than content to drink tea and eat cookies while he sketches and sleeps. He sent this along, Katrin."

He produced a box from his inner coat pocket. Katrin fluttered a bit as she opened it and took out a lovely miniature ceramic sculpture of The Shadows.

"He says now you have your old home in your new home," Stevahn smiled.

"Look everyone – isn't it perfect?" Katrin said happily, showing it around before she placed it out of harm's way on the mantelpiece.

"I'm for a cigar," Villison said abruptly, letting himself out into the Tower garden, Sunny alongside him. Menders watched with amusement as Villison lit up, took only two puffs, waved the cigar about and then dropped it on the ground, extinguishing it under his foot. He came in immediately.

"Too cold out there," he said, rubbing his hands together. "When do we eat?"

"We're just waiting for Hemmett and Flori," Katrin explained, standing with Menders and looking at the exquisitely detailed sculpture. "I haven't found any errors yet," she said happily.

"We should go out to The Shadows soon – everyone would be very happy to see you," Menders replied, turning the sculpture around again. "Look, it even has the cracked window!"

"I can't wait to go," Katrin smiled.

Conversation buzzed around as everyone chatted and the ladies fussed with the dinner things. Then definite and powerful footsteps approached on the Staircase. A moment later, Hemmett thumped the door resoundingly.

Katrin was nearest and swung it open.

"Yes, Old Toad?" she laughed at him. "Come in Flori – let me give that to Varnia and take your coat…"

Hemmett put his hand on her arm.

"I found someone we both know and brought them along," he said. "I hope you have enough food for another guest."

"Of course, I cooked enough for an army," Katrin laughed. She tried to look around him.

Hemmett stepped aside.

Katrin looked puzzled for a moment until Lorein removed her fur hat. Her hair caught the light from the Staircase lanterns.

"Why it's Lorein Spartz!" Katrin cried. "Oh, come in! Varnia, look! Lorein, I haven't seen you in so long – how are you?"

Hemmett stepped over and put an arm around Lorein.

"This is Mistress Captain Greinholz," he said resoundingly.

Everyone was stunned to silence, except for Villison, who smirked with self-satisfaction. Of course, Menders thought. He was signaling Hemmett down in the Courtyard with that cigar, letting him know we were all here!

"You didn't! You did! Oh, how wonderful!" Katrin cried, throwing her arms around Lorein. "Oh, when did you do it? Why didn't you let me know – I would have put on a wonderful wedding for you!"

"We were married two weeks ago," Hemmett said, looking tremendously proud of himself. "We didn't want a great farfumboozala, so we did a runaway match. I hope there's room in the planning of the New Mordania for two of us instead of one of us."

Katrin put her arms around him in answer. Hemmett held her close for a moment and then when she looked up at him, smiling for all she was worth, he started to laugh.

***

Menders circulated around the room after dinner, pleased to be spending some time with people socially for a change, rather than giving orders or discussing strategy. Katrin's meal had been delicious, the company delightful and the addition of newlyweds had led to all the old toasts and blessings being given.

Katrin had done very well with her first party in her home. She was glowing with happiness, discussing orphanage reform and charitable endeavors with Varnia, Petra and Lorein while Flori listened intently. Hemmett was relating some humorous story to Stevahn with Villison leaning on the mantelpiece, only giving half an ear to the conversation. He'd probably heard the joke several times before.

Menders finally found himself near a western facing window and looked outside. Clouds that had been driven across the sunset earlier in the evening had cleared, leaving the starry sky unshrouded. The Weaver hung high in the sky, the three brightest stars brilliant in the frosty air.

He thought of Katrin, determinedly claiming her right to health and happiness as well as discovering her power. She was brilliant tonight, full of ideas and plans. Hemmett was her match, his marriage giving him new confidence. He and Lorein seemed perfect together and very, very happy.

His mind moved on to Borsen, as his gaze moved toward Borsen's home. It was so like him to send Stevahn here tonight, complete with the perfect gift. It had to be a solitary evening for him, away from this vibrant group of young people.

Menders saw Katrin rise to put on a second pot of coffee and followed her into the kitchen.

"If you don't mind, I'd like to walk up to see Borsen for a while," he said as she measured coffee grounds and put the water kettle on to boil. "I'll leave you younger folks to your planning. I won't be very long."

"Of course, Menders," Katrin replied. Suddenly things seemed awkward – the rift between them had made private moments awkward. At one time she would have called him Papa, particularly at a family event like this. Now it was invariably Menders.

"I'm trying to think if I can send any of the food to him, but I'm not sure just what he can have at this point," she said uncertainly.

"That's fine – best not to risk having Franz after us if you sent something he can't tolerate yet," Menders agreed. "I'll let him know how much you liked his gift."

He made his goodbyes to everyone, picked up his hat and put on his coat before letting himself out of the suite.

The Staircase was a perfect place to think, if only to break the monotony of climbing down and down and down. Menders' mind was sorting over many things, but kept returning to the distance between Katrin and himself.

Eiren said it was inevitable. After the events of the last six years and more, yes – but that made it no less tragic. His emotional reactions during Borsen's illness and his frustration with Katrin's abnormal mental state had erupted in more than one incident he would give anything to live over again, so he could choose a different path. At times, he could tell Katrin felt chagrin about her own behavior during those days, though her illness had made her unable to control her actions.

Several times during the evening Menders felt that they were close to restoring their father-daughter bond – but each time it had slipped elusively away. It would take time, if the estrangement could ever be entirely healed.

The blast of winter cold greeting him at ground level turned his thoughts to more immediate matters – such as the fact that he'd forgotten his gloves and scarf in the suite.

He swore softly to himself and turned up his collar, then thrust his hands into his pockets. If something got left behind at the top of the Tower, you did without or went out and bought another one. Making a trip up and back down the Staircase now was something he simply wouldn't consider. That elevator could not be built soon enough.

As he walked through the archway into the Courtyard, the sentry on duty began swinging open the heavy, iron gate leading to the Promenade.

That's odd, Menders thought. This is the archway I walked through all those years ago on the night Katrin was born, carrying her. I've never considered it, but this bitter cold brings it all right back. It was so cold that the stars seemed very bright and close enough to touch – just like tonight.

"Papa? Papa!"

Menders stood stock still for a moment. Katrin's voice had rung out high above him. He turned and looked up, shielding his eyes from the light of the lanterns on the Palace walls.

"You forgot your gloves and scarf!" she called. He could just see her, leaning over the edge of the garden wall. "Catch!"

She dropped a small bundle toward him. Two steps, a slight jump and he caught it in midair.

His gloves and scarf were bundled and tied around a little packet, paper wrapped around something light and crisp. He opened it to find two fragrant spice cookies, the kind Cook made at The Shadows – his favorite and Katrin's. She had prepared the recipe earlier in the day, to go with the evening coffee.

Something was inscribed on the paper - a heart and a note,

I love you, Papa.

Katrin

He looked up.

"Everything is all right," he called softly. "Sleep well, little princess."

Katrin kissed her hand to him and was gone.

Menders drew on his gloves, wrapped the scarf around his neck and walked through the open gate, nodding to the sentry's salute and greeting. Then he was on his way down the Promenade on what had turned out to be a beautiful night, walking toward his son's house, the fragrance and flavor of home safe in the packet in his hand.

UNTIL THE CIRCLE TURNS AGAIN

CHETIGRÉ'S SAMORSAN SEVEN SPICE SOUP

Using Earth Ingredients

Ingredients

Soup Base

½ medium onion

1 garlic clove

4 – 5 boneless chicken breasts, diced

6 cups chicken stock/broth

2 T olive oil

The Seven Spices

1 t thyme

1 bay leaf

½ t cinnamon

Dash of cloves

1 t coriander

¼ - ½ t cayenne

1 tsp cumin

Lagniappe

Salt and pepper to taste (salt and pepper are a *given*!)
2 t lime or lemon juice.

Cream Sauce for Thickening

2 T butter

¼ cup flour

1 ½ cup milk

The Original Decadent Cream Thickening (optional)

1 ½ cup cream (heavy cream or whipping cream – Mexican table cream is also excellent for thickening.)

Directions

Chop your onion and garlic finely. Dice chicken in 1 inch cubes.
Heat your olive oil in the bottom of a heavy pot. Add the onion and garlic and sauté until soft. Add diced chicken and sauté until lightly browned.
Add chicken stock and bring to a boil, then lower to a simmer.
Add the seven spices, salt and pepper and lime or lemon juice.
Let your soup simmer covered for ½ hour or until chicken is tender.
You may thicken your soup by adding 1 ½ cup of heavy or whipping cream. Bring soup to a hard simmer before serving.

If you prefer to use a cream sauce to thicken your soup, this is the way to do it:

Melt the butter in a saucepan. When it bubbles, add the ¼ cup of flour. Stir until the flour has absorbed all the butter and is a very light golden color. Stir in the 1 ½ cup of milk gradually, using a whisk so there are no lumps. Stir the cream sauce into the soup, bring to a hard simmer before serving.